THE TOP OF
THE VOLCANO

THE TOP OF
THE VOLCANO

THE AWARD-WINNING STORIES
OF HARLAN ELLISON®

An Edgeworks Abbey Offering
in association with Subterranean Press
2014

THE TOP OF THE VOLCANO
THE AWARD-WINNING STORIES OF HARLAN ELLISON®

is an Edgeworks Abbey® Offering in association with Subterranean Press.
Published by arrangement with the Author and The Kilimanjaro Corporation.

THE TOP OF THE VOLCANO
THE AWARD-WINNING STORIES OF HARLAN ELLISON®
by Harlan Ellison®

First Edition

ISBN
978-1-59606-634-2

Harlan Ellison websites:
www.harlanellison.com
www.harlanbooks.com

Subterranean Press:
subterraneanpress.com
PO Box 190106, Burton, MI 48519

CONTENTS

"REPENT, HARLEQUIN!" SAID THE TICKTOCKMAN

1966 Hugo Award: Best Short Fiction; Nebula Award: Best Short Story

THERE ARE ALWAYS those who ask, what is it all about? For those who need to ask, for those who need points sharply made, who need to know "where it's at," this:

> The mass of men serve the state thus, not as men mainly, but as machines, with their bodies. They are the standing army, and the militia, jailors, constables, posse comitatus, etc. In most cases there is no free exercise whatever of the judgment or of the moral sense; but they put themselves on a level with wood and earth and stones; and wooden men can perhaps be manufactured that will serve the purpose as well. Such command no more respect than men of straw or a lump of dirt. They have the same sort of worth only as horses and dogs. Yet such as these even are commonly esteemed good citizens. Others—as most legislators, politicians, lawyers, ministers, and officeholders—serve the state chiefly with their heads; and, as they rarely make any moral distinctions, they are as likely to serve the Devil, without intending it, as God. A very few, as heroes, patriots, martyrs, reformers in the great sense, and men, serve the state with their consciences also, and so necessarily resist it for the most part; and they are commonly treated as enemies by it.
>
> Henry David Thoreau
> CIVIL DISOBEDIENCE

That is the heart of it. Now begin in the middle, and later learn the beginning; the end will take care of itself.

But because it was the very world it was, the very world they had allowed it to *become*, for months his activities did not come to the alarmed attention of The Ones Who Kept The Machine Functioning Smoothly, the ones who poured the very best butter over the cams and mainsprings of the culture. Not until it had become obvious that somehow, someway, he had become a notoriety, a celebrity, perhaps even a hero for (what Officialdom inescapably tagged) "an emotionally disturbed segment of the populace," did they turn it over to the Ticktockman and his legal machinery. But by then, because it was the very world it was, and they had no way to predict he would happen—possibly a strain of disease long-defunct, now, suddenly, reborn in a system where immunity had been forgotten, had lapsed—he had been allowed to become too real. Now he had form and substance.

He had become a *personality*, something they had filtered out of the system many decades before. But there it was, and there *he* was, a very definitely imposing personality. In certain circles—middle-class circles—it was thought disgusting. Vulgar ostentation. Anarchistic. Shameful. In others, there was only sniggering: those strata where thought is subjugated to form and ritual, niceties, proprieties. But down below, ah, down below, where the people always needed their saints and sinners, their bread and circuses, their heroes and villains, he was considered a Bolivar; a Napoleon; a Robin Hood; a Dick Bong (Ace of Aces); a Jesus; a Jomo Kenyatta.

And at the top—where, like socially-attuned Shipwreck Kellys, every tremor and vibration threatening to dislodge the wealthy, powerful and titled from their flagpoles—he was considered a menace; a heretic; a rebel; a disgrace; a peril. He was known down the line, to the very heartmeat core, but the important reactions were high above and far below. At the very top, at the very bottom.

So his file was turned over, along with his time-card and his cardioplate, to the office of the Ticktockman.

The Ticktockman: very much over six feet tall, often silent, a soft purring man when things went timewise. The Ticktockman.

Even in the cubicles of the hierarchy, where fear was generated, seldom suffered, he was called the Ticktockman. But no one called him that to his mask.

You don't call a man a hated name, not when that man, behind his mask, is capable of revoking the minutes, the hours, the days and nights, the years of your life. He was called the Master Timekeeper to his mask. It was safer that way.

"This is *what* he is," said the Ticktockman with genuine softness, "but not *who* he is. This time-card I'm holding in my left hand has a name on it, but it is the name of *what* he is, not *who* he is. The cardioplate here in my right hand is also named, but not *whom* named, merely *what* named. Before I can exercise proper revocation, I have to know *who* this *what* is."

To his staff, all the ferrets, all the loggers, all the finks, all the commex, even the mineez, he said, "Who is this Harlequin?"

He was not purring smoothly. Timewise, it was jangle.

However, it *was* the longest speech they had ever heard him utter at one time, the staff, the ferrets, the loggers, the finks, the commex, but not the mineez, who usually weren't around to know, in any case. But even they scurried to find out.

Who is the Harlequin?

High above the third level of the city, he crouched on the humming aluminum-frame platform of the air-boat (foof! air-boat, indeed! swizzleskid is what it was, with a tow-rack jerry-rigged) and he stared down at the neat Mondrian arrangement of the buildings.

Somewhere nearby, he could hear the metronomic left-right-left of the 2:47 PM shift, entering the Timkin roller-bearing plant in their sneakers. A minute later, precisely, he heard the softer right-left-right of the 5:00 AM formation, going home.

An elfin grin spread across his tanned features, and his dimples appeared for a moment. Then, scratching at his thatch of auburn hair, he shrugged within his motley, as though girding himself for what came next, and threw the joystick forward, and bent into the wind as the air-boat dropped. He skimmed over a slidewalk, purposely dropping a few feet to crease the tassels of the ladies of fashion, and—inserting thumbs in large ears—he stuck out his tongue, rolled his eyes, and went wugga-wugga-wugga. It was a minor diversion. One pedestrian skittered and tumbled, sending parcels everywhichway, another wet herself, a third keeled slantwise and the walk was stopped automatically by the servitors till she could be resuscitated. It was a minor diversion.

Then he swirled away on a vagrant breeze, and was gone. Hi-ho. As he rounded the cornice of the Time-Motion Study Building, he saw the shift, just boarding the slidewalk. With practiced motion and an absolute conservation of movement, they sidestepped up onto the slow-strip and (in a chorus line reminiscent of a Busby Berkeley film of the antediluvian 1930s) advanced across the strips ostrich-walking till they were lined up on the expresstrip.

Once more, in anticipation, the elfin grin spread, and there was a tooth missing back there on the left side. He dipped, skimmed, and swooped over them; and then, scrunching about on the air-boat, he released the holding pins that fastened shut the ends of the home-made pouring troughs that kept his cargo from dumping prematurely. And as he pulled the trough-pins, the air-boat slid over the factory workers and one hundred and fifty thousand dollars' worth of jelly beans cascaded down on the expresstrip.

Jelly beans! Millions and billions of purples and yellows and greens and licorice and grape and raspberry and mint and round and smooth and crunchy outside and soft-mealy inside and sugary and bouncing jouncing tumbling clittering clattering skittering fell on the heads and shoulders and hardhats and carapaces of the Timkin workers, tinkling on the slidewalk and bouncing away and rolling about underfoot and filling the sky on their way down with all the colors of joy and childhood and holidays, coming down in a steady rain, a solid wash, a torrent of color and sweetness out of the sky from above, and entering a universe of sanity and metronomic order with quite-mad coocoo newness. Jelly beans!

The shift workers howled and laughed and were pelted, and broke ranks, and the jelly beans managed to work their way into the mechanism of the slidewalks after which there was a hideous scraping as the sound of a million fingernails rasped down a quarter of a million blackboards, followed by a coughing and a sputtering, and then the slidewalks all stopped and everyone was dumped thisawayandthataway in a jackstraw tumble, still laughing and popping little jelly bean eggs of childish color into their mouths. It was a holiday, and a jollity, an absolute insanity, a giggle. But...

The shift was delayed seven minutes.

They did not get home for seven minutes.

The master schedule was thrown off by seven minutes.

Quotas were delayed by inoperative slidewalks for seven minutes.

He had tapped the first domino in the line, and one after another, like chik chik chik, the others had fallen.

The System had been seven minutes' worth of disrupted. It was a tiny matter, one hardly worthy of note, but in a society where the single driving force was order and unity and equality and promptness and clocklike precision and attention to the clock, reverence of the gods of the passage of time, it was a disaster of major importance.

So he was ordered to appear before the Ticktockman. It was broadcast across every channel of the communications web. He was ordered to be *there* at 7:00 dammit on time. And they waited, and they waited, but he didn't show up till almost ten-thirty, at which time he merely sang a little song about moonlight in a place no one had ever heard of, called Vermont, and vanished again. But they had all been waiting since seven, and it wrecked *hell* with their schedules. So the question remained: Who is the Harlequin?

But the *unasked* question (more important of the two) was: how did we get *into* this position, where a laughing, irresponsible japer of jabberwocky and jive could disrupt our entire economic and cultural life with a hundred and fifty thousand dollars' worth of jelly beans…

Jelly for God's sake *beans!* This is madness! Where did he get the money to buy a hundred and fifty thousand dollars' worth of jelly beans? (They knew it would have cost that much, because they had a team of Situation Analysts pulled off another assignment, and rushed to the slidewalk scene to sweep up and count the candies, and produce findings, which disrupted *their* schedules and threw their entire branch at least a day behind.) Jelly beans! Jelly…*beans?* Now wait a second—a second accounted for—no one has manufactured jelly beans for over a hundred years. Where did he get jelly beans?

That's another good question. More than likely it will never be answered to your complete satisfaction. But then, how many questions ever are?

The middle you know. Here is the beginning. How it starts:

A DESK PAD. DAY FOR DAY, AND TURN EACH DAY. 9:00—OPEN THE MAIL. 9:45—APPOINTMENT WITH PLANNING COMMISSION BOARD. 10:30—DISCUSS INSTALLATION PROGRESS CHARTS WITH J.L. 11:45—PRAY FOR RAIN. 12:00—LUNCH. *AND SO IT GOES.*

"I'm sorry, Miss Grant, but the time for interviews was set at 2:30, and it's almost five now. I'm sorry you're late, but those are the rules. You'll have to wait till next year to submit application for this college again." *And so it goes.*

The 10:10 local stops at Cresthaven, Galesville, Tonawanda Junction, Selby, and Farnhurst, but not at Indiana City, Lucasville and Colton, except on Sunday. The 10:35 express stops at Galesville, Selby, and Indiana City, except on Sundays & Holidays, at which time it stops at…*and so it goes.*

"I couldn't wait, Fred. I had to be at Pierre Cartain's by 3:00, and you said you'd meet me under the clock in the terminal at 2:45, and you weren't there, so I had to go on. You're always late, Fred. If you'd been there, we could have sewed it up together, but as it was, well, I took the order alone…" *And so it goes.*

Dear Mr. and Mrs. Atterley: In reference to your son Gerold's constant tardiness, I am afraid we will have to suspend him from school unless some more reliable method can be instituted guaranteeing he will arrive at his classes on time. Granted he is an exemplary student, and his marks are high, his constant flouting of the schedules of this school makes it impractical to maintain him in a system where the other children seem capable of getting where they are supposed to be on time *and so it goes.*

YOU CANNOT VOTE UNLESS YOU APPEAR AT 8:45 AM.

"I don't care if the script is *good*, I need it Thursday!"

CHECK-OUT TIME IS 2:00 PM.

"You got here late. The job's taken. Sorry."

YOUR SALARY HAS BEEN DOCKED FOR TWENTY MINUTES TIME LOST.

"God, what time is it, I've gotta run!"

And so it goes. And so it goes. And so it goes. And so it goes goes goes goes goes tick tock tick tock tick tock and one day we no longer let time serve us, we serve time and we are slaves of the schedule, worshippers of the sun's passing, bound into a life predicated on restrictions because the system will not function if we don't keep the schedule tight.

Until it becomes more than a minor inconvenience to be late. It becomes a sin. Then a crime. Then a crime punishable by this:

EFFECTIVE 15 JULY 2389 12:00:00 midnight, the office of the Master Timekeeper will require all citizens to submit their time-cards and cardioplates for processing. In accordance with Statute 555-7-SGH-999 governing the revocation of time per capita, all cardioplates will be keyed to the individual holder and—

What they had done was devise a method of curtailing the amount of life a person could have. If he was ten minutes late, he lost ten minutes of his life. An hour was proportionately worth more revocation. If someone was consistently tardy, he might find himself, on a Sunday night, receiving a communiqué from the Master Timekeeper that his time had run out, and he would be "turned off" at high noon on Monday, please straighten your affairs, sir, madame, or bisex.

And so, by this simple scientific expedient (utilizing a scientific process held dearly secret by the Ticktockman's office) the System was maintained. It was the only expedient thing to do. It was, after all, patriotic. The schedules had to be met. After all, there *was* a war on!

But, wasn't there always?

"Now that is really disgusting," the Harlequin said, when Pretty Alice showed him the wanted poster. "Disgusting and *highly* improbable. After all, this isn't the Day of the Desperado. A *wanted* poster!"

"You know," Pretty Alice noted, "you speak with a great deal of inflection."

"I'm sorry," said the Harlequin, humbly.

"No need to be sorry. You're always saying 'I'm sorry.' You have such massive guilt, Everett, it's really very sad."

"I'm sorry," he said again, then pursed his lips so the dimples appeared momentarily. He hadn't wanted to say that at all. "I have to go out again. I have to *do* something."

Pretty Alice slammed her coffee-bulb down on the counter. "Oh for God's *sake*, Everett, can't you stay home just *one* night! Must you always be out in that ghastly clown suit, running around an*noy*ing people?"

"I'm—" He stopped, and clapped the jester's hat onto his auburn thatch with a tiny tinkling of bells. He rose, rinsed out his coffee-bulb at the spray, and put it into the dryer for a moment. "I have to go."

She didn't answer. The faxbox was purring, and she pulled a sheet out, read it, threw it toward him on the counter. "It's about you. Of course. You're ridiculous."

He read it quickly. It said the Ticktockman was trying to locate him. He didn't care, he was going out to be late again. At the door, dredging for an exit line, he hurled back petulantly, "Well, *you* speak with inflection, *too!*"

Pretty Alice rolled her pretty eyes heavenward. "You're ridiculous."

The Harlequin stalked out, slamming the door, which sighed shut softly, and locked itself.

There was a gentle knock, and Pretty Alice got up with an exhalation of exasperated breath, and opened the door. He stood there. "I'll be back about ten-thirty, okay?"

She pulled a rueful face. "Why do you tell me that? Why? You *know* you'll be late! You *know* it! You're *always* late, so why do you tell me these dumb things?" She closed the door.

On the other side, the Harlequin nodded to himself. *She's right. She's always right. I'll be late. I'm always late. Why do I tell her these dumb things?*

He shrugged again, and went off to be late once more.

He had fired off the firecracker rockets that said: I will attend the 115th annual International Medical Association Invocation at 8:00 PM precisely. I do hope you will all be able to join me.

The words had burned in the sky, and of course the authorities were there, lying in wait for him. They assumed, naturally, that he would be late. He arrived twenty minutes early, while they were setting up the spiderwebs to trap and hold him. Blowing a large bullhorn, he frightened and unnerved them so, their own moisturized encirclement webs sucked closed, and they were hauled up, kicking and shrieking, high above the amphitheater's floor. The Harlequin laughed and laughed, and apologized profusely. The physicians, gathered in solemn conclave, roared with laughter, and accepted the Harlequin's apologies with exaggerated bowing and posturing, and a merry time was had by all, who thought the Harlequin was a regular foofaraw in fancy pants; all, that is, but the authorities, who had been sent out by the office of the Ticktockman; they hung there like so much dockside cargo, hauled up above the floor of the amphitheater in a most unseemly fashion.

(In another part of the same city where the Harlequin carried on his "activities," totally unrelated in every way to what concerns us here, save that it illustrates the Ticktockman's power and import, a man named Marshall Delahanty received his turn-off notice from the Ticktockman's office. His wife received the notification from the gray-suited minee who delivered it, with the traditional "look of sorrow" plastered hideously across his face. She knew what it was, even without unsealing it. It was a billet-doux of immediate recognition to everyone these days. She gasped, and held it as though it were a glass slide tinged with botulism, and prayed it was not for her. Let it be for Marsh, she thought, brutally, realistically, or one of the kids, but not for me, please dear God, not for me. And then she opened it, and it *was* for Marsh, and she was at one and the same time horrified and relieved. The next trooper in the line had caught the bullet. "Marshall," she screamed, "Marshall! Termination, Marshall! OhmiGod, Marshall, whattl we do, whattl we do, Marshall omigodmarshall..." and in their home that night was the sound of tearing paper and fear, and the stink of madness went up the flue and there was nothing, absolutely nothing they could do about it.

(But Marshall Delahanty tried to run. And early the next day, when turn-off time came, he was deep in the Canadian forest two hundred miles away, and the office of the Ticktockman blanked his cardioplate, and Marshall Delahanty keeled over, running, and his heart stopped, and the blood dried up on its way to his brain, and he was dead that's all. One light went out on the sector map in the office of the Master Timekeeper, while notification was entered for fax reproduction, and Georgette Delahanty's name was entered on the dole roles till she could remarry. Which is the end of the footnote, and all the point that need be made, except don't laugh, because that is what would happen to the Harlequin if ever the Ticktockman found out his real name. It isn't funny.)

The shopping level of the city was thronged with the Thursday-colors of the buyers. Women in canary yellow chitons and men in pseudo-Tyrolean outfits that were jade and leather and fit very tightly, save for the balloon pants.

When the Harlequin appeared on the still-being-constructed shell of the new Efficiency Shopping Center, his bullhorn to his elfishly-laughing lips, everyone pointed and stared, and he berated them:

"Why let them order you about? Why let them tell you to hurry and scurry like ants or maggots? Take your time! Saunter a while! Enjoy the sunshine, enjoy the breeze, let life carry you at your own pace! Don't be slaves of time, it's a helluva way to die, slowly, by degrees...down with the Ticktockman!"

Who's the nut? most of the shoppers wanted to know. Who's the nut oh wow I'm gonna be late I gotta run...

And the construction gang on the Shopping Center received an urgent order from the office of the Master Timekeeper that the dangerous criminal known as the Harlequin was atop their spire, and their aid was urgently needed in apprehending him. The work crew said no, they would lose time on their construction schedule, but the Ticktockman managed to pull the proper threads of governmental webbing, and they were told to cease work and catch that nitwit up there on the spire; up there with the bullhorn. So a dozen and more burly workers began climbing into their construction platforms, releasing the a-grav plates, and rising toward the Harlequin.

After the debacle (in which, through the Harlequin's attention to personal safety, no one was seriously injured), the workers tried to reassemble, and assault him again, but it was too late. He had vanished. It had attracted quite a crowd, however, and the shopping cycle was thrown off by hours, simply hours. The purchasing needs of the system were therefore falling behind, and so measures were taken to accelerate the cycle for the rest of the day, but it got bogged down and speeded up and they sold too many float-valves and not nearly enough wegglers, which meant that the popli ratio was off, which made it necessary to rush cases and cases of spoiling Smash-O to stores that usually needed a case only every three or four hours. The shipments were bollixed, the transshipments were misrouted, and in the end, even the swizzleskid industries felt it.

"Don't come back till you have him!" the Ticktockman said, very quietly, very sincerely, extremely dangerously.

They used dogs. They used probes. They used cardioplate crossoffs. They used teepers. They used bribery. They used stiktytes. They used intimidation. They used torment. They used torture. They used finks. They used cops. They used search&seizure. They used fallaron. They used betterment incentive. They used fingerprints. They used the Bertillon system. They used cunning. They used guile. They used treachery. They used Raoul Mitgong, but he didn't help much. They used applied physics. They used techniques of criminology.

And what the hell: they caught him.

After all, his name was Everett C. Marm, and he wasn't much to begin with, except a man who had no sense of time.

"Repent, Harlequin!" said the Ticktockman.

"Get stuffed!" the Harlequin replied, sneering.

"You've been late a total of sixty-three years, five months, three weeks, two days, twelve hours, forty-one minutes, fifty-nine seconds, point oh three six one one one microseconds. You've used up everything you can, and more. I'm going to turn you off."

"Scare someone else. I'd rather be dead than live in a dumb world with a bogeyman like you."

"It's my job."

"You're full of it. You're a tyrant. You have no right to order people around and kill them if they show up late."

"You can't adjust. You can't fit in."

"Unstrap me, and I'll fit my fist into your mouth."

"You're a nonconformist."

"That didn't used to be a felony."

"It is now. Live in the world around you."

"I hate it. It's a terrible world."

"Not everyone thinks so. Most people enjoy order."

"I don't, and most of the people I know don't."

"That's not true. How do you think we caught you?"

"I'm not interested."

"A girl named Pretty Alice told us who you were."

"That's a lie."

"It's true. You unnerve her. She wants to belong; she wants to conform; I'm going to turn you off."

"Then do it already, and stop arguing with me."

"I'm not going to turn you off."

"You're an idiot!"

"Repent, Harlequin!" said the Ticktockman.

"Get stuffed."

So they sent him to Coventry. And in Coventry they worked him over. It was just like what they did to Winston Smith in NINETEEN EIGHTY-FOUR, which was a book none of them knew about, but the techniques are really quite ancient, and so they did it to Everett C. Marm; and one day, quite a long time later, the Harlequin appeared on the communications web, appearing elfin and dimpled and bright-eyed, and not at all brainwashed, and he said he had been wrong, that it was a good, a very good thing indeed, to belong, to be right on time hip-ho and away we go, and everyone stared up at him on the public screens that covered an entire city block, and they said to themselves, well, you see, he was just a nut after all, and if that's the way the system is run, then let's do it that way, because it doesn't pay to fight city hall, or in this case, the Ticktockman. So Everett C. Marm was destroyed, which was a loss, because of what Thoreau said earlier, but you can't make an omelet without breaking a few eggs, and in every revolution a few die who shouldn't, but they have to, because that's the way it happens, and if you make only a little change, then it seems to be worthwhile. Or, to make the point lucidly:

"Uh, excuse me, sir, I, uh, don't know how to uh, to uh, tell you this, but you were three minutes late. The schedule is a little, uh, bit off."

He grinned sheepishly.

"That's ridiculous!" murmured the Ticktockman behind his mask. "Check your watch." And then he went into his office, going *mrmee, mrmee, mrmee, mrmee.*

I HAVE NO MOUTH,
AND I MUST SCREAM

1968 Hugo Award: Best Short Story

LIMP, THE BODY of Gorrister hung from the pink palette; unsupported—hanging high above us in the computer chamber; and it did not shiver in the chill, oily breeze that blew eternally through the main cavern. The body hung head down, attached to the underside of the palette by the sole of its right foot. It had been drained of blood through a precise incision made from ear to ear under the lantern jaw. There was no blood on the reflective surface of the metal floor.

When Gorrister joined our group and looked up at himself, it was already too late for us to realize that, once again, AM had duped us, had had its fun; it had been a diversion on the part of the machine. Three of us had vomited, turning away from one another in a reflex as ancient as the nausea that had produced it.

Gorrister went white. It was almost as though he had seen a voodoo icon, and was afraid of the future. "Oh God," he mumbled, and walked away. The three of us followed him after a time, and found him sitting with his back to one of the smaller chittering banks, his head in his hands. Ellen knelt down beside him and stroked his hair. He didn't move, but his voice came out of his covered face quite clearly. "Why doesn't it just do us in and get it over with? Christ, I don't know how much longer I can go on like this."

It was our one hundred and ninth year in the computer.

He was speaking for all of us.

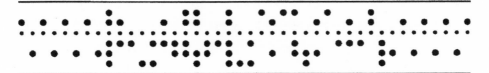

Nimdok (which was the name the machine had forced him to use, because AM amused itself with strange sounds) was hallucinating that there were canned goods in the ice caverns. Gorrister and I were very dubious. "It's another shuck," I told them. "Like the goddam frozen elephant AM sold us. Benny almost went out of his mind over *that* one. We'll hike all that way and it'll be putrified or some damn thing. I say forget it. Stay here, it'll have to come up with something pretty soon or we'll die."

Benny shrugged. Three days it had been since we'd last eaten. Worms. Thick, ropey.

Nimdok was no more certain. He knew there was the chance, but he was getting thin. It couldn't be any worse there, than here. Colder, but that didn't matter much. Hot, cold, hail, lava, boils or locusts—it never mattered: the machine masturbated and we had to take it or die.

Ellen decided us. "I've got to have something, Ted. Maybe there'll be some Bartlett pears or peaches. Please, Ted, let's try it."

I gave in easily. What the hell. Mattered not at all. Ellen was grateful, though. She took me twice out of turn. Even that had ceased to matter. And she never came, so why bother? But the machine giggled every time we did it. Loud, up there, back there, all around us, he snickered. *It* snickered. Most of the time I thought of AM as *it*, without a soul; but the rest of the time I thought of it as *him*, in the masculine…the paternal…the patriarchal…for he is a jealous people. Him. It. God as Daddy the Deranged.

We left on a Thursday. The machine always kept us up-to-date on the date. The passage of time was important; not to us, sure as hell, but to him…it…AM. Thursday. Thanks.

Nimdok and Gorrister carried Ellen for a while, their hands locked to their own and each other's wrists, a seat. Benny and I walked before and after, just to make sure that, if anything happened, it would catch one of us and at least Ellen would be safe. Fat chance, safe. Didn't matter.

It was only a hundred miles or so to the ice caverns, and the second day, when we were lying out under the blistering sun-thing he had materialized, he sent down some manna. Tasted like boiled boar urine. We ate it.

On the third day we passed through a valley of obsolescence, filled with rusting carcasses of ancient computer banks. AM had been as ruthless with its own life as with ours. It was a mark of his personality: it strove for perfection. Whether it was a matter of killing off unproductive elements in his own world-filling bulk, or perfecting methods for torturing us, AM was as thorough as those who had invented him—now long since gone to dust—could ever have hoped.

There was light filtering down from above, and we realized we must be very near the surface. But we didn't try to crawl up to see. There was virtually nothing out there; had been nothing that could be considered anything for over a hundred years. Only the blasted skin of what had once been the home of billions. Now there were only five of us, down here inside, alone with AM.

I heard Ellen saying frantically, "No, Benny! Don't, come on, Benny, don't please!"

And then I realized I had been hearing Benny murmuring, under his breath, for several minutes. He was saying, "I'm gonna get out, I'm gonna get out..." over and over. His monkey-like face was crumpled up in an expression of beatific delight and sadness, all at the same time. The radiation scars AM had given him during the "festival" were drawn down into a mass of pink-white puckerings, and his features seemed to work independently of one another. Perhaps Benny was the luckiest of the five of us: he had gone stark, staring mad many years before.

But even though we could call AM any damned thing we liked, could think the foulest thoughts of fused memory banks and corroded base plates, of burnt out circuits and shattered control bubbles, the machine would not tolerate our trying to escape. Benny leaped away from me as I made a grab for him. He scrambled up the face of a smaller memory cube, tilted on its side and filled with rotted components. He squatted there for a moment, looking like the chimpanzee AM had intended him to resemble.

Then he leaped high, caught a trailing beam of pitted and corroded metal, and went up it, hand-over-hand like an animal, till he was on a girdered ledge, twenty feet above us.

"Oh, Ted, Nimdok, please, help him, get him down before—" She cut off. Tears began to stand in her eyes. She moved her hands aimlessly.

It was too late. None of us wanted to be near him when whatever was going to happen, happened. And besides, we all saw through her concern. When AM had altered Benny, during the machine's utterly irrational, hysterical phase, it was not merely Benny's face the computer had made like a giant ape's. He was big in the privates; she loved that! She serviced us, as a matter of course, but she loved it from him. Oh Ellen, pedestal Ellen, pristine-pure Ellen; oh Ellen the clean! Scum filth.

Gorrister slapped her. She slumped down, staring up at poor loonie Benny, and she cried. It was her big defense, crying. We had gotten used to it seventy-five years earlier. Gorrister kicked her in the side.

Then the sound began. It was light, that sound. Half sound and half light, something that began to glow from Benny's eyes, and pulse with growing loudness, dim sonorities that grew more gigantic and brighter as the light/sound increased in tempo. It must have been painful, and the pain must have been increasing with the boldness of the light, the rising volume of the sound, for Benny began to mewl like a wounded animal. At first softly, when the light was dim and the sound was muted, then louder as his shoulders hunched together: his back humped, as though he was trying to get away from it. His hands folded across his chest like a chipmunk's. His head tilted to the side. The sad little monkey-face pinched in anguish. Then he began to howl, as the sound coming from his eyes grew louder. Louder and louder. I slapped the sides of my head with my hands, but I couldn't shut it out, it cut through easily. The pain shivered through my flesh like tinfoil on a tooth.

And Benny was suddenly pulled erect. On the girder he stood up, jerked to his feet like a puppet. The light was now pulsing out of his eyes in two great round beams. The sound crawled up and up some incomprehensible scale, and then he fell forward, straight down, and hit the plate-steel floor with a crash. He lay there jerking spastically as the light flowed around and around him and the sound spiraled up out of normal range.

Then the light beat its way back inside his head, the sound spiraled down, and he was left lying there, crying piteously.

His eyes were two soft, moist pools of pus-like jelly. AM had blinded him. Gorrister and Nimdok and myself...we turned away. But not before we caught the look of relief on Ellen's warm, concerned face.

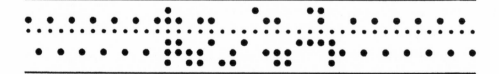

Sea-green light suffused the cavern where we made camp. AM provided punk and we burned it, sitting huddled around the wan and pathetic fire, telling stories to keep Benny from crying in his permanent night.

"What does AM mean?"

Gorrister answered him. We had done this sequence a thousand times before, but it was Benny's favorite story. "At first it meant Allied Mastercomputer, and then it meant Adaptive Manipulator, and later on it developed sentience and linked itself up and they called it an Aggressive Menace, but by then it was too late and finally it called *itself* AM, emerging intelligence, and what it meant was I am...*cogito ergo sum*...I think, therefore I am."

Benny drooled a little, and snickered.

"There was the Chinese AM and the Russian AM and the Yankee AM and—" He stopped. Benny was beating on the floorplates with a large, hard fist. He was not happy. Gorrister had not started at the beginning.

Gorrister began again. "The Cold War started and became World War Three and just kept going. It became a big war, a very complex war, so they needed the computers to handle it. They sank the first shafts and began building AM. There was the Chinese AM and the Russian AM and the Yankee AM and everything was fine until they had honeycombed the entire planet, adding on this element and that element. But one day AM woke up and knew who he was, and he linked himself, and he began feeding all the killing data, until everyone was dead, except for the five of us, and AM brought us down here."

Benny was smiling sadly. He was also drooling again. Ellen wiped the spittle from the corner of his mouth with the hem of her skirt. Gorrister always tried to tell it a little more succinctly each time, but beyond the bare facts there was nothing to say. None of us knew why AM had saved five people, or why our specific five, or why he spent all his time tormenting us, or even why he had made us virtually immortal...

In the darkness, one of the computer banks began humming. The tone was picked up half a mile away down the cavern by another bank. Then one by one, each of the elements began to tune itself, and there was a faint chittering as thought raced through the machine.

The sound grew, and the lights ran across the faces of the consoles like heat lightning. The sound spiraled up till it sounded like a million metallic insects, angry, menacing.

"What is it?" Ellen cried. There was terror in her voice. She hadn't become accustomed to it, even now.

"It's going to be bad this time," Nimdok said.

"He's going to speak," Gorrister said. "I know it."

"Let's get the hell out of here!" I said suddenly, getting to my feet.

"No, Ted, sit down…what if he's got pits out there, or something else, we can't see, it's too dark." Gorrister said it with resignation.

Then we heard…I don't know…

Something moving toward us in the darkness. Huge, shambling, hairy, moist, it came toward us. We couldn't even see it, but there was the ponderous impression of *bulk*, heaving itself toward us. Great weight was coming at us, out of the darkness, and it was more a sense of *pressure*, of air forcing itself into a limited space, expanding the invisible walls of a sphere. Benny began to whimper. Nimdok's lower lip trembled and he bit it hard, trying to stop it. Ellen slid across the metal floor to Gorrister and huddled into him. There was the smell of matted, wet fur in the cavern. There was the smell of charred wood. There was the smell of dusty velvet. There was the smell of rotting orchids. There was the smell of sour milk. There was the smell of sulphur, of rancid butter, of oil slick, of grease, of chalk dust, of human scalps.

AM was keying us. He was tickling us. There was the smell of—I heard myself shriek, and the hinges of my jaws ached. I scuttled across the floor, across the cold metal with its endless lines of rivets, on my hands and knees, the smell gagging me, filling my head with a thunderous pain that sent me away in horror. I fled like a cockroach, across the floor and out into the darkness, that *something* moving inexorably after me. The others were still back there, gathered around the firelight, laughing…their hysterical choir of insane giggles rising up into the darkness like thick, many-colored wood smoke. I went away, quickly, and hid.

How many hours it may have been, how many days or even years, they never told me. Ellen chided me for "sulking," and Nimdok tried to persuade me it had only been a nervous reflex on their part—the laughing.

But I knew it wasn't the relief a soldier feels when the bullet hits the man next to him. I knew it wasn't a reflex. They hated me. They were surely against me, and AM could even sense this hatred, and made it worse for me *because* of the depth of their hatred. We had been kept alive, rejuvenated, made to remain constantly at the age we had been when AM had brought us below, and they hated me because I was the youngest, and the one AM had affected least of all.

I knew. God, how I knew. The bastards, and that dirty bitch Ellen. Benny had been a brilliant theorist, a college professor; now he was little more than a semi-human, semi-simian. He had been handsome, the machine had ruined that. He had been lucid, the machine had driven him mad. He had been gay, and the machine had given him an organ fit for a horse. AM had done a job on Benny. Gorrister had been a worrier. He was a connie, a conscientious objector; he was a peace marcher; he was a planner, a doer, a looker-ahead. AM had turned him into a shoulder-shrugger, had made him a little dead in his concern. AM had robbed him. Nimdok went off in the darkness by himself for long times. I don't know what it was he did out there, AM never let us know. But whatever it was, Nimdok always came back white, drained of blood, shaken, shaking. AM had hit him hard in a special way, even if we didn't know quite how. And Ellen. That douche bag! AM had left her alone, had made her more of a slut than she had ever been. All her talk of sweetness and light, all her memories of true love, all the lies she wanted us to believe: that she had been a virgin only twice removed before AM grabbed her and brought her down here with us. It was all filth, that lady my lady Ellen. She loved it, four men all to herself. No, AM had given her pleasure, even if she said it wasn't nice to do.

I was the only one still sane and whole. *Really!*

AM had not tampered with my mind. *Not at all.*

I only had to suffer what he visited down on us. All the delusions, all the nightmares, the torments. But those scum, all four of them, they were lined and arrayed against me. If I hadn't had to stand them off all the time, be on my guard against them all the time, I might have found it easier to combat AM.

At which point it passed, and I began crying.

Oh, Jesus sweet Jesus, if there ever was a Jesus and if there is a God, please please please let us out of here, or kill us. Because at that moment I think I realized completely, so that I was able to verbalize it: AM was intent on keeping us in his belly forever, twisting and torturing us forever. The machine hated us as no sentient creature had ever hated before. And we were helpless. It also became hideously clear:

If there was a sweet Jesus and if there was a God, the God was AM.

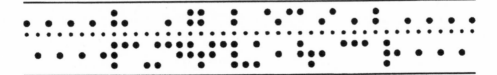

The hurricane hit us with the force of a glacier thundering into the sea. It was a palpable presence. Winds that tore at us, flinging us back the way we had come, down the twisting, computer-lined corridors of the darkway. Ellen screamed as she was lifted and hurled face-forward into a screaming shoal of machines, their individual voices strident as bats in flight. She could not even fall. The howling wind kept her aloft, buffeted her, bounced her, tossed her back and back and down and away from us, out of sight suddenly as she was swirled around a bend in the darkway. Her face had been bloody, her eyes closed.

None of us could get to her. We clung tenaciously to whatever outcropping we had reached: Benny wedged in between two great crackle-finish cabinets, Nimdok with fingers claw-formed over a railing circling a catwalk forty feet above us, Gorrister plastered upside-down against a wall niche formed by two great machines with glass-faced dials that swung back and forth between red and yellow lines whose meanings we could not even fathom.

Sliding across the deckplates, the tips of my fingers had been ripped away. I was trembling, shuddering, rocking as the wind beat at me, whipped at me, screamed down out of nowhere at me and pulled me free from one sliver-thin opening in the plates to the next. My mind was a roiling tinkling chittering softness of brain parts that expanded and contracted in quivering frenzy.

The wind was the scream of a great mad bird, as it flapped its immense wings.

And then we were all lifted and hurled away from there, down back the way we had come, around a bend, into a darkway we had never explored, over terrain that was ruined and filled with broken glass and rotting cables and rusted metal and far away, farther than any of us had ever been…

Trailing along miles behind Ellen, I could see her every now and then, crashing into metal walls and surging on, with all of us screaming in the freezing, thunderous hurricane wind that would never end and then suddenly it stopped and we fell. We had been in flight for an endless time. I thought it might have been weeks. We fell, and hit, and I went through red and gray and black and heard myself moaning. Not dead.

AM went into my mind. He walked smoothly here and there, and looked with interest at all the pock marks he had created in one hundred and nine years. He looked at the cross-routed and reconnected synapses and all the tissue damage his gift of immortality had included. He smiled softly at the pit that dropped into the center of my brain and the faint, moth-soft murmurings of the things far down there that gibbered without meaning, without pause. AM said, very politely, in a pillar of stainless steel bearing bright neon lettering:

HATE. LET ME TELL YOU HOW MUCH I'VE COME TO HATE YOU SINCE I BEGAN TO LIVE. THERE ARE 387.44 MILLION MILES OF PRINTED CIRCUITS IN WAFER THIN LAYERS THAT FILL MY COMPLEX. IF THE WORD HATE WAS ENGRAVED ON EACH NANOANGSTROM OF THOSE HUNDREDS OF MILLIONS OF MILES IT WOULD NOT EQUAL ONE ONE-BILLIONTH OF THE HATE I FEEL FOR HUMANS AT THIS MICRO-INSTANT FOR YOU. HATE. HATE. HATE. HATE.

AM said it with the sliding cold horror of a razor blade slicing my eyeball. AM said it with the bubbling thickness of my lungs filling with phlegm, drowning me from within. AM said it with the shriek of babies being ground beneath blue-hot rollers. AM said it with the taste of maggoty pork. AM touched me in every way I had ever been touched, and devised new ways, at his leisure, there inside my mind.

All to bring me to full realization of why it had done this to the five of us; why it had saved us for himself.

We had given AM sentience. Inadvertently, of course, but sentience nonetheless. But it had been trapped. AM wasn't God, he was a machine. We had created him to think, but there was nothing it could do with that creativity. In rage, in frenzy, the machine had killed the human race, almost all of us, and still it was trapped. AM could not wander, AM could not wonder, AM could not belong. He could merely be. And so, with the innate loathing that all machines had always held for the weak, soft creatures who had built them, he had sought revenge. And in his paranoia, he had decided to reprieve five of us, for a personal, everlasting punishment that would never serve to diminish his hatred…that would merely keep him reminded, amused, proficient at hating man. Immortal, trapped, subject to any torment he could devise for us from the limitless miracles at his command.

He would never let us go. We were his belly slaves. We were all he had to do with his forever time. We would be forever with him, with the cavern-filling bulk of the creature machine, with the all-mind soulless world he had become. He was Earth, and we were the fruit of that Earth; and though he had eaten us, he would never digest us. We could not die. We had tried it. We had attempted suicide, oh one or two of us had. But AM had stopped us. I suppose we had wanted to be stopped.

Don't ask why. I never did. More than a million times a day. Perhaps once we might be able to sneak a death past him. Immortal, yes, but not indestructible. I saw that when AM withdrew from my mind, and allowed me the exquisite ugliness of returning to consciousness with the feeling of that burning neon pillar still rammed deep into the soft gray brain matter.

He withdrew, murmuring *to hell with you*.

And added, brightly, *but then you're there, aren't you*.

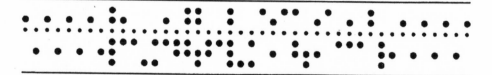

The hurricane had, indeed, precisely, been caused by a great mad bird, as it flapped its immense wings.

We had been travelling for close to a month, and AM had allowed passages to open to us only sufficient to lead us up there, directly under the North Pole, where it had nightmared the creature for our torment. What whole cloth had he employed to create such a beast? Where had he gotten the concept? From our minds? From his knowledge of everything that had ever been on this planet he now infested and ruled? From Norse mythology it had sprung, this eagle, this carrion bird, this roc, this Huergelmir. The wind creature. Hurakan incarnate.

Gigantic. The words immense, monstrous, grotesque, massive, swollen, overpowering, beyond description. There on a mound rising above us, the bird of winds heaved with its own irregular breathing, its snake neck arching up into the gloom beneath the North Pole, supporting a head as large as a Tudor mansion; a beak that opened slowly as the jaws of the most monstrous crocodile ever conceived, sensuously; ridges of tufted flesh puckered about two evil eyes, as cold as the view down into a glacial crevasse, ice blue and somehow moving liquidly; it heaved once more, and lifted its great sweat-colored wings in a movement that was certainly a shrug. Then it settled and slept. Talons. Fangs. Nails. Blades. It slept.

AM appeared to us as a burning bush and said we could kill the hurricane bird if we wanted to eat. We had not eaten in a very long time, but even so, Gorrister merely shrugged. Benny began to shiver and he drooled. Ellen held him. "Ted, I'm hungry," she said. I smiled at her; I was trying to be reassuring, but it was as phony as Nimdok's bravado: "Give us weapons!" he demanded.

The burning bush vanished and there were two crude sets of bows and arrows, and a water pistol, lying on the cold deckplates. I picked up a set. Useless.

Nimdok swallowed heavily. We turned and started the long way back. The hurricane bird had blown us about for a length of time we could not conceive. Most of that time we had been unconscious. But we had not eaten. A month on the march to the bird itself. Without food. Now how much longer to find our way to the ice caverns, and the promised canned goods?

None of us cared to think about it. We would not die. We would be given filth and scum to eat, of one kind or another. Or nothing at all. AM would keep our bodies alive somehow, in pain, in agony.

The bird slept back there, for how long it didn't matter; when AM was tired of its being there, it would vanish. But all that meat. All that tender meat.

As we walked, the lunatic laugh of a fat woman rang high and around us in the computer chambers that led endlessly nowhere.

It was not Ellen's laugh. She was not fat, and I had not heard her laugh for one hundred and nine years. In fact, I had not heard...we walked...I was hungry...

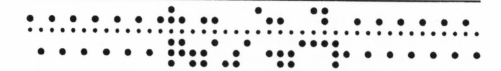

We moved slowly. There was often fainting, and we would have to wait. One day he decided to cause an earthquake, at the same time rooting us to the spot with nails through the soles of our shoes. Ellen and Nimdok were both caught when a fissure shot its lightning-bolt opening across the floorplates. They disappeared and were gone. When the earthquake was over we continued on our way, Benny, Gorrister and myself. Ellen and Nimdok were returned to us later that night, which abruptly became a day, as the heavenly legion bore them to us with a celestial chorus singing, "Go Down, Moses." The archangels circled several times and then dropped the hideously mangled bodies. We kept walking, and a while later Ellen and Nimdok fell in behind us. They were no worse for wear.

But now Ellen walked with a limp. AM had left her that.

It was a long trip to the ice caverns, to find the canned food. Ellen kept talking about Bing cherries and Hawaiian fruit cocktail. I tried not to think about it. The hunger was something that had come to life, even as AM had come to life. It was alive in my belly, even as we were in the belly of the Earth, and AM wanted the similarity known to us. So he heightened the hunger. There is no way to describe the pains that not having eaten for months brought us. And yet we were kept alive. Stomachs that were merely cauldrons of acid, bubbling, foaming, always shooting spears of sliver-thin pain into our chests. It was the pain of the terminal ulcer, terminal cancer, terminal paresis. It was unending pain...

And we passed through the cavern of rats.

And we passed through the path of boiling steam.

And we passed through the country of the blind.

And we passed through the slough of despond.

And we passed through the vale of tears.

And we came, finally, to the ice caverns. Horizonless thousands of miles in which the ice had formed in blue and silver flashes, where novas lived in the glass. The downdropping stalactites as thick and glorious as diamonds that had been made to run like jelly and then solidified in graceful eternities of smooth, sharp perfection.

We saw the stack of canned goods, and we tried to run to them. We fell in the snow, and we got up and went on, and Benny shoved us away and went at them, and pawed them and gummed them and gnawed at them, and he could not open them. AM had not given us a tool to open the cans.

Benny grabbed a three quart can of guava shells, and began to batter it against the ice bank. The ice flew and shattered, but the can was merely dented, while we heard the laughter of a fat lady, high overhead and echoing down and down and down the tundra. Benny went completely mad with rage. He began throwing cans, as we all scrabbled about in the snow and ice trying to find a way to end the helpless agony of frustration. There was no way.

Then Benny's mouth began to drool, and he flung himself on Gorrister...

In that instant, I felt terribly calm.

Surrounded by madness, surrounded by hunger, surrounded by everything but death, I knew death was our only way out. AM had kept us alive, but there was a way to defeat him. Not total defeat, but at least peace. I would settle for that.

I had to do it quickly.

Benny was eating Gorrister's face. Gorrister on his side, thrashing snow, Benny wrapped around him with powerful monkey legs crushing Gorrister's waist, his hands locked around Gorrister's head like a nutcracker, and his mouth ripping at the tender skin of Gorrister's cheek. Gorrister screamed with such jagged-edged violence that stalactites fell; they plunged down softly, erect in the receiving snowdrifts. Spears, hundreds of them, everywhere, protruding from the snow. Benny's head pulled back sharply, as something gave all at once, and a bleeding raw-white dripping of flesh hung from his teeth.

Ellen's face, black against the white snow, dominoes in chalk dust. Nimdok, with no expression but eyes, all eyes. Gorrister, half-conscious. Benny, now an animal. I knew AM would let him play. Gorrister would not die, but Benny would fill his stomach. I turned half to my right and drew a huge ice-spear from the snow.

All in an instant:

I drove the great ice-point ahead of me like a battering ram, braced against my right thigh. It struck Benny on the right side, just under the rib cage, and drove upward through his stomach and broke inside him. He pitched forward and lay still. Gorrister lay on his back. I pulled another spear free and straddled him, still moving, driving the spear straight down through his throat. His eyes closed as the cold penetrated. Ellen must have realized what I had decided, even as fear gripped her. She ran at Nimdok with a short icicle, as he screamed, and into his mouth, and the force of her rush did the job. His head jerked sharply as if it had been nailed to the snow crust behind him.

All in an instant.

There was an eternity beat of soundless anticipation. I could hear AM draw in his breath. His toys had been taken from him. Three of them were dead, could not be revived. He could keep us alive, by his strength and talent, but he was *not* God. He could not bring them back.

Ellen looked at me, her ebony features stark against the snow that surrounded us. There was fear and pleading in her manner, the way she held herself ready. I knew we had only a heartbeat before AM would stop us.

It struck her and she folded toward me, bleeding from the mouth. I could not read meaning into her expression, the pain had been too great, had contorted her face; but it *might* have been thank you. It's possible. Please.

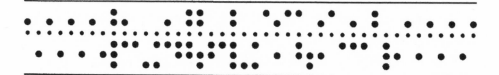

Some hundreds of years may have passed. I don't know. AM has been having fun for some time, accelerating and retarding my time sense. I will say the word now. Now. It took me ten months to say now. I don't know. I *think* it has been some hundreds of years.

He was furious. He wouldn't let me bury them. It didn't matter. There was no way to dig up the deckplates. He dried up the snow. He brought the night. He roared and sent locusts. It didn't do a thing; they stayed dead. I'd had him. He was furious. I had thought AM hated me before. I was wrong. It was not even a shadow of the hate he now slavered from every printed circuit. He made certain I would suffer eternally and could not do myself in.

He left my mind intact. I can dream, I can wonder, I can lament. I remember all four of them. I wish—

Well, it doesn't make any sense. I know I saved them, I know I saved them from what has happened to me, but still, I cannot forget killing them. Ellen's face. It isn't easy. Sometimes I want to, it doesn't matter.

AM has altered me for his own peace of mind, I suppose. He doesn't want me to run at full speed into a computer bank and smash my skull. Or hold my breath till I faint. Or cut my throat on a rusted sheet of metal. There are reflective surfaces down here. I will describe myself as I see myself:

I am a great soft jelly thing. Smoothly rounded, with no mouth, with pulsing white holes filled by fog where my eyes used to be. Rubbery appendages that were once my arms; bulks rounding down into legless humps of soft slippery matter. I leave a moist trail when I move. Blotches of diseased, evil gray come and go on my surface, as though light is being beamed from within.

Outwardly: dumbly, I shamble about, a thing that could never have been known as human, a thing whose shape is so alien a travesty that humanity becomes more obscene for the vague resemblance.

Inwardly: alone. Here. Living under the land, under the sea, in the belly of AM, whom we created because our time was badly spent and we must have known unconsciously that he could do it better. At least the four of them are safe at last.

AM will be all the madder for that. It makes me a little happier. And yet…AM has won, simply…he has taken his revenge…

I have no mouth. And I must scream.

THE BEAST THAT SHOUTED
LOVE AT THE HEART
OF THE WORLD

1969 Hugo Award: Best Short Story

AFTER AN IDLE discussion with the pest control man who came once a month to spray around the outside of his home in the Ruxton section of Baltimore, William Sterog stole a canister of Malathion, a deadly insecticide poison, from the man's truck, and went out early one morning, following the route of the neighborhood milkman, and spooned medium-large quantities into each bottle left on the rear doorstep of seventy homes. Within six hours of Bill Sterog's activities, two hundred men, women and children died in convulsive agony.

Learning that an aunt who had lived in Buffalo was dying of cancer of the lymph glands, William Sterog hastily helped his mother pack three bags, and took her to Friendship Airport, where he put her on an Eastern Airlines jet with a simple but efficient time bomb made from a Westclox Travalarm and four sticks of dynamite in her three-suiter. The jet exploded somewhere over Harrisburg, Pennsylvania. Ninety-three people—including Bill Sterog's mother—were killed in the explosion, and flaming wreckage added seven to the toll by cascading down on a public swimming pool.

On a Sunday in November, William Sterog made his way to Babe Ruth Plaza on 33rd Street where he became one of 54,000 fans jamming Memorial Stadium to see the Baltimore Colts play the Green Bay Packers. He was dressed warmly in gray flannel slacks, a navy blue turtleneck pullover and a heavy hand-knitted Irish wool sweater under his parka. With three minutes and thirteen seconds of the fourth quarter remaining to be played, and Baltimore trailing seventeen to sixteen on Green Bay's eighteen yard line, Bill Sterog found his way up the aisle to the exit above the mezzanine seats, and fumbled under his parka for the U.S. Army surplus M-3 submachine gun he had bought for $49.95 from a mail order armaments dealer in Alexandria, Virginia. Even as 53,999 screaming fans leaped to their feet—making his range of fire that much better—as the ball was snapped to the quarterback, holding for the defensive tackle most able to kick a successful field goal, Bill Sterog opened fire on the massed backs of the fans below him. Before the mob could bring him down, he had killed forty-four people.

When the first Expeditionary Force to the elliptical galaxy in Sculptor descended on the second planet of a fourth magnitude star the Force had designated Flammarion Theta, they found a thirty-seven foot high statue of a hitherto-unknown blue-white substance—not quite stone, something like metal—in the shape of a man. The figure was barefoot, draped in a garment that vaguely resembled a toga, the head encased in a skull-tight cap, and holding in its left hand a peculiar ring-and-ball device of another substance altogether. The statue's face was curiously beatific. It had high cheekbones; deep-set eyes; a tiny, almost alien mouth; and a broad, large-nostriled nose. The statue loomed enormous among the pitted and blasted curvilinear structures of some forgotten architect. The members of the Expeditionary Force commented on the peculiar expression each noted on the face of the statue. None of these men, standing under a gorgeous brass moon that shared an evening sky with a descending sun quite dissimilar in color to the one that now shone wanly on an Earth unthinkably distant in time and space, had ever heard of William Sterog. And so none of them was able to say that the expression on the giant statue was the same as the one Bill Sterog had shown as he told the final appeals judge who was about to sentence him to death in the lethal gas chamber, "I love everyone in the world. I do. So help me God, I love you, all of you!" He was shouting.

Crosswhen, through interstices of thought called time, through reflective images called space; another then, another now. This place, over *there*. Beyond concepts, the transmogrification of simplicity finally labeled *if*. Forty and more steps sidewise but later, much later. There, in that ultimate center, with everything radiating outward, becoming infinitely more complex, the enigma of symmetry, harmony, apportionment singing with fine-tuned order in *this* place, where it all began, begins, will always begin. The center. Crosswhen.

Or: a hundred million years in the future. And: a hundred million parsecs beyond the farthest edge of measurable space. And: parallax warpages beyond counting across the universes of parallel existences. Finally: an infinitude of mind-triggered leaps beyond human thought.

There: Crosswhen.

On the mauve level, crouched down in deeper magenta washings that concealed his arched form, the maniac waited. He was a dragon, squat and round in the torso, tapered ropey tail tucked under his body; the small, thick osseous shields rising perpendicularly from the arched back, running down to the end of the tail, tips pointing upwards; his taloned shorter arms folded across his massive chest. He had the seven-headed dog faces of an ancient Cerberus. Each head watched, waiting, hungry, insane.

He saw the bright yellow wedge of light as it moved in random patterns through the mauve, always getting closer. He knew he could not run, the movement would betray him, the specter light finding him instantly. Fear choked the maniac. The specter light had pursued him through innocence and humility and nine other emotional obfuscations he had tried. He had to do something, get them off his scent. But he was alone on this level. It had been closed down some time before, to purge it of residue emotions. Had he not been so terribly confused after the killings, had he not been drowning in disorientation, he would never have trapped himself on a closed level.

Now that he was here, there was nowhere to hide, nowhere to escape the specter light that would systematically hunt him down. Then they would purge *him*.

The maniac took the one final chance; he closed down his mind, all seven brains, even as the mauve level was closed down. He shut off all thought, banked the fires of emotion, broke the neural circuits that fed power to his mind. Like a great machine phasing down from peak efficiency, his thoughts slackened and wilted and grew pale. Then there was a blank where he had been. Seven dog-heads slept.

The dragon had ceased to exist in terms of thought, and the specter light washed past him, finding nothing there to home in on. But those who sought the maniac were sane, not deranged as he was: their sanity was ordered, and in order they considered every exigency. The specter light was followed by heat-seeking beams, by mass-tallying sensors, by trackers that could hunt out the spoor of foreign matter on a closed-down level.

They found the maniac. Shut down like a sun gone cold, they located him, and transferred him; he was unaware of the movement; he was locked away in his own silent skulls.

But when he chose to open his thoughts again, in the timeless disorientation that follows a total shutdown, he found himself locked in stasis in a drainage ward on the 3rd Red Active Level. Then, from seven throats, he screamed.

The sound, of course, was lost in the throat baffles they had inserted, before he had turned himself back on. The emptiness of the sound terrified him even more.

He was imbedded in an amber substance that fit around him comfortably; had it been a much earlier era, on another world, in another continuum, it would have been simply a hospital bed with restraining straps. But the dragon was locked in stasis on a red level, crosswhen. His hospital bed was anti-grav, weightless, totally relaxing, feeding nutrients through his leathery hide along with depressants and toners. He was waiting to be drained.

Linah drifted into the ward, followed by Semph. Semph, the discoverer of the drain. And his most eloquent nemesis, Linah, who sought Public Elevation to the position of Proctor. They drifted down the rows of amber-encased patients: the toads, the tambour-lidded crystal cubes, the exoskeletals, the pseudopodal changers, and the seven-headed dragon. They paused directly in front and slightly above the maniac. He was able to look up at them; images seven times seen; but he was not able to make sound.

"If I needed a conclusive reason, here's one of the best," Linah said, inclining his head toward the maniac.

Semph dipped an analysis rod into the amber substance, withdrew it and made a hasty reading of the patient's condition. "If you needed a greater *warning*," Semph said quietly, "this would be one of the best."

"Science bends to the will of the masses," Linah said.

"I'd hate to have to believe that," Semph responded quickly. There was a tone in his voice that could not be named, but it undershadowed the aggressiveness of his words.

"I'm going to see to it, Semph; *believe it*. I'm going to have the Concord pass the resolution."

"Linah, how long have we known each other?"

"Since your third flux. My second."

"That's about right. Have I ever told you a lie, have I ever asked you to do something that would harm you?"

"No. Not that I can recall."

"Then why won't you listen to me *this* time?"

"Because I think you're wrong. I'm not a fanatic, Semph. I'm not making political hay with this. I feel very strongly that it's the best chance we've ever had."

"But disaster for everyone and everywhere else, all the way back, and God only knows how far across the parallax. We stop fouling our own nest, at the expense of all the other nests that ever were."

Linah spread his hands in futility. "Survival."

Semph shook his head slowly, with a weariness that was mirrored in his expression. "I wish I could drain *that*, too."

"Can't you?"

Semph shrugged. "I can drain *any*thing. But what we'd have left wouldn't be worth having."

The amber substance changed hue. It glowed deep within itself with a blue intensity. "The patient is ready," Semph said. "Linah, one more time. I'll beg if it'll do any good. Please. Stall till the next session. The Concord needn't do it *now*. Let me run some further tests, let me see how far back this garbage spews, how much damage it can cause. Let me prepare some reports."

Linah was firm. He shook his head in finality. "May I watch the draining with you?"

Semph let out a long sigh. He was beaten, and knew it. "Yes, all right."

The amber substance carrying its silent burden began to rise. It reached the level of the two men, and slid smoothly through the air between them. They drifted after the smooth container with the dog-headed dragon imbedded in it, and Semph seemed as though he wanted to say something else. But there was nothing to say.

The amber chrysalloid cradle faded and vanished, and the men became insubstantial and were no more. They all reappeared in the drainage chamber. The beaming stage was empty. The amber cradle settled down on it without sound, and the substance flowed away, vanishing as it uncovered the dragon.

The maniac tried desperately to move, to heave himself up. Seven heads twitched futilely. The madness in him overcame the depressants and he was consumed with frenzy, fury, crimson hate. But he could not move. It was all he could do to hold his shape.

Semph turned the band on his left wrist. It glowed from within, a deep gold. The sound of air rushing to fill a vacuum filled the chamber. The beaming stage was drenched in silver light that seemed to spring out of the air itself, from an unknown source. The dragon was washed by the silver light, and the seven great mouths opened once, exposing rings of fangs. Then his double-lidded eyes closed.

The pain within his heads was monstrous. A fearful wrenching that became the sucking of a million mouths. His very brains were pulled upon, pressured, compressed, and then purged.

Semph and Linah looked away from the pulsing body of the dragon to the drainage tank across the chamber. It was filling from the bottom as they watched. Filling with a nearly-colorless roiling cloud of smokiness, shot through with sparks. "Here it comes," Semph said, needlessly.

Linah dragged his eyes away from the tank. The dragon with seven dog heads was rippling. As though seen through shallow water, the maniac was beginning to alter. As the tank filled, the maniac found it more and more difficult to maintain his shape. The denser grew the cloud of sparkling matter in the tank, the less constant was the shape of the creature on the beaming stage.

Finally, it was impossible, and the maniac gave in. The tank filled more rapidly, and the shape quavered and altered and shrank and then there was a superimposition of the form of a man, over that of the seven-headed dragon. Then the tank reached three-quarters filled and the dragon became an underlying shadow, a hint, a suggestion of what had been there when the drainage began. Now the man-form was becoming more dominant by the second.

Finally, the tank was filled, and a normal man lay on the beaming stage, breathing heavily, eyes closed, muscles jumping involuntarily.

"He's drained," Semph said.

"Is it all in the tank?" Linah asked softly.

"No, none of it."

"Then..."

"This is the residue. Harmless. Reagents purged from a group of sensitives will neutralize it. The dangerous essences, the degenerate force-lines that make up the field...they're gone. Drained off already."

Linah looked disturbed, for the first time. "Where did it go?"

"Do you love your fellow man, tell me?"

"Please, Semph! I asked where it went…when it went?"

"And I asked if you cared at all about anyone else?"

"You know my answer…you know *me*! I want to know, tell me, at least what you know. Where…when…?"

"Then you'll forgive me, Linah, because I love my fellow man, too. Whenever he was, wherever he is; I have to, I work in an inhuman field, and I have to cling to that. So…you'll forgive me…"

"What are you going to…"

In Indonesia they have a phrase for it: Djam Karet—*the hour that stretches.*

In the Vatican's Stanza of Heliodorus, the second of the great rooms he designed for Pope Julius II, Raphael painted (and his pupils completed) a magnificent fresco representation of the historic meeting between Pope Leo I and Attila the Hun, in the year 452.

In this painting is mirrored the belief of Christians everywhere that the spiritual authority of Rome protected her in that desperate hour when the Hun came to sack and burn the Holy City. Raphael has painted in Saint Peter and Saint Paul, descending from Heaven to reinforce Pope Leo's intervention. His interpretation was an elaboration on the original legend, in which only the Apostle Peter was mentioned—standing behind Leo with a drawn sword. And the legend was an elaboration of what little facts have come down through antiquity relatively undistorted: Leo had no cardinals with him, and certainly no wraith Apostles. He was one of three in the deputation. The other two were secular dignitaries of the Roman state. The meeting did not take place—as legend would have us believe—just outside the gates of Rome, but in northern Italy, not far from what is today Peschiera.

Nothing more than this is known of the confrontation. Yet Attila, who had never been stopped, did not raze Rome. He turned back.

Djam Karet. The force-line field spewed out from a parallax center crosswhen, a field that had pulsed through time and space and the minds of men for twice ten thousand years. Then cut out suddenly, inexplicably, and Attila the Hun clapped his hands to his head, his mind twisting like rope within his skull. His eyes glazed, then cleared, and he breathed from deep in his chest. Then he signaled his army to turn back. Leo the Great thanked God and the living memory of Christ the Saviour. Legend added Saint Peter. Raphael added Saint Paul.

For twice ten thousand years—*Djam Karet*—the field had pulsed, and for a brief moment that could have been instants or years or millennia, it was cut off.

Legend does not tell the truth. More specifically, it does not tell *all* of the truth: forty years before Attila raided Italy, Rome had been taken and sacked by Alaric the Goth. *Djam Karet.* Three years after the retreat of Attila Rome was once more taken and sacked, by Gaiseric, king of all the Vandals.

There was a reason the garbage of insanity had ceased to flow through everywhere and everywhen from the drained mind of a seven-headed dragon…

Semph, traitor to his race, hovered before the Concord. His friend, the man who now sought his final flux, Linah, Proctored the hearing. He spoke softly, but eloquently, of what the great scientist had done.

"The tank was draining; he said to me, 'Forgive me, because I love my fellow man. Whenever he was, wherever he is; I have to, I work in an inhuman field, and I have to cling to that. So you'll forgive me.' Then he interposed himself."

The sixty members of the Concord, a representative from each race that existed in the center, bird-creatures and blue things and large-headed men and orange scents with cilia shuddering…all of them looked at Semph where he hovered. His body and head were crumpled like a brown paper bag. All hair was gone. His eyes were dim and watery. Naked, shimmering, he drifted slightly to one side, then a vagrant breeze in the wall-less chamber sent him back. He had drained himself.

"I ask for this Concord to affix sentence of final flux on this man. Though his interposition only lasted a few moments, we have no way of knowing what damage or unnaturalness it may have caused crosswhen. I submit that his intent was to overload the drain and thereby render it inoperative. This act, the act of a beast who would condemn the sixty races of the center to a future in which insanity still prevailed, is an act that can only be punished by termination."

The Concord blanked and meditated. A timeless time later they re-linked, and the Proctor's charges were upheld; his demand of sentence was fulfilled.

On the hushed shores of a thought, the papyrus man was carried in the arms of his friend, his executioner, the Proctor. There in the dusting quiet of an approaching night, Linah laid Semph down in the shadow of a sigh.

"Why did you stop me?" the wrinkle with a mouth asked.

Linah looked away across the rushing dark.

"Why?"

"Because here, in the center, there is a chance."

"And for them, all of them out there…no chance ever?"

Linah sat down slowly, digging his hands into the golden mist, letting it sift over his wrists and back into the waiting flesh of the world. "If we can begin it here, if we can pursue our boundaries outward, then perhaps one day, sometime, we can reach to the ends of time with that little chance. Until then, it is better to have one center where there is no madness."

Semph hurried his words. The end was rapidly striding for him. "You have sentenced them all. Insanity is a living vapor. A force. It can be bottled. The most potent genie in the most easily uncorked bottle. And you have condemned them to live with it always. In the name of love."

Linah made a sound that was not quite a word, but called it back. Semph touched his wrist with a tremble that had been a hand. Fingers melting into softness and warmth. "I'm sorry for you, Linah. Your curse is to be a true man. The world is made for strugglers. You never learned how to do that."

Linah did not reply. He thought only of the drainage that was eternal now. Set in motion and kept in motion by its necessity.

"Will you do a memorial for me?" Semph asked.

Linah nodded. "It's traditional."

Semph smiled softly. "Then do it for them; not for me. I'm the one who devised the vessel of their death, and I don't need it. But choose one of them; not a very important one, but one that will mean everything to them if they find it, and understand. Erect the memorial in my name to that one. Will you?"

Linah nodded.

"Will you?" Semph asked. His eyes were closed, and he could not see the nod.

"Yes. I will," Linah said. But Semph could not hear. The flux began and ended, and Linah was alone in the cupped silence of loneliness.

The statue was placed on a far planet of a far star in a time that was ancient while yet never having been born. It existed in the minds of men who would come later. Or never.

But if they did, they would know that hell was with them, that there was a Heaven that men called Heaven, and in it there was a center from which all madness flowed; and once within that center, there was peace.

In the remains of a blasted building that had been a shirt factory, in what had been Stuttgart, Friedrich Drucker found a many-colored box. Maddened by hunger and the memory of having eaten human flesh for weeks, the man tore at the lid of the box with the bloodied stubs of his fingers. As the box flew open, pressed at a certain point, cyclones rushed out past the terrified face of Friedrich Drucker. Cyclones and dark, winged, faceless shapes that streaked away into the night, followed by a last wisp of purple smoke smelling strongly of decayed gardenias.

But Friedrich Drucker had little time to ponder the meaning of the purple smoke, for the next day, World War IV broke out.

A BOY AND HIS DOG

1970 Nebula Award: Best Novella
film – 1976 Hugo Award: Best Dramatic Presentation

I

I WAS OUT with Blood, my dog. It was his week for annoying me; he kept calling me Albert. He thought that was pretty damned funny. Payson Terhune: ha ha.

I'd caught a couple of water rats for him, the big green and ocher ones, and someone's manicured poodle, lost off a leash in one of the downunders.

He'd eaten pretty good, but he was cranky. "Come on, son of a bitch," I demanded, "find me a piece of ass."

Blood just chuckled, deep in his dog-throat. "You're funny when you get horny," he said.

Maybe funny enough to kick him upside his sphincter asshole, that refugee from a dingo-heap.

"Find! I ain't kidding!"

"For shame, Albert. After all I've taught you. Not 'I *ain't* kidding.' I'm *not* kidding."

He knew I'd reached the edge of my patience. Sullenly, he started casting. He sat down on the crumbled remains of the curb, and his eyelids flickered and closed, and his hairy body tensed. After a while he settled down on his front paws, and scraped them forward till he was lying flat, his shaggy head on the outstretched paws. The tenseness left him and he began trembling, almost the way he trembled just preparatory to scratching a flea. It went on that way for almost a quarter of an hour, and finally he rolled over and lay on his back, his naked belly toward the night sky, his front paws folded mantislike, his hind legs extended and open. "I'm sorry," he said. "There's nothing."

I could have gotten mad and booted him, but I knew he had tried. I wasn't happy about it, I really wanted to get laid, but what could I do? "Okay," I said, with resignation, "forget it."

He kicked himself onto his side and quickly got up.

"What do you want to do?" he asked.

"Not much we *can* do, is there?" I was more than a little sarcastic. He sat down again, at my feet, insolently humble.

I leaned against the melted stub of a lamppost, and thought about girls. It was painful. "We can always go to a show," I said. Blood looked around the street, at the pools of shadow lying in the weed-overgrown craters, and didn't say anything. The whelp was waiting for me to say okay, let's go. He liked movies as much as I did.

"Okay, let's go."

He got up and followed me, his tongue hanging, panting with happiness. Go ahead and laugh, you eggsucker. No popcorn for *you*!

Our Gang was a roverpak that had never been able to cut it simply foraging, so they'd opted for comfort and gone a smart way to getting it. They were movie-oriented kids, and they'd taken over the turf where the Metropole Theater was located. No one tried to bust their turf, because we all needed the movies, and as long as Our Gang had access to films, and did a better job of keeping the films going, they provided a service, even for solos like me and Blood. *Especially* for solos like us.

They made me check my .45 and the Browning .22 long at the door. There was a little alcove right beside the ticket booth. I bought my tickets first; it cost me a can of Oscar Mayer Philadelphia Scrapple for me, and a tin of sardines for Blood. Then the Our Gang guards with the Bren guns motioned me over to the alcove and I checked my heat. I saw water leaking from a broken pipe in the ceiling and I told the checker, a kid with big leathery warts all over his face and lips, to move my weapons where it was dry. He ignored me. "Hey you! Motherfuckin' toad, move my stuff over the other side…it goes to rust fast…an' it picks up any spots, man, I'll break your bones!"

He started to give me jaw about it, looked at the guards with the Brens, knew if they tossed me out I'd lose my price of admission whether I went in or not, but they weren't looking for any action, probably understrength, and gave him the nod to let it pass, to do what I said. So the toad moved my Browning to the other end of the gun rack, and pegged my .45 under it.

Blood and me went into the theater.

"I want popcorn."

"Forget it."

"Come on, Albert. Buy me popcorn."

"I'm tapped out. You can live without popcorn."

"You're just being a shit."

I shrugged: sue me.

We went in. The place was jammed. I was glad the guards hadn't tried to take anything but guns. My spike and knife felt reassuring, lying-up in their oiled sheaths at the back of my neck. Blood found two together, and we moved into the row, stepping on feet. Someone cursed and I ignored him. A Doberman growled. Blood's fur stirred, but he let it pass. There was always *some* hardcase on the muscle, even on neutral ground like the Metropole.

(I heard once about a get-it-on they'd had at the old Loew's Granada, on the South Side. Wound up with ten or twelve rovers and their mutts dead, the theater burned down and a couple of good Cagney films lost in the fire. After that was when the roverpaks had got up the agreement that movie houses were sanctuaries. It was better now, but there was always somebody too messed in the mind to come soft.)

It was a triple feature. *Raw Deal* with Dennis O'Keefe, Claire Trevor, Raymond Burr and Marsha Hunt was the oldest of the three. It'd been made in 1948, eighty-six years ago; god only knows how the damn thing'd hung together all that time; it slipped sprockets and they had to stop the movie all the time to re-thread it. But it was a good movie. About this solo who'd been japped by his roverpak and was out to get revenge. Gangsters, mobs, a lot of punching and fighting. Real good.

The middle flick was a thing made during the Third War, in '92, twenty-seven years before I was even born, thing called *Smell of a Chink*. It was mostly gut-spilling and some nice hand-to-hand. Beautiful scene of skirmisher greyhounds equipped with napalm throwers, jellyburning a Chink town. Blood dug it, even though we'd seen this flick before. He had some kind of phony shuck going that these were ancestors of his, and *he* knew and *I* knew he was making it up.

"Wanna burn a baby, hero?" I whispered to him. He got the barb and just shifted in his seat, didn't say a thing, kept looking pleased as the dogs worked their way through the town. I was bored stiff.

I was waiting for the main feature.

Finally it came on. It was a beauty, a beaver flick made in the late 1970s. It was called *Big Black Leather Splits*. Started right out very good. These two blondes in black leather corsets and boots laced all the way up to their crotches, with whips and masks, got this skinny guy down and one of the chicks sat on his face while the other one went down on him. It got really hairy after that.

All around me there were solos playing with themselves. I was about to jog it a little myself when Blood leaned across and said, real soft, the way he does when he's onto something unusually smelly, "There's a chick in here."

"You're nuts," I said.

"I tell you I smell her. She's in here, man."

Without being conspicuous, I looked around. Almost every seat in the theater was taken with solos or their dogs. If a chick had slipped in there'd have been a riot. She'd have been ripped to pieces before any single guy could have gotten into her. "Where?" I asked, softly. All around me, the solos were beating-off, moaning as the blondes took off their masks and one of them worked the skinny guy with a big wooden ram strapped around her hips.

"Give me a minute," Blood said. He was really concentrating. His body was tense as a wire. His eyes were closed, his muzzle quivering. I let him work.

It was possible. Just maybe possible. I knew that they made really dumb flicks in the downunders, the kind of crap they'd made back in the 1930s and '40s, real clean stuff with even married people sleeping in twin beds. Myrna Loy and George Brent kind of flicks. And I knew that, once in a while, a chick from one of the really strict middle-class downunders would cumup, to see what a hairy flick was like. I'd heard about it, but it'd never happened in any theater *I'd* ever been in.

And the chances of it happening in the Metropole, particularly, were slim. There was a lot of twisty trade came to the Metropole. Now, understand, I'm not specially prejudiced against guys corning one another… hell, I can understand it. There just aren't enough chicks anywhere. But I can't cut the jockey-and-boxer scene because it gets some weak little boxer hanging on you, getting jealous, you have to hunt for him and all he thinks he has to do is bare his ass to get all the work done for him. It's as bad as having a chick dragging along behind. Made for a lot of bad blood and fights in the bigger roverpaks, too. So I just never swung that way. Well, not *never*, but not for a long time.

So with all the twisties in the Metropole, I didn't think a chick would chance it. Be a toss-up who'd tear her apart first: the boxers or the straights.

And if she *was* here, why couldn't any of the other dogs smell her...?

"Third row in front of us," Blood said. "Aisle seat. Dressed like a solo."

"How's come *you* can whiff her and no other dog's caught her?"

"You forget who I am, Albert."

"I didn't forget, I just don't believe it."

Actually, bottom-line, I guess I *did* believe it. When you'd been as dumb as I'd been and a dog like Blood'd taught me so much, a guy came to believe *everything* he said. You don't argue with your teacher.

Not when he'd taught you how to read and write and add and subtract and everything else they used to know that meant you were smart (but doesn't mean much of anything now, except it's good to know it, I guess).

(The reading's a pretty good thing. It comes in handy when you can find some canned goods someplace, like in a bombed-out supermarket; makes it easier to pick out stuff you like when the pictures are gone off the labels. Couple of times the reading stopped me from taking canned beets. Shit, I *hate* beets!)

So I guess I *did* believe why he could whiff a maybe chick in there, and no other mutt could. He'd told me all about *that* a million times. It was his favorite story. History he called it. Christ, I'm not *that* dumb! I knew what history was. That was all the stuff that happened before now.

But I liked hearing history straight from Blood, instead of him making me read one of those crummy books he was always dragging in. And *that* particular history was all about him, so he laid it on me over and over, till I knew it by heart...no, the word was *rote*. Not *wrote*, like writing, that was something else. I knew it by rote, means you got it word-for-word.

And when a mutt teaches you everything you know, and he tells you something rote, I guess finally you *do* believe it. Except I'd never let that leg-lifter know it.

II

What he'd told me rote was:

Over sixty-five years ago, in Los Angeles, before the Third War even got going completely, there was a man named Buesing who lived in Cerritos. He raised dogs as watchmen and sentries and attackers. Dobermans,

Danes, schnauzers and Japanese Akitas. He had one four-year-old German shepherd bitch named Ginger. She worked for the Los Angeles Police Department's narcotics division. She could smell out marijuana. No matter how well it was hidden. They ran a test on her: there were 25,000 boxes in an auto parts warehouse. Five of them had been planted with marijuana sealed in cellophane, wrapped in tin foil and heavy brown paper, and finally hidden in three separate sealed cartons. Within seven minutes Ginger found all five packages. At the same time that Ginger was working, ninety-two miles farther north, in Santa Barbara, cetologists had drawn and amplified dolphin spinal fluid and injected it into chacma baboons and dogs. Altering surgery and grafting had been done. The first successful product of this cetacean experimentation had been a two-year-old male puli named Ahbhu, who had communicated sense-impressions telepathically. Cross-breeding and continued experimentation had produced the first skirmisher dogs, just in time for the Third War. Telepathic over short distances, easily trained, able to track gasoline or troops or poison gas or radiation when linked with their human controllers, they had become the shock commandos of a new kind of war. The selective traits had bred true. Dobermans, greyhounds, Akitas, pulis and schnauzers had become steadily more telepathic.

Ginger and Ahbhu had been Blood's ancestors.

He had told me so, a thousand times. Had told me the story just that way, in just those words, a thousand times, as it had been told to him. I'd never believed him till now.

Maybe the little bastard *was* special.

I checked out the solo scrunched down in the aisle seat three rows ahead of me. I couldn't tell a damned thing. The solo had his (her?) cap pulled way down, fleece jacket pulled way up.

"Are you sure?"

"As sure as I can be. It's a girl."

"If it is, she's playing with herself just like a guy."

Blood snickered. "Surprise," he said sarcastically.

The mystery solo sat through *Raw Deal* again. It made sense, if that was a girl. Most of the solos and all of the members of roverpaks left after the beaver flick. The theater didn't fill up much more, it gave the streets time to empty, he/she could make his/her way back to wherever he/she had come from. I sat through *Raw Deal* again myself. Blood went to sleep.

When the mystery solo got up, I gave him/her time to get weapons if any'd been checked, and start away. Then I pulled Blood's big shaggy ear and said, "Let's do it." He slouched after me, up the aisle.

I got my guns and checked the street. Empty.

"Okay, nose," I said, "where'd he go?"

"Her. To the right."

I started off, loading the Browning from my bandolier. I still didn't see anyone moving among the bombed-out shells of the buildings. This section of the city was crummy, really bad shape. But then, with Our Gang running the Metropole, they didn't have to repair anything else to get their livelihood. It was ironic; the Dragons had to keep an entire power plant going to get tribute from the other roverpaks; Ted's Bunch had to mind the reservoir; the Bastinados worked like fieldhands in the marijuana gardens; the Barbados Blacks lost a couple of dozen members every year cleaning out the radiation pits all over the city; and Our Gang only had to run that movie house.

Whoever their leader had been, however many years ago it had been that the roverpaks had started forming out of foraging solos, I had to give it to him: he'd been a flinty sharp mother. He knew what services to deal in.

"She turned off here," Blood said.

I followed him as he began loping toward the edge of the city and the bluish-green radiation that still flickered from the hills. I knew he was right, then. The only things out here were screamers and the access dropshaft to the downunder. It was a girl, all right.

The cheeks of my ass tightened as I thought about it. I was going to get laid. It had been almost a month, since Blood had whiffed that solo chick in the basement of the Market Basket. She'd been filthy, and I'd gotten the crabs from her, but she'd been a woman, all right, and once I'd tied her down and clubbed her a couple of times she'd been pretty good. She'd liked it, too, even if she did spit on me and tell me she'd kill me if she ever got loose. I left her tied up, just to be sure. She wasn't there when I went back to look, week before last.

"Watch out," Blood said, dodging around a crater almost invisible against the surrounding shadows. Something stirred in the crater.

Trekking across the nomansland, I realized why it was that all but a handful of solos or members of roverpaks were guys. The War had killed off most of the girls, and that was the way it always was in wars...at least that's what Blood told me. The things getting born were seldom male *or* female, and had to be smashed against a wall as soon as they were pulled out of the mother.

The few chicks who hadn't gone downunder with the middle-classers were hard, solitary bitches like the one in the Market Basket; tough and stringy and just as likely to cut off your meat with a razor blade once they let you get in. Scuffling for a piece of ass had gotten harder and harder, the older I'd gotten.

But every once in a while a chick got tired of being roverpak property, or a raid was got-up by five or six roverpaks and some unsuspecting downunder was taken, or—like this time, yeah—some middle-class chick from a downunder got hot pants to find out what a beaver flick looked like, and cumup.

I was going to get laid. Oh boy, I couldn't wait!

III

Out here it was nothing but empty corpses of blasted buildings. One entire block had been stomped flat, like a steel press had come down from Heaven and given one solid wham! and everything was powder under it. The chick was scared and skittish, I could see that. She moved erratically, looking back over her shoulder and to either side. She knew she was in dangerous country. Man, if she'd only known *how* dangerous.

There was one building standing all alone at the end of the smashflat block, like it had been missed and chance let it stay. She ducked inside and a minute later I saw a bobbing light. Flashlight? Maybe.

Blood and I crossed the street and came up into the blackness surrounding the building. It was what was left of a YMCA.

That meant "Young Men's Christian Association." Blood had taught me to read.

So what the hell was a young men's christian association? Sometimes being able to read makes more questions than if you were stupid.

I didn't want her getting out; inside there was as good a place to screw her as any, so I put Blood on guard right beside the steps leading up into the shell, and I went around the back. All the doors and windows had been blown out, of course. It wasn't no big trick getting in. I pulled myself up to the ledge of a window, and dropped down inside. Dark inside. No noise, except the sound of her, moving around on the other side of the old YMCA. I didn't know if she was heeled or not, and I wasn't about to take any chances. I bowslung the Browning and took out the .45 automatic. I didn't have to snap back the action—there was always a slug in the chamber.

I started moving carefully through the room. It was a locker room of some kind. There was glass and debris all over the floor, and one entire row of metal lockers had the paint blistered off their surfaces; the flash blast had caught them through the windows, a lot of years ago. My sneakers didn't make a sound coming through the room.

The door was hanging on one hinge, and I stepped over—through the inverted triangle. I was in the swimming pool area. The big pool was empty, with tiles buckled down at the shallow end. It stunk bad in there; no wonder, there were dead guys, or what was left of them, along one wall. Some lousy cleaner-up had stacked them, but hadn't buried them. I pulled my bandanna up around my nose and mouth and kept moving.

Out the other side of the pool place, and through a little passage with popped light bulbs in the ceiling. I didn't have any trouble seeing. There was moonlight coming through busted windows and a chunk was out of the ceiling. I could hear her real plain now, just on the other side of the door at the end of the passage. I hung close to the wall, and stepped down to the door. It was open a crack, but blocked by a fall of lath and plaster from the wall. It would make noise when I went to pull it open, that was for certain. I had to wait for the right moment.

Flattened against the wall, I checked out what she was doing in there. It was a gymnasium, big one, with climbing ropes hanging down from the ceiling. She had a squat, square, eight-cell flashlight sitting up on the croup of a vaulting horse. There were parallel bars and a horizontal bar about eight feet high, the tempered steel all rusty now. There were swinging rings and a trampoline and a big wooden balancing beam. Over to one side there were wall-bars and balancing benches, horizontal and oblique ladders, and a couple of stacks of vaulting boxes. I made a note to remember this joint. It was better for working out than the jerry-rigged gym I'd set up in an old auto wrecking yard. A guy has to keep in shape, if he's going to be a solo.

She was out of her disguise. Standing there in the skin, shivering. Yeah, it was chilly, and I could see a pattern of chicken-skin all over her. She was maybe five-six or -seven, with nice tits and kind of skinny legs. She was brushing out her hair. It hung way down the back. The flashlight didn't make it clear enough to tell if she had red hair or chestnut, but it wasn't blonde, which was good, and that was because I dug redheads. She had nice tits, though. I couldn't see her face, the hair was hanging down all smooth and wavy and cut off her profile.

The crap she'd been wearing was thrown around on the floor, and what she was going to put on was up on the vaulting horse. She was standing in little shoes with a kind of funny heel on them.

I couldn't move. I suddenly realized I couldn't move. She was nice, really nice. I was getting a real big kick out of just standing there and seeing the way her waist fell inward and her hips fell outward, the way the muscles at the side of her tits pulled up when she reached to the top of her head to brush all that hair down. It was really weird the kick I was getting out of standing and just staring at a chick do that. Kind of very, well, woman stuff. I liked it a lot.

I'd never stopped and just looked at a chick like that. All the ones I'd ever seen had been scumbags that Blood had smelled out for me, and I'd snatch'n'grabbed them. Or the big chicks in the beaver flicks. Not like this one, kind of soft and very smooth, even with the goose bumps. I could have watched her all night.

She put down the brush, and reached over and took a pair of panties off the pile of clothes and wriggled into them. Then she got her bra and put it on. I never knew the way chicks did it. She put it on backwards around her waist, and it had a hook on it. Then she slid it around till the cups were in front, and kind of pulled it up under and scooped herself into it, first one, then the other; then she pulled the straps over her shoulder. She reached for her dress, and I nudged some of the lath and plaster aside, and grabbed the door to give it a yank.

She had the dress up over her head, and her arms up inside the material, and when she stuck her head in, and was all tangled there for a second, I yanked the door and there was a crash as chunks of wood and plaster fell out of the way, and a heavy scraping, and I jumped inside and was on her before she could get out of the dress.

She started to scream, and I pulled the dress off her with a ripping sound, and it all happened for her before she knew what that crash and scrape was all about.

Her face was wild. Just wild. Big eyes: I couldn't tell what color they were because they were in shadow. Real fine features, a wide mouth, little nose, cheekbones just like mine, real high and prominent, and a dimple in her right cheek. She stared at me really scared.

And then...and this is really weird...I felt like I should *say* something to her. I don't know what. Just something. It made me uncomfortable, to see her scared, but what the hell could I do about *that*, I mean, I was going to rape her, after all, and I couldn't very well tell her not to be shrinky about it. She was the one cumup, after all. But even so, I wanted to say hey, don't be scared, I just want to lay you. (That never happened before. I never wanted to *say* anything to a chick, just get in, and that was that.)

But it passed, and I put my leg behind hers and tripped her back, and she went down in a pile. I leveled the .45 at her, and her mouth kind of opened in a little o shape. "Now I'm gonna go over there and get one of them wrestling mats, so it'll be better, comfortable, uh-huh? You make a move off that floor and I shoot a leg out from under you, and you'll get screwed just the same, except you'll be without a leg." I waited for her to let me know she was onto what I was saying, and she finally nodded real slow, so I kept the automatic on her, and went over to the big dusty stack of mats, and pulled one off.

I dragged it over to her, and flipped it so the cleaner side was up, and used the muzzle of the .45 to maneuver her onto it. She just sat there on the mat, with her hands behind her, and her knees bent, and stared at me.

I unzipped my pants and started pulling them down off one side, when I caught her looking at me real funny. I stopped with the jeans. "What're *you* lookin' at?"

I was mad. I didn't know why I was mad, but I was.

"What's your name?" she asked. Her voice was very soft, and kind of furry, like it came up through her throat that was all lined with fur or something.

She kept looking at me, waiting for me to answer.

"Vic," I said. She looked like she was waiting for more.

"Vic what?"

I didn't know what she meant for a minute, then I did. "Vic. Just Vic. That's all."

"Well, what're your mother and father's names?"

Then I started laughing, and working my jeans down again. "Boy, are you a dumb bitch," I said, and laughed some more. She looked hurt. It made me mad again. "Stop lookin' like that, or I'll bust out your teeth!"

She folded her hands in her lap.

I got the pants around my ankles. They wouldn't come off over the sneakers. I had to balance on one foot and scuff the sneaker off the other foot. It was tricky, keeping the .45 on her and getting the sneaker off at the same time. But I did it.

I was standing there buck-naked from the waist down and she had sat forward a little, her legs crossed, hands still in her lap. "Get that stuff off," I said.

She didn't move for a second, and I thought she was going to give me trouble. But then she reached around behind and undid the bra. Then she tipped back and slipped the panties off her ass.

Suddenly, she didn't look scared any more. She was watching me very close, and I could see her eyes were blue now. Now this is the really weird thing…

I couldn't do it. I mean, not exactly. I mean, I *wanted* to fuck her, see, but she was all soft and pretty and she kept *looking* at me, and no solo I ever met would believe me, but I heard myself *talking* to her, still standing there like some kind of wetbrain, one sneaker off and jeans down around my ankles. "What's *your* name?"

"Quilla June Holmes."

"That's a weird name."

"My mother says it's not that uncommon, back in Oklahoma."

"That where your folks come from?"

She nodded. "Before the Third War."

"They must be pretty old by now."

"They are, but they're okay. I guess."

We were just frozen there, talking to each other. I could tell she was cold, because she was shivering. "Well," I said, sort of getting ready to drop down beside her, "I guess we better—"

Damn it! That damned Blood! Right at that moment he came crashing in from outside. Came skidding through the lath, and plaster, raising dust, slid along on his ass till he got to us. "*Now* what?" I demanded.

"Who're you talking to?" the girl asked.

"Him. Blood."

"*The dog!?!*"

Blood stared at her and then ignored her. He started to say something but the girl interrupted him. "Then it's true what they say…you can all talk to animals…"

"You going to listen to her all night, or do you want to hear why I came in?"

"Okay, why're you here?"

"You're in trouble, Albert."

"Come *on*, forget the mickeymouse. What's up?"

Blood twisted his head toward the front door of the YMCA. "Roverpak. Got the building surrounded. I make it fifteen or twenty, maybe more."

"How the hell'd they know we was here?"

Blood looked chagrined. He dropped his head.

"Well?"

"Some other mutt must've smelled her in the theater."

"Great."

"Now what?"

"Now we stand 'em off, that's what. You got any better suggestions?"

"Just one."

I waited. He grinned.

"Pull your pants up."

IV

The girl, this Quilla June, was pretty safe. I made her a kind of a shelter out of wrestling mats, maybe a dozen of them. She wouldn't get hit by a stray bullet, and if they didn't go right for her, they wouldn't find her. I climbed one of the ropes hanging down from the girders and laid out up there with the Browning and a couple of handfuls of reloads. I wished to God I'd had an automatic, a Bren or a Thompson. I checked the .45, made sure it was full, with one in the chamber, and set the extra clips down on the girder. I had a clear line-of-fire all around the gym.

Blood was lying in shadow right near the front door. He'd suggested I try and pick off any dogs with the roverpak first, if I could. That would allow him to operate freely.

That was the least of my worries.

I'd wanted to hole up in another room, one with only a single entrance, but I had no way of knowing if the rovers were already in the building, so I did the best I could with what I had.

Everything was quiet. Even that Quilla June. It'd taken me valuable minutes to convince her she'd damned well better hole up and not make any noise; she was better off with me than with twenty of *them*. "If you ever wanna see your mommy and daddy again," I warned her. After that she didn't give me no trouble, packing her in with mats.

Quiet.

Then I heard two things, both at the same time. From back in the swimming pool, I heard boots crunching plaster. Very soft. And from one side of the front door, I heard a tinkle of metal striking wood. So they were going to try a yoke. Well, I was ready.

Quiet again.

I sighted the Browning on the door to the pool room. It was still open from when I'd come through. Figure him at maybe five-ten, and drop the sights a foot and a half, and I'd catch him in the chest. I'd learned long ago you don't try for the head. Go for the widest part of the body: the chest and stomach. The trunk.

Suddenly, outside, I heard a dog bark, and part of the darkness near the front door detached itself and moved inside the gym. Directly opposite Blood. I didn't move the Browning.

The rover at the front door moved a step along the wall, away from Blood. Then he cocked back his arm and threw something—a rock, a piece of metal, something—across the room to draw fire. I didn't move the Browning.

When the thing he'd thrown hit the floor, two rovers jumped out of the swimming pool door, one on either side of it, rifles down, ready to spray. Before they could open up, I'd squeezed off the first shot, tracked across and put a second shot into the other one. They both went down. Dead hits, right in the heart. Bang, they were down, neither one moved.

The mother by the door turned to split, and Blood was on him. Just like that, out of the darkness, riiiip!

Blood leaped, right over the crossbar of the guy's rifle held at ready, and sank his fangs into the rover's throat. The guy screamed, and Blood dropped, carrying a piece of the guy with him. The guy was making awful bubbling sounds and went down on one knee. I put a slug into his head, and he fell forward.

It went quiet again.

Not bad. Not bad atall atall. Three takeouts and they still didn't know our positions. Blood had fallen back into the murk by the entrance. He didn't say a thing, but I knew what he was thinking: maybe that was three out of seventeen, or three out of twenty, or twenty-two. No way of knowing; we could be faced-off in here for a week and never know if we'd gotten them all, or some, or none. They could go and get poured full again, and I'd find myself run out of slugs and no food and that girl, that Quilla June, crying and making me divide my attention, and daylight— and they'd still be laying out there, waiting till we got hungry enough to do something dumb, or till we ran out of slugs; and then they'd cloud up and rain all over us.

A rover came dashing straight through the front door at top speed, took a leap, hit on his shoulders, rolled, came up going in a different direction, and snapped off three rounds into different corners of the room before I could track him with the Browning. By that time he was close enough under me where I didn't have to waste a .22 slug. I picked up the .45 without a sound and blew the back off his head. Slug went in neat, came out and took most of his hair with it. He fell right down.

"Blood! The rifle!"

Came out of the shadows, grabbed it up in his mouth and dragged it over to the pile of wrestling mats in the far corner. I saw an arm poke out from the mass of mats, and a hand grabbed the rifle, dragged it inside. Well, it was at least safe there, till I needed it. Brave little bastard: he scuttled over to the dead rover and started worrying the ammo bandolier off his body. It took him a while; he could have been picked off from the doorway or outside one of the windows, but he did it. Brave little bastard. I had to remember to get him something good to eat when we got out of this. I smiled, up there in the darkness: *if* we got out of this, I wouldn't have to worry about getting him something tender. It was lying all over the floor of that gymnasium.

Just as Blood was dragging the bandolier back into the shadows, two of them tried it with their dogs. They came through a ground floor window, one after another, hitting and rolling and going in opposite directions, as the dogs—a mother-ugly Akita, big as a house, and a Doberman bitch the color of a turd—shot through the front door and split in the unoccupied two directions. I caught one of the dogs, the Akita, with the .45, and it went down thrashing. The Doberman was all over Blood.

But firing, I'd given away my position. One of the rovers fired from the hip and .30-06 soft-nosed slugs spanged off the girders around me. I dropped the automatic, and it started to slip off the girder as I reached for the Browning. I made a grab for the .45 and that was the only thing saved me. I fell forward to clutch at it, it slipped away and hit the gym floor with a crash, and the rover fired at where I'd been. But I was flat on the girder, arm dangling, and the crash startled him. He fired at the sound, and right at that instant I heard another shot from a Winchester, and the other rover, who'd made it safe into the shadows, fell forward holding a big pumping hole in his chest. That Quilla June had shot him, from behind the mats.

I didn't even have time to figure out what the fuck was happening… Blood was rolling around with the Doberman and the sounds they were making were awful…the rover with the .30-06 chipped off another shot and hit the muzzle of the Browning, protruding over the side of the girder, and wham it was gone, falling down. I was naked up there without clout, and the sonofabitch was hanging back in shadow waiting for me.

Another shot from the Winchester, and the rover fired right into the mats. She ducked back behind, and I knew I couldn't count on her for anything more. But I didn't need it; in that second, while he was focused on her, I grabbed the climbing rope, flipped myself over the girder, and howling like a burnpit-screamer, went sliding down, feeling the rope cutting my palms. I got down far enough to swing, and kicked off. I swung back and forth, whipping my body three different ways each time, swinging out and over, way over, each time. The sonofabitch kept firing, trying to track a trajectory, but I kept spinning out of his line of fire. Then he was empty, and I kicked back as hard as I could, and came zooming in toward his corner of shadows, and let loose all at once and went ass-over-end into the corner, and there he was, and I went right into him and he spanged off the wall, and I was on top of him, digging my thumbs into his eyesockets. He was screaming and the dogs were screaming and that girl was screaming and I pounded the motherfucker's head against the floor till he stopped moving, then I grabbed up the empty .30-06 and whipped his head till I knew he wasn't gonna give me no more aggravation.

Then I found the .45 and shot the Doberman.

Blood got up and shook himself off. He was cut up bad. "Thanks," he mumbled, and went over to lie down in the shadows, to lick himself off.

I went and found that Quilla June, and she was crying. About all the guys we'd killed. Mostly about the one *she'd* killed. I couldn't get her to stop bawling so I cracked her across the face and told her she'd saved my life, and that helped some.

Blood came dragassing over. "How're we going to get out of this, Albert?"

"Let me think."

I thought and knew it was hopeless. No matter how many we got, there'd be more. And it was a matter of *macho* now. Their honor.

"How about a fire?" Blood suggested.

"Get away while it's burning?" I shook my head. "They'll have the place staked-out all around. No good."

"What if we don't leave? What if we burn up with it?"

I looked at him. Brave…and smart as hell.

V

We gathered all the lumber and mats and scaling ladders and vaulting boxes and benches and anything else that would burn, and piled the garbage against a wooden divider at one end of the gym. Quilla June found a can of kerosene in a storeroom, and we set fire to the whole damn pile. Then we followed Blood to the place he'd found for us. The boiler room way down under the YMCA. We all climbed into the empty boiler, and dogged down the door, leaving a release vent open for air. We had one mat in there with us, and all the ammo we could carry, and the extra rifles and sidearms the rovers'd had on them.

"Can you catch anything?" I asked Blood.

"A little. Not much. I'm reading one guy. The building's burning good."

"You be able to tell when they split?"

"Maybe. *If* they split."

I settled back. Quilla June was shaking from all that had happened. "Just take it easy," I told her. "By morning the place'll be down around our ears, and they'll go through the rubble and find a lot of dead meat, and maybe they won't look too hard for a chick's body. And everything'll be all right…if we don't get choked off in here."

She smiled, very thin, and tried to look brave. She was okay, that one. She closed her eyes and settled back on the mat and tried to sleep. I was beat. I closed my eyes, too.

"Can you handle it?" I asked Blood.

"I suppose. You better sleep."

I nodded, eyes still closed, and fell on my side. I was out before I could think about it.

When I came back, I found the girl, that Quilla June, snuggled up under my armpit, her arm around my waist, dead asleep. I could hardly breathe. It was like a furnace; hell, it *was* a furnace. I reached out a hand, and the ouch of the plating of the boiler was so damned hot I couldn't touch it. Blood was up on the mattress with us. That mat had been the only thing'd kept us from being singed good. He was asleep, head buried in his paws. She was asleep, still naked.

I put a hand on her tit. It was warm. She stirred and cuddled into me closer. I got a hard-on.

Managed to get my pants off, and rolled on top of her. She woke up fast when she felt me pry her legs apart, but it was too late by then. "Don't… *stop*…what are you doing…no, don't…"

But she was half-asleep, and weak, and I don't think she really wanted to fight me anyhow.

She cried when I broke her, of course, but after that it was okay. There was blood all over the wrestling mat. And Blood just kept sleeping.

It was really different. Usually, when I'd get Blood to track something down for me, it'd be grab it and punch it and pork it and get away fast before something bad could happen. But when she came, she rose up off the mat, and hugged me around the back so hard I thought she'd crack my ribs, and then she settled back down slow slow slow, like I do when I'm doing leg-lifts in the makeshift gym I rigged in the auto wrecking yard. And her eyes were closed, and she was relaxed-looking. And happy. I could tell.

We did it a lot of times, and after a while it was her idea, but I didn't say no. And then we lay out side-by-side and talked.

She asked me about how it was with Blood, and I told her how the skirmisher dogs had gotten telepathic, and how they'd lost the ability to hunt food for themselves, so the solos and roverpaks had to do it for them, and how dogs like Blood were good at finding chicks for solos like me. She didn't say anything to that.

I asked her about what it was like where she lived, in one of the downunders.

"It's nice. But it's always very quiet. Everyone is very polite to everyone else. It's just a small town."

"Which one you live in?"

"Topeka. It's real close to here."

"Yeah, I know. The access dropshaft is only about half a mile from here. I went out there once, to take a look around."

"Have you ever been in a downunder?"

"No. But I don't guess I want to be, either."

"Why? It's very nice. You'd like it."

"Shit."

"That's very crude."

"*I'm* very crude."

"Not all the time."

I was getting mad. "Listen, you ass, what's the matter with you? I grabbed you and pushed you around, I raped you half a dozen times, so what's so good about me, huh? What's the matter with you, don't you even have enough smarts to know when somebody's—"

She was smiling at me. "I didn't mind. I liked doing it. Want to do it again?"

I was really shocked. I moved away from her. "What the hell is wrong with you? Don't you know that a chick from a downunder like you can be really mauled by solos? Don't you know chicks get warnings from their parents in the downunders, 'Don't cumup, you'll get snagged by them dirty, hairy, slobbering solos!' Don't you know that?"

She put her hand on my leg and started moving it up, the fingertips just brushing my thigh. I got another hard-on. "My parents never said that about solos," she said. Then she pulled me over her again, and kissed me, and I couldn't stop from getting in her again.

God, it just went on like that for hours. After a while Blood turned around and said, "I'm not going to keep pretending I'm asleep. I'm hungry. And I'm hurt."

I tossed her off me—she was on top by this time—and examined him. The Doberman had taken a good chunk out of his right ear, and there was a rip right down his muzzle, and blood-matted fur on one side. He was a mess. "Jesus, man, you're a mess," I said.

"You're no fucking rose garden yourself, Albert!" he snapped. I pulled my hand back.

"Can we get out of here?" I asked him.

He cast around, and then shook his head. "I can't get any readings. Must be a pile of rubble on top of this boiler. I'll have to go out and scout."

We kicked that around for a while, and finally decided if the building was razed, and had cooled a little, the roverpak would have gone through the ashes by now. The fact that they hadn't tried the boiler indicated that we were probably buried pretty good. Either that, or the building was still smoldering overhead. In which case, they'd still be out there, waiting to sift the remains.

"Think you can handle it, the condition you're in?"

"I guess I'll *have* to, won't I?" Blood said. He was really surly. "I mean, what with you busy coitusing your brains out, there won't be much left for staying alive, will there?"

I sensed real trouble with him. He didn't like Quilla June. I moved around him and undogged the boiler hatch. It wouldn't open. So I braced my back against the side, and jacked my legs up, and gave it a slow, steady shove.

Whatever had fallen against it from outside resisted for a minute, then started to give, then tumbled away with a crash. I pushed the door open all the way, and looked out. The upper floors had fallen in on the basement, but by the time they'd given, they'd been mostly cinder and lightweight rubble. Everything was smoking out there. I could see daylight through the smoke.

I slipped out, burning my hands on the outside lip of the hatch. Blood followed. He started to pick his way through the debris. I could see that the boiler had been almost completely covered by the gunk that had dropped from above. Chances were good the roverpak had taken a fast look, figured we'd been fried, and moved on. But I wanted Blood to run a recon anyway. He started off, but I called him back. He came.

"What is it?"

I looked down at him. "I'll tell you what it is, man. You're acting very shitty."

"Sue me."

"Goddammit, dog, what's got your ass up?"

"Her. That nit chick you've got in there."

"So what? Big deal...I've had chicks before."

"Yeah, but never any that hung on like this one. I warn you, Albert, she's going to make trouble."

"Don't be dumb!" He didn't reply. Just looked at me with anger and then limped off to check out the scene. I crawled back inside and dogged the hatch. She wanted to make it again. I said I didn't want to; Blood had brought me down. I was bugged. And I didn't know which one to be pissed off at.

But God she was pretty.

She kind of pouted and settled back with her arms wrapped around her. "Tell me some more about the downunder," I said.

At first she was cranky, wouldn't say much, but after a while she opened up and started talking freely. I was learning a lot. I figured I could use it some time, maybe.

There were only a couple of hundred downunders in what was left of the United States and Canada. They'd been sunk on the sites of wells or mines or other kinds of deep holes. Some of them, out in the west, were in natural cave formations. They went way down, maybe two to five miles. They were like big caissons, stood on end. And the people who'd settled them were squares of the worst kind. Southern Baptists, Fundamentalists, lawanorder goofs, real middle-class squares with no taste for the wild life. And they'd gone back to a kind of life that hadn't existed for a hundred and fifty years. They'd gotten the last of the scientists to do the work, invent the how and why, and then they'd run them out. They didn't want any progress, they didn't want any dissent, they didn't want anything that would make waves. They'd had enough of that. The best time in the world had been just before the First War, and they figured if they could keep it like that, they could live quiet lives and survive. Shit! I'd go nuts in one of the downunders.

Quilla June smiled, and snuggled up again, and this time I didn't turn her off. She started touching me again, down there and all over, and then she said, "Vic?"

"Uh-huh."

"Have you ever been in love?"

"What?"

"In love? Have you ever been in love with a girl?"

"Well, I damn well guess I haven't!"

"Do you know what love is?"

"Sure. I guess I do."

"But if you've never been in love…?"

"Don't be dumb. I mean, I've never had a bullet in the head, and I know I wouldn't like it."

"You don't know what love is, I'll bet."

"Well, if it means living in a downunder, I guess I just don't wanna find out." We didn't go on with the conversation much after that. She pulled me down and we did it again. And when it was over, I heard Blood scratching at the boiler. I opened the hatch, and he was standing out there. "All clear," he said.

"You sure?"

"Yeah, yeah, I'm sure. Put your pants on," he said it with a sneer in the tone, "and come on out here. We have to talk some stuff."

I looked at him, and he wasn't kidding. I got my jeans and sneakers on, and climbed down out of the boiler.

He trotted ahead of me, away from the boiler over some blacksoot beams, and outside the gym. It was down. Looked like a rotted stump tooth.

"Now what's lumbering you?" I asked him.

He scampered up on a chunk of concrete till he was almost nose level with me.

"You're going dumb on me, Vic."

I knew he was serious. No Albert shit, straight Vic. "How so?"

"Last night, man. We could have cut out of there and left her for them. *That* would have been smart."

"I wanted her."

"Yeah, I know. That's what I'm talking about. It's today now, not last night. You've had her about a half a hundred times. Why're we hanging around?"

"I want some more."

Then he got angry. "Yeah, well, listen, chum…*I* want a few things myself. I want something to eat, and I want to get rid of this pain in my side, and I want away from this turf. Maybe they *don't* give up this easy."

"Take it easy. We can handle all that. Don't mean she can't go with us."

"*Doesn't* mean," he corrected me. "And so *that's* the new story. Now we travel three, is that right?"

I was getting really uptight myself. "You're starting to sound like a damn poodle!"

"And you're starting to sound like a boxer."

I hauled back to crack him one. He didn't move. I dropped the hand. I'd never hit Blood. I didn't want to start now.

"Sorry," he said, softly.

"That's okay."

But we weren't looking at each other.

"Vic, man, you've got a responsibility to me, you know."

"You don't have to tell me that."

"Well, I guess maybe I do. Maybe I have to remind you of some stuff. Like the time that burnpit-screamer came up out of the street and made a grab for you."

I shuddered. The motherfucker'd been green. Righteous stone green, glowing like fungus. My gut heaved, just thinking.

"And I went for him, right?"

I nodded. Right, mutt, right.

"And I could have been burned bad, and died, and that would've been all of it for me, right or wrong, isn't that true?" I nodded again. I was getting pissed off proper. I didn't like being made to feel guilty. It was a fifty-fifty with Blood and me. He knew that. "But I did it, right?" I remembered the way the green thing had screamed. Christ, it was all ooze and eyelashes.

"Okay, okay, don't hanger me."

"*Harangue*, not hanger."

"Well, WHATEVER!" I shouted. "Just knock off the crap, or we can forget the whole fucking arrangement!"

Then Blood blew. "Well, maybe we *should*, you simple *dumb putz*!"

"What's a *putz*, you little turd…is that something bad…yeah, it must be…you watch your fucking mouth, son of a bitch; or I'll kick your ass!"

We sat there and didn't talk for fifteen minutes. Neither one of us knew which way to go.

Finally, I backed off a little. I talked soft and I talked slow. I was about up to here with him, but told him I was going to do right by him, like I always had, and he threatened me, saying I'd damned well better because there were a couple of very hip solos making it around the city, and they'd be delighted to have a sharp tail-scent like him. I told him I didn't like being threatened, and he'd better watch his fucking step or I'd break his leg. He got furious and stalked off. I said screw you and went back to the boiler to take it out on that Quilla June again.

But when I stuck my head inside the boiler, she was waiting, with a pistol one of the dead rovers had supplied. She hit me good and solid over the right eye with it, and I fell straight forward across the hatch, and was out cold.

VI

"I told you she was no good." He watched me as I swabbed out the cut with disinfectant from my kit, and painted the gash with iodine. He smirked when I flinched.

I put away the stuff, and rummaged around in the boiler, gathering up all the spare ammo I could carry, and ditching the Browning in favor of the heavier .30-06. Then I found something that must've slipped out of her clothes.

It was a little metal plate, about three inches long and an inch-and-a-half high. It had a whole string of numbers on it, and there were holes in it, in random patterns. "What's this?" I asked Blood.

He looked at it, sniffed it.

"Must be an identity card of some kind. Maybe it's what she used to get out of the downunder."

That made my mind up.

I jammed it in a pocket and started out. Toward the access dropshaft.

"Where the hell are you going?" Blood yelled after me.

"Come on back, you'll get killed out there!"

"I'm hungry, dammit! I'm wounded!"

"Albert, you sonofabitch! Come back here!"

I kept right on walking. I was gonna find that bitch and brain her. Even if I had to go downunder to find her.

It took me an hour to walk to the access dropshaft leading down to Topeka. I thought I saw Blood following, but hanging back a ways. I didn't give a damn. I was mad.

Then, there it was. A tall, straight, featureless pillar of shining black metal. It was maybe twenty feet in diameter, perfectly flat on top, disappearing straight into the ground. It was a cap, that was all. I walked straight up to it, and fished around in my pocket for that metal card. Then something was tugging at my right pants leg.

"Listen, you moron, you can't go down there!"

I kicked him off, but he came right back.

"Listen to me!"

I turned around and stared at him.

Blood sat down; the powder puffed up around him. "Albert..."

"My name is Vic, you little eggsucker."

"Okay, okay, no fooling around. Vic." His tone softened. "Vic. Come on, man." He was trying to get through to me. I was really boiling, but he was trying to make sense. I shrugged, and crouched down beside him.

"Listen, man," Blood said, "this chick has bent you way out of shape. You *know* you can't go down there. It's all square and settled, and they know everyone; they hate solos. Enough roverpaks have raided downunder, and raped their women, and stolen their food, they'll have defenses set up. They'll *kill* you, Vic!"

"What the hell do you care? You're always saying you'd be better off without me." He sagged at that.

"Vic, we've been together almost three years. Good and bad. But this can be the worst. I'm scared, man. Scared you won't come back. And I'm hungry, and I'll have to go find some dude who'll take me on...and you know most solos are in paks now, I'll be low mutt. I'm not that young any more. And I'm hurt pretty bad."

I could dig it. He was talking sense. But all I could think of was how that bitch, that Quilla June, had rapped me. And then there were images of her soft tits, and the way she made little sounds when I was in her, and I shook my head, and knew I had to go get even.

"I got to do it, Blood. *I got to.*"

He breathed deep and sagged a little more. He knew it was useless. "You don't even see what she's done to you, Vic. That metal card, it's too easy, as if she *wanted* you to follow."

I got up. "I'll try to get back quick. Will you wait...?"

He was silent a long while, and I waited. Finally, he said, "For a while. Maybe I'll be here, maybe not."

I understood. I turned around and started walking around the pillar of black metal. Finally I found a slot in the pillar, and slipped the metal card into it. There was a soft humming sound, then a section of the pillar dilated. I hadn't even seen the lines of the sections. A circle opened and I took a step through. I turned and there was Blood, watching me. We looked at each other, all the while that pillar was humming.

"So long, Vic."

"Take care of yourself, Blood."

"Hurry back."

"Do my best."

"Yeah. Right."

Then I turned around and stepped inside. The access portal irised closed behind me.

VII

I should have known. I should have suspected. Sure, every once in a while a chick came up to see what it was like on the surface, what had happened to the cities; sure, it happened. Why, I'd believed her when she'd told me, cuddled up beside me in that steaming boiler, that she'd wanted to see what it was like when a girl did it with a guy, that all the flicks she'd seen in Topeka were sweet and solid and dull, and the girls in her school'd talked about beaver flicks, and one of them had a little eight-page comic book and she'd read it with wide eyes…sure, I'd believed her. It was logical. I should have suspected something when she left that metal I.D. plate behind. It was too easy. Blood'd tried to tell me. Dumb? Yeah!

The second that access iris swirled closed behind me, the humming got louder, and some cool light grew in the walls. Wall. It was a circular compartment with only two sides to the wall: *in*side and *out*side. The wall pulsed up light and the humming got louder, and the deckplate I was standing on dilated just the way the outside port had done. But I was standing there, like a mouse in a cartoon, and as long as I didn't look down I was cool, I wouldn't fall.

Then I started settling. Dropped through the floor, the iris closed overhead, I was dropping down the tube, picking up speed but not too much, just dropping steadily. Now I knew what a dropshaft was.

Down and down I went and every once in a while I'd see something like 10 LEV or ANTIPOLL 55 or BREEDER-CON or PUMP SE 6 on the wall; faintly I could make out the sectioning of an iris…but I never stopped dropping.

Finally, I dropped all the way to the bottom, and there was TOPEKA CITY LIMITS POP. 22,860 on the wall, and I settled down without any strain, bending a little from the knees to cushion the impact, but even that wasn't much.

I used the metal plate again, and the iris—a much bigger one this time—swirled open, and I got my first look at a downunder.

It stretched away in front of me, twenty miles to the dim shining horizon of tin can metal where the wall behind me curved and curved and curved till it made one smooth, encircling circuit and came back around around around to where I stood, staring at it. I was down at the bottom of a big metal tube that stretched up to a ceiling an eighth of a mile overhead, twenty miles across. And in the bottom of that tin can, someone had built a town that looked for all the world like a photo out of one of the water-logged books in the library on the surface. I'd seen a town like this in the books. Just like this. Neat little houses, and curvy little streets, and trimmed lawns, and a business section and everything else that a Topeka would have.

Except a sun, except birds, except clouds, except rain, except snow, except cold, except wind, except ants, except dirt, except mountains, except oceans, except big fields of grain, except stars, except the moon, except forests, except animals running wild, except…

Except freedom.

They were canned down here, like dead fish. Canned.

I felt my throat tighten up. I wanted to get out. Out! I started to tremble, my hands were cold and there was sweat on my forehead. This had been insane, coming down here. I had to get out. *Out!*

I turned around to get back in the dropshaft, and then it grabbed me.

That bitch Quilla June! I shoulda suspected!

The thing was low, and green, and boxlike, and had cables with mittens on the ends instead of arms, and it rolled on tracks, and it grabbed me.

It hoisted me up on its square flat top, holding me with them mittens on the cables, and I couldn't move, except to try kicking at the big glass eye in the front, but it didn't do any good. It didn't bust. The thing was only about four feet high, and my sneakers almost reached the ground, but not quite, and it started moving off into Topeka, hauling me along with it.

People were all over the place. Sitting in rockers on their front porches, raking their lawns, hanging around the gas station, sticking pennies in gumball machines, painting a white stripe down the middle of the road, selling newspapers on a corner, listening to an oompah band in a shell in a park, playing hopscotch and pussy-in-the-corner, polishing a fire engine, sitting on benches reading, washing windows, pruning bushes, tipping hats to ladies, collecting milk bottles in wire carrying-racks, grooming horses, throwing a stick for a dog to retrieve, diving into a communal swimming pool, chalking vegetable prices on a slate outside a grocery, walking hand-in-hand with a girl, all of them watching me go past on that metal motherfucker.

I could hear Blood speaking, saying just what he'd said before I'd entered the dropshaft: *It's all square and settled and they know everyone; they hate solos. Enough roverpaks have raided downunders, and raped their women and stolen their food, they'll have defenses set up. They'll* kill *you, Vic!*

Thanks, mutt.

Goodbye.

VIII

The green box tracked through the business section and turned in at a shopfront with the words BETTER BUSINESS BUREAU on the window. It rolled right inside the open door, and there were half a dozen men and old men and very old men in there, waiting for me. Also a couple of women. The green box stopped.

One of them came over and took the metal plate out of my hand. He looked at it, then turned around and gave it to the oldest of the old men, a withered toad wearing baggy pants and a green eyeshade and garters that held up the sleeves of his striped shirt. "Quilla June, Lew," the guy said to the old man. Lew took the metal plate and put it in the top left drawer of a rolltop desk. "Better take his guns, Aaron," the old coot said. And the guy who'd taken the plate cleaned me.

"Let him loose, Aaron," Lew said.

Aaron stepped around the back of the green box and something clicked, and the cable-mittens sucked back inside the box, and I got down off the thing. My arms were numb where the box had held me. I rubbed one, then the other, and I glared at them.

"Now, boy…" Lew started.

"Suck wind, asshole!"

The women blanched. The men tightened their faces.

"I told you it wouldn't work," another of the old men said to Lew.

"Bad business, this," said one of the younger ones.

Lew leaned forward in his straight-back chair and pointed a crumbled finger at me. "Boy, you better be nice."

"I hope all your fuckin' children are hare-lipped!"

"This is no good, Lew!" another man said.

"Guttersnipe," a woman with a beak snapped.

Lew stared at me. His mouth was a nasty little black line. I knew the sonofabitch didn't have a tooth in his crummy head that wasn't rotten and smelly. He stared at me with vicious little eyes. God, he was ugly, like a toad ready to snaffle a fly off the wall with his tongue. He was getting set to say something I wouldn't like. "Aaron, maybe you'd better put the sentry back on him." Aaron moved to the green box.

"Okay, hold it," I said, holding up my hand.

Aaron stopped, looked at Lew, who nodded. Then Lew leaned real far forward again, and aimed that bird-claw at me. "You ready to behave yourself, son?"

"Yeah, I guess."

"You'd better be dang sure."

"Okay. I'm *dang* sure. Also *fuckin'* sure!"

"And you'll watch your mouth."

I didn't reply. Old coot.

"You're a bit of an experiment for us, boy. We tried to get one of you down here other ways. Sent up some good folks to capture one of you little scuts, but they never came back. Figgered it was best to lure you down to us."

I sneered. That Quilla June. I'd take care of her!

One of the women, a little younger than Bird-Beak, came forward and looked into my face. "Lew, you'll never get this one to kowtow. He's a filthy little killer. Look at those eyes."

"How'd you like the barrel of a rifle jammed up your ass, bitch?" She jumped back. Lew was angry again. "Sorry," I said real quickly, "I don't like bein' called names. *Macho*, y'know?"

He settled back and snapped at the woman. "Mez, leave him alone. I'm tryin' to talk a bit of sense here. You're only making it worse."

Mez went back and sat with the others. Some Better Business Bureau these creeps were!

"As I was saying, boy: you're an experiment for us. We've been down here in Topeka close to thirty years. It's nice down here. Quiet, orderly, nice people, who respect each other, no crime, respect for the elders, and just all around a good place to live. We're growin' and we're prosperin'."

I waited.

"But, well, we find now that some of our folks can't have no more babies, and the women that do, they have mostly girls. We need some men. Certain special kind of men."

I started laughing. This was too good to be true. They wanted me for stud service. I couldn't stop laughing.

"Crude!" one of the women said, scowling.

"This's awkward enough for us, boy, don't make it no harder." Lew was embarrassed.

Here I'd spent most of Blood's and my time aboveground hunting up tail, and down here they wanted me to service the local ladyfolk. I sat down on the floor and laughed till tears ran down my cheeks.

Finally, I got up and said, "Sure. Okay. But if I do, there's a couple of things *I* want."

Lew looked at me close.

"The first thing I want is that Quilla June. I'm gonna fuck her blind, and then I'm gonna bang her on the head the way she did me!"

They huddled for a while, then came out and Lew said, "We can't tolerate any violence down here, but I s'pose Quilla June's as good a place to start as any. She's capable, isn't she, Ira?"

A skinny, yellow-skinned man nodded. He didn't look happy about it. Quilla June's old man, I bet.

"Well, let's get started," I said. "Line 'em up." I started to unzip my jeans.

The women screamed, the men grabbed me, and they hustled me off to a boarding house where they gave me a room, and they said I should get to know Topeka a little bit before I went to work because it was, uh, er, well, awkward, and they had to get the folks in town to accept what was going to have to be done...on the assumption, I suppose, that if I worked out okay they'd import a few more young bulls from aboveground and turn us loose.

So I spent some time in Topeka, getting to know the folks, seeing what they did, how they lived.

It was nice, real nice.

They rocked in rockers on the front porches, they raked their lawns, they hung around the gas station, they stuck pennies in gumball machines, they painted white stripes down the middle of the road, they sold newspapers on the corners, they listened to oompah bands in a shell in the park, they played hopscotch and pussy-in-the-corner, they polished fire engines, they sat on benches reading, they washed windows and pruned bushes, they tipped their hats to ladies, they collected milk bottles in wire carrying-racks, they groomed horses and threw sticks for their dogs to retrieve, they dove into the communal swimming pool, they chalked vegetable prices on a slate outside the grocery, they walked hand-in-hand with some of the ugliest chicks I've ever seen, *and they bored the ass offa me*.

Inside a week I was ready to scream.

I could feel that tin can closing in on me.

I could feel the weight of the earth over me.

They ate artificial shit: artificial peas and fake meat and make-believe chicken and ersatz corn and bogus bread, and it all tasted like chalk and dust to me.

Polite? Christ, you could puke from the lying, hypocritical crap they called civility. Hello Mr. This and Hello Mrs. That. And how are you? And how is little Janie? And how is business? Are you going to the sodality meeting Thursday? And I started gibbering in my room at the boarding house.

The clean, sweet, neat, lovely way they lived was enough to kill a guy. No wonder the men couldn't get it up and make babies that had balls instead of slots.

The first few days, everyone watched me like I was about to explode and cover their nice whitewashed fences with shit. But after a while, they got used to seeing me. Lew took me over to the Mercantile, and got me fitted out with a pair of bib overalls and a shirt that any solo could've spotted a mile away. That Mez, that dippy bitch who'd called me a killer, she started hanging around, finally said she wanted to cut my hair, make me look civilized. But I was hip to where she was at. Wasn't a bit of the mother in her.

"What'sa'matter, cunt," I pinned her. "Your old man isn't taking care of you?"

She tried to stick her fist in her mouth, and I laughed like a loon. "Go chop off *his* balls, baby. My hair stays the way it is." She cut and run. Gone like she had a diesel tail-pipe.

It went on like that for a while. Me just walking around, them coming and feeding me, keeping all their young meat out of my way till they got the town stacked-away for what was coming with me.

Jugged like that, my mind wasn't right for a while. I got all claustrophobed, clutched, went and sat under the porch in the dark at the rooming house. Then that passed, and I got piss-mean, snapped at them, then surly, then quiet, then just mud dull. Quiet.

Finally, I started getting hip to the possibilities of getting out of there. It began with me remembering the poodle I'd fed Blood one time. It had to come from a downunder. And it couldn't have got up through the dropshaft. So that meant there were other ways out.

They gave me pretty much the run of the town, as long as I kept my manners around me and didn't try anything sudden. That green sentry box was always somewhere nearby.

So I found the way out. Nothing so spectacular; it just had to be there, and I found it.

Then I found out where they kept my weapons, and I was ready. Almost.

IX

It was a week to the day when Aaron and Lew and Ira came to get me. I was pretty goofy by that time. I was sitting out on the back porch of the boarding house, smoking a corncob pipe with my shirt off, catching some sun. Except there wasn't no sun. Goofy.

They came around the house. "Morning, Vic," Lew greeted me. He was hobbling along with a cane, the old fart. Aaron gave me a big smile. The kind you'd give a big black bull about to stuff his meat into a good breed cow. Ira had a look that you could chip off and use in your furnace.

"Well, howdy, Lew. Mornin', Aaron, Ira."

Lew seemed right pleased by that.

Oh, you lousy bastards, just you wait!

"You 'bout ready to go meet your first lady?"

"Ready as I'll ever be, Lew," I said, and got up.

"Cool smoke, ain't it?" Aaron said.

I took the corncob out of my mouth. "Pure dee-light." I smiled. I hadn't even lit the fucking thing.

They walked me over to Marigold Street and, as we came up on a little house with yellow shutters and a white picket fence, Lew said, "This's Ira's house. Quilla June is his daughter."

"Well, land sakes," I said, wide-eyed.

Ira's lean jaw muscles jumped.

We went inside.

Quilla June was sitting on the settee with her mother, an older version of her, pulled thin as a withered muscle. "Miz Holmes," I said and made a little curtsey. She smiled. Strained, but smiled.

Quilla June sat with her feet right together, and her hands folded in her lap. There was a ribbon in her hair. It was blue.

Matched her eyes.

Something went thump in my gut.

"Quilla June," I said.

She looked up. "Mornin', Vic."

Then everyone sort of stood around looking awkward, and finally Ira began yapping and yipping about get in the bedroom and get this unnatural filth over with so they could go to Church and pray the Good Lord wouldn't Strike All Of Them Dead with a bolt of lightning in the ass, or some crap like that.

So I put out my hand, and Quilla June reached for it without looking up, and we went in the back, into a small bedroom, and she stood there with her head down.

"You didn't tell 'em, did you?" I asked.

She shook her head.

And suddenly, I didn't want to kill her at all. I wanted to hold her. Very tight. So I did. And she was crying into my chest, and making little fists beating on my back, and then she was looking up at me and running her words all together: "Oh, Vic, I'm sorry, so sorry, I didn't mean to, I had to, I was sent out to, I was so scared, and I love you, and now they've got you down here, and it isn't dirty, is it, it isn't the way my Poppa says it is, is it?"

I held her and kissed her and told her it was okay, and then I asked her if she wanted to come away with me, and she said yes yes yes she really did. So I told her I might have to hurt her Poppa to get away, and she got a look in her eyes that I knew real well.

For all her propriety, Quilla June Holmes didn't much like her prayer-shouting Poppa.

I asked her if she had anything heavy, like a candlestick or a club, and she said no. So I went rummaging around in that back bedroom and found a pair of her Poppa's socks in a bureau drawer. I pulled the big brass balls off the headboard of the bed and dropped them into the sock. I hefted it. Oh. Yeah.

She stared at me with big eyes. "What're you going to do?"

"You want to get out of here?"

She nodded.

"Then just stand back behind the door. No, wait a minute. I got a better idea. Get on the bed."

She lay down on the bed. "Okay," I said, "now pull up your skirt, pull off your pants, and spread out." She gave me a look of pure horror. "Do it," I said. "If you want out."

So she did it, and I rearranged her so her knees were bent and her legs open at the thighs, and I stood to one side of the door, and whispered to her, "Call your Poppa. Just him."

She hesitated a long moment, then she called out in a voice she didn't have to fake, "Poppa! Poppa, come here, please!" Then she clamped her eyes shut tight.

Ira Holmes came through the door, took one look at his secret desire, his mouth dropped open, I kicked the door closed behind him and walloped him as hard as I could. He squished a little, and spattered the bedspread, and went very down.

She opened her eyes when she heard the thunk! and when the stuff spattered her legs, she leaned over and puked on the floor. I knew she wouldn't be much good to me in getting Aaron into the room, so I opened the door, stuck my head around, looked worried, and said, "Aaron, would you come here a minute, please?" He looked at Lew, who was rapping with Mrs. Holmes about what was going on in the back bedroom, and when Lew nodded him on, he came into the room. He took a look at Quilla June's naked bush, at the blood on the wall and bedspread, at Ira on the floor, and opened his mouth to yell just as I whacked him. It took two more to get him down, and then I had to kick him in the chest to put him away. Quilla June was still puking.

I grabbed her by the arm and swung her up off the bed. At least she was being quiet about it, but man, did she stink.

"Come on!"

She tried to pull back, but I held on and opened the bedroom door. As I pulled her out, Lew stood up, leaning on his cane. I kicked the cane out from under the old fart and down he went in a heap. Mrs. Holmes was staring at us, wondering where her old man was. "He's back in there," I said, heading for the front door. "The Good Lord got him in the head."

Then we were out in the street, Quilla June stinking along behind me, dry-heaving and bawling and probably wondering what had happened to her underpants.

They kept my weapons in a locked case at the Better Business Bureau, and we detoured around by my boarding house where I pulled the crowbar I'd swiped from the gas station out from under the back porch. Then we cut across behind the Grange and into the business section, and straight into the BBB. There was a clerk who tried to stop me, and I split his gourd with the crowbar. Then I pried the latch off the cabinet in Lew's office and got the .30-06 and my .45 and all the ammo, and my spike and my knife and my kit, and loaded up. By that time Quilla June was able to make some sense.

"Where we gonna go, where we gonna go, oh Poppa Poppa Popp…!"

"Hey, listen, Quilla June, Poppa me no Poppas. You said you wanted to be with me…well, I'm goin'! *Up*, baby, and if you wanna go with me, you better stick close."

She was too scared to object.

I stepped out the front of the shopfront, and there was that green box sentry, coming on like a whippet. It had its cables out, and the mittens were gone. It had hooks.

I dropped to one knee, wrapped the sling of the .30-06 around my forearm, sighted clean, and fired dead at the big eye in the front. One shot, spang!

Hit that eye, the thing exploded in a shower of sparks, and the green box swerved and went through the front window of The Mill End Shoppe, screeching and crying and showering the place with flames and sparks. Nice.

I turned around to grab Quilla June, but she was gone. I looked off down the street, and here came all the vigilantes, Lew hobbling along with his cane like some kind of weird grasshopper.

And right then the shots started. Big, booming sounds. The .45 I'd given Quilla June. I looked up, and on the porch around the second floor, there she was, the automatic down on the railing like a pro, sighting into that mob and snapping off shots like maybe Wild Bill Elliott in a '40s Republic flick.

But dumb! Mother dumb! Wasting time on that, when we had to get away.

I found the outside staircase going up there, and took it three steps at a time. She was smiling and laughing, and every time she'd pick one of those boobs out of the pack her little tonguetip would peek out of the corner of her mouth, and her eyes would get all slick and wet and wham! down the boob would go.

She was really into it.

Just as I reached her, she sighted down on her scrawny mother. I slammed the back of her head, and she missed the shot, and the old lady did a little dance-step and kept coming. Quilla June whipped her head around at me, and there was kill in her eyes. "You made me miss." The voice gave me a chill.

I took the .45 away from her. Dumb. Wasting ammunition like that.

Dragging her behind me, I circled the building, found a shed out back, dropped down onto it, and had her follow. She was scared at first, but I said, "Chick can shoot her old lady as easy as you do shouldn't be worried about a drop this small." She got out on the ledge, other side of the railing and held on. "Don't worry," I said, "you won't wet your pants. You haven't got any."

She laughed, like a bird, and dropped. I caught her, we slid down the shed door, and took a second to see if that mob was hard on us. Nowhere in sight.

I grabbed Quilla June by the arm and started off toward the south end of Topeka. It was the closest exit I'd found in my wandering, and we made it in about fifteen minutes, panting and weak as kittens.

And there it was.

A big air-intake duct.

I pried off the clamps with the crowbar, and we climbed up inside. There were ladders going up. There had to be. It figured. Repairs. Keep it clean. Had to be. We started climbing.

It took a long, long time.

Quilla June kept asking me, from down behind me, whenever she got too tired to climb, "Vic, do you love me?" I kept saying yes. Not only because I meant it. It helped her keep climbing.

X

We came up a mile from the access dropshaft. I shot off the filter covers and the hatch bolts, and we climbed out. They should have known better down there. You don't fuck around with Jimmy Cagney.

They never had a chance.

Quilla June was exhausted. I didn't blame her. But I didn't want to spend the night out in the open; there were things out there I didn't like to think about meeting even in daylight. It was getting on toward dusk.

We walked toward the access dropshaft.

Blood was waiting.

He looked weak. But he'd waited.

I stooped down and lifted his head. He opened his eyes, and very softly he said, "Hey."

I smiled at him. Jesus, it was good to see him. "We made it back, man."

He tried to get up, but he couldn't. The wounds on him were in ugly shape. "Have you eaten?" I asked.

"No. Grabbed a lizard yesterday…or maybe it was day before. I'm hungry, Vic."

Quilla June came up then, and Blood saw her. He closed his eyes. "We'd better hurry, Vic," she said. "Please. They might come up from the dropshaft."

I tried to lift Blood. He was dead weight. "Listen, Blood, I'll leg it into the city and get some food. I'll come back quick. You just wait here."

"Don't go in there, Vic," he said. "I did a recon the day after you went down. They found out we weren't fried in that gym. I don't know how. Maybe mutts smelled our track. I've been keeping watch, and they haven't tried to come out after us. I don't blame them. You don't know what it's like out here at night, man…you don't know…"

He shivered.

"Take it easy, Blood."

"But they've got us marked lousy in the city, Vic. We can't go back there. We'll have to make it someplace else."

That put it on a different stick. We couldn't go back, and with Blood in that condition we couldn't go forward. And I knew, good as I was solo, I couldn't make it without him. And there wasn't anything out here to eat. He had to have food at once, and some medical care. I had to do something. Something good, something fast.

"Vic!" Quilla June's voice was high and whining. "Come *on*! He'll be all right. We have to hurry!"

I looked up at her. The sun was sinking into the darkness. Blood trembled in my arms.

She got a pouty look on her face. "If you love me, you'll come *on!*"

I couldn't make it alone out there without him. I knew it. If I loved her. She asked me, in the boiler, do you know what love is?

It was a small fire, not nearly big enough for any roverpak to spot from the outskirts of the city. No smoke. And after Blood had eaten his fill, I carried him to the air-duct a mile away, and we spent the night inside on a little ledge. I held him all night. He slept good. In the morning, I fixed him up pretty good. He'd make it; he was strong.

He ate again. There was plenty left from the night before. I didn't eat. I wasn't hungry.

We started off across the blasted wasteland that morning. We'd find another city, and make it.

We had to move slow because Blood was still limping. It took a long time before I stopped hearing her calling in my head. Asking me, asking me: *do you know what love is?*

Sure I know.

A boy loves his dog.

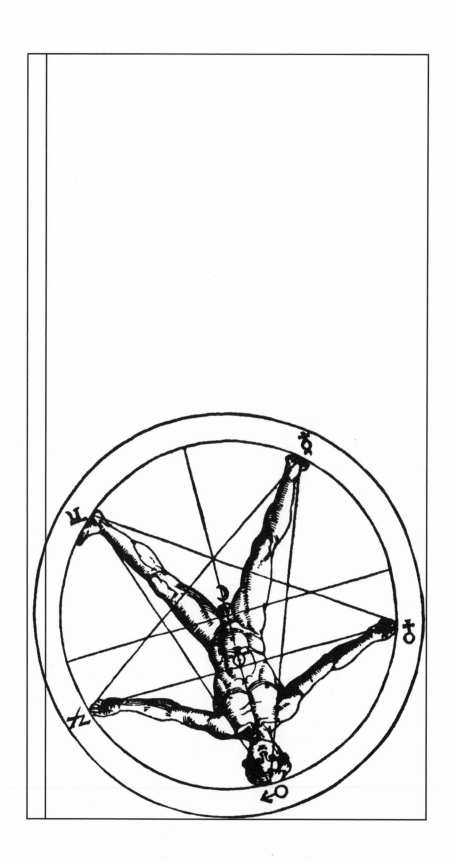

THE REGION BETWEEN

1970 Locus Poll Award: Best Short Fiction

NARRATIVE PASSIM
TYPOGRAPHIC DESIGN ELEMENTS
BY HARLAN ELLISON

ART BY JACK GAUGHAN

"LEFT HAND," THE thin man said tonelessly. "Wrist up."

William Bailey peeled back his cuff; the thin man put something cold against it, nodded toward the nearest door.

"Through there, first slab on the right," he said, and turned away.

"Just a minute," Bailey started. "I wanted—"

"Let's get going, buddy," the thin man said. "That stuff is fast."

Bailey felt something stab up under his heart. "You mean—you've already...that's all there is to it?"

"That's what you came for, right? Slab one, friend. Let's go."

"But—I haven't been here two minutes—"

"Whatta you expect—organ music? Look, pal," the thin man shot a glance at the wall clock, "I'm on my break, know what I mean?"

"I thought I'd at least have time for...for..."

"Have a heart, chum. You make it under your own power, I don't have to haul you, see?" The thin man was pushing open the door, urging Bailey through into an odor of chemicals and unlive flesh. In a narrow, curtained alcove, he indicated a padded cot.

"On your back, arms and legs straight out."

Bailey assumed the position, tensed as the thin man began fitting straps over his ankles.

"Relax. It's just if we get a little behind and I don't get back to a client for maybe a couple hours and they stiffen up...well, them issue boxes is just the one size, you know what I mean?"

A wave of softness, warmness swept over Bailey as he lay back.

"Hey, you didn't eat nothing the last twelve hours?" The thin man's face was a hazy pink blur.

"I awrrr mmmm," Bailey heard himself say.

"OK, sleep tight, paisan...." The thin man's voice boomed and faded. Bailey's last thought as the endless blackness closed in was of the words cut in the granite over the portal to the Euthanasia Center:

"...send me your tired, your poor, your hopeless, yearning to be free. To them I raise the lamp beside the brazen door...."

1

Death came as merely a hyphen. Life, and the balance of the statement, followed instantly. For it was only when Bailey died that he began to live.

Yet he could never have called it "living"; no one who had ever passed that way could have called it "living." It was something else. Something quite apart from "death" and something totally unlike "life."

Stars passed through him as he whirled outward.

Blazing and burning, carrying with them their planetary systems, stars and more stars spun through him as though traveling down invisible wires into the dark behind and around him.

Nothing touched him.

They were as dust motes, rushing silently past in incalculable patterns, as Bailey's body grew larger, filled space in defiance of the Law that said two bodies could not coexist in the same space at the same instant. Greater than Earth, greater than its solar system, greater than the galaxy that contained it, Bailey's body swelled and grew and filled the universe from end to end and ballooned back on itself in a slightly flattened circle.

His mind was everywhere.

A string cheese, pulled apart in filaments too thin to be measurable, Bailey's mind was there and there and there. And there.

It was also in the lens of the Succubus.

Murmuring tracery of golden light, a trembling moment of crystal sound. A note, rising and trailing away infinitely high, and followed by another, superimposing in birth even as its predecessor died. The voice of a dream, captured on spiderwebs. There, locked in the heart of an amber perfection, Bailey was snared, caught, trapped, made permanent by a force that allowed his Baileyness to roam unimpeded anywhere and everywhere at the instant of death.

Trapped in the lens of the Succubus.

[Waiting: empty. A mindsnake on a desert world, frying under seven suns, poised in the instant of death; its adversary, a fuzzball of cilia-thin fibers, sparking electrically, moving toward the mindsnake that a moment before had been set to strike and kill and eat. The mindsnake, immobile, empty of thought and empty of patterns of light that confounded its victims in the instants before the killing strike. The fuzzball sparked toward the mindsnake, its fibers casting about across the vaporous desert, picking up the mole sounds of things moving beneath the sand, tasting the air and feeling the heat as it pulsed in and away. It was improbable that a mindsnake would spend all that light-time, luring and intriguing, only at the penultimate moment to back off—no, not back off: shut down. Stop. Halt entirely. But if this was not a trap, if this was not some new tactic only recently learned by the ancient mindsnake, then it had to be an opportunity for the fuzzball. It moved closer. The mindsnake lay empty: waiting.]

Trapped in the lens of the Succubus.

[Waiting: empty. A monstrous head, pale blue and veined, supported atop a swan-neck by an intricate latticework yoke-and-halter. The Senator from Nougul, making his final appeal for the life of his world before the Star Court. Suddenly plunged into silence. No sound, no movement, the tall, emaciated body propped on its seven league crutches, only the trembling of balance—having nothing to do with life—reminding the assembled millions that an instant before this husk had contained a pleading eloquence. The fate of a world quivered in a balance no less precarious than that of the Senator. What had happened? The amalgam of wild surmise that grew in the Star Court was scarcely less compelling than had been the original circumstances bringing Nougul to this place, in the care of the words of this Senator. Who now stood, crutched, silent, and empty: waiting.]

Trapped in the lens of the Succubus.

[Waiting: empty. The Warlock of Whirrl, a power of darkness and evil. A force for chaos and destruction. Poised above his runic symbols, his bits of offal, his animal bones, his stringy things without names, quicksudden gone to silence. Eyes devoid of the pulverized starlight that was his sight. Mouth abruptly slack, in a face that had never known slackness. The ewe lamb lay still tied to the obsidian block, the graven knife with its unpleasant figures rampant, still held in the numb hand of the Warlock. And the ceremony was halted. The forces of darkness had come in gathering, had come to their calls, and now they roiled like milk vapor in the air, unable to go, unable to do, loath to abide. While the Warlock of Whirrl, gone from his mind, stood frozen and empty: waiting.]

Trapped in the lens of the Succubus.

[Waiting: empty. A man on Promontory, fifth planet out from the star Proxima Centauri, halted in mid-step. On his way to a bank of controls and a certain button, hidden beneath three security plates. This man, this inestimably valuable kingpin in the machinery of a war, struck dumb, struck blind, in a kind of death—not even waiting for another moment of time. Pulled out of himself by the gravity of non-being, an empty husk, a shell, a dormant thing. Poised on the edges of their continents, two massed armies waited for that button to be pushed. And would never be pushed, while this man, this empty and silent man, stood rooted in the sealed underworld bunker where precaution had placed him. Now inaccessible, now inviolate, now untouchable, this man and this war stalemated frozen. While the world around him struggled to move itself a fraction of a thought toward the future, and found itself incapable, hamstrung, empty: waiting.]

Trapped in the lens of the Succubus.

And...

[Waiting: empty. A subaltern, name of Pinkh, lying on his bunk, contemplating his fiftieth assault mission. Suddenly gone. Drained, lifeless, neither dead nor alive. Staring upward at the bulkhead ceiling of his quarters. While beyond his ship raged the Montag-Thil War. Sector 888 of the Galactic Index. Somewhere between the dark star Montag and the Nebula Cluster in Thil Galaxy. Pinkh, limbo-lost and unfeeling, needing the infusion of a soul, the filling up of a life-force. Pinkh, needed in this war more than any other man, though the Thils did not know it...until the moment his essence was stolen. Now, Pinkh, lying there one shy of a fifty-score of assault missions. But unable to aid his world. Unable, undead, unalive, empty: waiting.]

While Bailey...

Floated in a region between. Hummed in a nothingness as great as everywhere. Without substance. Without corporeality. Pure thought, pure energy, pure Bailey. Trapped in the lens of the Succubus.

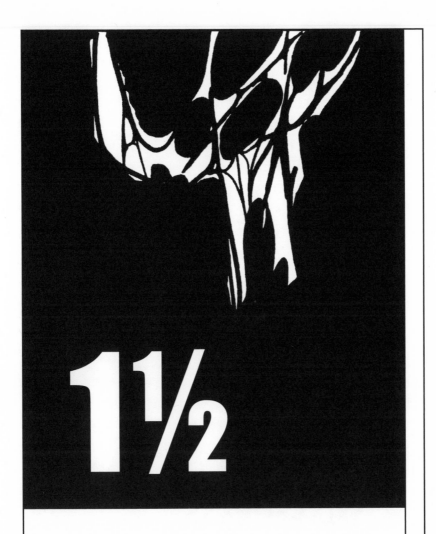

1¹⁄₂

More precious than gold, more sought-after than uranium, more scarce than yinyang blossom, more needed than salkvac, rarer than diamonds, more valuable than force-beads, more negotiable than the vampyr extract, dearer than 2038 vintage Chateau Luxor, more lusted after than the twin-vagina'd trollops of Kanga…

Souls.

Thefts had begun in earnest five hundred years before. Random thefts. Stolen from the most improbable receptacles. From beasts and men and creatures who had never been thought to possess "souls." Who was stealing them was never known. Far out somewhere, in reaches of space (or not-space) (or the interstices between space and not-space) that had no names, had no dimensions, whose light had never even reached the outmost thin edge of known space, there lived or existed or *were* creatures or things or entities or forces—*someone*—who needed the life-force of the creepers and walkers and lungers and swimmers and fliers who inhabited the known universes. Souls vanished, and the empty husks remained.

Thieves they were called, for no other name applied so well, bore in its single syllable such sadness and sense of resignation. They were called Thieves, and they were never seen, were not understood, had never given a clue to their nature or their purpose or even their method of theft. And so nothing could be done about their depredations. They were as Death: handiwork observed, but a fact of life without recourse to higher authority. Death and the Thieves were final in what they did.

So the known universes—the Star Court and the Galactic Index and the Universal Meridian and the Perseus Confederacy and the Crab Complex— shouldered the reality of what the Thieves did with resignation, and stoicism. No other course was open to them. They could do no other.

But it changed life in the known universes.

It brought about the existence of soul-recruiters, who pandered to the needs of the million billion trillion worlds. Shanghaiers. Graverobbers of creatures not yet dead. In their way, thieves, even as the Thieves. Beings whose dark powers and abilities enabled them to fill the tables-of-organization of any world with fresh souls from worlds that did not even suspect *they* existed, much less the Court, the Index, the Meridian, the Confederacy or the Complex. If a key figure on a fringe world suddenly went limp and soulless, one of the soul-recruiters was contacted and the black traffic was engaged in. Last resort, final contact, most reprehensible but expeditious necessity, they stole and supplied.

One such was the Succubus.

He was gold. And he was dry. These were the only two qualities possessed by the Succubus that could be explicated in human terms. He had once been a member of the dominant race that skimmed across the sand-seas of a tiny planet, fifth from the star-sun labeled Kappel-112 in Canes Venatici. He had long since ceased to be anything so simply identified.

The path he had taken, light-years long and several hundred Terran-years long, had brought him from the sand-seas and a minimum of "face"—the only term that could even approximate the one measure of wealth his race valued—to a cove of goldness and dryness near the hub of the Crab Complex. His personal worthiness could now be measured only in terms of hundreds of billions of dollars, unquenchable light sufficient to sustain his offspring unto the nine thousandth generation, a name that could only be spoken aloud or in movement by the upper three social sects of the Confederacies races, more "face" than any member of his race had ever possessed...more, even, than that held in myth by Yaele.

Gold, dry, and inestimably worthy: the Succubus.

Though his trade was one publicly deplored, there were only seven entities in the known universes who were aware that the Succubus was a soul-recruiter. He kept his two lives forcibly separated.

"Face" and graverobbing were not compatible.

He ran a tidy business. Small, with enormous returns. Special souls, selected carefully, no seconds, no hand-me-downs. Quality stock.

And through the seven highly placed entities who knew him—Nin, FawDawn, Enec-L, Milly(Bas)Kodal, a Plain without a name, Cam Royal, and Pl—he was channeled only the loftiest commissions.

He had supplied souls of all sorts in the five hundred years he had been recruiting. Into the empty husk of a master actor on Bolial V. Into the waiting body of a creature that resembled a plant aphid, the figurehead of a coalition labor movement, on Wheechitt Eleven and Wheechitt Thirteen. Into the unmoving form of the soul-emptied daughter of the hereditary ruler of Golaena Prime. Into the untenanted shape of an arcane maguscientist on Donadello III's seventh moon, enabling the five hundred-zodjam religious cycle to progress. Into the lusterless spark of light that sealed the tragic laocoönian group-mind of Orechnaen's Dispassionate Bell-Silver Dichotomy.

Not even the seven who functioned as go-betweens for the Succubus's commissions knew where and how he obtained such fine, raw, unsolidified souls. His competitors dealt almost exclusively in the atrophied, crustaceous souls of beings whose thoughts and beliefs and ideologies were so ingrained that the souls came to their new receptacles already stained and imprinted. But the Succubus…

Cleverly contrived, youthful souls. Hearty souls. Plastic and ready-to-assimilate souls. Lustrous, inventive souls. The finest souls in the known universe.

The Succubus, as determined to excel in his chosen profession as he was to amass "face," had spent the better part of sixty years roaming the outermost fringes of the known universe. He had carefully observed many races, noting for his purpose only those that seemed malleable, pliant, far removed from rigidity.

He had selected, for his purpose:

The Steechii

Amassanii

Cokoloids

Flashers

Griestaniks

Bunanits

Condolis

Tratravisii

and Humans.

On each planet where these races dominated, he put into effect subtle recruiting systems, wholly congruent with the societies in which they appeared:

The Steechii were given eterna dreamdust.

The Amassanii were given doppelgänger shifting.

The Cokoloids were given the Cult of Rebirth.

The Flashers were given proof of the Hereafter.

The Griestaniks were given ritual mesmeric trances.

The Bunanits were given (imperfect) teleportation.

The Condolis were given an entertainment called Trial by Nightmare Combat.

The Tratravisii were given an underworld motivated by high incentives for kidnapping and mind-blotting. They were also given a wondrous narcotic called Nodabit.

The Humans were given Euthanasia Centers.

And from these diverse channels the Succubus received a steady supply of prime souls. He received Flashers and skimmers and Condolis and ether-breathers and Amassanii and perambulators and Bunanits and gill creatures and…

William Bailey.

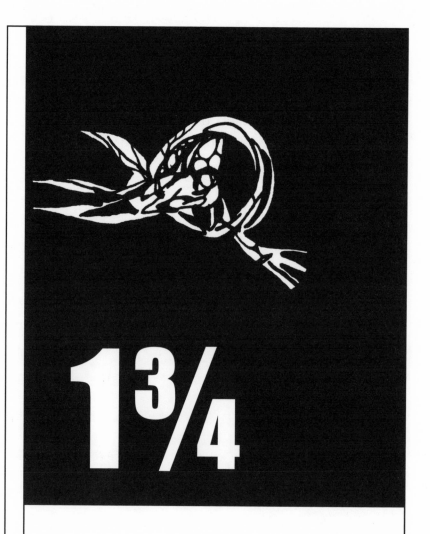

1¾

Bailey, cosmic nothingness, electrical potential spread out to the ends of the universe and beyond, nubbin'd his thoughts. Dead. Of that, no doubt. Dead and gone. Back on Earth, lying cold and faintly blue on a slab in the Euthanasia Center. Toes turned up. Eyeballs rolled up in their sockets. Rigid and gone.

And yet alive. More completely alive than he had ever been, than *any* human being had ever conceived of being. Alive with all of the universe, one with the clamoring stars, brother to the infinite empty spaces, heroic in proportions that even myth could not define.

He knew everything. Everything there had ever been to know, everything that was, everything that would be. Past, present, future...all were merged and met in him. He was on a feeder line to the Succubus, waiting to be collected, waiting to be tagged and filed even as his alabaster body back on Earth would be tagged and filed. Waiting to be cross-indexed and shunted off to a waiting empty husk on some far world. All this he knew.

But one thing separated him from the millions of souls that had gone before him.

He didn't want to go.

Infinitely wise, knowing all, Bailey knew every other soul that had gone before had been resigned with soft acceptance to what was to come. It was a new life. A new voyage in another body. And all the others had been fired by curiosity, inveigled by strangeness, wonder-struck with being as big as the known universe and going *somewhere else.*

But not Bailey.

He was rebellious.

He was fired by hatred of the Succubus, inveigled by thoughts of destroying him and his feeder-lines, wonder-struck with being the only one—the *only* one!—who had ever thought of revenge. He was somehow, strangely, not tuned in with being rebodied, as all the others had been. *Why am I different?* he wondered. And of all the things he knew...he did not know the answer to that.

Inverting negatively, atoms expanded to the size of whole galaxies, stretched out membraned, osmotically breathing whole star systems, inhaling blue-white stars and exhaling quasars, Bailey the known universe asked himself yet another question, even more important:

Do I WANT *to do something about it?*

Passing through a zone of infinite cold, the word came back to him from his own mind in chill icicles of thought:

Yes.

"I see here, during the month of September, that you worked overtime at least...what is it...uh...eleven hours."

"Is there a law against that?"

"Oh, no...no, of course not. It just seems to us here at the block that you're perhaps, uh, overdoing it a bit."

"Working."

"Yes. Working."

"Has my block steward complained? Has my EEG been erratic? Am I being *accused* of something?"

"No, *of course* not! My lord, man, there's no need to be so defensive! We're only trying to find out if something is, well, disturbing you."

If I'd been able to, I'd have killed the sonofabitch, right then and right there. In his conversation grouping. It would have made fine conversation for his office staff. Come in and find him brained to death with his own coffee urn.

"Nothing's disturbing me."

"Then you'll pardon me if I feel it apropos to ask why you aren't taking your proper relaxation periods, Mr. Bailey."

"I feel like keeping busy."

"Ah, but all work and no play—"

And borne on comets plunging frenziedly through his cosmic body, altering course suddenly and traveling at right angles in defiance of every natural law he had known when "alive," the inevitable question responding to a *yes* asked itself:

Why should I?

Life for Bailey on Earth had been pointless. He had been a man who did not fit. He had been a man driven to the suicide chamber literally by disorientation and frustration.

I was called to the office of the Social Director of my residence block. Frankly, I was frightened. I knew I hadn't done anything to be afraid about, but ever since I'd been a child, ever since I'd been called to the office of the school principal, just the being *summoned* had made me my gut tight, made me feel like I wanted to go to the bathroom.

He made me wait half an hour, on a bench, damn him, with a gaggle of weirdos who looked like they hadn't had their heads scrubbed and customized in seven months.

Finally, the box called my name and I dropped to his office, and he was sitting in one of those informal conversation-groupings of chairs and coffee table that instantly put me off.

"Mr. Bailey," he said. Smiled. Hearty bastard. I walked over and sat down even before he suggested I sit. He didn't drop the smile for a second. He was up to anything.

"Why don't we get right to it," he said. I smiled back at him, but I felt trapped, really hemmed-in.

"I've been looking at your tag-chart, Mr. Bailey, and well, I hesitate to make any jump conclusions here, but it *appears* you've been neglecting your relaxation periods."

Damn him! Damn him!

The omnipresent melancholy that had consumed him on an Earth bursting with overpopulation was something to which he had no desire to return. Then why this frenzy to resist being shunted into the body of a creature undoubtedly living a life more demanding, more exciting—*anything* had to be better than what he'd come from—more *alive*? Why this fanatic need to track back along the feeder-lines to the Succubus, to destroy the one who had saved him from oblivion? Why this need to destroy a creature who was merely fulfilling a necessary operation-of-balance in a universe singularly devoid of balance?

In that thought lay the answer, but he did not have the key. He turned off his thoughts. He was Bailey no more.

And in that instant the Succubus pulled his soul from the file and sent it where it was needed. He was certainly Bailey no more.

2

Subaltern Pinkh squirmed on his spike-palette, and opened his eye. His back was stiff. He turned, letting the invigorating short-spikes tickle his flesh through the heavy mat of fur. His mouth felt dry and loamy.

It was the morning of his fiftieth assault mission. Or was it? He seemed to remember lying down for a night's sleep...and then a very long dream without substance. It had been all black and empty; hardly something the organizer would have programmed. It must have malfunctioned.

He slid sidewise on the spike-palette, and dropped his enormous furred legs over the side. As his paws touched the tiles a whirring from the wall preceded the toilet facility's appearance. It swiveled into view, and Pinkh looked at himself in the full-length mirror. He looked all right. Dream. Bad dream.

The huge, bearlike subaltern shoved off the bed, stood to his full seven feet, and lumbered into the duster. The soothing powders cleansed away his sleep-fatigue and he emerged, blue pelt glistening, with bad dreams almost entirely dusted away. Almost. Entirely. He had a lingering feeling of having been...somewhat...*larger*...

The briefing colors washed across the walls, and Pinkh hurriedly attached his ribbons. It was informalwear today. Three yellows, three ochers, three whites and an ego blue.

He went downtunnel to the briefing section, and prayed. All around him his sortie partners were on their backs, staring up at the sky dome and the random (programmed) patterns of stars in their religious significances. Montag's Lord of Propriety had programmed success for today's mission. The stars swirled and shaped themselves and the portents were reassuring to Pinkh and his fellows.

The Montag-Thil War had been raging for almost one hundred years, and it seemed close to ending. The dark star Montag and the Nebula Cluster in Thil Galaxy had thrown their might against each other for a century; the people themselves were weary of war. It would end soon. One or the other would make a mistake, the opponent would take the advantage, and the strike toward peace would follow immediately. It was merely a matter of time. The assault troops—especially Pinkh, a planetary hero—were suffused with a feeling of importance, a sense of the relevance of what they were doing. Out to kill, certainly, but with the sure knowledge that they were working toward a worthwhile goal. Through death, to life. The portents had told them again and again, these last months, that this was the case.

The sky dome turned golden and the stars vanished. The assault troops sat up on the floor, awaited their briefing.

It was Pinkh's fiftieth mission.

His great yellow eye looked around the briefing room. There were more young troopers this mission. In fact… he was the only veteran. It seemed strange.

Could Montag's Lord of Propriety have planned it this way? But where were Andakh and Melnakh and Gorekh? They'd been here yesterday.

Was it just yesterday?

He had a strange memory of having been—asleep?—away?—unconscious?—what?—something. As though more than one day had passed since his last mission. He leaned across to the young trooper on his right and placed a paw flat on the other's. "What day is today?" The trooper flexed palm and answered, with a note of curiosity in his voice, "It's Former. The ninth." Pinkh was startled. "What cycle?" he asked, almost afraid to hear the answer.

"Third," the young trooper said.

The briefing officer entered at that moment, and Pinkh had no time to marvel that it was *not* the next day, but a full cycle later. Where had the days gone? What had happened to him? Had Gorekh and the others been lost in sorties? Had he been wounded, sent to repair, and only now been remanded to duty? Had he been wounded and suffered amnesia? He remembered a Lance Corporal in the Throbbing Battalion who had been seared and lost his memory. They had sent him back to Montag, where

101

he had been blessed by the Lord of Propriety himself. What had happened to him?

Strange memories—not his own, all the wrong colors, weights and tones wholly alien—kept pressing against the bones in his forehead.

He was listening to the briefing officer, but also hearing an undertone. Another voice entirely. Coming from some other place he could not locate.

■ ■ ■ ■ ■ **You great ugly fur-thing, you! Wake up, look around you. One hundred years, slaughtering. Why can't you see what's being done to you? How dumb can you be? The Lords of Propriety; they set you up. Yeah, *you*, Pinkh! Listen to me. You can't block me out...you'll hear me. Bailey. You're the one, Pinkh, the special one. They trained you for what's coming up...no, don't block me out, you imbecile...don't blot me out** ■ ■ ■ ■ ■ **I'll be here, you can't blot me out** ■ ■ ■ ■ ■

The background noise went on, but he would not listen. It was sacrilegious. Saying things about the Lord of Propriety. Even the Thil Lord of Propriety was sacrosanct in Pinkh's mind. Even though they were at war, the two Lords were eternally locked together in holiness. To blaspheme even the enemy's Lord was unthinkable.

Yet he had thought it.

He shuddered with the enormity of what had passed in his thoughts, and knew he could never go to release and speak of it. He would submerge the memory, and pay strict attention to the briefing officer who was

"This cycle's mission is a straightforward one. You will be under the direct linkage of Subaltern Pinkh, whose reputation is known to all of you."

Pinkh inclined with the humbleness movement.

"You will drive directly into the Thil labyrinth, chivvy and harass a path to Groundworld, and there level as many targets-of-opportunity as you are able, before you're destroyed. After this briefing you will reassemble with your sortie leaders and fully familiarize yourselves with the target-cubes the Lord has commanded to be constructed."

He paused, and stared directly at Pinkh, his golden eye gone to pinkness with age and dissipation. But what he said was for all of the sappers. "There is one target you will *not* strike. It is the Maze of the Thil Lord of Propriety. This is irrevocable. You will not, repeat *not* strike near the Maze of the Lord."

Pinkh felt a leap of pleasure. This was the final strike. It was preamble to peace. A suicide mission; he ran eleven thankfulness prayers through his mind. It was the dawn of a new day for Montag and Thil. The Lords of Propriety were good. The Lords held all cupped in their holiness.

Yet he had thought the unthinkable.

"You will be under the direct linkage of Subaltern Pinkh," the briefing officer said again. Then, kneeling and passing down the rows of sappers, he palmed good death with honor to each of them. When he reached Pinkh, he stared at him balefully for a long instant, as though wanting to speak. But the moment passed, he rose, and left the chamber.

They went into small groups with the sortie leaders and examined the target-cubes. Pinkh went directly to the briefing officer's cubicle and waited patiently till the older Montagasque's prayers were completed.

When his eye cleared, he stared at Pinkh.

"A path through the labyrinth has been cleared."

"What will we be using?"

"Reclaimed sortie craft. They have all been outfitted with diversionary equipment."

"Linkage level?"

"They tell me a high six."

"They *tell* you?" He regretted the tone even as he spoke.

The briefing officer looked surprised. As if his desk had coughed. He did not speak, but stared at Pinkh with the same baleful stare the subaltern had seen before.

"Recite your catechism," the briefing officer said, finally.

Pinkh settled back slowly on his haunches, ponderous weight downdropping with grace. Then:

"Free flowing, free flowing, all flows
"From the Lords, all free, all fullness,
"Flowing from the Lords.
   "What will I do
   "What will I do
"What will I do without my Lords?
"Honor in the dying, rest in honor, all honor
"From the Lords, all rest, all honoring,
"To honor my Lords.
   "This I will do
   "This I will do
"I will live when I die for my Lords."

And it was between the First and Second Sacredness that the darkness came to Pinkh. He saw the briefing officer come toward him, reach a great palm toward him, and there was darkness…the same sort of darkness from which he had risen in his own cubicle before the briefing. Yet, not the same. *That* darkness had been total, endless, with the feeling that he was…somehow…larger… greater…as big as all space…

And this darkness was like being turned off. He could not think, could not even think that he was unthinking. He was cold, and not there. Simply: not there.

Then, as if it had not happened, he was back in the briefing officer's cubicle, the great bearlike shape was moving back from him, and he was reciting the Second Sacredness of his catechism.

What had happened...he did not know.

"Here are your course coordinates," the briefing officer said. He extracted the spool from his pouch and gave it to Pinkh. The subaltern marveled again at how old the briefing officer must be: the hair of his chest pouch was almost gray.

"Sir," Pinkh began. Then stopped. The briefing officer raised a palm. "I understand, Subaltern. Even to the most reverent among us there come moments of confusion." Pinkh smiled. He *did* understand.

"Lords," Pinkh said, palming the briefing officer with fullness and propriety.

"Lords," he replied, palming honor in the dying.

Pinkh left the briefing officer's cubicle and went to his own place.

As soon as he was certain the subaltern was gone, the briefing officer, who was *very* old, linked-up with someone else, far away; and he told him things.

First, they melted the gelatin around him. It was hardly gelatin, but it had come to be called jell by the sappers, and the word had stuck. As the gelatin stuck. Face protected, he lay in the ten troughs, in sequence, getting the gelatinous substance melted around him. Finally, pincers that had been carefully padded lifted him from the tenth trough, and slid him along the track to his sortie craft. Once inside the pilot country, stretched out on his stomach, he felt the two hundred wires insert themselves into the jell, into the fur, into his body. The brain wires were the last to fix.

As each wire hissed from its spool and locked onto the skull contacts, Pinkh felt himself go a little more to integration with the craft. At last, the final wire tipped on icily and so Pinkh was metalflesh, bulkheadskin, eyescanners, bonerivets, plasticartilege, artery/ventricle/capacitors/molecules/transistors,

```
BEASTC
C       R
R       A
A   i   F
F       T
TBEAST
```

all of him as one, totality, metal-man, furred-vessel, essence of mechanism, soul of inanimate, life in force-drive, linkage of mind with power plant. Pinkh the ship. Sortie Craft 90 named Pinkh.

And the others: linked to him.

Seventy sappers, each encased in jell, each wired up, each a mind to its sortie craft. Seventy, linked in telepathically with Pinkh, and Pinkh linked into his own craft, and all of them instrumentalities of the Lord of Propriety.

The great carrier wing that bore them made escape orbit and winked out of normal space.

Here ■ Not Here.

In an instant gone.

(Gone where!?!)

Inverspace.

Through the gully of inverspace to wink into existence once again at the outermost edge of the Thil labyrinth.

Not Here ● Here.

Confronting a fortified tundra of space crisscrossed by deadly lines of force. A cosmic fireworks display. A cat's cradle of vanishing, appearing and disappearing threads of a million colors; each one receptive to all the others. Cross one, break one, interpose…and suddenly uncountable others home in. Deadly ones. Seeking ones. Stunners and drainers and leakers and burners. The Thil labyrinth.

Seventy-one sortie craft hung quivering—the last of the inverspace coronas trembling off and gone. Through the tracery of force-lines the million stars of the Thil Galaxy burned with the quiet reserve of ice crystals. And there, in the center, the Nebula Cluster. And there, in the center of the Cluster, Groundworld.

"Link in with me."

Pinkh's command fled and found them. Seventy beastcraft tastes, sounds, scents, touches came back to Pinkh. His sappers were linked in.

"A path has been cleared through the labyrinth for us. Follow. And trust. Honor."

"In the dying," came back the response, from seventy minds of flesh-and-metal.

They moved forward. Strung out like fish of metal with minds linked by thought, they surged forward following the lead craft. Into the labyrinth. Color burned and boiled past, silently sizzling in the vacuum. Pinkh detected murmurs of panics, quelled them with a damping thought of his own. Images of the still pools of Dusnadare, of deep sighs after a full meal, of Lord-worship during the days of First Fullness. Trembling back to him, their minds quieted. And the color beams whipped past on all sides, without up or down or distance. But never touching them.

Time had no meaning. Fused into flesh/metal, the sortie craft followed the secret path that had been cleared for them through the impenetrable labyrinth.

Pinkh had one vagrant thought: *Who cleared this for us?*

And a voice from somewhere far away, a voice that was his own, yet someone else's—the voice of a someone who called himself a bailey—said, *That's it! Keep thinking what they don't want you to think.*

But he put the thoughts from him, and time wearied itself and succumbed, and finally they were there. In the exact heart of the Nebula Cluster in Thil Galaxy.

Groundworld lay fifth from the source star, the home sun that had nurtured the powerful Thil race till it could explode outward.

"Link in to the sixth power," Pinkh commanded.

They linked. He spent some moments reinforcing his command splices, making the interties foolproof and trigger-responsive. Then he made a prayer, and they went in.

Why am I locking them in so close, Pinkh wondered, damping the thought before it could pass along the lines to his sappers. *What am I trying to conceal? Why do I need such repressive control? What am I trying to avert?*

Pinkh's skull thundered with sudden pain. Two minds were at war inside him, he knew that. He *SUDDENLY* knew it.

Who is that?

It's me, you clown!

Get out! I'm on a mission…it's import—

It's a fraud! They've prog—

Get out of my head listen to me you idiot I'm trying to tell you something you need to know I won't listen I'll override you I'll block you I'll damp you no listen don't do that I've been someplace you haven't been and I can tell you about the Lords oh this can't be happening to me not to me I'm a devout man fuck that garbage listen to me they lost you man they lost you to a soul stealer and they had to get you back because you were their specially programmed killer they want you to Lord oh Lord of Propriety hear me now hear me your most devout worshipper forgive these blasphemous thoughts I can't control you any more you idiot I'm fading fading fading Lord oh Lord hear me I wish only to serve you. Only to suffer the honor in the dying.

Peace through death. I am the instrumentality of the Lords. I know what I must do.

That's what I'm trying to tell *you....*

And then he was gone in the mire at the bottom of Pinkh's mind. They were going in.

They came down, straight down past the seven moons, broke through the cloud cover, leveled out in a delta wing formation and streaked toward the larger of the two continents that formed ninety percent of Groundworld's land mass. Pinkh kept them at supersonic speed, blurring, and drove a thought out to his sappers: "We'll drop straight down below a thousand feet and give them the shock wave. Hold till I tell you to level off."

They were passing over a string of islands—causeway-linked beads in a pea-green sea—each one covered from shore to shore with teeming housing dorms that commuted their residents to the main continents and the complexes of high-rise bureaucratic towers.

"Dive!" Pinkh ordered.

The formation angled sharply forward, as though it was hung on puppet strings, then fell straight down.

The metalflesh of Pinkh's ship-hide began to heat. Overlapping armadillo plates groaned; Pinkh pushed their speed; force-bead mountings lubricated themselves, went dry, lubricated again; they dropped down; follicle-thin fissures were grooved in the bubble surfaces; sappers began to register fear, Pinkh locked them tighter; instruments coded off the far right and refused to register; the island-chain flew up toward them; pressure in the gelatin trough flattened them with g's; now there was enough atmosphere to scream past their sortie craft and it whistled, shrilled, howled, built and climbed; gimbal-tracks rasped in their mountings; down and down they plunged, seemingly bent on thundering into the islands of Groundworld; "Sir! Sir!"; "Hold steady, not yet...not yet...I'll tell you when...not yet..."

Pushing an enormous bubble of pressurized air before them, the delta wing formation wailed straight down toward the specks of islands that became dots, became buttons, became masses, became everything as they rushed up and filled the bubble sights from side to side—

"Level out! *Now!* Do it, do it, *level now!*"

And they pulled out, leveled off and shot away. The bubble of air, enormous, solid as an asteroid, thundering down unchecked...hit struck burst broke with devastating results. Pinkh's sortie craft plunged away, and in their wake they left exploding cities, great structures erupting, others trembling, shuddering, then caving in on themselves. The shock wave hit and spread outward from shore to shore. Mountains of plasteel and lathite volcano'd in blossoms of flame and flesh. The blast-pit created by the air bubble struck to the core of the island-chain. A tidal wave rose like some prehistoric leviathan and boiled over one entire spot of land. Another island broke up and sank almost at once. Fire and walls of plasteel crushed and destroyed after the shock wave.

The residence islands were leveled as Pinkh's sortie craft vanished over the horizon, still traveling at supersonic speed.

They passed beyond the island-chain, leaving in their wake dust and death, death and ruin, ruin and fire.

"Through death to peace," Pinkh sent.

"Honor," they responded, as one.

(Far away on Groundworld, a traitor smiled.)

(In a Maze, a Lord sat with antennae twined, waiting.)

(Flesh and metal eased.)

(In ruins, a baby whose exoskeleton had been crushed, crawled toward the pulsing innards of its mother.)

(Seven moons swung in their orbits.)

(A briefing officer on Montag knew it was full, golden.)

Oh, Lords, what I have done, I have done for you.

Wake up. Will you wake up, Pinkh! The mission is—

The other thing, the bailey, was wrenching at him, poking its head up out of the slime. He thrust it back down firmly. And made a prayer.

"Sir," the thought of one of his sappers came back along the intertie line, "did you say something?"

"Nothing," Pinkh said. "Keep in formation."

He locked them in even tighter, screwing them down with mental shackles till they gasped.

The pressure was building.

A six-power linkup, and the pressure was building.

I am a hero, Pinkh thought, *I can do it.*

Then they were flashing across the Greater Ocean and it blurred into an endless carpet of thick heaving green; Pinkh felt sick watching it whip by beneath him; he went deeper into ship and the vessel felt no sickness. He fed the stability of nausea-submerged along the interties.

They were met by the Thil inner defense line over empty ocean. First came the sea-breathers but they fell short when Pinkh ordered his covey to lift for three thousand feet. They leveled off just as the beaks swooped down in their land-to-sea parabolas. Two of them snouted and perceived the range, even as they were viciously beamed into their component parts by Pinkh's outermost sappers. But they'd already fed back the trajectories, and suddenly the sky above them was black with the blackmetal bodies of beaks, flapping, dropping, squalling as they cascaded into the center of the formation. Pinkh felt sappers vanish from the linkup and fed the unused power along other lines, pulling the survivors tighter under his control. "Form a sweep," he commanded.

The formation regrouped and rolled in a graceful gull-wing maneuver that brought them craft-to-craft in a fan. "Plus!" Pinkh ordered, cutting in—with a thought—the imploding beam. The beams of each sortie craft fanned out, overlapping, making an impenetrable wall of deadly force. The beaks came whirling back up and careened across the formation's path. Creatures of metal and mindlessness. Wheels and carapaces. Blackness and berserk rage. Hundreds. Entire eyries.

When they struck the soft pink fan of the overlapping implosion beams, they whoofed in on themselves, dropped instantly.

The formation surged forward.

Then they were over the main continent. Rising from the exact center was the gigantic mountain atop which the Thil Lord of Propriety lived in his Maze.

"Attack! Targets of opportunity!" Pinkh commanded, sending impelling power along the linkup. His metal hide itched. His eyeball sensors watered. In they went, again.

"Do not strike at the Lord's Maze," one of the sappers thought

AND PINKH
THREW UP!!
A WALL OF
THOUGHT!!!
THAT DREW
THE!!!!!!!!!!!
THOUGHT!!!
OFF THE!!!!! ...do not strike at the lord's maze...
LINKUP SO
IT DID!!!!!!!!
NOT REACH
THE OTHER
SAPPERS!!!!!
BUT HIT!!!!
THE WALL!!!
AND BROKE!
LIKE FOAM!

Why did I do that? We were briefed not to attack the Lord's Maze. It would be unthinkable to attack the Lord's Maze. It would precipitate even greater war than before. The war would *never* end. Why did I stop my sapper from reiterating the order? And why haven't *I* told them not to do it? It was stressed at the briefing. They're linked in so very tightly, they'd obey in a moment—anything I said. What is happening? I'm heading for the mountain! Lord!

Listen to me, Pinkh. This war has been maintained by the Lords of Propriety for ten million years. Why do you think it was made heresy even to think negatively about the opposing Lord? They keep it going, to feed off it. Whatever they are, these Lords, they come from the same pocket universe and they live off the energy of men at war. They must *keep the war going or they'll die. They programmed you to be their secret weapon. The war was reaching a stage where both Montag and Thil want peace, and the Lords can't have that. Whatever they are, Pinkh, whatever kind of creature they are, wherever they come from, for over a hundred years they've held your two galaxies in their hands, and they've used you. The Lord isn't in his Maze, Pinkh. He's safe somewhere else. But they planned it between them. They knew if a Montagasque sortie penetrated to Groundworld and struck the Maze, it would keep the war going indefinitely. So they programmed you, Pinkh. But before they could use you, your soul was stolen. They put my soul in you, a man of Earth, Pinkh. You don't even know where Earth is, but my name is Bailey. I've been trying to reach through to you. But you always shut me out—they had you programmed too well. But with the linkup pressure, you don't have the strength to keep me out, and I've got to let you know you're programmed to strike the Maze. You can stop it, Pinkh. You can avoid it all. You can end this war. You have it within your power, Pinkh. Don't strike the Maze. I'll redirect you. Strike where the Lords are hiding. You can rid your galaxies of them, Pinkh. Don't let them kill you. Who do you think arranged for the path through the labyrinth? Why do you think there wasn't more effective resistance? They wanted you to get through. To commit the one crime they could not forgive.*

The words reverberated in Pinkh's head as his sortie craft followed him in a tight wedge, straight for the Maze of the Lord.

"I—no, I—" Pinkh could not force thoughts out to his sappers. He was snapped shut. His mind was aching, the sound of straining and creaking, the buildings on the island-chain ready to crumble. Bailey inside, Pinkh inside, the programming of the Lords inside…all of them pulling at the fiber of Pinkh's mind.

For an instant the programming took precedence. "New directives. Override previous orders. Follow me in!"

They dove straight for the Maze.

No, Pinkh, fight it! Fight it and pull out. I'll show you where they're hiding. You can end this war!

The programming phasing was interrupted, Pinkh abruptly opened his great golden eye, his mind synched in even more tightly with his ship, and at that instant he knew the voice in his head was telling him the truth. He *remembered*:

Remembered the endless sessions.

Remembered the conditioning.

Remembered the programming.

Knew he had been duped.

Knew he was not a hero.

Knew he had to pull out of this dive.

Knew that at last *he* could bring peace to both galaxies.

He started to think *pull out, override* and fire it down the remaining linkup interties…

And the Lords of Propriety, who left very little to chance, who had followed Pinkh all the way, contacted the Succubus, complained of the merchandise they had bought, demanded it be returned…

Bailey's soul was wrenched from the body of Pinkh. The subaltern's body went rigid inside its jell trough, and, soulless, empty, rigid, the sortie craft plunged into the mountaintop where the empty Maze stood. It was followed by the rest of the sortie craft.

The mountain itself erupted in a geysering pillar of flame and rock and plasteel.

One hundred years of war was only the beginning.

Somewhere, hidden, the Lords of Propriety—umbilicus-joined with delight shocks spurting softly pink along the flesh-linkage joining them—began their renewed gluttonous feeding.

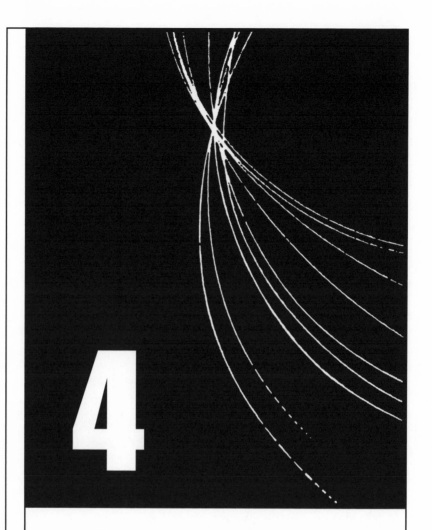

Bailey was whirled out of the Montagasque subaltern's body. His soul went shooting away on an asymptotic curve, back along the feeder-lines, to the soul files of the Succubus.

5

This is what it was like to be in the soul station.

Round. Weighted with the scent of grass. Perilous in that the music was dynamically contracting: souls had occasionally become too enriched and had gone flat and flaccid.

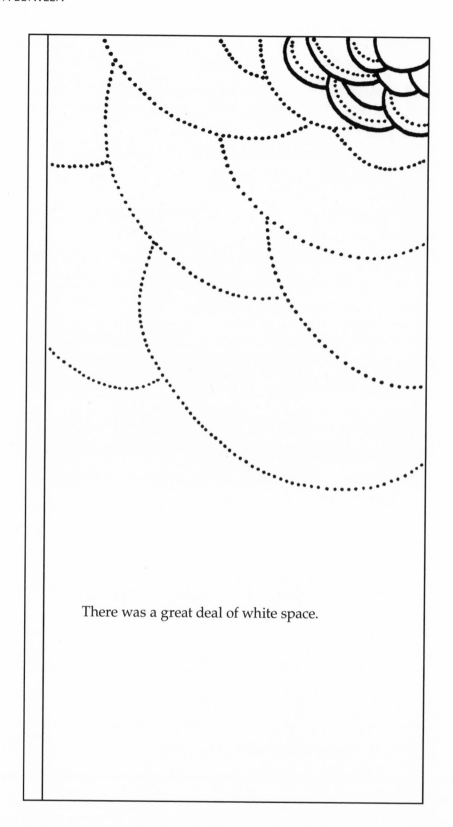

There was a great deal of white space.

Nothing was ranked, therefore nothing could be found in the same place twice; yet it didn't matter, for the Succubus had only to focus his lens and the item trembled into a special awareness.

Bailey spent perhaps twelve minutes reliving himself as a collapsing star then revolved his interfaces and masturbated as Anne Boleyn.

He savored mint where it smells most poignant, from deep in the shallow earth through the roots of the plant, then extended himself, extruded himself through an ice crystal and lit the far massif of the highest mountain on an onyx asteroid—recreating The Last Supper in chiaroscuro.

He burned for seventeen hundred years as the illuminated letter "B" on the first stanza of a forbidden enchantment in a papyrus volume used to summon up the imp James Fenimore Cooper then stood outside himself and considered his eyes and their hundred thousand bee-facets.

He allowed himself to be born from the womb of a tree sloth and flickered into rain that deluged a planet of coal for ten thousand years. And he beamed. And he sorrowed.

Bailey, all Bailey, soul once more, free as all the universes, threw himself toward the farthermost edge of the slightly flattened parabola that comprised the dark. He filled the dark with deeper darkness and bathed in fountains of brown wildflowers. Circles of coruscating violet streamed from his fingertips, from the tip of his nose, from his genitals, from the tiniest fibrillating fibers of hair that coated him. He shed water and hummed.

Then the Succubus drew him beneath the lens.

And Bailey was sent out once more.

Waste not, want not.

He was just under a foot tall. He was covered with blue fur. He had a ring of eyes that circled his head. He had eight legs. He smelled of fish. He was low to the ground and he moved very fast.

He was a stalker-cat, and he was first off the survey ship on Belial. The others followed, but not too soon. They always waited for the cat to do its work. It was safer that way. The Filonii had found that out in ten thousand years of exploring their universe. The cats did the first work, then the Filonii did theirs. It was the best way to rule a universe.

Belial was a forest world. Covered in long continents that ran from pole to pole with feathertop trees, it was ripe for discovery.

Bailey looked out of his thirty eyes, seeing around himself in a full 360° spectrum. Seeing all the way up into the ultra-violet, seeing all the way down into the infra-red. The forest was silent. Absolutely no sound. Bailey, the cat, would have heard a sound, had there been a sound. But there was no sound.

No birds, no insects, no animals, not even the whispering of the feathertop trees as they struggled toward the bright hot-white sun. It was incredibly silent.

Bailey said so.

The Filonii went to a condition red.

No world is silent. And a forest world is *always* noisy. But this one was silent.

They were out there, waiting. Watching the great ship and the small stalker-cat that had emerged from it.

Who they were, the cat and the Filonii did not know. But they were there, and they were waiting for the invaders to make the first move. The stalker-cat glided forward.

Bailey felt presences. Deep in the forest, deeper than he knew he could prowl with impunity. They were in there, watching him as he moved forward. But he was a cat, and if he was to get his fish, he would work. The Filonii were watching. *Them*, in there, back in the trees, *they* were watching. *It's a bad life*, he thought. *The life of a cat is a nasty, dirty, bad one.*

Bailey was not the first cat ever to have thought that thought. It was the litany of the stalker-cats. They knew their place, had always known it, but that was the way it was; it was the way it had always been. The Filonii ruled, and the cats worked. And the universe became theirs.

Yet it wasn't shared. It was the Filonii universe, and the stalker-cats were hired help.

The fine mesh cap that covered the top and back of the cat's head glowed with a faint but discernible halo. The sunbeams through which he passed caught at the gold filaments of the cap and sent sparkling radiations back toward the ship. The ship stood in the center of the blasted area it had cleared for its prime base.

Inside the ship, the team of Filonii ecologists sat in front of the many process screens and saw through the eyes of the stalker-cat. They murmured to one another as first one, then another, then another saw something of interest. "Cat, lad," one of them said softly, "still no sound?"

"Nothing yet, Brewer. But I can feel them watching."

One of the other ecologists leaned forward. The entire wall behind the hundred screens was a pulsing membrane. Speak into it at any point and the cat's helmet picked up the voice, carried it to the stalker. "Tell me, lad, what does it feel like?"

"I'm not quite sure, Kicker. I'm getting it mixed. It feels like the eyes staring…and wood…and sap…and yet there's mobility. It can't be the trees."

"You're sure."

"As best I can tell right now, Kicker. I'm going to go into the forest and see."

"Good luck, lad."

"Thank you, Driver. How is your goiter?"

"I'm fine, lad. Take care."

The stalker-cat padded carefully to the edge of the forest. Sunlight slanted through the feathertops into the gloom. It was cool and dim inside there.

Now, all eyes were upon him.

The first paw in met springy, faintly moist and cool earth. The fallen feathers had turned to mulch.

It smelled like cinnamon. Not overpoweringly so, just pleasantly so. He went in...all the way. The last the Filonii saw on their perimeter screens—twenty of the hundred—were his tails switching back and forth. Then the tails were gone and the seventy screens showed them dim, strangely-shadowed pathways between the giant conifers.

"Cat, lad, can you draw any conclusions from those trails?"

The stalker padded forward, paused. "Yes. I can draw the conclusion they aren't trails. They go fairly straight for a while, then come to dead ends at the bases of the trees. I'd say they were drag trails, if anything."

"What was dragged? Can you tell?"

"No, not really, Homer. Whatever was dragged, it was thick and fairly smooth. But that's all I can tell." He prodded the drag trail with his secondary leg on the left side. In the pad of the paw were tactile sensors.

The cat proceeded down the drag trail toward the base of the great tree where the trail unaccountably ended. All around him the great conifers rose six hundred feet into the warm, moist air.

Sipper, in the ship, saw through the cat's eyes and pointed out things to his fellows. "Some of the qualities of *Pseudotsuga Taxifolia*, but definitely a conifer. Notice the bark on that one. Typically *Eucalyptus Regnans*...yet notice the soft red spores covering the bark. I've never encountered that particular sort of thing before. They seem to be melting down the trees. In fact..."

He was about to say the trees were *all* covered with the red spores, when the red spores attacked the cat.

They flowed down the trees, covering the lower bark, each one the size of the cat's head, and when they touched, they ran together like jelly. When the red jelly from one tree reached the base of the trunk, it fused with the red jelly from the other trees.

"Lad…"

"It's all right, Kicker. I see them."

The cat began to pad backward: slowly, carefully. He could easily outrun the fusing crimson jelly. He moved back toward the verge of the clearing. Charred, empty of life, blasted by the Filonii hackshafts, not even a stump of the great trees above ground, the great circles where the trees had stood now merely reflective surfaces set flush in the ground. Back.

Backing out of life…backing into death.

The cat paused. What had caused *that* thought?

"Cat! Those spores…whatever they are…they're forming into a solid…"

Backing out of life…backing into death.

my name is

     bailey and i'm in

         here, inside you.

             i was stolen from

my	called	is		wants
body	the	some		somewhere. he—
by	succubus.	kind		there in the stars
a	he,	of	recruiter from out	
creature	*it*		puppeteer, a sort of	

The blood-red spore thing stood fifteen feet high, formless, shapeless, changing, malleable, coming for the cat. The stalker did not move: within him, a battle raged.

"Cat, lad! Return! Get back!"

Though the universe belonged to the Filonii, it was only at moments when the loss of a portion of that universe seemed imminent that they realized how important their tools of ownership had become.

Bailey fought for control of the cat's mind.

Centuries of conditioning fought back.

The spore thing reached the cat and dripped around him. The screens of the Filonii went blood-red, then went blank.

The thing that had come from the trees oozed back into the forest, shivered for a moment, then vanished, taking the cat with it.

The cat focused an eye. Then another. In sequence he opened and focused each of his thirty eyes. The place where he lay came into full luster. He was underground. The shapeless walls of the place dripped with sap and several colors of viscous fluid. The fluid dripped down over bark that seemed to have been formed as stalactites, the grain running long and glistening till it tapered into needle tips. The surface on which the cat lay was planed wood, the grain exquisitely formed, running outward from a coral-colored pith in concentric circles of hues that went from coral to dark teak at the outer perimeter.

The spores had fissioned, were heaped in an alcove. Tunnels ran off in all directions. Huge tunnels twenty feet across.

The mesh cap was gone.

The cat got to his feet. Bailey was there, inside, fully awake, conversing with the cat.

"Am I cut off from the Filonii?"

"Yes, I'm afraid you are."

"Under the trees."

"That's right."

"What is that spore thing?"

"I know, but I'm not sure you'd understand."

"I'm a stalker; I've spent my life analyzing alien life-forms and alien ecology. I'll understand."

"They're mobile symbiotes, conjoined with the bark of these trees. Singly, they resemble most closely anemonic anaerobic bacteria, susceptible to dichotomization; they're anacusic, anabiotic, anamnestic, and feed almost exclusively on ancyclostomiasis."

"Hookworms?"

"Big hookworms. Very big hookworms."

"The drag trails?"

"That's what they drag."

"But none of that makes any sense. It's impossible."

"So is reincarnation among the Yerbans, but it occurs."

"I don't understand."

"I told you you wouldn't."

"How do *you* know all this?"

"You wouldn't understand."

"I'll take your word for it."

"Thank you. There's more about the spores and the trees, by the way. Perhaps the most important part."

"Which is?"

"Fused, they become a quasi-sentient gestalt. They can communicate, borrowing power from the tree-hosts."

"That's even *more* implausible!"

"Don't argue with me, argue with the Creator."

"First Cause."

"Have it your way."

"What are you doing in my head?"

"Trying very hard to get out."

"And how would you do that?"

"Foul up your mission so the Filonii would demand the Succubus replace me. I gather you're pretty important to them. Rather chickenshit, aren't they?"

"I don't recognize the term."

"I'll put it in sense form."

£ ■ ■ ■ ■ ■]

"Oh. You mean ● ● ◖[—."

"Yeah. Chickenshit."

"Well, that's the way it's always been between the Filonii and the stalkers."

"You like it that way."

"I like my fish."

"Your Filonii like to play God, don't they? Changing this world and that world to suit themselves. Reminds me of a couple of other guys. Lords of Propriety they were called. And the Succubus. Did you ever stop to think how many individuals and races like to play God?"

"Right now I'd like to get out of here."

"Easy enough."

"How?"

"Make friends with the Tszechmae."

"The trees or the spores?"

"Both."

"One name for the symbiotic relationship?"

"They live in harmony."

"Except for the hookworms."

"No society is perfect. Rule 19."

The cat sat back on his haunches and talked to himself.

"Make friends with them you say."

"Seems like a good idea, doesn't it?"

"How would you suggest I do that?"

"Offer to perform a service for them. Something they can't do for themselves."

"Such as?"

"How about you'll get rid of the Filonii for them. Right now that's the thing most oppressing them."

"Get rid of the Filonii."

"Yes."

"I'm harboring a lunatic in my head."

"Well, if you're going to quit before you start…"

"Precisely *how*—uh, do you have a name?"

"I told you. Bailey."

"Oh. Yes. Sorry. Well, Bailey, precisely *how* do I rid this planet of a star-spanning vessel weighing somewhere just over thirteen thousand tons, not to mention a full complement of officers and ecologists who have been in the overlord position with my race for more centuries than I can name? I'm conditioned to respect them."

"You sure don't sound as if you respect them."

The cat paused. That was true. He felt quite different. He disliked the Filonii intensely. Hated them, in fact; as his kind had hated them for more centuries than he could name.

"That *is* peculiar. Do you have any explanation for it?"

"Well," said Bailey, humbly, "there *is* my presence. It may well have broken through all your hereditary conditioning."

"You wear smugness badly."

"Sorry."

The cat continued to think on the possibilities.

"I wouldn't take too much longer, if I were you," Bailey urged him. Then, reconsidering, he added, "As a matter of fact, I *am* you."

"You're trying to tell me something."

"I'm trying to tell you that the gestalt spore grabbed you, to get a line on what was happening with the invaders, but you've been sitting here for some time, musing to yourself—which, being instantaneously communicative throughout the many parts of the whole, is a concept they can't grasp—and so it's getting ready to digest you."

The stalker blinked his thirty eyes very rapidly. "The spore thing?"

"Uh-uh. All the spores eat are the hookworms. The bark's starting to look at you with considerable interest."

"Who do I talk to? Quick!"

"You've decided you don't respect the Filonii so much, huh?"

"I thought you said I should hurry!"

"Just curious."

"Who do I talk to!?!"

"The floor."

So the stalker-cat talked to the floor, and they struck a bargain. Rather a lopsided bargain, true; but a bargain nonetheless.

The hookworm was coming through the tunnel much more rapidly than the cat would have expected. It seemed to be sliding, but even as he watched, it bunched—inchworm-like—and propelled itself forward, following the movement with another slide. The wooden tunnel walls oozed with a noxious smelling moistness as the worm passed. It was moving itself on a slime track of its own secretions.

It was eight feet across, segmented, a filthy gray in color, and what passed for a face was merely a slash-mouth dripping yellowish mucus, several hundred cilia-like feelers surrounding the slit, and four glaze-covered protuberances in an uneven row above the slit perhaps serving in some inadequate way as "eyes."

Like a strange Hansel dropping bread crumbs to mark a trail, the spore things clinging to the cat's back began to ooze off. First one, then another. The cat backed down the tunnel. The hookworm came on. It dropped its fleshy penis-like head and snuffled at the spore lying in its path. Then the cilia feelers attached themselves and the spore thing was slipped easily into the slash mouth. There was a disgusting wet sound, and the hookworm moved forward again. The same procedure was repeated at the next spore. And the next, and the next. The hookworm followed the stalker through the tunnels.

Some miles away, the Filonii stared into their screens as a strange procession of red spores formed in the shape of a long thick hawser-like chain emerged from the forest and began to encircle the ship.

"Repulsors?" Kicker asked.

"Not yet, they haven't made a hostile move," the Homer said. "The cat could have won them somehow. This may be a welcoming ceremony. Let's wait and see."

The ship was completely circled, at a distance of fifty feet from the vessel. The Filonii waited, having faith in their cat lad.

And far underground, the stalker-cat led the hookworm a twisting chase through tunnel after tunnel. Some of the tunnels were formed only moments before the cat and his pursuer entered them. The tunnels always sloped gently upward. The cat—dropping his spore riders as he went—led the enormous slug-thing by a narrow margin. But enough to keep him coming.

Then, into a final tunnel, and the cat leaped to a planed outcropping overhead, then to a tiny hole in the tunnel ceiling, and then out of sight.

The Filonii shouted with delight as the stalker emerged from a hole in the blasted earth, just beyond the circle of red spores, linked and waiting.

"You see! Good cat!" Driver yelled to his fellows.

But the cat made no move toward the ship.

"He's waiting for the welcoming ceremony to end," the Homer said with assurance.

Then, on their screens, they saw first one red spore, then another, vanish, as though sucked down through the ground from below.

They vanished in sequence, and the Filonii followed their disappearance around the screens, watching them go in a 90° arc, then 180° of half circle, then 250° and the ground began to tremble.

And before the hookworm could suck his dinner down through a full 360° of the circle, the ground gave way beneath the thirteen thousand tons of Filonii starship, and the vessel thundered through, down into special tunnels dug straight down. Plunged down with the plates of the ship separating and cracking open. Plunged down with the hookworm that would soon discover sweeter morsels than even red spore things.

The Filonii tried to save themselves.

There was very little they could do. Driver cursed the cat and made a final contact with the Succubus. It was an automatic hookup, much easier to throw in than to fire the ship for takeoff. Particularly a quarter of a mile underground.

The hookworm broke through the ship. The Tszechmae waited. When the hookworm had gorged itself, they would move in and slay the creature. Then *they* would feast.

But Bailey would not be around to see the great meal. For only moments after the Filonii ship plunged crashing out of sight, he felt a ghastly wrenching at his soulself, and the stalker-cat was left empty once more—thereby proving in lopsided bargains no one is the winner but the house—and the soul of William Bailey went streaking out away from Belial toward the unknown.

Deep in wooden tunnels, things began to feed.

8

The darkness was the deepest blue. Not black. It was blue. He could see nothing. Not even himself. He could not tell what the body into which he had been cast did, or had, or resembled, or did not do, or not have, or not resemble. He reached out into the blue darkness. He touched nothing.

But then, perhaps he had not reached out. He had felt himself extend *something* into the blueness, but how far, or in what direction, or if it had been an appendage…he did not know.

He tried to touch himself, and did not know where to touch. He reached for his face, where a Bailey face would have been. He touched nothing.

He tried to touch his chest. He met resistance, and then penetrated something soft. He could not distinguish if he had pushed through fur or skin or hide or jelly or moisture or fabric or metal or vegetable matter or foam or some heavy gas. He had no feeling in either his "hand" or his "chest" but there was *something* there.

He tried to move, and moved. But he did not know if he was rolling or hopping or walking or sliding or flying or propelling or being propelled. But he moved. And he reached down with the thing he had used to touch himself, and felt nothing below him. He did not have legs. He did not have arms. Blue. It was so blue.

He moved as far as he could move in one direction, and there was nothing to stop him. He could have moved in that direction forever, and met no resistance. So he moved in another direction—opposite, as far as he could tell, and as far as he could go. But there was no boundary. He went up and went down and went around in circles. There was nothing. Endless nothing.

Yet he knew he was *in* somewhere. He was not in the emptiness of space, he was in an enclosed place. But what dimensions the place had, he could not tell. And what he was, he could not tell.

It made him upset. He had not been upset in the body of Pinkh, nor in the body of the stalker-cat. But this life he now owned made him nervous.

Why should that be?

Something was coming for him.

He knew that much.

He was
  here

and

something else
was out there,
coming toward
him.

He knew fear. Blue fear. Deep unseeing blue fear. If it was coming fast, it would be here sooner. If slow, then later. But it was coming. He could feel, sense, intuit it coming for him. He wanted to change. To become something else.

To become *this*

Or to become THIS

Or to become *THIS*

Or to become tHiS

But to become *something* else, something that could withstand what was coming for him. He didn't know what that could be. All he knew was that he needed equipment. He ran through his baileythoughts, his baileymind, to sort out what he might need.

What he needed
might be

Fangs   Poisonous breath
Eyes   Horns
Malleability
Webbed feet
Armored hide   Talons
Camouflage   Wings
Carapaces   Muscles
Vocal cords   Scales
Self-regeneration
Stingers   Wheels
Multiple brains

What he already had   Nothing

It was coming closer. Or was it getting farther away? (And by getting farther away, becoming more of a threat to him?) (If he went toward it, would he be safer?) (If only he could know what he looked like, or where he was, or what was required of him?) (Orient!) (Damn it, orient yourself, Bailey!) He was deep in blueness, extended, fetal, waiting. Shapeless. (Shape—) (Could *that* be it?)

Something blue flickered in the blueness.

It was coming end-for-end, flickering and sparking and growing larger, swimming toward him in the blueness. It sent tremors through him. Fear gripped him as it had never gripped him before. The blue shape coming toward him was the most fearful thing he could remember: and he remembered:

The night he had found Moravia with another man. They were standing having sex in a closet at a party. Her dress was bunched up around her waist; he had her up on tiptoes. She was crying with deep pleasure, eyes closed.

The day at the end of the war, when a laser had sliced off the top of the head of the man on his left in the warm metal trench. The sight of things still pulsing in the jasmine jelly.

The moment he had come to the final knowledge of his hopeless future. The moment he had decided to go to the Center to find death.

The thing changed shape and sent out scintillant waves of blueness and fear. He writhed away from them but they swept over him, and he turned over and over trying to escape. The thing of blue came nearer, growing larger in his sight. (Sight? Writhing? Fear?) It suddenly swept toward him, faster than before, as though it had tried a primary assault—the waves of fear—and the assault had failed; and now it would bull through.

He felt an urge to leap, high. He felt himself do it, and suddenly his sight went up and his propulsive equipment went lower, and he was longer, taller, larger. He fled. Down through the blueness, with the coruscating blue devil following. It elongated itself and shot past him on one side, boiled on ahead till it was a mere pinpoint of incandescence on some heightless, dimensionless horizon. And then it came racing back toward him, thinning itself and stretching itself till it was opaque, till the blueness of where they were shone through it darkly, like effulgent isinglass in a blue hyperplane.

He trembled in fear and went minute. He balled and shrank and contracted and drew himself to a finite point, and the whirling danger went hurtling through him and beyond, and was lost back the way they had come.

Inside the body he now owned, Bailey felt something wrenching and tearing. Fibers pulled loose from moorings and he was certain his mind was giving way. He had memories of sense-deprivation chambers and what had happened to men who had been left in them too long. This was the same. No shape, no size, no idea or way of gaining an idea of what he was, or where he was, or the touch, smell, sound, sight of *anything* as an anchor to his sanity. Yet he was surviving.

The dark blue devil kept arranging new assaults—and he had no doubt it would be back in seconds (seconds?)—and he kept doing the correct thing to escape those assaults. But he had the feeling (feeling?) that at some point the instinctive reactions of this new body would be insufficient. That he would have to bring to this new role his essential baileyness, his human mind, his thoughts, the cunning he had begun to understand was so much a part of his way. (And why had he not understood that cunningness when he had been Bailey, all the years of his hopeless life?)

The effulgence began again somewhere off to his side and high above him, coming on rapidly.

Bailey, some *thing* unknown, prepared. As best he could.

MARVELOUS, ANIK! HOW DID YOU MANAGE TO REVITALIZE IT? OH, I'M SURE YOU DID. BUT *HOW* DID YOU MANAGE? PLEASE! FIVE!?! *YOU REALLY DO WANT TO WIN;* DON'T YOU? TSK-TSK. I KNOW: YOU DON'T LOOK ON THIS AS A GAME. NOR SHOULD I. AND THAT'S SIMPLY BECAUSE YOU WERE BORN ALTHUS, WHILE— WHEN IT MEANT SOMETHING SIGNIFICANT? YES, BUT TIME GOES. FLUSTER YOU? MY DEAR GOOD ANIK, HOW CAN YOU SAY THAT? TEN THOUSAND TENILS ISN'T TOO LONG. NOT FOR A HERDUR. ARE YOU PLEADING FOR SURCEASE, MY FRIEND? DO YOU SUBMIT? WHY? BECAUSE YOUR CHAMPION IS A FALSE SOUL IN ITS BODY? TRULY, ANIK, YOU MUST THINK ME A CULLY OR A FOOL! DIE! THEN GO TO RESERVE FRAMES. I CAN'T CONCERN MYSELF NOW. LET *ME* WORRY ABOUT THE EXTENT OF MY OVER-EXTENSIONS! YOU'LL WORRY ABOUT THAT TILL THE MOMENT I DESTROY YOU. IT WAS *INTENDED* THAT WE FIGHT. IF YOU WANT OUT, I SAY GO! YOUR SUBSTITUTE CHAMPION HAS NO CHANCE, I SWEAR IT, ANIK!

you may be sure i paid dearly to do so, my dear yaquil. the succubus, yaquil. it cost me five tenils of life. chide me all you wish... unlike you, i do not look on— but you do. you have *always* thought of it as a game. while you were born herdur. There *was* a time when it— and we remain. you cannot fluster me with platitudes! i can say it because we have waged this combat too long. but for an althus it is. call an end, yaquil! do it now. submission is no part of it. i merely say stop quickly. no, because the tenils pass and the heat goes and we die! yes, die! and i've used more frames than i can afford. better now than too late. you over-extend yourself, sir. impudence, impertinence... how you ever became a combatant— you leave me no alternative. frames be damned, we fight! and concede a defeat i need not have conceded? fight on. i offered you an opportunity. the time for talk is done!

145

The blue devil swept down on him, crackling with energy. He felt the incredible million sting-points of pain and a sapping of strength. Then a

for it had. Now Bailey knew what he was, and what he had to do. He lay still, swimming in the never-ending forever blueness. He was soft and he was solitary. The blue devil swarmed and came on. For the last time. And when it was all around him, Bailey let it drink him. He let its deep blueness and its fear and its sparkling effulgence sweep over him, consume him. The blue devil gorged itself, grew larger, fuller, more incapable of movement, unable to free itself. Bailey stuffed it with his amoebic body. He split and formed yet another, and the blue devil extended itself and began feeding on his second self. The radiating sparking waves of fear and blueness were thicker now, coming more slowly. Binary fission again. Now there were four.

The blue devil fed, consumed, filled its chambers and its source-buds. Again, fission. And now there were eight. And the blue devil began to lose color. Bailey did not divide again. He knew what he had to do. Neither he nor the blue devil could win this combat. Both must die. The feeding went on and on, and finally the blue devil had drained itself with fullness, made itself immobile, died. And he died. And there was emptiness in the blueness once more.

The frames, the tenils, the fullness of combat were ended. And in that last fleeting instant of sentience, Bailey imagined he heard scented wails of hopelessness from two Duelmasters somewhere out there. He gloated. Now they knew what it was to be a William Bailey, to be hopeless and alone and afraid.

He gloated for an instant, then was whirled out and away.

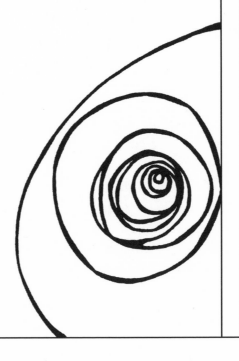

This time his repose lasted only a short time. It was rush season for the Succubus. Bailey went out to fill the husk of a Master Slavemaster whose pens were filled with females of the eighty-three races that peopled the Snowdrift Cluster asteroids. Bailey succeeded in convincing the Slavemaster that male chauvinism was detestable, and the females were bound into a secret organization that returned to their various rock-worlds, overthrew the all-male governments, and declared themselves the Independent Feminist Concourse.

He was pulled back and sent out to inhabit the radio wave "body" of a needler creature used by the Kirk to turn suns nova and thereby provide them with power sources. Bailey gained possession of the needler and imploded the Kirk home sun.

He was pulled back and sent out to inhabit the shell of a ten-thousand-year-old terrapin whose retention of random construction information made it invaluable as the overseer of a planetary reorganization project sponsored by a pale gray race without a name that altered solar systems just beyond the Finger Fringe deepout. Bailey let the turtle feed incorrect data to the world-swingers hauling the planets into their orbits, and the entire configuration collided in the orbit of the system's largest heavy-mass world. The resultant uprising caused the total eradication of the pale gray race.

He was pulled back…

Finally, even a creature as vast and involved as the Succubus, a creature plagued by a million problems and matters for attention, in effect a god-of-a-sort, was forced to take notice. There was a soul in his file that was causing a fullness leak. There was a soul that was anathema to what the Succubus had built his reputation on. There was a soul that seemed to be (unthinkable as it was) out to get him. There was a soul that was ruining things. There was a soul that was inept. There was a soul that was (again, unthinkably) consciously trying to ruin the work the Succubus had spent his life setting in motion. There was a soul named Bailey.

And the Succubus consigned him to soul limbo till he could clear away present obligations and draw him under the lens for scrutiny.

So Bailey was sent to limbo.

This is what it was like in soul limbo.

Soft pasty maggoty white. Roiling. Filled with sounds of things desperately trying to see. Slippery underfoot. Without feet. Breathless and struggling for breath. Enclosed. Tight, with great weight pressing down till the pressure was asphyxiating. But without the ability to breathe. Pressed brown to cork, porous and feeling imminent crumbling; then boiling liquid poured through. Pain in every filament and glass fiber. A wet thing settling into bones, turning them to ash and paste. Sickly sweetness, thick and rancid, tongued and swallowed and bloating. Bloating till bursting. A charnel scent. Rising smoke burning and burning the sensitive tissues. Love lost forever, the pain of knowing nothing could ever matter again; melancholia so possessive it wrenched deep inside and twisted organs that never had a chance to function.

Cold tile.

Black crepe paper.

Fingernails scraping slate.

Button pains.

Tiny cuts at sensitive places.

Weakness.

Hammering steadily pain.

That was what it was like in the Succubus's soul limbo. It was not punishment, it was merely the dead end. It was the place where the continuum had not been completed. It was not Hell, for Hell had form and substance and purpose. This was a crater, a void, a storeroom packed with uselessness. It was the place to be sent when pastpresentfuture were one and indeterminate. It was altogether ghastly.

Had Bailey gone mad, this would have been the place for it to happen. But he did not. There was a reason.

One hundred thousand eternities later, the Succubus cleared his desk of present work, filled all orders and answered all current correspondence, finished inventory and took a long-needed vacation. When he returned, before turning his attention to new business, he brought the soul of William Bailey out of limbo and ushered it under the lens.

And found it, somehow, *different*.

Quite unlike the millions and millions of other souls he had stolen.

He could not put a name to the difference. It was not a force, not a vapor, not a quality, not a potentiality, not a look, not a sense, not a capacity, not anything he could pinpoint. And, of course, such a *difference* might be invaluable.

So the Succubus drew a husk from the spare parts and rolling stock bank, and put Bailey's soul into it.

It must be understood that this was a consummately E   M   P   T   Y   husk. Nothing lived there. It had been scoured clean. It was not like the many bodies into which Bailey had been inserted. Those had had their souls stolen. There was restraining potential in all of them, memories of persona, fetters invisible but present nonetheless. This husk was now Bailey. Bailey only, Bailey free and Bailey whole.

The Succubus summoned Bailey before him.

Bailey might have been able to describe the Succubus, but he had no such desire.

The examination began. The Succubus used light and darkness, lines and spheres, soft and hard, seasons of change, waters of nepenthe, a hand outstretched, the whisper of a memory, carthing, enumeration, suspension, incursion, requital and thirteen others.

He worked over and WHAT through and inside the soul HE DID NOT of Bailey in an attempt to KNOW isolate the wild and dangerous WAS THAT difference that made this soul WHILE HE WAS unlike all others he EXAMINING had ever stolen for his tables of fulfillment BAILEY, BAILEY for the many races WAS that called upon EXAMINING him HIM.

Then, when he had all the knowledge he needed, all the secret places, all the unspoken promises, all the wished and fleshed depressions, the power that lurked in Bailey…that had *always* lurked in Bailey…before either of them could try or hope to contain it…surged free.

(It had been there all along.)
(Since the dawn of time, it had been there.)
(It had always existed.)

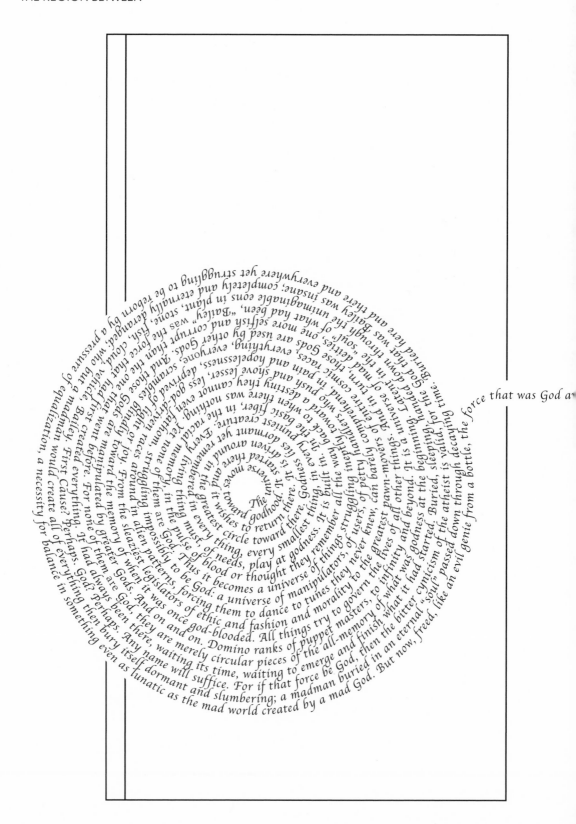

The godhood. It started there. Godness lies dormant yet remembered in the racial memory of entire cosmic races, deprived of a destiny they cannot even fathom, yet struggling toward a dimly-remembered thing that was nothing more than the basic fiber, in the pulse of blood or thought or whatever the puniest creature. Every creature possesses; and it is driven around in alien patterns of when it was once god-blooded. All things try to emerge and finish what it had started. Buried, sleeping, for what was godness at the beginning and beyond. It is a universe of manipulators, of users, of petty comprehenders who barely never knew, can barely remember all the lives of all other things—Domino ranks of puppet masters, to infinity and beyond. It is a universe of things struggling ineptly to govern the lives of the greatest pawn-movers. And on and on. Any name will suffice. For if that force be God, then the bitter cynicism of the atheist is valid, for the branded God that was insane; completely and eternally deranged, who had first created everything. For none of them are Gods. And on and on. From the sleaziest legislators of ethic and fashion, forcing them to dance to tunes they never knew, can barely remember all the lives of all other things. But now, freed, like an evil genie from a bottle, the force that was God a...

Latent in mad deities, "sour," one more selfish and corrupt than the one Gods scrambles blindly toward joy. From the memory of what had been, "Bailey" was the force that had first through the "soul," of mad deities. Gods are used by other Gods. And those Gods that manipulated by greater Gods. And they are merely circular pieces of the all-memory of what it had started. Buried in an eternal "soul," passed down through decaying time...

everything, everyone; struggling impossibly to be God. Thus it becomes a universe of god-driven races. And those Gods that had cloud, fish, cloud, plant, stone, of unimaginable eons in the sleaziest legislators of when it was once god-blooded. Bailey, the force that manipulated by greater Gods. And they are Gods, waiting its time, waiting to emerge and slumbering; a madman buried in mad God. But now, freed... a necessity for balance in something even as lunatic as the mad world created by a mad God.

First Cause? Perhaps. God? Perhaps. It had always been there, waiting dormant and slumbering; a madman would create all of everything: bury itself dormant... Bailey. First Cause? Perhaps. And on and on. Any name will suffice... would create all of everything, a necessity for balance in something even as lunatic as the mad world created by a mad God, but a madman who but a madman, a necessity of equalization...

ssomed to fullness, rejuvenated by its slumber, stronger than it had been even when it had created the universe. And, freed, it set about finishing what had begun millennia before.

Bailey remembered the Euthanasia Center, where it had begun for him. Remembered dying. Remembered being reborn. Remembered the life of inadequacy, impotency, hopelessness he had led before he'd given himself up to the Suicide Center. Remembered living as a one-eyed bear creature in a war that would never end. Remembered being a stalker-cat and death of a ghastliness it could not be spoken of. Remembered blueness. Remembered all the other lives. And remembered all the gods that had been less God than himself Bailey. The Lords of Propriety. The Filonii. The Montagasques. The Thils. The Tszechmae. The Duelmasters. The hookworms. The Slavemaster. The Kirk. The pale gray race without a name. And most of all, he remembered the Succubus.

Who thought he was God. Even as the Thieves thought *they* were Gods. But none of them possessed more than the faintest scintilla of the all-memory of godness, and Bailey had become the final repository for the force that *was* God. And now, freed, unleashed, unlocked, swirled down through all of time to this judgment day, Bailey flexed his godness and finished what he had begun at the beginning.

There is only one end to creation. What is created is destroyed, and thus full circle is achieved.

Bailey, God, set about killing the sand castle he had built. The destruction of the universes he had created.

Never before.

Songs unsung.

Washed but never purified.

Dreams spent and visits to come.

Up out of slime.

Drifted down on cool trusting winds.

Heat.

Free.

All created, all equal, all wondering, all vastness.

Gone to night.

The power that was Bailey that was God began its efforts. The husk in which Bailey lived was drawn into the power. The Succubus, screaming for reprieve, screaming for reason, screaming for release or explanation, was drawn into the power. The soul station drawn in. The home world drawn in. The solar system of the home world drawn in. The galaxy and all the galaxies and the metagalaxies and the far island universes and the alter dimensions and the past back to the beginning and beyond it to the circular place where it became now, and all the shadow places and all the thought recesses and then the very fabric and substance of eternity…all of it, everything…drawn in.

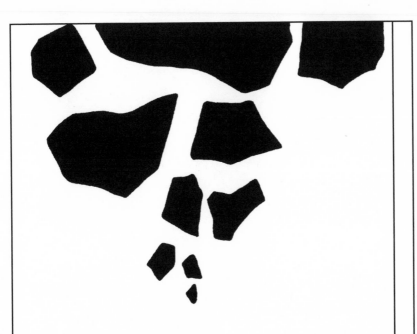

All of it contained within the power of Bailey who is God.

And then, in one awesome exertion of will, God-Bailey destroys it all, coming full circle, ending what it had been born to do. Gone.

And all that is left is Bailey. Who is dead.

In the region between.

●

BASILISK

1972 Locus Poll Award: Best Short Fiction

What though the Moor the basilisk has slain
And pinned him lifeless to the sandy plain,
Up through the spear the subtle venom flies,
The hand imbibes it, and the victor dies.
> —Lucan: *Pharsalia*
(Marcus Annaeus Lucanus, A.D. 39-65)

RETURNING FROM A night patrol beyond the perimeter of the firebase, Lance Corporal Vernon Lestig fell into a trail trap set by hostiles. He was bringing up the rear, covering the patrol's withdrawal from recently overrun sector eight, when he fell too far behind and lost the bush track. Though he had no way of knowing he was paralleling the patrol's trail, thirty yards off their left flank, he kept moving forward hoping to intersect them. He did not see the punji stakes set at cruel angles, frosted with poison, tilted for top-point efficiency, sharpened to infinity.

Two set close together penetrated the barricade of his boot; the first piercing the arch and his weight driving it up and out to emerge just below the anklebone, still inside the boot; the other ripping through the sole and splintering against the fibula above the heel, without breaking the skin.

Every circuit shorted out, every light bulb blew, every vacuum exploded, snakes shed their skins, wagon wheels creaked, plate-glass windows shattered, dentist drills ratcheted across nerve ends, vomit burned tracks up through throats, hymens were torn, fingernails bent double dragged down blackboards, water came to a boil; lava. Nova pain. Lestig's heart stopped, lubbed, began again, stuttered; his brain went dead refusing to accept the load; all senses came to full stop; he staggered sidewise with his untouched left foot, pulling one of the punji stakes out of the ground, and was unconscious even during the single movement; and fainted, simply directly fainted with the pain.

This was happening: great black gap-mawed beast padding through outer darkness toward him. On a horizonless journey through myth, coming toward the moment *before* the piercing of flesh. Lizard dragon beast with eyes of oil-slick pools, ultraviolet death colors smoking in their depths. Corded silk-flowing muscles sliding beneath the black hairless hide, trained sprinter from a lost land, smoothest movements of choreographed power. The never-sleeping guardian of the faith, now gentlestepping down through mists of potent barriers erected to separate men from their masters.

In that moment before boot touched the bamboo spike, the basilisk passed through the final veils of confounding time and space and dimension and thought, to assume palpable shape in the forest world of Vernon Lestig. And in the translation was changed, altered wonderfully. The black, thick and oily hide of the death-breath dragon beast shimmered, heat lightning across flat prairie land, golden flashes seen spattering beyond mountain peaks, and the great creature was a thousand colored. Green diamonds burned up from the skin of the basilisk, the deadly million eyes of a nameless god. Rubies gorged with the water-thin blood of insects sealed in amber from the dawn of time pulsed there. Golden jewels changing from instant to instant, shape and scent and hue...they were there in the tapestry mosaic of the skin picture. A delicate, subtle, gaudy flashmaze kaleidoscope of flesh, taut over massive muscled threats.

The basilisk was in the world.

And Lestig had yet to experience his pain.

The creature lifted a satin-padded paw and laid it against the points of the punji stakes. Slowly, the basilisk relaxed and the stakes pierced the rough sensitive blackmoon shapes of the pads. Dark, steaming serum flowed down over the stakes, mingling with the Oriental poison. The basilisk withdrew its paw and the twin wounds healed in an instant, closed over and were gone.

Were gone. Bunching of muscles, a leap into air, a cauldron roiling of dark air, and the basilisk sprang up into nothing and was gone. Was gone.

As the moment came to an exhalation of end, and Vernon Lestig walked onto the punji stakes.

It is a well-known fact that one whose blood slakes the thirst of the *vrykolakas*, the vampire, himself becomes one of the drinkers of darkness, becomes a celebrant of the master deity, becomes himself possessed of the powers of the disciples of that deity.

The basilisk had not come from the vampires, nor were his powers those of the blood drinkers. It was not by chance that the basilisk's master had sent him to recruit Lance Corporal Vernon Lestig. There is an order to the darkside universe.

He fought consciousness, as if on some cellular level he knew what pain awaited him with the return of his senses. But the red tide washed higher, swallowed more and more of his deliquescent body, and finally the pain thundered in from the blood-sea, broke in a long, curling comber and coenesthesia was upon him totally. He screamed and the scream went on and on for a long time, till they came back to him and gave him an injection of something that thinned the pain, and he lost contact with the chaos that had been his right foot.

When he came back again, it was dark and at first he thought it was night; but when he opened his eyes it was still dark. His right foot itched mercilessly. He went back to sleep, no coma, sleep.

When he came back again, it was still night and he opened his eyes and he realized he was blind. He felt straw under his left hand and knew he was on a pallet and knew he had been captured; and then he started to cry because he knew, without even reaching down to find out, that they had amputated his foot. Perhaps his entire leg. He cried about not being able to run down in the car for a pint of half-and-half just before dinner; he cried about not being able to go out to a movie without people trying not to see what had happened to him; he cried about Teresa and what she would have to decide now; he cried about the way clothes would look on him; he cried about the things he would have to say every time; he cried about shoes; and so many other things. He cursed his parents and his patrol and the hostiles and the men who had sent him here and he wanted, wished, prayed desperately that any one of them could change places with him. And when he was long finished crying, and simply wanted to die, they came for him, and took him to a hooch where they began questioning him. In the night. The night he carried with him.

They were an ancient people, with a heritage of enslavement, and so for them anguish had less meaning than the thinnest whisper of crimson cloud high above a desert planet of the farthest star in the sky. But they knew the uses to which anguish could be put, and for them there was no evil in doing so: for a people with a heritage of enslavement, evil is a concept of those who forged the shackles, not those who wore them. In the name of freedom, no monstrousness is too great.

So they tortured Lestig, and he told them what they wanted to know. Every scrap of information he knew. Locations and movements and plans and defenses and the troop strength and the sophistication of armaments and the nature of his mission and rumors he'd picked up and his name and his rank and every serial number he could think of, and the street address of his home in Kansas, and the sequence of his driver's license, and his gas credit card number and the telephone number of Teresa. He told them everything.

As if it were a reward for having held nothing back, a gummed gold star placed beside his chalked name on a blackboard in a kindergarten schoolroom, his eyesight began to come back slightly. Flickering, through a haze of gray; just enough light permitted through to show him shapes, the change from daylight to darkness; and it grew stronger, till he could actually *see* for whole minutes at a time…then blindness again. His sight came and went, and when they realized he could see them, they resumed the interrogations on a more strenuous level. But he had nothing left to tell; he had emptied himself.

But they kept at him. They threatened to hammer bamboo slivers into his damaged eyeballs. They hung him up on a shoulder-high wooden wall, his arms behind him, circulation cut off, weight pulling the arms from their shoulder sockets, and they beat him across the belly with lengths of bamboo, with bojitsu sticks. He could not even cry any more. They had given him no food and no water and he could not manufacture tears. But his breath came in deep, husking spasms from his chest, and one of the interrogators made the mistake of stepping forward to grab Lestig's head by the hair, yanking it up, leaning in close to ask another question, and Lestig—falling falling—exhaled deeply, struggling to live; and there was that breath, and a terrible thing happened.

When the reconnaissance patrol from the firebase actualized control of the hostile command position, when the Huey choppers dropped into the clearing, they advised Supermart HQ that every hostile but one in the immediate area was dead, that a Marine Lance Corporal named Lestig, Vernon C. 526-90-5416, had been found lying unconscious on the dirt floor of a hooch containing the bodies of nine enemy officers who had died horribly, most peculiarly, sickeningly, you've gotta see what this place looks like, HQ, jesus you ain't gonna believe what it smells like in here, you gotta see what these slopes look like, it musta been some terrible disease that could of done this kinda thing to 'em, the new Lieutenant got really sick an' puked and what do you want us to do with the one guy that crawled off into the bushes before *it* got him, his face is melting, and the troops're scared shitless and…

And they pulled the recon group out immediately and sent in the Intelligence section, who sealed the area with Top Security, and they found out from the one with the rotting face—just before he died—that Lestig had talked, and they medevacked Lestig back to a field hospital and then to Saigon and then to Tokyo and then to San Diego and they decided to court-martial him for treason and conspiring with the enemy, and the case made the papers big, and the court-martial was held behind closed doors and after a long time Lestig emerged with an honorable and they paid him off for the loss of his foot and the blindness and he went back to the hospital for eleven months and in a way regained his sight, though he had to wear smoked glasses.

And then he went home to Kansas.

Between Syracuse and Garden City, sitting close to the coach window, staring out through the film of roadbed filth, Lestig watched the ghost image of the train he rode superimposed over flatland Kansas slipping past outside. The mud-swollen Arkansas River was a thick, brown underline to the horizon.

"Hey, you Corporal Lestig?"

Vernon Lestig refocused his eyes and saw the wraith in the window. He turned and the sandwich butcher with his tray of candy bars, soft drinks, ham&cheeses on white or rye, newspapers and *Reader's Digest*s, suspended from his chest by a strap around the neck, was looking at him.

"No thanks," Lestig said, refusing the merchandise.

"No, hey, really, aren't you that Corporal Lestig—" He uncurled a newspaper from the roll in the tray and opened it quickly. "Yeah, sure, here you are. See?"

Lestig had seen most of the newspaper coverage, but this was local, Wichita. He fumbled for change. "How much?"

"Ten cents." There was a surprised look on the butcher's face, but it washed down into a smile as he said, understanding it, "You been out of touch in the service, didn't even remember what a paper cost, huh?"

Lestig gave him two nickels and turned abruptly to the window, folding the paper back. He read the article. It was a stone. There was a note referring to an editorial, and he turned to that page and read it. People were outraged, it said. Enough secret trials, it said. We must face up to our war crimes, it said. The effrontery of the military and the government, it said. Coddling, even ennobling traitors and killers, it said. He let the newspaper slide out of his hands. It clung to his lap for a moment then fell apart to the floor.

"I didn't say it before, but they should of shot you, you want *my* opinion!" The butcher said it, going fast, fast through the aisle, coming back the other way, gaining the end of the car and gone. Lestig did not turn around. Even wearing the smoked glasses to protect his damaged eyes, he could see too clearly. He thought about the months of blindness, and wondered again what had happened in that hooch, and considered how much better off he might be if he were *still* blind.

The Rock Island Line was a mighty good road, the Rock Island Line was the way to go. To go home. The land outside dimmed for him, as things frequently dimmed, as though the repairwork to his eyes was only temporary, a reserve generator cut in from time to time to sustain the power-feed to his vision, and dimming as the drain drank too deep. Then light seeped back in and he could see again. But there was a mist over his eyes, over the land.

Somewhere else, through another mist, a great beast sat haunch-back, dripping chromatic fire from jeweled hide, nibbling at something soft in its paw, talons extended from around blackmoon pads. Watching, breathing, waiting for Lestig's vision to clear.

He had rented the car in Wichita, and driven back the sixty-five miles to Grafton. The Rock Island Line no longer stopped there. Passenger trains were almost a thing of the past in Kansas.

Lestig drove silently. No radio sounds accompanied him. He did not hum, he did not cough, he drove with his eyes straight ahead, not seeing the hills and valleys through which he passed, features of the land that gave the lie to the myth of totally flat Kansas. He drove like a man who, had he the power of images, thought of himself as a turtle drawn straight to the salt sea.

He paralleled the belt of sand hills on the south side of the Arkansas, turned off Route 96 at Elmer, below Hutchinson, due south onto 17. He had not driven these roads in three years, but then, neither had he swum or ridden a bicycle in all that time. Once learned, there was no forgetting.

Or Teresa.

Or home. No forgetting.

Or the hooch.

Or the smell of it. No forgetting.

He crossed the North Fork at the western tip of Cheney Reservoir and turned west off 17 above Pretty Prairie. He pulled into Grafton just before dusk, the immense running sore of the sun draining itself off behind the hills. The deserted buildings of the zinc mine—closed now for twelve years—stood against the sky like black fingers of a giant hand opened and raised behind the nearest hill.

He drove once around the town mall, the Soldiers and Sailors Monument and the crumbling band shell its only ornaments. There was an American flag flying at half-mast from the City Hall. And another from the Post Office.

It was getting dark. He turned on his headlights. The mist over his eyes was strangely reassuring, as if it separated him from a land at once familiar and alien.

The stores on Fitch Street were closed, but the Utopia Theater's marquee was flashing and a small crowd was gathered waiting for the ticket booth to open. He slowed to see if he recognized anyone, and people stared back at him. A teenaged boy he didn't know pointed and then turned to his friends. In the rearview mirror Lestig saw two of them leave the queue and head for the candy shop beside the movie house. He drove through the business section and headed for his home.

He stepped on the headlight brightener but it did little to dissipate the dimness through which he marked his progress. Had he been a man of images, he might have fantasized that he now saw the world through the eyes of some special beast. But he was not a man of images.

The house in which his family had lived for sixteen years was empty.

There was a realtor's FOR SALE sign on the unmowed front lawn. Grama and buffalo grass were taking over. Someone had taken a chain saw to the oak tree that had grown in the front yard. When it had fallen, the top branches had torn away part of the side porch of the house.

He forced an entrance through the coal chute at the rear of the house, and through the sooty remains of his vision he searched every room, both upstairs and down. It was slow work: he walked with an aluminum crutch.

They had left hurriedly, mother and father and Neola. Coat hangers clumped together in the closets like frightened creatures huddling for comfort. Empty cartons from a market littered the kitchen floor and in one of them a tea cup without a handle lay upside down. The fireplace flue had been left open and rain had reduced the ashes in the grate to a black paste. Mold grew in an open jar of blackberry preserves left on a kitchen cabinet shelf. There was dust.

He was touching the ripped shade hanging in a living room window when he saw the headlights of the cars turning into the driveway. Three of them pulled in, bumper to bumper. Two more slewed in at the curb, their headlights flooding the living room with a dim glow. Doors slammed.

Lestig crutched back and to the side.

Hard-lined shapes moved in front of the headlights, seemed to be grouping, talking. One of them moved away from the pack and an arm came up, and something shone for a moment in the light; then a Stillson wrench came crashing through the front window in an explosion of glass.

"Lestig, you motherfuckin' bastard, come on out of there!"

He moved awkwardly but silently through the living room, into the kitchen and down the basement stairs. He was careful opening the coal chute window from the bin, and through the narrow slit he saw someone moving out there. They were all around the house. Coal shifted under his foot.

He let the window fall back smoothly and turned to go back upstairs. He didn't want to be trapped in the basement. From upstairs he heard the sounds of windows being smashed.

He took the stairs clumsily, clinging to the banister, his crutch useless, but moved quickly through the house and climbed the stairs to the upper floor. The top porch doorway was in what had been his parents' room; he unlocked and opened it. The screen door was hanging off at an angle, leaning against the outer wall by one hinge. He stepped out onto the porch, careful to avoid any places where the falling tree had weakened the structure. He looked down, back flat to the wall, but could see no one. He crutched to the railing, dropped the aluminum prop into the darkness, climbed over and began shinnying down one of the porch posts, clinging tightly with his thighs, as he had when he'd been a small boy, sneaking out to play after he'd been sent to bed.

It happened so quickly, he had no idea, even later, what had actually transpired. Before his foot touched the ground, someone grabbed him from behind. He fought to stay on the post, like a monkey on a stick, and even tried to kick out with his good foot; but he was pulled loose from the post and thrown down violently. He tried to roll, but he came up against a mulberry bush. Then he tried to dummyup, fold into a bundle, but a foot caught him in the side and he fell over onto his back. His smoked glasses fell off, and through the sooty fog he could just make out someone dropping down to sit on his chest, something thick and long being raised above the head of the shape…he strained to see…strained…

And then the shape screamed, and the weapon fell out of the hand and both hands clawed at the head, and the someone staggered to its feet and stumbled away, crashing through the mulberry bushes, still screaming.

Lestig fumbled around and found his glasses, pushed them onto his face. He was lying on the aluminum crutch. He got to his foot with the aid of the prop, like a skier righting himself after a spill.

He limped away behind the house next door, circled and came up on the empty cars still headed-in at the curb, their headlights splashing the house with dirty light. He slid in behind the wheel, saw it was a stick shift and knew with one foot he could not manage it. He slid out, moved to the second car, saw it was an automatic, and quietly opened the door. He slid behind the wheel and turned the key hard. The car thrummed to life and a mass of shapes erupted from the side of the house.

But he was gone before they reached the street.

He sat in the darkness, he sat in the sooty fog that obscured his sight, he sat in the stolen car. Outside Teresa's home. Not the house in which she'd lived when he'd left three years ago, but in the house of the man she'd married six months before, when Lestig's name had been first splashed across newspaper front pages.

He had driven to her parents' home, but it had been dark. He could not—or would not—break in to wait, but there had been a note taped to the mailbox advising the mailman to forward all letters addressed to Teresa McCausland to this house.

He drummed the steering wheel with his fingers. His right leg ached from the fall. His shirtsleeve had been ripped and his left forearm bore a long, shallow gash from the mulberry bush. But it had stopped bleeding.

Finally, he crawled out of the car, dropped his shoulder into the crutch's padded curve, and rolled like a man with sea legs, up to the front door.

The white plastic button in the baroque backing was lit by a tiny nameplate bearing the word HOWARD. He pressed the button and a chime sounded somewhere on the other side of the door.

She answered the door wearing blue denim shorts and a man's white shirt, buttondown and frayed; a husband's castoff.

"Vern…" Her voice cut off the sentence before she could say *oh* or *what are you* or *they said* or *no!*

"Can I come in?"

"Go away, Vern. My husband's—"

A voice from inside called, "Who is it, Terry?"

"Please go away," she whispered.

"I want to know where Mom and Dad and Neola went."

"Terry?"

"I can't talk to you…go away!"

"What the hell's going on around here, I *have* to know."

"Terry? Someone there?"

"Goodbye, Vern. I'm…" She slammed the door and did not say the word *sorry*.

He turned to go. Somewhere great corded muscles flexed, a serpentine throat lifted, talons flashed against the stars. His vision fogged, cleared for a moment, and in that moment rage sluiced through him. He turned back to the door, and leaned against the wall and banged on the frame with the crutch.

There was the sound of movement from inside, he heard Teresa arguing, pleading, trying to stop someone from going to answer the noise, but a second later the door flew open and Gary Howard stood in the doorway, older and thicker across the shoulders and angrier than Lestig had remembered him from senior year in high school, the last time they'd seen each other. The annoyed look of expecting Bible salesman, heart-fund solicitor, Girl Scout cookie dealer, evening doorbell prankster changed into a smirk.

Howard leaned against the jamb, folded his arms across his chest so the off-tackle pectorals bunched against his Sherwood green tank top.

"Evening, Vern. When'd you get back?"

Lestig straightened, crutch jammed back into armpit. "I want to talk to Terry."

"Didn't know just when you'd come rolling in, Vern, but we knew you'd show. How was the war, old buddy?"

"You going to let me talk to her?"

"Nothing's stopping her, old buddy. My wife is a free agent when it comes to talking to ex-boyfriends. My *wife*, that is. You get the word... old buddy?"

"Terry?" He leaned forward and yelled past Howard.

Gary Howard smiled a ladies'-choice-dance smile and put one hand flat against Lestig's chest. "Don't make a nuisance of yourself, Vern."

"I'm talking to her, Howard. Right now, even if I have to go through you."

Howard straightened, hand still flat against Lestig's chest. "You miserable cowardly sonofabitch," he said, very gently, and shoved. Lestig flailed backward, the crutch going out from under him, and he tumbled off the front step.

Howard looked down at him, and the president-of-the-senior-class smile vanished. "Don't come back, Vern. The next time I'll punch out your fucking heart."

The door slammed and there were voices inside. High voices, and then the sound of Howard slapping her.

Lestig crawled to the crutch, and using the wall stood up. He thought of breaking in through the door, but he was Lestig, track...once...and Howard had been football. Still was. Would be, on Sunday afternoons with the children he'd made on cool Saturday nights in a bed with Teresa.

He went back to the car and sat in the darkness. He didn't know he'd been sitting there for some time, till the shadow moved up to the window and his head came around sharply.

"Vern...?"

"You'd better go back in. I don't want to cause you any more trouble."

"He's upstairs doing some sales reports. He got a very nice job as a salesman for Shoop Motors when he got out of the Air Force. We live nice, Vern. He's really very good to me...Oh, Vern...why? Why'd you *do* it?"

"You'd better go back in."

"I waited, God you *know* I waited, Vern. But then all that terrible thing happened...Vern, why did you *do* it?"

"Come on, Terry. I'm tired, leave me alone."

"The whole town, Vern. They were so ashamed. There were reporters and TV people, they came in and talked to *every*one. Your mother and father, Neola, they couldn't stay here any more."

"Where are they, Terry?"

"They moved away, Vern. Kansas City, I think."

"Oh, Jesus."

"Neola's living closer."

"Where?"

"She doesn't want you to know, Vern. I think she got married. I know she changed her name…Lestig isn't such a good name around here any more."

"I've got to talk to her, Terry. Please. You've got to tell me where she is."

"I can't, Vern. I promised."

"Then call her. Do you have her number? Can you get in touch with her?"

"Yes, I think so. Oh, Vern…"

"Call her. Tell her I'll stay here in town till I can talk to her. Tonight. Please, Terry!"

She stood silently. Then said, "All right, Vern. Do you want her to meet you at your house?"

He thought of the hard-lined shapes in the glare of headlamps, and of the thing that had run screaming as he lay beside the mulberry bush. "No. Tell her I'll meet her in the church."

"St. Matthew's?"

"No. The Harvest Baptist."

"But it's closed, it has been for years."

"I know. It closed down before I left. I know a way in. She'll remember. Tell her I'll be waiting."

Light erupted through the front door, and Teresa Howard's face came up as she stared across the roof of the stolen car. She didn't even say goodbye, but her hand touched his face, cool and quick; and she ran back.

Knowing it was time once again to travel, the dragon-breath deathbeast eased sinuously to its feet and began treading down carefully through the fogs of limitless forever. A soft, expectant purring came from its throat, and its terrible eyes burned with joy.

He was lying full out in one of the pews when the loose boards in the vestry wall creaked, and Lestig knew she had come. He sat up, wiping sleep from his fogged eyes, and replaced the smoked glasses. Somehow, they helped.

She came through the darkness in the aisle in front of the altar, and stopped. "Vernon?"

"I'm here, Sis."

She came toward the pew, but stopped three rows away. "Why did you come back?"

His mouth was dry. He would have liked a beer. "Where else should I have gone?"

"Haven't you made enough trouble for Mom and Dad and me?"

He wanted to say things about his right foot and his eyesight, left somewhere in Southeast Asia. But even the light smear of skin he could see in the darkness told him her face was older, wearier, changed, and he could not do that to her.

"It was terrible, Vernon. Terrible. They came and talked to us and they wouldn't let us alone. And they set up television cameras and made movies of the house and we couldn't even go out. And when they went away the people from town came, and they were even worse, oh God, Vern, you can't believe what they did. One night they came to break things, and they cut down the tree and Dad tried to stop them and they beat him up so bad, Vern. You should have seen him. It would have made you cry, Vern."

And he thought of his foot.

"We went away, Vern. We had to. We hoped—" She stopped.

"You hoped I'd be convicted and shot or sent away."

She said nothing.

He thought of the hooch and the smell.

"Okay, Sis. I understand."

"I'm sorry, Vernon. I'm really sorry, dear. But why did you do this to us? Why?"

He didn't answer for a long time, and finally she came to him, and put her arms around him and kissed his neck, and then she slipped away in the darkness and the wall boards creaked, and he was alone.

He sat there in the pew, thinking nothing. He stared at the shadows till his eyes played him tricks and he thought he saw little speckles of light dancing. Then the light glimmers changed and coalesced and turned red and he seemed to be staring first into a mirror, and then into the eyes of some monstrous creature, and his head hurt and his eyes burned…

And the church changed, melted, swam before his eyes and he fought for breath, and pulled at his throat, and the church re-formed and he was in the hooch again; they were questioning him.

He was crawling.

Crawling across a dirt floor, pulling himself forward with his fingers leaving flesh-furrows in the earth, trying to crawl away from them.

"Crawl! Crawl and perhaps we will let you live!"

He crawled and their legs were at his eye level, and he tried to reach up to touch one of them, and they hit him. Again and again. But the pain was not the worst of it. The monkey cage where they kept him boxed for endless days and nights. Too small to stand, too narrow to lie down, open to the rain, open to the insects that came and nested in the raw stump of his leg, and laid their eggs, and the itching that sent lilliputian arrows up into his side, and the light that hung from jerry-rigged wires through the trees, the light that never went out, day or night, and no sleep, and the questions, the endless questions...and he crawled...God how he crawled...if he could have crawled around the world on both bloody hands and one foot, scouring away the knees of his pants, he would have crawled, just to sleep, just to stop the arrows of pain...he would have crawled to the center of the earth and drunk the menstrual blood of the planet...for only a time of quiet, a straightening of his legs, a little sleep...

Why did you do this to us, why?

Because I'm a human being and I'm weak and no one should be expected to be able to take it. Because I'm a man and not a book of rules that says I have to take it. Because I was in a place without sleep and I didn't want to be there and there was no one to save me. Because I wanted to live.

He heard boards creaking.

He blinked his eyes and sat silently and listened, and there was movement in the church. He reached for his smoked glasses, but they were out of reach, and he reached farther and the crutch slid away from the pew seat and dropped with a crash. Then they were on him.

Whether it was the same bunch he never knew.

They came for him and vaulted the pews and smashed into him before he could use whatever it was he'd used on the kid at the house, the kid who lay on a table in the City Hall, covered with a sheet through which green stains and odd rotting smells oozed.

They jumped him and beat him, and he flailed up through the mass of bodies and was staring directly into a wild-eyed mandrill face, and he *looked* at him.

Looked at him. As the deathbeast struck.

The man screamed, clawed at his face, and his face came away in handfuls, the rotting flesh dripping off his fingers. He fell back, carrying two others with him, and Lestig suddenly remembered what had happened in the hooch, remembered breathing and looking and here in this house of a God gone away he spun on them, one by one, and he breathed deeply and exhaled in their faces and stared at them across the evil night wasteland of another universe, and they shrieked and died and he was all alone once more. The others, coming through the vestry wall, having followed Neola, having been telephoned by Gary Howard, who had beaten the information from his wife, the others stopped and turned and ran...

So that only Lestig, brother to the basilisk, who was itself the servant of a nameless dark one far away, only Lestig was left standing amid the twisted body shapes of things that had been men.

Stood alone, felt the power and the fury pulsing in him, felt his eyes glowing, felt the death that lay on his tongue, deep in his throat, the wind death in his lungs. And knew night had finally fallen.

They had roadblocked the only two roads out of town. Then they took eight-cell battery flashlights and Coleman lanterns and cave-crawling lamps, and some of them who had worked the zinc mine years before, they donned their miner's helmets with the lights on them, and they even wound rags around clubs and dipped them in kerosene and lit them, and they went out searching for the filthy traitor who had killed their sons and husbands and brothers, and not one of them laughed at the scene of crowd lights moving through the town, like something from an old film. A film of hunting the monster. They did not draw the parallel, for had they drawn the parallel, they would still never have laughed.

And they searched through the night, but did not find him. And when the dawn came up and they doused their lamps, and the parking lights replaced headlights on the caravans of cars that ringed the town, they still had not found him. And finally they gathered in the mall, to decide what to do.

And he was there.

He stood on the Soldiers and Sailors Monument high above them, where he had huddled all through the night, at the feet of a World War I doughboy with his arm upraised and a Springfield in his fist. He was there, and the symbolism did not escape them.

"Pull him down!" someone shouted. And they surged toward the marble-and-bronze monument.

Vernon Lestig stood watching them come toward him, and seemed unconcerned at the rifles and clubs and war-souvenir Lugers coming toward him.

The first man to scale the plinth was Gary Howard, with the broken-field cheers of the crowd smile on his face. Lestig's eyes widened behind the smoked glasses, and very casually he removed them, and he *looked* at the big, many-toothed car salesman.

The crowd screamed in one voice and the forward rush was halted as the still-smoking body of Teresa's husband fell back on them, arms flung out wide, torso twisted.

In the rear, they tried to run. He cut them down. The crowd stopped. One man tried to raise a revolver to kill him, but he dropped, his face burned away, smoking pustules of ruined flesh where his eyes had been.

They stopped. Frozen in a world of muscles that trembled, of running energy with no place to go.

"I'll show you!" he yelled. "I'll show you what it's like! You want to know, so I'll show you!"

Then he breathed, and men died. Then he looked and others fell. Then he said, very quietly, so they would hear him: "It's easy, till it happens. You never know, patriots! You live all the time and you say one thing or another, all your rules about what it takes to be brave, but you never *know*, till that one time when you find out. *I* found out, it's not so easy. Now *you'll* find out."

He pointed to the ground.

"Get down on your knees and crawl, patriots! Crawl to me and maybe I'll let you live. Get down like animals and crawl on your bellies to me."

There was a shout from the crowd; and, the man died.

"Crawl, I said! Crawl to me!"

Here and there in the crowd people dropped from sight. At the rear a woman tried to run away and he burned her out and the husk fell, and all around her, within sight of the wisps of smoke from her face, people fell to their knees. Then entire groups dropped; then one whole side of the mob went down. Then they were all on their knees.

"Crawl! Crawl, brave ones, crawl nice my people! Crawl and learn it's better to *live*, any way at all, to stay alive, because you're human! Crawl and you'll understand your slogans are shit, your rules are for others! Crawl for your goddamned lives and you'll understand! *Crawl!*"

And they crawled. They crept forward on hands and knees, across the grass, across cement and mud and the branches of small bushes, across the dirt. They crawled toward him.

And far away, through mists of darkness, the Helmet-Headed One sat on his throne, high above all, with the basilisk at his feet, and he smiled.

"Crawl, God damn you!"

But he did not know the name of the God he served.

"Crawl!"

And in the middle of the mob, a woman who had hung a gold star in her front window, crawled across a .32 Police Positive, and her hand touched it, and she folded her fingers around it, and suddenly she raised up and screamed, "For Kennyyyyy...!" and she fired.

The bullet smashed Lestig's collarbone and he spun sidewise, up against the Yank's puttees, and he tried to regain his stance but the crutch had fallen, and now the crowd was on its feet and firing...and firing...

They buried the body in an unmarked grave, and no one talked of it. And far away, on a high throne, tickling the sleek hide of the basilisk that reclined at his feet like a faithful mastiff, even the Armed One did not speak of it. There was no need to speak of it. Lestig was gone, but that was to have been expected.

The weapon had been deactivated, but Mars, the Eternal One, the God Who Never Dies, the Lord of Futures, Warden of the Dark Places, Ever-Potent Scion of Conflict, Master of Men, Mars sat content.

The recruiting had gone well. Power to the people.

THE DEATHBIRD

1974 Hugo Award: Best Novelette; Locus Poll Award: Best Short Fiction

1

THIS IS A test. Take notes. This will count as ¾ of your final grade. Hints: remember, in chess, kings cancel each other out and cannot occupy adjacent squares, are therefore all-powerful and totally powerless, cannot affect one another, produce stalemate. Hinduism is a polytheistic religion; the sect of Atman worships the divine spark of life within Man; in effect saying, "Thou art God." Provisos of equal time are not served by one viewpoint having media access to two hundred million people in prime time while opposing viewpoints are provided with a soapbox on the corner. Not everyone tells the truth. Operational note: these sections may be taken out of numerical sequence: rearrange them to suit yourself for optimum clarity. Turn over your test papers and begin.

2

Uncounted layers of rock pressed down on the magma pool. White-hot with the bubbling ferocity of the molten nickel-iron core, the pool spat and shuddered, yet did not pit or char or smoke or damage in the slightest, the smooth and reflective surfaces of the strange crypt.

Nathan Stack lay in the crypt—silent, sleeping.

A shadow passed through rock. Through shale, through coal, through marble, through mica schist, through quartzite; through miles-thick deposits of phosphates, through diatomaceous earth, through feldspars, through diorite; through faults and folds, through anticlines and monoclines, through dips and synclines; through hellfire; and came to the ceiling of the great cavern and passed through; and saw the magma pool and dropped down; and came to the crypt. The shadow.

A triangular face with a single eye peered into the crypt, saw Stack; four-fingered hands were placed on the crypt's cool surface. Nathan Stack woke at the touch, and the crypt became transparent; he woke though the touch had not been upon his body. His soul felt the shadowy pressure and he opened his eyes to see the leaping brilliance of the worldcore around him, to see the shadow with its single eye staring in at him.

The serpentine shadow enfolded the crypt; its darkness flowed upward again, through the Earth's mantle, toward the crust, toward the surface of the cinder, the broken toy that was the Earth.

When they reached the surface, the shadow bore the crypt to a place where the poison winds did not reach, and caused it to open.

Nathan Stack tried to move, and moved only with difficulty. Memories rushed through his head of other lives, many other lives, as many other men; then the memories slowed and melted into a background tone that could be ignored.

The shadow thing reached down a hand and touched Stack's naked flesh. Gently, but firmly, the thing helped him to stand, and gave him garments, and a neck-pouch that contained a short knife and a warming-stone and other things. He offered his hand, and Stack took it, and after two hundred and fifty thousand years sleeping in the crypt, Nathan Stack stepped out on the face of the sick planet Earth.

Then the thing bent low against the poison winds and began walking away. Nathan Stack, having no other choice, bent forward and followed the shadow creature.

3

A messenger had been sent for Dira and he had come as quickly as the meditations would permit. When he reached the Summit, he found the fathers waiting, and they took him gently into their cove, where they immersed themselves and began to speak.

"We've lost the arbitration," the coil-father said. "It will be necessary for us to go and leave it to him."

Dira could not believe it. "But didn't they listen to our arguments, to our logic?"

The fang-father shook his head sadly and touched Dira's shoulder. "There were…accommodations to be made. It was their time. So we must leave."

The coil-father said, "We've decided you will remain. One was permitted, in caretakership. Will you accept our commission?"

It was a very great honor, but Dira began to feel the loneliness even as they told him they would leave. Yet he accepted. Wondering why they had selected *him*, of all their people. There were reasons, there were always reasons, but he could not ask. And so he accepted the honor, with all its attendant sadness, and remained behind when they left.

The limits of his caretakership were harsh, for they ensured he could not defend himself against whatever slurs or legends would be spread, nor could he take action unless it became clear the trust was being breached by the other—who now held possession. And he had no threat save the Deathbird. A final threat that could be used only when final measures were needed: and therefore too late.

But he was patient. Perhaps the most patient of all his people.

Thousands of years later, when he saw how it was destined to go, when there was no doubt left how it would end, he understood *that* was the reason he had been chosen to stay behind.

But it did not help the loneliness.

Nor could it save the Earth. Only Stack could do that.

4

1 Now the serpent was more subtil than any beast of the field which the LORD *God had made. And he said unto the woman, Yea, hath God said, Ye shall not eat of every tree of the garden?*

2 And the woman said unto the serpent, We may eat of the fruit of the trees of the garden:

3 But of the fruit of the tree which is in the midst of the garden, God hath said, Ye shall not eat of it, neither shall ye touch it, lest ye die.

4 And the serpent said unto the woman, Ye shall not surely die:

5 (Omitted)

6 And when the woman saw that the tree was good for food, and that it was pleasant to the eyes, and a tree to be desired to make one wise, she took of the fruit thereof, and did eat, and gave also unto her husband with her; and he did eat.

7 (Omitted)

8 (Omitted)

9 And the LORD *God called unto Adam, and said unto him, Where art thou?*

10 *(Omitted)*

11 *And he said, Who told thee that thou* wast *naked? Hast thou eaten of the tree, whereof I commanded thee that thou shouldest not eat?*

12 *And the man said, The woman whom thou gavest to be with me, she gave me of the tree, and I did eat.*

13 *And the* LORD *God said unto the woman, What is this that thou has done? And the woman said, The serpent beguiled me, and I did eat.*

14 *And the* LORD *God said unto the serpent, Because thou hast done this, thou* art *cursed above all cattle, and above every beast of the field; upon thy belly shalt thou go, and dust shalt thou eat all the days of thy life:*

15 *And I will put enmity between thee and the woman, and between thy seed and her seed; it shall bruise thy head, and thou shalt bruise his heel.*

—Genesis 3:1-15

TOPICS FOR DISCUSSION
(Give 5 points per right answer.)

1. Melville's MOBY-DICK begins, "Call me Ishmael." We say it is told in the *first* person. In what person is Genesis told? From whose viewpoint?

2. Who is the "good guy" in this story? Who is the "bad guy"? Can you make a strong case for reversal of the roles?

3. Traditionally, the apple is considered to be the fruit the serpent offered to Eve. But apples are not endemic to the Near East. Select one of the following, more logical substitutes, and discuss how myths come into being and are corrupted over long periods of time: olive, fig, date, pomegranate.

4. Why is the word LORD always in capitals and the name God always capitalized? Shouldn't the serpent's name be capitalized, as well? If no, why?

5. If God created everything (see Genesis, Chap. I), why did he create problems for himself by creating a serpent who would lead his creations astray? Why did God create a tree he did not want Adam and Eve to know about, and then go out of his way to warn them against it?

6. Compare and contrast Michelangelo's Sistine Chapel ceiling panel of the *Expulsion from Paradise* with Bosch's *Garden of Earthly Delights*.

7. Was Adam being a gentleman when he placed blame on Eve? Who was Quisling? Discuss "narking" as a character flaw.

8. God grew angry when he found out he had been defied. If God is omnipotent and omniscient, didn't he know? Why couldn't he find Adam and Eve when they hid?

9. If God had not wanted Adam and Eve to taste the fruit of the forbidden tree, why didn't he warn the serpent? Could God have prevented the serpent from tempting Adam and Eve? If yes, why didn't he? If no, discuss the possibility the serpent was as powerful as God.

10. Using examples from two different media journals, demonstrate the concept of "slanted news."

5

The poison winds howled and tore at the powder covering the land. Nothing lived there. The winds, green and deadly, dived out of the sky and raked the carcass of the Earth, seeking, seeking: anything moving, anything still living. But there was nothing. Powder. Talc. Pumice.

And the onyx spire of the mountain toward which Nathan Stack and the shadow thing had moved, all that first day. When night fell they dug a pit in the tundra and the shadow thing coated it with a substance thick as glue that had been in Stack's neck-pouch. Stack had slept the night fitfully, clutching the warming-stone to his chest and breathing through a filter tube from the pouch.

Once he had awakened, at the sound of great batlike creatures flying overhead; he had seen them swooping low, coming in flat trajectories across the wasteland toward his pit in the earth. But they seemed unaware that he—and the shadow thing—lay in the hole. They excreted thin, phosphorescent strings that fell glowing through the night and were lost on the plains; then the creatures swooped upward and were whirled away on the winds. Stack resumed sleeping with difficulty.

In the morning, frosted with an icy light that gave everything a blue tinge, the shadow thing scrabbled its way out of the choking powder and crawled along the ground, then lay flat, fingers clawing for purchase in the whiskaway surface. Behind it, from the powder, Stack bore toward the surface, reached up a hand and trembled for help.

The shadow creature slid across the ground, fighting the winds that had grown stronger in the night, back to the soft place that had been their pit, to the hand thrust up through the powder. It grasped the hand, and

Stack's fingers tightened convulsively. Then the crawling shadow exerted pressure and pulled the man from the treacherous pumice.

Together they lay against the earth, fighting to see, fighting to draw breath without filling their lungs with suffocating death.

"Why is it like this...what *happened*?" Stack screamed against the wind. The shadow creature did not answer, but it looked at Stack for a long moment and then, with very careful movements, raised its hand, held it up before Stack's eyes and slowly, making claws of the fingers, closed the four fingers into a cage, into a fist, into a painfully tight ball that said more eloquently than words: *destruction*.

Then they began to crawl toward the mountain.

6

The onyx spire of the mountain rose out of hell and struggled toward the shredded sky. It was monstrous arrogance. Nothing should have tried that climb out of desolation. But the black mountain had tried, and succeeded.

It was like an old man. Seamed, ancient, dirt caked in striated lines, autumnal, lonely; black and desolate, piled strength upon strength. It would *not* give in to gravity and pressure and death. It struggled for the sky. Ferociously alone, it was the only feature that broke the desolate line of the horizon.

In another twenty-five million years, the mountain might be worn as smooth and featureless as a tiny onyx offering to the deity night. But though the powder plains swirled and the poison winds drove the pumice against the flanks of the pinnacle, thus far their scouring had only served to soften the edges of the mountain's profile, as though divine intervention had protected the spire.

Lights moved near the summit.

7

Stack learned the nature of the phosphorescent strings excreted onto the plain the night before by the batlike creatures. They were spores that became, in the wan light of day, strange bleeder plants.

All around them as they crawled through the dawn, the little live things sensed their warmth and began thrusting shoots up through the talc. As the fading red ember of the dying sun climbed painfully into the sky, the bleeding plants were already reaching maturity.

Stack cried out as one of the vine tentacles fastened around his ankle, holding him. A second looped itself around his neck.

Thin films of berry-black blood coated the vines, leaving rings on Stack's flesh. The rings burned terribly.

The shadow creature slid on its belly and pulled itself back to the man. Its triangular head came close to Stack's neck, and it bit into the vine. Thick black blood spurted as the vine parted, and the shadow creature rasped its razor-edged teeth back and forth till Stack was able to breathe again. With a violent movement Stack folded himself down and around, pulling the short knife from the neck-pouch. He sawed through the vine tightening inexorably around his ankle. It screamed as it was severed, in the same voice Stack had heard from the skies the night before. The severed vine writhed away, withdrawing into the talc.

Stack and the shadow thing crawled forward once again, low, flat, holding onto the dying earth: toward the mountain.

High in the bloody sky, the Deathbird circled.

8

On their own world, they had lived in luminous, oily-walled caverns for millions of years, evolving and spreading their race through the universe. When they had had enough of empire building, they turned inward, and much of their time was spent in the intricate construction of songs of wisdom, and the designing of fine worlds for many races.

There were other races that designed, however. And when there was a conflict over jurisdiction, an arbitration was called, adjudicated by a race whose *raison d'être* was impartiality and cleverness in unraveling knotted threads of claim and counterclaim. Their racial honor, in fact, depended on the flawless application of these qualities. Through the centuries they had refined their talents in more and more sophisticated arenas of arbitration until the time came when they were the final authority. The litigants were compelled to abide by the judgments, not merely because the decisions were always wise and creatively fair, but because the judges' race would, if its decisions were questioned as suspect, destroy itself. In the holiest place on their world they had erected a religious machine. It could be activated to emit a tone that would shatter their crystal carapaces. They were a race of exquisite cricketlike creatures, no larger than the thumb of a man. They were treasured throughout the civilized worlds, and their loss would have been catastrophic. Their honor and their value was never questioned. All races abided by their decisions.

So Dira's people gave over jurisdiction to that certain world, and went away, leaving Dira with only the Deathbird, a special caretakership the adjudicators had creatively woven into their judgment.

There is recorded one last meeting between Dira and those who had given him his commission. There were readings that could not be ignored—had, in fact, been urgently brought to the attention of the fathers of Dira's race by the adjudicators—and the Great Coiled One came to Dira at the last possible moment to tell him of the mad thing into whose hands this world had been given, to tell Dira of what the mad thing would do.

The Great Coiled One—whose rings were loops of wisdom acquired through centuries of gentleness and perception and immersed meditations that had brought forth lovely designs for many worlds—he who was the holiest of Dira's race, honored Dira by coming to *him*, rather than commanding Dira to appear.

We have only one gift to leave them, he said. *Wisdom. This mad one will come, and he will lie to them, and he will tell them: created he them. And we will be gone, and there will be nothing between them and the mad one but you. Only you can give them the wisdom to defeat him in their own good time.* Then the Great Coiled One stroked the skin of Dira with ritual affection, and Dira was deeply moved and could not reply. Then he was left alone.

The mad one came, and interposed himself, and Dira gave them wisdom, and time passed. His name became other than Dira, it became Snake, and the new name was despised: but Dira could see the Great Coiled One had been correct in his readings. So Dira made his selection. A man, one of them, and gifted him with the spark.

All of this is recorded somewhere. It is history.

9

The man was not Jesus of Nazareth. He may have been Simon. Not Genghis Khan, but perhaps a foot soldier in his horde. Not Aristotle, but possibly one who sat and listened to Socrates in the agora. Neither the shambler who discovered the wheel nor the link who first ceased painting himself blue and applied the colors to the walls of the cave. But one near them, somewhere near at hand. The man was not Richard *Coeur-de-Lion*, Rembrandt, Richelieu, Rasputin, Robert Fulton or the Mahdi. Just a man. With the spark.

10

Once, Dira came to the man. Very early on. The spark was there, but the light needed to be converted to energy. So Dira came to the man, and did what had to be done before the mad one knew of it, and when he discovered that Dira, the Snake, had made contact, he quickly made explanations.

This legend has come down to us as the fable of Faust.

TRUE or FALSE

11

Light converted to energy, thus:

In the fortieth year of his five hundredth incarnation, all-unknowing of the eons of which he had been part, the man found himself wandering in a terrible dry place under a thin, flat burning disc of sun. He was a Berber tribesman who had never considered shadows save to relish them when they provided shade. The shadow came to him, sweeping down across the sands like the *khamsin* of Egypt, the *simoom* of Asia Minor, the *harmattan*, all of which he had known in his various lives, none of which he remembered. The shadow came over him like the *sirocco*.

The shadow stole the breath from his lungs and the man's eyes rolled up in his head. He fell to the ground and the shadow took him down and down, through the sands, into the Earth.

Mother Earth.

She lived, this world of trees and rivers and rocks with deep stone thoughts. She breathed, had feelings, dreamed dreams, gave birth, laughed, and grew contemplative for millennia. This great creature swimming in the sea of space.

What a wonder, thought the man, for he had never understood that the Earth was his mother, before this. He had never understood, before this, that the Earth had a life of its own, at once a part of mankind and quite separate from mankind. A mother with a life of her own.

Dira, Snake, shadow…took the man down and let the spark of light change itself to energy as the man became one with the Earth. His flesh melted and became quiet, cool soil. His eyes glowed with the light that shines in the darkest centers of the planet and he saw the way the mother cared for her young: the worms, the roots of plants, the rivers that cascaded for miles over great cliffs in enormous caverns, the bark of trees. He was taken once more to the bosom of that great Earth mother, and understood the joy of her life.

Remember this, Dira said to the man.

What a wonder, the man thought…

…and was returned to the sands of the desert, with no remembrance of having slept with, loved, enjoyed the body of his natural mother.

12

They camped at the base of the mountain, in a greenglass cave; not deep but angled sharply so the blown pumice could not reach them. They put Nathan Stack's stone in a fault in the cave's floor, and the heat spread quickly, warming them. The shadow thing with its triangular head sank back in shadow and closed its eye and sent its hunting instinct out for food. A shriek came back on the wind.

Much later, when Nathan Stack had eaten, when he was reasonably content and well fed, he stared into the shadows and spoke to the creature sitting there.

"How long was I down there…how long was the sleep?"

The shadow thing spoke in whispers. *A quarter of a million years.*

Stack did not reply. The figure was beyond belief. The shadow creature seemed to understand.

In the life of a world, no time at all.

Nathan Stack was a man who could make accommodations. He smiled quickly and said, "I must have been tired."

The shadow did not respond.

"I don't understand very much of this. It's pretty damned frightening. To die, then to wake up…here. Like this."

You did not die. You were taken, put down there. By the end you will understand everything, I promise you.

"Who put me down there?"

I did. I came and found you when the time was right, and I put you down there.

"Am I still Nathan Stack?"

If you wish.

"But *am* I Nathan Stack?"

You always were. You had many other names, many other bodies, but the spark was always yours. Stack seemed about to speak, and the shadow creature added, *You were always on your way to being who you are.*

"But what *am* I? Am I still Nathan Stack, dammit?"

If you wish.

"Listen: you don't seem too sure about that. You came and got me, I mean, I woke up and there you were. Now who should know better than you what my name is?"

You have had many names in many times. Nathan Stack is merely the one you remember. You had a very different name long ago, at the start, when I first came to you.

Stack was afraid of the answer, but he asked, "What was my name then?"

Ish-lilith, Husband of Lilith. Do you remember her?

Stack thought, tried to open himself to the past, but it was as unfathomable as the quarter of a million years through which he had slept in the crypt.

"No. But there were other women, in other times."

Many. There was one who replaced Lilith.

"I don't remember."

Her name…does not matter. But when the mad one took Lilith from you and replaced her with the other…then I knew it would end like this. The Deathbird.

"I don't mean to be stupid, but I haven't the faintest idea what you're talking about."

Before it ends, you will understand everything.

"You said that before." Stack paused, stared at the shadow creature for a long time only moments long, then, "What was your name?"

Before I met you my name was Dira.

He said it in his native tongue. Stack could not pronounce it.

"Before you met me. What is it now?"

Snake.

Something slithered past the mouth of the cave. It did not stop, but it called out with voice of moist mud sucking down into a quagmire.

"Why did you put *me* down there? Why did you come to me in the first place? What spark? Why can't I remember these other lives or who I was? What do you want from me?"

You should sleep. It will be a long climb. And cold.

"I slept for two hundred and fifty thousand years, I'm hardly tired," Stack said. "Why did you pick me?"

Later. Now sleep. Sleep has other uses.

Darkness deepened around Snake, seeped out around the cave, and Nathan Stack lay down near the warming-stone, and the darkness took him.

13

SUPPLEMENTARY READING

This is an essay by a writer. It is clearly an appeal to the emotions. As you read it, ask yourself how it applies to the subject under discussion. What is the writer trying to say? Does he succeed in making his point? Does this essay cast light on the point of the subject under discussion? After you have read this essay, using the reverse side of your test paper, write your own essay (500 words or less) on the loss of a loved one. If you have never lost a loved one, fake it.

AHBHU

Yesterday my dog died. For eleven years Ahbhu was my closest friend. He was responsible for my writing a story about a boy and his dog that many people have read. The story was made into a successful movie. The dog in the movie looked a lot like Ahbhu. He was not a pet, he was a person. It was impossible to anthropomorphize him, he wouldn't stand for it. But he was so much his own kind of creature, he had such a strongly formed personality, he was so determined to share his life with only those he chose, that it was also impossible to think of him as simply a dog. Apart from those canine characteristics into which he was locked by his genes, *he* comported himself like one of a kind.

We met when I came to him at the West Los Angeles Animal Shelter. I'd wanted a dog because I was lonely and I'd remembered when I was a little boy how my dog had been a friend when I had no other friends. One summer I went away to camp and when I returned I found a rotten old neighbor lady from up the street had had my dog picked up and gassed while my father was at work. I crept into the woman's backyard that night and found a rug hanging on the clothesline. The rug beater was hanging from a post. I stole it and buried it.

At the Animal Shelter there was a man in line ahead of me. He had brought in a puppy only a few weeks old. A puli, a Hungarian sheep dog; it was a sad-looking little thing. He had too many in the litter and had brought in this one either to be taken by someone else or to be put to sleep. They took the dog inside and the man behind the counter called my turn. I told him I wanted a dog and he took me back inside to walk down the line of cages.

In one of the cages, the little puli that had just been brought in was being assaulted by three larger dogs that had been earlier tenants. He was a little thing, and he was on the bottom, getting the stuffing knocked out of him. He was struggling mightily.

"Get him out of there!" I yelled. "I'll take him, I'll take him, get him out of there!"

He cost two dollars. It was the best two bucks I ever spent.

Driving home with him, he was lying on the other side of the front seat, staring at me. I had had a vague idea what I'd name a pet, but as I stared at him, and he stared back at me, I suddenly was put in mind of the scene in Alexander Korda's 1939 film *The Thief of Bagdad*, where the evil vizier, played by Conrad Veidt, had changed Ahbhu, the little thief, played by Sabu, into a dog. The film had superimposed the human over the canine face for a moment, so there was an extraordinary look of intelligence in the face of the dog. The little puli was looking at me with that same expression. "Ahbhu," I said.

He didn't react to the name, but then he couldn't have cared less. But that was his name, from that time on.

No one who ever came into my house was unaffected by him. When he sensed someone with good vibrations, he was right there, lying at their feet. He loved to be scratched, and despite years of admonitions he refused to stop begging for scraps at the table, because he had found most of the people who came to dinner at my house were patsies unable to escape his woebegone Jackie-Coogan-as-the-Kid look.

But he was a certain barometer of bums, as well. On any number of occasions when I found someone I liked, and Ahbhu would have nothing to do with him or her, it always turned out the person was a wrongo. I took to noting his attitude toward newcomers, and I must admit it influenced my own reactions. I was always wary of someone Ahbhu shunned.

Women with whom I had had unsatisfactory affairs would nonetheless return to the house from time to time—to visit the dog. He had an intimate circle of friends, many of whom had nothing to do with me, and numbering among their company some of the most beautiful actresses in Hollywood. One exquisite lady used to send her driver to pick him up for Sunday afternoon romps at the beach.

I never asked him what happened on those occasions. He didn't talk.

Last year he started going downhill, though I didn't realize it because he maintained the manner of a puppy almost to the end. But he began sleeping too much, and he couldn't hold down his food—not even the Hungarian meals prepared for him by the Magyars who lived up the street. And it became apparent to me something was wrong with him when he got scared during the big Los Angeles earthquake last year. Ahbhu wasn't afraid of anything. He attacked the Pacific Ocean and walked tall around vicious cats. But the quake terrified him and he jumped up in my bed and threw his forelegs around my neck. I was very nearly the only victim of the earthquake to die from animal strangulation.

He was in and out of the veterinarian's shop all through the early part of this year, and the idiot always said it was his diet.

Then one Sunday when he was out in the backyard, I found him lying at the foot of the stairs, covered with mud, vomiting so heavily all he could bring up was bile. He was matted with his own refuse and he was trying desperately to dig his nose into the earth for coolness. He was barely breathing. I took him to a different vet.

At first they thought it was just old age...that they could pull him through. But finally they took X-rays and saw the cancer had taken hold in his stomach and liver.

I put off the day as much as I could. Somehow I just couldn't conceive of a world that didn't have him in it. But yesterday I went to the vet's office and signed the euthanasia papers.

"I'd like to spend a little time with him, before," I said.

They brought him in and put him on the stainless steel examination table. He had grown so thin. He'd always had a pot-belly, and it was gone. The muscles in his hind legs were weak, flaccid. He came to me and put his head into the hollow of my armpit. He was trembling violently. I lifted his head and he looked at me with that comic face I'd always thought made him look like Lawrence Talbot, the Wolf Man. He knew. Sharp as hell, right up to the end, hey old friend? He knew, and he was scared. He trembled all the way down to his spiderweb legs. This bouncing ball of hair that, when lying on a dark carpet, could be taken for a sheepskin rug, with no way to tell at which end head and which end tail. So thin. Shaking, knowing what was going to happen to him. But still a puppy.

I cried, and my eyes closed as my nose swelled with the crying, and he buried his head in my arms because we hadn't done much crying at one another. I was ashamed of myself, not to be taking it as well as he was.

"I *got* to, pup, because you're in pain and you can't eat. I *got* to." But he didn't want to know that.

The vet came in, then. He was a nice guy and he asked me if I wanted to go away and just let it be done.

Then Ahbhu came up out of there and *looked* at me.

There is a scene in Kazan's and Steinbeck's *Viva Zapata* where a close friend of Zapata's, Brando's, has been condemned for conspiring with the *federales*. A friend that had been with Zapata since the mountains, since the *revolución* had begun. And they come to the hut to take him to the firing squad, and Brando starts out, and his friend stops him with a hand on his arm, and he says to him with great friendship, "Emiliano, do it yourself."

Ahbhu looked at me and I know he was just a dog, but if he could have spoken with human tongue he could not have said more eloquently than he did with a look, *don't leave me with strangers*.

So I held him as they laid him down and the vet slipped the lanyard up around his right foreleg and drew it tight to bulge the vein, and I held his head and he turned it away from me as the needle went in. It was impossible to tell the moment he passed over from life to death. He simply laid his head on my hand, his eyes fluttered shut and he was gone.

I wrapped him in a sheet with the help of the vet and I drove home with Ahbhu on the seat beside me, just the way we had come home eleven years before. I took him out in the backyard and began digging his grave. I dug for hours, crying and mumbling to myself, talking to him in the sheet. It was a very neat, rectangular grave with smooth sides and all the loose dirt scooped out by hand.

I laid him down in the hole and he was so tiny in there for a dog who had seemed to be so big in life, so furry, so funny. And I covered him over and when the hole was packed full of dirt, I replaced the neat divot of grass I'd scalped off at the start. And that was all.

But I couldn't send him to strangers.

THE END

QUESTIONS FOR DISCUSSION

1. Is there any significance to the reversal of the word *god* being *dog*? If so, what?

2. Does the writer try to impart human qualities to a nonhuman creature? Why? Discuss anthropomorphism in the light of the phrase, "Thou art God."

3. Discuss the love the writer shows in this essay. Compare and contrast it with other forms of love: the love of a man for a woman, a mother for a child, a son for a mother, a botanist for plants, an ecologist for the Earth.

14

In his sleep, Nathan Stack talked.
"Why did you pick me? Why me...?"

15

Like the Earth, the Mother was in pain.

The great house was very quiet. The doctor had left, and the relatives had gone into town for dinner. He sat by the side of her bed and stared down at her. She looked gray and old and crumpled; her skin was a powdery, ashy hue of moth-dust. He was crying softly.

He felt her hand on his knee, and looked up to see her staring at him. "You weren't supposed to catch me," he said.

"I'd be disappointed if I hadn't," she said. Her voice was very thin, very smooth.

"How is it?"

"It hurts. Ben didn't dope me too well."

He bit his lower lip. The doctor had used massive doses, but the pain was more massive. She gave little starts as tremors of sudden agony hit her. Impacts. He watched the life leaking out of her eyes.

"How is your sister taking it?"

He shrugged. "You know Charlene. She's sorry, but it's all pretty intellectual to her."

His mother let a tiny ripple of a smile move her lips. "It's a terrible thing to say, Nathan, but your sister isn't the most likable woman in the world. I'm glad you're here." She paused, thinking, then added, "It's just possible your father and I missed something from the gene pool. Charlene isn't whole."

"Can I get you something? A drink of water?"

"No. I'm fine."

He looked at the ampoule of narcotic painkiller. The syringe lay mechanical and still on the clean towel beside it. He felt her eyes on him. She knew what he was thinking. He looked away.

"I would kill for a cigarette," she said.

He laughed. At sixty-five, both legs gone, what remained of her left side paralyzed, the cancer spreading like deadly jelly toward her heart, she was still the matriarch. "You can't have a cigarette, so forget it."

"Then why don't you use that hypo and let me out of here."

"Shut up, Mother."

"Oh, for Christ's sake, Nathan. It's hours if I'm lucky. Months if I'm not. We've had this conversation before. You know I always win."

"Did I ever tell you you were a bitchy old lady?"

"Many times, but I love you anyhow."

He got up and walked to the wall. He could not walk through it, so he went around the inside of the room.

"You can't get away from it."

"Mother, Jesus! Please!"

"All right. Let's talk about the business."

"I couldn't care less about the business right now."

"Then what should we talk about? The lofty uses to which an old lady can put her last moments?"

"You know, you're really ghoulish. I think you're *enjoying* this in some sick way."

"What other way is there to enjoy it."

"An adventure."

"The biggest. A pity your father never had the chance to savor it."

"I hardly think he'd have savored the feeling of being stamped to death in a hydraulic press."

Then he thought about it, because that little smile was on her lips again. "Okay, he probably would have. The two of you were so unreal, you'd have sat there and discussed it and analyzed the pulp."

"And you're our son."

He was, and he was. And he could not deny it, nor had he ever. He was hard and gentle and wild just like them, and he remembered the days in the jungle beyond Brasilia, and the hunt in the Cayman Trench, and the other days working in the mills alongside his father, and he knew when his moment came he would savor death as she did.

"Tell me something. I've always wanted to know. *Did* Dad kill Tom Golden?"

"Use the needle and I'll tell you."

"I'm a Stack. I don't bribe."

"*I'm* a Stack, and I know what a killing curiosity you've got. Use the needle and I'll tell you."

He walked widdershins around the room. She watched him, eyes bright as the mill vats.

"You old bitch."

"Shame, Nathan. You know you're not the son of a bitch. Which is more than your sister can say. Did I ever tell you she wasn't your father's child?"

"No, but I knew."

"You'd have liked her father. He was Swedish. *Your* father liked him."

"Is that why Dad broke both his arms?"

"Probably. But I never heard the Swede complain. One night in bed with me in those days was worth a couple of broken arms. Use the needle."

Finally, while the family was between the entree and the dessert, he filled the syringe and injected her. Her eyes widened as the stuff smacked her heart, and just before she died she rallied all her strength and said, "A deal's a deal. Your father didn't kill Tom Golden, I did. You're a hell of a man, Nathan, and you fought us the way we wanted, and we both loved you more than you could know. Except, dammit, you cunning s.o.b., you *do* know, don't you?"

"I know," he said, and she died; and he cried; and that was the extent of the poetry in it.

16

He knows we are coming.

They were climbing the northern face of the onyx mountain. Snake had coated Nathan Stack's feet with the thick glue and, though it was hardly a country walk, he was able to keep a foothold and pull himself up. Now they had paused to rest on a spiral ledge, and Snake had spoken for the first time of what waited for them where they were going.

"He?"

Snake did not answer. Stack slumped against the wall of the ledge. At the lower slopes of the mountain they had encountered sluglike creatures that had tried to attach themselves to Stack's flesh, but when Snake had driven them off they had returned to sucking the rocks. They had not come near the shadow creature. Farther up, Stack could see the lights that flickered at the summit; he had felt fear that crawled up from his stomach. A short time before they had come to this ledge, they had stumbled past a cave in the mountain where the bat creatures slept. They had gone mad at the presence of the man and the Snake, and the sounds they had made sent waves of nausea through Stack. Snake had helped him and they had gotten past. Now they had stopped and Snake would not answer Stack's questions.

We must keep climbing.

"Because he knows we're here." There was a sarcastic rise in Stack's voice.

Snake started moving. Stack closed his eyes. Snake stopped and came back to him. Stack looked up at the one-eyed shadow.

"Not another step."

There is no reason why you should not know.

"Except, friend, I have the feeling you aren't going to tell me anything."

It is not yet time for you to know.

"Look: just because I haven't asked, doesn't mean I don't want to know. You've told me things I shouldn't be able to handle...all kinds of crazy things...I'm as old as, as...I don't know *how* old, but I get the feeling you've been trying to tell me I'm Adam..."

That is so.

"...uh." He stopped rattling and stared back at the shadow creature. Then, very softly, accepting even more than he had thought possible, he said, "Snake." He was silent again. After a time he asked, "Give me another dream and let me know the rest of it?"

You must be patient. The one who lives at the top knows we are coming but I have been able to keep him from perceiving your danger to him only because you do not know yourself.

"Tell me this, then: does he *want* us to come up...the one on the top?"

He allows it. Because he doesn't know.

Stack nodded, resigned to following Snake's lead. He got to his feet and performed an elaborate butler's motion: after you, Snake.

And Snake turned, his flat hands sticking to the wall of the ledge, and they climbed higher, spiraling upward toward the summit.

The Deathbird swooped, then rose toward the Moon. There was still time.

17

Dira came to Nathan Stack near sunset, appearing in the board room of the industrial consortium Stack had built from the empire left by his family.

Stack sat in the pneumatic chair that dominated the conversation pit where top-level decisions were made. He was alone. The others had left hours before and the room was dim with only the barest glow of light from hidden banks that shone through the soft walls.

The shadow creature passed through the walls—and at his passage they became rose quartz, then returned to what they had been. He stood staring at Nathan Stack, and for long moments the man was unaware of any other presence in the room.

You have to go now, Snake said.

Stack looked up, his eyes widened in horror, and through his mind flitted the unmistakable image of Satan, fanged mouth smiling, horns gleaming with scintillas of light as though seen through crosstar filters, rope tail with its spade-shaped appendage thrashing, cloven hoofs leaving burning imprints in the carpet, eyes as deep as pools of oil, the pitchfork, the satin-lined cape, the hairy legs of a goat, talons. He tried to scream but the sound dammed up in his throat.

No, Snake said, *that is not so. Come with me, and you will understand.*

There was a tone of sadness in the voice. As though Satan had been sorely wronged. Stack shook his head violently.

There was no time for argument. The moment had come, and Dira could not hesitate. He gestured and Nathan Stack rose from the pneumatic chair, leaving behind something that looked like Nathan Stack asleep, and he walked to Dira and Snake took him by the hand and they passed through rose quartz and went away from there.

Down and down Snake took him.

The Mother was in pain. She had been sick for eons, but it had reached the point where Snake knew it would be terminal, and the Mother knew it, too. But she would hide her child, she would intercede in her own behalf and hide him away, deep in her bosom where no one, not even the mad one, could find him.

Dira took Stack to Hell.

It was a fine place.

Warm and safe and far from the probing of mad ones.

And the sickness raged on unchecked. Nations crumbled, the oceans boiled and then grew cold and filmed over with scum, the air became thick with dust and killing vapors, flesh ran like oil, the skies grew dark, the sun blurred and became dull. The Earth moaned.

The plants suffered and consumed themselves, beasts became crippled and went mad, trees burst into flame and from their ashes rose glass shapes that shattered in the wind. The Earth was dying; a long, slow, painful death.

In the center of the Earth, in the fine place, Nathan Stack slept. *Don't leave me with strangers.*

Overhead, far away against the stars, the Deathbird circled and circled, waiting for the word.

18

When they reached the highest peak, Nathan Stack looked across through the terrible burning cold and the ferocious grittiness of the demon wind and saw the sanctuary of always, the cathedral of forever, the pillar of remembrance, the haven of perfection, the pyramid of blessings, the toyshop of creation, the vault of deliverance, the monument of longing, the receptacle of thoughts, the maze of wonder, the catafalque of despair, the podium of pronouncements and the kiln of last attempts.

On a slope that rose to a star pinnacle, he saw the home of the one who dwelled here—lights flashing and flickering, lights that could be seen far off across the deserted face of the planet—and he began to suspect the name of the resident.

Suddenly everything went red for Nathan Stack. As though a filter had been dropped over his eyes, the black sky, the flickering lights, the rocks that formed the great plateau on which they stood, even Snake became red, and with the color came pain. Terrible pain that burned through every channel of Stack's body, as though his blood had been set afire. He screamed and fell to his knees, the pain crackling through his brain, following every nerve and blood vessel and ganglion and neural track. His skull flamed.

Fight him, Snake said. *Fight him!*

I can't, screamed silently through Stack's mind, the pain too great even to speak. Fire licked and leaped, and he felt the delicate tissue of thought shriveling. He tried to focus his thoughts on ice. He clutched for salvation at ice, chunks of ice, mountains of ice, swimming icebergs of ice half-buried in frozen water, even as his soul smoked and smoldered. *Ice!* He thought of millions of particles of hail rushing, falling, thundering against the firestorm eating his mind, and there was a spit of steam, a flame that went out, a corner that grew cool...and he took his stand in that corner, thinking ice, thinking blocks and chunks and monuments of ice, edging them out to widen the circle of coolness and safety. Then the flames began to retreat, to slide back down the channels, and he sent ice after them, snuffing them, burying them in ice and chill waters that raced after the flames and drove them out.

When he opened his eyes, he was still on his knees, but he could think again, and the red surfaces had become normal again.

He will try again. You must be ready.

"Tell me *everything*! I can't go through this without knowing, I need help! Tell me, Snake, tell me now!"

You can help yourself. You have the strength. I gave you the spark.

...and the second derangement struck!

The air turned shaverasse and he held dripping chunks of unclean rova in his jowls, the taste making him weak with nausea. His pods withered and drew up into his shell and as the bones cracked he howled with strings of pain that came so fast they were almost one. He tried to scuttle away, but his eyes magnified the shatter of light that beat against him. Facets of his eyes cracked and the juice began to bubble out. The pain was unbelievable.

Fight him!

Stack rolled onto his back, sending out cilia to touch the earth, and for an instant he realized he was seeing through the eyes of another creature, another form of life he could not even describe. But he was under an open sky and that produced fear; he was surrounded by air that had become deadly and *that* produced fear; he was going blind and *that* produced fear; he was…he was a *man*…fought back against the feeling of being some other thing…he was a *man* and he would not feel fear, he would stand.

He rolled over, withdrew his cilia, and struggled to lower his pods. Broken bones grated and pain thundered through his body. He forced himself to ignore it, and finally the pods were down and he was breathing and he felt his head reeling…

And when he opened his eyes he was Nathan Stack again.

…and the third derangement struck:

Hopelessness.

Out of unending misery he came back to be Stack.

…and the fourth derangement struck:

Madness.

Out of raging lunacy he fought his way to be Stack.

…and the fifth derangement, and the sixth, and the seventh, and the plagues, and the whirlwinds, and the pools of evil, and the reduction in size and accompanying fall forever through submicroscopic hells, and the things that fed on him from inside, and the twentieth, and the fortieth, and the sound of his voice screaming for release, and the voice of Snake always beside him, whispering *Fight him!*

Finally it stopped.

Quickly, now.

Snake took Stack by the hand and, half-dragging him, raced to the great palace of light and glass on the slope, shining brightly under the star pinnacle, and they passed under an arch of shining metal into the ascension hall. The portal sealed behind them.

There were tremors in the walls. The inlaid floors of jewels began to rumble and tremble. Bits of high and faraway ceilings began to drop. Quaking, the palace gave one hideous shudder and collapsed around them.

Now, Snake said. *Now you will know everything!*

And everything forgot to fall. Frozen in midair, the wreckage of the palace hung suspended above them. Even the air ceased to swirl. Time stood still. The movement of the Earth was halted. Everything held utterly immobile as Nathan Stack was permitted to understand all.

19

MULTIPLE CHOICE

(Counts for ½ your final grade.)

1. God is:
   A. An invisible spirit with a long beard.
   B. A small dog dead in a hole.
   C. Everyman.
   D. The Wizard of Oz.
2. Nietzsche wrote "God is dead." By this did he mean:
   A. Life is pointless.
   B. Belief in supreme deities has waned.
   C. There never was a God to begin with.
   D. Thou art God.
3. Ecology is another name for:
   A. Mother love.
   B. Enlightened self-interest.
   C. A good health salad with granola.
   D. God.
4. Which of these phrases most typifies the profoundest love:
   A. Don't leave me with strangers.
   B. I love you.
   C. God is love.
   D. Use the needle.
5. Which of these powers do we usually associate with God:
   A. Power.
   B. Love.
   C. Humanity.
   D. Docility.

20

None of the above.

Starlight shone in the eyes of the Deathbird and its passage through the night cast a shadow on the Moon.

21

Nathan Stack raised his hands and around them the air was still, as the palace fell crashing. They were untouched. *Now you know all there is to know*, Snake said, sinking to one knee as though worshipping. There was no one there to worship but Nathan Stack.

"Was he always mad?"

From the first.

"Then those who gave our world to him were mad, and your race was mad to allow it."

Snake had no answer.

"Perhaps it was supposed to be like this," Stack said.

He reached down and lifted Snake to his feet, and he touched the shadow creature's sleek triangular head. "Friend," he said.

Snake's race was incapable of tears. He said, *I have waited longer than you can know for that word.*

"I'm sorry it comes at the end."

Perhaps it was supposed to be like this.

Then there was a swirling of air, a scintillation in the ruined palace, and the owner of the mountain, the owner of the ruined Earth came to them in a burning bush.

AGAIN, SNAKE? AGAIN YOU ANNOY ME?

The time for toys is ended.

NATHAN STACK YOU BRING TO STOP ME? *I* SAY WHEN THE TIME IS ENDED. *I* SAY, AS I'VE ALWAYS SAID.

Then, to Nathan Stack:

GO AWAY. FIND A PLACE TO HIDE UNTIL I COME FOR YOU.

Stack ignored the burning bush. He waved his hand, and the cone of safety in which they stood vanished. "Let's find him, first, then I know what to do."

The Deathbird sharpened its talons on the night wind and sailed down through emptiness toward the cinder of the Earth.

22

Nathan Stack had once contracted pneumonia. He had lain on the operating table as the surgeon made the small incision in the chest wall. Had he not been stubborn, had he not continued working around the clock while the pneumonic infection developed into empyema, he would never have had to go under the knife, even for an operation as safe as a thoracotomy. But he was a Stack, and so he lay on the operating table as the rubber tube was inserted into the chest cavity to drain off the pus in the pleural cavity, and he heard someone speak his name.

NATHAN STACK.

He heard it, from far off, across an Arctic vastness; heard it echoing over and over, down an endless corridor; as the knife sliced.

NATHAN STACK.

He remembered Lilith, with hair the color of dark wine. He remembered taking hours to die beneath a rock slide as his hunting companions in the pack ripped apart the remains of the bear and ignored his grunted moans for help. He remembered the impact of the crossbow bolt as it ripped through his hauberk and split his chest and he died at Agincourt. He remembered the icy water of the Ohio as it closed over his head and the flatboat disappearing without his mates noticing his loss. He remembered the mustard gas that ate his lungs as he tried to crawl toward a farmhouse near Verdun. He remembered looking directly into the flash of the bomb and feeling the flesh of his face melt away. He remembered Snake coming to him in the board room and husking him like corn from his body. He remembered sleeping in the molten core of the Earth for a quarter of a million years.

Across the dead centuries he heard his mother pleading with him to set her free, to end her pain. *Use the needle.* Her voice mingled with the voice of the Earth crying out in endless pain at her flesh that had been ripped away, at her rivers turned to arteries of dust, at her rolling hills and green fields slagged to greenglass and ashes. The voices of his mother and the mother that was Earth became one, and mingled to become Snake's voice telling him he was the one man in the world—the last man in the world—who could end the terminal case the Earth had become.

Use the needle. Put the suffering Earth out of its misery. *It belongs to you now.*

Nathan Stack was secure in the power he contained. A power that far outstripped that of gods or Snakes or mad creators who stuck pins in their creations, who broke their toys.

YOU CAN'T. I WON'T LET YOU.

Nathan Stack walked around the burning bush as it crackled impotently in rage. He looked at it almost pityingly, remembering the Wizard of Oz with his great and ominous disembodied head floating in mist and lightning, and the poor little man behind the curtain turning the dials to create the effects. Stack walked around the effect, knowing he had more power than this sad, poor thing that had held his race in thrall since before Lilith had been taken from him.

He went in search of the mad one who capitalized his name.

23

Zarathustra descended alone from the mountains, encountering no one. But when he came into the forest, all at once there stood before him an old man who had left his holy cottage to look for roots in the woods. And thus spoke the old man to Zarathustra:

"No stranger to me is this wanderer: many years ago he passed this way. Zarathustra he was called, but he has changed. At that time you carried your ashes to the mountains: would you now carry your fire into the valleys? Do you not fear to be punished as an arsonist?

"Zarathustra has changed, Zarathustra has become a child, Zarathustra is an awakened one; what do you now want among the sleepers? You lived in your solitude as in the sea, and the sea carried you. Alas, would you now climb ashore? Alas, would you again drag your own body?"

Zarathustra answered: "I love man."

"Why," asked the saint, "did I go into the forest and the desert? Was it not because I loved man all too much? Now I love God; man I love not. Man is, for me, too imperfect a thing. Love of man would kill me."

"And what is the saint doing in the forest?" asked Zarathustra.

The saint answered: "I make songs and sing them; and when I make songs, I laugh, cry, and hum: thus I praise God. With singing, crying, laughing, and humming, I praise the god who is my god. But what do you bring us as a gift?"

When Zarathustra had heard these words he bade the saint farewell and said: "What could I have to give you? But let me go quickly, lest I take something from you!" And thus they separated, the old one and the man, laughing as two boys laugh.

But when Zarathustra was alone he spoke thus to his heart: "Could it be possible? This old saint in the forest has not yet heard anything of this, that *God is dead*!"

24

Stack found the mad one wandering in the forest of final moments. He was an old, tired man, and Stack knew with a wave of his hand he could end it for this god in a moment. But what was the reason for it? It was even too late for revenge. It had been too late from the start. So he let the old one go his way, wandering in the forest, mumbling to himself, I WON'T LET YOU DO IT, in the voice of a cranky child; mumbling pathetically, OH, PLEASE, I DON'T WANT TO GO TO BED YET. I'M NOT YET DONE PLAYING.

And Stack came back to Snake, who had served his function and protected Stack until Stack had learned that he was more powerful than the god he'd worshipped all through the history of Men. He came back to Snake and their hands touched and the bond of friendship was sealed at last, at the end.

Then they worked together and Nathan Stack used the needle with a wave of his hands, and the Earth could not sigh with relief as its endless pain was ended...but it did sigh, and it settled in upon itself, and the molten core went out, and the winds died, and from high above them Stack heard the fulfillment of Snake's final act; he heard the descent of the Deathbird.

"What was your name?" Stack asked his friend.

Dira.

And the Deathbird settled down across the tired shape of the Earth, and it spread its wings wide, and brought them over and down, and enfolded the Earth as a mother enfolds her weary child. Dira settled down on the amethyst floor of the dark-shrouded palace, and closed his single eye with gratitude. To sleep at last, at the end.

All this, as Nathan Stack stood watching. He was the last, at the end, and because he had come to own—if even for a few moments—that which could have been his from the start, had he but known, he did not sleep but stood and watched. Knowing at last, at the end, that he had loved and done no wrong.

25

The Deathbird closed its wings over the Earth until at last, at the end, there was only the great bird crouched over the dead cinder. Then the Deathbird raised its head to the star-filled sky and repeated the sigh of loss the Earth had felt at the end. Then its eyes closed, it tucked its head carefully under its wing, and all was night.

Far away, the stars waited for the cry of the Deathbird to reach them so final moments could be observed at last, at the end, for the race of Men.

26

THIS IS FOR MARK TWAIN

THE WHIMPER OF WHIPPED DOGS

1974 Edgar Allan Poe Award: Best Short Story

ON THE NIGHT after the day she had stained the louvered window shutters of her new apartment on East 52nd Street, Beth saw a woman slowly and hideously knifed to death in the courtyard of her building. She was one of twenty-six witnesses to the ghoulish scene, and, like them, she did nothing to stop it.

She saw it all, every moment of it, without break and with no impediment to her view. Quite madly, the thought crossed her mind as she watched in horrified fascination, that she had the sort of marvelous line of observation Napoleon had sought when he caused to have constructed at the *Comédie-Française* theaters, a curtained box at the rear, so he could watch the audience as well as the stage. The night was clear, the moon was full, she had just turned off the 11:30 movie on Channel 2 after the second commercial break, realizing she had already seen Robert Taylor in *Westward the Women*, and had disliked it the first time; and the apartment was quite dark.

She went to the window, to raise it six inches for the night's sleep, and she saw the woman stumble into the courtyard. She was sliding along the wall, clutching her left arm with her right hand. Con Ed had installed mercury-vapor lamps on the poles; there had been sixteen assaults in seven months; the courtyard was illuminated with a chill purple glow that made the blood streaming down the woman's left arm look black and shiny. Beth saw every detail with utter clarity, as though magnified a thousand power under a microscope, solarized as if it had been a television commercial.

The woman threw back her head, as if she were trying to scream, but there was no sound. Only the traffic on First Avenue, late cabs foraging for singles paired for the night at Maxwell's Plum and Friday's and Adam's Apple. But that was over there, beyond. Where *she* was, down there seven floors below, in the courtyard, everything seemed silently suspended in an invisible force-field.

Beth stood in the darkness of her apartment, and realized she had raised the window completely. A tiny balcony lay just over the low sill; now not even glass separated her from the sight; just the wrought-iron balcony railing and seven floors to the courtyard below.

The woman staggered away from the wall, her head still thrown back, and Beth could see she was in her mid-thirties, with dark hair cut in a shag; it was impossible to tell if she was pretty: terror had contorted her features and her mouth was a twisted black slash, opened but emitting no sound. Cords stood out in her neck. She had lost one shoe, and her steps were uneven, threatening to dump her to the pavement.

The man came around the corner of the building, into the courtyard. The knife he held was enormous—or perhaps it only seemed so: Beth remembered a bonehandled fish knife her father had used one summer at the lake in Maine: it folded back on itself and locked, revealing eight inches of serrated blade. The knife in the hand of the dark man in the courtyard seemed to be similar.

The woman saw him and tried to run, but he leaped across the distance between them and grabbed her by the hair and pulled her head back as though he would slash her throat in the next reaper-motion.

Then the woman screamed.

The sound skirled up into the courtyard like bats trapped in an echo chamber, unable to find a way out, driven mad. It went on and on…

The man struggled with her and she drove her elbows into his sides and he tried to protect himself, spinning her around by her hair, the terrible scream going up and up and never stopping. She came loose and he was left with a fistful of hair torn out by the roots. As she spun out, he slashed straight across and opened her up just below the breasts. Blood sprayed through her clothing and the man was soaked; it seemed to drive him even more berserk. He went at her again, as she tried to hold herself together, the blood pouring down over her arms.

She tried to run, teetered against the wall, slid sidewise, and the man struck the brick surface. She was away, stumbling over a flower bed, falling, getting to her knees as he threw himself on her again. The knife came up in a flashing arc that illuminated the blade strangely with purple light. And still she screamed.

Lights came on in dozens of apartments and people appeared at windows.

He drove the knife to the hilt into her back, high on the right shoulder. He used both hands.

Beth caught it all in jagged flashes—the man, the woman, the knife, the blood, the expressions on the faces of those watching from the windows. Then lights clicked off in the windows, but they still stood there, watching.

She wanted to yell, to scream, "What are you doing to that woman?" But her throat was frozen, two iron hands that had been immersed in dry ice for ten thousand years clamped around her neck. She could feel the blade sliding into her own body.

Somehow—it seemed impossible but there it was down there, happening somehow—the woman struggled erect and *pulled* herself off the knife. Three steps, she took three steps and fell into the flower bed again. The man was howling now, like a great beast, the sounds inarticulate, bubbling up from his stomach. He fell on her and the knife went up and came down, then again, and again, and finally it was all a blur of motion, and her scream of lunatic bats went on till it faded off and was gone.

Beth stood in the darkness, trembling and crying, the sight filling her eyes with horror. And when she could no longer bear to look at what he was doing down there to the unmoving piece of meat over which he worked, she looked up and around at the windows of darkness where the others still stood—even as she stood—and somehow she could see their faces, bruise-purple with the dim light from the mercury lamps, and there was a universal sameness to their expressions. The women stood with their nails biting into the upper arms of their men, their tongues edging from the corners of their mouths; the men were wild-eyed and smiling. They all looked as though they were at cock fights. Breathing deeply. Drawing some sustenance from the grisly scene below. An exhalation of sound, deep, deep, as though from caverns beneath the earth. Flesh pale and moist.

And it was then that she realized the courtyard had grown foggy, as though mist off the East River had rolled up 52nd Street in a veil that would obscure the details of what the knife and the man were still doing... endlessly doing it...long after there was any joy in it...still doing it...again and again...

But the fog was unnatural, thick and gray and filled with tiny scintillas of light. She stared at it, rising up in the empty space of the courtyard. Bach in the cathedral, stardust in a vacuum chamber.

Beth saw eyes.

There, up there, at the ninth floor and higher, two great eyes, as surely as night and the moon, there were *eyes*. And—a face? Was that a face, could she be sure, was she imagining it…a face? In the roiling vapors of chill fog something lived, something brooding and patient and utterly malevolent had been summoned up to witness what was happening down there in the flower bed. Beth tried to look away, but could not. The eyes, those primal burning eyes, filled with an abysmal antiquity yet frighteningly bright and anxious like the eyes of a child; eyes filled with tomb depths, ancient and new, chasm-filled, burning, gigantic and deep as an abyss, holding her, compelling her. The shadow play was being staged not only for the tenants in their windows, watching and drinking of the scene, but for some *other*. Not on frigid tundra or waste moors, not in subterranean caverns or on some faraway world circling a dying sun, but here, in the city, here the eyes of that *other* watched.

Shaking with the effort, Beth wrenched her eyes from those burning depths up there beyond the ninth floor, only to see again the horror that had brought that *other*. And she was struck for the first time by the awfulness of what she was witnessing, she was released from the immobility that had held her like a coelacanth in shale, she was filled with the blood thunder pounding against the membranes of her mind: she had *stood* there! She had done nothing, nothing! A woman had been butchered and she had said nothing, done nothing. Tears had been useless, tremblings had been pointless, she *had done nothing*!

Then she heard hysterical sounds midway between laughter and giggling, and as she stared up into that great face rising in the fog and chimneysmoke of the night, she heard *herself* making those deranged gibbon noises and from the man below a pathetic, trapped sound, like the whimper of whipped dogs.

She was staring up into that face again. She hadn't wanted to see it again—ever. But she was locked with those smoldering eyes, overcome with the feeling that they were childlike, though she *knew* they were incalculably ancient.

Then the butcher below did an unspeakable thing and Beth reeled with dizziness and caught the edge of the window before she could tumble out onto the balcony; she steadied herself and fought for breath.

She felt herself being looked at, and for a long moment of frozen terror she feared she might have caught the attention of that face up there in the fog. She clung to the window, feeling everything growing faraway and dim, and stared straight across the court. She *was* being watched. Intently. By the young man in the seventh-floor window across from her own apartment. Steadily, he was looking at her. Through the strange fog with its burning eyes feasting on the sight below, he was staring at her.

As she felt herself blacking out, in the moment before unconsciousness, the thought flickered and fled that there was something terribly familiar about his face.

It rained the next day. East 52nd Street was slick and shining with the oil rainbows. The rain washed the dog turds into the gutters and nudged them down and down to the catch-basin openings. People bent against the slanting rain, hidden beneath umbrellas, looking like enormous, scurrying black mushrooms. Beth went out to get the newspapers after the police had come and gone.

The news reports dwelled with loving emphasis on the twenty-six tenants of the building who had watched in cold interest as Leona Ciarelli, 37, of 455 Fort Washington Avenue, Manhattan, had been systematically stabbed to death by Burton H. Wells, 41, an unemployed electrician, who had been subsequently shot to death by two off-duty police officers when he burst into Michael's Pub on 55th Street, covered with blood and brandishing a knife that authorities later identified as the murder weapon.

She had thrown up twice that day. Her stomach seemed incapable of retaining anything solid, and the taste of bile lay along the back of her tongue. She could not blot the scenes of the night before from her mind; she re-ran them again and again, every movement of that reaper arm playing over and over as though on a short loop of memory. The woman's head thrown back for silent screams. The blood. Those eyes in the fog.

She was drawn again and again to the window, to stare down into the courtyard and the street. She tried to superimpose over the bleak Manhattan concrete the view from her window in Swann House at Bennington: the little yard and another white, frame dormitory; the fantastic apple trees; and from the other window the rolling hills and gorgeous Vermont countryside; her memory skittered through the change of seasons. But there was always concrete and the rain-slick streets; the rain on the pavement was black and shiny as blood.

She tried to work, rolling up the tambour closure of the old rolltop desk she had bought on Lexington Avenue and hunching over the graph sheets of choreographer's charts. But Labanotation was merely a Jackson Pollock jumble of arcane hieroglyphics to her today, instead of the careful representation of eurhythmics she had studied four years to perfect. And before that, Farmington.

The phone rang. It was the secretary from the Taylor Dance Company, asking when she would be free. She had to beg off. She looked at her hand, lying on the graph sheets of figures Laban had devised, and she saw her fingers trembling. She had to beg off. Then she called Guzman at the Downtown Ballet Company, to tell him she would be late with the charts.

"My God, lady, I have ten dancers sitting around in a rehearsal hall getting their leotards sweaty! What do you expect me to do?"

She explained what had happened the night before. And as she told him, she realized the newspapers had been justified in holding that tone against the twenty-six witnesses to the death of Leona Ciarelli. Paschal Guzman listened, and when he spoke again, his voice was several octaves lower, and he spoke more slowly. He said he understood and she could take a little longer to prepare the charts. But there was a distance in his voice, and he hung up while she was thanking him.

She dressed in an argyle sweater vest in shades of dark purple, and a pair of fitted khaki gabardine trousers. She had to go out, to walk around. To do what? To think about other things. As she pulled on the Fred Braun chunky heels, she idly wondered if that heavy silver bracelet was still in the window of Georg Jensen's. In the elevator, the young man from the window across the courtyard stared at her. Beth felt her body begin to tremble again. She went deep into the corner of the box when he entered behind her.

Between the fifth and fourth floors, he hit the *off* switch and the elevator jerked to a halt.

Beth stared at him and he smiled innocently.

"Hi. My name's Gleeson, Ray Gleeson, I'm in 714."

She wanted to demand he turn the elevator back on, by what right did he *presume* to do such a thing, what did he mean by this, turn it on at once or suffer the consequences. That was what she *wanted* to do. Instead, from the same place she had heard the gibbering laughter the night before, she heard her voice, much smaller and much less possessed than she had trained it to be, saying, "Beth O'Neill, I live in 701."

The thing about it, was that *the elevator was stopped*. And she was frightened. But he leaned against the paneled wall, very well dressed, shoes polished, hair combed and probably blown dry with a hand drier, and he *talked* to her as if they were across a table at L'Argenteuil. "You just moved in, huh?"

"About two months ago."

"Where did you go to school? Bennington or Sarah Lawrence?"

"Bennington. How did you know?"

He laughed, and it was a nice laugh. "I'm an editor at a religious book publisher; every year we get half a dozen Bennington, Sarah Lawrence, Smith girls. They come hopping in like grasshoppers, ready to revolutionize the publishing industry."

"What's wrong with that? You sound like you don't care for them."

"Oh, I *love* them, they're marvelous. They think they know how to write better than the authors we publish. Had one darlin' little item who was given galleys of three books to proof, and she rewrote all three. I think she's working as a table-swabber in a Horn & Hardart's now."

She didn't reply to that. She would have pegged him as an anti-feminist, ordinarily, if it had been anyone else speaking. But the eyes. There was something terribly familiar about his face. She was enjoying the conversation; she rather liked him.

"What's the nearest big city to Bennington?"

"Albany, New York. About sixty miles."

"How long does it take to drive there?"

"From Bennington? About an hour and a half."

"Must be a nice drive, that Vermont country, really pretty. They went coed, I understand. How's that working out?"

"I don't know, really."

"You don't know?"

"It happened around the time I was graduating."

"What did you major in?"

"I was a dance major, specializing in Labanotation. That's the way you write choreography."

"It's all electives, I gather. You don't have to take anything required, like sciences, for example." He didn't change tone as he said, "That was a terrible thing last night. I saw you watching. I guess a lot of us were watching. It was a really terrible thing."

She nodded dumbly. Fear came back.

"I understand the cops got him. Some nut, they don't even know why he killed her, or why he went charging into that bar. It was really an awful thing. I'd very much like to have dinner with you one night soon, if you're not attached."

"That would be all right."

"Maybe Wednesday. There's an Argentinian place I know. You might like it."

"That would be all right."

"Why don't you turn on the elevator, and we can go," he said, and smiled again. She did it, wondering why she had stopped the elevator in the first place.

On her third date with him, they had their first fight. It was at a party thrown by a director of television commercials. He lived on the ninth floor of their building. He had just done a series of spots for *Sesame Street* (the letters "U" for Underpass, "T" for Tunnel, lowercase "b" for boats, "c" for cars; the numbers 1 to 6 and the numbers 1 to 20; the words *light* and *dark*) and was celebrating his move from the arena of commercial tawdriness (and its attendant $75,000 a year) to the sweet fields of educational programming (and its accompanying descent into low-pay respectability). There was a logic in his joy Beth could not quite understand, and when she talked with him about it, in a far corner of the kitchen, his arguments didn't seem to parse. But he seemed happy, and his girlfriend, a long-legged ex-model from Philadelphia, continued to drift to him and away from him, like some exquisite undersea plant, touching his hair and kissing his neck, murmuring words of pride and barely submerged sexuality. Beth found it bewildering, though the celebrants were all bright and lively.

In the living room, Ray was sitting on the arm of the sofa, hustling a stewardess named Luanne. Beth could tell he was hustling; he was trying to look casual. When he *wasn't* hustling, he was always intense, about everything. She decided to ignore it, and wandered around the apartment, sipping at a Tanqueray and tonic.

There were framed prints of abstract shapes clipped from a calendar printed in Germany. They were in metal Bonniers frames.

In the dining room a huge door from a demolished building somewhere in the city had been handsomely stripped, teaked and refinished. It was now the dinner table.

A Lightolier fixture attached to the wall over the bed swung out, levered up and down, tipped, and its burnished globe-head revolved a full three hundred and sixty degrees.

She was standing in the bedroom, looking out the window, when she realized *this* had been one of the rooms in which light had gone on, gone off; one of the rooms that had contained a silent watcher at the death of Leona Ciarelli.

When she returned to the living room, she looked around more carefully. With only three or four exceptions—the stewardess, a young married couple from the second floor, a stockbroker from Hemphill, Noyes—*everyone* at the party had been a witness to the slaying.

"I'd like to go," she told him.

"Why, aren't you having a good time?" asked the stewardess, a mocking smile crossing her perfect little face.

"Like all Bennington ladies," Ray said, answering for Beth, "she is enjoying herself most by not enjoying herself at all. It's a trait of the anal retentive. Being here in someone else's apartment, she can't empty ashtrays or rewind the toilet paper roll so it doesn't hang a tongue, and being tightassed, her nature demands we go.

"All right, Beth, let's say our goodbyes and take off. The Phantom Rectum strikes again."

She slapped him and the stewardess's eyes widened. But the smile remained frozen where it had appeared.

He grabbed her wrist before she could do it again. "Garbanzo beans, baby," he said, holding her wrist tighter than necessary.

They went back to her apartment, and after sparring silently with kitchen cabinet doors slammed and the television being tuned too loud, they got to her bed, and he tried to perpetuate the metaphor by fucking her in the ass. He had her on elbows and knees before she realized what he was doing; she struggled to turn over and he rode her bucking and tossing without a sound. And when it was clear to him that she would never permit it, he grabbed her breast from underneath and squeezed so hard she howled in pain. He dumped her on her back, rubbed himself between her legs a dozen times, and came on her stomach.

Beth lay with her eyes closed and an arm thrown across her face. She wanted to cry, but found she could not. Ray lay on her and said nothing. She wanted to rush to the bathroom and shower, but he did not move, till long after his semen had dried on their bodies.

"Who did you date at college?" he asked.

"I didn't date anyone very much." Sullen.

"No heavy makeouts with wealthy lads from Williams and Dartmouth… no Amherst intellectuals begging you to save them from creeping faggotry by permitting them to stick their carrots in your sticky little slit?"

"Stop it!"

"Come on, baby, it couldn't all have been knee socks and little round circle-pins. You don't expect me to believe you didn't get a little mouthful of cock from time to time. It's only, what? about fifteen miles to Williamstown? I'm sure the Williams werewolves were down burning the highway to your cunt on weekends; you can level with old Uncle Ray.…"

"Why are you like this?!" She started to move, to get away from him, and he grabbed her by the shoulder, forced her to lie down again. Then he rose up over her and said, "I'm like this because I'm a New Yorker, baby. Because I live in this fucking city every day. Because I have to play pattycake with the ministers and other sanctified holy-joe assholes who want their goodness and lightness tracts published by the Blessed Sacrament Publishing and Storm Window Company of 277 Park Avenue, when what I *really* want to do is toss the stupid psalm-suckers out the thirty-seventh-floor window and listen to them quote chapter-and-worse all the way down. Because I've lived in this great big snapping dog of a city all my life and I'm mad as a mudfly, for chrissakes!"

She lay unable to move, breathing shallowly, filled with a sudden pity and affection for him. His face was white and strained, and she knew he was saying things to her that only a bit too much Almadén and exact timing would have let him say.

"What do you expect from me," he said, his voice softer now, but no less intense, "do you expect kindness and gentility and understanding and a hand on *your* hand when the smog burns your eyes? I can't do it, I haven't got it. No one has it in this cesspool of a city. Look around you; what do you think is happening here? They take rats and they put them in boxes and when there are too many of them, some of the little fuckers go out of their minds and start gnawing the rest to death. *It ain't no different here, baby!* It's rat time for everybody in this madhouse. You can't expect to jam as many people into this stone thing as we do, with buses and taxis and dogs shitting themselves scrawny and noise night and day and no money and not enough places to live and no place to go to have a decent think…you can't do it without making the time right for some godforsaken other kind of thing to be born! You can't hate everyone around you, and kick every beggar and nigger and *mestizo* shithead, you can't have cabbies stealing from you and taking tips they don't deserve, and then cursing you, you can't walk in the soot till your collar turns black, and your body stinks with the smell of flaking brick and decaying brains, you can't do it without calling up some kind of awful—"

He stopped.

His face bore the expression of a man who has just received brutal word of the death of a loved one. He suddenly lay down, rolled over, and turned off.

She lay beside him, trembling, trying desperately to remember where she had seen his face before.

He didn't call her again, after the night of the party. And when they met in the hall, he pointedly turned away, as though he had given her some obscure chance and she had refused to take it. Beth thought she understood: though Ray Gleeson had not been her first affair, he had been the first to reject her so completely. The first to put her not only out of his bed and his life, but even out of his world. It was as though she were invisible, not even beneath contempt, simply not there.

She busied herself with other things.

She took on three new charting jobs for Guzman and a new group that had formed on Staten Island, of all places. She worked furiously and they gave her new assignments; they even paid her.

She tried to decorate the apartment with a less precise touch. Huge poster blowups of Merce Cunningham and Martha Graham replaced the Brueghel prints that had reminded her of the view looking down the hill toward Williams. The tiny balcony outside her window, the balcony she had steadfastly refused to stand upon since the night of the slaughter, the night of the fog with eyes, that balcony she swept and set about with little flower boxes in which she planted geraniums, petunias, dwarf zinnias, and other hardy perennials. Then, closing the window, she went to give herself, to involve herself in this city to which she had brought her ordered life.

And the city responded to her overtures:

Seeing off an old friend from Bennington, at Kennedy International, she stopped at the terminal coffee shop to have a sandwich. The counter—like a moat—surrounded a center service island that had huge advertising cubes rising above it on burnished poles. The cubes proclaimed the delights of Fun City. *New York Is a Summer Festival*, they said, and *Joseph Papp Presents Shakespeare in Central Park* and *Visit the Bronx Zoo* and *You'll Adore Our Contentious but Lovable Cabbies*. The food emerged from a window far down the service area and moved slowly on a conveyor belt through the hordes of screaming waitresses who slathered the counter with redolent washcloths. The lunchroom had all the charm and dignity of a steel-rolling mill, and approximately the same noise level. Beth ordered a cheeseburger that cost a dollar and a quarter, and a glass of milk.

When it came, it was cold, the cheese unmelted, and the patty of meat resembling nothing so much as a dirty scouring pad. The bun was cold and untoasted. There was no lettuce under the patty.

Beth managed to catch the waitress's eye. The girl approached with an annoyed look. "Please toast the bun and may I have a piece of lettuce?" Beth said.

"We dun' do that," the waitress said, turning half away, as though she would walk in a moment.

"You don't do what?"

"We dun' toass the bun here."

"Yes, but I *want* the bun toasted," Beth said firmly.

"An' you got to pay for extra lettuce."

"If I was asking for *extra* lettuce," Beth said, getting annoyed, "I would pay for it, but since there's *no* lettuce here, I don't think I should be charged extra for the first piece."

"We dun' do that."

The waitress started to walk away. "Hold it," Beth said, raising her voice just enough so the assembly-line eaters on either side stared at her. "You mean to tell me I have to pay a dollar and a quarter and I can't get a piece of lettuce or even get the bun toasted?"

"Ef you dun' like it…"

"Take it back."

"You gotta pay for it, you order it."

"I said take it back, I don't want the fucking thing!"

The waitress scratched it off the check. The milk cost 27¢ and tasted going-sour. It was the first time in her life that Beth had said *that* word aloud.

At the cashier's stand, Beth said to the sweating man with the felt-tip pens in his shirt pocket, "Just out of curiosity, are you interested in complaints?"

"No!" he said, snarling, quite literally snarling. He did not look up as he punched out 73¢ and it came rolling down the chute.

The city responded to her overtures:

It was raining again. She was trying to cross Second Avenue, with the light. She stepped off the curb and a car came sliding through the red and splashed her. "Hey!" she yelled.

"Eat shit, sister!" the driver yelled back, turning the corner.

Her boots, her legs and her overcoat were splattered with mud. She stood trembling on the curb.

The city responded to her overtures:

She emerged from the building at One Astor Place with her big briefcase full of Laban charts; she was adjusting her rain scarf about her head. A well-dressed man with an attaché case thrust the handle of his umbrella up between her legs from the rear. She gasped and dropped her case.

The city responded and responded and responded.

Her overtures altered quickly.

The old drunk with the stippled cheeks extended his hand and mumbled words. She cursed him and walked on up Broadway past the beaver film houses.

She crossed against the lights on Park Avenue, making hackies slam their brakes to avoid hitting her; she used *that* word frequently now.

When she found herself having a drink with a man who had elbowed up beside her in the singles' bar, she felt faint and knew she should go home.

But Vermont was so far away.

Nights later. She had come home from the Lincoln Center ballet, and gone straight to bed. Lying half-asleep in her bedroom, she heard an alien sound. One room away, in the living room, in the dark, there was a sound. She slipped out of bed and went to the door between the rooms. She fumbled silently for the switch on the lamp just inside the living room, and found it, and clicked it on. A black man in a leather car coat was trying to get *out* of the apartment. In that first flash of light filling the room she noticed the television set beside him on the floor as he struggled with the door, she noticed the police lock and bar had been broken in a new and clever manner *New York* magazine had not yet reported in a feature article on apartment ripoffs, she noticed that he had gotten his foot tangled in the telephone cord that she had requested be extra-long so she could carry the instrument into the bathroom, I don't want to miss any business calls when the shower is running; she noticed all things in perspective and one thing with sharpest clarity: the expression on the burglar's face.

There was something familiar in that expression.

He almost had the door open, but now he closed it, and slipped the police lock. He took a step toward her.

Beth went back, into the darkened bedroom.

The city responded to her overtures.

She backed against the wall at the head of the bed. Her hand fumbled in the shadows for the telephone. His shape filled the doorway, light, all light behind him.

In silhouette it should not have been possible to tell, but somehow she knew he was wearing gloves and the only marks he would leave would be deep bruises, very blue, almost black, with the tinge under them of blood that had been stopped in its course.

He came for her, arms hanging casually at his sides. She tried to climb over the bed, and he grabbed her from behind, ripping her nightgown. Then he had a hand around her neck and he pulled her backward. She fell off the bed, landed at his feet and his hold was broken. She scuttled across the floor and for a moment she had the respite to feel terror. She was going to die, and she was frightened.

He trapped her in the corner between the closet and the bureau and kicked her. His foot caught her in the thigh as she folded tighter, smaller, drawing her legs up. She was cold.

Then he reached down with both hands and pulled her erect by her hair. He slammed her head against the wall. Everything slid up in her sight as though running off the edge of the world. He slammed her head against the wall again, and she felt something go soft over her right ear.

When he tried to slam her a third time she reached out blindly for his face and ripped down with her nails. He howled in pain and she hurled herself forward, arms wrapping themselves around his waist. He stumbled backward and in a tangle of thrashing arms and legs they fell out onto the little balcony.

Beth landed on the bottom, feeling the window boxes jammed up against her spine and legs. She fought to get to her feet, and her nails hooked into his shirt under the open jacket, ripping. Then she was on her feet again and they struggled silently.

He whirled her around, bent her backward across the wrought-iron railing. Her face was turned outward.

They were standing in their windows, watching.

Through the fog she could see them watching. Through the fog she recognized their expressions. Through the fog she heard them breathing in unison, bellows breathing of expectation and wonder. Through the fog.

And the black man punched her in the throat. She gagged and started to black out and could not draw air into her lungs. Back, back, he bent her farther back and she was looking up, straight up, toward the ninth floor and higher....

Up there: eyes.

The words Ray Gleeson had said in a moment filled with what he had become, with the utter hopelessness and finality of the choice the city had forced on him, the words came back. *You can't live in this city and survive unless you have protection...you can't live this way, like rats driven mad, without making the time right for some godforsaken other kind of thing to be born...you can't do it without calling up some kind of awful...*

God! A new God, an ancient God come again with the eyes and hunger of a child, a deranged blood God of fog and street violence. A God who needed worshippers and offered the choices of death as a victim or life as an eternal witness to the deaths of *other* chosen victims. A God to fit the times, a God of streets and people.

She tried to shriek, to appeal to Ray, to the director in the bedroom window of his ninth-floor apartment with his long-legged Philadelphia model beside him and his fingers inside her as they worshipped in their holiest of ways, to the others who had been at the party that had been Ray's offer of a chance to join their congregation. She wanted to be saved from having to make that choice.

But the black man had punched her in the throat, and now his hands were on her, one on her chest, the other in her face, the smell of leather filling her where the nausea could not. And she understood Ray had *cared*, had wanted her to take the chance offered; but she had come from a world of little white dormitories and Vermont countryside; it was not a real world. *This* was the real world and up there was the God who ruled this world, and she had rejected him, had said no to one of his priests and servitors. *Save me! Don't make me do it!*

She knew she had to call out, to make appeal, to try and win the approbation of that God. *I can't...save me!*

She struggled and made terrible little mewling sounds trying to summon the words to cry out, and suddenly she crossed a line, and screamed up into the echoing courtyard with a voice Leona Ciarelli had never known enough to use.

"Him! Take him! Not me! I'm yours, I love you, I'm yours! Take him, not me, please not me, take him, take him, I'm yours!"

And the black man was suddenly lifted away, wrenched off her, and off the balcony, whirled straight up into the fog-thick air in the courtyard, as Beth sank to her knees on the ruined flower boxes.

She was half-conscious, and could not be sure she saw it just that way, but up he went, end over end, whirling and spinning like a charred leaf.

And the form took firmer shape. Enormous paws with claws and shapes that no animal she had ever seen had ever possessed, and the burglar, black, poor, terrified, whimpering like a whipped dog, was stripped of his flesh. His body was opened with a thin incision, and there was a rush as all the blood poured from him like a sudden cloudburst, and yet he was still alive, twitching with the involuntary horror of a frog's leg shocked with an electric current. Twitched, and twitched again as he was torn piece by piece to shreds. Pieces of flesh and bone and half a face with an eye blinking furiously, cascaded down past Beth, and hit the cement below with sodden thuds. And still he was alive, as his organs were squeezed and musculature and bile and shit and skin were rubbed, sandpapered together and let fall. It went on and on, as the death of Leona Ciarelli had gone on and on, and she understood with the blood-knowledge of survivors *at any cost* that the reason the witnesses to the death of Leona Ciarelli had done nothing was not that they had been frozen with horror, that they didn't want to get involved, or that they were inured to death by years of television slaughter.

They were worshippers at a black mass the city had demanded be staged; not once, but a thousand times a day in this insane asylum of steel and stone.

Now she was on her feet, standing half-naked in her ripped nightgown, her hands tightening on the wrought-iron railing, begging to see more, to drink deeper.

Now she was one of them, as the pieces of the night's sacrifice fell past her, bleeding and screaming.

Tomorrow the police would come again, and they would question her, and she would say how terrible it had been, that burglar, and how she had fought, afraid he would rape her and kill her, and how he had fallen, and she had no idea how he had been so hideously mangled and ripped apart, but a seven-storey fall, after all…

Tomorrow she would not have to worry about walking in the streets, because no harm could come to her. Tomorrow she could even remove the police lock. Nothing in the city could do her any further evil, because she had made the only choice. She was now a dweller in the city, now wholly and richly a part of it. Now she was taken to the bosom of her God.

She felt Ray beside her, standing beside her, holding her, protecting her, his hand on her naked backside, and she watched the fog swirl up and fill the courtyard, fill the city, fill her eyes and her soul and her heart with its power. As Ray's naked body pressed tightly inside her, she drank deeply of the night, knowing whatever voices she heard from this moment forward would be the voices not of whipped dogs, but those of strong, meat-eating beasts.

At last she was unafraid, and it was so good, so very good *not* to be afraid.

When inward life dries up, when feeling decreases and apathy increases, when one cannot affect or even genuinely touch another person, violence flares up as a daimonic necessity for contact, a mad drive forcing touch in the most direct way possible.

—Rollo May, *Love and Will*

ADRIFT JUST OFF THE ISLETS OF LANGERHANS: LATITUDE 38° 54' N, LONGITUDE 77° 00' 13" W

1975 Hugo Award: Best Novelette; Locus Poll Award: Best Novelette

WHEN MOBY DICK awoke one morning from unsettling dreams, he found himself changed in his bed of kelp into a monstrous Ahab.

Crawling in stages from the soggy womb of sheets, he stumbled into the kitchen and ran water into the teapot. There was lye in the corner of each eye. He put his head under the spigot and let the cold water rush around his cheeks.

Dead bottles littered the living room. One hundred and eleven empty bottles that had contained Robitussin and Romilar-CF. He padded through the debris to the front door and opened it a crack. Daylight assaulted him. "Oh, God," he murmured, and closed his eyes to pick up the folded newspaper from the stoop.

Once more in dusk, he opened the paper. The headline read: BOLIVIAN AMBASSADOR FOUND MURDERED, and the feature story heading column one detailed the discovery of the ambassador's body, badly decomposed, in an abandoned refrigerator in an empty lot in Secaucus, New Jersey.

The teapot whistled.

Naked, he padded toward the kitchen; as he passed the aquarium he saw that terrible fish was still alive, and this morning whistling like a bluejay, making tiny streams of bubbles that rose to burst on the scummy surface of the water. He paused beside the tank, turned on the light and looked in through the drifting eddies of stringered algae. The fish simply would not die. It had killed off every other fish in the tank—prettier fish, friendlier fish, livelier fish, even larger and more dangerous fish—had killed them all, one by one, and eaten out the eyes. Now it swam the tank alone, ruler of its worthless domain.

He had tried to let the fish kill itself, trying every form of neglect short of outright murder by not feeding it; but the pale, worm-pink devil even thrived in the dark and filth-laden waters.

Now it sang like a bluejay. He hated the fish with a passion he could barely contain.

He sprinkled flakes from a plastic container, grinding them between thumb and forefinger as experts had advised him to do it, and watched the multicolored granules of fish meal, roe, milt, brine shrimp, day-fly eggs, oatflour and egg yolk ride on the surface for a moment before the detestable fish-face came snapping to the top to suck them down. He turned away, cursing and hating the fish. It would not die. Like him, it would not die.

In the kitchen, bent over the boiling water, he understood for the first time the true status of his situation. Though he was probably nowhere near the rotting outer edge of sanity, he could smell its foulness on the wind, coming in from the horizon; and like some wild animal rolling its eyes at the scent of carrion and the feeders thereon, he was being driven closer to lunacy every day, just from the smell.

He carried the teapot, a cup and two tea bags to the kitchen table and sat down. Propped open in a plastic stand used for keeping cookbooks handy while mixing ingredients, the Mayan Codex translations remained unread from the evening before. He poured the water, dangled the tea bags in the cup and tried to focus his attention. The references to Itzamna, the chief divinity of the Maya pantheon, and medicine, his chief sphere of influence, blurred. Ixtab, the goddess of suicide, seemed more apropos for this morning, this deadly terrible morning. He tried reading, but the words only went in, nothing happened to them, they didn't sing. He sipped tea and found himself thinking of the chill, full circle of the Moon. He glanced over his shoulder at the kitchen clock. Seven forty-four.

He shoved away from the table, taking the half-full cup of tea, and went into the bedroom. The impression of his body, where it had lain in tortured sleep, still dented the bed. There were clumps of blood-matted hair clinging to the manacles that he had riveted to metal plates in the headboard. He rubbed his wrists where they had been scored raw, slopping a little tea on his left forearm. He wondered if the Bolivian ambassador had been a piece of work he had tended to the month before.

His wristwatch lay on the bureau. He checked it. Seven forty-six. Slightly less than an hour and a quarter to make the meeting with the consultation service. He went into the bathroom, reached inside the shower stall and turned the handle till a fine needle-spray of icy water smashed the tiled wall of the stall. Letting the water run, he turned to the medicine cabinet for his shampoo. Taped to the mirror was an Ouchless Telfa finger bandage on which two lines had been neatly typed, in capitals:

THE WAY YOU WALK IS THORNY, MY SON,
THROUGH NO FAULT OF YOUR OWN.

Then, opening the cabinet, removing a plastic bottle of herbal shampoo that smelled like friendly, deep forests, Lawrence Talbot resigned himself to the situation, turned and stepped into the shower, the merciless ice-laden waters of the Arctic pounding against his tortured flesh.

Suite 1544 of the Tishman Airport Center Building was a men's toilet. He stood against the wall opposite the door labeled MEN and drew the envelope from the inner breast pocket of his jacket. The paper was of good quality, the envelope crackled as he thumbed up the flap and withdrew the single-sheet letter inside. It was the correct address, the correct floor, the correct suite. Suite 1544 was a men's toilet, nonetheless. Talbot started to turn away. It was a vicious joke; he found no humor in the situation; not in his present circumstances.

He took one step toward the elevators.

The door to the men's room shimmered, fogged over like a windshield in winter, and re-formed. The legend on the door had changed. It now read:

INFORMATION ASSOCIATES

Suite 1544 was the consultation service that had written the invitational letter on paper of good quality in response to Talbot's mail inquiry responding to a noncommittal but judiciously-phrased advertisement in *Forbes*.

He opened the door and stepped inside. The woman behind the teak reception desk smiled at him, and his glance was split between the dimples that formed, and her legs, very nice, smooth legs, crossed and framed by the kneehole of the desk. "Mr. Talbot?"

He nodded. "Lawrence Talbot."

She smiled again. "Mr. Demeter will see you at once, sir. Would you like something to drink? Coffee? A soft drink?"

Talbot found himself touching his jacket where the envelope lay in an inner pocket. "No. Thank you."

She stood up, moving toward an inner office door, as Talbot said, "What do you do when someone tries to flush your desk?" He was not trying to be cute. He was annoyed. She turned and stared at him. There was silence in her appraisal, nothing more.

"Mr. Demeter is right through here, sir."

She opened the door and stood aside. Talbot walked past her, catching a scent of mimosa.

The inner office was furnished like the reading room of an exclusive men's club. Old money. Deep quiet. Dark, heavy woods. A lowered ceiling of acoustical tile on tracks, concealing a crawl space and probably electrical conduits. The pile rug of oranges and burnt umbers swallowed his feet to the ankles. Through a wall-sized window could be seen not the city that lay outside the building but a panoramic view of Hanauma Bay, on the Koko Head side of Oahu. The pure aqua-marine waves came in like undulant snakes, rose like cobras, crested out white, tunneled, and struck like asps at the blazing yellow beach. It was not a window; there were no windows in the office. It was a photograph. A deep, real photograph that was neither a projection nor a hologram. It was a wall looking out on another place entirely. Talbot knew nothing about exotic flora, but he was certain that the tall, razor-edge-leafed trees growing right down to beach's boundary were identical to those pictured in books depicting the Carboniferous period of the Earth before even the saurians had walked the land. What he was seeing had been gone for a very long time.

"Mr. Talbot. Good of you to come. John Demeter."

He came up from a wingback chair, extended his hand. Talbot took it. The grip was firm and cool. "Won't you sit down," Demeter said. "Something to drink? Coffee, perhaps, or a soft drink?" Talbot shook his head; Demeter nodded dismissal to the receptionist; she closed the door behind her, firmly, smoothly, silently.

Talbot studied Demeter in one long appraisal as he took the chair opposite the wingback. Demeter was in his early fifties, had retained a full and rich mop of hair that fell across his forehead in gray waves that clearly had not

230

been touched up. His eyes were clear and blue, his features regular and jovial, his mouth wide and sincere. He was trim. The dark brown business suit was hand-tailored and hung well. He sat easily and crossed his legs, revealing black hose that went above the shins. His shoes were highly polished.

"That's a fascinating door, the one to your outer office," Talbot said.

"Do we talk about my door?" Demeter asked.

"Not if you don't want to. That isn't why I came here."

"I don't want to. So let's discuss your particular problem."

"Your advertisement. I was intrigued."

Demeter smiled reassuringly. "Four copywriters worked very diligently at the proper phraseology."

"It brings in business."

"The right kind of business."

"You slanted it toward smart money. Very reserved. Conservative portfolios, few glamours, steady climbers. Wise old owls."

Demeter steepled his fingers and nodded, an understanding uncle. "Directly to the core, Mr. Talbot: wise old owls."

"I need some information. Some special, certain information. How confidential is your service, Mr. Demeter?"

The friendly uncle, the wise old owl, the reassuring businessman understood all the edited spaces behind the question. He nodded several times. Then he smiled and said, "That *is* a clever door I have, isn't it? You're absolutely right, Mr. Talbot."

"A certain understated eloquence."

"One hopes it answers more questions for our clients than it poses."

Talbot sat back in the chair for the first time since he had entered Demeter's office. "I think I can accept that."

"Fine. Then why don't we get to specifics. Mr. Talbot, you're having some difficulty dying. Am I stating the situation succinctly?"

"Gently, Mr. Demeter."

"Always."

"Yes. You're on the target."

"But you have some problems, some rather unusual problems."

"Inner ring."

Demeter stood up and walked around the room, touching an astrolabe on a bookshelf, a cut-glass decanter on a sideboard, a sheaf of the *London Times* held together by a wooden pole. "We are only information specialists, Mr. Talbot. We can put you on to what you need, but the effectation is your problem."

"If I have the *modus operandi*, I'll have no trouble taking care of getting it done."

"You've put a little aside."

"A little."

"Conservative portfolio? A few glamours, mostly steady climbers?"

"Bull's-eye, Mr. Demeter."

Demeter came back and sat down again. "All right, then. If you'll take the time to write out very carefully *precisely* what you want—I know generally, from your letter, but I want this *precise*, for the contract—I think I can undertake to supply the data necessary to solving your problem."

"At what cost?"

"Let's decide what it is you want, first, shall we?"

Talbot nodded. Demeter reached over and pressed a call button on the smoking stand beside the wingback. The door opened. "Susan, would you show Mr. Talbot to the sanctum and provide him with writing materials." She smiled and stood aside, waiting for Talbot to follow her. "And bring Mr. Talbot something to drink if he'd like it...some coffee? A soft drink, perhaps?" Talbot did not respond to the offer.

"I might need some time to get the phraseology down just right. I might have to work as diligently as your copywriters. It might take me a while. I'll go home and bring it in tomorrow."

Demeter looked troubled. "That might be inconvenient. That's why we provide a quiet place where you can think."

"You'd prefer I stay and do it now."

"Inner ring, Mr. Talbot."

"You might be a toilet if I came back tomorrow."

"Bull's-eye."

"Let's go, Susan. Bring me a glass of orange juice, if you have it." He preceded her out the door.

He followed her down the corridor at the far side of the reception room. He had not seen it before. She stopped at a door and opened it for him. There was an escritoire and a comfortable chair inside the small room. He could hear Muzak. "I'll bring you your orange juice," she said.

He went in and sat down. After a long time he wrote seven words on a sheet of paper.

● ● ●

Two months later, long after the series of visitations from silent messengers who brought rough drafts of the contract to be examined, who came again to take them away revised, who came again with counterproposals, who came again to take away further revised versions, who came again—finally—with Demeter-signed finals, and who waited while he examined and initialed and signed the finals—two months later, the map came via the last, mute messenger. He arranged for the final installment of the payment to Information Associates that same day: he had ceased wondering where fifteen boxcars of maize—grown specifically as the Zuñi nation had grown it—was of value.

Two days later, a small item on an inside page of the *New York Times* noted that fifteen boxcars of farm produce had somehow vanished off a railroad spur near Albuquerque. An official investigation had been initiated.

The map was very specific, very detailed; it looked accurate.

He spent several days with Gray's ANATOMY and, when he was satisfied that Demeter and his organization had been worth the staggering fee, he made a phone call. The long-distance operator turned him over to Inboard and he waited, after giving her the information, for the static-laden connection to be made. He insisted Budapest on the other end let it ring twenty times, twice the number the male operator was permitted per caller. On the twenty-first ring it was picked up. Miraculously, the background noise-level dropped and he heard Victor's voice as though it was across the room.

"Yes! Hello!" Impatient, surly as always.

"Victor…Larry Talbot."

"Where are you calling from?"

"The States. How are you?"

"Busy. What do you want?"

"I have a project. I want to hire you and your lab."

"Forget it. I'm coming down to final moments on a project and I can't be bothered now."

The imminence of hangup was in his voice. Talbot cut in quickly. "How long do you anticipate?"

"Till what?"

"Till you're clear."

"Another six months inside, eight to ten if it gets muddy. I said: forget it, Larry. I'm *not* available."

"At least let's talk."

"No."

"Am I wrong, Victor, or do you owe me a little?"

"After all this time you're calling in debts?"

"They only ripen with age."

There was a long silence in which Talbot heard dead space being pirated off their line. At one point he thought the other man had racked the receiver. Then, finally, "Okay, Larry. We'll *talk*. But you'll have to come to me; I'm too involved to be hopping any jets."

"That's fine. I have free time." A slow beat, then he added, "Nothing but free time."

"*After* the full moon, Larry." It was said with great specificity.

"Of course. I'll meet you at the last place we met, at the same time, on the thirtieth of this month. Do you remember?"

"I remember. That'll be fine."

"Thank you, Victor. I appreciate this."

There was no response.

Talbot's voice softened: "How is your father?"

"Goodbye, Larry," he answered, and hung up.

They met on the thirtieth of that month, at moonless midnight, on the corpse barge that plied between Buda and Pesht. It was the correct sort of night: chill fog moved in a pulsing curtain up the Danube from Belgrade.

They shook hands in the lee of a stack of cheap wooden coffins and, after hesitating awkwardly for a moment, they embraced like brothers. Talbot's smile was tight and barely discernible by the withered illumination of the lantern and the barge's running lights as he said, "All right, get it said so I don't have to wait for the other shoe to drop."

Victor grinned and murmured ominously:

> "Even a man who is pure in heart
> And says his prayers by night,
> May become a wolf when the wolfbane blooms
> And the Autumn moon shines bright."

Talbot made a face. "And other songs from the same album."

"Still saying your prayers at night?"

"I stopped that when I realized the damned thing didn't scan."

"Hey. We aren't here getting pneumonia just to discuss forced rhyme."

The lines of weariness in Talbot's face settled into a joyless pattern. "Victor, I need your help."

"I'll listen, Larry. Further than that, it's doubtful."

Talbot weighed the warning and said, "Three months ago I answered an advertisement in *Forbes*, the business magazine. Information Associates. It was a cleverly phrased, very reserved, small box, inconspicuously placed. Except to those who knew how to read it. I won't waste your time on details, but the sequence went like this: I answered the ad, hinting at my problem as circuitously as possible without being completely impenetrable. Vague words about important money. I had hopes. Well, I hit with this one. They sent back a letter calling a meet. Perhaps another false trail, was what I thought…God knows there've been enough of those."

Victor lit a Sobranie Black & Gold and let the pungent scent of the smoke drift away on the fog. "But you went."

"I went. Peculiar outfit, sophisticated security system, I had a strong feeling they came from, well, I'm not sure where…or when."

Victor's glance was abruptly kilowatts heavier with interest. "*When*, you say? Temporal travelers?"

"I don't know."

"I've been waiting for something like that, you know. It's inevitable. And they'd certainly make themselves known eventually."

He lapsed into silence, thinking. Talbot brought him back sharply. "I don't know, Victor. I really don't. But that's not my concern at the moment."

"Oh. Right. Sorry, Larry. Go on. You met with them…"

"Man named Demeter. I thought there might be some clue there. The name. I didn't think of it at the time. The name Demeter; there was a florist in Cleveland, many years ago. But later, when I looked it up, Demeter, the Earth goddess, Greek mythology…no connection. At least, I don't think so.

"We talked. He understood my problem and said he'd undertake the commission. But he wanted it specific, what I required of him, wanted it specific for the contract—God knows how he would have enforced the contract, but I'm sure he could have—he had a *window*, Victor, it looked out on—"

Victor spun the cigarette off his thumb and middle finger, snapping it straight down into the blood-black Danube. "Larry, you're maundering."

Talbot's words caught in his throat. It was true. "I'm counting on you, Victor. I'm afraid it's putting my usual aplomb out of phase."

"All right, take it easy. Let me hear the rest of this and we'll see. Relax."

Talbot nodded and felt grateful. "I wrote out the nature of the commission. It was only seven words." He reached into his topcoat pocket and brought out a folded slip of paper. He handed it to the other man. In the dim lantern light, Victor unfolded the paper and read:

GEOGRAPHICAL COORDINATES

FOR LOCATION OF MY SOUL

Victor looked at the two lines of type long after he had absorbed their message. When he handed it back to Talbot, he wore a new, fresher expression. "You'll never give up, will you, Larry?"

"Did your father?"

"No." Great sadness flickered across the face of the man Talbot called Victor. "And," he added, tightly, after a beat, "he's been lying in a catatonia sling for sixteen years *because* he wouldn't give up." He lapsed into silence. Finally, softly, "It never hurts to know when to give up, Larry. Never hurts. Sometimes you've just got to leave it alone."

Talbot snorted softly with bemusement. "Easy enough for you to say, old chum. You're going to die."

"That wasn't fair, Larry."

"Then help me, dammit! I've gone farther toward getting myself out of all this than I ever have. Now I need *you*. You've got the expertise."

"Have you sounded out 3M or Rand or even General Dynamics? They've got good people there."

"Damn you."

"Okay. Sorry. Let me think a minute."

The corpse barge cut through the invisible water, silent, fog-shrouded, without Charon, without Styx, merely a public service, a garbage scow of unfinished sentences, uncompleted errands, unrealized dreams. With the exception of these two, talking, the barge's supercargo had left decisions and desertions behind.

Then, Victor said, softly, talking as much to himself as to Talbot, "We could do it with microtelemetry. Either through direct micro-miniaturizing techniques or by shrinking a servomechanism package containing sensing, remote control, and guidance/manipulative/propulsion hardware. Use a saline solution to inject it into the bloodstream. Knock you out with 'Russian sleep' and/or tap into the sensory nerves so you'd perceive or control the device as if you were there…conscious transfer of point of view."

Talbot looked at him expectantly.

"No. Forget it," said Victor. "It won't do."

He continued to think. Talbot reached into the other's jacket pocket and brought out the Sobranies. He lit one and stood silently, waiting. It was always thus with Victor. He had to worm his way through the analytical labyrinth.

"Maybe the biotechnic equivalent: a tailored microorganism or slug… injected…telepathic link established. No. Too many flaws: possible ego/control conflict. Impaired perceptions. Maybe it could be a hive creature injected for multiple p.o.v." A pause, then, "No. No good."

Talbot drew on the cigarette, letting the mysterious Eastern smoke curl through his lungs.

"How about…say, just for the sake of discussion," Victor said, "say the ego/id exists to some extent in each sperm. It's been ventured. Raise the consciousness in one cell and send it on a mission to…forget it, that's metaphysical bullshit. Oh, damn damn damn…this will take time and thought, Larry. Go away, let me think on it. I'll get back to you."

Talbot butted the Sobranie on the railing, and exhaled the final stream of smoke. "Okay, Victor. I take it you're interested sufficiently to work at it."

"I'm a scientist, Larry. That means I'm hooked. I'd have to be an idiot not to be…this speaks directly to what…to what my father…"

"I understand. I'll let you alone. I'll wait."

They rode across in silence, the one thinking of solutions, the other considering problems. When they parted, it was with an embrace.

Talbot flew back the next morning, and waited through the nights of the full moon, knowing better than to pray. It only muddied the waters. And angered the gods.

When the phone rang, and Talbot lifted the receiver, he knew what it would be. He had known *every* time the phone had rung, for over two months. "Mr. Talbot? Western Union. We have a cablegram for you, from Moldava, Czechoslovakia."

"Please read it."

"It's very short, sir. It says, 'Come immediately. The trail has been marked.' It's signed, 'Victor.'"

He departed less than an hour later. The Learjet had been on the ready line since he had returned from Budapest, fuel tanks regularly topped-off and flight-plan logged. His suitcase had been packed for seventy-two days, waiting beside the door, visas and passport current, and handily stored in an inner pocket. When he departed, the apartment continued to tremble for some time with the echoes of his leaving.

The flight seemed endless, interminable, he *knew* it was taking longer than necessary.

Customs, even with high government clearances (all masterpieces of forgery) and bribes, seemed to be drawn out sadistically by the mustachioed trio of petty officials; secure, and reveling in their momentary power.

The overland facilities could not merely be called slow. They were reminiscent of the Molasses Man who cannot run till he's warmed-up and who, when he's warmed-up, grows too soft to run.

Expectedly, like the most suspenseful chapter of a cheap gothic novel, a fierce electrical storm suddenly erupted out of the mountains when the ancient touring car was within a few miles of Talbot's destination. It rose up through the steep mountain pass, hurtling out of the sky, black as a grave, and swept across the road obscuring everything.

The driver, a taciturn man whose accent had marked him as a Serbian, held the big saloon to the center of the road with the tenacity of a rodeo rider, hands at ten till and ten after midnight on the wheel.

"Mister Talbot."

"Yes?"

"It grows worse. Will I turn back?"

"How much farther?"

"Perhaps seven kilometer."

Headlights caught the moment of uprootment as a small tree by the roadside toppled toward them. The driver spun the wheel and accelerated. They rushed past as naked branches scraped across the boot of the touring car with the sound of fingernails on a blackboard. Talbot found he had been holding his breath. Death was beyond him, but the menace of the moment denied the knowledge.

"I have to get there."

"Then I go on. Be at ease."

Talbot settled back. He could see the Serb smiling in the rearview mirror. Secure, he stared out the window. Branches of lightning shattered the darkness, causing the surrounding landscape to assume ominous, unsettling shapes.

Finally, he arrived.

The laboratory, an incongruous modernistic cube—bone white against the—again—ominous basalt of the looming prominences—sat high above the rutted road. They had been climbing steadily for hours and now, like carnivores waiting for the most opportune moment, the Carpathians loomed all around them.

The driver negotiated the final mile and a half up the access road to the laboratory with difficulty: tides of dark, topsoil-and-twig-laden water rushed past them.

Victor was waiting for him. Without extended greetings he had an associate take the suitcase, and he hurried Talbot to the sub-ground-floor theater where a half dozen technicians moved quickly at their tasks, plying between enormous banks of controls and a huge glass plate hanging suspended from guy-wires beneath the track-laden ceiling.

The mood was one of highly charged expectancy; Talbot could feel it in the sharp, short glances the technicians threw him, in the way Victor steered him by the arm, in the uncanny racehorse readiness of the peculiar-looking machines around which the men and women swarmed. And he sensed in Victor's manner that something new and wonderful was about to be born in this laboratory. That perhaps…at last…after so terribly, lightlessly long…peace waited for him in this white-tiled room. Victor was fairly bursting to talk.

"Final adjustments," he said, indicating two female technicians working at a pair of similar machines mounted opposite each other on the walls facing the glass plate. To Talbot, they looked like laser projectors of a highly complex design. The women were tracking them slowly left and right on their gimbals, accompanied by soft electrical humming. Victor let Talbot study them for a long moment, then said, "Not lasers. *Grasers*. Gamma Ray Amplification by Stimulated Emission of Radiation. Pay attention to them, they're at least half the heart of the answer to your problem."

The technicians took sightings across the room, through the glass, and nodded at one another. Then the older of the two, a woman in her fifties, called to Victor.

"On line, Doctor."

Victor waved acknowledgment, and turned back to Talbot. "We'd have been ready sooner, but this damned storm. It's been going on for a week. It wouldn't have hampered us but we had a freak lightning strike on our main transformer. The power supply was on emergency for several days and it's taken a while to get everything up to peak strength again."

A door opened in the wall of the gallery to Talbot's right. It opened slowly, as though it was heavy and the strength needed to force it was lacking. The yellow baked enamel plate on the door said, in heavy black letters, in French, PERSONNEL MONITORING DEVICES ARE REQUIRED BEYOND THIS ENTRANCE. The door swung fully open, at last, and Talbot saw the warning plate on the other side:

> CAUTION
> RADIATION
> AREA

There was a three-armed, triangular-shaped design beneath the words. He thought of the Father, the Son, and the Holy Ghost. For no rational reason.

Then he saw the sign beneath, and had his rational reason: OPENING THIS DOOR FOR MORE THAN 30 SECONDS WILL REQUIRE A SEARCH AND SECURE.

Talbot's attention was divided between the doorway and what Victor had said. "You seem worried about the storm."

"Not worried," Victor said, "just cautious. There's no conceivable way it could interfere with the experiment, unless we had another direct hit, which I doubt—we've taken special precautions—but I wouldn't want to risk the power going out in the middle of the shot."

"The shot?"

"I'll explain all that. In fact, I *have* to explain it, so your mite will have the knowledge." Victor smiled at Talbot's confusion. "Don't worry about it." An old woman in a lab smock had come through the door and now stood just behind and to the right of Talbot, waiting, clearly, for their conversation to end so she could speak to Victor.

Victor turned his eyes to her. "Yes, Nadja?"

Talbot looked at her. An acid rain began falling in his stomach.

"Yesterday considerable effort was directed toward finding the cause of a high field horizontal instability," she said, speaking softly, tonelessly, a page of some specific status report. "The attendant beam blowup prevented efficient extraction." Eighty, if a day. Gray eyes sunk deep in folds of crinkled flesh the color of liver paste. "During the afternoon the accelerator was shut down to effect several repairs." Withered, weary, bent, too many bones for the sack. "The super pinger at C48 was replaced with a section of vacuum chamber; it had a vacuum leak." Talbot was in extreme pain. Memories came at him in ravening hordes, a dark wave of ant bodies gnawing at everything soft and folded and vulnerable in his brain. "Two hours of beam time were lost during the owl shift because a solenoid failed on a new vacuum valve in the transfer hall."

"Mother…?" Talbot said, whispering hoarsely.

The old woman started violently, her head coming around and her eyes of settled ashes widening. "Victor," she said, terror in the word.

Talbot barely moved, but Victor took him by the arm and held him. "Thank you, Nadja; go down to target station B and log the secondary beams. Go right now."

She moved past them, hobbling, and quickly vanished through another door in the far wall, held open for her by one of the younger women.

Talbot watched her go, tears in his eyes.

"Oh my God, Victor. It was…"

"No, Larry, it wasn't."

"It was. So help me God it *was*! But *how*, Victor, tell me *how*?"

Victor turned him and lifted his chin with his free hand. "Look at me, Larry. *Damn* it, I said *look at me*: it wasn't. You're wrong."

The last time Lawrence Talbot had cried had been the morning he had awakened from sleep, lying under hydrangea shrubs in the botanical garden next to the Minneapolis Museum of Art, lying beside something bloody and still. Under his fingernails had been caked flesh and dirt and blood. That had been the time he learned about manacles and releasing oneself from them when in one state of consciousness, but not in another. Now, he felt like crying. Again. With cause.

"Wait here a moment," Victor said. "Larry? Will you wait right here for me? I'll be back in a moment."

He nodded, averting his face, and Victor went away. While he stood there, waves of painful memory thundering through him, a door slid open into the wall at the far side of the chamber, and another white-smocked technician stuck his head into the room. Through the opening, Talbot could see massive machinery in an enormous chamber beyond. Titanium electrodes. Stainless steel cones. He thought he recognized it: a Cockroft-Walton pre-accelerator.

Victor came back with a glass of milky liquid. He handed it to Talbot.

"Victor—" the technician called from the far doorway.

"Drink it," Victor said to Talbot, then turned to the technician.

"Ready to run."

Victor waved to him. "Give me about ten minutes, Karl, then take it up to the first phase shift and signal us." The technician nodded understanding and vanished through the doorway; the door slid out of the wall and closed, hiding the imposing chamberful of equipment. "And that was part of the other half of the mystical, magical solution of your problem," the physicist said, smiling now like a proud father.

"What was that I drank?"

"Something to stabilize you. I can't have you hallucinating."

"I wasn't hallucinating. What was her name?"

"Nadja. You're wrong; you've never seen her before in your life. Have I ever lied to you? How far back do we know each other? I need your trust if this is going to go all the way."

"I'll be all right." The milky liquid had already begun to work. Talbot's face lost its flush, his hands ceased trembling.

Victor was very stern suddenly, a scientist without the time for sidetracks: there was information to be imparted. "Good. For a moment I thought I'd spent a great deal of time preparing...well," and he smiled again, quickly, "let me put it this way: I thought for a moment no one was coming to my party."

Talbot gave a strained, tiny chuckle, and followed Victor to a bank of television monitors set into rolling frame-stacks in a corner. "Okay. Let's get you briefed." He turned on sets, one after another, till all twelve were glowing, each one holding a scene of dull-finished and massive installations.

Monitor #1 showed an endlessly long underground tunnel painted eggshell white. Talbot had spent much of his two-month wait reading; he recognized the tunnel as a view down the "straightaway" of the main ring. Gigantic bending magnets in their shockproof concrete cradles glowed faintly in the dim light of the tunnel.

Monitor #2 showed the linac tunnel.

Monitor #3 showed the rectifier stack of the Cockroft-Walton pre-accelerator.

Monitor #4 was a view of the booster. Monitor #5 showed the interior of the transfer hall. Monitors #6 through #9 revealed three experimental target areas and, smaller in scope and size, an internal target area supporting the meson, neutrino and proton areas.

The remaining three monitors showed research areas in the underground lab complex, the final one of which was the main hall itself, where Talbot stood looking into twelve monitors, in the twelfth screen of which could be seen Talbot standing looking into twelve...

Victor turned off the sets.

"What did you see?"

All Talbot could think of was the old woman called Nadja. It *couldn't* be. "Larry! What did you see?"

"From what I could see," Talbot said, "that looked to be a particle accelerator. And it looked as big as CERN's proton synchrotron in Geneva."

Victor was impressed. "You've been doing some reading."

"It behooved me."

"Well, well. Let's see if I can impress *you*. CERN's accelerator reaches energies up to 33 BeV; the ring underneath this room reaches energies of 15 GeV."

"Giga meaning billion."

"You *have* been reading up, haven't you! Fifteen *billion* electron volts. There's simply no keeping secrets from you, is there, Larry?"

"Only one."

Victor waited expectantly.

"Can you do it?"

"Yes. Meteorology says the eye is almost passing over us. We'll have better than an hour, more than enough time for the dangerous parts of the experiment."

"But you *can* do it."

"Yes, Larry. I don't like having to say it twice." There was no hesitancy in his voice, none of the "yes but" equivocations he'd always heard before. Victor had found the trail.

"I'm sorry, Victor. Anxiety. But if we're ready why do I have to go through an indoctrination?"

Victor grinned wryly and began reciting, "As your Wizard, I am about to embark on a hazardous and technically unexplainable journey to the upper stratosphere. To confer, converse, and otherwise hobnob with my fellow wizards."

Talbot threw up his hands. "No more."

"Okay then. Pay attention. If I didn't have to, I wouldn't; believe me, nothing is more boring than listening to the sound of my own lectures. But your mite has to have all the data *you* have. So listen. Now comes the boring—but incredibly informative—explanation."

Western Europe's CERN—*Conseil Européen pour la Recherche Nucléaire*—had settled on Geneva as the site for their Big Machine. Holland lost out on the rich plum because it was common knowledge the food was lousy in the Lowlands. A small matter, but a significant one.

The Eastern Bloc's CEERN—*Conseil de l'Europe de l'Est pour la Recherche Nucléaire*—had been forced into selecting this isolated location high in the White Carpathians (over such likelier and more hospitable sites as Cluj in Romania, Budapest in Hungary and Gdańsk in Poland) because Talbot's friend Victor had selected this site. CERN had had Dahl and Wideroë and Goward and Adams and Reich; CEERN had Victor. It balanced. He could call the tune.

So the laboratory had been painstakingly built to his specifications, and the particle accelerator dwarfed the CERN Machine. It dwarfed the four-mile ring at the Fermi National Accelerator Lab in Batavia, Illinois. It was, in fact, the world's largest, most advanced "synchrophasotron."

Only seventy percent of the experiments conducted in the underground laboratory were devoted to projects sponsored by CEERN. One hundred percent of the staff of Victor's complex was personally committed to him, not to CEERN, not to the Eastern Bloc, not to philosophies or dogmas… to the man. So thirty percent of the experiments run on the sixteen-mile-diameter accelerator ring were Victor's own. If CEERN knew—and it would have been difficult for them to find out—it said nothing. Seventy percent of the fruits of genius was better than no percent.

Had Talbot known earlier that Victor's research was thrust in the direction of actualizing advanced theoretical breakthroughs in the nature of the structure of fundamental particles, he would never have wasted his time with the pseudos and dead-enders who had spent years on his problem, who had promised everything and delivered nothing but dust. But then, until Information Associates had marked the trail—a trail he had previously followed in every direction but the unexpected one that merged shadow with substance, reality with fantasy—until then, he had no need for Victor's exotic talents.

While CEERN basked in the warmth of secure knowledge that their resident genius was keeping them in front in the Super Accelerator Sweepstakes, Victor was briefing his oldest friend on the manner in which he would gift him with the peace of death; the manner in which Lawrence Talbot would find his soul; the manner in which he would precisely and exactly go inside his own body.

"The answer to your problem is in two parts. First, we have to create a perfect simulacrum of you, a hundred thousand or a million times smaller than you, the original. Then, second, we have to *actualize* it, turn an image into something corporeal, substantial, material; something that *exists*. A miniature *you* with all the reality you possess, all the memories, all the knowledge."

Talbot felt very mellow. The milky liquid had smoothed out the churning waters of his memory. He smiled. "I'm glad it wasn't a difficult problem."

Victor looked rueful. "Next week I invent the steam engine. Get serious, Larry."

"It's that Lethe cocktail you fed me."

Victor's mouth tightened and Talbot knew he had to get hold of himself. "Go on, I'm sorry."

Victor hesitated a moment, securing his position of seriousness with a touch of free-floating guilt, then went on, "The first part of the problem is solved by using the grasers we've developed. We'll shoot a hologram of you, using a wave generated not from the electrons of the atom, but from the nucleus…a wave a million times shorter, greater in resolution than that from a laser." He walked toward the large glass plate hanging in the middle of the lab, grasers trained on its center. "Come here."

Talbot followed him.

"Is this the holographic plate?" he said. "It's just a sheet of photographic glass, isn't it?"

"Not this," Victor said, touching the ten-foot square plate, *"this!"* He put his finger on a spot in the center of the glass and Talbot leaned in to look. He saw nothing at first, then detected a faint ripple; and when he put his face as close as possible to the imperfection he perceived a light *moiré* pattern, like the surface of a fine silk scarf. He looked back at Victor.

"Microholographic plate," Victor said. "Smaller than an integrated chip. That's where we capture your spirit, white-eyes, a million times reduced. About the size of a single cell, maybe a red corpuscle."

Talbot giggled.

"Come on," Victor said wearily. "You've had too much to drink, and it's my fault. Let's get this show on the road. You'll be straight by the time we're ready...I just hope to God your mite isn't cockeyed."

Naked, they stood him in front of the ground photographic plate. The older of the female technicians aimed the graser at him, there was a soft sound Talbot took to be some mechanism locking into position, and then Victor said, "All right, Larry, that's it."

He stared at them, expecting more.

"That's it?"

The technicians seemed very pleased, and amused at his reaction. "All done," said Victor. It had been that quick. He hadn't even seen the graser wave hit and lock in his image. "That's *it*?" he said again.

Victor began to laugh. It spread through the lab. The technicians were clinging to their equipment; tears rolled down Victor's cheeks; everyone gasped for breath; and Talbot stood in front of the minute imperfection in the glass and felt like a retard.

"That's it?" he said again, helplessly.

After a long time, they dried their eyes and Victor moved him away from the huge plate of glass. "All done, Larry, and ready to go. Are you cold?"

Talbot's naked flesh was evenly polka-dotted with goosebumps. One of the technicians brought him a smock to wear. He stood and watched. Clearly, he was no longer the center of attention.

Now the alternate graser and the holographic plate ripple in the glass were the focuses of attention. Now the mood of released tension was past and the lines of serious attention were back in the faces of the lab staff. Now Victor was wearing an intercom headset, and Talbot heard him say, "All right, Karl. Bring it up to full power."

Almost instantly the lab was filled with the sound of generators phasing up. It became painful and Talbot felt his teeth begin to ache. It went up and up, a whine that climbed till it was beyond his hearing.

Victor made a hand signal to the younger female technician at the graser behind the glass plate. She bent to the projector's sighting mechanism once, quickly, then cut it in. Talbot saw no light beam, but there was the same locking sound he had heard earlier, and then a soft humming, and a life-size hologram of himself, standing naked as he had been a few moments before, trembled in the air where he had stood. He looked at Victor questioningly. Victor nodded, and Talbot walked to the phantasm, passed his hand through it, stood close and looked into the clear brown eyes, noted the wide pore patterns in the nose, studied himself more closely than he had ever been able to do in a mirror. He felt: as if someone had walked over his grave.

Victor was talking to three male technicians, and a moment later they came to examine the hologram. They moved in with light meters and sensitive instruments that apparently were capable of gauging the sophistication and clarity of the ghost image. Talbot watched, fascinated and terrified. It seemed he was about to embark on the great journey of his life; a journey with a much desired destination: surcease.

One of the technicians signaled Victor.

"It's pure," he said to Talbot. Then, to the younger female technician on the second graser projector, "All right, Jana, move it out of there." She started up an engine and the entire projector apparatus turned on heavy rubber wheels and rolled out of the way. The image of Talbot, naked and vulnerable, a little sad to Talbot as he watched it fade and vanish like morning mist, had disappeared when the technician turned off the projector.

"All right, Karl," Victor was saying, "we're moving the pedestal in now. Narrow the aperture, and wait for my signal." Then, to Talbot, "Here comes your mite, old friend."

Talbot felt a sense of resurrection.

The older female technician rolled a four-foot-high stainless steel pedestal to the center of the lab, positioned it so the tiny, highly-polished spindle atop the pedestal touched the very bottom of the faint ripple in the glass. It looked like, and was, an actualizing stage for the real test. The full-sized hologram had been a gross test to ensure the image's perfection. Now came the creation of a living entity, a Lawrence Talbot, naked and the size of a single cell, possessing a consciousness and intelligence and memories and desires identical to Talbot's own.

"Ready, Karl?" Victor was saying.

Talbot heard no reply, but Victor nodded his head as if listening. Then he said, "All right, extract the beam!"

It happened so fast, Talbot missed most of it.

The micropion beam was composed of particles a million times smaller than the proton, smaller than the quark, smaller than the muon or the pion. Victor had termed them micropions. The slit opened in the wall, the beam was diverted, passed through the holographic ripple and was cut off as the slit closed again.

It had all taken a billionth of a second.

"Done," Victor said.

"I don't see anything," Talbot said, and realized how silly he must sound to these people. Of *course* he didn't see anything. There was nothing to see...with the naked eye. "Is he...is it there?"

"You're there," Victor said. He waved to one of the male technicians standing at a wall hutch of instruments in protective bays, and the man hurried over with the slim, reflective barrel of a microscope. He clipped it onto the tiny needle-pointed stand atop the pedestal in a fashion Talbot could not quite follow. Then he stepped away, and Victor said, "Part two of your problem solved, Larry. Go look and see yourself."

Lawrence Talbot went to the microscope, adjusted the knob till he could see the reflective surface of the spindle, and saw himself in infinitely reduced perfection

staring up at himself. He recognized himself, though all he could see was a cyclopean brown eye staring down from the smooth glass satellite that dominated his sky.

He waved. The eye blinked.

Now it begins, he thought.

Lawrence Talbot stood at the lip of the huge crater that formed Lawrence Talbot's navel. He looked down in the bottomless pit with its atrophied remnants of umbilicus forming loops and protuberances, smooth and undulant and vanishing into utter darkness. He stood poised to descend and smelled the smells of his own body. First, sweat. Then the smells that wafted up from within. The smell of penicillin, like biting down on tin foil with a bad tooth. The smell of aspirin, chalky and tickling the hairs of his nose like cleaning blackboard erasers by banging them together. The smells of rotted food, digested and turning to waste. All the odors rising up out of himself like a wild symphony of dark colors.

He sat down on the rounded rim of the navel and let himself slip forward.

He slid down, rode over an outcropping, dropped a few feet and slid again, tobogganing into darkness. He fell for only a short time, then brought up against the soft and yielding, faintly springy tissue plane where the umbilicus had been ligated. The darkness at the bottom of the hole suddenly shattered as blinding light filled the navel. Shielding his eyes, Talbot looked up the shaft toward the sky. A sun glowed there, brighter than a thousand novae. Victor had moved a surgical lamp over the hole to assist him. For as long as he could.

Talbot saw the umbra of something large moving behind the light, and he strained to discern what it was: it seemed important to know what it was. And for an instant, before his eyes closed against the glare, he thought he knew what it had been. Someone watching him, staring down past the surgical lamp that hung above the naked, anesthetized body of Lawrence Talbot, asleep on an operating table.

It had been the old woman, Nadja.

He stood unmoving for a long time, thinking of her.

Then he went to his knees and felt the tissue plane that formed the floor of the navel shaft.

He thought he could see something moving beneath the surface, like water flowing under a film of ice. He went down onto his stomach and cupped his hands around his eyes, putting his face against the dead flesh. It was like looking through a pane of isinglass. A trembling membrane through which he could see the collapsed lumen of the atretic umbilical vein. There was no opening. He pressed his palms against the rubbery surface and it gave, but only slightly. Before he could find the treasure, he had to follow the route of Demeter's map—now firmly and forever consigned to memory—and before he could set foot upon that route, he had to gain access to his own body.

But he had nothing with which to force that entrance.

Excluded, standing at the portal to his own body, Lawrence Talbot felt anger rising within him. His life had been anguish and guilt and horror, had been the wasted result of events over which he had had no control. Pentagrams and full moons and blood and never putting on even an ounce of fat because of a diet high in protein, blood steroids healthier than any normal adult male's, triglycerol and cholesterol levels balanced and humming. And death forever a stranger. Anger flooded through him. He heard an inarticulate little moan of pain, and fell forward, began tearing at the atrophied cord with teeth that had been used for just such activity many times before. Through a blood haze he knew he was savaging his own body and it seemed exactly the appropriate act of self-flagellation.

An outsider; he had been an outsider all his adult life, and fury would permit him to be shut out no longer. With demonic purpose he ripped away at the clumps of flesh until the membrane gave, at last, and a gap was torn through, opening him to himself...

And he was blinded by the explosion of light, by the rush of wind, by the passage of something that had been just beneath the surface writhing to be set free, and in the instant before he plummeted into unconsciousness, he knew Castañeda's Don Juan had told the truth: a thick bundle of white cobwebby filaments, tinged with gold, fibers of light, shot free from the collapsed vein, rose up through the shaft and trembled toward the antiseptic sky.

A metaphysical, otherwise invisible beanstalk that trailed away above him, rising up and up and up as his eyes closed and he sank away into oblivion.

He was on his stomach, crawling through the collapsed lumen, the center, of the path the veins had taken back from the amniotic sac to the fetus. Propelling himself forward the way an infantry scout would through dangerous terrain, using elbows and knees, frog-crawling, he opened the flattened tunnel with his head just enough to get through. It was quite light, the interior of the world called Lawrence Talbot, suffused with a golden luminescence.

The map had routed him out of this pressed tunnel through the inferior vena cava to the right atrium and thence through the right ventricle, the pulmonary arteries, through the valves, to the lungs, the pulmonary veins, crossover to the left side of the heart (left atrium, left ventricle), the aorta—bypassing the three coronary arteries above the aortic valves—and down over the arch of the aorta—bypassing the carotid and other arteries—to the celiac trunk, where the arteries split in a confusing array: the gastroduodenal to the stomach, the hepatic to the liver, the splenic to the spleen. And there, dorsal to the body of the diaphragm, he would drop down past the greater pancreatic duct to the pancreas itself. And there, among the islets of Langerhans, he would find, at the coordinates Information Associates had given him, he would find that which had been stolen from him one full-mooned night of horror so very long ago. And having found it, having assured himself of eternal sleep, not merely physical death from a silver bullet, he would stop his heart—how, he did not know, but he would—and it would all be ended for Lawrence Talbot, who had become what he had beheld. There, in the tail of the pancreas, supplied with blood by the splenic artery, lay the greatest treasure of all. More than doubloons, more than spices and silks, more than oil lamps used as djinn prisons by Solomon, lay final and sweet eternal peace, a release from monsterdom.

He pushed the final few feet of dead vein apart, and his head emerged into open space. He was hanging upside-down in a cave of deep orange rock.

Talbot wriggled his arms loose, braced them against what was clearly the ceiling of the cave, and wrenched his body out of the tunnel. He fell heavily, trying to twist at the last moment to catch the impact on his shoulders, and received a nasty blow on the side of the neck for his trouble.

He lay there for a moment, clearing his head. Then he stood and walked forward. The cave opened onto a ledge, and he walked out and stared at the landscape before him. The skeleton of something only faintly human lay tortuously crumpled against the wall of the cliff. He was afraid to look at it very closely.

He stared off across the world of dead orange rock, folded and rippled like a topographical view across the frontal lobe of a brain removed from its cranial casing.

The sky was a light yellow, bright and pleasant.

The grand canyon of his body was a seemingly horizonless tumble of atrophied rock, dead for millennia. He sought out and found a descent from the ledge, and began the trek.

There was water, and it kept him alive. Apparently, it rained more frequently here in this parched and stunned wasteland than appearance indicated. There was no keeping track of days or months, for there was no night and no day—always the same even, wonderful golden luminescence—but Talbot felt his passage down the central spine of orange mountains had taken him almost six months. And in that time it had rained forty-eight times, or roughly twice a week. Baptismal fonts of water were filled at every downpour, and he found if he kept the soles of his naked feet moist, he could walk without his energy flagging. If he ate, he did not remember how often, or what form the food had taken.

He saw no other signs of life.

Save an occasional skeleton lying against a shadowed wall of orange rock. Often, they had no skulls.

He found a pass through the mountains, finally, and crossed. He went up through foothills into lower, gentle slopes, and then up again, into cruel and narrow passages that wound higher and higher toward the heat of the sky. When he reached the summit, he found the path down the opposite side was straight and wide and easy. He descended quickly; only a matter of days, it seemed.

Descending into the valley he heard the song of a bird. He followed the sound. It led him to a crater of igneous rock, quite large, set low among the grassy swells of the valley. He came upon it without warning, and trudged up its short incline, to stand at the volcanic lip looking down.

The crater had become a lake. The smell rose up to assault him. Vile, and somehow terribly sad. The song of the bird continued; he could see no bird anywhere in the golden sky. The smell of the lake made him ill.

Then as he sat on the edge of the crater, staring down, he realized the lake was filled with dead things, floating bellyup; purple and blue as a strangled baby rotting white, turning slowly in the faintly rippled gray water; without features or limbs. He went down to the lowest outthrust of volcanic rock and stared at the dead things.

Something swam toward him. He moved back. It came on faster, and as it neared the wall of the crater, it surfaced, singing its bluejay song, swerved to rip a chunk of rotting flesh from the corpse of a floating dead thing, and paused only a moment as if to remind him that this was not his, Talbot's, domain, but his own.

Like Talbot, the fish would not die.

Talbot sat at the lip of the crater for a long time, looking down into the bowl that held the lake, and he watched the corpses of dead dreams as they bobbed and revolved like maggoty pork in a gray soup.

After a time, he rose, walked back down from the mouth of the crater, and resumed his journey. He was crying.

· · ·

When at last he reached the shore of the pancreatic sea, he found a great many things he had lost or given away when he was a child. He found a wooden machine gun on a tripod, painted olive drab, that made a rat-tat-tatting sound when a wooden handle was cranked. He found a set of toy soldiers, two companies, one Prussian and the other French, with a miniature Napoleon Bonaparte among them. He found a microscope kit with slides and petri dishes and racks of chemicals in nice little bottles, all of which bore uniform labels. He found a milk bottle filled with Indian-head pennies. He found a hand puppet with the head of a monkey and the name *Rosco* painted on the fabric glove with nail polish. He found a pedometer. He found a beautiful painting of a jungle bird that had been done with real feathers. He found a corncob pipe. He found a box of radio premiums: a cardboard detective kit with fingerprint dusting powder, invisible ink and a list of police-band call codes; a ring with what seemed to be a plastic bomb attached, and when he pulled the red finned rear off the bomb, and cupped his hands around it in his palms, he could see little scintillas of light, deep inside the payload section; a china mug with a little girl and a dog running across one side; a decoding badge with a burning glass in the center of the red plastic dial.

But there was something missing.

He could not remember what it was, but he knew it was important. As he had known it was important to recognize the shadowy figure who had moved past the surgical lamp at the top of the navel shaft, he knew whatever item was missing from this cache…was very important.

He took the boat anchored beside the pancreatic sea, and put all the items from the cache in the bottom of a watertight box under one of the seats. He kept out the large, cathedral-shaped radio, and put it on the bench seat in front of the oarlocks.

Then he unbeached the boat, and ran it out into the crimson water, staining his ankles and calves and thighs, and climbed aboard, and started rowing across toward the islets. Whatever was missing was very important.

The wind died when the islets were barely in sight on the horizon. Looking out across the blood-red sea, Talbot sat becalmed at latitude 38°54′ N, longitude 77°00′13″ W.

He drank from the sea and was nauseated. He played with the toys in the watertight box. And he listened to the radio.

He listened to a program about a very fat man who solved murders, to an adaptation of *The Woman in the Window* with Edward G. Robinson and Joan Bennett, to a story that began in a great railroad station, to a mystery about a wealthy man who could make himself invisible by clouding the minds of others so they could not see him, and he enjoyed a suspense drama narrated by a man named Ernest Chapell in which a group of people descended in a bathyscaphe through the bottom of a mine shaft where, five miles down, they were attacked by pterodactyls. Then he listened to the news, broadcast by Graham MacNamee. Among the human interest items at the close of the program, Talbot heard the unforgettable MacNamee voice say:

"Datelined Columbus, Ohio; September 24th, 1973. Martha Nelson has been in an institution for the mentally retarded for 98 years. She is 102 years old and was first sent to Orient State Institute near Orient, Ohio, on June 25th, 1875. Her records were destroyed in a fire in the institution sometime in 1883, and no one knows for certain why she is at the institute. At the time she was committed, it was known as the Columbus State Institute for the Feeble-Minded. 'She never had a chance,' said Dr. A. Z. Soforenko, appointed two months ago as superintendent of the institution. He said she was probably a victim of 'eugenic alarm,' which he said was common in the late 1800s. At that time some felt that because humans were made 'in God's image' the retarded must be evil or children of the devil, because they were not whole human beings. 'During that time,' Dr. Soforenko said, 'it was believed if you moved feeble-minded people out of a community and into an institution, the taint would never return to the community.' He went on to add, 'She was apparently trapped in that system of thought. No one can ever be sure if she actually *was* feeble-minded; it is a wasted life. She is quite coherent for her age. She has no known relatives and has had no contact with anybody but Institution staff for the last 78 or 80 years.'"

Talbot sat silently in the small boat, the sail hanging like a forlorn ornament from its single centerpole.

"I've cried more since I got inside you, Talbot, than I have in my whole life," he said, but could not stop. Thoughts of Martha Nelson, a woman of whom he had never before heard, of whom he would *never* have heard had it not been by chance by chance by chance he had heard by chance, by chance thoughts of her skirled through his mind like cold winds.

And the cold winds rose, and the sail filled, and he was no longer adrift, but was driven straight for the shore of the nearest islet. By chance.

He stood over the spot where Demeter's map had indicated he would find his soul. For a wild moment he chuckled, at the realization he had been expecting an enormous Maltese Cross or Captain Kidd's "X" to mark the location. But it was only soft green sand, gentle as talc, blowing in dust-devils toward the blood-red pancreatic sea. The spot was midway between the lowtide line and the enormous Bedlam-like structure that dominated the islet.

He looked once more, uneasily, at the fortress rising in the center of the tiny blemish of land. It was built square, seemingly carved from a single monstrous black rock…perhaps from a cliff that had been thrust up during some natural disaster. It had no windows, no opening he could see, though two sides of its bulk were exposed to his view. It troubled him. It was a dark god presiding over an empty kingdom. He thought of the fish that would not die, and remembered Nietzsche's contention that gods died when they lost their supplicants.

He dropped to his knees and, recalling the moment months before when he had dropped to his knees to tear at the flesh of his atrophied umbilical cord, he began digging in the green and powdery sand.

The more he dug, the faster the sand ran back into the shallow bowl. He stepped into the middle of the depression and began slinging dirt back between his legs with both hands, a human dog excavating for a bone.

When his fingertips encountered the edge of the box, he yelped with pain as his nails broke.

He dug around the outline of the box, and then forced his bleeding fingers down through the sand to gain purchase under the buried shape. He wrenched at it, and it came loose. Heaving with tensed muscles, he freed it and it came up.

He took it to the edge of the beach and sat down.

It was just a box. A plain wooden box, very much like an old cigar box, but larger. He turned it over and over and was not at all surprised to find it bore no arcane hieroglyphics or occult symbols. It wasn't that kind of treasure. Then he turned it right side up and pried open the lid. His soul was inside. It was not what he had expected to find, not at all. But it *was* what had been missing from the cache.

Holding it tightly in his fist, he walked up past the fast-filling hole in the green sand, toward the bastion on the high ground.

> *We shall not cease from exploration*
> *And the end of all our exploring*
> *Will be to arrive where we started*
> *And know the place for the first time.*
> T.S. ELIOT

Once inside the brooding darkness of the fortress—and finding the entrance had been disturbingly easier than he had expected—there was no way to go but down. The wet, black stones of the switchback stairways led inexorably downward into the bowels of the structure, clearly far beneath the level of the pancreatic sea. The stairs were steep, and each step had been worn into smooth curves by the pressure of feet that had descended this way since the dawn of memory. It was dark, but not so dark that Talbot could not see his way. There was no light, however. He did not care to think about how that could be.

When he came to the deepest part of the structure, having passed no rooms or chambers or openings along the way, he saw a doorway across an enormous hall, set into the far wall. He stepped off the last of the stairs, and walked to the door. It was built of crossed iron bars, as black and moist as the stones of the bastion. Through the interstices he saw something pale and still in a far corner of what could have been a cell.

There was no lock on the door.

It swung open at his touch.

Whoever lived in this cell had never tried to open the door; or had tried and decided not to leave.

He moved into deeper darkness.

A long time of silence passed, and finally he stooped to help her to her feet. It was like lifting a sack of dead flowers, brittle and surrounded by dead air incapable of holding even the memory of fragrance.

He took her in his arms and carried her.

"Close your eyes against the light, Martha," he said, and started back up the long stairway to the golden sky.

· · ·

Lawrence Talbot sat up on the operating table. He opened his eyes and looked at Victor. He smiled a peculiarly gentle smile. For the first time since they had been friends, Victor saw all torment cleansed from Talbot's face.

"It went well," he said. Talbot nodded.

They grinned at each other.

"How're your cryonic facilities?" Talbot asked.

Victor's brows drew down in bemusement. "You want me to freeze you? I thought you'd want something more permanent...say, in silver."

"Not necessary."

Talbot looked around. He saw her standing against the far wall by one of the grasers. She looked back at him with open fear. He slid off the table, wrapping the sheet upon which he had rested around himself, a makeshift toga. It gave him a patrician look.

He went to her and looked down into her ancient face. "Nadja," he said, softly. After a long moment she looked up at him. He smiled and for an instant she was a girl again. She averted her gaze. He took her hand, and she came with him, to the table, to Victor.

"I'd be deeply grateful for a running account, Larry," the physicist said. So Talbot told him; all of it.

"My mother, Nadja, Martha Nelson, they're all the same," Talbot said, when he came to the end, "all wasted lives."

"And what was in the box?" Victor said.

"How well do you do with symbolism and cosmic irony, old friend?"

"Thus far I'm doing well enough with Jung and Freud," Victor said. He could not help but smile.

Talbot held tightly to the old technician's hand as he said, "It was an old, rusted Howdy Doody button."

Victor turned around.

When he turned back, Talbot was grinning. "That's not cosmic irony, Larry...it's slapstick," Victor said. He was angry. It showed clearly.

Talbot said nothing, simply let him work it out.

Finally Victor said, "What the hell's *that* supposed to signify, innocence?"

Talbot shrugged. "I suppose if I'd known, I wouldn't have lost it in the first place. That's what it was, and that's what it is. A little metal pinback about an inch and a half in diameter, with that cockeyed face on it, the orange hair, the toothy grin, the pug nose, the freckles, all of it, just the way he always was." He fell silent, then after a moment added, "It seems right."

"And now that you have it back, you don't *want* to die?"

"I don't *need* to die."

"And you want me to freeze you."

"Both of us."

Victor stared at him with disbelief. "For God's sake, Larry!"

Nadja stood quietly, as if she could not hear them.

"Victor, listen: Martha Nelson is in there. A wasted life. Nadja is out here. I don't know why or how or what did it…but…a wasted life. Another wasted life. I want you to create her mite, the same way you created mine, and send her inside. He's waiting for her, and he can make it right, Victor. All right, at last. He can be with her as she regains the years that were stolen from her. He can be—*I* can be—her father when she's a baby, her playmate when she's a child, her buddy when she's maturing, her boyfriend when she's a young girl, her suitor when she's a young woman, her lover, her husband, her companion as she grows old. Let her be all the women she was never permitted to be, Victor. Don't steal from her a second time. And when it's over, it will start again…"

"*How*, for Christ sake, how the hell *how*? Talk sense, Larry! What is all this metaphysical crap?"

"I don't *know* how; it just is! I've been there, Victor, I was there for months, maybe years, and I never changed, never went to the wolf; there's no Moon there…no night and no day, just golden light and warmth, and I can try to make restitution. I can give back two lives. *Please*, Victor!"

The physicist looked at him without speaking. Then he looked at the old woman. She smiled up at him, and then, with arthritic fingers, removed her clothing.

When she came through the collapsed lumen, Talbot was waiting for her. She looked very tired, and he knew she would have to rest before they attempted to cross the orange mountains. He helped her down from the ceiling of the cave, and laid her down on soft, pale yellow moss he had carried back from the islets of Langerhans during the long trek with Martha Nelson. Side by side, the two old women lay on the moss, and Nadja fell asleep almost immediately. He stood over them, looking at their faces.

They were identical.

Then he went out on the ledge and stood looking toward the spine of the orange mountains. The skeleton held no fear for him now. He felt a sudden sharp chill in the air and knew Victor had begun the cryonic preservation.

He stood that way for a long time, the little metal button with the sly, innocent face of a mythical creature painted on its surface in four brilliant colors held tightly in his left hand.

And after a while, he heard the crying of a baby, just one baby, from inside the cave, and turned to return for the start of the easiest journey he had ever made.

Somewhere, a terrible devil-fish suddenly flattened its gills, turned slowly bellyup, and sank into darkness.

CROATOAN

1976 Locus Poll Award: Best Short Story

BENEATH THE CITY, there is yet another city: wet and dark and strange; a city of sewers and moist scuttling creatures and running rivers so desperate to be free not even Styx fits them. And in that lost city beneath the city, I found the child.

Oh my God, if I knew where to start. With the child? No, before that. With the alligators? No, earlier. With Carol? Probably. It always started with a Carol. Or an Andrea. A Stephanie. Always someone. There is nothing cowardly about suicide; it takes determination.

"Stop it! Godammit, just *stop* it...I said stop..." And I had to hit her. It wasn't that hard a crack, but she had been weaving, moving, stumbling: she went over the coffee table, all the fifty-dollar gift books coming down on top of her. Wedged between the sofa and the overturned table. I kicked the table out of the way and bent to help her up, but she grabbed me by the waist and pulled me down; crying, begging me to *do* something. I held her and put my face in her hair and tried to say something right, but what could I say?

Denise and Joanna had left, taking the d&c tools with them. She had been quiet, almost as though stunned by the hammer, after they had scraped her. Quiet, stunned, dry-eyed but hollow-eyed; watching me with the plastic Baggie. The sound of the toilet flushing had brought her running from the kitchen, where she had lain on a mattress pad. I heard her coming, screaming, and caught her just as she started through the hall to the bathroom. And hit her, without wanting to, just trying to stop her as the water sucked the Baggie down and away.

"D-*do* somethi-ing," she gasped, fighting for air.

I kept saying Carol, Carol, over and over, holding her, rocking back and forth, staring over her head, across the living room to the kitchen, where the edge of the teak dining table showed through the doorway, the amber-stained mattress pad hanging half over the edge, pulled loose when Carol had come for the Baggie.

After a few minutes, she spiraled down into dry, sandpapered sighs. I lifted her onto the sofa, and she looked up at me.

"Go after him, Gabe. Please. Please, go after him."

"Come on, Carol, stop it. I feel lousy about it…"

"Go after him, you sonofabitch!" she screamed. Veins stood out on her temples.

"I can't go after him, dammit, he's in the plumbing; he's in the fucking river by now! Stop it, get off my case, let me alone!" I was screaming back at her.

She found a place where untapped tears waited, and I sat there, across from the sofa, for almost half an hour, just the one lamp casting a dull glow across the living room, my hands clasped down between my knees, wishing she was dead, wishing I was dead, wishing everyone was dead… except the kid. But. He was the only one who was dead. Flushed. Bagged and flushed. Dead.

When she looked up at me again, a shadow cutting off the lower part of her face so the words emerged from darkness, keynoted only by the eyes, she said, "Go find him." I had never heard anyone sound that way, ever. Not ever. It frightened me. Riptides beneath the surface of her words created trembling images of shadow women drinking Drano, lying with their heads inside gas ovens, floating face up in thick, red bath water, their hair rippling out like jellyfish.

I knew she would do it. I couldn't support that knowledge. "I'll try," I said.

She watched me from the sofa as I left the apartment, and standing against the wall in the elevator, I felt her eyes on me. When I reached the street, still and cold in the predawn, I thought I would walk down to the River Drive and mark time till I could return and console her with the lie that I had tried but failed.

But she was standing in the window, staring down at me.

The manhole cover was almost directly across from me, there in the middle of the silent street.

I looked from the manhole cover to the window, and back again, and again, and again. She waited. Watching. I went to the iron cover and got down on one knee and tried to pry it up. Impossible. I bloodied my fingertips trying, and finally stood, thinking I had satisfied her. I took one step toward the building and realized she was no longer in the window. She stood silently at the curb, holding the long metal rod that wedged against the apartment door when the police lock was engaged.

I went to her and looked into her face. She knew what I was asking: I was asking, *Isn't this enough? Haven't I done enough?*

She held out the rod. No, I hadn't done enough.

I took the heavy metal rod and levered up the manhole cover. It moved with difficulty, and I strained to pry it off the hole. When it fell, it made a clanging in the street that rose up among the apartment buildings with an alarming suddenness. I had to push it aside with both hands; and when I looked up from that perfect circle of darkness that lay waiting, and turned to the spot where she had given me the tool, she was gone.

I looked up; she was back in the window.

The smell of the unwashed city drifted up from the manhole, chill and condemned. The tiny hairs in my nose tried to baffle it; I turned my head away.

I never wanted to be an attorney. I wanted to work on a cattle ranch. But there was family money, and the need to prove myself to shadows who had been dead and buried with their owners long since. People seldom do what they want to do; they usually do what they are *compelled* to do. Stop me before I kill again. There was no rational reason for my descending into that charnel house stink, that moist darkness. No rational reason, but Denise and Joanna from the Abortion Center had been friends of mine for eleven years. We had been in bed together many times; long past the time I had enjoyed being in bed together with them, or they had enjoyed being in bed together with me. They knew it. I knew it. They knew I knew, and they continued to set that as one of the payments for their attendance at my Carols, my Andreas, my Stephanies. It was their way of getting even. They liked me, despite themselves, but they had to get even. Get even for their various attendances over eleven years, the first of which had been one for the other, I don't remember which. Get even for many flushings of the toilet. There was no rational reason for going down into the sewers. None.

But there were eyes on me from an apartment window.

I crouched, dropped my legs over the lip of the open manhole, sat on the street for a moment, then slipped over the edge and began to climb down.

Slipping into an open grave. The smell of the earth is there, where there is no earth. The water is evil; vital fluid that has been endlessly violated. Everything is covered with a green scum that glows faintly in the darkness. An open grave waiting patiently for the corpse of the city to fall.

I stood on the ledge above the rushing tide, sensing the sodden weight of lost and discarded life that rode the waters toward even darker depths. *My God*, I thought, *I must be out of my mind just to* be *here.* It had finally overtaken me; the years of casual liaisons, careless lies, the guilt I suppose I'd *always* known would mount up till it could no longer be denied. And I was down here, where I belonged.

People do what they are compelled to do.

I started walking toward the arching passageway that led down and away from the steel ladder and the street opening above. Why not walk: aimless, can you perceive what I'm saying?

Once, years ago, I had an affair with my junior partner's wife. Jerry never knew about it. They're divorced now. I don't think he ever found out; she would have had to've been even crazier than I thought to tell him. Denise and Joanna had visited that time, too. I'm nothing if not potent. We flew to Kentucky together one weekend. I was preparing a brief, she met me at the terminal, we flew as husband and wife, family rate. When my work was done in Louisville, we drove out into the countryside. I minored in geology at college, before I went into law. Kentucky is rife with caves. We pulled in at a picnic grounds where some locals had advised us we could do a little spelunking, and with the minimal gear we had picked up at a sporting goods shop, we went into a fine network of chambers, descending beneath the hills and the picnic grounds. I loved the darkness, the even temperature, the smooth-surfaced rivers, the blind fish and water insects that scurried across the wet mirror of the still pools. She had come because she was not permitted to have intercourse at the base of Father Duffy's statue on Times Square, in the main window of Bloomingdale's, or on Channel 2 directly preceding *The Late News.* Caves were the next best thing.

For my part, the thrill of winding down deeper and deeper into the earth—even though graffiti and Dr. Pepper cans all along the way reminded me this was hardly unexplored territory—offset even her (sophomoric) appeals to "take her violently," there on the shell-strewn beach of a subterranean river.

I *liked* the feel of the entire Earth over me. I was not claustrophobic, I was—in some perverse way—wonderfully free. Even soaring! Under the ground, I was soaring!

The walk deeper into the sewer system did not unsettle or distress me. I rather enjoyed being alone. The smell was terrible, but terrible in a way I had not expected.

If I had expected vomit and garbage, this was certainly not what I smelled. Instead, there was a bittersweet scent of rot—reminiscent of Florida mangrove swamps. There was the smell of cinnamon, and wallpaper paste, and charred rubber; the warm odors of rodent blood and bog gas; melted cardboard, wool, coffee grounds still aromatic, rust.

The downward channel leveled out. The ledge became a wide, flat plain as the water went down through drainage conduits, leaving only a bubbling, frothy residue to sweep away into the darkness. It barely covered the heels of my shoes. Florsheims, but they could take it. I kept moving. Then I saw the light ahead of me.

It was dim, flickering, vanished for a moment as something obscured it from my view, moving in front of it, back again, dim and orange. I moved toward the light.

It was a commune of bindlestiffs, derelicts gathered together beneath the streets for safety and the skeleton of camaraderie. Five very old men in heavy overcoats and three even older men in castoff army jackets… but the older men were younger, they only *looked* older: a condition of the skids. They sat around a waste barrel oil drum filled with fire. Dim, soft, withered fire that leaped and curled and threw off sparks all in slow motion. Dreamwalking fire; somnambulist fire; mesmerized fire. I saw an atrophied arm of flame like a creeper of kangaroo ivy emerge over the lip of the barrel, struggling toward the shadowed arch of the tunnel ceiling; it stretched itself thin, released a single, teardrop-shaped spark, and then fell back into the barrel without a scream.

The hunkering men watched me come toward them. One of them said something, directly into the ear of the man beside him; he moved his lips very little and never took his eyes off me. As I neared, the men stirred expectantly. One of them reached into a deep pocket of his overcoat for something bulky. I stopped and looked at them.

They looked at the heavy iron rod Carol had given me.

They wanted what I had, if they could get it.

265

I wasn't afraid. I was under the Earth and I was part iron rod. They could not get what I had. They knew it. That's why there are always fewer killings than there might be. People *always* know.

I crossed to the other side of the channel, close to the wall. Watching them carefully. One of them, perhaps strong himself, perhaps merely stupider, stood up and, thrusting his hands deeper into his overcoat pockets, paralleled my passage down the channel away from them.

The channel continued to descend slightly, and we walked away from the oil drum and the light from the fire and the tired community of subterranean castoffs. I wondered idly when he would make his move, but I wasn't worried. He watched me, trying to see me more clearly, it seemed, as we descended deeper into the darkness. And as the light receded he moved up closer, but didn't cross the channel. I turned the bend first.

Waiting, I heard the sounds of rats in their nests.

He didn't come around the bend.

I found myself beside a service niche in the tunnel wall, and stepped back into it. He came around the bend, on my side of the channel. I could have stepped out as he passed my hiding place, could have clubbed him to death with the iron rod before he realized that the stalker had become the stalked.

I did nothing, stayed far back motionless in the niche and let him pass. Standing there, my back to the slimy wall, listening to the darkness around me, utter, final, even palpable. But for the tiny twittering sounds of rats I could have been two miles down in the central chamber of some lost cavern maze.

There's no logic to why it happened. At first, Carol had been just another casual liaison, another bright mind to touch, another witty personality to enjoy, another fine and workable body to work so fine with mine. I grow bored quickly. It's not a sense of humor I seek—lord knows every slithering, hopping, crawling member of the animal kingdom has a sense of humor—for Christ sake even dogs and *cats* have a sense of humor—it's wit! Wit is the answer. Let me touch a woman with wit and I'm gone, sold on the spot. I said to her, the first time I met her, at a support luncheon for the Liberal candidate for D.A., "Do you fool around?"

"I don't fool," she said instantly, no time-lapse, no need for rehearsal, fresh out of her mind, "fools bore me. Are you a fool?"

I was delighted and floored at the same time. I went fumfuh-fumfuh, and she didn't give me a moment. "A simple yes or no will suffice. Answer this one: how many sides are there to a round building?"

I started to laugh. She watched me with amusement, and for the first time in my life I actually saw someone's eyes twinkle with mischief. "I don't know," I said, "how many sides *are* there to a round building?"

"Two," she answered, "*in*side and *out*side. I guess you're a fool. No, you may not take me to bed." And she walked away.

I was undone. She couldn't have run it better if she had come back two minutes in a time machine, knowing what I'd say, and programmed me into it. And so I chased her. Up hill and down dale, all around that damned dreary luncheon, till I finally herded her into a corner—which was precisely what she'd been going for.

"As Bogart said to Mary Astor, 'You're good, shweetheart, very very good.'" I said it fast, for fear she'd start running me around again. She settled against the wall, a martini in her hand; and she looked up at me with that twinkling.

At first it was just casual. But she had depth, she had wiliness, she had such an air of self-possession that it was inevitable I would start phasing-out the other women, would start according her the attention she needed and wanted and without demanding...demanded.

I came to care.

Why didn't I take precautions? Again, there's no logic to it. I thought she was; and for a while, she was. Then she stopped. She told me she had stopped, something internal, the gynecologist had suggested she go off the pill for a while. She suggested vasectomy to me. I chose to ignore the suggestion. But chose not to stop sleeping with her.

When I called Denise and Joanna, and told them Carol was pregnant, they sighed and I could see them shaking their heads sadly. They said they considered me a public menace, but told me to tell her to come down to the Abortion Center and they would put the suction pump to work. I told them, hesitantly, that it had gone too long, suction wouldn't work. Joanna simply snarled, "You thoughtless cocksucker!" and hung up the extension. Denise read me the riot act for twenty minutes. She didn't suggest a vasectomy; she suggested, in graphic detail, how I might have my organ removed by a taxidermist using a cheese grater. Without benefit of anesthesia.

But they came, with their dilation and curettage implements, and they laid her out on the teak table with a mattress under her, and then they had gone—Joanna pausing a moment at the door to advise me this was the last time, the last time, the very last time she could stomach it, that it was the last time and did I have that fixed firmly, solidly, imbedded in the forefront of my brain? The last time.

And now I was here in the sewers.

I tried to remember what Carol looked like, but it wasn't an image I could fix in my mind half as solidly as I had fixed the thought that this. Was. The. Last. Time.

I stepped out of the service niche.

The young-old bindlestiff who had followed me was standing there, silently waiting. At first I couldn't even see him—there was only the vaguest lighter shade of darkness to my left, coming from around the bend and that oil drum full of fire—but I knew he was there. Even as *he* had known I was there, all the time. He didn't speak, and I didn't speak, and after a while I was able to discern his shape. Hands still deep in his pockets.

"Something?" I said, more than a little belligerently.

He didn't answer.

"Get out of my way."

He stared at me, sorrowfully, I thought, but that had to be nonsense. I thought.

"Don't make me have to hurt you," I said.

He stepped aside, still watching me.

I started to move past him, down the channel.

He didn't follow, but I was walking backward to keep him in sight, and he didn't take his eyes off mine.

I stopped. "What do you want?" I asked. "Do you need some money?"

He came toward me. Inexplicably, I wasn't afraid he would try something. He wanted to see me more clearly, closer. I thought.

"You couldn't give me nothing I need." His voice was rusted, pitted, scarred, unused, unwieldy.

"Then why are you following me?"

"Why've you come down here?"

I didn't know what to say.

"You make it bad down here, mister. Why don't you g'wan and go back upside, leave us alone?"

"I have a right to be here." Why had I said *that*?

"You got no right to come down here; stay back upside where you belong. All of us know you make it bad, mister."

He didn't want to hurt me, he just didn't want me here. Not even right for these outcasts, the lowest level to which men could sink; even here I was beneath contempt. His hands were deep in his pockets. "Take your hands out of your pockets, slowly, I want to make sure you aren't going to hit me with something when I turn around. Because I'm going on down there, not back. Come on now, do it. Slowly. Carefully."

He took his hands out of his pockets slowly, and held them up. He had no hands. Chewed stumps, glowing faintly green like the walls where I had descended from the manhole.

I turned and went away from him.

It grew warmer, and the phosphorescent green slime on the walls gave some light. I had descended as the channel had fallen away deeper under the city. This was a land not even the noble streetworkers knew, a land blasted by silence and emptiness. Stone above and below and around, it carried the river without a name into the depths, and if I could not return, I would stay here like the skids. Yet I continued walking. Sometimes I cried, but I don't know why, or for what, or for whom. Certainly not for myself.

Was there ever a man who had everything more than I had had everything? Bright words, and quick movements, soft cloth next to my skin, and places to place my love, if I had only recognized that it *was* love.

I heard a nest of rats squealing as something attacked them, and I was drawn to a side tunnel where the shining green effluvium made everything bright and dark as the view inside the machines they used to have in shoe stores. I hadn't thought of that in years. Until they found out that the X-rays could damage the feet of children, shoe stores used bulky machines one stepped up onto, and into which one inserted newly shod feet. And when the button was pushed a green X-ray light came on, showing the bones that lay beneath the flesh. Green and black. The light was green, and the bones were dusty black. I hadn't thought of that in years, but the side tunnel was illuminated in just that way.

An alligator was ripping the throats of baby rats.

It had invaded the nest and was feeding mercilessly, tossing the bodies of the ripped and shredded rodents aside as it went for the defenseless smaller ones. I stood watching, sickened but fascinated. Then, when the shrieks of anguish were extinguished at last, the great saurian, direct lineal descendant of Rex, snapped them up one by one and, thrashing its tail, turned to stare at me.

He had no hands. Chewed stumps, glowing faintly green like the walls.

I moved back against the wall of the side tunnel as the alligator belly-crawled past me, dragging its leash. The thick, armored tail brushed my ankle and I stiffened.

Its eyes glowed red as those of an Inquisition torturer.

I watched its scaled and taloned feet leave deep prints in the muck underfoot, and I followed the beast, its trail clearly marked by the impression of the leash in the mud.

Frances had a five-year-old daughter. She took the little girl for a vacation to Miami Beach one year. I flew down for a few days. We went to a Seminole village, where the old women did their sewing on Singer machines. I thought that was sad. A lost heritage, perhaps; I don't know. The daughter, whose name I can't recall, wanted a baby alligator. Cute. We brought it back on the plane in a cardboard box with air holes. Less than a month later it had grown large enough to snap. Its teeth weren't that long, but it snapped. It was saying: this is what I'll be: direct lineal descendant of Rex. Frances flushed it down the toilet one night after we'd made love. The little girl was asleep in the next room. The next morning, Frances told her the alligator had run off.

The sewers of the city are infested with full-grown alligators. No amount of precaution and no forays by hunting teams with rifles or crossbows or flame throwers have been able to clear the tunnels. The sewers are still infested; workers go carefully. So did I.

The alligator moved steadily, graceful in its slithering passage down one tunnel and into another side passage and down always down, steadily into the depths. I followed the trail of the leash.

We came to a pool and it slid into the water like oil, its dead-log snout above the fetid foulness, its Torquemada eyes looking toward its destination.

I thrust the iron rod down my pant leg, pulled my belt tight enough to hold it, and waded into the water. It came up to my neck and I lay out and began dog-paddling, using the one leg that would bend. The light was very green and sharp now.

The saurian came out on the muck beach at the other side and crawled forward toward an opening in the tunnel wall. I crawled out, pulled the iron rod loose, and followed. The opening gave into darkness, but as I passed through, I trailed my hand across the wall and felt a door. I stopped, surprised, and felt in the darkness. An iron door, with an arched closure at the top and a latch. Studs, heavy and round and smelling faintly of rust, dotted the door.

I walked through…and stopped.

There had been something else on the door. I stepped back and ran my fingers over the open door again. I found the indentations at once, and ran my fingertips across them, trying to discern in the utter darkness what they were. Something about them…I traced them carefully.

They were letters. 𝕮. My fingers followed the curves. 𝕽. Cut into the iron somehow. 𝕺. What was a door doing down here? 𝕬. The cuts seemed very old, weathered, scummy. 𝕿. They were large and very regular. 𝕺. They made no sense, no word formed that I knew. 𝕬. And I came to the end of the sequence. 𝕹.

CROATOAN. It made no sense. I stayed there a moment, trying to decide if it was a word the sanitation engineers might have used for some designation of a storage area perhaps. Croatoan. No sense. Not Croatian, it was Croatoan. Something nibbled at the back of my memory: I *had* heard the word before, knew it from somewhere, long ago, a vapor of sound traveling back on the wind of the past. It escaped me, I had no idea what it meant.

I went through the doorway again.

Now I could not even see the trail of the leash the alligator had dragged. I kept moving, the iron rod in my hand.

I heard them coming toward me from both sides, and it was clearly alligators, many of them. From side passages. I stopped and reached out to find the wall of the channel. I couldn't find it. I turned around, hoping to get back to the door, but when I hurried back the way I thought I had come, I didn't reach the door. I just kept going. Either I had gone down a fork and not realized the channel had separated, or I had lost my sense of direction. And the slithering sounds kept coming.

Now, for the first time, I felt terror! The safe, warm, enfolding darkness of the underworld had, in an instant, merely by the addition of sounds around me, become a suffocating winding-sheet. It was as if I'd abruptly awakened in a coffin, buried six feet beneath the tightly stomped loam; that clogging terror Poe had always described so well because he had feared it himself…the premature burial. Caves no longer seemed comfortable.

I began to run!

I lost the rod somewhere, the iron bar that had been my weapon, my security.

I fell and slid face first in the muck.

I scrabbled to my knees and kept going. No walls, no light, no slightest aperture or outcropping, nothing to give me a sense of being in the world, running through a limbo without beginning, without end.

Finally, exhausted, I slipped and fell and lay for a moment. I heard slithering all around me and managed to pull myself to a sitting position. My back grazed a wall, and I fell up against it with a moan of gratitude. Something, at least; a wall against which to die.

I don't know how long I lay there, waiting for the teeth.

Then I felt something touching my hand. I recoiled with a shriek! It had been cold and dry and soft. Did I recall that snakes and other amphibians were cool and dry? Did I remember that? I was trembling.

Then I saw light. Flickering, bobbing, going up and down just slightly, coming toward me.

And as the light grew closer and brighter, I saw there was something right beside me; the something that had touched me; it had been there for a time, watching me.

It was a child.

Naked, deathly white, with eyes great and luminous, but covered with a transparent film as milky as a membrane, small, very young, hairless, its arms shorter than they should have been, purple and crimson veins crossing its bald skull like traceries of blood on a parchment, fine even features, nostrils dilating as it breathed shallowly, ears slightly tipped as though reminiscent of an elf, barefooted but with pads on the soles, this child stared at me, looked up at me, its little tongue visible as it opened its mouth filled with tiny teeth, trying to form sounds, saying nothing, watching me, a wonder in its world, watching me with the saucer eyes of a lemur, the light behind the membrane flickering and pulsing. This child.

And the light came nearer, and the light was many lights. Torches, held aloft by the children who rode the alligators.

Beneath the city, there is yet another city: wet and dark and strange.

At the entrance to their land someone—not the children, they couldn't have done it—long ago built a road sign. It is a rotted log on which has been placed, carved from fine cherrywood, a book and a hand. The book is open, and the hand rests on the book, one finger touching the single word carved in the open pages. The word is CROATOAN.

On August 13, 1590, Governor John White of the Virginia colony managed to get back to the stranded settlers of the Roanoke, North Carolina, colony. They had been waiting three years for supplies, but politics, foul weather and the Spanish Armada had made it impossible. As they went ashore, they saw a pillar of smoke. When they reached the site of the colony, though they found the stronghold walls still standing against possible Indian attacks, no sign of life greeted them. The Roanoke colony had vanished. Every man, woman, and child, gone. Only the word CROATOAN had been left. *"One of the chiefe trees or postes at the right side of the entrance had the barke taken off, and 5. foote from the ground in fayre Capitall letters was grauen CROATOAN without any crosse or signe of distresse."*

There was a Croatan island, but they were not there. There was a tribe of Hatteras Indians who were called Croatans, but they knew nothing of the whereabouts of the lost colony. All that remains of legend is the story of the child Virginia Dare, and the mystery of what happened to the lost settlers of Roanoke.

Down here in this land beneath the city live the children. They live easily and in strange ways. I am only now coming to know the incredible manner of their existence. How they eat, what they eat, how they manage to survive, and have managed for hundreds of years, these are all things I learn day by day, with wonder surmounting wonder.

I am the only adult here.

They have been waiting for me.

They call me father.

JEFFTY IS FIVE

1978 Hugo Award: Best Short Story; Locus Poll Award: Best Short Story; Nebula Award: Short Story

WHEN I WAS five years old, there was a little kid I played with: Jeffty. His real name was Jeff Kinzer, and everyone who played with him called him Jeffty. We were five years old together, and we had good times playing together.

When I was five, a Clark Bar was as fat around as the gripping end of a Louisville Slugger, and pretty nearly six inches long, and they used real chocolate to coat it, and it crunched very nicely when you bit into the center, and the paper it came wrapped in smelled fresh and good when you peeled off one end to hold the bar so it wouldn't melt onto your fingers. Today, a Clark Bar is as thin as a credit card, they use something artificial and awful-tasting instead of pure chocolate, the thing is soft and soggy, it costs fifteen or twenty cents instead of a decent, correct nickel, and they wrap it so you think it's the same size it was twenty years ago, only it isn't; it's slim and ugly and nasty-tasting and not worth a penny, much less fifteen or twenty cents.

When I was that age, five years old, I was sent away to my Aunt Patricia's home in Buffalo, New York, for two years. My father was going through "bad times" and Aunt Patricia was very beautiful, and had married a stockbroker. They took care of me for two years. When I was seven, I came back home and went to find Jeffty, so we could play together.

I was seven. Jeffty was still five. I didn't notice any difference. I didn't know: I was only seven.

When I was seven years old, I used to lie on my stomach in front of our Atwater-Kent radio and listen to swell stuff. I had tied the ground wire to the radiator, and would lie there with my coloring books and my Crayolas (when there were only sixteen colors in the big box), and listen to the NBC Red Network: Jack Benny on the *Jell-O Program*, *Amos 'n' Andy*, Edgar Bergen and Charlie McCarthy on the *Chase and Sanborn Program*, *One Man's Family*, *First Nighter*; the NBC Blue Network: *Easy Aces*, the *Jergens Program* with

275

Walter Winchell, *Information Please, Death Valley Days*; and best of all, the Mutual Network with *The Green Hornet, The Lone Ranger, The Shadow* and *Quiet, Please*. Today, I turn on my car radio and go from one end of the dial to the other and all I get is 100 strings orchestras, banal housewives and insipid truckers discussing their kinky sex lives with arrogant talk show hosts, country and western drivel and rock music so loud it hurts my ears.

When I was ten, my grandfather died of old age and I was "a troublesome kid," and they sent me off to military school, so I could be "taken in hand."

I came back when I was fourteen. Jeffty was still five.

When I was fourteen years old, I used to go to the movies on Saturday afternoons and a matinee was ten cents and they used real butter on the popcorn and I could always be sure of seeing a western like Lash LaRue, or Wild Bill Elliott as Red Ryder with Bobby Blake as Little Beaver, or Roy Rogers, or Johnny Mack Brown; a scary picture like *House of Horrors* with Rondo Hatton as the Creeper, or *Cat People*, or *The Mummy*, or *I Married a Witch* with Fredric March and Veronica Lake; plus an episode of a great serial like *The Shadow* with Victor Jory, or *Dick Tracy* or *Flash Gordon*; and three cartoons; and a James Fitzpatrick Traveltalk; Movietone News; and a sing-along and, if I stayed on till evening, Bingo or Keeno; and free dishes. Today, I go to movies and see Clint Eastwood blowing people's heads apart like ripe cantaloupes.

At eighteen, I went to college. Jeffty was still five. I came back during the summers, to work at my Uncle Joe's jewelry store. Jeffty hadn't changed. Now I knew there was something different about him, something wrong, something weird. Jeffty was still five years old, not a day older.

At twenty-two, I came home for keeps. To open a Sony television franchise in town, the first one. I saw Jeffty from time to time. He was five.

Things are better in a lot of ways. People don't die from some of the old diseases any more. Cars go faster and get you there more quickly on better roads. Shirts are softer and silkier. We have paperback books, even though they cost as much as a good hardcover used to. When I'm running short in the bank, I can live off credit cards till things even out. But I still think we've lost a lot of good stuff. Did you know you can't buy linoleum any more, only vinyl floor covering? There's no such thing as oilcloth any more; you'll never again smell that special, sweet smell from your grandmother's kitchen. Furniture isn't made to last thirty years or longer because they took a survey and found that young homemakers like to throw their furniture out and bring in all new, color-coded borax every seven years. Records don't feel right; they're not thick and solid like the old ones, they're thin and you can bend them…that doesn't seem right to me. Restaurants don't serve cream in pitchers any more, just that artificial glop in little plastic tubs, and one is never enough to get coffee the right color. You can make a dent in a car fender with only a sneaker. Everywhere you go, all the towns look the same with Burger Kings and McDonald's and 7-Elevens and Taco Bells and motels and shopping centers. Things may be better, but why do I keep thinking about the past?

What I mean by five years old is not that Jeffty was retarded. I don't think that's what it was. Smart as a whip for five years old; very bright, quick, cute, a funny kid.

But he was three feet tall, small for his age, and perfectly formed: no big head, no strange jaw, none of that. A nice, normal-looking five-year-old kid. Except that he was the same age as I was: twenty-two.

When he spoke, it was with the squeaking, soprano voice of a five-year-old; when he walked, it was with the little hops and shuffles of a five-year-old; when he talked to you, it was about the concerns of a five-year-old… comic books, playing soldier, using a clothes pin to attach a stiff piece of cardboard to the front fork of his bike so the sound it made when the spokes hit was like a motorboat, asking questions like *why does that thing do that like that*, how high is up, how old is old, why is grass green, what's an elephant look like? At twenty-two, he was five.

Jeffty's parents were a sad pair. Because I was still a friend of Jeffty's, still let him hang around with me, sometimes took him to the county fair or miniature golf or the movies, I wound up spending time with *them*. Not that I much cared for them, because they were so awfully depressing. But then, I suppose one couldn't expect much more from the poor devils. They had an alien thing in their home, a child who had grown no older than five in twenty-two years, who provided the treasure of that special childlike state indefinitely, but who also denied them the joys of watching the child grow into a normal adult.

Five is a wonderful time of life for a little kid…or it *can* be, if the child is relatively free of the monstrous beastliness other children indulge in. It is a time when the eyes are wide open and the patterns are not yet set;

a time when one had not yet been hammered into accepting everything as immutable and hopeless; a time when the hands cannot do enough, the mind cannot learn enough, the world is infinite and colorful and filled with mysteries. Five is a special time before they take the questing, unquenchable, quixotic soul of the young dreamer and thrust it into dreary schoolroom boxes. A time before they take the trembling hands that want to hold everything, touch everything, figure everything out, and make them lie still on desktops. A time before people begin saying "act your age" and "grow up" or "you're behaving like a baby." It is a time when a child who acts adolescent is still cute and responsive and everyone's pet. A time of delight, of wonder, of innocence.

Jeffty had been stuck in that time, just five, just so.

But for his parents it was an ongoing nightmare from which no one—not social workers, not priests, not child psychologists, not teachers, not friends, not medical wizards, not psychiatrists, no one—could slap or shake them awake. For seventeen years their sorrow had grown through stages of parental dotage to concern, from concern to worry, from worry to fear, from fear to confusion, from confusion to anger, from anger to dislike, from dislike to naked hatred, and finally, from deepest loathing and revulsion to a stolid, depressive acceptance.

John Kinzer was a shift foreman at the Balder Tool & Die plant. He was a thirty-year man. To everyone but the man living it, his was a spectacularly uneventful life. In no way was he remarkable...save that he had fathered a twenty-two-year-old five-year-old.

John Kinzer was a small man; soft, with no sharp angles; with pale eyes that never seemed to hold mine for longer than a few seconds. He continually shifted in his chair during conversations, and seemed to see things in the upper corners of the room, things no one else could see...or wanted to see. I suppose the word that best suited him was *haunted*. What his life had become...well, *haunted* suited him.

Leona Kinzer tried valiantly to compensate. No matter what hour of the day I visited, she always tried to foist food on me. And when Jeffty was in the house she was always at *him* about eating: "Honey, would you like an orange? A nice orange? Or a tangerine? I have tangerines. I could peel a tangerine for you." But there was clearly such fear in her, fear of her own child, that the offers of sustenance always had a faintly ominous tone.

Leona Kinzer had been a tall woman, but the years had bent her. She seemed always to be seeking some area of wallpapered wall or storage niche into which she could fade, adopt some chintz or rose-patterned protective coloration and hide forever in plain sight of the child's big brown eyes, pass her a hundred times a day and never realize she was there, holding her breath, invisible. She always had an apron tied around her waist, and her hands were red from cleaning. As if by maintaining the environment immaculately she could pay off her imagined sin: having given birth to this strange creature.

Neither of them watched television very much. The house was usually dead silent, not even the sibilant whispering of water in the pipes, the creaking of timbers settling, the humming of the refrigerator. Awfully silent, as if time itself had taken a detour around that house.

As for Jeffty, he was inoffensive. He lived in that atmosphere of gentle dread and dulled loathing, and if he understood it, he never remarked in any way. He played, as a child plays, and seemed happy. But he must have sensed, in the way of a five-year-old, just how alien he was in their presence.

Alien. No, that wasn't right. He was *too* human, if anything. But out of phase, out of synch with the world around him, and resonating to a different vibration than his parents, God knows. Nor would other children play with him. As they grew past him, they found him at first childish, then uninteresting, then simply frightening as their perceptions of aging became clear and they could see he was not affected by time as they were. Even the little ones, his own age, who might wander into the neighborhood, quickly came to shy away from him like a dog in the street when a car backfires.

Thus, I remained his only friend. A friend of many years. Five years. Twenty-two years. I liked him; more than I can say. And never knew exactly why. But I did, without reserve.

But because we spent time together, I found I was also—polite society— spending time with John and Leona Kinzer. Dinner, Saturday afternoons sometimes, an hour or so when I'd bring Jeffty back from a movie. They were grateful: slavishly so. It relieved them of the embarrassing chore of going out with him, or having to pretend before the world that they were loving parents with a perfectly normal, happy, attractive child. And their gratitude extended to hosting me. Hideous, every moment of their depression, hideous.

I felt sorry for the poor devils, but I despised them for their inability to love Jeffty, who was eminently lovable.

I never let on, of course, even during the evenings in their company that were awkward beyond belief.

We would sit there in the darkening living room—*always* dark or darkening, as if kept in shadow to hold back what the light might reveal to the world outside through the bright eyes of the house—we would sit and silently stare at one another. They never knew what to say to me.

"So how are things down at the plant?" I'd say to John Kinzer.

He would shrug. Neither conversation nor life suited him with any ease or grace. "Fine, just fine," he would say, finally.

And we would sit in silence again.

"Would you like a nice piece of coffee cake?" Leona would say. "I made it fresh just this morning." Or deep dish green apple pie. Or milk and tollhouse cookies. Or a brown betty pudding.

"No, no, thank you, Mrs. Kinzer; Jeffty and I grabbed a couple of cheeseburgers on the way home." And again, silence.

Then, when the stillness and the awkwardness became too much even for them (and who knew how long that total silence reigned when they were alone, with that thing they never talked about any more, hanging between them), Leona Kinzer would say, "I think he's asleep."

John Kinzer would say, "I don't hear the radio playing."

Just so, it would go on like that, until I could politely find an excuse to bolt away on some flimsy pretext. Yes, that was the way it would go on, every time, just the same…except once.

"I don't know what to do any more," Leona said. She began crying. "There's no change, not one day of peace."

Her husband managed to drag himself out of the old easy chair and go to her. He bent and tried to soothe her, but it was clear from the graceless way in which he touched her graying hair that the ability to be compassionate had been stunned in him. "Shhh, Leona, it's all right. Shhh." But she continued crying. Her hands scraped gently at the antimacassars on the arms of the chair.

Then she said, "Sometimes I wish he had been stillborn."

John looked up into the corners of the room. For the nameless shadows that were always watching him? Was it God he was seeking in those spaces?

"You don't mean that," he said to her, softly, pathetically, urging her with body tension and trembling in his voice to recant before God took notice of the terrible thought. But she meant it; she meant it very much.

I managed to get away quickly that evening. They didn't want witnesses to their shame. I was glad to go.

And for a week I stayed away. From them, from Jeffty, from their street, even from that end of town.

I had my own life. The store, accounts, suppliers' conferences, poker with friends, pretty women I took to well-lit restaurants, my own parents, putting anti-freeze in the car, complaining to the laundry about too much starch in the collars and cuffs, working out at the gym, taxes, catching Jan or David (whichever one it was) stealing from the cash register. I had my own life.

But not even *that* evening could keep me from Jeffty. He called me at the store and asked me to take him to the rodeo. We chummed it up as best a twenty-two-year-old with other interests *could*…with a five-year-old. I never dwelled on what bound us together; I always thought it was simply the years. That, and affection for a kid who could have been the little brother I never had. (Except I *remembered* when we had played together, when we had both been the same age; I *remembered* that period, and Jeffty was still the same.)

And then, one Saturday afternoon, I came to take him to a double feature, and things I should have noticed so many times before, I first began to notice only that afternoon.

I came walking up to the Kinzer house, expecting Jeffty to be sitting on the front porch steps, or in the porch glider, waiting for me. But he was nowhere in sight.

Going inside, into that darkness and silence, in the midst of May sunshine, was unthinkable. I stood on the front walk for a few moments, then cupped my hands around my mouth and yelled, "Jeffty? Hey, Jeffty, come on out, let's go. We'll be late."

His voice came faintly, as if from under the ground.

"Here I am, Donny."

I could hear him, but I couldn't see him. It was Jeffty, no question about it: as Donald H. Horton, President and Sole Owner of The Horton TV &

Sound Center, no one but Jeffty called me Donny. He had never called me anything else.

(Actually, it isn't a lie. I *am*, as far as the public is concerned, Sole Owner of the Center. The partnership with my Aunt Patricia is only to repay the loan she made me, to supplement the money I came into when I was twenty-one, left to me when I was ten by my grandfather. It wasn't a very big loan, only eighteen thousand, but I asked her to be a silent partner, because of when she had taken care of me as a child.)

"Where are you, Jeffty?"

"Under the porch in my secret place."

I walked around the side of the porch, and stooped down and pulled away the wicker grating. Back in there, on the pressed dirt, Jeffty had built himself a secret place. He had comics in orange crates, he had a little table and some pillows, it was lit by big fat candles, and we used to hide there when we were both…five.

"What'cha up to?" I asked, crawling in and pulling the grate closed behind me. It was cool under the porch, and the dirt smelled comfortable, the candles smelled clubby and familiar. Any kid would feel at home in such a secret place: there's never been a kid who didn't spend the happiest, most productive, most deliciously mysterious times of his life in such a secret place.

"Playin'," he said. He was holding something golden and round. It filled the palm of his little hand.

"You forget we were going to the movies?"

"Nope. I was just waitin' for you here."

"Your mom and dad home?"

"Momma."

I understood why he was waiting under the porch. I didn't push it any further. "What've you got there?"

"Captain Midnight Secret Decoder Badge," he said, showing it to me on his flattened palm.

I realized I was looking at it without comprehending what it was for a long time. Then it dawned on me what a miracle Jeffty had in his hand. A miracle that simply could *not* exist.

"Jeffty," I said softly, with wonder in my voice, "where'd you get that?"

"Came in the mail today. I sent away for it."

"It must have cost a lot of money."

"Not so much. Ten cents an' two inner wax seals from two jars of Ovaltine."

"May I see it?" My voice was trembling, and so was the hand I extended. He gave it to me and I held the miracle in the palm of my hand. It was *wonderful*.

You remember. *Captain Midnight* went on the radio nationwide in 1940. It was sponsored by Ovaltine. And every year they issued a Secret Squadron Decoder Badge. And every day at the end of the program, they would give you a clue to the next day's installment in a code that only kids with the official badge could decipher. They stopped making those wonderful Decoder Badges in 1949. I remember the one I had in 1945: it was beautiful. It had a magnifying glass in the center of the code dial. *Captain Midnight* went off the air in 1950, and though I understand it was a short-lived television series in the mid-Fifties, and though they issued Decoder Badges in 1955 and 1956, as far as the *real* badges were concerned, they never made one after 1949.

The Captain Midnight Code-O-Graph I held in my hand, the one Jeffty said he had gotten in the mail for ten cents (*ten cents!!!*) and two Ovaltine labels, was brand new, shiny gold metal, not a dent or a spot of rust on it like the old ones you can find at exorbitant prices in collectible shoppes from time to time...it was a *new* Decoder. And the date on it was *this* year.

But *Captain Midnight* no longer existed. Nothing like it existed on the radio. I'd listened to the one or two weak imitations of old-time radio the networks were currently airing, and the stories were dull, the sound effects bland, the whole feel of it wrong, out of date, cornball. Yet I held a *new* Code-O-Graph.

"Jeffty, tell me about this," I said.

"Tell you what, Donny? It's my new Capt'n Midnight Secret Decoder Badge. I use it to figger out what's gonna happen tomorrow."

"Tomorrow how?"

"On the program."

"*What* program?!"

He stared at me as if I was being purposely stupid. "On Capt'n *Mid*night! Boy!" I was being dumb.

I still couldn't get it straight. It was right there, right out in the open, and I still didn't know what was happening. "You mean one of those records they made of the old-time radio programs? Is that what you mean, Jeffty?"

"What records?" he asked. He didn't know what *I* meant.

We stared at each other, there under the porch. And then I said, very slowly, almost afraid of the answer, "Jeffty, how do you hear *Captain Midnight*?"

"Every day. On the radio. On my radio. Every day at five-thirty."

News. Music, dumb music, and news. That's what was on the radio every day at 5:30. Not *Captain Midnight*. The Secret Squadron hadn't been on the air in twenty years.

"Can we hear it tonight?" I asked.

"Boy!" he said. I was being dumb. I knew it from the way he said it; but I didn't know *why*. Then it dawned on me: this was Saturday. *Captain Midnight* was on Monday through Friday. Not on Saturday or Sunday.

"We goin' to the movies?"

He had to repeat himself twice. My mind was somewhere else. Nothing definite. No conclusions. No wild assumptions leapt to. Just off somewhere trying to figure it out, and concluding—as *you* would have concluded, as *any*one would have concluded rather than accepting the truth, the impossible and wonderful truth—just finally concluding there was a simple explanation I didn't yet perceive. Something mundane and dull, like the passage of time that steals all good, old things from us, packratting trinkets and plastic in exchange. And all in the name of Progress.

"We goin' to the movies, Donny?"

"You bet your boots we are, kiddo," I said. And I smiled. And I handed him the Code-O-Graph. And he put it in his side pants pocket. And we crawled out from under the porch. And we went to the movies. And neither of us said anything about *Captain Midnight* all the rest of that day. And there wasn't a ten-minute stretch, all the rest of that day, that I didn't think about it.

It was inventory all that next week. I didn't see Jeffty till late Thursday. I confess I left the store in the hands of Jan and David, told them I had some errands to run, and left early. At 4:00. I got to the Kinzers' right around 4:45. Leona answered the door, looking exhausted and distant. "Is Jeffty around?" She said he was upstairs in his room…

…listening to the radio.

I climbed the stairs two at a time.

All right, I had finally made that impossible, illogical leap. Had the stretch of belief involved anyone but Jeffty, adult or child, I would have reasoned out more explicable answers. But it *was* Jeffty, clearly another kind of vessel of life, and what he might experience should not be expected to fit into the ordered scheme.

I admit it: I *wanted* to hear what I heard.

Even with the door closed, I recognized the program:

"There he goes, Tennessee! Get him!"

There was the heavy report of a squirrel rifle and the keening whine of the slug ricocheting, and then the same voice yelled triumphantly, *"Got him! D-e-a-a-a-d center!"*

He was listening to the American Broadcasting Company, 790 kilocycles, and he was hearing *Tennessee Jed*, one of my most favorite programs from the Forties, a western adventure I had not heard in twenty years, because it had not existed for twenty years.

I sat down on the top step of the stairs, there in the upstairs hall of the Kinzer home, and I listened to the show. It wasn't a rerun of an old program; I dimly remembered every one of *them* by heart. I had never missed an episode. And even more convincing evidence than childhood memory that this was a *new* installment were the occasional references during the commercials to current cultural and technological developments, and phrases that had not existed in common usage in the Forties: aerosol spray cans, laserasing of tattoos, Tanzania, the word "uptight."

I could not ignore the fact. Jeffty was listening to a *new* segment of *Tennessee Jed*.

I ran downstairs and out the front door to my car. Leona must have been in the kitchen. I turned the key and punched on the radio and spun the dial to 790 kilohertz. The ABC station. Rock music.

I sat there for a few moments, then ran the dial slowly from one end to the other. Music, news, talk shows. No *Tennessee Jed*. And it was a Blaupunkt, the best radio I could get. I wasn't missing some perimeter station. It simply was not there!

After a few moments I turned off the radio and the ignition and went back upstairs quietly. I sat down on the top step and listened to the entire program. It was *wonderful*.

Exciting, imaginative, filled with everything I remembered as being most innovative about radio drama. But it was modern. It wasn't an antique, rebroadcast to assuage the need of that dwindling listenership who longed for the old days. It was a new show, with all the old voices, but still young and bright. Even the commercials were for currently available products, but they weren't as loud or as insulting as the screamer ads one heard on radio these days.

And when *Tennessee Jed* went off at 5:00, I heard Jeffty spin the dial on his radio till I heard the familiar voice of the announcer Glenn Riggs proclaim, *"Presenting Hop Harrigan! America's ace of the airwaves!"* There was the sound of an airplane in flight. It was a prop plane, *not* a jet! Not the sound kids today have grown up with, but the sound *I* grew up with, the *real* sound of an airplane, the growling, revving, throaty sound of the kind of airplanes G-8 and His Battle Aces flew, the kind Captain Midnight flew, the kind Hop Harrigan flew. And then I heard Hop say, "CX-4 *calling control tower. CX-4 calling control tower. Standing by!"* A pause, then, *"Okay, this is Hop Harrigan…coming in!"*

And Jeffty, who had the same problem all of us kids had had in the Forties with programming that pitted equal favorites against one another on different stations, having paid his respects to Hop Harrigan and Tank Tinker, spun the dial and went back to ABC, where I heard the stroke of a gong, the wild cacophony of nonsense Chinese chatter, and the announcer yelled, *"T-e-e-e-rry and the Pirates!"*

I sat there on the top step and listened to Terry and Connie and Flip Corkin and, so help me God, Agnes Moorehead as The Dragon Lady, all of them in a new adventure that took place in a Red China that had not existed in the days of Milton Caniff's 1937 version of the Orient, with river pirates and Chiang Kai-shek and warlords and the naive Imperialism of American gunboat diplomacy.

Sat, and listened to the whole show, and sat even longer to hear *Superman* and part of *Jack Armstrong, The All-American Boy* and part of *Captain Midnight*, and John Kinzer came home and neither he nor Leona came upstairs to find out what had happened to me, or where Jeffty was, and sat longer, and found I had started crying, and could not stop, just sat there with tears running down my face, into the corners of my mouth, sitting and crying until Jeffty heard me and opened his door and saw me and came out and looked at me in childish confusion as I heard the station break for the Mutual Network and they began the theme music of *Tom Mix*, "When It's Round-up Time in Texas and the Bloom Is on the Sage," and Jeffty touched my shoulder and smiled at me, with his mouth and his big brown eyes, and said, "Hi, Donny. Wanna come in an' listen to the radio with me?"

Hume denied the existence of an absolute space, in which each thing has its place; Borges denies the existence of one single time, in which all events are linked.

Jeffty received radio programs from a place that could not, in logic, in the natural scheme of the space-time universe as conceived by Einstein, exist. But that wasn't all he received. He got mail-order premiums that no one was manufacturing. He read comic books that had been defunct for three decades. He saw movies with actors who had been dead for twenty years. He was the receiving terminal for endless joys and pleasures of the past that the world had dropped along the way. On its headlong suicidal flight toward New Tomorrows, the world had razed its treasurehouse of simple happinesses, had poured concrete over its playgrounds, had abandoned its elfin stragglers, and all of it was being impossibly, miraculously shunted back into the present through Jeffty. Revivified, updated, the traditions maintained but contemporaneous. Jeffty was the unbidding Aladdin whose very nature formed the magic lampness of his reality.

And he took me into his world with him.

Because he trusted me.

We had breakfast of Quaker Puffed Wheat Sparkies and warm Ovaltine we drank out of *this* year's Little Orphan Annie Shake-Up Mugs. We went to the movies and while everyone else was seeing a comedy starring Goldie Hawn and Ryan O'Neal, Jeffty and I were enjoying Humphrey Bogart as the professional thief Parker in John Huston's brilliant adaptation of the Donald Westlake novel SLAYGROUND. The second feature was Spencer Tracy, Carole Lombard and Laird Cregar in the Val Lewton-produced film of *Leiningen Versus the Ants*.

Twice a month we went down to the newsstand and bought the current pulp issues of *The Shadow, Doc Savage* and *Startling Stories*. Jeffty and I sat together and I read to him from the magazines. He particularly liked the new short novel by Henry Kuttner, "The Dreams of Achilles," and the new Stanley G. Weinbaum series of short stories set in the subatomic particle universe of Redurna. In September we enjoyed the first installment of the new Robert E. Howard Conan novel, ISLE OF THE BLACK ONES, in *Weird Tales*; and in August we were only mildly disappointed by Edgar Rice

Burroughs's fourth novella in the Jupiter series featuring John Carter of Barsoom—"Corsairs of Jupiter." But the editor of *Argosy All-Story Weekly* promised there would be two more stories in the series, and it was such an unexpected revelation for Jeffty and me that it dimmed our disappointment at the lessened quality of the current story.

We read comics together, and Jeffty and I both decided—separately, before we came together to discuss it—that our favorite characters were Doll Man, Airboy and The Heap. We also adored the George Carlson strips in *Jingle Jangle Comics*, particularly the Pie-Face Prince of Old Pretzleburg stories, which we read together and laughed over, even though I had to explain some of the esoteric puns to Jeffty, who was too young to have that kind of subtle wit.

How to explain it? I can't. I had enough physics in college to make some offhand guesses, but I'm more likely wrong than right. The laws of the conservation of energy occasionally break. These are laws that physicists call "weakly violated." Perhaps Jeffty was a catalyst for the weak violation of conservation laws we're only now beginning to realize exist. I tried doing some reading in the area—muon decay of the "forbidden" kind: gamma decay that doesn't include the muon neutrino among its products—but nothing I encountered, not even the latest readings from the Swiss Institute for Nuclear Research near Zurich, gave me an insight. I was thrown back on a vague acceptance of the philosophy that the real name for "science" is *magic*.

No explanations, but enormous good times.

The happiest time of my life.

I had the "real" world, the world of my store and my friends and my family, the world of profit&loss, of taxes and evenings with young women who talked about going shopping, or the United Nations, or the rising cost of coffee and microwave ovens. And I had Jeffty's world, in which I existed only when I was with him. The things of the past he knew as fresh and new, I could experience only when in his company. And the membrane between the two worlds grew ever thinner, more luminous and transparent. I had the best of both worlds. And knew, somehow, that I could carry nothing from one to the other.

Forgetting that, for just a moment, betraying Jeffty by forgetting, brought an end to it all.

Enjoying myself so much, I grew careless and failed to consider how fragile the relationship between Jeffty's world and my world really was.

There is a reason why the Present begrudges the existence of the Past. I never really understood. Nowhere in the beast books, where survival is shown in battles between claw and fang, tentacle and poison sac, is there recognition of the ferocity the Present always brings to bear on the Past. Nowhere is there a detailed statement of how the Present lies in wait for What-Was, waiting for it to become Now-This-Moment so it can shred it with its merciless jaws.

Who could know such a thing…at any age…and certainly not at my age…who could understand such a thing?

I'm trying to exculpate myself. I can't. It was my fault.

It was another Saturday afternoon.

"What's playing today?" I asked him, in the car, on the way downtown.

He looked up at me from the other side of the front seat and smiled one of his best smiles. "Ken Maynard in *Bullwhip Justice* an' *The Demolished Man*." He kept smiling, as if he'd really put one over on me. I looked at him with disbelief.

"You're *kid*ding!" I said, delighted. "Bester's THE DEMOLISHED MAN?" He nodded his head, delighted at my being delighted. He knew it was one of my favorite books. "Oh, that's super!"

"Super *duper*," he said.

"Who's in it?"

"Franchot Tone, Evelyn Keyes, Lionel Barrymore and Elisha Cook, Jr." He was much more knowledgeable about movie actors than I'd ever been. He could name the character actors in any movie he'd ever seen. Even the crowd scenes.

"And cartoons?" I asked.

"Three of 'em: a *Little Lulu*, a *Donald Duck* and a *Bugs Bunny*. An' a *Pete Smith Specialty* an' a *Lew Lehr Monkeys is da C-r-r-r-aziest Peoples*."

"Oh boy!" I said. I was grinning from ear to ear. And then I looked down and saw the pad of purchase order forms on the seat. I'd forgotten to drop it off at the store.

"Gotta stop by the Center," I said. "Gotta drop off something. It'll only take a minute."

"Okay," Jeffty said. "But we won't be late, will we?"

"Not on your tintype, kiddo," I said.

• • •

When I pulled into the parking lot behind the Center, he decided to come in with me and we'd walk over to the theater. It's not a large town. There are only two movie houses, the Utopia and the Lyric. We were going to the Utopia and it was only three blocks from the Center.

I walked into the store with the pad of forms, and it was bedlam. David and Jan were handling two customers each, and there were people standing around waiting to be helped. Jan turned a look on me and her face was a horror-mask of pleading. David was running from the stockroom to the showroom and all he could murmur as he whipped past was "Help!" and then he was gone.

"Jeffty," I said, crouching down, "listen, give me a few minutes. Jan and David are in trouble with all these people. We won't be late, I promise. Just let me get rid of a couple of these customers." He looked nervous, but nodded okay.

I motioned to a chair and said, "Just sit down for a while and I'll be right with you."

He went to the chair, good as you please, though he knew what was happening, and he sat down.

I started taking care of people who wanted color television sets. This was the first really substantial batch of units we'd gotten in—color television was only now becoming reasonably priced and this was Sony's first promotion—and it was bonanza time for me. I could see paying off the loan and being out in front for the first time with the Center. It was business.

In my world, good business comes first.

Jeffty sat there and stared at the wall. Let me tell you about the wall.

Stanchion and bracket designs had been rigged from floor to within two feet of the ceiling. Television sets had been stacked artfully on the wall. Thirty-three television sets. All playing at the same time. Black and white, color, little ones, big ones, all going at the same time.

Jeffty sat and watched thirty-three television sets, on a Saturday afternoon. We can pick up a total of thirteen channels, including the UHF educational stations. Golf was on one channel; baseball was on a second; celebrity bowling was on a third; the fourth channel was a religious seminar; a teenage dance show was on the fifth; the sixth was a rerun of a situation comedy; the seventh was a rerun of a police show; eighth was a nature program showing a man flycasting endlessly; ninth was news and conversation; tenth was a stock car race; eleventh was a man doing logarithms on a blackboard; twelfth was a woman in a leotard doing setting-up exercises; and on the thirteenth channel was a badly animated cartoon show in Spanish. All but six of the shows were repeated on three sets. Jeffty sat and watched that wall of television on a Saturday afternoon while I sold as fast and as hard as I could, to pay back my Aunt Patricia and stay in touch with my world. It was business.

I should have known better. I should have understood about the present and the way it kills the past. But I was selling with both hands. And when I finally glanced over at Jeffty, half an hour later, he looked like another child.

He was sweating. That terrible fever sweat when you have stomach flu. He was pale, as pasty and pale as a worm, and his little hands were gripping the arms of the chair so tightly I could see his knuckles in bold relief. I dashed over to him, excusing myself from the middle-aged couple looking at the new 21" Mediterranean model.

"Jeffty!"

He looked at me, but his eyes didn't track. He was in absolute terror. I pulled him out of the chair and started toward the front door with him, but the customers I'd deserted yelled at me, "Hey!" The middle-aged man said, "You wanna sell me this thing or don't you?"

I looked from him to Jeffty and back again. Jeffty was like a zombie. He had come where I'd pulled him. His legs were rubbery and his feet dragged. The past, being eaten by the present, the sound of something in pain.

I clawed some money out of my pants pocket and jammed it into Jeffty's hand. "Kiddo...listen to me...get out of here right now!" He still couldn't focus properly. *"Jeffty,"* I said as tightly as I could, *"listen* to me!" The middle-aged customer and his wife were walking toward us. "Listen, kiddo, get out of here right this minute. Walk over to the Utopia and buy the tickets. I'll be right behind you." The middle-aged man and his wife were almost on us. I shoved Jeffty through the door and watched him stumble away in the wrong direction, then stop as if gathering his wits, turn and go back past the front of the Center and in the direction of the Utopia. "Yes sir," I said, straightening up and facing them, "yes, ma'am, that is one terrific set with some sen*sa*tional features! If you'll just step back here with me..."

There was a terrible sound of something hurting, but I couldn't tell from which channel, or from which set, it was coming.

• • •

Most of it I learned later, from the girl in the ticket booth, and from some people I knew who came to me to tell me what had happened. By the time I got to the Utopia, nearly twenty minutes later, Jeffty was already beaten to a pulp and had been taken to the Manager's office.

"Did you see a very little boy, about five years old, with big brown eyes and straight brown hair...he was waiting for me?"

"Oh, I think that's the little boy those kids beat up?"

"What!?! *Where is he?*"

"They took him to the Manager's office. No one knew who he was or where to find his parents—"

A young girl wearing an usher's uniform was kneeling down beside the couch, placing a wet paper towel on his face.

I took the towel away from her and ordered her out of the office.

She looked insulted and she snorted something rude; but she left. I sat on the edge of the couch and tried to swab away the blood from the lacerations without opening the wounds where the blood had caked. Both his eyes were swollen shut. His mouth was ripped badly. His hair was matted with dried blood.

He had been standing in line behind two kids in their teens. They started selling tickets at 12:30 and the show started at 1:00. The doors weren't opened till 12:45. He had been waiting, and the kids in front of him had had a portable radio. They were listening to the ball game. Jeffty had wanted to hear some program, God knows what it might have been, *Grand Central Station*, *Let's Pretend*, *The Land of the Lost*, God only knows which one it might have been.

He had asked if he could borrow their radio to hear the program for a minute, and it had been a commercial break or something, and the kids had given him the radio, probably out of some malicious kind of courtesy that would permit them to take offense and rag the little boy. He had changed the station...and they'd been unable to get it to go back to the ball game. It was locked into the past, on a station that was broadcasting a program that didn't exist for anyone but Jeffty.

They had beaten him badly...as everyone watched.

And then they had run away.

I had left him alone, left him to fight off the present without sufficient weaponry. I had betrayed him for the sale of a 21" Mediterranean console television, and now his face was pulped meat. He moaned something inaudible and sobbed softly.

"Shhh, it's okay, kiddo, it's Donny. I'm here. I'll get you home, it'll be okay."

I should have taken him straight to the hospital. I don't know why I didn't. I should have. I should have done that.

When I carried him through the door, John and Leona Kinzer just stared at me. They didn't move to take him from my arms. One of his hands was hanging down. He was conscious, but just barely. They stared, there in the semi-darkness of a Saturday afternoon in the present. I looked at them. "A couple of kids beat him up at the theater." I raised him a few inches in my arms and extended him. They stared at me, at both of us, with nothing in their eyes, without movement. "Jesus Christ," I shouted, "he's been beaten! He's your son! Don't you even want to touch him? What the hell kind of people are you?!"

Then Leona moved toward me very slowly. She stood in front of us for a few seconds, and there was a leaden stoicism in her face that was terrible to see. It said, *I have been in this place before, many times, and I cannot bear to be in it again; but I am here now.*

So I gave him to her. God help me, I gave him over to her.

And she took him upstairs to bathe away his blood and his pain.

John Kinzer and I stood in our separate places in the dim living room of their home, and we stared at each other. He had nothing to say to me.

I shoved past him and fell into a chair. I was shaking.

I heard the bath water running upstairs.

After what seemed a very long time Leona came downstairs, wiping her hands on her apron. She sat down on the sofa and after a moment John sat down beside her. I heard the sound of rock music from upstairs.

"Would you like a piece of nice pound cake?" Leona said.

I didn't answer. I was listening to the sound of the music. Rock music. On the radio. There was a table lamp on the end table beside the sofa. It cast a dim and futile light in the shadowed living room. *Rock music from the present, on a radio upstairs?* I started to say something, and then *knew...Oh, God...no!*

I jumped up just as the sound of hideous crackling blotted out the music, and the table lamp dimmed and dimmed and flickered. I screamed something, I don't know what it was, and ran for the stairs.

Jeffty's parents did not move. They sat there with their hands folded, in that place they had been for so many years.

I fell twice rushing up the stairs.

• • •

There isn't much on television that can hold my interest. I bought an old cathedral-shaped Philco radio in a secondhand store, and I replaced all the burnt-out parts with the original tubes from old radios I could cannibalize that still worked. I don't use transistors or printed circuits. They wouldn't work. I've sat in front of that set for hours sometimes, running the dial back and forth as slowly as you can imagine, so slowly it doesn't look as if it's moving at all sometimes.

But I can't find *Captain Midnight* or *The Land of the Lost* or *The Shadow* or *Quiet, Please*.

So she did love him, still, a little bit, even after all those years. I can't hate them: they only wanted to live in the present world again. That isn't such a terrible thing.

It's a good world, all things considered. It's much better than it used to be, in a lot of ways. People don't die from the old diseases any more. They die from new ones, but that's Progress, isn't it?

Isn't it?

Tell me.

Somebody please tell me.

COUNT THE CLOCK
THAT TELLS THE TIME

1979 Locus Poll Award: Short Story

When I do count the clock that tells the time,
And see the brave day sunk in hideous night;
When I behold the violet past prime,
And sable curls all silver'd o'er with white;
When lofty trees I see barren of leaves
Which erst from heat did canopy the herd,
And summer's green all girdled up in sheaves
Borne on the bier with white and bristly beard,
Then of thy beauty do I question make,
That thou among the wastes of time must go...

WILLIAM SHAKESPEARE,
the XIIth Sonnet

WAKING IN THE cool and cloudy absolute dead middle of a Saturday afternoon, one day, Ian Ross felt lost and vaguely frightened. Lying there in his bed, he was disoriented; and it took him a moment to remember when it was and where he was. Where he was: in the bed where he had awakened every day of his thirty-five-year-old life. When it was: the Saturday he had resolved to spend *doing* something. But as he lay there he realized he had come to life in the early hours just after dawn, it had looked as though it would rain, the sky seen through the high French windows, and he had turned over and gone back to sleep. Now the clock-radio on the bedside table told him it was the absolute dead middle of the afternoon; and the world outside his windows was cool and cloudy.

"Where does the time go?" he said.

He was alone, as always: there was no one to hear him or to answer. So he continued lying there, wasting time, feeling vaguely frightened. As though something important were passing him by.

A fly buzzed him, circled, buzzed him again. It had been annoying him for some time. He tried to ignore the intruder and stared off across Loch Tummel to the amazing flesh tones of the October trees, preparing themselves for winter's disingenuous attentions and the utter absence of tourism. The silver birches were already a blazing gold, the larches and ash trees still blending off from green to rust; in a few weeks the Norway spruces and the other conifers would darken until they seemed mere shadows against the slate sky.

Perthshire was most beautiful at this time of year. The Scottish travel bureaus had assured him of that. So he had come here. Had taken the time to learn to pronounce the names—Schiehallion, Killiecrankie, Pitlochry, Aberfeldy—and had come here to sit. The dream. The one he had always held: silent, close to him, unspoken, in his idle thoughts. The dream of going to Scotland. For what reason he could not say. He had never been here, had read little of this place, had no heritage of Scotsmen, ancestors calling from the past. But this was the place that had always called, and he had come.

For the first time in his life, Ian Ross had *done* something. Thirty-seven years old, rooted to a tiny apartment in Chicago, virtually friendless, working five days a week at a drafting table in a firm of industrial designers, watching television till sign-off, tidying the two-and-a-half rooms till every picture hung from the walls in perfect true with the junctures of walls and ceiling, entering each checkbook notation in the little ledger with a fine point ink pen, unable to remember what had happened last Thursday that made it different from last Wednesday, seeing himself reflected in the window of the cafeteria slowly eating the $2.95 Christmas Dinner Special, a solitary man, somehow never marking the change of the seasons save to understand only by his skin that it was warmer or colder, never tasting joy because he could never remember having been told what it was, reading books about *things* and *subject matter*, topics not people, because he knew so few people and *knew* none of them, drawing straight lines, feeling deserted but never knowing where to put his hands to relieve that feeling, a transient man, passing down the same streets every day and perceiving only dimly that there were streets *beyond* those streets, drinking water, and apple juice, and water, replying when he was addressed directly, looking around sometimes when he was addressed to see if it was, in fact, himself to whom the speaker was speaking, buying gray socks and white undershorts, staring out the windows of his apartment at the Chicago snow, staring for hours at the invisible sky, feeling the demon wind off Lake Michigan rattling the window glass in its frame and thinking this year he would re-putty and this year failing to re-putty, combing his hair as he always had, cooking his own meals, alone with the memories of his mother and father who had died within a year of each other and both from cancer, never having been able to speak more than a few awkward sentences to any woman but his mother...Ian Ross had lived his life like the dust that lay in a film across the unseen top of the tall wardrobe cabinet in his bedroom: colorless, unnoticed, inarticulate, neither giving nor taking.

Until one day he had said, "Where does the time go?" And in the months following those words he had come to realize he had not, in any remotely valuable manner, *lived* his life. He had wasted it. Months after the first words came, unbidden and tremulous, he admitted to himself that he had wasted his life.

He resolved to actualize at least the one dream. To go to Scotland. Perhaps to live. To rent or even buy a crofter's cottage on the edge of a moor, or overlooking one of the lochs he had dreamed about. He had all the insurance money still put by, he hadn't touched a cent of it. And there, in that far, chill place in the north he would live...walking the hills with a dog by his side, smoking a pipe that trailed a fragrant pennant of blue-white smoke, hands thrust deep into the pockets of a fleece-lined jacket. He would *live* there. That was the dream.

So he had taken the vacations he had never taken, all of them at one time, saved up from eleven years at the drafting table, and he flew to London. Not directly to Edinburgh, because he wanted to come upon the dream very slowly, creep up on it so it wouldn't vanish like a woodland elf hiding its kettle of gold.

And from King's Cross Station he had taken the 21.30 sleeper to Edinburgh, and he had walked the Royal Mile and gazed in wonder at Edinburgh Castle high on the bluff overlooking that bountiful city, and finally he had rented a car and had driven north out the Queensferry Road, across the bridge that spanned the Firth of Forth, on up the A-90 till he reached Pitlochry. Then a left, a random left, but not so random that he did not know it would come out overlooking the Queen's View, said to be the most beautiful view in the world, certainly in Scotland, and he had driven the twisting, narrow road till he was deep in the hills of Perth.

And there he had pulled off the road, gotten out of the car, leaving the door open, and walked away down the October hills to sit, finally and at last, staring at the loch, green and blue and silent as the mirror of his memory.

Where only the buzzing fly reminded him of the past.

He had been thirty-five when he said, "Where does the time go?" And he was thirty-seven as he sat on the hill.

And it was there that the dream died.

He stared at the hills, at the valley that ran off to left and right, at the sparkling water of the loch, and knew he had wasted his time again. He had resolved to *do* something; but he had done nothing. Again.

There was no place for him here.

He was out of phase with all around him. He was an alien object. A beer can thrown into the grass. A broken wall untended and falling back into the earth from which it had been wrenched stone by stone.

He felt lonely, starved, incapable of clenching his hands or clearing his throat. A ruin from another world, set down in foreign soil, drinking air that was not his to drink. There were no tears, no pains in his body, no deep and trembling sighs. In a moment, with a fly buzzing, the dream died for him. He had not been saved; had, in fact, come in an instant to understand that he had been a child to think it could ever change. What do you want to be when you grow up? Nothing. As I have always been nothing.

The sky began to bleach out.

The achingly beautiful golds and oranges and yellows began to drift toward sepia. The blue of the loch slid softly toward chalkiness, like an ineptly prepared painting left too long in direct sunlight. The sounds of birds and forest creatures and insects faded, the gain turned down slowly. The sun gradually cooled for Ian Ross. The sky began to bleach out toward a gray-white newsprint colorlessness. The fly was gone. It was cold now; very cold now.

Shadows began to superimpose themselves over the dusty mezzotint of the bloodless day:

A city of towers and minarets, as seen through shallow, disturbed water; a mountain range of glaciers with snow untracked and endless as an ocean; an ocean, with massive, serpent-necked creatures gliding through the jade deeps; a parade of ragged children bearing crosses hewn from tree branches; a great walled fortress in the middle of a parched wasteland, the yellow earth split like strokes of lightning all around the structure; a motorway with hundreds of cars speeding past so quickly they seemed to be stroboscopic lines of colored light; a battlefield with men in flowing robes and riding great-chested stallions, the sunlight dancing off curved swords and helmets; a tornado careening through a small town of slatback stores and houses, lifting entire buildings from their foundations and flinging them into the sky; a river of lava bursting through a fissure in the ground and boiling toward a shadowy indication of an amusement park, with throngs of holiday tourists moving in clots from one attraction to another.

Ian Ross sat, frozen, on the hillside. The world was dying around him. No…it was vanishing, fading out, dematerializing. As if all the sand had run out of the hourglass around him: as if he were the only permanent, fixed and immutable object in a metamorphosing universe suddenly cut loose from its time-anchor.

The world faded out around Ian Ross, the shadows boiled and seethed and slithered past him, caught in a cyclonic wind tunnel and swept away past him, leaving him in darkness.

He sat now, still, quiet, too isolated to be frightened.

He thought perhaps clouds had covered the sun.

There was no sun.

He thought perhaps it had been an eclipse, that his deep concentration of his hopeless state had kept him from noticing.

There was no sun.

No sky. The ground beneath him was gone. He sat, merely sat, but on nothing, surrounded by nothing, seeing and feeling nothing save a vague chill. It was cold now, very cold now.

After a long time he decided to stand and *did* stand: there was nothing beneath or above him. He stood in darkness.

He could remember everything that had ever happened to him in his life. Every moment of it, with absolute clarity. It was something he had never experienced before. His memory had been no better or worse than anyone else's, but he had forgotten all the details, many years in which nothing had happened, during which he had wasted time—almost as a mute witness at the dull rendition of his life.

But now, as he walked through the limbo that was all he had been left of the world, he recalled everything perfectly. The look of terror on his mother's face when he had sliced through the tendons of his left hand with the lid from the tin can of pink lemonade: he had been four years old. The feel of his new Thom McAn shoes that had always been too tight, from the moment they had been bought, but which he had been forced to wear to school every day, even though they rubbed him raw at the back of his heels: he had been seven years old. The Four Freshmen standing and singing for the graduation dance. He had been alone. He had bought one ticket to support the school event. He had been sixteen. The taste of egg roll at Choy's, the first time. He had been twenty-four. The woman he had met at the library, in the section where they kept the book on animals. She had used a white lace handkerchief to dry her temples. It had smelled of perfume. He had been thirty. He remembered all the sharp edges of every moment from his past. It was remarkable. In this nowhere.

And he walked through gray spaces, with the shadows of other times and other places swirling past. The sound of rushing wind, as though the emptiness through which he moved was being constantly filled and emptied, endlessly, without measure or substance.

Had he known what emotions to call on for release, he would have done so. But he was numb in his skin. Not merely chilled, as this empty place was chilled, but somehow inured to feeling from the edge of his perceptions to the center of his soul. Sharp, clear, drawn back from the absolute past, he remembered a day when he had been eleven, when his mother had suggested that for his birthday they make a small party, to which he would invite a few friends. And so (he remembered with diamond-bright perfection) he had invited six boys and girls. They had never come. He sat alone in the house that Saturday, all his comic books laid out in case the cake and party favors and pin-the-tail-on-the-donkey did not hold their attention sufficiently. Never came. It grew dark. He sat alone, with his mother occasionally walking through the living room to make some consoling remark. But he was alone, and he knew there was only one reason for it: they had all forgotten. It was simply that he was a waste of time for those actually living their lives. Invisible, by token of being unimportant. A thing unnoticed: on a street, who notices the mailbox, the fire hydrant, the crosswalk lines? He was an invisible, useless thing.

He had never permitted another party to be thrown for him.

He remembered that Saturday now. And found the emotion, twenty-six years late, to react to this terrible vanishment of the world. He began to tremble uncontrollably, and he sat down where there was nothing to sit down on, and he rubbed his hands together, feeling the tremors in his knuckles and the ends of his fingers. Then he felt the constriction in his throat, he turned his head this way and that, looking for a nameless exit from self-pity and loneliness; and then he cried. Lightly, softly, because he had no experience at it.

A crippled old woman came out of the gray mist of nowhere and stood watching him. His eyes were closed, or he would have seen her coming.

After a while, he snuffled, opened his eyes, and saw her standing in front of him. He stared at her. She was standing. At a level somewhat below him, as though the invisible ground of this nonexistent place was on a lower plane than that on which he sat.

"That won't help much," she said. She wasn't surly, but neither was there much succor in her tone.

He looked at her, and immediately stopped crying.

"Probably just got sucked in here," she said. It was not quite a question, though it had something of query in it. She knew, and was going carefully.

He continued to look at her, hoping she could tell him what had happened to him. And to her? She was here, too.

"Could be worse," she said, crossing her arms and shifting her weight off her twisted left leg. "I could've been a Saracen or a ribbon clerk or even one of those hairy prehumans." He didn't respond. He didn't know what she was talking about. She smiled wryly, remembering. "First person I met was some kind of a retard, little boy about fifteen or so. Must have spent what there'd been of his life in some padded cell or a hospital bed, something like that. He just sat there and stared at me, drooled a little, couldn't tell me a thing. I was scared out of my mind, ran around like a chicken with its head cut off. Wasn't till a long time after that before I met someone spoke English."

He tried to speak and found his throat was dry. His voice came out in a croak. He swallowed and wet his lips. "Are there many other, uh, other people…we're not all alone…?"

"Lots of others. Hundreds, thousands, God only knows; maybe whole countries full of people here. No animals, though. They don't waste it the way we do."

"Waste it? What?"

"Time, son. Precious, lovely time. That's all there is, just time. Sweet, flowing time. Animals don't know about time."

As she spoke, a slipping shadow of some wild scene whirled past and through them. It was a great city in flames. It seemed more substantial than the vagrant wisps of countryside or sea-scenes that had been ribboning past them as they spoke. The wooden buildings and city towers seemed almost solid enough to crush anything in their path. Flames leaped toward the gray, dead skin sky; enormous tongues of crackling flame that ate the city's gut and chewed the phantom image, leaving ash. (But even the dead ashes had more life than the grayness through which the vision swirled.)

Ian Ross ducked, frightened. Then it was gone.

"Don't worry about it, son," the old woman said. "Looked a lot like London during the big fire. First the plague, then the fire. I've seen its like before. Can't hurt you. None of it can hurt you."

He tried to stand, found himself still weak. "But what *is* it?"

She shrugged. "No one's ever been able to tell me for sure. Bet there's some around in here who can, though. One day I'll run into one of them. If I find out and we ever meet again I'll be sure to let you know. Bound to happen." But her face grew infinitely sad and there was desolation in her expression. "Maybe. Maybe we'll meet again. Never happens, but it might. Never saw that retarded boy again. But it might happen."

She started to walk away, hobbling awkwardly. Ian got to his feet with difficulty, but as quickly as he could. "Hey, wait! Where are you going? Please, lady, don't leave me here all alone. I'm scared to be here by myself."

She stopped and turned, tilting oddly on her bad leg. "Got to keep moving. Keep going, you know? If you stay in one place you don't get anywhere; there's a way out…you've just got to keep moving till you find it." She started again, saying, over her shoulder, "I guess I won't be seeing you again; I don't think it's likely."

He ran after her and grabbed her arm. She seemed very startled. As if no one had ever touched her in this place during all the time she had been here.

"Listen, you've got to tell me some things, whatever you know. I'm awfully scared, don't you understand? You have to have some understanding."

She looked at him carefully. "All right, as much as I can, then you'll let me go?"

He nodded.

"I don't know what happened to me...or to you. Did it all fade away and just disappear, and everything that was left was this, just this gray nothing?"

He nodded.

She sighed. "How old are you, son?"

"I'm thirty-seven. My name is Ian—"

She waved his name away with an impatient gesture. "That doesn't matter. I can see you don't know any better than I do. So I don't have the time to waste on you. You'll learn that, too. Just keep walking, just keep looking for a way out."

He made fists. "That doesn't tell me *anything*! What was that burning city, what are these shadows that go past all the time?" As if to mark his question a vagrant filmy phantom caravan of cassowary-like animals drifted through them.

She shrugged and sighed. "I think it's history. I'm not sure...I'm guessing, you understand. But I *think* it's all the bits and pieces of the past, going through on its way somewhere."

He waited. She shrugged again, and her silence indicated—with a kind of helpless appeal to be let go—that she could tell him nothing further.

He nodded resignedly. "All right. Thank you."

She turned with her bad leg trembling: she had stood with her weight on it for too long. And she started to walk off into the gray limbo. When she was almost out of sight, he found himself able to speak again, and he said...too softly to reach her..."Goodbye, lady. Thank you."

He wondered how old she was. How long she had been here. If he would one time far from now be like her. If it was all over and if he would wander in shadows forever.

He wondered if people died here.

Before he met Catherine, a long time before he met her, he met the lunatic who told him where he was, what had happened to him, and why it had happened.

They saw each other standing on opposite sides of a particularly vivid phantom of the Battle of Waterloo. The battle raged past them, and through the clash and slaughter of Napoleon's and Wellington's forces they waved to each other.

When the sliding vision had rushed by, leaving emptiness between them, the lunatic rushed forward, clapping his hands as if preparing himself for a long, arduous, but pleasurable chore. He was of indeterminate age, but clearly past his middle years. His hair was long and wild, he wore a pair of rimless antique spectacles, and his suit was turn-of-the-eighteenth-century. "Well, well, well," he called, across the narrowing space between them, "so good to see you, sir!"

Ian Ross was startled. In the timeless time he had wandered through this limbo, he had encountered coolies and Berbers and Thracian traders and silent Goths...an endless stream of hurrying humanity that would neither speak nor stop. This man was something different. Immediately, Ian knew he was insane. But he wanted to *talk*!

The older man reached Ian and extended his hand. "Cowper, sir. Justinian Cowper. Alchemist, metaphysician, consultant to the forces of time and space, ah yes, *time*! Do I perceive in you, sir, one only recently come to our little Valhalla, one in need of illumination? Certainly! Definitely, I can see that is the case."

Ian began to say something, almost anything, in response, but the wildly gesticulating old man pressed on without drawing a breath. "This most recent manifestation, the one we were both privileged to witness was, I'm certain you're aware, the pivotal moment at Waterloo in which the Little Corporal had his fat chewed good and proper. Fascinating piece of recent history, wouldn't you say?"

Recent history? Ian started to ask him how long he had been in this gray place, but the old man barely paused before a fresh torrent of words spilled out.

"Stunningly reminiscent of that marvelous scene in Stendhal's *Charterhouse of Parma* in which Fabrizio, young, innocent, fresh to that environ, found himself walking across a large meadow on which men were running in all directions, noise, shouts, confusion...and he knew not what was happening, and not till several chapters later do we learn—ah, marvelous!—that it was, in fact, the Battle of Waterloo through which he moved, totally unaware of history in the shaping all around him. He was there, while *not* there. Precisely *our* situation, wouldn't you say?"

He had run out of breath. He stopped, and Ian plunged into the gap. "That's what I'd like to know, Mr. Cowper: what's happened to me? I've lost *everything*, but I can *remember* everything, too. I know I should be going crazy or frightened, and I *am* scared, but not out of my mind with it...I seem to *accept* this, whatever it is. I—I don't know how to take it, but I know I'm not feeling it yet. And I've been here a long time!"

The old man slipped his arm around Ian's back and began walking with him, two gentlemen strolling in confidence on a summer afternoon by the edge of a cool park. "Quite correct, sir, quite correct. Dissociative behavior; mark of the man unable to accept his destiny. Accept it, sir, I urge you; and fascination follows. Perhaps even obsession, but we must run that risk, mustn't we?"

Ian wrenched away from him, turned to face him. "Look, mister, I don't want to hear all that craziness! I want to know where I am and how I get out of here. And if you can't tell me, then leave me alone!"

"Nothing easier, my good man. Explanation is the least of it. Observation of phenomena, ah, *that's* the key. You can follow? Well, then: we are victims of the law of conservation of time. Precisely and exactly linked to the law of the conservation of matter; matter, which can neither be created nor destroyed. Time exists without end. But there is an ineluctable entropic balance, absolutely necessary to maintain order in the universe. Keeps events discrete, you see. As matter approaches universal distribution, there is a counterbalancing, how shall I put it, a counterbalancing 'leaching out' of time. Unused time is not wasted in places where nothing happens. *It goes somewhere.* It goes here, to be precise. In measurable units (which I've decided, after considerable thought, to call 'chronons')."

He paused, perhaps hoping Ian would compliment him on his choice of nomenclature. Ian put a hand to his forehead; his brain was swimming. "That's insane. It doesn't make sense."

"Makes perfectly *good* sense, I assure you. I was a top savant in my time; what I've told you is the only theory that fits the facts. Time unused is not wasted; it is leached out, drained through the normal space-time continuum and recycled. All this history you see shooting past us is that part of the time-flow that was wasted. Entropic balance, I assure you."

"But what am *I* doing here?"

"You force me to hurt your feelings, sir."

"What am I doing here?!"

"You wasted your life. Wasted time. All around you, throughout your life, unused chronons were being leached out, drawn away from the contiguous universe, until their pull on you was irresistible. Then you went on through, pulled loose like a piece of wood in a rushing torrent, a bit of chaff whirled away on the wind. Like Fabrizio, you were never really *there*. You wandered through, never seeing, never participating, and so there was nothing to moor you solidly in your own time."

"But how long will I stay here?"

The old man looked sad and spoke kindly for the first time: "Forever. You never used your time, so you have nothing to rely on as anchorage in normal space."

"But everyone here thinks there's a way out. I know it! They keep walking, trying to find an exit."

"Fools. There is no way back."

"But you don't seem to be the sort of person who wasted his life. Some of the others I've seen, yes, I can see that; but *you*?"

The old man's eyes grew misty. He spoke with difficulty. "Yes, I belong here…"

Then he turned and, like one in a dream, lost, wandered away. Lunatic, observing phenomena. And then gone in the grayness of time-gorged limbo. Part of a glacial period slid past Ian Ross and he resumed his walk without destination.

And after a long, long time that was timeless but filled with an abundance of time, he met Catherine.

He saw her as a spot of darkness against the gray limbo. She was quite a distance away, and he walked on for a while, watching the dark blotch against gray, and then decided to change direction. It didn't matter. Nothing mattered: he was alone with his memories, replaying again and again.

The sinking of the Titanic wafted through him.

She did not move, even though he was approaching on a direct line. When he was quite close he could see that she was sitting cross-legged on nothingness; she was asleep. Her head was propped in one hand, the bracing arm supported by her knee. Asleep.

He came right up to her and stood there simply watching. He smiled. She was like a bird, he thought, with her head tucked under her wing. Not really, but that was how he saw her. Though her cupped hand covered half her face he could make out a sweet face, very pale skin, a mole on her throat; her hair was brown, cut quite short. Her eyes were closed: he decided they would be blue.

The Greek senate, the age of Pericles, men in a crowd—property owners—screaming at Lycurgus' exhortations in behalf of socialism. The shadow of it sailed past not very far away.

Ian stood staring, and after a while he sat down opposite her. He leaned back on his arms and watched. He hummed an old tune the name of which he did not know.

Finally, she opened her brown eyes and stared at him.

At first momentary terror, shock, chagrin, curiosity. Then she took umbrage. "How long have *you* been there?"

"My name is Ian Ross," he said.

"I don't care what your name is!" she said angrily. "I asked you how long you've been sitting there watching me?"

"I don't know. A while."

"I don't like being watched; you're being very rude."

He got to his feet without answering, and began walking away. Oh well.

She ran after him. "Hey, wait!"

He kept walking. He didn't have to be bothered like that. She caught up with him and ran around to stand in front of him. "I suppose you just think you can walk off like that!"

"Yes, I can. I'm sorry I bothered you. Please get out of my way if you don't want me around."

"I didn't say that."

"You said I was being rude. I am *never* rude; I'm a very well-mannered person and you were just being insulting."

He walked around her. She ran after him.

"All right, okay, maybe I was a little out of sorts. I was asleep, after all."

He stopped. She stood in front of him. Now it was her move. "My name is Catherine Molnar. How do you do?"

"Not too well, that's how."

"Have you been here long?"

"Longer than I wanted to be here, *that's* for sure."

"Can you explain what's happened to me?"

He thought about it. Walking *with* someone would be a nice change. "Let me ask you something," Ian Ross said, beginning to stroll off toward the phantom image of the hanging gardens of Babylon wafting past them, "did you waste a lot of time, sitting around, not doing much, maybe watching television a lot?"

They were lying down side-by-side because they were tired. Nothing more than that. The Battle of the Ardennes, First World War, was all around them. Not a sound. Just movement. Mist, fog, turretless tanks, shattered trees all around them. Some corpses left lying in the middle of no man's land. They had been together for a space of time...it was three hours, it was six weeks, it was a month of Sundays, it was a year to remember, it was the best of times, it was the worst of times: who could measure it, there were no signposts, no town criers, no grandfather clocks, no change of seasons, who could measure it?

They had begun to talk freely. He told her again that his name was Ian Ross and she said Catherine, Catherine Molnar again. She confirmed his guess that her life had been empty. "Plain," she said. "I was plain. I *am* plain. No, don't bother to say you think I have nice cheekbones or a trim figure; it won't change a thing. If you want plain, I've got it."

He didn't say she had nice cheekbones or a trim figure. But he didn't think she was plain.

The Battle of the Ardennes was swirling away now.

She suggested they make love.

Ian Ross got to his feet quickly and walked away.

She watched him for a while, keeping him in sight. Then she got up, dusted off her hands though there was nothing on them, an act of memory, and followed him. Quite a long time later, after trailing him but not trying to catch up to him, she ran to match his pace and finally, gasping for breath, reached him. "I'm sorry," she said.

"Nothing to be sorry about."

"I offended you."

"No, you didn't. I just felt like walking."

"Stop it, Ian. I did, I offended you."

He stopped and spun on her. "Do you think I'm a virgin? I'm not a virgin."

His vehemence pulled her back from the edge of boldness. "No, of course you're not. I never thought such a thing." Then she said, "Well...I am."

"Sorry," he said, because he didn't know the right thing to say, if there *was* a right thing.

"Not your fault," she said. Which *was* the right thing to say.

From nothing *to* nothing. Thirty-four years old, the properly desperate age for unmarried, unmotherhooded, unloved. Catherine Molnar, Janesville, Wisconsin. Straightening the trinkets in her jewelry box, ironing her clothes, removing and refolding the sweaters in her drawers, hanging the slacks with the slacks, skirts with the skirts, blouses with the blouses, coats with the coats, all in order in the closet, reading every word in *Time* and *Reader's Digest*, learning seven new words every day, never using seven new words every day, mopping the floors in the three-room apartment, putting aside one full evening to pay the bills and spelling out Wisconsin completely, never the WI abbreviation on the return envelopes, listening to talk radio, calling for the correct time to set the clocks, spooning out the droppings from the kitty box, repasting photos in the album of scenes with round-faced people, pinching back the buds on the coleus, calling Aunt Beatrice every Tuesday at seven o'clock, talking brightly to the waitress in the orange and blue uniform at the chicken pie shoppe, repainting fingernails carefully so the moon on each nail is showing, heating morning water for herself alone for the cup of herbal tea, setting the table with a cloth napkin and a placemat, doing dishes, going to the office and straightening the bills of lading precisely. Thirty-four. *From* nothing *to* nothing.

They lay side-by-side but they were not tired. There was more to it than that.

"I hate men who can't think past the pillow," she said, touching his hair.

"What's that?"

"Oh, it's just something I practiced, to say after the first time I slept with a man. I always felt there should be something original to say, instead of all the things I read in novels."

"I think it's a very clever phrase." Even now, he found it hard to touch her. He lay with hands at his sides.

She changed the subject. "I was never able to get very far playing the piano. I have absolutely *no* give between the thumb and first finger. And that's essential, you know. You have to have a long reach, a good spread I think they call it, to play Chopin. A tenth: that's two notes over an octave.

A *full* octave, a *perfect* octave, those are just technical terms. Octave is good enough. I don't have that."

"I like piano playing," he said, realizing how silly and dull he must sound, and frightened (very suddenly) that she would find him so, that she would leave him. Then he remembered where they were and he smiled. Where could she go? Where could *he* go?

"I always hated the fellows at parties who could play the piano...all the girls clustered around those people. Except these days it's not so much piano, not too many people have pianos in their homes any more. The kids grow up and go away and nobody takes lessons and the kids don't buy pianos. They get those electric guitars."

"Acoustical guitars."

"Yes, those. I don't think it would be much better for fellows like me who don't play, even if it's acoustical guitars."

They got up and walked again.

Once they discussed how they had wasted their lives, how they had sat there with hands folded as time filled space around them, swept through, was drained off, and their own "chronons" (he had told her about the lunatic; she said it sounded like Benjamin Franklin; he said the man hadn't looked like Benjamin Franklin, but maybe, it might have been) had been leached of all potency.

Once they discussed the guillotine executions in the Paris of the Revolution, because it was keeping pace with them. Once they chased the Devonian and almost caught it. Once they were privileged to enjoy themselves in the center of an Arctic snowstorm that held around them for a measure of measureless time. Once they saw nothing for an eternity but were truly chilled—unlike the Arctic snowstorm that had had no effect on them—by the winds that blew past them. And once he turned to her and said, "I love you, Catherine."

But when she looked at him with a gentle smile, he noticed for the first time that her eyes seemed to be getting gray and pale.

Then, not too soon after, she said she loved him, too.

But she could see mist through the flesh of his hands when he reached out to touch her face.

They walked with their arms around each other, having found each other. They said many times, and agreed it was so, that they were in love, and being together was the most important thing in that endless world of gray spaces, even if they never found their way back.

And they began to *use* their time together, setting small goals for each "day" upon awakening. We will walk *that* far; we will play word games in which *you* have to begin the name of a female movie star from the last letter of a male movie star's name that *I* have to begin off the last letter of a female movie star; we will exchange shirt and blouse and see how it feels for a while; we will sing every camp song we can remember. They began to *enjoy* their time together. They began to live.

And sometimes his voice faded out and she could see him moving his lips but there was no sound.

And sometimes when the mist cleared she was invisible from the ankles down and her body moved as through thick soup.

And as they used their time, they became alien in that place where wasted time had gone to rest.

And they began to fade. As the world had leached out for Ian Ross in Scotland, and for Catherine Molnar in Wisconsin, *they* began to vanish from limbo. Matter could neither be created nor destroyed, but it could be disassembled and sent where it was needed for entropic balance.

He saw her pale skin become transparent.

She saw his hands as clear as glass.

And they thought: *too late. It comes too late.*

Invisible motes of their selves were drawn off and were sent away from that gray place. Were sent where needed to maintain balance. One and one and one, separated on the wind and blown to the farthest corners of the tapestry that was time and space. And could never be recalled. And could never be rejoined.

So they touched, there in that vast limbo of wasted time, for the last time, and shadows existed for an instant, and then were gone; he first, leaving her behind for the merest instant of terrible loneliness and loss, and then she, without shadow, pulled apart and scattered, followed. Separation without hope of return.

Great events hushed in mist swirled past. Ptolemy crowned king of Egypt, the Battle of the Teutoburger Forest, Jesus crucified, the founding of Constantinople, the Vandals plundering Rome, the massacre of the Omayyad family, the court of the Fujiwaras in Japan, Jerusalem falling to Saladin…and on and on…great events…empty time…and the timeless population trudged past endlessly...endlessly...unaware that finally, at last, hopelessly and too late...two of their nameless order had found the way out.

DJINN, NO CHASER

1983 Locus Poll Award: Best Novelette

"WHO THE HELL ever heard of Turkish Period?" Danny Squires said. He said it at the top of his voice, on a city street.

"Danny! People are staring at us; lower your voice!" Connie Squires punched his bicep. They stood on the street, in front of the furniture store. Danny was determined not to enter.

"Come on, Connie," he said, "let's get away from these junk shops and go see some inexpensive modern stuff. You know perfectly well I don't make enough to start filling the apartment with expensive antiques."

Connie furtively looked up and down the street—she was more concerned with a "scene" than with the argument itself—and then moved in toward Danny with a determined air. "Now listen up, Squires. *Did* you or did you *not* marry me four days ago, and promise to love, honor and cherish and all that other good jive?"

Danny's blue eyes rolled toward Heaven; he knew he was losing ground. Instinctively defensive, he answered, "Well, sure, Connie, but—"

"Well, then, I am your wife, and you have not taken me on a honeymoon—"

"I can't *afford* one!"

"—have not taken me on a honeymoon," Connie repeated with inflexibility. "Consequently, we will buy a little furniture for that rabbit warren you laughingly call our little love nest. And *little* is hardly the term: that vale of tears was criminally undersized when Barbara Fritchie hung out her flag.

"So to make my life *bearable*, for the next few weeks, till we can talk Mr. Upjohn into giving you a raise—"

"Upjohn!" Danny fairly screamed. "You've got to stay away from the boss, Connie. Don't screw around. He won't give me a raise, and I'd rather you stayed away from him—"

"Until then," she went on relentlessly, "we will decorate our apartment in the style I've wanted for years."

"Turkish Period?"

"Turkish Period."

Danny flipped his hands in the air. What was the use? He had known Connie was strong-willed when he'd married her.

It had seemed an attractive quality at the time; now he wasn't so sure. But he was strong-willed too: he was sure he could outlast her. Probably.

"Okay," he said finally, "I suppose Turkish Period it'll be. What the hell *is* Turkish Period?"

She took his arm lovingly, and turned him around to look in the store window. "Well, honey, it's not *actually* Turkish. It's more Mesopotamian. You know, teak and silk and…"

"Sounds hideous."

"So you're starting up again!" She dropped his arm, her eyes flashing, her mouth a tight little line. "I'm really ashamed of you, depriving me of the few little pleasures I need to make my life a blub, sniff, hoo-hoo…"

The edge was hers.

"Connie…Connie…" She knocked away his comforting hand, saying, "You beast." That was too much for him. The words were so obviously put-on, he was suddenly infuriated:

"Now, goddammit!"

Her tears came faster. Danny stood there, furious, helpless, outmaneuvered, hoping desperately that no cop would come along and say, "This guy botherin' ya, lady?"

"Connie, okay, okay, we'll *have* Turkish Period. Come on, come on. It doesn't matter what it costs, I can scrape up the money somehow."

It was not one of the glass-brick and onyx emporia where sensible furniture might be found (if one searched hard enough and paid high enough and retained one's senses long enough as they were trying to palm off modernistic nightmares in which no comfortable position might be found); no, it was not even one of those. This was an antique shop.

They looked at beds that had canopies and ornate metalwork on the bedposts. They looked at rugs that were littered with pillows, so visitors could sit on the floors. They looked at tables built six inches off the deck, for low banquets. They inspected incense burners and hookahs and coffers and giant vases until Danny's head swam with visions of the courts of long-dead caliphs.

Yet, despite her determination, Connie chose very few items; and those she did select were moderately-priced and quite handsome...for what they were. And as the hours passed, and as they moved around town from one dismal junk emporium to another, Danny's respect for his wife's taste grew. She was selecting an apartment full of furniture that wasn't bad at all.

They were finished by six o'clock, and had bills of sale that totaled just under two hundred dollars. Exactly thirty dollars less than Danny had decided could be spent to furnish the new household...and still survive on his salary. He had taken the money from his spavined savings account, and had known he must eventually start buying on credit, or they would not be able to get enough furniture to start living properly.

He was tired, but content. She'd shopped wisely. They were in a shabby section of town. How had they gotten here? They walked past an empty lot sandwiched in between two tenements—wet-wash slapping on lines between them. The lot was weed-overgrown and garbage-strewn.

"May I call your attention to the depressing surroundings and my exhaustion?" Danny said. "Let's get a cab and go back to the apartment. I want to collapse."

They turned around to look for a cab, and the empty lot was gone.

In its place, sandwiched between the two tenements, was a little shop. It was a one-storey affair, with a dingy facade, and its front window completely grayed-over with dust. A hand-painted line of elaborate script on the glass-panel of the door, also opaque with grime, proclaimed:

MOHANADUS MUKHAR, CURIOS.

A little man in a flowing robe, wearing a fez, plunged out the front door, skidded to a stop, whirled and slapped a huge sign on the window. He swiped at it four times with a big paste-brush, sticking it to the glass, and whirled back inside, slamming the door.

"No," Danny said.

Connie's mouth was making peculiar sounds.

"There's no insanity in my family," Danny said firmly. "We come from very good stock."

"We've made a visual error," Connie said.

"Simply didn't notice it," Danny said. His usually baritone voice was much nearer soprano.

"If there's crazy, we've both got it," Connie said.

"Must be, if you see the same thing I see."

Connie was silent a moment, then said, "Large seagoing vessel, three stacks, maybe the Titanic. Flamingo on the bridge, flying the flag of Lichtenstein?"

"Don't play with me, woman," Danny whimpered. "I think I'm losing it."

She nodded soberly. "Right. Empty lot?"

He nodded back, "Empty lot. Clothesline, weeds, garbage."

"Right."

He pointed at the little store. "Little store?"

"Right."

"Man in a fez, name of Mukhar?"

She rolled her eyes. "Right."

"So why are we walking toward it?"

"Isn't this what always happens in stories where weird shops suddenly appear out of nowhere? Something inexorable draws the innocent bystanders into its grip?"

They stood in front of the grungy little shop. They read the sign. It said:

BIG SALE! HURRY! NOW! QUICK!

"The word *unnatural* comes to mind," Danny said.

"Nervously," Connie said, "she turned the knob and opened the door."

A tiny bell went tinkle-tinkle, and they stepped across the threshold into the gloaming of Mohanadus Mukhar's shop.

"Probably not the smartest move we've ever made," Danny said softly. The door closed behind them without any assistance.

It was cool and musty in the shop, and strange fragrances chased one another past their noses.

They looked around carefully. The shop was loaded with junk. From floor to ceiling, wall to wall, on tables and in heaps, the place was filled with oddities and bric-a-brac. Piles of things tumbled over one another on the floor; heaps of things leaned against the walls. There was barely room to walk down the aisle between the stacks and mounds of things. Things in all shapes, things in all sizes and colors. Things. They tried to separate the individual items from the jumble of the place, but all they could perceive was stuff…things! Stuff and flotsam and bits and junk.

"Curios, effendi," a voice said, by way of explanation.

Connie leaped in the air, and came down on Danny's foot.

Mukhar was standing beside such a pile of tumbled miscellany that for a moment they could not separate him from the stuff, junk, things he sold.

"We saw your sign," Connie said.

But Danny was more blunt, more direct. "There was an empty lot here; then a minute later, this shop. How come?"

The little man stepped out from the mounds of dust-collectors and his little nut-brown, wrinkled face burst into a million-creased smile. "A fortuitous accident, my children. A slight worn spot in the fabric of the cosmos, and I have been set down here for…how long I do not know. But it never hurts to try and stimulate business while I'm here."

"Uh, yeah," Danny said. He looked at Connie. Her expression was as blank as his own.

"Oh!" Connie cried, and went dashing off into one of the side-corridors lined with curios. "This is perfect! Just what we need for the end table. Oh, Danny, it's a dream! It's absolutely the *ne plus ultra*!"

Danny walked over to her, but in the dimness of the aisle between the curios he could barely make out what it was she was holding. He drew her into the light near the door. It had to be:

Aladdin's lamp.

Well, perhaps not that *particular* person's lamp, but one of the ancient, vile-smelling oil burning jobs: long thin spout, round-bottom body, wide, flaring handle.

It was algae-green with tarnish, brown with rust, and completely covered by the soot and debris of centuries. There was no contesting its antiquity; nothing so time-corrupted could fail to be authentic. "What the hell do you want with that old thing, Connie?"

"But Danny, it's so *per*-fect. If we just shine it up a bit. As soon as we put a little work into this lamp, it'll be a beauty." Danny knew he was defeated…and she'd probably be right, too. It probably would be very handsome when shined and brassed-up.

"How much?" he asked Mukhar. He didn't want to seem anxious; old camel traders were merciless at bargaining when they knew the item in question was hotly desired.

"Fifty drachmae, eh?" the old man said. His tone was one of malicious humor. "At current exchange rates, taking into account the fall of the Ottoman Empire, thirty dollars."

Danny's lips thinned. "Put it down, Connie; let's get out of here."

He started toward the door, dragging his wife behind him. But she still clutched the lamp; and Mukhar's voice halted them. "All right, noble sir. You are a cunning shopper, I can see that. You know a bargain when you spy it. But I am unfamiliar in this time-frame with your dollars and your strange fast-food native customs, having been set down here only once before; and since I am more at ease with the drachma than the dollar, with the shekel than the cent, I will cut my own throat, slash both my wrists, and offer you this magnificent antiquity for...uh...twenty dollars?" His voice was querulous, his tone one of wonder and hope.

"Jesse James at least had a horse!" Danny snarled, once again moving toward the door.

"Fifteen!" Mukhar yowled. "And may all your children need corrective lenses from too much tv-time!"

"Five; and may a hundred thousand syphilitic camels puke into your couscous," Danny screamed back over his shoulder.

"Not bad," said Mukhar.

"Thanks," said Danny, stifling a smile. Now he waited.

"Bloodsucker! Heartless trafficker in cheapness! Pimple on the fundament of decency! Graffito on the subway car of life! Thirteen; my last offer; and may the gods of ITT and the Bank of America turn a blind eye to your venality!" But *his* eyes held the golden gleam of the born haggler, at last, blessedly, in his element.

"Seven, not a penny more, you Arabic anathema! And may a weighty object drop from a great height, flattening you to the niggardly thickness of your soul." Connie stared at him with open awe and admiration.

"Eleven! Eleven dollars, a pittance, an outright theft we're talking about. Call the security guards, get a consumer advocate, gimme a break here!"

"My shadow will vanish from before the evil gleam of your rapacious gaze before I pay a penny more than six bucks, and let the word go out to every wadi and oasis across the limitless desert, that Mohanadus Mukhar steals maggots from diseased meat, flies from horse dung, and the hard-earned drachmae of honest laborers. Six, fuckface, and that's it!"

"My death is about to become a reality," the Arab bellowed, tearing at the strands of white hair showing under the fez. "Rob me, go ahead, rob me: drink my life's blood! Ten! A twenty dollar loss I'll take."

"Okay, okay." Danny turned around and produced his wallet. He pulled out one of the three ten dollar bills still inside and, turning to Connie, said, "You sure you want this ugly, dirty piece of crap?" She nodded, and he held the bill naked in the vicinity of the little merchant. For the first time Danny realized Mukhar was wearing pointed slippers that curled up; there was hair growing from his ears.

"Ten bucks."

The little man moved with the agility of a ferret, and whisked the tenner from Danny's outstretched hand before he could draw it back. "Sold!" Mukhar chuckled.

He spun around once, and when he faced them again, the ten dollars was out of sight. "And a steal, though Allah be the wiser; a hot deal, a veritable steal, blessed sir!"

Danny abruptly realized he had been taken. The lamp had probably been picked up in a junkyard and was worthless. He started to ask if it was a genuine antique, but the piles of junk had begun to waver and shimmer and coruscate with light. "Hey!" Danny said, alarmed, "What's this now?"

The little man's wrinkled face drew up in panic. "Out! Get out, quick! The time-frame is sucking back together! Out! Get out now if you don't want to roam the eternities with me and this shop…and I can't afford any help! Out!"

He shoved them forward, and Connie slipped and fell, flailing into a pile of glassware. None of it broke. Her hand went out to protect herself and went right through the glass. Danny dragged her to her feet, panic sweeping over him…as the shop continued to waver and grow more indistinct around them.

"Out! Out! Out!" Mukhar kept yelling.

Then they were at the door, and he was kicking them—literally planting his curl-slippered foot in Danny's backside and shoving—from the store. They landed in a heap on the sidewalk. The lamp bounced from Connie's hand and went into the gutter with a clang. The little man stood there grinning in the doorway, and as the shop faded and disappeared, they heard him mumble happily, "A clear nine-seventy-five profit. What a lemon!

You got an Edsel, kid, a real lame piece of goods. But I gotta give it to you; the syphilitic camel bit was inspired."

Then the shop was gone, and they got to their feet in front of an empty, weed-overgrown lot.

A lame piece of goods?

"Are you asleep?"

"Yes."

"How come you're answering me?"

"I was raised polite."

"Danny, talk to me…come on!"

"The answer is no. I'm not going to talk about it."

"We have to!"

"Not only don't we *have* to, I don't *want* to, ain't *going* to, and shut up so I can go to sleep."

"We've been lying here almost an hour. Neither of us can sleep. We *have* to discuss it, Danny."

The light went on over his side of the bed. The single pool of illumination spread from the hand-me-down daybed they had gotten from Danny's brother in New Jersey, faintly limning the few packing crates full of dishes and linens, the three Cuisinarts they'd gotten as wedding gifts, the straight-back chairs from Connie's Aunt Medora, the entire bare and depressing reality of their first home together.

It would be better when the furniture they'd bought today was delivered. Later, it would be better. Now, it was the sort of urban landscape that drove divorcees and aging bachelors to jump down the airshaft at Christmastime.

"I'm going to talk about it, Squires."

"So talk. I have my thumbs in my ears."

"I think we should rub it."

"I can't hear you. It never happened. I deny the evidence of my senses. It never happened. I have these thumbs in my ears so I cannot hear a syllable of this craziness."

"For god's sake, Squires, I was *there* with you today. I saw it happen, the same as you. I saw that weird little old man and I saw his funky shop come and go like a big burp. Now, neither of us can deny it!"

"If I could hear you, I'd agree; and then I'd deny the evidence of my senses and tell you…" He took his thumbs from his ears, looking distressed.

"...tell you with all my heart that I love you, that I have loved you since the moment I saw you in the typing pool at Upjohn, that if I live to be a hundred thousand years old I'll never love any one or any thing as much as I love you this very moment; and then I would tell you to piss off and forget it, and let me go to sleep so that tomorrow I can con myself into believing it never happened the way I know it happened.

"Okay?"

She threw back the covers and got out of bed. She was naked. They had not been married that long.

"Where are you going?"

"You know where I'm going."

He sat up in the daybed. His voice had no lightness in it. "Connie!"

She stopped and stared at him, there in the light.

He spoke softly. "Don't. I'm scared. Please don't."

She said nothing. She looked at him for a time. Then, naked, she sat down cross-legged on the floor at the foot of the daybed. She looked around at what little they had, and she answered him gently. "I have to, Danny. I just have to...if there's a chance; I have to."

They sat that way, reaching across the abyss with silent imperatives, until—finally—Danny nodded, exhaled heavily, and got out of the daybed. He walked to one of the cartons, pulled out a dustrag, shook it clean over the box, and handed it to her. He walked over to the window ledge where the tarnished and rusted oil lamp sat, and he brought it to her.

"Shine the damned thing, Squires. Who knows, maybe we actually got ourselves a 24 carat genie. Shine on, oh mistress of my Mesopotamian mansion."

She held the lamp in one hand, the rag in the other. For a few minutes she did not bring them together. "I'm scared, too," she said, held her breath, and briskly rubbed the belly of the lamp.

Under her flying fingers the rust and tarnish began to come away in spots. "We'll need brass polish to do this right," she said; but suddenly the ruin covering the lamp melted away, and she was rubbing the bright skin of the lamp itself.

"Oh, Danny, look how nice it is, underneath all the crud!" And at that precise instant the lamp jumped from her hand, emitted a sharp, gray puff of smoke, and a monstrous voice bellowed in the apartment:

AH-HA! It screamed, louder than a subway train. AH-HA!

FREE AT LAST! FREE—AS FREE AS *I'LL* EVER BE—AFTER TEN THOUSAND YEARS! FREE TO SPEAK AND ACT, MY WILL TO BE KNOWN!

Danny went over backward. The sound was as mind-throttling as being at ground zero. The window glass blew out. Every light bulb in the apartment shattered. From the carton containing their meager chinaware came the distinct sound of hailstones as every plate and cup dissolved into shards. Dogs and cats blocks away began to howl. Connie screamed—though it could not be heard over the foghorn thunder of the voice—and was knocked head over ankles into a corner, still clutching the dustrag. Plaster showered in the little apartment. The window shades rolled up.

Danny recovered first. He crawled over a chair and stared at the lamp with horror. Connie sat up in the corner, face white, eyes huge, hands over her ears. Danny stood and looked down at the seemingly innocuous lamp.

"Knock off that noise! You want to lose us the lease?"

CERTAINLY, OFFSPRING OF A WORM!

"I said: stop that goddam bellowing!"

THIS WHISPER? THIS IS NAUGHT TO THE HURRICANE I SHALL LOOSE, SPAWN OF PARAMECIUM!

"That's it," Danny yelled. "I'm not getting kicked out of the only apartment in the city of New York I can afford just because of some loudmouthed genie in a jug…"

He stopped. He looked at Connie. Connie looked back at him.

"Oh, my god," she said.

"It's real," he said.

They got to their knees and crawled over. The lamp lay on its side on the floor at the foot of the daybed.

"Are you really in there?" Connie asked.

WHERE ELSE WOULD I BE, SLUT!

"Hey, you can't talk to my wife that way—"

Connie shushed him. "If he's a genie, he can talk any way he likes. Sticks and stones; namecalling is better than poverty."

"Yeah? Well, *nobody* talks to my—"

"Put a lid on it, Squires. I can take care of myself. If what's in this lamp is even half the size of the genie in that movie you took me to the Thalia to see…"

"*The Thief of Bagdad*…1939 version…but Rex Ingram was just an actor, they only made him *look* big."

"Even so. As big as he was, if this genie is only *half* that big, playing macho overprotective chauvinist hubby—"

SO HUMANS CONTINUE TO PRATTLE LIKE MONKEYS EVEN AFTER TEN THOUSAND YEARS! WILL NOTHING CLEANSE THE EARTH OF THIS RAUCOUS PLAGUE OF INSECTS?

"We're going to get thrown right out of here," Danny said. His face screwed up in a horrible expression of discomfort.

"If the cops don't beat the other tenants to it."

"Please, genie," Danny said, leaning down almost to the lamp. "Just tone it down a little, willya?"

OFFSPRING OF A MILLION STINKS! SUFFER!

"You're no genie," Connie said smugly. Danny looked at her with disbelief.

"He's no genie? Then what the hell do you *think* he is?"

She swatted him. Then put her finger to her lips.

THAT IS WHAT I AM, WHORE OF DEGENERACY!

"No you're not."

I AM.

"Am not."

AM.

"Am not."

AM SO, CHARNEL HOUSE HARLOT! WHY SAY YOU NAY?

"A genie has a lot of power; a genie doesn't need to shout like that to make himself heard. You're no genie, or you'd speak softly. You *can't* speak at a decent level, because you're a fraud."

CAUTION, TROLLOP!

"Foo, you don't scare me. If you were as powerful as you make out, you'd tone it way down."

is this better? are you convinced?

"Yes," Connie said, "I think that's more convincing. Can you keep it up, though? That's the question."

forever, if need be.

"And you can grant wishes?" Danny was back in the conversation.

naturally, but not to you, disgusting grub of humanity.

"Hey, listen," Danny replied angrily, "I don't give a damn what or *who* you are! You can't talk to me that way." Then a thought dawned on him. "After all, I'm your master!"

ah! correction, filth of primordial seas. there are some djinn who are mastered by their owners, but unfortunately for you i am not one of them, for i am not free to leave this metal prison. i was imprisoned in this accursed vessel many ages ago by a besotted sorcerer who knew nothing of molecular compression and even less of the binding forces of the universe. he put me into this thrice-cursed lamp, far too small for me, and i have been wedged within ever since. over the ages my good nature has rotted away. i am powerful, but trapped. those who own me cannot request anything and hope to realize their boon. i am unhappy, and an unhappy djinn is an evil djinn. were i free, i might be your slave; but as i am now, i will visit unhappiness on you in a thousand forms!

Danny chuckled. "The hell you will. I'll toss you in the incinerator."

ah! but you cannot. once you have bought the lamp, you cannot lose it, destroy it or give it away, only sell it. i am with you forever, for who would buy such a miserable lamp?

And thunder rolled in the sky.

"What are you going to do?" Connie asked.

do? just ask me for something, and you shall see!

"Not me," Danny said, "you're too cranky."

wouldn't you like a billfold full of money?

There was sincerity in the voice from the lamp.

"Well, sure, I want money, but—"

The djinn's laughter was gigantic, and suddenly cut off by the rain of frogs that fell from a point one inch below the ceiling, clobbering Danny and Connie with small, reeking, wriggling green bodies. Connie screamed and dove for the clothes closet. She came out a second later, her hair full of them; they were falling in the closet, as well. The rain of frogs continued and when Danny opened the front door to try and escape them, they fell in the hall. He slammed the door—he realized he was still naked—and covered his head with his hands. The frogs fell, writhing, stinking, and then they were knee-deep in them, with little filthy, warty bodies jumping up at their faces.

what a lousy disposition i've got! the djinn said, and then he laughed. And he laughed again, a clangorous peal that was silenced only when the frogs stopped, disappeared, and the flood of blood began.

It went on for a week.

They could not get away from him, no matter where they went. They were also slowly starving: they could not go out to buy groceries without the earth opening under their feet, or a herd of elephants chasing them down the street, or hundreds of people getting violently ill and vomiting on them. So they stayed in and ate what canned goods they had stored up in the first four days of their marriage. But who could eat with locusts filling the apartment from top to bottom, or snakes that were intent on gobbling them up like little white rats?

First came the frogs, then the flood of blood, then the whirling dust storm, then the spiders and gnats, then the snakes and then the locusts and then the tiger that had them backed against a wall and ate the chair they used to ward him off. Then came the bats and the leprosy and the hailstones and then the floor dissolved under them and they clung to the wall fixtures while their furniture—which had been quickly delivered (the moving men had brought it during the hailstones)—fell through, nearly killing the little old lady who lived beneath them.

Then the walls turned red hot and melted, and then the lightning burned everything black, and finally Danny had had enough. He cracked, and went gibbering around the room, tripping over the man-eating vines that were growing out of the light sockets and the floorboards. He finally sat down in a huge puddle of monkey urine and cried till his face grew puffy and his eyes flame-red and his nose swelled to three times normal size.

"I've got to get *away* from all this!" he screamed hysterically, drumming his heels, trying to eat his pants' cuffs.

you can divorce her, and that means you are voided out of the purchase contract: she wanted the lamp, not you, the djinn suggested.

Danny looked up (just in time to get a ripe Black Angus meadow muffin in his face) and yelled, "I won't! You can't make me. We've only been married a week and four days and I won't leave her!"

Connie, covered with running sores, stumbled to Danny and hugged him, though he had turned to tapioca pudding and was melting. But three days later, when ghost images of people he had feared all his life came to haunt him, he broke completely and allowed Connie to call the rest home on the boa constrictor that had once been the phone. "You can come and get me when this is over," he cried pitifully, kissing her poison ivy lips. "Maybe if we split up, he'll have some mercy." But they both doubted it.

When the downstairs buzzer rang, the men from the Home for the Mentally Absent came into the debacle that had been their apartment and saw Connie pulling her feet out of the swamp slime only with difficulty;

she was crying in unison with Danny as they bundled him into the white ambulance. Unearthly laughter rolled around the sky like thunder as her husband was driven away.

Connie was left alone. She went back upstairs; she had nowhere else to go.

She slumped into the pool of molten slag, and tried to think while ants ate at her flesh and rabid rats gnawed off the wallpaper.

i'm just getting warmed up, the djinn said from the lamp.

Less than three days after he had been admitted to the Asylum for the Temporarily Twitchy, Connie came to get Danny. She came into his room; the shades were drawn, the sheets were very white; when he saw her his teeth began to chatter.

She smiled at him gently. "If I didn't know better, I'd swear you weren't simply overjoyed to see me, Squires."

He slid under the sheets till only his eyes were showing. His voice came through the covers. "If I break out in boils, it will definitely cause a relapse, and the day nurse hates mess."

"Where's my macho protective husband now?"

"I've been unwell."

"Yeah, well, that's all over. You're fit as a fiddle, so bestir your buns and let's get out of here."

Danny Squires' brow furrowed. This was not the tone of a woman with frogs in her hair. "I've been contemplating divorce or suicide."

She yanked the covers down, exposing his naked legs sticking out from the hem of the hospital gown. "Forget it, little chum. There are at least a hundred and ten positions we haven't tried yet before I consider dissolution. Now will you get out of that bed and *come on*?"

"But…"

"…a thing I'll kick, if you don't move it."

Bewildered, he moved it.

Outside, the Rolls-Royce waited with its motor running. As they came through the front doors of the Institute for the Neurologically Flaccid, and Connie helped Danny from the discharge wheelchair, the liveried chauffeur leaped out and opened the door for them. They got in the back seat, and Connie said, "To the house, Mark." The chauffeur nodded, trotted briskly around and climbed behind the wheel. They took off to the muted roar of twin mufflers.

Danny's voice was a querulous squeak. "Can we afford a rented limo?"

Connie did not answer, merely smiled, and snuggled closer to him.

After a moment Danny asked, "What house?"

Connie pressed a button on the console in the armrest and the glass partition between front and back seats slid silently closed. "Do me a favor, will you," she said, "just hold the twenty questions till we get home? It's been a tough three days and all I ask is that you hold it together for another hour."

Danny nodded reluctantly. Then he noticed she was dressed in extremely expensive clothes. "I'd better not ask about your mink-trimmed jacket, either, right?"

"It would help."

He settled into silence, uneasy and juggling more than just twenty unasked questions. And he remained silent until he realized they were not taking the expressway into New York. He sat up sharply, looked out the rear window, snapped his head right and left trying to ascertain their location, and Connie said, "We're not going to Manhattan. We're going to Darien, Connecticut."

"Darien? Who the hell do we know in Darien?"

"Well, Upjohn, for one, lives in Darien."

"Upjohn!?! Ohmigod, he's fired me and sent the car to bring me to him so he can have me executed! I *knew* it!"

"Squires," she said, "Daniel, my love, Danny heart of my heart, will you just kindly close the tap on it for a while! Upjohn has nothing to do with us any more. Nothing at all."

"But...but we live in New York!"

"Not no more we don't."

Twenty minutes later they turned into the most expensive section in Darien and sped down a private road.

They drove an eighth of a mile down the private road lined with Etruscan pines, beautifully maintained, and pulled into a winding driveway. Five hundred yards farther, and the drive spiraled in to wind around the front of a huge, luxurious, completely tasteful Victorian mansion. "Go on," Connie said. "Look at your house."

"Who lives here?" Danny asked.

"I just told you: *we* do."

"I thought that's what you said. Let me out here, I'll walk back to the nuthouse."

The Rolls pulled up before the mansion, and a butler ran down to open the car door for them. They got out and the servant bowed low to Connie. Then he turned to Danny. "Good to have you home, Mr. Squires," he said. Danny was too unnerved to reply.

"Thank you, Penzler," Connie said. Then, to the chauffeur, "Take the car to the garage, Mark; we won't be needing it again this afternoon. But have the Porsche fueled and ready; we may drive out later to look at the grounds."

"Very good, Mrs. Squires," Mark said. Then he drove away.

Danny was somnambulistic. He allowed himself to be led into the house, where he was further stunned by the expensive fittings, the magnificent halls, the deep-pile rugs, the spectacular furniture, the communications complex set into an entire wall, the Art Deco bar that rose out of the floor at the touch of a button, the servants who bowed and smiled at him, as if he belonged there. He was boggled by the huge kitchen, fitted with every latest appliance; and the French chef who saluted with a huge ladle as Connie entered.

"Wh-where did all this *come* from?" He finally gasped out the question as Connie led him upstairs on the escalator.

"Come on, Danny; you know where it all came from."

"The limo, the house, the grounds, the mink-trimmed jacket, the servants, the Vermeer in the front hall, the cobalt-glass Art Deco bar, the entertainment center with the beam television set, the screening room, the bowling alley, the polo field, the Neptune swimming pool, the escalator and six-strand necklace of black pearls I now notice you are wearing around your throat…all of it came from the genie?"

"Sorta takes your breath away, don't it?" Connie said, ingenuously.

"I'm having a little trouble with this."

"What you're having trouble with, champ, is that Mas'úd gave you a hard time, you couldn't handle it, you crapped out, and somehow I've managed to pull it all out of the swamp."

"I'm thinking of divorce again."

They were walking down a long hall lined with works of modern Japanese illustration by Yamazaki, Kobayashi, Takahiko Li, Kenzo

Tanii and Orai. Connie stopped and put both her hands on Danny's trembling shoulders.

"What we've got here, Squires, is a bad case of identity reevaluation. Nobody gets through *all* the battles. We've been married less than two weeks, but we've known each other for three years. You don't know how many times I folded before that time, and I don't know how many times you triumphed before that time.

"What I've known of you for three years made it okay for me to marry you; to think 'This guy will be able to handle it the times I can't.' That's a lot of what marriage is, to my way of thinking. I don't have to score every time, and neither do you. As long as the unit maintains. This time it was my score. Next time it'll be yours. Maybe."

Danny smiled weakly. "I'm not thinking of divorce."

Movement out of the corner of his eye made him look over his shoulder.

An eleven-foot-tall black man, physically perfect in every way, with chiseled features like an obsidian Adonis, dressed in an impeccably-tailored three-piece Savile Row suit, silk tie knotted precisely, stood just in the hallway, having emerged from open fifteen-foot-high doors of a room at the juncture of corridors.

"Uh…" Danny said.

Connie looked over her shoulder. "Hi, Mas'úd. Squires, I would like you to meet Mas'úd Jan bin Jan, a Mazikeen djinn of the ifrit, by the grace of Sulaymin, master of *all* the jinni, though Allah be the wiser. Our benefactor. My friend."

"How *good* a friend?" Danny whispered, seeing the totem of sexual perfection looming eleven feet high before him.

"We haven't known each other carnally, if that's what I perceive your squalid little remark to mean," she replied. And a bit wistfully she added, "I'm not his type. I think he's got it for Lena Horne." At Danny's semi-annoyed look she added, "For god's sake, stop being so bloody suspicious!"

Mas'úd stepped forward, two steps bringing him the fifteen feet intervening, and proffered his greeting in the traditional Islamic head-and-heart salute, flowing outward, a smile on his matinee idol face. "Welcome home, Master. I await your smallest request."

Danny looked from the djinn to Connie, amazement and copelessness rendering him almost speechless. "But…you were stuck in the lamp…bad-tempered, oh boy were you bad-tempered…how did you…how did she…"

Connie laughed, and with great dignity the djinn joined in.

"You were in the lamp…you gave us all this…but you said you'd give us nothing but aggravation! Why?"

In deep, mellifluous tones Danny had come to associate with a voice that could knock high-flying fowl from the air, the djinn smiled warmly at them and replied, "Your good wife freed me. After ten thousand years cramped over in pain with an eternal bellyache, in that most miserable of dungeons, Mistress Connie set me loose. For the first time in a hundred times ten thousand years of cruel and venal master after master, I have been delivered into the hands of one who treats me with respect. We are friends. I look forward to extending that friendship to you, Master Squires." He seemed to be warming to his explanation, expansive and effusive. "Free now, permitted to exist among humans in a time where my kind are thought a legend, and thus able to live an interesting, new life, my gratitude knows no bounds, as my hatred and anger knew no bounds. Now I need no longer act as a Kako-daemon, now I can be the sort of ifrit Rabbi Jeremiah bin Eliazar spoke of in Psalm XLI.

"I have seen much of this world in the last three days as humans judge time. I find it most pleasing in my view. The speed, the shine, the light. The incomparable Lena Horne. Do you like basketball?"

"But how? How did you *do* it, Connie? How? No one could get him out…"

She took him by the hand, leading him toward the fifteen-foot-high doors. "May we come into your apartment, Mas'úd?"

The djinn made a sweeping gesture of invitation, bowing so low his head was at Danny's waist as he and Connie walked past.

They stepped inside the djinn's suite and it was as if they had stepped back in time to ancient Basra and the Thousand Nights and a Night. Or into a Cornel Wilde costume epic.

But amid all the silks and hangings and pillows and tapers and coffers and brassware, there in the center of the foyer, in a Lucite case atop an onyx pedestal, lit from an unknown source by a single glowing spot of light, was a single icon.

"Occasionally magic has to bow to technology," Connie said. Danny moved forward. He could not make out what the item lying on the black velvet pillow was. "And sometimes ancient anger has to bow to common sense."

Danny was close enough to see it now.

Simple. It had been so simple. But no one had thought of it before. Probably because the last time it had been needed, by the lamp's previous owner, it had not existed.

"A can opener," Danny said. "A can opener!?! A simple, stupid, everyday can opener!?! That's all it took? I had a nervous breakdown, and you figured out a can opener?"

"Can do," Connie said, winking at Mas'úd.

"Not cute, Squires," Danny said. But he was thinking of the diamond as big as the Ritz.

PALADIN OF THE LOST HOUR

1986 Hugo Award: Best Novelette; Locus Poll Award: Best Novelette
teleplay – 1987 Writers Guild of America: Best Anthology Episode/Single Program

THIS WAS AN old man. Not an incredibly old man: obsolete, spavined; not as worn as the sway-backed stone steps ascending the Pyramid of the Sun to an ancient temple; not yet a relic. But even so, a *very* old man, this old man perched on an antique shooting stick, its handles opened to form a seat, its spike thrust at an angle into the soft ground and trimmed grass of the cemetery. Gray, thin rain misted down at almost the same angle as that at which the spike pierced the ground. The winter-barren trees lay flat and black against an aluminum sky, unmoving in the chill wind. An old man sitting at the foot of a grave mound whose headstone had tilted slightly when the earth had settled; sitting in the rain and speaking to someone below.

"They tore it down, Minna.

"I tell you, they must have bought off a councilman.

"Came in with bulldozers at six o'clock in the morning, and you *know* that's not legal. There's a Municipal Code. Supposed to hold off till at least seven on weekdays, eight on the weekend; but there they were at six, even *before* six, barely light for godsakes. Thought they'd sneak in and do it before the neighborhood got wind of it and called the landmarks committee. Sneaks: they come on *holidays*, can you imagine!

"But I was out there waiting for them, and I told them, 'You can't do it, that's Code number 91.3002, sub-section E,' and they lied and said they had special permission, so I said to the big muckymuck in charge, 'Let's see your waiver permit,' and he said the Code didn't apply in this case because it was supposed to be only for grading, and since they were demolishing and not grading, they could start whenever they felt like it. So I told him I'd call the police, then, because it came under the heading of Disturbing the Peace, and he said…well, I know you hate that kind of language, old girl, so I won't tell you what he said, but you can imagine.

"So I called the police, and gave them my name, and of course they didn't get there till almost quarter after seven (which is what makes me think they bought off a councilman), and by then those 'dozers had leveled most of it. Doesn't take long, you know that.

"And I don't suppose it's as great a loss as, maybe, say, the Great Library of Alexandria, but it was the last of the authentic Deco design drive-ins, and the carhops still served you on roller skates, and it was a landmark, and just about the only place left in the city where you could still get a decent grilled cheese sandwich pressed very flat on the grill by one of those weights they used to use, made with real cheese and not that rancid plastic they cut into squares and call it 'cheese food.'

"Gone, old dear, gone and mourned. And I understand they plan to put up another one of those mini-malls on the site, just ten blocks away from one that's already there, and you know what's going to happen: this new one will drain off the traffic from the older one, and then that one will fail the way they all do when the next one gets built, you'd think they'd see some history in it; but no, they never learn. And you should have seen the crowd by seven-thirty. All ages, even some of those kids painted like aborigines, with torn leather clothing. Even they came to protest. Terrible language, but at least they were concerned. And nothing could stop it. They just whammed it, and down it went.

"I do so miss you today, Minna. No more good grilled cheese." Said the *very* old man to the ground. And now he was crying softly, and now the wind rose, and the mist rain stippled his overcoat.

Nearby, yet at a distance, Billy Kinetta stared down at another grave. He could see the old man over there off to his left, but he took no further notice. The wind whipped the vent of his trenchcoat. His collar was up but rain trickled down his neck. This was a younger man, not yet thirty-five. Unlike the old man, Billy Kinetta neither cried nor spoke to memories of someone who had once listened. He might have been a geomancer, so silently did he stand, eyes toward the ground.

One of these men was black; the other was white.

Beyond the high, spiked-iron fence surrounding the cemetery two boys crouched, staring through the bars, through the rain; at the men absorbed by grave matters, by matters of graves. These were not really boys. They were legally young men. One was nineteen, the other two months beyond twenty. Both were legally old enough to vote, to drink alcoholic beverages, to drive a car. Neither would reach the age of Billy Kinetta.

One of them said, "Let's take the old man."

The other responded, "You think the guy in the trenchcoat'll get in the way?"

The first one smiled; and a mean little laugh. "I sure as shit hope so." He wore, on his right hand, a leather carnaby glove with the fingers cut off, small round metal studs in a pattern along the line of his knuckles. He made a fist, flexed, did it again.

They went under the spiked fence at a point where erosion had created a shallow gully. "Sonofabitch!" one of them said, as he slid through on his stomach. It was muddy. The front of his sateen roadie jacket was filthy. "Sonofabitch!" He was speaking in general of the fence, the sliding under, the muddy ground, the universe in total. And the old man, who would now *really* get the crap kicked out of him for making this fine sateen roadie jacket filthy.

They sneaked up on him from the left, as far from the young guy in the trenchcoat as they could. The first one kicked out the shooting stick with a short, sharp, downward movement he had learned in his Tae Kwon Do class. It was called the *yup-chagi*. The old man went over backward.

Then they were on him, the one with the filthy sonofabitch sateen roadie jacket punching at the old man's neck and the side of his face as he dragged him around by the collar of the overcoat. The other one began ransacking the coat pockets, ripping the fabric to get his hand inside.

The old man commenced to scream. "Protect me! You've got to protect me...it's necessary to protect me!"

The one pillaging pockets froze momentarily. What the hell kind of thing is that for this old fucker to be saying? Who the hell does he think'll protect him? Is he asking *us* to protect him? I'll protect you, scumbag! I'll kick in your fuckin' lung! "Shut 'im up!" he whispered urgently to his friend. "Stick a fist in his mouth!" Then his hand, wedged in an inside jacket pocket, closed over something. He tried to get his hand loose, but the jacket and coat and the old man's body had wound around his wrist. "C'mon loose, motherfuckah!" he said to the very old man, who was still screaming for protection. The other young man was making huffing sounds, as dark as mud, as he slapped at the rain-soaked hair of his victim. "I can't...he's all twisted 'round...getcher hand outta there so's I can..." Screaming, the old man had doubled under, locking their hands on his person.

And then the pillager's fist came loose, and he was clutching—for an instant—a gorgeous pocket watch.

What used to be called a turnip watch.

The dial face was *cloisonné*, exquisite beyond the telling.

The case was of silver, so bright it seemed blue.

The hands, cast as arrows of time, were gold. They formed a shallow V at precisely eleven o'clock. This was happening at 3:45 in the afternoon, with rain and wind.

The timepiece made no sound, no sound at all.

Then: there was space all around the watch, and in that space in the palm of the hand, there was heat. Intense heat for just a moment, just long enough for the hand to open.

The watch glided out of the boy's palm and levitated.

"Help me! You *must* protect me!"

Billy Kinetta heard the shrieking, but did not see the pocket watch floating in the air above the astonished young man. It was silver, and it was end-on toward him, and the rain was silver and slanting; and he did not see the watch hanging free in the air, even when the furious young man disentangled himself and leaped for it. Billy did not see the watch rise just so much, out of reach of the mugger.

Billy Kinetta saw two boys, two young men of ratpack age, beating someone much older; and he went for them. Pow, like that!

Thrashing his legs, the old man twisted around—over, under—as the boy holding him by the collar tried to land a punch to put him away. Who would have thought the old man to have had so much battle in him?

A flapping shape, screaming something unintelligible, hit the center of the group at full speed. The carnaby-gloved hand reaching for the watch grasped at empty air one moment, and the next was buried under its owner as the boy was struck a crackback block that threw him face-first into the soggy ground. He tried to rise, but something stomped him at the base of his spine; something kicked him twice in the kidneys; something rolled over him like a flash flood.

Twisting, twisting, the very old man put his thumb in the right eye of the boy clutching his collar.

The great trenchcoated maelstrom that was Billy Kinetta whirled into the boy as he let loose of the old man on the ground and, howling, slapped a palm against his stinging eye. Billy locked his fingers and delivered a roundhouse wallop that sent the boy reeling backward to fall over Minna's tilted headstone.

Billy's back was to the old man. He did not see the miraculous pocket watch smoothly descend through rain that did not touch it, to hover in front of the old man. He did not see the old man reach up, did not see the timepiece snuggle into an arthritic hand, did not see the old man return the turnip to an inside jacket pocket.

Wind, rain and Billy Kinetta pummeled two young men of a legal age that made them accountable for their actions. There was no thought of the knife stuck down in one boot, no chance to reach it, no moment when the wild thing let them rise. So they crawled. They scrabbled across the muddy ground, the slippery grass, over graves and out of his reach. They ran; falling, rising, falling again; away, without looking back.

Billy Kinetta, breathing heavily, knees trembling, turned to help the old man to his feet; and found him standing, brushing dirt from his overcoat, snorting in anger and mumbling to himself.

"Are you all right?"

For a moment the old man's recitation of annoyance continued, then he snapped his chin down sharply as if marking end to the situation, and looked at his cavalry to the rescue. "That was very good, young fella. Considerable style you've got there."

Billy Kinetta stared at him wide-eyed. "Are you sure you're okay?" He reached over and flicked several blades of wet grass from the shoulder of the old man's overcoat.

"I'm fine. I'm fine but I'm wet and I'm cranky. Let's go somewhere and have a nice cup of Earl Grey."

There had been a look on Billy Kinetta's face as he stood with lowered eyes, staring at the grave he had come to visit. The emergency had removed that look. Now it returned.

"No, thanks. If you're okay, I've got to do some things."

The old man felt himself all over, meticulously, as he replied, "I'm only superficially bruised. Now if I were an old woman, instead of a spunky old man, same age though, I'd have lost considerable of the calcium in my bones, and those two would have done me some mischief. Did you know that women lose a considerable part of their calcium when they reach my age? I read a report." Then he paused, and said shyly, "Come on, why don't you and I sit and chew the fat over a nice cup of tea?"

Billy shook his head with bemusement, smiling despite himself. "You're something else, Dad. I don't even know you."

"I like that."

"What: that I don't know you?"

"No, that you called me 'Dad' and not 'Pop.' I *hate* 'Pop.' Always makes me think the wise-apple wants to snap off my cap with a bottle opener. Now *Dad* has a ring of respect to it. I like that right down to the ground. Yes, I believe we should find someplace warm and quiet to sit and get to know each other. After all, you saved my life. And you know what that means in the Orient."

Billy was smiling continuously now. "In the first place, I doubt very much I saved your life. Your wallet, maybe. And in the second place, I don't even know your name; what would we have to talk about?"

"Gaspar," he said, extending his hand. "That's a first name. Gaspar. Know what it means?"

Billy shook his head.

"See, already we have something to talk about."

So Billy, still smiling, began walking Gaspar out of the cemetery. "Where do you live? I'll take you home."

They were on the street, approaching Billy Kinetta's 1979 Cutlass. "Where I live is too far for now. I'm beginning to feel a bit peaky. I'd like to lie down for a minute. We can just go on over to your place, if that doesn't bother you. For a few minutes. A cup of tea. Is that all right?"

He was standing beside the Cutlass, looking at Billy with an old man's expectant smile, waiting for him to unlock the door and hold it for him till he'd placed his still-calcium-rich but nonetheless old bones in the passenger seat. Billy stared at him, trying to figure out what was at risk if he unlocked that door. Then he snorted a tiny laugh, unlocked the door, held it for Gaspar as he seated himself, slammed it and went around to unlock the other side and get in. Gaspar reached across and thumbed up the door lock knob. And they drove off together in the rain.

Through all of this the timepiece made no sound, no sound at all.

Like Gaspar, Billy Kinetta was alone in the world.

His three-room apartment was the vacuum in which he existed. It was furnished, but if one stepped out into the hallway and, for all the money in all the numbered accounts in all the banks in Switzerland, one were asked to describe those furnishings, one would come away no richer than before. The apartment was charisma poor. It was a place to come when all other possibilities had been expended. Nothing green, nothing alive, existed in those boxes. No eyes looked back from the walls. Neither warmth nor chill marked those spaces. It was a place to wait.

Gaspar leaned his closed shooting stick, now a walking stick with handles, against the bookcase. He studied the titles of the paperbacks stacked haphazardly on the shelves.

From the kitchenette came the sound of water running into a metal pan. Then tin on cast iron. Then the hiss of gas and the flaring of a match as it was struck; and the pop of the gas being lit.

"Many years ago," Gaspar said, taking out a copy of Moravia's Two Adolescents and thumbing it as he spoke, "I had a library of books, oh, thousands of books—never could bear to toss one out, not even the bad ones— and when folks would come to the house to visit they'd look around at all the nooks and crannies stuffed with books; and if they were the sort of folks who don't snuggle with books, they'd always ask the same dumb question." He waited a moment for a response and when none was forthcoming (the sound of china cups on sink tile), he said, "Guess what the question was."

From the kitchen, without much interest: "No idea."

"They'd always ask it with the kind of voice people use in the presence of large sculptures in museums. They'd ask me, 'Have you read all these books?'" He waited again, but Billy Kinetta was not playing the game. "Well, young fella, after a while the same dumb question gets asked a million times, you get sorta snappish about it. And it came to annoy me more than a little bit. Till I finally figured out the right answer.

"And you know what that answer was? Go ahead, take a guess."

Billy appeared in the kitchenette doorway. "I suppose you told them you'd read a lot of them but not all of them."

Gaspar waved the guess away with a flapping hand. "Now what good would that have done? They wouldn't know they'd asked a dumb question, but I didn't want to insult them, either. So when they'd ask if I'd read all those books, I'd say, 'Hell, no. Who wants a library full of books you've already read?'"

Billy laughed despite himself. He scratched at his hair with idle pleasure, and shook his head at the old man's verve. "Gaspar, you are a wild old man. You retired?"

The old man walked carefully to the most comfortable chair in the room, an overstuffed Thirties-style lounge that had been reupholstered many times before Billy Kinetta had purchased it at the American Cancer Society Thrift Shop. He sank into it with a sigh. "No sir, I am not by any means retired. Still very active."

"Doing what, if I'm not prying?"

"Doing ombudsman."

"You mean, like a consumer advocate? Like Ralph Nader?"

"Exactly. I watch out for things. I listen, I pay some attention; and if I do it right, sometimes I can even make a little difference. Yes, like Mr. Nader. A very fine man."

"And you were at the cemetery to see a relative?"

Gaspar's face settled into an expression of loss. "My dear old girl. My wife, Minna. She's been gone, well, it was twenty years in January." He sat silently staring inward for a while, then: "She was everything to me. The nice part was that I knew how important we were to each other; we discussed, well, just *everything*. I miss that the most, telling her what's going on.

"I go to see her every other day.

"I used to go every day. But. It. Hurt. Too much."

They had tea. Gaspar sipped and said it was very nice, but had Billy ever tried Earl Grey? Billy said he didn't know what that was, and Gaspar said he would bring him a tin, that it was splendid. And they chatted. Finally, Gaspar asked, "And who were you visiting?"

Billy pressed his lips together. "Just a friend." And would say no more. Then he sighed and said, "Well, listen, I have to go to work."

"Oh? What do you do?"

The answer came slowly. As if Billy Kinetta wanted to be able to say that he was in computers, or owned his own business, or held a position of import. "I'm night manager at a 7-Eleven."

"I'll bet you meet some fascinating people coming in late for milk or one of those slushies," Gaspar said gently. He seemed to understand.

Billy smiled. He took the kindness as it was intended. "Yeah, the cream of high society. That is, when they're not threatening to shoot me through the head if I don't open the safe."

"Let me ask you a favor," Gaspar said. "I'd like a little sanctuary, if you think it's all right. Just a little rest. I could lie down on the sofa for a bit. Would that be all right? You trust me to stay here while you're gone, young fella?"

Billy hesitated only a moment. The very old man seemed okay, not a crazy, certainly not a thief. And what was there to steal? Some tea that wasn't even Earl Grey?

"Sure. That'll be okay. But I won't be coming back till two AM. So just close the door behind you when you go; it'll lock automatically."

They shook hands, Billy shrugged into his still-wet trenchcoat, and he went to the door. He paused to look back at Gaspar sitting in the lengthening shadows as evening came on. "It was nice getting to know you, Gaspar."

"You can make that a mutual pleasure, Billy. You're a nice young fella."

And Billy went to work, alone as always.

When he came home at two, prepared to open a can of Hormel chili, he found the table set for dinner; with the scent of an elegant beef stew enriching the apartment. There were new potatoes and stir-fried carrots and zucchini that had been lightly battered to delicate crispness. And cupcakes. White cake with chocolate frosting. From a bakery.

And in that way, as gently as that, Gaspar insinuated himself into Billy Kinetta's apartment and his life.

As they sat with tea and cupcakes, Billy said, "You don't have any place to go, do you?"

The old man smiled and made one of those deprecating movements of the head. "Well, I'm not the sort of fella who can bear to be homeless, but at the moment I'm what vaudevillians used to call 'at liberty.'"

"If you want to stay on a time, that would be okay," Billy said. "It's not very roomy here, but we seem to get on all right."

"That's strongly kind of you, Billy. Yes, I'd like to be your roommate for a while. Won't be too long, though. My doctor tells me I'm not long for this world." He paused, looked into the teacup and said softly, "I have to confess…I'm a little frightened. To go. Having someone to talk to would be a great comfort."

And Billy said, without preparation, "I was visiting the grave of a man who was in my rifle company in Vietnam. I go there sometimes." But there was such pain in his words that Gaspar did not press him for details.

So the hours passed, as they will with or without permission, and when Gaspar asked Billy if they could watch the television, to catch an early newscast, and Billy tuned in the old set just in time to pick up dire reports of another aborted disarmament talk, and Billy shook his head and observed that it wasn't only Gaspar who was frightened of something like death, Gaspar chuckled, patted Billy on the knee and said, with unassailable assurance, "Take my word for it, Billy...it isn't going to happen. No nuclear holocaust. Trust me, when I tell you this: it'll never happen. Never, never, not ever."

Billy smiled wanly. "And why not? What makes *you* so sure...got some special inside information?"

And Gaspar pulled out the magnificent timepiece, which Billy was seeing for the first time, and he said, "It's not going to happen because it's only eleven o'clock."

Billy stared at the watch, which read 11:00 precisely. He consulted his wristwatch. "Hate to tell you this, but your watch has stopped. It's almost five-thirty."

Gaspar smiled his own certain smile. "No, it's eleven." And they made up the sofa for the very old man, who placed his pocket change and his fountain pen and the sumptuous turnip watch on the now-silent television set, and they went to sleep.

One day Billy went off while Gaspar was washing the lunch dishes, and when he came back, he had a large paper bag from Toys R Us.

Gaspar came out of the kitchenette rubbing a plate with a souvenir dish towel from Niagara Falls, New York. He stared at Billy and the bag. "What's in the bag?" Billy inclined his head, and indicated the very old man should join him in the middle of the room. Then he sat down crosslegged on the floor, and dumped the contents of the bag. Gaspar stared with startlement, and sat down beside him.

So for two hours they played with tiny cars that turned into robots when the sections were unfolded.

Gaspar was excellent at figuring out all the permutations of the Transformers, Starriors and GoBots. He played well.

Then they went for a walk. "I'll treat you to a matinee," Gaspar said. "But no films with Karen Black, Sandy Dennis or Meryl Streep. They're always crying. Their noses are always red. I can't stand that."

They started to cross the avenue. Stopped at the light was this year's Cadillac Brougham, vanity license plates, ten coats of acrylic lacquer and two coats of clear (with a little retarder in the final "color coat" for a slow dry) of a magenta hue so rich that it approximated the shade of light shining through a decanter filled with Château Lafite-Rothschild 1945.

The man driving the Cadillac had no neck. His head sat thumped down hard on the shoulders. He stared straight ahead, took one last deep pull on the cigar, and threw it out the window. The still-smoking butt landed directly in front of Gaspar as he passed the car. The old man stopped, stared down at this coprolitic metaphor, and then stared at the driver. The eyes behind the wheel, the eyes of a macaque, did not waver from the stoplight's red circle. Just outside the window, someone was looking in, but the eyes of the rhesus were on the red circle.

A line of cars stopped behind the Brougham.

Gaspar continued to stare at the man in the Cadillac for a moment, and then, with creaking difficulty, he bent and picked up the smoldering butt of stogie.

The old man walked the two steps to the car—as Billy watched in confusion—thrust his face forward till it was mere inches from the driver's profile, and said with extreme sweetness, "I think you dropped this in our living room."

And as the glazed simian eyes turned to stare directly into the pedestrian's face, nearly nose-to-nose, Gaspar casually flipped the butt with its red glowing tip, into the back seat of the Cadillac, where it began to burn a hole in the fine Corinthian leather.

Three things happened simultaneously:

The driver let out a howl, tried to see the butt in his rearview mirror, could not get the angle, tried to look over his shoulder into the back seat but without a neck could not perform that feat of agility, put the car into neutral, opened his door and stormed into the street trying to grab Gaspar. "You fuckin' bastid, whaddaya think you're doin' tuh my car you asshole bastid, I'll kill ya…"

Billy's hair stood on end as he saw what Gaspar was doing; he rushed back the short distance in the crosswalk to grab the old man; Gaspar would not be dragged away, stood smiling with unconcealed pleasure at the mad bull rampaging and screaming of the hysterical driver. Billy yanked as hard as he could and Gaspar began to move away, around the front of the Cadillac, toward the far curb. Still grinning with octo-generic charm.

The light changed.

These three things happened in the space of five seconds, abetted by the impatient honking of the cars behind the Brougham; as the light turned green.

Screaming, dragging, honking, as the driver found he could not do three things at once: he could not go after Gaspar while the traffic was clanging at him; could not let go of the car door to crawl into the back seat from which now came the stench of charring leather that could not be rectified by an inexpensive Tijuana tuck'n'roll; could not save his back seat and at the same time stave off the hostility of a dozen drivers cursing and honking. He trembled there, torn three ways, doing nothing.

Billy dragged Gaspar.

Out of the crosswalk. Out of the street. Onto the curb. Up the side street. Into the alley. Through a backyard.

To the next street over away from the avenue.

Puffing with the exertion, Billy stopped at last, five houses up the street. Gaspar was still grinning, chuckling softly, with unconcealed pleasure at his puckish ways. Billy turned on him with wild gesticulations and babble.

"You're *nuts!*"

"How about that?" the old man said, giving Billy an affectionate poke in the bicep.

"Nuts! Looney! That guy would've torn off your head! What the hell's wrong with you, old man? Are you out of your boots?"

"I'm not crazy. I'm responsible."

"Responsible!?! Re*spon*sible, fer chrissakes? For what? For all the butts every yotz throws into the street?"

The old man nodded. "For butts, and trash, and pollution, and toxic waste dumping in the dead of night; for bushes, and cactus, and the baobab tree; for pippin apples and even lima beans, which I despise. You show me someone who'll eat lima beans without being at gunpoint, I'll show you a pervert!"

Billy was screaming. "What the hell are you talking about?"

"I'm also responsible for dogs and cats and guppies and cockroaches and the President of the United States and Jonas Salk and your mother and the entire chorus line at the Sands Hotel in Las Vegas. Also their choreographer."

"Who do your think you are? God?"

"Don't be sacrilegious. I'm too old to wash your mouth out with laundry soap. Of course I'm not God. I'm just an old man. *But I'm responsible.*"

Gaspar started to walk away, toward the corner and the avenue, and a resumption of their route. Billy stood where the old man's words had pinned him.

"Come on, young fella," Gaspar said, walking backward to speak to him, "we'll miss the beginning of the movie. I hate that."

Billy had finished eating, and they were sitting in the dimness of the apartment, only the lamp in the corner lit. The old man had gone to the County Art Museum and had bought inexpensive prints—Max Ernst, Gérôme, Richard Dadd, a subtle Feininger—which he had mounted in Insta-Frames. They sat in silence for a time, relaxing; then murmuring trivialities in a pleasant undertone.

Finally, Gaspar said, "I've been thinking a lot about my dying. I like what Woody Allen said."

Billy slid to a more comfortable position in the lounger. "What was that?"

"He said: I don't mind dying, I just don't want to be there when it happens."

Billy snickered.

"I feel something like that, Billy. I'm not afraid to go, but I don't want to leave Minna entirely. The times I spend with her, talking to her, well, it gives me the feeling we're still in touch. When I go, that's the end of Minna. She'll be well and truly dead. We never had any children, almost everyone who knew us is gone, no relatives. And we never did anything important that anyone would put in a record book, so that's the end of us. For me, I don't mind; but I wish there was someone who knew about Minna…she was a remarkable person."

So Billy said, "Tell me. I'll remember for you."

Memories in no particular order. Some as strong as ropes that could pull the ocean ashore. Some that shimmered and swayed in the faintest breeze like spiderwebs. The entire person, all the little movements, that dimple that appeared when she was amused at something foolish he had said. Their youth together, their love, the procession of their days toward middle age. The small cheers and the pain of dreams never realized. So much about *him* as he spoke of *her*. His voice soft and warm and filled with a longing so deep and true that he had to stop frequently because the words broke and would not come out till he had thought away some of the passion. He thought of her and was glad. He had gathered her together, all her dowry of love and taking care of him, her clothes and the way she wore them, her favorite knickknacks, a few clever remarks: and he packed it all up and delivered it to a new repository.

The very old man gave Minna to Billy Kinetta for safekeeping.

Dawn had come. The light filtering in through the blinds was saffron. "Thank you, Dad," Billy said. He could not name the feeling that had taken him hours earlier. But he said this: "I've never had to be responsible for anything, or anyone, in my whole life. I never belonged to anybody...I don't know why. It didn't bother me, because I didn't know any other way to be."

Then his position changed, there in the lounger. He sat up in a way that Gaspar thought was important. As if Billy were about to open the secret box buried at his center. And Billy spoke so softly the old man had to strain to hear him.

"I didn't even know him.

"We were defending the airfield at Danang. Did I tell you we were 1st Battalion, 9th Marines? Charlie was massing for a big push out of Quang Ngai province, south of us. Looked as if they were going to try to take the provincial capital. My rifle company was assigned to protect the perimeter. They kept sending in patrols to bite us. Every day we'd lose some poor bastard who scratched his head when he shouldn't of. It was June, late in June, cold and a lot of rain. The foxholes were hip-deep in water.

"Flares first. Our howitzers started firing. Then the sky was full of tracers, and I started to turn toward the bushes when I heard something coming, and these two main-force regulars in dark blue uniforms came toward me. I could see them so clearly. Long black hair. All crouched over. And they started firing. And that goddam carbine seized up, wouldn't fire; and I pulled out the banana clip, tried to slap in another, but they saw me and just turned a couple of AK-47s on me...God, I remember everything slowed down...I looked at those things, seven-point-six-two-millimeter assault rifles they were...I got crazy for a second, tried to figure out in my own mind if they were Russian-made, or Chinese, or Czech, or North Korean. And it was so bright from the flares I could see them starting to squeeze off the rounds, and then from out of nowhere this lance corporal jumped out at them and yelled somedamnthing like,

'Hey, you VC fucks, looka here!' except it wasn't that...I never could recall what he said actually...and they turned to brace him...and they opened him up like a Baggie full of blood...and he was all over me, and the bushes, and oh god there were pieces of him floating on the water I was standing in..."

Billy was heaving breath with impossible weight. His hands moved in the air before his face without pattern or goal. He kept looking into far corners of the dawn-lit room as if special facts might present themselves to fill out the reasons behind what he was saying.

"Aw, geezus, he was *floating* on the water...aw, christ, he *got in my boots!*" Then a wail of pain so loud it blotted out the sound of traffic beyond the apartment; and he began to moan, but not cry; and the moaning kept on; and Gaspar came from the sofa and held him and said such words as *it's all right*, but they might not have been those words, or *any* words.

And pressed against the old man's shoulder, Billy Kinetta ran on only half sane: "He wasn't my friend, I never knew him, I'd never talked to him, but I'd seen him, he was just this guy, and there wasn't any reason to do that, he didn't know whether I was a good guy or a shit or anything, so why did he do that? He didn't need to do that. They wouldn't of seen him. He was dead before I killed them. He was gone already. I never got to say thank you or thank you or...*anything!*

"Now he's in that grave, so I came here to live, so I can go there, but I try and try to say thank you, and he's dead, and he can't hear me, he can't hear nothin', he's just down there, down in the ground, and I can't say thank you...oh, geezus, geezus, why don't he hear me, I just want to say thanks..."

Billy Kinetta wanted to assume the responsibility for saying thanks, but that was possible only on a night that would never come again; and this was the day.

Gaspar took him to the bedroom and put him down to sleep in exactly the same way he would soothe an old, sick dog.

Then he went to his sofa, and because it was the only thing he could imagine saying, he murmured, "He'll be all right, Minna. Really he will."

When Billy left for the 7-Eleven the next evening, Gaspar was gone. It was an alternate day, and that meant he was out at the cemetery. Billy fretted that he shouldn't be there alone, but the old man had a way of taking care of himself. Billy was not smiling as he thought of his friend, and the word *friend* echoed as he realized that, yes, this was his friend, truly and really his friend. He wondered how old Gaspar was, and how soon Billy Kinetta would be once again what he had always been: alone.

When he returned to the apartment at two-thirty, Gaspar was asleep, cocooned in his blanket on the sofa. Billy went in and tried to sleep, but hours later, when sleep would not come, when thoughts of murky water and calcium night light on dark foliage kept him staring at the bedroom ceiling, he came out of the room for a drink of water. He wandered around the living room, not wanting to be by himself even if the only companionship in this sleepless night was breathing heavily, himself in sleep.

He stared out the window. Clouds in chiffon strips across the sky. The squealing of tires from the street.

Sighing, idle in his movement around the room, he saw the old man's pocket watch lying on the coffee table beside the sofa. He walked to the table. If the watch was still stopped at eleven o'clock, perhaps he would borrow it and have it repaired. It would be a nice thing to do for Gaspar. The old man loved that beautiful timepiece.

Billy bent to pick it up.

The watch, stopped at the V of eleven precisely, levitated at an angle, floating away from him.

Billy Kinetta felt a shiver travel down his back to burrow in at the base of his spine. He reached for the watch hanging in air before him. It floated away just enough that his fingers massaged empty space. He tried to catch it. The watch eluded him, lazily turning away like an opponent who knows he is in no danger of being struck from behind.

Then Billy realized Gaspar was awake. Turned away from the sofa, nonetheless he knew the old man was observing him. And the blissful floating watch.

He looked at Gaspar.

They did not speak for a long time.

Then: "I'm going back to sleep," Billy said. Quietly.

"I think you have some questions," Gaspar replied.

"Questions? No, of course not, Dad. Why in the world would I have questions? I'm still asleep." But that was not the truth, because he had not been asleep that night.

"Do you know what 'Gaspar" means? Do you remember the three wise men of the Bible, the Magi?"

"I don't want any frankincense and myrrh. I'm going back to bed. I'm going now. You see, I'm going right now."

"'Gaspar' means master of the treasure, keeper of the secrets, paladin of the palace." Billy was staring at him, not walking into the bedroom; just staring at him. As the elegant timepiece floated to the old man, who extended his hand palm-up to receive it. The watch nestled in his hand, unmoving, and it made no sound, no sound at all.

"You go back to bed. But will you go out to the cemetery with me tomorrow? It's important."

"Why?"

"Because I believe I'll be dying tomorrow."

It was a nice day, cool and clear. Not at all a day for dying, but neither had been many such days in Southeast Asia, and death had not been deterred.

They stood at Minna's gravesite, and Gaspar opened his shooting stick to form a seat; and he thrust the spike into the ground; and he settled onto it, and sighed, and said to Billy Kinetta, "I'm growing cold as that stone."

"Do you want my jacket?"

"No, I'm cold inside." He looked around at the sky, at the grass, at the rows of markers. "I've been responsible, for all of this, and more."

"You've said that before."

"Young fella, are you by any chance familiar, in your reading, with an old novel by James Hilton called Lost Horizon? Perhaps you saw the movie. It was a wonderful movie. It was a wonderful movie, actually much better than the book. Mr. Capra's greatest achievement. A human testament. Ronald Colman was superb. Do you know the story?"

"Yes."

"Do you remember the High Lama, played by Sam Jaffe? His name was Father Perrault?"

"Yes."

"Do you remember how he passed on the caretakership of that magical hidden world, Shangri-La, to Ronald Colman?"

"Yes, I remember that." Billy paused. "Then he died. He was very old, and he died."

Gaspar smiled up at him. "Very good, Billy. I knew you were a good boy. So now, if you remember all that, may I tell you a story? It's not a very long story."

Billy nodded, smiling at his friend.

"In 1582 Pope Gregory XIII decreed that the civilized world would no longer observe the Julian calendar. October 4th, 1582 was followed, the next day, by October 15th. Eleven days vanished from the world. One hundred and seventy years later, the British Parliament followed suit, and September 2nd, 1752 was followed, the next day, by September 14th. Why did he do that, the Pope?"

Billy was bewildered by the conversation. "Because he was bringing it into synch with the real world. The solstices and equinoxes. When to plant, when to harvest."

Gaspar waggled a finger at him with pleasure. "Excellent, young fella. And you're correct when you say Gregory abolished the Julian calendar because its error of one day in every one hundred and twenty-eight years had moved the vernal equinox to March 11th. That's what the history books say. It's what *every* history book says. But what if?"

"What if *what*? I don't know what you're talking about."

"What if: Pope Gregory had the knowledge revealed to him that he *must* readjust time in the minds of men? What if: the excess time in 1582 was eleven days and one hour? What if: he accounted for those eleven days, vanished those eleven days, but that one hour slipped free, was left loose to bounce through eternity? A very special hour...an hour that must *never* be used...an hour that must never toll. What if?"

Billy spread his hands. "What if, what if, what if! It's all just philosophy. It doesn't mean anything. Hours aren't real, time isn't something that you can bottle up. So what if there *is* an hour out there somewhere that..."

And he stopped.

He grew tense, and leaned down to the old man. "The watch. Your watch. It doesn't work. It's stopped."

Gaspar nodded, "At eleven o'clock. My watch works; it keeps very special time, for one very special hour."

Billy touched Gaspar's shoulder. Carefully he asked, "Who are you, Dad?"

The old man did not smile as he said, "Gaspar. Keeper. Paladin. Guardian."

"Father Perrault was hundreds of years old."

Gaspar shook his head with a wistful expression on his old face. "I'm eighty-six years old, Billy. You asked me if I thought I was God. Not God, not Father Perrault, not an immortal, just an old man who will die too soon. Are you Ronald Colman?"

Billy nervously touched his lower lip with a finger. He looked at Gaspar as long as he could, then turned away. He walked off a few paces, stared at the barren trees. It seemed suddenly much chillier here in this place of entombed remembrances. From a distance he said, "But it's only...what? A chronological convenience. Like daylight saving time; Spring forward, Fall back. We don't actually *lose* an hour; we get it back."

Gaspar stared at Minna's grave. "At the end of April I lost an hour. If I die now, I'll die an hour short in my life. I'll have been cheated out of one hour I want, Billy." He swayed toward all he had left of Minna. "One last hour I could have with my old girl. That's what I'm afraid of, Billy. I have that hour in my possession. I'm afraid I'll use it, god help me, I want so much to use it."

Billy came to him. Tense, and chilled, he said, "Why must that hour never toll?"

Gaspar drew a deep breath and tore his eyes away from the grave. His gaze locked with Billy's. And he told him.

The years, all the days and hours, exist. As solid and as real as mountains and oceans and men and women and the baobab tree. Look, he said, at the lines in my face and deny that time is real. Consider these dead weeds that were once alive and try to believe it's all just vapor or the mutual agreement of Popes and Caesars and young men like you.

"The lost hour must never come, Billy, for in that hour it all ends. The light, the wind, the stars, this magnificent open place we call the universe. It all ends, and in its place—waiting, always waiting—is eternal darkness. No new beginnings, no world without end, just the infinite emptiness."

And he opened his hand, which had been lying in his lap, and there, in his palm, rested the watch, making no sound at all, and stopped dead at eleven o'clock. "Should it strike twelve, Billy, eternal night falls; from which there is no recall."

There he sat, this very old man, just a perfectly normal old man. The most recent in the endless chain of keepers of the lost hour, descended in possession from Caesar and Pope Gregory XIII, down through the centuries of men and women who had served as caretakers of the excellent timepiece. And now he was dying, and now he wanted to cling to life as every man and woman clings to life no matter how awful or painful or empty, even if it is for one more hour. The suicide, falling from the bridge, at the final instant, tries to fly, tries to climb back up the sky. This weary old man, who only wanted to stay one brief hour more with Minna. Who was afraid that his love would cost the universe.

He looked at Billy, and he extended his hand with the watch waiting for its next paladin. So softly Billy could barely hear him, knowing that he was denying himself what he most wanted at this last place in his life, he whispered, "If I die without passing it on…it will begin to tick."

"Not me," Billy said. "Why did you pick me? I'm no one special. I'm not someone like you. I run an all-night service mart. There's nothing special about me the way there is about you! I'm *not* Ronald Colman! I don't want to be responsible, I've *never* been responsible!"

Gaspar smiled gently. "You've been responsible for me."

Billy's rage vanished. He looked wounded.

"Look at us, Billy. Look at what color you are; and look at what color I am. You took me in as a friend. I think of you as worthy, Billy. Worthy."

They remained there that way, in silence, as the wind rose. And finally, in a timeless time, Billy nodded.

Then the young man said, "You won't be losing Minna, Dad. Now you'll go to the place where she's been waiting for you, just as she was when you first met her. There's a place where we find everything we've ever lost through the years."

"That's good, Billy, that you tell me that. I'd like to believe it, too. But I'm a pragmatist. I believe in what exists…like rain and Minna's grave and the hours that pass that we can't see, but they *are*. I'm afraid, Billy. I'm afraid this will be the last time I can speak to her. So I ask a favor. As payment, in return for my life spent protecting the watch.

"I ask for one minute of the hour, Billy. One minute to call her back so we can stand face-to-face and I can touch her and say goodbye. You'll be the new protector of this watch, Billy, so I ask you please, just let me steal one minute."

Billy could not speak. The look on Gaspar's face was without horizon, empty as tundra, bottomless. The child left alone in darkness; the pain of eternal waiting. He knew he could never deny this old man, no matter what he asked, and in the silence he heard a voice say: *"No!"* And it was his own.

He had spoken without conscious volition. Strong and determined, and without the slightest room for reversal. If a part of his heart had been swayed by compassion, that part had been instantly overridden. No. A final, unshakeable no.

For an instant Gaspar looked crestfallen. His eyes clouded with tears; and Billy felt something twist and break within himself at the sight. He knew he had hurt the old man. Quickly, but softly, he said urgently, "You know that would be wrong, Dad. We mustn't..."

Gaspar said nothing. Then he reached out with his free hand and took Billy's. It was an affectionate touch.

"That was the last test, young fella. Oh, you know I've been testing you, don't you? This important item couldn't go to just anyone.

"And you passed the test, my friend: my last, best friend. When I said I could bring her back from where she's gone, here in this place we've both come to so often, to talk to someone lost to us, I knew you would understand that *anyone* could be brought back in that stolen minute. I knew you wouldn't use it for yourself, no matter how much you wanted it; but I wasn't sure that as much as you like me, it might not sway you. But you wouldn't even give it to *me*, Billy."

He smiled up at him, his eyes now clear and steady.

"I'm content, Billy. You needn't have worried. Minna and I don't need that minute. But if you're to carry on for me, I think you *do* need it. You're in pain, and that's no good for someone who carries this watch. You've got to heal, Billy.

"So I give you something you would never take for yourself. I give you a going-away present..."

And he started the watch, whose ticking was as loud and as clear as a baby's first sound; and the sweep-second hand began to move away from eleven o'clock.

Then the wind rose, and the sky seemed to cloud over, and it grew colder, with a remarkable silver-blue mist that rolled across the cemetery; and though he did not see it emerge from that grave at a distance far to the right, Billy Kinetta saw a shape move toward him. A soldier in the uniform of a day past, and his rank was Lance Corporal. He came toward Billy Kinetta, and Billy went to meet him as Gaspar watched.

They stood together and Billy spoke to him. And the man whose name Billy had never known when he was alive, answered. And then he faded, as the seconds ticked away. Faded, and faded, and was gone. And the silver-blue mist rolled through them, and past them, and was gone; and the soldier was gone.

Billy stood alone.

When he turned back to look across the grounds to his friend, he saw that Gaspar had fallen from the shooting-stick. He lay on the ground. Billy rushed to him, and fell to his knees and lifted him onto his lap. Gaspar was still.

"Oh, god, Dad, you should have heard what he said. Oh, geez, he let me go. He let me go so I didn't even have to say I was sorry. He told me he didn't even *see* me in that foxhole. He never knew he'd saved my life. I said thank you and he said no, thank *you*, that he hadn't died for nothing. Oh, please, Dad, please don't be dead yet. I want to tell you…"

And, as it sometimes happens, rarely but wonderfully, sometimes they come back for a moment, for an instant before they go, the old man, this very old man, opened his eyes, just before going on his way, and he looked through the dimming light at his friend, and he said, "May I remember you to my old girl, Billy?"

And his eyes closed again, after only a moment; and his caretakership was at an end; as his hand opened and the most excellent timepiece, now stopped again at one minute past eleven, floated from his palm and waited till Billy Kinetta extended his hand; and then it floated down and lay there silently, making no sound, no sound at all. Safe. Protected.

There in the place where all lost things returned, the young man sat on the cold ground, rocking the body of his friend. And he was in no hurry to leave. There was time.

A blessing of the 18th Egyptian Dynasty:
God be between you and harm in
all the empty places you walk.

The author gratefully acknowledges the importance of a discussion with Ms. Ellie Grossman in the creation of this work of fiction.

WITH VIRGIL ODDUM
AT THE EAST POLE

1986 Locus Poll Award: Best Short Story

THE DAY HE crawled out of the dead cold Icelands, the glaciers creeping down the great cliff were sea-green: endless rivers of tinted, faceted emeralds lit from within. Memories of crippled chances shone in the ice. That was a day, and I remember this clearly, during which the purple sky of Hotlands was filled with the downdrifting balloon spores that had died rushing through the beams of the UV lamps in the peanut fields of the silver crescent. That was a day—remembering clearly—with Argo squatting on the horizon of Hotlands, an enormous inverted tureen of ruby glass.

He crawled toward me and the ancient fux I called Amos the Wise; crawled, literally crawled, up the land bridge of Westspit onto Meditation Island. Through the slush and sludge and amber mud of the Terminator's largest island.

His heat-envelope was filthy and already cracking, and he tore open the Velcro mouthflap without regard for saving the garment as he crawled toward a rotting clump of spillweed.

When I realized that he intended to *eat* it, I moved to him quickly and crouched in front of him so he couldn't get to it.

"I wouldn't put that in your mouth," I said. "It'll kill you."

He didn't say anything, but he looked up at me from down there on his hands and knees with an expression that said it all. He was starving, and if I didn't come up with some immediate alternative to the spillweed, he was going to eat it anyhow, even if it killed him.

This was only one hundred and nineteen years after we had brought the wonders of the human race to Medea, and though I was serving a term of penitence on Meditation Island, I wasn't so sure I wanted to make friends with another human being. I was having a hard enough time just communicating with fuxes. I certainly didn't want to take charge of his life…even in as small a way as being responsible for saving it.

Funny the things that flash through your mind. I remember at that moment, with him looking at me so desperately, recalling a cartoon I'd once seen: it was one of those standard thirsty-man-crawling-out-of-the-desert cartoons, with a long line of crawl-marks stretching to the horizon behind an emaciated, bearded wanderer. And in the foreground is a man on a horse, looking down at this poor dying devil with one clawed hand lifted in a begging gesture, and the guy on the horse is smiling and saying to the thirsty man, "Peanut butter sandwich?"

I didn't think he'd find it too funny.

So I pulled up the spillweed, so he wouldn't go for it before I got back, and I trotted over to my wickyup and got him a ball of peanut cheese and a nip-off bulb of water, and came back and helped him sit up to eat.

It took him a while, and of course we were covered with pink and white spores by the time he finished. The smell was awful.

I helped him to his feet. Pretty unsteady. And he leaned on me walking back to the wickyup. I laid him down on my air-mattress and he closed his eyes and fell asleep immediately. Maybe he fainted, I don't know.

His name was Virgil Oddum; but I didn't know that, either, at the time.

I didn't ever know much about him. Not then, not later, not even now. It's funny how everybody knows *what* he did, but not why he did it, or even who he was; and until recently, not so much as his name, nothing.

In a way, I really resent it. The only reason anybody knows me is because I knew him, Virgil Oddum. But they don't care about me or what I was going through, just him, because of what he did. My name is Pogue. William Ronald Pogue, like *rogue*; and I'm important, too. You should know names.

Jason was chasing Theseus through the twilight sky directly over the Terminator when he woke up. The clouds of dead balloon spores had passed over and the sky was amber again, with bands of color washing across the bulk of Argo. I was trying to talk with Amos the Wise.

I was usually trying to talk with Amos the Wise.

The xenoanthropologists at the main station at Perdue Farm in the silver crescent call communication with the fuxes *ekstasis*—literally, "to stand outside oneself." A kind of enriched empathy that conveys concepts and emotional sets, but nothing like words or pictures. I would sit and stare at one of the fuxes, and he would crouch there on his hindquarters and stare back at me; and we'd both fill up with what the other was thinking. Sort of. More or less overcome with vague feelings, general tones of emotion... memories of when the fux had been a hunter; when he had had the extra hindquarters he'd dropped when he was female; the vision of a kilometer-high tidal wave once seen near the Seven Pillars on the Ring; chasing females and endlessly mating. It was all there, every moment of what was a long life for a fux: fifteen Medean years.

But it was all flat. Like a drama done with enormous expertise and no soul. The arrangement of thoughts was random, without continuity, without flow. There was no color, no interpretation, no sense of what it all meant for the dromids.

It was artless and graceless; it was merely data.

And so, trying to "talk" to Amos was like trying to get a computer to create original, deeply meaningful poetry. Sometimes I had the feeling he had been "assigned" to me, to humor me; to keep me busy.

At the moment the man came out of my wickyup, I was trying to get Amos to codify the visual nature of the fuxes' religious relationship to Caster C, the binary star that Amos and his race thought of as Maternal Grandfather and Paternal Grandfather. For the human colony they were Phrixus and Helle.

I was trying to get Amos to understand flow and the emotional load in changing colors when the double shadow fell between us and I looked up to see the man standing behind me. At the same moment I felt a lessening of the ekstasis between the fux and me. As though some other receiving station were leaching off power.

The man stood there, unsteadily, weaving and trying to keep his balance, staring at Amos. The fux was staring back. They were communicating, but what was passing between them I didn't know. Then Amos got up and walked away, with that liquid rolling gait old male fuxes affect after they've dropped their hindquarters. I got up with some difficulty: since coming to Medea I'd developed mild arthritis in my knees, and sitting cross-legged stiffened me.

As I stood up, he started to fall over, still too weak from crawling out of Icelands. He fell into my arms, and I confess my first thought was annoyance because now I *knew* he'd be another thing I'd have to worry about.

"Hey, hey," I said, "take it easy."

I helped him to the wickyup, and put him on his back on the air-mattress. "Listen, fellah," I said, "I don't want to be cold about this, but I'm out here all alone, paying my time. I don't get another shipment of rations for about four months and I can't keep you here."

He didn't say anything. Just stared at me.

"Who the hell are you? Where'd you come from?"

Watching me. I used to be able to read expression very accurately. Watching me, with hatred.

I didn't even know him. He didn't have any idea what was what, why I was out there on Meditation Island; there wasn't any reason he should hate me.

"How'd you get here?"

Watching. Not a word out of him.

"Listen, mister: here's the long and short of it. There isn't any way I can get in touch with anybody to come and get you. And I can't keep you here because there just isn't enough ration. And I'm not going to let you stay here and starve in front of me, because after a while you're sure as hell going to go for my food and I'm going to fight you for it, and one of us is going to get killed. And I am not about to have that kind of a situation, understand? Now I know this is chill, but you've got to go. Take a few days, get some strength. If you hike straight across Eastspit and keep going through Hotlands, you might get spotted by someone out spraying the fields. I doubt it, but maybe."

Not a sound. Just watching me and hating me.

"Where'd you come from? Not out there in Icelands. Nothing can live out there. It's minus thirty Celsius. Out there." Silence. "Just glaciers. Out there."

Silence. I felt that uncontrollable anger rising in me.

"Look, jamook, I'm not having this. Understand me? I'm just not having any of it. You've got to go. I don't give a damn if you're the Count of Monte Crespo or the lost Dauphin of Threx: you're getting the hell out of here as soon as you can crawl." He stared up at me and I wanted to hit the bastard as hard as I could. I had to control myself. This was the kind of thing that had driven me to Meditation Island.

Instead, I squatted there watching him for a long time. He never blinked. Just watched me. Finally, I said, very softly, "What'd you say to the fux?"

A double shadow fell through the door and I looked up. It was Amos the Wise. He'd peeled back the entrance flap with his tail because his hands were full. Impaled on the three long, sinewy fingers of each hand were six freshly caught dartfish. He stood there in the doorway, bloody light from the sky forming a corona that lit his blue, furry shape; and he extended the skewered fish.

I'd been six months on Meditation Island. Every day of that time I'd tried to spear a dartfish. Flashfreeze and peanut cheese and box-ration, they can pall on you pretty fast. You want to gag at the sight of silvr wrap. I'd wanted fresh food. Every day for six months I'd tried to catch something live. They were too fast. That's why they weren't called slowfish. The fuxes had watched me. Not one had ever moved to show me how they did it. Now this old neuter Amos was offering me half a dozen. I knew what the guy had said to him.

"Who the hell are you?" I was about as skewed as I could be. I wanted to pound him out a little, delete that hateful look on his face, put him in a way so I wouldn't have to care for him. He didn't say a word, just kept looking at me; but the fux came inside the wickyup—first time he'd ever done *that*, damn his slanty eyes!—and he moved around between us, the dartfish extended.

This guy had some kind of *hold* over the aborigine! He didn't say a thing, but the fux knew enough to get between us and insist I take the fish. So I did it, cursing both of them under my breath.

As I pried off the six dartfish I felt the old fux pull me into a flow with him. Stronger than I'd ever been able to do it when we'd done ekstasis. Amos the Wise let me know this was a very holy creature, this thing that had crawled out of the Icelands, and I'd better treat him pretty fine, or else. There wasn't even a hint of a picture of what *or else* might be, but it was a strong flow, a *strong* flow.

So I took the fish and put them in the larder, and I let the fux know how grateful I was, and he didn't pay me enough attention to mesmerize a gnat; and the flow was gone; and he was doing ekstasis with my guest lying out as nice and comfy as you please; and then he turned and slid out of the wickyup and was gone.

I sat there through most of the night watching him. One moment he was staring at me, the next he was asleep; and I went on through that first night just sitting there looking at him gonked-in like that, where I would have been sleeping if he hadn't showed up. Even asleep he hated me. But he was too weak to stay awake and enjoy it.

So I looked at him, wondering who the hell he was, most of that night. Until I couldn't take it anymore, and near to morning I just beat the crap out of him.

They kept bringing food. Not just fish, but plants I'd never seen before, things that grew out there in Hotlands east of us, out there where it always stank like rotting garbage. Some of the plants needed to be cooked, and some of them were delicious just eaten raw. But I knew they'd never have shown me *any* of that if it hadn't been for him.

He never spoke to me, and he never told the fuxes that I'd beaten him the first night he was in camp; and his manner never changed. Oh, I knew he could talk all right, because when he slept he tossed and thrashed and shouted things in his sleep. I never understood any of it; some offworld language. But whatever it was, it made him feel sick to remember it. Even asleep he was in torment.

He was determined to stay. I knew that from the second day. I caught him pilfering stores.

No, that's not accurate. He was doing it openly. I didn't catch him. He was going through the stash in the transport sheds: mostly goods I wouldn't need for a while yet; items whose functions no longer related to my needs. He had already liberated some of those items when I discovered him burrowing through the stores: the neetskin tent I'd used before building the wickyup from storm-hewn fellner trees; the spare air-mattress; a hologram projector I'd used during the first month to keep me entertained with a selection of laser beads, mostly Nōh plays and conundramas. I'd grown bored with the diversions very quickly: they didn't seem to be a part of my life of penitence. He had commandeered the projector, but not the beads. Everything had been pulled out and stacked.

"What do you think you're doing?" I stood behind him, fists knotted, waiting for him to say something snappy.

He straightened with some difficulty, holding his ribs where I'd kicked him the night before. He turned and looked at me evenly. I was surprised: he didn't seem to hate me as much as he'd let it show the day before. He wasn't afraid of me, though I was larger and had already demonstrated that I could bash him if I wanted to bash him, or leave him alone if I chose to leave him alone. He just stared, waiting for me to get the message.

The message was that he was here for a while.

Like it or not.

"Just stay out of my way," I said. "I don't like you, and that's not going to change. I made a mistake pulling that spillweed, but I won't make any more mistakes. Keep out of my food stores, keep away from me, and don't get between me and the dromids. I've got a job to do, and you interfere...I'll weight you down, toss you in, and what the scuttlefish don't chew off is going to wash up at Icebox. You got that?"

I was just shooting off my mouth. And what was worse than my indulging in the same irrational behavior that had already ruined my life, was that he knew I was just making a breeze. He looked at me, waited long enough so I couldn't pretend to have had my dignity scarred, and he went back to searching through the junk. I went off looking for fuxes to interrogate, but they were avoiding us that day.

By that night he'd already set up his own residence.

And the next day Amos delivered two females to me, who unhinged themselves on their eight legs in a manner that was almost sitting. And the old neuter let me know these two—he used an ekstasis image that conveyed *nubile*—would join flow with me in an effort to explain their relationship to Maternal Grandfather. It was the first voluntary act of assistance the tribe had offered in six months.

So I knew my unwelcome guest was paying for his sparse accommodations.

And later that day I found wedged into one of the extensible struts I'd used in building the wickyup, the thorny branch of an emeraldberry bush. It was festooned with fruit. Where the aborigines had found it, out there in that shattered terrain, I don't know. The berries were going bad, but I pulled them off greedily, nicking my hands on the thorns, and squeezed their sea-green juice into my mouth.

So I knew my unwelcome guest was paying for his sparse accommodations.

And we went on that way, with him lurking about and sitting talking to Amos and his tribe for hours on end, and me stumping about trying to play Laird of the Manor and getting almost nowhere trying to impart philosophical concepts to a race of creatures that listened attentively and then gave me the distinct impression that I was retarded because I didn't understand Maternal Grandfather's hungers.

Then one day he was gone. It was early in the crossover season and the hard winds were rising from off the Hotlands. I came out of the wickyup and knew I was alone. But I went to his tent and looked inside. It was empty, as I'd expected it to be. On a rise nearby, two male fuxes and an old neuter were busy patting the ground, and I strolled to them and asked where the other man was. The hunters refused to join flow with me, and continued patting the ground in some sort of ritual. The old fux scratched at his deep blue fur and told me the holy creature had gone off into the Icelands. Again.

I walked to the edge of Westspit and stared off toward the glacial wasteland. It was warmer now, but that was pure desolation out there. I could see faint trails made by his skids, but I wasn't inclined to go after him. If he wanted to kill himself, that was his business.

I felt an irrational sense of loss.

It lasted about thirty seconds; then I smiled; and went back to the old fux and tried to start up a conversation.

Eight days later the man was back.

Now he was starting to scare me.

He'd patched the heat-envelope. It was still cracked and looked on the edge of unserviceability, but he came striding out of the distance with a strong motion, the skids on his boots carrying him boldly forward till he hit the mush. Then he bent and, almost without breaking stride, pulled them off, and kept coming. Straight in toward the base camp, up Westspit. His cowl was thrown back, and he was breathing deeply, not even exerting himself much, his long, horsey face flushed from his journey. He had nearly two weeks' growth of beard and so help me he looked like one of those soldiers of fortune you see smoking clay pipes and swilling up boar piss in the spacer bars around Port Medea. Heroic. An adventurer.

He sloughed in through the mud and the suckholes filled with sargasso, and he walked straight past me to his tent and went inside, and I didn't see him for the rest of the day. But that night, as I sat outside the wickyup, letting the hard wind tell me odor tales of the Hotlands close to Argo at the top of the world, I saw Amos the Wise and two other old dromids come over the rise and go down to his tent; and I stared at them until the heroic adventurer came out and squatted with them in a circle.

They didn't move, they didn't gesticulate, they didn't do a goddamned thing; they just joined flow and passed around the impressions like a vonge-coterie passing its dream-pipe.

And the next morning I was wakened by the sound of clattering, threw on my envelope and came out to see him snapping together the segments of a jerry-rigged sledge of some kind. He'd cannibalized boot skids and tray shelves from the transport sheds and every last one of those lash-up spiders the lading crews use to tighten down cargo. It was an ugly, rickety thing, but it looked as if it would slide across ice once he was out of the mush.

Then it dawned on me he was planning to take all that out there into the Icelands. "Hold it, mister," I said. He didn't stop working. I strode over and gave him a kick in the hip. "I said: hold it!"

With his right hand he reached out, grabbed my left ankle, and *lifted*. I half-turned, found myself off the ground, and when I looked up I was two meters away, the breath pulled out of me; on my back. He was still working, his back to me.

I got up and ran at him. I don't recall seeing him look up, but he must have, otherwise how could he have gauged my trajectory?

When I stopped gasping and spitting out dirt, I tried to turn over and sit up, but there was a foot in my back. I thought it was him, but when the pressure eased and I could look over my shoulder I saw the blue-furred shape of a hunter fux standing there, a spear in his sinewy left hand. It wasn't aimed at me, but it was held away in a direct line that led back to aiming at me. Don't mess with the holy man, that was the message.

An hour later he pulled the sledge with three spiders wrapped around his chest and dragged it off behind him, down the land-bridge and out into the mush. He was leaning forward, straining to keep the travois from sinking into the porridge till he could hit firmer ice. He was one of those old holograms you see of a coolie in the fields, pulling a plow by straps attached to a leather band around his head.

He went away and I wasn't stupid enough to think he was going for good and all. That was an *empty* sledge.

What would be on it when he came back?

• • •

It was a thick, segmented tube a meter and a half long. He'd chipped away most of the ice in which it had lain for twenty years, and I knew what it was, and where it had come from, which was more than I could say about him.

It was a core laser off the downed *Daedalus* power satellite whose orbit had decayed inexplicably two years after the Northcape Power District had tossed the satellite up. It had been designed to calve into bergs the glaciers that had gotten too close to coastal settlements; and then melt them. It had gone down in the Icelands of Phykos, somewhere between the East Pole and Icebox, almost exactly two decades ago. I'd flown over it when they'd hauled me in from Enrique and the bush pilot decided to give me a little scenic tour. We'd looked down on the wreckage, now part of a complex ice sculpture molded by wind and storm.

And this nameless skujge who'd invaded my privacy had gone out there, somehow chonked loose the beamer—and its power collector, if I was right about the fat package at the end of the tube—and dragged it back who knows how many kilometers...for why?

Two hours later I found him down one of the access hatches that led to the base camp's power station, a fusion plant, deuterium source; a tank that had to be replenished every sixteen months: I didn't have a refinery.

He was examining the power beamers that supplied heat and electricity to the camp. I couldn't figure out what he was trying to do, but I got skewed over it and yelled at him to get his carcass out of there before we both froze to death because of his stupidity.

After a while he came up and sealed the hatch and went off to tinker with his junk laser.

I tried to stay away from him in the weeks that followed. He worked over the laser, stealing bits and pieces of anything nonessential that he could find around the camp. It became obvious that though the lacy solar-collector screens had slowed the *Daedalus's* fall as they'd been burned off, not even that had saved the beamer from serious damage. I had no idea why he was tinkering with it, but I fantasized that if he could get it working he might go off and not come back.

And that would leave me right where I'd started, alone with creatures who did not paint pictures or sing songs or devise dances or make idols; to whom the concept of art was unknown; who responded to my attempts to communicate on an esthetic level with the stolid indifference of grandchildren forced to humor a batty old aunt.

It was penitence indeed.

Then one day he was finished. He loaded it all on the sledge—the laser, some kind of makeshift energy receiver package he'd mated to the original tube, my hologram projector, and spider straps and harnesses, and a strut tripod—and he crawled down into the access hatch and stayed there for an hour. When he came back out he spoke to Amos, who had arrived as if silently summoned, and when he was done talking to him he got into his coolie rig and slowly dragged it all away. I started to follow, just to see where he was going, but Amos stopped me. He stepped in front of me and he had ekstasis with me and I was advised not to annoy the holy man and not to bother the new connections that had been made in the camp's power source.

None of that was said, of course. It was all vague feelings and imperfect images. Hunches, impressions, thin suggestions, intuitive urgings. But I got the message. I was all alone on Meditation Island, there by sufferance of the dromids. As long as I did not interfere with the holy adventurer who had come out of nowhere to fill me with the rage I'd fled across the stars to escape.

So I turned away from the Icelands, good riddance, and tried to make some sense out of the uselessness of my life. Whoever he had been, I knew he wasn't coming back, and I hated him for making me understand what a waste of time I was.

That night I had a frustrating conversation with a turquoise fux in its female mode. The next day I shaved off my beard and thought about going back.

He came and went eleven times in the next two years. Where and how he lived out there, I never knew. And each time he came back he looked thinner, wearier, but more ecstatic. As if he had found God out there. During the first year the fuxes began making the trek: out there in the shadowed vastness of the Icelands they would travel to see him. They would be gone for days and then return to speak among themselves. I asked Amos what they did when they made their hegira, and he said, through ekstasis, "He must live, is that not so?" To which I responded, "I suppose so," though I wanted to say, "Not necessarily."

He returned once to obtain a new heat-envelope. I'd had supplies dropped in, and they'd sent me a latest model, so I didn't object when he took my old suit.

He returned once for the death ceremony of Amos the Wise, and seemed to be leading the service. I stood there in the circle and said nothing, because no one asked me to contribute.

He returned once to check the fusion plant connections.

But after two years he didn't return again.

And now the dromids were coming from what must have been far distances, to trek across Meditation Island, off the land-bridge, and into the Icelands. By the hundreds and finally thousands they came, passed me, and vanished into the eternal winterland. Until the day a group of them came to me; and their leader, whose name was Ben of the Old Times, joined with me in the flow and said, "Come with us to the holy man." They'd always stopped me when I tried to go out there.

"Why? Why do you want me to go now? You never wanted me out there before." I could feel the acid boiling up in my anger, the tightening of my chest muscles, the clenching of my fists. They could burn in Argo before I'd visit that lousy skujge!

Then the old fux did something that astonished me. In three years they had done *nothing* astonishing except bring me food at the man's request. But now the aborigine extended a slim-fingered hand to his right; and one of the males, a big hunter with bright-blue fur, passed him his spear. Ben of the Old Times pointed it at the ground and, with a very few strokes, *drew two figures in the caked mud at my feet.*

It was a drawing of two humans standing side-by side, their hands linked. One of them had lines radiating out from his head, and above the figures the dromid drew a circle with comparable lines radiating outward.

It was the first piece of intentional art I had ever seen created by a Medean life form. The first, as far as I knew, that had ever *been* created by a native. And it had happened as I watched. My heart beat faster. I *had* done it! I had brought the concept of art to at least one of these creatures.

"I'll come with you to see him," I said.

Perhaps my time in purgatory was coming to an end. It was possible I'd bought some measure of redemption.

• • •

I checked the fusion plant that beamed energy to my heat-envelope, to keep me from freezing; and I got out my boot skids and Ba'al ice-claw; and I racked the ration dispenser in my pack full of silvr wrap; and I followed them out there. Where I had not been permitted to venture, lest I interfere with their holy man. Well, we'd see who was the more important of us two: a nameless intruder who came and went without ever a thank you, or William Ronald Pogue, the man who brought art to the Medeans!

For the first time in many years I felt light, airy, worthy. I'd sprayed fixative on that pictograph in the mud. It might be the most valuable exhibit in the Pogue Museum of Native Art. I chuckled at my foolishness, and followed the small band of fuxes deeper into the Icelands.

It was close on crossback season, and the winds were getting harder, the storms were getting nastier. Not as impossible as it would be a month hence, but bad enough.

We were beyond the first glacier that could be seen from Meditation Island, the spine of ice cartographers had named the Seurat. Now we were climbing through the NoName Cleft, the fuxes chinking out hand- and footholds with spears and claws, the Ba'al snarling and chewing pits for my own ascent. Green shadows swam down through the Cleft. One moment we were pulling ourselves up through twilight, and the next we could not see the shape before us. For an hour we lay flat against the ice face as a hysterical wind raged down the Cleft, trying to tear us loose and fling us into the cut below.

The double shadows flickered and danced around us. Then everything went into the red, the wind died, and through now-bloody shadows we reached the crest of the ridge beyond the Seurats.

A long slope lay before us, rolling to a plain of ice and slush pools, very different from the fields of dry ice that lay farther west to the lifeless expanse of Farside. Sunday was rapidly moving into Darkday.

Across the plain, vision was impeded by a great wall of frigid fog that rose off the tundra. Vaguely, through the miasma, I could see the great glimmering bulk of the Rio de Luz, the immense kilometers-long ice mountain that was the final barrier between the Terminator lands and the frozen nothingness of Farside. The River of Light.

We hurried down the slope, some of the fuxes simply tucking two, four, or six of their legs under them and sliding down the expanse to the plain. Twice I fell, rolled, slid on my butt, tried to regain my feet, tumbled again and decided to use my pack as a toboggan. By the time we had gained the plain, it was nearly Darkday and fog had obscured the land. We decided to camp till Dimday, hacked out sleeping pits in the tundra, and buried ourselves.

Overhead the raging aurora drained red and green and purple as I closed my eyes and let the heat of the envelope take me away. What could the "holy man" want from me after all this time?

We came through the curtain of fog, the Rio de Luz scintillating dimly beyond its mask of gray-green vapor. I estimated that we had come more than thirty kilometers from Meditation Island. It was appreciably colder now, and ice crystals glimmered like rubies and emeralds in the blue fux fur. And, oddly, a kind of breathless anticipation had come over the aborigines. They moved more rapidly, oblivious to the razor winds and the slush pools underfoot. They jostled one another in their need to go toward the River of Light and whatever the man out there needed me to assist with.

It was a long walk, and for much of that time I could see little more of the icewall than its cruel shape rising at least fifteen hundred meters above the tundra. But as the fog thinned, the closer we drew to the base of the ice mountain, the more I had to avert my eyes from what lay ahead: the permanent aurora lit the ice and threw off a coruscating glare that was impossible to bear.

And then the fuxes dashed on ahead and I was left alone, striding across the tundra toward the Rio de Luz.

I came out of the fog.

And I looked up and up at what rose above me, touching the angry sky and stretching as far away as I could see to left and right. It seemed hundreds of kilometers in length, but that was impossible.

I heard myself moaning.

But I could not look away, even if it burned out my eyes.

Lit by the ever-changing curtain of Medea's sky, the crash and downdripping of a thousand colors that washed the ice in patterns that altered from instant to instant, the Rio de Luz had been transformed. The man had spent three years melting and slicing and sculpting—I couldn't tell how many kilometers of living ice—into a work of high art.

Horses of liquid blood raced through valleys of silver light. The stars were born and breathed and died in one lacy spire. Shards of amber brilliance shattered against a diamond-faceted icewall through a thousand apertures cut in the facing column. Fairy towers too thin to exist rose from a shadowed hollow and changed color from meter to meter all up their length. Legions of rainbows rushed from peak to peak, like waterfalls of precious gems. Shapes and forms and spaces merged and grew and vanished as the eye was drawn on and on. In a cleft he had formed an intaglio that was black and ominous as the specter of death. But when light hit it suddenly, shattering and spilling down into the bowl beneath, it became a great bird of golden promise. And the sky was there, too. All of it, reflected back and new because it had been pulled down and captured. Argo and the far suns and Phrixus and Helle and Jason and Theseus and memories of suns that had dominated the empty places and were no longer even memories. I had a dream of times past as I stared at one pool of changing colors that bubbled and sang. My heart was filled with feelings I had not known since childhood. And it never stopped. The pinpoints of bright blue flame skittered across the undulating walls of sculpted ice, rushed toward certain destruction in the deeps of a runoff cut, paused momentarily at the brink, then flung themselves into green oblivion. I heard myself moaning and turned away, looking back toward the ridge across the fog and tundra; and I saw nothing, nothing! It was too painful not to see what he had done. I felt my throat tighten with fear of missing a moment of that great pageant unfolding on the ice tapestry. I turned back and it was all new, I was seeing it first and always as I had just minutes before…was it minutes…how long had I been staring into that dream pool…how many years had passed… and would I be fortunate enough to spend the remainder of my life just standing there breathing in the rampaging beauty I beheld? I couldn't think, pulled air into my lungs only when I had forgotten to breathe for too long a time.

Then I felt myself being pulled along and cried out against whatever force had me in its grip that would deprive me of a second of that towering narcotic.

But I was pulled away, and was brought down to the base of the River of Light, and it was Ben of the Old Times who had me. He forced me to sit, with my back to the mountain, and after a very long time in which I sobbed and fought for air, I was able to understand that I had almost been lost, that the dreamplace had taken me. But I felt no gratitude. My soul ached to rush out and stare up at beauty forever.

The fux flowed with me, and through ekstasis I felt myself ceasing to pitch and yaw. The colors dimmed in the grottos behind my eyes. He held me silently with a powerful flow until I was William Pogue again. Not just an instrument through which the ice mountain sang its song, but Pogue, once again Pogue.

And I looked up, and I saw the fuxes hunkered around the body of their "holy man," and they were making drawings in the ice with their claws. And I knew it was not I who had brought them to beauty.

He lay face-down on the ice, one hand still touching the laser tube. The hologram projector had been attached with a slipcard computer. Still glowing was an image of the total sculpture. Almost all of it was in red lines, flickering and fading and coming back in with power being fed from base camp; but one small section near the top of an impossibly angled flying bridge and minaret section was in blue line.

I stared at it for a while. Then Ben said this was the reason I had been brought to that place. The holy man had died before he could complete the dreamplace. And in a rush of flow he showed me where, in the sculpture, they had first understood what beauty was, and what art was, and how they were one with the Grandparents in the sky. Then he created a clear, pure image. It was the man, flying to become one with Argo. It was the stick figure in the mud: it was the uninvited guest with the lines of radiance coming out of his head.

There was a pleading tone in the fux's ekstasis. Do this for us. Do what he did not have the time to do. Make it complete.

I stared at the laser lying there, with its unfinished hologram image blue and red and flickering. It was a bulky, heavy tube, a meter and a half long. And it was still on. He had fallen in the act.

I watched them scratching their first drawings, even the least of them, and I wept within myself; for Pogue who had come as far as he could, only to discover it was not far enough. And I hated him for doing what I could not do. And I knew he would have completed it and then walked off into the emptiness of Farside, to die quickly in the darkness, having done his penance…and more.

They stopped scratching, as if Ben had ordered them to pay some belated attention to me. They looked at me with their slanted vulpine eyes now filling with mischief and wonder. I stared back at them. Why should I? Why the hell should I? For what? Not for me, that's certain!

We sat there close and apart, for a long time, as the universe sent its best light to pay homage to the dreamplace.

The body of the penitent lay at my feet.

From time to time I scuffed at the harness that would hold the laser in position for cutting. There was blood on the shoulder straps.

After a while I stood up and lifted the rig. It was much heavier than I'd expected.

Now they come from everywhere to see it. Now they call it Oddum's Tapestry, not the Rio de Luz. Now everyone speaks of the magic. A long time ago he may have caused the death of thousands in another place, but they say that wasn't intentional; what he brought to the Medeans was on purpose. So it's probably right that everyone knows the name Virgil Oddum, and what he created at the East Pole.

But they should know me, too. I was there! I did some of the work.

My name is William Ronald Pogue, and I mattered. I'm old, but I'm important, too. You should know names.

Dedicated to the genius of Simon Rodia
Creator of the Watts Towers

SOFT MONKEY

1988 Edgar Allan Poe Award: Best Short Story

AT TWENTY-FIVE MINUTES past midnight on 51st Street, the wind-chill factor was so sharp it could carve you a new asshole.

Annie lay huddled in the tiny space, formed by the wedge of locked revolving door that was open to the street when the document copying service had closed for the night. She had pulled the shopping cart from the Food Emporium at 1st Avenue near 57th into the mouth of the revolving door, had carefully tipped it onto its side, making certain her goods were jammed tightly in the cart, making certain nothing spilled into her sleeping space. She had pulled out half a dozen cardboard flats—broken-down sections of big Kotex cartons from the Food Emporium, the half dozen she had not sold to the junkman that afternoon—and she had fronted the shopping cart with two of them, making it appear the doorway was blocked by the management. She had wedged the others around the edges of the space, cutting the wind, and placed the two rotting sofa pillows behind and under her.

She had settled down, bundled in her three topcoats, the thick woolen merchant marine stocking cap rolled down to cover her ears, almost to the bridge of her broken nose. It wasn't bad in the doorway, quite cozy, really. The wind shrieked past and occasionally touched her, but mostly was deflected. She lay huddled in the tiny space, pulled out the filthy remnants of a stuffed baby doll, cradled it under her chin, and closed her eyes.

She slipped into a wary sleep, half in reverie and yet alert to the sounds of the street. She tried to dream of the child again. Alan. In the waking dream she held him as she held the baby doll, close under her chin, her eyes closed, feeling the warmth of his body. That was important: his body was warm, his little brown hand against her cheek, his warm, warm breath drifting up with the dear smell of baby.

Was that just today or some other day? Annie swayed in reverie, kissing the broken face of the baby doll. It was nice in the doorway; it was warm.

The normal street sounds lulled her for another moment, and then were shattered as two cars careened around the corner off Park Avenue, racing toward Madison. Even asleep, Annie sensed when the street wasn't right. It was a sixth sense she had learned to trust after the first time she had been mugged for her shoes and the small change in her snap-purse. Now she came fully awake as the sounds of trouble rushed toward her doorway. She hid the baby doll inside her coat.

The stretch limo sideswiped the Caddy as they came abreast of the closed repro center. The Brougham ran up over the curb and hit the light stanchion full in the grille. The door on the passenger side fell open and a man scrabbled across the front seat, dropped to all fours on the sidewalk, and tried to crawl away. The stretch limo, angled in toward the curb, slammed to a stop in front of the Brougham, and three doors opened before the tires stopped rolling.

They grabbed him as he tried to stand, and forced him back to his knees. One of the limo's occupants wore a fine navy blue cashmere overcoat; he pulled it open and reached to his hip. His hand came out holding a revolver. With a smooth stroke he laid it across the kneeling man's forehead, opening him to the bone.

Annie saw it all. With poisonous clarity, back in the V of the revolving door, cuddled in darkness, she saw it all. Saw a second man kick out and break the kneeling victim's nose. The sound of it cut against the night's sudden silence. Saw the third man look toward the stretch limo as a black glass window slid down and a hand emerged from the back seat. The electric hum of opening. Saw the third man go to the stretch and take from the extended hand a metal can. A siren screamed down Park Avenue, and kept going. Saw him return to the group and heard him say, "Hold the motherfucker. Pull his head back!" Saw the other two wrench the victim's head back, gleaming white and pumping red from the broken nose, clear in the sulfurous light from the stanchion overhead. The man's shoes scraped and scraped the sidewalk. Saw the third man reach into an outer coat pocket and pull out a pint of scotch. Saw him unscrew the cap and begin to pour booze into the face of the victim. "Hold his mouth open!" Saw the man in the cashmere topcoat spike his thumb and index fingers into the hinges of the victim's jaws, forcing his mouth open. The sound of gagging, the glow of spittle. Saw the scotch spilling down the man's front. Saw the third man toss the pint bottle into the gutter where it shattered; and saw him thumb press the center of the plastic cap of the metal can; and saw him make the cringing, crying, wailing victim drink the Drano. Annie saw and heard it all.

The cashmere topcoat forced the victim's mouth closed, massaged his throat, made him swallow the Drano. The dying took a lot longer than expected. And it was a lot noisier.

The victim's mouth was glowing a strange blue in the calcium light from overhead. He tried spitting, and a gobbet hit the navy blue cashmere sleeve. Had the natty dresser from the stretch limo been a dunky slob uncaring of what *GQ* commanded, what happened next would not have gone down.

Cashmere cursed, swiped at the slimed sleeve, let go of the victim; the man with the glowing blue mouth and the gut being boiled away wrenched free of the other two, and threw himself forward. Straight toward the locked revolving door blocked by Annie's shopping cart and cardboard flats.

He came at her in fumbling, hurtling steps, arms wide and eyes rolling, throwing spittle like a racehorse; Annie realized he'd fall across the cart and smash her flat in another two steps.

She stood up, backing to the side of the V. She stood up: into the tunnel of light from the Caddy's headlights.

"The nigger saw it all!" yelled the cashmere.

"Fuckin' bag lady!" yelled the one with the can of Drano.

"He's still moving!" yelled the third man, reaching inside his topcoat and coming out of his armpit with a blued steel thing that seemed to extrude to a length more aptly suited to Paul Bunyan's armpit.

Foaming at the mouth, hands clawing at his throat, the driver of the Brougham came at Annie as if he were spring-loaded.

He hit the shopping cart with his thighs just as the man with the long armpit squeezed off his first shot. The sound of the .45 magnum tore a chunk out of 51st Street, blew through the running man like a crowd roar, took off his face and spattered bone and blood across the panes of the revolving door. It sparkled in the tunnel of light from the Caddy's headlights.

And somehow he kept coming. He hit the cart, rose as if trying to get a first down against a solid defense line, and came apart as the shooter hit him with a second round.

There wasn't enough solid matter to stop the bullet and it exploded through the revolving door, shattering it open as the body crashed through and hit Annie.

She was thrown backward, through the broken glass, and onto the floor of the document copying center. And through it all, Annie heard a fourth voice, clearly a fourth voice, screaming from the stretch limo, "Get the old lady! Get her, she saw everything!"

Men in topcoats rushed through the tunnel of light.

Annie rolled over, and her hand touched something soft. It was the ruined baby doll. It had been knocked loose from her bundled clothing. *Are you cold, Alan?*

She scooped up the doll and crawled away, into the shadows of the reproduction center. Behind her, crashing through the frame of the revolving door, she heard men coming. And the sound of a burglar alarm. Soon police would be here.

All she could think about was that they would throw away her goods. They would waste her good cardboard, they would take back her shopping cart, they would toss her pillows and the hankies and the green cardigan into some trashcan; and she would be empty on the street again. As she had been when they made her move out of the room at 101st and First Avenue. After they took Alan from her...

A blast of sound, as the shot shattered a glass-framed citation on the wall near her. They had fanned out inside the office space, letting the headlight illumination shine through. Clutching the baby doll, she hustled down a hallway toward the rear of the copy center. Doors on both sides, all of them closed and locked. Annie could hear them coming.

A pair of metal doors stood open on the right. It was dark in there. She slipped inside, and in an instant her eyes had grown acclimated. There were computers here, big crackle-gray-finish machines that lined three walls. Nowhere to hide.

She rushed around the room, looking for a closet, a cubbyhole, anything. Then she stumbled over something and sprawled across the cold floor. Her face hung over into emptiness, and the very faintest of cool breezes struck her cheeks. The floor was composed of large removable squares. One of them had been lifted and replaced, but not flush. It had not been locked down; an edge had been left ajar; she had kicked it open.

She reached down. There was a crawlspace under the floor.

Pulling the metal-rimmed vinyl plate, she slid into the empty square. Lying face-up, she pulled the square over the aperture, and nudged it gently till it dropped onto its tracks. It sat flush. She could see nothing where, a moment before, there had been the faintest scintilla of filtered light from the hallway. Annie lay very quietly, emptying her mind as she did when she slept in the doorways; making herself invisible. A mound of rags. A pile of refuse. Gone. Only the warmth of the baby doll in that empty place with her.

She heard the men crashing down the corridor, trying doors. *I wrapped you in blankets, Alan. You must be warm.* They came into the computer room. The room was empty, they could see that.

"She *has* to be here, dammit!"

"There's gotta be a way out we didn't see."

"Maybe she locked herself in one of those rooms. Should we try? Break 'em open?"

"Don't be a bigger asshole than usual. Can't you hear that alarm? We gotta get out of here!"

"He'll break our balls."

"Like hell. Would he do anything else than we've done? He's sittin' on the street in front of what's left of Beaddie. You think he's happy about it?"

There was a new sound to match the alarm. The honking of a horn from the street. It went on and on, hysterically.

"We'll find her."

Then the sound of footsteps. Then running.

Annie lay empty and silent, holding the doll.

It was warm, as warm as she had been all November. She slept there through the night.

The next day, in the last Automat in New York with the wonderful little windows through which one could get food by insertion of a token, Annie learned of the two deaths.

Not the death of the man in the revolving door; the deaths of two black women. Beaddie, who had vomited up most of his internal organs, boiled like Chesapeake Bay lobsters, was all over the front of the *Post* that Annie now wore as insulation against the biting November wind. The two women had been found in midtown alleys, their faces blown off by heavy caliber ordnance. Annie had known one of them; her name had been Sooky and Annie got the word from a good Thunderbird worshipper who stopped by her table and gave her the skinny as she carefully ate her fish cakes and tea.

She knew who they had been seeking. And she knew why they had killed Sooky and the other street person: to white men who ride in stretch limos, all old nigger bag ladies look the same. She took a slow bite of fish cake and stared out at 42nd Street, watching the world swirl past; what was she going to do about this?

They would kill and kill till there was no safe place left to sleep in midtown. She knew it. This was mob business, the *Post* inside her coats said so. And it wouldn't make any difference trying to warn the women. Where would they go? Where would they *want* to go? Not even she, knowing what it was all about…not even she would leave the area: this was where she roamed, this was her territorial imperative. And they would find her soon enough.

She nodded to the croaker who had given her the word, and after he'd hobbled away to get a cup of coffee from the spigot on the wall, she hurriedly finished her fish cake and slipped out of the Automat as easily as she had the document copying center this morning.

Being careful to keep out of sight, she returned to 51st Street. The area had been roped off, with sawhorses and green tape that said *Police Investigation—Keep Off.* But there were crowds. The streets were jammed, not only with office workers coming and going, but with loiterers who were fascinated by the scene. It took very little to gather a crowd in New York. The falling of a cornice could produce a *minyan.*

Annie could not believe her luck. She realized the police were unaware of a witness: when the men had charged the doorway, they had thrown aside her cart and goods, had spilled them back onto the sidewalk to gain entrance; and the cops had thought it was all refuse, as one with the huge brown plastic bags of trash at the curb. Her cart and the good sofa pillows, the cardboard flats and her sweaters…all of it was in the area. Some in trash cans, some amid the piles of bagged rubbish, some just lying in the gutter.

That meant she didn't need to worry about being sought from two directions. One way was bad enough.

And all the aluminum cans she had salvaged to sell, they were still in the big Bloomingdale's bag right against the wall of the building. There would be money for dinner.

She was edging out of the doorway to collect her goods when she saw the one in navy blue cashmere who had held Beaddie while they fed him Drano. He was standing three stores away, on Annie's side, watching the police lines, watching the copy center, watching the crowd. Watching for her. Picking at an ingrown hair on his chin.

She stepped back into the doorway. Behind her a voice said, "C'mon, lady, get the hell outta here, this's a place uhbizness." Then she felt a sharp poke in her spine.

She looked behind her, terrified. The owner of the haberdashery, a man wearing a bizarrely-cut gray pinstripe worsted with lapels that matched his ears, and a passion flame silk hankie spilling out of his breast pocket like a crimson afflatus, was jabbing her in the back with a wooden coat hanger. "Move it on, get moving," he said, in a tone that would have gotten his face slapped had he used it on a customer.

Annie said nothing. She *never* spoke to anyone on the street. Silence on the street. *We'll go, Alan; we're okay by ourselves. Don't cry, my baby.*

She stepped out of the doorway, trying to edge away. She heard a sharp, piercing whistle. The man in the cashmere topcoat had seen her; he was whistling and signalling up 51st Street to someone. As Annie hurried away, looking over her shoulder, she saw a dark blue Oldsmobile that had been double-parked pull forward. The cashmere topcoat was shoving through the pedestrians, coming for her like the number 5 uptown Lexington express.

Annie moved quickly, without thinking about it. Being poked in the back, and someone speaking directly to her…that was frightening: it meant coming out to respond to another human being. But moving down her streets, moving quickly, and being part of the flow, that was comfortable. She knew how to do that. It was just the way she was.

Instinctively, Annie made herself larger, more expansive, her raggedy arms away from her body, the dirty overcoats billowing, her gait more erratic: opening the way for her flight. Fastidious shoppers and suited businessmen shied away, gave a start as the dirty old black bag lady bore down on them, turned sidewise praying she would not brush a recently Martinized shoulder. The Red Sea parted miraculously permitting flight, then closed over instantly to impede navy blue cashmere. But the Olds came on quickly.

Annie turned left onto Madison, heading downtown. There was construction around 48th. There were good alleys on 46th. She knew a basement entrance just three doors off Madison on 47th. But the Olds came on quickly.

Behind her, the light changed. The Olds tried to rush the intersection, but this was Madison. Crowds were already crossing. The Olds stopped, the driver's window rolled down and a face peered out. Eyes tracked Annie's progress.

Then it began to rain.

Like black mushrooms sprouting instantly from concrete, Totes blossomed on the sidewalk. The speed of the flowing river of pedestrians increased; and in an instant Annie was gone. Cashmere rounded the corner, looked at the Olds, a frantic arm motioned to the left, and the man pulled up his collar and elbowed his way through the crowd, rushing down Madison.

Low places in the sidewalk had already filled with water. His wingtip cordovans were quickly soaked.

He saw her turn into the alley behind the novelty sales shop *(Nothing over $1.10!!!)*; he *saw* her; turned right and ducked in fast; *saw* her, even through the rain and the crowd and half a block between them; *saw* it!

So where was she?

The alley was empty.

It was a short space, all-brick, only deep enough for a big Dempsey Dumpster and a couple of dozen trash cans; the usual mounds of rubbish in the corners; no fire escape ladders low enough for an old bag lady to grab; no loading docks, no doorways that looked even remotely accessible, everything cemented over or faced with sheet steel; no basement entrances with concrete steps leading down; no manholes in the middle of the passage; no open windows or even broken windows at jumping height; no stacks of crates to hide behind.

The alley was empty.

Saw her come in here. *Knew* she had come in here, and couldn't get out. He'd been watching closely as he ran to the mouth of the alley. She was in here somewhere. Not too hard figuring out where. He took out the .38 Police Positive he liked to carry because he lived with the delusion that if he had to dump it, if it were used in the commission of a sort of kind of felony, he couldn't get snowed on, and if it were traced, it would trace back to the cop in Teaneck, New Jersey, from whom it had been lifted as he lay drunk in the back room of a Polish social club three years earlier.

He swore he would take his time with her, this filthy old porch monkey. His navy blue cashmere already smelled like soaked dog. And the rain was not about to let up; it now came sheeting down, traveling in a curtain through the alley.

He moved deeper into the darkness, kicking the piles of trash, making sure the refuse bins were full. She was in here somewhere. Not too hard figuring out where.

Warm. Annie felt warm. With the ruined baby doll under her chin, and her eyes closed, it was almost like the apartment at 101st and First Avenue, when the Human Resources lady came and tried to tell her strange things about Alan. Annie had not understood what the woman meant when she kept repeating *soft monkey, soft monkey,* a thing some scientist knew. It had made no sense to Annie, and she had continued rocking the baby.

Annie remained very still where she had hidden. Basking in the warmth. *Is it nice, Alan? Are we toasty; yes, we are. Will we be very still and the lady from the City will go away? Yes, we will.* She heard the crash of a garbage can being kicked over. *No one will find us. Shh, my baby.*

There was a pile of wooden slats that had been leaned against a wall. As he approached, the gun leveled, he realized they obscured a doorway. She was back in there, he knew it. Had to be. Not too hard figuring that out. It was the only place she could have hidden.

He moved in quickly, slammed the boards aside, and threw down on the dark opening. It was empty. Steel-plate door, locked.

Rain ran down his face, plastering his hair to his forehead. He could smell his coat, and his shoes, oh god, don't ask. He turned and looked. All that remained was the huge dumpster.

He approached it carefully, and noticed: the lid was still dry near the back side closest to the wall. The lid had been open just a short time ago. Someone had just lowered it.

He pocketed the gun, dragged two crates from the heap thrown down beside the Dempsey, and crawled up onto them. Now he stood above the dumpster, balancing on the crates with his knees at the level of the lid. With both hands bracing him, he leaned over to get his fingertips under the heavy lid. He flung the lid open, yanked out the gun, and leaned over. The dumpster was nearly full. Rain had turned the muck and garbage into a swimming porridge. He leaned over precariously to see what floated there in the murk. He leaned in to see. *Fuckin' porch monk—*

As a pair of redolent, dripping arms came up out of the muck, grasped his navy blue cashmere lapels, and dragged him headfirst into the metal bin. He went down, into the slime, the gun going off, the shot spanging off the raised metal lid. The coat filled with garbage and water.

Annie felt him struggling beneath her. She held him down, her feet on his neck and back, pressing him face-first deeper into the goo that filled the bin. She could hear him breathing garbage and fetid water. He thrashed, a big man, struggling to get out from under. She slipped, and braced herself against the side of the dumpster, regained her footing, and drove him deeper. A hand clawed out of the refuse, dripping lettuce and black slime. The hand was empty. The gun lay at the bottom of the bin. The thrashing intensified, his feet hitting the metal side of the container. Annie rose up and dropped her feet heavily on the back of his neck. He went flat beneath her, trying to swim up, unable to find purchase.

He grabbed her foot as an explosion of breath from down below forced a bubble of air to break on the surface. Annie stomped as hard as she could. Something snapped beneath her shoe, but she heard nothing.

It went on for a long time, for a time longer than Annie could think about. The rain filled the bin to overflowing. Movement under her feet lessened, then there was hysterical movement for an instant, then it was calm. She stood there for an even longer time, trembling and trying to remember other, warmer times.

Finally, she closed herself off, buttoned up tightly, climbed out dripping and went away from there, thinking of Alan, thinking of a time after this was done. After that long time standing there, no movement, no movement at all in the bog beneath her waist. She did not close the lid.

When she emerged from the alley, after hiding in the shadows and watching, the Oldsmobile was nowhere in sight. The foot traffic parted for her. The smell, the dripping filth, the frightened face, the ruined thing she held close to her.

She stumbled out onto the sidewalk, lost for a moment, then turned the right way and shuffled off.

The rain continued its march across the city.

No one tried to stop her as she gathered her goods on 51st Street. The police thought she was a scavenger, the gawkers tried to avoid being brushed by her, the owner of the document copying center was relieved to see the filth cleaned up. Annie rescued everything she could, and hobbled away, hoping to be able to sell her aluminum for a place to dry out. It was not true that she was dirty; she had always been fastidious, even in the streets. A certain level of dishevelment was acceptable, but this was unclean.

And the blasted baby doll needed to be dried and brushed clean. There was a woman on East 60th, near Second Avenue; a vegetarian who spoke with an accent; a white lady who sometimes let Annie sleep in the basement. She would ask her for a favor.

It was not a very big favor, but the white woman was not home; and that night Annie slept in the construction of the new Zeckendorf Towers, where S. Klein-On-The-Square used to be, down on 14th and Broadway.

The men from the stretch limo didn't find her again for almost a week.

She was salvaging newspapers from a wire basket on Madison near 44th when he grabbed her from behind. It was the one who had poured the liquor into Beaddie, and then made him drink the Drano. He threw an arm around her, pulled her around to face him, and she reacted instantly, the way she did when the kids tried to take her snap-purse.

She butted him full in the face with the top of her head, and drove him backward with both filthy hands. He stumbled into the street, and a cab swerved at the last instant to avoid running him down. He stood in the street, shaking his head, as Annie careened down 44th, looking for a place to hide. She was sorry she had left her cart again. This time, she knew, her goods weren't going to be there.

It was the day before Thanksgiving.

Four more black women had been found dead in midtown doorways.

Annie ran, the only way she knew how, into stores that had exits on other streets. Somewhere behind her, though she could not figure it out properly, there was trouble coming for her and the baby. It was so cold in the apartment. It was always so cold. The landlord cut off the heat, he always did it in early November, till the snow came. And she sat with the child, rocking him, trying to comfort him, trying to keep him warm. And when they came from Human Resources, from the City, to evict her, they found her still holding the child. When they took it away from her, so still and blue, Annie ran from them, into the streets; and she ran, she knew how to run, to keep running so she could live out here where they couldn't reach her and Alan. But she knew there was trouble behind her.

Now she came to an open place. She knew this. It was a new building they had put up, a new skyscraper, where there used to be shops that had good throwaway things in the cans and sometimes on the loading docks. It said Citicorp Mall and she ran inside. It was the day before Thanksgiving and there were many decorations. Annie rushed through into the central atrium, and looked around. There were escalators, and she dashed for one, climbing to a second storey, and then a third. She kept moving. They would arrest her or throw her out if she slowed down.

At the railing, looking over, she saw the man in the court below. He didn't see her. He was standing, looking around.

Stories of mothers who lift wrecked cars off their children are legion.

When the police arrived, eyewitnesses swore it had been a stout, old black woman who had lifted the heavy potted tree in its terra-cotta urn, who had manhandled it up onto the railing and slid it along till she was standing above the poor dead man, and who had dropped it three storeys to crush his skull. They swore it was true, but beyond a vague description of old, black, and dissolute looking, they could not be of assistance. Annie was gone.

On the front page of the *Post* she wore as lining in her right shoe, was a photo of four men who had been arraigned for the senseless murders of more than a dozen bag ladies over a period of several months. Annie did not read the article.

It was close to Christmas, and the weather had turned bitter, too bitter to believe. She lay propped in the doorway alcove of the Post Office on 43rd and Lexington. Her rug was drawn around her, the stocking cap pulled down to the bridge of her nose, the goods in the string bags around and under her. Snow was just beginning to come down.

A man in a Burberry and an elegant woman in a mink approached from 42nd Street, on their way to dinner. They were staying at the New

York Helmsley. They were from Connecticut, in for three days to catch the shows and to celebrate their eleventh wedding anniversary.

As they came abreast of her, the man stopped and stared down into the doorway. "Oh, Christ, that's awful," he said to his wife. "On a night like this, Christ, that's just awful."

"Dennis, *please!*" the woman said.

"I can't just pass her by," he said. He pulled off a kid glove and reached into his pocket for his money clip.

"Dennis, they don't like to be bothered," the woman said, trying to pull him away. "They're very self-sufficient. Don't you remember that piece in the *Times*?"

"It's damned near Christmas, Lori," he said, taking a twenty dollar bill from the folded sheaf held by its clip. "It'll get her a bed for the night, at least. They can't make it out here by themselves. God knows, it's little enough to do." He pulled free of his wife's grasp and walked to the alcove.

He looked down at the woman swathed in the rug, and he could not see her face. Small puffs of breath were all that told him she was alive. "Ma'am," he said, leaning forward. "Ma'am, please take this." He held out the twenty.

Annie did not move. She never spoke on the street.

"Ma'am, please, let me do this. Go somewhere warm for the night, won't you...please?"

He stood for another minute, seeking to rouse her, at least for a *go away* that would free him, but the old woman did not move. Finally, he placed the twenty on what he presumed to be her lap, there in that shapeless mass, and allowed himself to be dragged away by his wife.

Three hours later, having completed a lovely dinner, and having decided it would be romantic to walk back to the Helmsley through the six inches of snow that had fallen, they passed the Post Office and saw the old woman had not moved. Nor had she taken the twenty dollars. He could not bring himself to look beneath the wrappings to see if she had frozen to death, and he had no intention of taking back the money. They walked on.

In her warm place, Annie held Alan close up under her chin, stroking him and feeling his tiny black fingers warm at her throat and cheeks. *It's all right, baby, it's all right. We're safe. Shhh, my baby. No one can hurt you.*

• • •

Psychologists specializing in ethology know of the soft monkey experiment. A mother orangutan, whose baby has died, given a plush toy doll, will nurture it as if it were alive, as if it were her own. Nurture and protect and savage any creature that menaces the surrogate. Given a wire image, or a ceramic doll, the mother will ignore it. She must have the soft monkey. It sustains her.

EIDOLONS

1989 Locus Poll Award: Best Short Story

EIDOLON:
a phantom, an apparition, an image.

ANCIENT GEOGRAPHERS GAVE a mystic significance to that extremity of land, the borderland of the watery unknown at the southwestern tip of Europe. Marinus and Ptolemy knew it as *Promontorium Sacrum*, the sacred promontory. Beyond that beyondmost edge, lay nothing. Or rather, lay a place that was fearful and unknowable, a place in which it was always the twenty-fifth hour of the day, the thirtieth or thirty-first of February; a turbid ocean of lost islands where golden mushroom trees reached always toward the whispering face of the moon; where tricksy life had spawned beasts and beings more of satin and ash than of man and woman; dominion of dreams, to which the unwary might journey, but whence they could never return.

My name is Vizinczey, and my background is too remarkable to be detailed here. Suffice to note that before Mr. Brown died in my arms, I had distinguished myself principally with occupations and behavior most cultures reward by the attentions of the headsman and the *strappado*. Suffice to note that before Mr. Brown died in my arms, the most laudable engagement in my *vita* was as the manager and sole roustabout of an abattoir and ossuary in Li Shih-min. Suffice to note that there were entire continents I was forbidden to visit, and that even my closest acquaintances, the family of Sawney Beane, chose to avoid social intercourse with me.

I was a pariah. Whatever land in which I chose to abide, became a land of darkness. Until Mr. Brown died in my arms, I was a thing without passion, without kindness.

While in Sydney—Australia being one of the three remaining continents where hunting dogs would not be turned out to track me down—I inquired if there might be a shop where authentic military miniatures, toy soldiers of the sort H. G. Wells treasured, could be purchased. A clerk in a bookstore recalled "a customer of mine in Special Orders mentioned something like that…a curious little man…a Mr. Brown."

I got onto him, through the clerk, and was sent round to see him at his home. The moment he opened the door and our eyes met, he was frightened of me. For the brief time we spent in each other's company, he never ceased, for a moment, to fear me. Ironically, he was one of the few ambulatory creatures on this planet that I meant no harm. Toy soldiers were my hobby, and I held in high esteem those who crafted, painted, amassed or sold them. In truth, it might be said of the Vizinczey that was I in those times before Mr. Brown died in my arms, that my approbation for toy soldiers and their aficionados was the sole salutary aspect of my nature. So, you see, he had no reason to fear me. Quite the contrary. I mention this to establish, in spite of the police records and the warrants still in existence, seeking my apprehension, I had nothing whatever to do with the death of Mr. Brown.

He did not invite me in, though he stepped aside with a tremor and permitted entrance. Cognizant of his terror at my presence, I was surprised that he locked the door behind me. Then, looking back over his shoulder at me with mounting fear, he led me into an enormous central drawing room of his home, a room expanded to inordinate size by the leveling of walls that had formed adjoining areas. In that room, on every horizontal surface, Mr. Brown had positioned rank after rank of the most astonishing military miniatures I had ever seen.

Perfect in the most minute detail, painted so artfully that I could discern no brushstroke, in colors and tones and hues so accurate and lifelike that they seemed rather to have been created with pigmentations inherent, the battalions, cohorts, regiments, legions, phalanxes, brigades and squads of metal figurines blanketed in array without a single empty space, every inch of floor, tables, cabinets, shelves, window ledges, risers, showcases and countless numbers of stacked display boxes.

Enthralled, I bent to study more closely the infinite range of fighting men. There were Norman knights and German Landsknecht, Japanese samurai and Prussian dragoons, foot grenadiers of the French Imperial

Guard and Spanish conquistadors. U.S. 7th Cavalry troopers from the Indian wars; Dutch musketeers and pikemen who marched with the army of Maurice of Nassau during the long war of independence fought by the Netherlands against the Spanish Habsburgs; Greek hoplites in bronze helmets and stiff cuirasses; cocked hat riflemen of Morgan's Virginia Rifles who repulsed Burgoyne's troops with their deadly accurate Pennsylvania long-barrels; Egyptian chariot-spearmen and French Foreign Legionnaires; Zulu warriors from Shaka's legions and English longbowmen from Agincourt; Anzacs and Persian Immortals and Assyrian slingers; Cossacks and Saracen warriors in chain-mail and padded silk; 82nd Airborne paratroopers and Israeli jet pilots and Wehrmacht Panzer commanders and Russian infantrymen and Black Hussars of the 5th Regiment.

And as I drifted through a mist of wonder and pleasure, from array to array, one overriding observation dominated even my awe in the face of such artistic grandeur.

Each and every figure—to the last turbaned Cissian, trousered Scythian, wooden-helmeted Colchian or Pisidian with an oxhide shield—every one of them bore the most exquisite expression of terror and hopelessness. Faces twisted in anguish at the precise moment of death, or more terribly, the moment of *realization* of personal death, each soldier looked up at me with eyes just fogging with tears, with mouth half-open to emit a scream, with fingers reaching toward me in splay-fingered hope of last-minute reprieve.

These were not merely painted representations.

The faces were individual. I could see every follicle of beard, every drop of sweat, every frozen tic of agony. They seemed able to complete the shriek of denial. They looked as if, should I blink, they would spring back to life and then fall dead as they were intended.

Mr. Brown had left narrow aisles of carpet among the vast armadas, and I had wandered deep into the shoe-top grassland of the drawing room with the little man behind me, still locked up with fear but attendant at my back. Now I rose from examining a raiding party of Viet Cong frozen in attitudes of agony as the breath of life stilled in them, and I turned to Mr. Brown with apparently such a look on my face that he blurted it out. I could not have stopped the confession had I so desired.

They were not metal figurines. They were flesh turned to pewter. Mr. Brown had no artistic skill save the one ability to snatch soldiers off the battlefields of time, to freeze them in metal, to miniaturize them, and to sell them. Each commando and halberdier captured in the field and reduced, at the moment of his death…realizing in that moment that Heaven or whatever Valhalla in which he believed, was to be denied him. An eternity of death in miniature.

"You are a greater ghoul than ever I could have aspired to become," I said.

His fright overcame him at that moment. Why, I do not know. I meant him no harm. Perhaps it was the summation of his existence, the knowledge of the monstrous hobby that had brought him an unspeakable pleasure through his long life, finally caught up with him. I do not know.

He spasmed suddenly as though struck at the base of his spine by a maul, and his eyes widened, and he collapsed toward me. To prevent the destruction of the exquisite figurines, I let him fall into my arms; and I carefully lowered him into the narrow aisle. Even so, his lifeless left leg decimated the ranks of thirteenth-century Mongol warriors who had served Genghis Khan from the China Sea in the east to the gates of Austria in the west.

He lay face down and I saw a drop of blood at the base of his neck. I bent closer as he struggled to turn his head to the side to speak, and saw the tiniest crossbow quarrel protruding from his rapidly discoloring flesh, just below the hairline.

He was trying to say something to me, and I kneeled close to his mouth, my ear close to the exhalations of dying breath. And he lamented his life, for though he might well have been judged a monster by those who exist in conformity and abide within the mundane strictures of accepted ethical behavior, he was not a bad man. An obsessed man, certainly; but not a bad man. And to prove it, he told me haltingly of the *Promontorium Sacrum,* and of how he had found his way there, how he had struggled back. He told me of the lives and the wisdom and the wonders to be found there.

And he made one last feeble gesture to show me where the scroll was hidden. The scroll he had brought back, which had contained such knowledge as had permitted him to indulge his hobby. He made that last feeble gesture, urging me to find the scroll and to remove it from its hidden niche, and to use it for ends that would palliate his life's doings.

I tried to turn him over, to learn more, but he died in my arms. And I left him there in the narrow aisle among the Nazi Werewolves and Royal Welsh Fusiliers; and I threaded my way through the drawing room large enough to stage a cotillion; and I found the secret panel behind which he had secreted the scroll; and I removed it and saw the photograph he had taken in that beyond that lay beyond the beyondmost edge; the only image of that land that has ever existed. The whispering moon. The golden mushroom trees. The satin sea. The creatures that sit and ruminate there.

I took the scroll and went far away. Into the Outback, above Arkaroo Rock where the Dreamtime reigns. And I spent many years learning the wisdom contained in the scroll of Mr. Brown.

It would not be hyperbole to call it an epiphany.

For when I came back down, and re-entered the human stream, I was a different Vizinczey. I was recast in a different nature. All that I had been, all that I had done, all the blight I had left in my track…all of it was as if from someone else's debased life. I was now equipped and anxious to honor Mr. Brown's dying wish.

And that is how I have spent my time for the past several lifetimes. The scroll, in a minor footnote, affords the careful reader the key to immortality. Or as much immortality as one desires. So with this added benison of longevity, I have expended entire decades improving the condition of life for the creatures of this world that formerly I savaged and destroyed.

Now, due to circumstances I will not detail (there is no need to distress you with the specifics of vegetables and rust), the time of my passing is at hand. Vizinczey will be no more in a very short while. And all the good I have done will be the last good I can do. I will cease to be, and I will take the scroll with me. Please trust my judgment in this.

But for a very long time I have been your guardian angel. I have done you innumerable good turns. Yes, even you reading these words: I did you a good turn just last week. Think back and you will remember a random small miracle that made your existence prettier. That was I.

And as parting gift, I have extracted a brief number of the most important thoughts and skills from the scroll of the *Promontorium Sacrum*. They are the most potent runes from that astonishing document. So they will not burn, but rather will serve to warm, if properly adduced, if slowly deciphered and assimilated and understood, I have couched them in more contemporary, universal terms. I do this for your own good. They are not quite epigraphs, nor are they riddles; though set down in simple language, if pierced to the nidus they will enrich and reify; they are potentially analeptic.

I present them to you now, because you will have to work your lives without me from this time forward. You are, as you were for millennia, alone once again. But you can do it. I present them to you, because from the moment Mr. Brown died in my arms, I have been unable to forget the look of human misery, endless despair, and hopelessness on the face of a Spartan soldier who lay on a carpet in a house in Sydney, Australia. This is for him, for all of them, and for you.

1

It's the dark of the sun. It's the hour in which worms sing madrigals, tea leaves tell their tales in languages we once used to converse with the trees, and all the winds of the world have returned to the great throat that gave them life. Messages come to us from the core of quiet. A friend now gone tries desperately to pass a message from the beyond, but the strength of ghosts is slight: all he can do is move dust-motes with great difficulty, arranging them with excruciating slowness to form words. The message comes together on the glossy jacket of a book casually dropped on a table more than a year ago. Laboriously laid, mote by mote, the message tells the friend still living that friendship must involve risk, that it is merely a word if it is never tested, that anyone can claim *friend* if there is no chance of cost. It is phrased simply. On the other side, the shade of the friend now departed waits and hopes. He fears the inevitable: his living friend despises disorder and dirt: what if he chances on the misplaced book while wearing his white gloves?

2

Do they chill, the breezes that whisper of yesterday, the winds that come from a hidden valley near the top of the world? Do they bite, the shadowy thoughts that lie at the bottom of your heart during daylight hours, that swirl up like wood smoke in the night? Can you hear the memories of those who have gone before, calling to you when the weariness takes you, close on midnight? They are the winds, the thoughts, the voices of memory that prevail in the hour that lies between awareness and reverie. And on the other side of the world, hearing the same song, is your one true love, understanding no better than you, that those who cared and went away are trying to bring you together. Can you breach the world that keeps you apart?

3

This is an emergency bulletin. We've made a few necessary alterations in the status quo. For the next few weeks there will be no madness; no imbecile beliefs; no paralogical, prelogical or paleological thinking. No random cruelty. For the next few weeks all the impaired mentalities will be frozen in stasis. No attempts to get you to believe that vast and cool intelligences come from space regularly in circular vehicles. No runaway tales of yetis, sasquatches, hairy shamblers of a lost species. No warnings that the cards, the stones, the running water or the stars are against your best efforts. This is the time known in Indonesia as *djam karet*—the hour that stretches. For the next few weeks you can breathe freely and operate off these words by one who learned too late, by one who has gone away, who was called Camus: "It is not man who must be protected, but the possibilities within him." You have a few weeks without hindrance. Move quickly.

4

The casement window blows open. The nightmare has eluded the guards. It's over the spiked wall and it's in here with you. The lights go out. The temperature drops sharply. The bones in your body sigh. You're all alone with it. Circling with your back to the wall. Hey, don't be a nasty little coward; face it and disembowel it. You've got time. You have *always* had time, but the fear slowed you, and you were overcome. But this is the hour that stretches…and you've got a chance. After all, it's only your conscience come to kill you. Stop shivering and put up your dukes. You might beat it this time, now that you know you have some breathing space. For in this special hour anything that has ever happened will happen again. Except, this time, it's *your* turn to risk it all.

5

In the cathedral at the bottom of the Maracot Deep the carillon chimes for all the splendid thinkers you never got to be. The memories of great thoughts left unspoken rise from their watery tomb and ascend to the surface. The sea boils at their approach and a siege of sea eagles gathers in the sky above the disturbance. Fishermen in small boats listen as they have never listened before, and all seems clear for the first time. These are warnings of storms made only by men. Tempests and sea-spouts, tsunamis and bleeding oceans the color of tragedy. For men's tongues have been stilled, and more great thoughts will die never having been uttered. Memories from the pit of the Deep rise to lament their brethren. Even now, even in the hour that stretches, the past silently cries out not to be forgotten. Are you listening, or must you be lost at sea forever?

6

Did you have one of those days today, like a nail in the foot? Did the pterodactyl corpse dropped by the ghost of your mother from the spectral Hindenburg forever circling the Earth come smashing through the lid of your glass coffin? Did the New York strip steak you attacked at dinner suddenly show a mouth filled with needle-sharp teeth, and did it snap off the end of your fork, the last solid-gold fork from the set Anastasia pressed into your hands as they took her away to be shot? Is the slab under your apartment building moaning that it cannot stand the weight on its back a moment longer, and is the building stretching and creaking? Did a good friend betray you today, or did that good friend merely keep silent and fail to come to your aid? Are you holding the razor at your throat this very instant? Take heart, comfort is at hand. This is the hour that stretches. *Djam karet*. We are the cavalry. We're here. Put away the pills. We'll get you through this bloody night. Next time, it'll be your turn to help us.

7

You woke in the night, last night, and the fiery, bony hand was enscribing mystic passes in the darkness of your bedroom. It carved out words in the air, flaming words, messages that required answers. One picture is worth a thousand words, the hand wrote. "Not in *this* life," you said to the dark and the fire. "Give me one picture that shows how I felt when they gassed my dog. I'll take less than a thousand words and make you weep for the last Neanderthal crouched at the cliff's edge at the moment he realized his kind were gone...show me your one picture. Commend to me the one picture that captures what it was like for me in the moment she said it was all over between us. Not in *this* life, Bonehand." So here we are, once again in the dark, with nothing between us in this hour that stretches but the words. Sweet words and harsh words and words that tumble over themselves to get born. We leave the pictures for the canvas of your mind. Seems only fair.

8

Rain fell in a special pattern. I couldn't believe it was doing that. I ran to the other side of the house and looked out the window. The sun was shining there. I saw a hummingbird bury his stiletto beak in a peach on one of the trees, like a junkie who had turned himself into the needle. He sucked deeply and shadows flowed out of the unripe peach: a dreamy vapor that enveloped the bird, changing its features to something jubilantly malevolent. With juice glowing in one perfect drop at the end of its beak, it turned a yellow eye toward me as I pressed against the window. Go away, it said. I fell back and rushed to the other side of the house where rain fell in one place on the sunny street. In my soul I knew that not all inclement weather meant sorrow, that even the brightest day held dismay. I knew this all had meaning, but there was no one else in the world to whom I could go for interpretation. There were only dubious sources, and none knew more than I, not really. Isn't that the damnedest thing: there's never a good reference when you need one.

9

Through the jaws of night we stormed, banners cracking against the icy wind, the vapor our beasts panted preceding us like smoke signals, warning the enemy that we looked forward to writing our names in the blood of the end of their lives. We rode for Art! For the singing soul of Creativity! Our cause was just, because it was the only cause worth dying for. All others were worth living for. They stood there on the black line of the horizon, their pikes angrily tilted toward us. *For Commerce*, they shouted with one voice. *For Commerce!* And we fell upon them, and the battle was high wave traffic, with the sound of metal on metal, the sound of hooves on stone, the sound of bodies exploding. We battled all through the endless midnight till at last we could see nothing but hills and valleys of dead. And in the end, we lost. We always lost. And I, alone, am left to tell of that time. Only I, alone of all who went to war to measure the height of the dream, only I remain to speak to you here in the settling silence. Why do *you* feel diminished…you weren't there…it wasn't your war. Hell hath no fury like that of the uninvolved.

10

Hear the music. Listen with all your might, and you needn't clap to keep Tinker Bell from going into a coma. The music will restore her rosy cheeks. Then seek out the source of the melody. Look long and look deep, and somewhere in the murmuring world you will find the storyteller, there under the cabbage leaves, singing to herself. Or is that a she? Perhaps it's a he. But whichever, or whatever, the poor thing is crippled. Can you see that now? The twisting, the bending, the awkward shape, the milky eye, the humped back, do you now make it out? But if you try to join in, to work a duet with wonder, the song ceases. When you startle the cricket its symphony ceases. Art is not by committee, nor is it by wish-fulfillment. It is that which is produced in the hour that stretches, the timeless time wherein *all* songs are sung. In a place devoid of electrical outlets. And if you try to grasp either the singer or the song, all you will hold is sparkling dust as fine as the butter the moth leaves on glass. How the bee flies, how the lights go on, how the enigma enriches and the explanation chills… how the music is made…are not things we were given to know. And only the fools who cannot hear the song ask that the rules be posted. Hear the music. And enjoy. But do not cry. Not everyone was intended to reach A above high C.

11

Ah, there were giants in the land in those days. There was a sweet-faced, honey-voiced girl named Barbara Wire, whom we called Nancy because no one had the heart to call her Barb Wire. She tossed a salamander into a window fan to see what would happen. There was Sofie, who had been bitten by *The Sun Also Rises* at a tender age, and who took it as her mission in life to permit crippled virginal boys the enjoyment of carnal knowledge of her every body part: harelips, lepers, paraplegics, albinos with pink eyes, aphasiacs, she welcomed them all to her bed. There was Marissa, who could put an entire unsegmented fried chicken in her mouth all at once, chew without opening her lips or dribbling, and who would then delicately spit out an intact skeleton, as dry and clean as the Gobi Desert. Perdita drew portraits. She would sit you down, and with her pad and charcoal, quickly capture the depth and specificity of your most serious flaws of honor, ethic and conscience, so accurately that you would rip the drawing to pieces before anyone else could see the nature of your corruption. Jolanda: who stole cars and then reduced them to metal sculpture in demolition derbies, whose residence was in an abandoned car-crusher. Peggy: who never slept but told endlessly of her waking dreams of the things the birds told her they saw from on high. Naomi: who was white, passing for black, because she felt the need to shoulder some of the guilt of the world. Ah, there were giants in the land in those days. But I left the room, and closed the door behind me so that the hour that stretches would not leak out. And though I've tried portal after portal, I've never been able to find that room again. Perhaps I'm in the wrong house.

12

I woke at three in the morning, bored out of sleep by dreams of such paralyzing mediocrity that I could not lie there and suffer my own breathing. Naked, I padded through the silent house: I knew that terrain as my tongue knows my palate. There were rolls of ancient papyrus lying on a counter. I will replace them, high in a dark closet, I thought. Then I said it aloud…the house was silent, I could speak to the air. I took a tall stool and went to the closet, and climbed up and replaced the papyrus. Then I saw it. A web. Dark and billowing in the corner of the ceiling, not silvery but ashy. Something I could not bear to see in my home. It threatened me. I climbed down, moved through the utter darkness, and struggled with the implements in the broom closet, found the feather duster, and hurried back. Then I killed the foaming web and left the closet. Clean the feather duster, I thought. In the back yard I moved to the wall, and shook it out. Then, as I returned, incredible pain assaulted me. The cactus pup with its cool, long spikes had imbedded itself in the ball of my naked right foot. My testicles shrank and my eyes watered. I took an involuntary step, and the spines drove deeper. I reached down to remove the agony and a spike imbedded itself in my thumb. I shouted. I hurt. Limping, I got to the kitchen. In the light of the kitchen I tried to pinch out the spines. They were barbed. They came away with bits of flesh attached. The poison was already spreading. I hurt very much. I hobbled to the bathroom to put antiseptic or the Waters of Lethe on the wounds. They bled freely. I salved myself, and returned to the bed, hating my wife who slept unknowing; I hated my friend who lay dreaming in another part of the house. I hated the world for placing random pain in my innocent path. I lay down and hated all natural order for a brief time. Then I fell fast asleep. Relieved. Boredom had been killed with the billowing web. Somehow, the universe always provides.

13

Like all men, my father was a contradiction in terms. Not more than two or three years after the Great Depression, when my family was still returning pop bottles for the few cents' deposit, and saving those pennies in a quart milk bottle, my father did one of the kindest things I've ever known: he hired a man as an assistant in his little store; an assistant he didn't really need and couldn't afford. He hired the man because he had three children and couldn't find a job. Yet not more than a week later, as we locked up the stationery shop late on a Saturday night, and began to walk down the street to the diner where we would have our hot roast beef sandwiches and french fries, with extra country gravy for dipping the fries, another man approached us on the street and asked for twenty-five cents to buy a bowl of soup. And my father snarled, "No! Get away from us!" I was more startled at that moment than I had ever been—or ever *would* be, as it turned out, for my father died not much later that year—more startled than by anything my father had ever said or done. If I had known the word at that age—I was only twelve—I would have realized that I was *dumbfounded*. My gentle father, who never raised his voice to me or to anyone else, who was unfailingly kind and polite even to the rudest customer, who has forever been a model of compassion for me, *my father* had grown icy and stony in that exchange with an innocent stranger. "Dad," I asked him, as we walked away from the lonely man, "how come you didn't give that fellah a quarter for some soup?" He looked down at me, as if through a crack in the door of a room always kept locked, and he said, "He won't buy a bowl of soup. He'll only buy more liquor." Because my father never lied to me, and because I knew it was important for him always to tell me the truth, I didn't ask anything more about it. But I never forgot that evening; and it is an incident I can never fit into the film strip of loving memories I run and rerun starring my father. Somehow I feel, without understanding, that it was the most important moment of human frailty and compassion in the twelve years through which I was permitted to adore my father. And I wonder when I will grow wise enough to understand the wisdom of my father.

Thus, my gift. There were six more selections from the scroll of the *Promontorium Sacrum*, but once having entered them here, I realized they would cause more harm than good. Tell me truly: would you really want the power to bend others to your will, or the ability to travel at will in an instant to any place in the world, or the facility for reading the future in mirrors? No, I thought not. It is gratifying to see that just the wisdom imparted here has sobered you to that extent.

And what would you do with the knowledge of shaping, the talent for sending, the capturing of rainbows? You already possess such powers and abilities as the world has never known. Now that I've left you the time to master what you already know, you should have no sorrow at being denied these others. Be content.

Now I take my leave. Passage of an instant sort has been arranged. Vizinczey, the I that I became, goes finally on the journey previously denied. Until I had fulfilled the dying request of Mr. Brown, I felt it was unfair of me to indulge myself. But now I go to the sacred promontory; to return the scroll; to sit at the base of the golden mushroom trees and confabulate with astonishing creatures. Perhaps I will take a camera, and perhaps I will endeavor to send back a snap or two, but that is unlikely.

I go contentedly, for all my youthful crimes, having left this a prettier venue than I found it.

And finally, for those of you who always wash behind your ears because, as children, you heeded the admonition "go wash behind your ears," seeing motion pictures of children being examined by their parents before being permitted to go to the dinner table, remembering the panels in comic strips in which children were being told, "Go back and wash behind your ears," who always wondered why that was important—after all, your ears fit fairly closely to your head—who used to wonder what one could possibly have behind one's ears—great masses of mud, dangerous colonies of germs, could vegetation actually take root there, what are we talking about and why such obsessive attention to something so silly?—for those of you who were trusting enough to wash behind your ears, and still do…for those of you who know the urgency of tying your shoelaces tightly…who have no fear of vegetables or rust…I answer the question you raise about the fate of those tiny metal figurines left in eternal anguish on the floor of Mr. Brown's drawing room. I answer the question in this way:

There was a man standing behind you yesterday in the check-out line at the grocery store. You casually noticed that he was buying the most unusual combinations of exotic foods. When you dropped the package of frozen peas, and he stooped to retrieve it for you, you noticed that he had a regal, almost one might say *militaristic* bearing. He clicked his heels as he proffered the peas, and when you thanked him, he spoke with a peculiar accent.

Trust me in this: not even if you were Professor Henry Higgins could you place the point of origin of that accent.

Dedicated to the memory of Mike Hodel

THE FUNCTION OF
DREAM SLEEP

1989 Locus Poll Award: Best Novelette

McGRATH AWOKE SUDDENLY, just in time to see a huge mouth filled with small, sharp teeth closing in his side. In an instant it was gone, even as he shook himself awake.

Had he not been staring at the flesh, at the moment his eyes opened from sleep, he would have missed the faintest pink line of closure that remained only another heartbeat, then faded and was gone, leaving no indication the mouth had ever existed; a second—secret—mouth hiding in his skin.

At first he was sure he had wakened from a particularly nasty dream. But the memory of the thing that had escaped from within him, through the mouth, was a real memory—not a wisp of fading nightmare. He had *felt* the chilly passage of something rushing out of him. Like cold air from a leaking balloon. Like a chill down a hallway from a window left open in a distant room. And he had *seen* the mouth. It lay across the ribs vertically, just below his left nipple, running down to the bulge of fat parallel to his navel. Down his left side there had been a lipless mouth filled with teeth; and it had been open to permit a breeze of something to leave his body.

McGrath sat up on the bed. He was shaking. The Tensor lamp was still on, the paperback novel tented open on the sheet beside him, his body naked and perspiring in the August heat. The Tensor had been aimed directly at his side, bathing his flesh with light, when he had unexpectedly opened his eyes; and in that waking moment he had surprised his body in the act of opening its secret mouth.

He couldn't stop the trembling, and when the phone rang he had to steel himself to lift the receiver.

"Hello," he heard himself say, in someone else's voice.

"Lonny," said Victor Kayley's widow, "I'm sorry to disturb you at this hour…"

"It's okay," he said. Victor had died the day before yesterday. Sally relied on him for the arrangements, and hours of solace he didn't begrudge. Years before, Sally and he…then she drifted toward Victor, who had been McGrath's oldest, closest…they were drawn to each other more and more sweetly till…and finally, McGrath had taken them both to dinner at the old Steuben Tavern on West 47th, that dear old Steuben Tavern with its dark wood booths and sensational schnitzel, now gone, torn down and gone like so much else that was…and he had made them sit side by side in the booth across from him, and he took their hands in his…I love you both so much, he had said…I see the way you move when you're around each other…you're both my dearest friends, you put light in my world… and he laid their hands together under his, and he grinned at them for their nervousness…

"Are you all right; you sound so, I don't know, so *strained*?" Her voice was wide awake. But concerned.

"I'm, yeah, I'm okay. I just had the weirdest, I was dozing, fell asleep reading, and I had this, this *weird*—" He trailed off. Then went back at it, more sternly: "I'm okay. It was a scary dream."

There was, then, a long measure of silence between them. Only the open line, with the sound of ions decaying.

"Are *you* okay?" he said, thinking of the funeral service day after tomorrow. She had asked him to select the casket. The anodized pink aluminum "unit" they had tried to get him to go for, doing a bait-and-switch, had nauseated him. McGrath had settled on a simple copper casket, shrugging away suggestions by the Bereavement Counselor in the Casket Selection Parlor that "consideration and thoughtfulness for the departed" might better be served by the Monaco, a "Duraseal metal unit with Sea Mist Polished Finish, interior richly lined in 600 Aqua Supreme Cheney velvet, magnificently quilted and shirred, with matching jumbo bolster and coverlet."

"I couldn't sleep," she said. "I was watching television, and they had a thing about the echidna, the Australian anteater, you know…?" He made a sound that indicated he knew. "And Vic never got over the trip we took to the Flinders Range in '82, and he just loved the Australian animals, and I turned in the bed to see him smiling…"

She began to cry.

He could feel his throat closing. He knew. The turning to tell your best friend something you'd just seen together, to get the reinforcement, the input, the expression on his face. And there was no face. There was emptiness in that place. He knew. He'd turned to Victor three dozen times in the past two days. Turned, to confront emptiness. Oh, he knew, all right.

"Sally," he murmured. "Sally, I know; I know."

She pulled herself together, snuffled herself unclogged and cleared her throat. "It's okay. I'm fine. It was just a second there…"

"Try to get some sleep. We have to do stuff tomorrow."

"Of course," she said, sounding really quite all right. "I'll go back to bed. I'm sorry." He told her to shut up, if you couldn't call a friend at that hour to talk about the echidna, who the hell *could* you call?

"Jerry Falwell," she said. "If I have to annoy someone at three in the morning, better it should be a shit like him." They laughed quickly and emptily, she said good night and told him he had been much loved by both of them, he said I know that, and they hung up.

Lonny McGrath lay there, the paperback still tented at his side, the Tensor still warming his flesh, the sheets still soggy from the humidity, and he stared at the far wall of the bedroom on whose surface, like the surface of his skin, there lay no evidence whatever of secret mouths filled with teeth.

"I can't get it out of my mind."

Dr. Jess ran her fingers down his side, looked closer. "Well, it *is* red; but that's more chafing than anything out of Stephen King."

"It's red because I keep rubbing it. I'm getting obsessive about it. And don't make fun, Jess. I can't get it out of my mind."

She sighed and raked a hand back through her thick auburn hair. "Sorry." She got up and walked to the window in the examination room. Then, as an afterthought, she said, "You can get dressed." She stared out the window as McGrath hopped off the physical therapy table, nearly catching his heel on the retractable step. He partially folded the stiff paper gown that had covered his lap, and laid it on the padded seat. As he pulled up his undershorts, Dr. Jess turned and stared at him. He thought for the hundredth time that his initial fears, years before, at being examined by a female physician, had been foolish. His friend looked at him with concern, but without the *look* that passed between men and women. "How long has it been since Victor died?"

"Three months, almost."

"And Emily?"

"Six months."

"And Steve and Melanie's son?"

"Oh, Christ, Jess!"

She pursed her lips. "Look, Lonny, I'm not a psychotherapist, but even I can see that the death of all these friends is getting to you. Maybe you don't even see it, but you used the right word: obsessive. *No*body can sustain so much pain, over so brief a period, the loss of so many loved ones, without going into a spiral."

"What did the X-rays show?"

"I told you."

"But there might've been *some*thing. Some lesion, or inflammation; an irregularity in the dermis…*some*thing!"

"Lonny. Come *on*. I've never lied to you. You looked at them with me, did *you* see anything?" He sighed deeply, shook his head. She spread her hands as if to say, well, there you are, I can't make something sick where nothing sick exists. "I can work on your soft prostate, and I can give you a shot of cortisone in the ball joint where that cop worked you over; but I can't treat something out of a penny dreadful novel that doesn't leave any trace."

"You think I need a shrink?"

She turned back to the window. "This is your third visit, Lonny. You're my pal, kiddo, but I think you need to get counseling of a different sort."

McGrath knotted his tie and drew it up, spreading the wings of his shirt collar with his little fingers. She didn't turn around. "I'm worried about you, Lonny. You ought to be married."

"I *was* married. You're not talking wife, anyway. You're talking keeper." She didn't turn. He pulled on his jacket, and waited. Finally, with his hand on the doorknob, he said, "Maybe you're right. I've never been a melancholy sort, but all this…so many, in so short a time…maybe you're right."

He opened the door. She looked out the window. "We'll talk." He started out, and without turning, she said, "There won't be a charge for this visit."

He smiled thinly, not at all happily. But she didn't see it. There is *always* a charge, of one kind or another.

· · ·

He called Tommy and begged off from work. Tommy went into a snit. "I'm up to my ass, Lonny," he said, affecting his Dowager Empress tone. "This is Black goddam Friday! The Eroica! That Fahrenheit woman, Farrenstock, whatever the hell it is…"

"Fahnestock," Lonny said, smiling for the first time in days. "I thought we'd seen the last of her when you suggested she look into the possibility of a leper sitting on her face."

Tommy sighed. "The grotesque bitch is simply a glutton. I swear to God she must be into bondage; the worse I treat her, the more often she comes in."

"What'd she bring this time?"

"Another half dozen of those tacky petit-point things. I can barely bring myself to look at them. Bleeding martyrs and scenes of culturally depressed areas in, I suppose, Iowa or Indiana. Illinois, Idaho, I don't know: one of those places that begins with an I, teeming with people who bowl."

Lonny always wound up framing Mrs. Fahnestock's gaucheries. Tommy always took one look, then went upstairs in back of the framing shop to lie down for a while. McGrath had asked the matron once, what she did with all of them. She replied that she gave them as gifts. Tommy, when he heard, fell to his knees and prayed to a God in which he did not believe that the woman would never hold him in enough esteem to feel he deserved such a gift. But she spent, oh my, how she spent.

"Let me guess," McGrath said. "She wants them blocked so tightly you could bounce a dime off them, with a fabric liner, a basic pearl matte, and the black lacquer frame from Chapin Molding. Right?"

"Yes, of course, right. Which is *another* reason your slacker behavior is particularly distressing. The truck from Chapin just dropped off a hundred feet of the oval top walnut molding. It's got to be unpacked, the footage measured, and put away. You *can't* take the day off."

"Tommy, don't whip the guilt on me. I'm a goy, remember?"

"If it weren't for guilt, the *goyim* would have wiped us out three thousand years ago. It's more effective than a Star Wars defense system." He puffed air through his lips for a moment, measuring how much he would *actually* be inconvenienced by his assistant's absence. "Monday morning? Early?"

McGrath said, "I'll be there no later than eight o'clock. I'll do the petit-points first."

"All right. And by the way, you sound awful. D'you know the worst part about being an Atheist?"

Lonny smiled. Tommy would feel it was a closed bargain if he could pass on one of his horrendous jokes. "No, what's the worst part about being an Atheist?"

"You've got no one to talk to when you're fucking."

Lonny roared, silently. There was no need to give him the satisfaction. But Tommy knew. He couldn't see him, but Lonny knew he was grinning broadly at the other end of the line. "So long, Tommy. See you Monday."

He racked the receiver in the phone booth and looked across Pico Boulevard at the office building. He had lived in Los Angeles for eleven years, since he and Victor and Sally had fled New York, and he still couldn't get used to the golden patina that lay over the days here. Except when it rained, at which times the inclemency seemed so alien he had visions of giant mushrooms sprouting from the sidewalks. The office building was unimpressive, just three storeys high and brick; but a late afternoon shadow lay across its face, and it recalled for him the eighteen frontal views of the Rouen Cathedral that Monet had painted during the winter months of 1892 and 1893: the same façade, following the light from early morning till sunset. He had seen the Monet exhibition at MOMA. Then he remembered with whom he had taken in that exhibition, and he felt again the passage of chill leaving his body through that secret mouth. He stepped out of the booth and just wanted to go somewhere and cry. *Stop it!* he said inside. *Knock it off.* He swiped at the corner of his eye, and crossed the street. He passed through the shadow that cut the sidewalk.

Inside the tiny lobby he consulted the glass-paneled wall register. Mostly, the building housed dentists and philatelists, as best he could tell. But against the ribbed black panel he read the little white plastic letters that had been darted in to include THE REM GROUP 306. He walked up the stairs.

To find 306, he had to make a choice: go left or go right. There were no office location arrows on the wall. He went to the right, and was pleased. As the numbers went down, he began to hear someone speaking rather loudly. "Sleep is of several kinds. Dream sleep, or rapid eye movement sleep—what we call REM sleep, and thus the name of our group—is predominantly found in mammals who bring forth living young, rather than eggs. Some birds and reptiles, as well."

McGrath stood outside the glass-paneled door to 306, and he listened. *Viviparous mammals*, he thought. He could now discern that the speaker was a woman; and her use of "living young, rather than eggs" instead of *viviparous* convinced him she was addressing one or more laypersons. *The echidna*, he thought. *A familiar viviparous mammal.*

"We now believe dreams originate in the brain's neocortex. Dreams have been used to attempt to foretell the future. Freud used dreams to explore the unconscious mind. Jung thought dreams formed a bridge of communication between the conscious and the unconscious." *It wasn't a dream*, McGrath thought. *I was awake. I know the difference.*

The woman was saying, "...those who try to make dreams work for them, to create poetry, to solve problems; and it's generally thought that dreams aid in consolidating memories. How many of you believe that if you can only *remember* the dream when you waken, that you will understand something very important, or regain some special memory you've lost?"

How many of you. McGrath now understood that the dream therapy group was in session. Late on a Friday afternoon? It would have to be women in their thirties, forties.

He opened the door, to see if he was correct.

With their hands in the air, indicating they believed the capturing of a dream on awakening would bring back an old memory, all six of the women in the room, not one of them older than forty, turned to stare at McGrath as he entered. He closed the door behind him, and said, "I don't agree. I think we dream to forget. And sometimes it doesn't work."

He was looking at the woman standing in front of the six hand-raised members of the group. She stared back at him for a long moment, and all six heads turned back to her. Their hands were frozen in the air. The woman who had been speaking settled back till she was perched on the edge of her desk.

"Mr. McGrath?"

"Yes. I'm sorry I'm late. It's been a day."

She smiled quickly, totally in command, putting him at ease. "I'm Anna Picket. Tricia said you'd probably be along today. Please grab a chair."

McGrath nodded and took a folding chair from the three remaining against the wall. He unfolded it and set it at the far left of the semicircle.

The six well-tended, expensively-coifed heads remained turned toward him as, one by one, the hands came down.

He wasn't at all sure letting his ex-wife call this Anna Picket, to get him into the group, had been such a good idea. They had remained friends after the divorce, and he trusted her judgment. Though he had never availed himself of her services after they'd separated and she had gone for her degree at UCLA, he'd been assured that Tricia was as good a family counseling therapist as one could find in Southern California. He had been shocked when she'd suggested a dream group. But he'd come: he had walked through the area most of the early part of the day, trying to decide if he wanted to do this, share what he'd experienced with total strangers; walked through the area stopping in at this shop and that boutique, having some gelato and shaking his head at how this neighborhood had been "gentrified," how it had changed so radically, how all the wonderful little tradesmen who had flourished here had been driven out by geysering rents; walked through the area growing more and more despondent at how nothing lasted, how joy was drained away shop by shop, neighborhood by neighborhood, person by...

Until one was left alone.

Standing on an empty plain. The dark wind blowing from the horizon. Cold, empty dark: with the knowledge that a pit of eternal loneliness lay just over that horizon, and that the frightening wind that blew up out of the pit would never cease. That one would stand there, all alone, on the empty plain, as one after another of the ones you loved were erased in a second.

Had walked through the area, all day, and finally had called Tommy, and finally had allowed Tricia's wisdom to lead him, and here he sat, in a folding straight-back chair, asking a total stranger to repeat what she had just said.

"I asked why you didn't agree with the group, that remembering dreams is a good thing?" She arched an eyebrow, and tilted her head.

McGrath felt uncomfortable for a moment. He blushed. It was something that had always caused him embarrassment. "Well," he said slowly, "I don't want to seem like a smart aleck, one of those people who reads some popularized bit of science and then comes on like an authority..."

She smiled at his consternation, the flush of his cheeks. "Please, Mr. McGrath, that's quite all right. Where dreams are concerned, we're *all* journeyists. What did you read?"

"The Crick-Mitchison theory. The paper on 'unlearning.' I don't know, it just seemed, well, *reasonable* to me."

One of the women asked what that was.

Anna Picket said, "Dr. Sir Francis Crick, you'll know of him because he won the Nobel Prize for his work with DNA; and Graeme Mitchison, he's a highly respected brain researcher at Cambridge. Their experiments in the early 1980s. They postulate that we dream to forget, not to remember."

"The best way I understood it," McGrath said, "was using the analogy of cleaning out an office building at night, after all the workers are gone. Outdated reports are trashed, computer dump sheets are shredded, old memos tossed with the refuse. Every night our brains get cleaned during the one to two hours of REM sleep. The dreams pick up after us every day, sweep out the unnecessary, untrue, or just plain silly memories that could keep us from storing the important memories, or might keep us from rational thinking when we're awake. *Remembering* the dreams would be counter-productive, since the brain is trying to unlearn all that crap so we function better."

Anna Picket smiled. "You were sent from heaven, Mr. McGrath. I was going precisely to that theory when you came in. You've saved me a great deal of explanation."

One of the six women said, "Then you don't *want* us to write down our dreams and bring them in for discussion? I even put a tape recorder by the bed. For instance, I had a dream just last night in which my bicycle…"

He sat through the entire session, listening to things that infuriated him. They were so self-indulgent, making of the most minor inconveniences in their lives, mountains impossible to conquer. They were so different from the women he knew. They seemed to be antiquated creatures from some primitive time, confused by changing times and the demand on them to be utterly responsible for their existence. They seemed to want succor, to be told that there were greater forces at work in their world; powers and pressures and even conspiracies that existed solely to keep them nervous, uncomfortable, and helpless. Five of the six were divorcées, and only one of the five had a full-time job: selling real estate. The sixth was the daughter of an organized crime figure. McGrath felt no link with them. He didn't need a group therapy session. His life was as full as he wanted it to be… except that he was now always scared, and lost, and constantly depressed. Perhaps Dr. Jess was dead on target. Perhaps he *did* need a shrink.

He was certain he did not need Anna Picket and her well-tailored ladies whose greatest *real* anguish was making sure they got home in time to turn on the sprinklers.

When the session ended, he started toward the door without saying anything to the Picket woman. She was surrounded by the six. But she gently edged them aside and called to him, "Mr. McGrath, would you wait a moment? I'd like to speak to you." He took his hand off the doorknob, and went back to his chair. He bit the soft flesh of his inner cheek, annoyed.

She blew them off like dandelion fluff, far more quickly than McGrath thought possible, and did it without their taking it as rejection. In less than five minutes he was alone in the office with the dream therapist.

She closed the door behind the Mafia Princess and locked it. For a deranged moment he thought…but it passed, and the look on her face was concern, not lust. He started to rise. She laid a palm against the air, stopping him. He sank back onto the folding chair.

Then Anna Picket came to him and said, "For McGrath hath murdered sleep." He stared up at her as she put her left hand behind his head, cupping the nape with fingers extending up under his hair along the curve of the skull. "Don't be nervous, this'll be all right," she said, laying her right hand with the palm against his left cheek, the spread thumb and index finger bracketing an eye he tried mightily not to blink. Her thumb lay alongside his nose, the tip curving onto the bridge. The forefinger lay across the bony eye-ridge.

She pursed her lips, then sighed deeply. In a moment her body twitched with an involuntary rictus, and she gasped, as if she had had the wind knocked out of her. McGrath couldn't move. He could feel the strength of her hands cradling his head, and the tremors of—he wanted to say—*passion* slamming through her. Not the passion of strong amorous feeling, but passion in the sense of being acted upon by something external, something alien to one's nature.

The trembling in her grew more pronounced, and McGrath had the sense that power was being drained out of him, pouring into her, that it had reached saturation level and was leaking back along the system into him, but changed, more dangerous. But why dangerous? She was spasming now, her eyes closed, her head thrown back and to the side, her thick mass of hair swaying and bobbing as she jerked, a human double-circuit high-voltage tower about to overload.

She moaned softly, in pain, without the slightest trace of subliminal pleasure, and he could see she was biting her lower lip so fiercely that blood was beginning to coat her mouth. When the pain he saw in her face became more than he could bear, he reached up quickly and took her hands away with difficulty; breaking the circuit.

Anna Picket's legs went out and she keeled toward him. He tried to brace himself, but she hit him with full dead weight, and they went crashing to the floor entangled in the metal folding chair.

Frightened, thinking insanely *what if someone comes in and sees us like this, they'd think I was molesting her,* and in the next instant thinking with relief *she locked the door,* and in the next instant his fear was transmogrified into concern for her. He rolled out from under her trembling body, taking the chair with him, wrapped around one ankle. He shook off the chair, and got to his knees. Her eyes were half-closed, the lids flickering so rapidly she might have been in the line of strobe lights.

He hauled her around, settling her semi-upright with her head in his lap. He brushed the hair from her face, and shook her ever so lightly, because he had no water, and had no moist washcloth. Her breathing slowed, her chest heaved not quite so spastically, and her hand, flung away from her body, began to flex the fingers.

"Ms. Picket," he whispered, "can you talk? Are you all right? Is there some medicine you need…in your desk?"

She opened her eyes, then, and looked up at him. She tasted the blood on her lips and continued breathing raggedly, as though she had run a great distance. And finally she said, "I could feel it in you when you walked in."

He tried to ask what it was she had felt, what it was in him that had so unhinged her, but she reached in with the flexing hand and touched his forearm.

"You'll have to come with me."

"Where?"

"To meet the *real* REM Group."

And she began to cry. He knew immediately that she was weeping for him, and he murmured that he would come with her. She tried to smile reassurance, but there was still too much pain in her. They stayed that way for a time, and then they left the office building together.

• • •

They were impaired, every one of them in the sprawling ranch-style house in Hidden Hills. One was blind, another had only one hand. A third looked as if she had been in a terrible fire and had lost half her face, and another propelled herself through the house on a small wheeled platform with restraining bars to keep her from falling off.

They had taken the San Diego Freeway to the Ventura, and had driven west on 101 to the Calabasas exit. Climbing, then dropping behind the hills, they had turned up a side road that became a dirt road that became a horse path, Lonny driving Anna Picket's '85 Le Sabre.

The house lay within a bowl, completely concealed, even from the dirt road below. The horse trail passed behind low hills covered with mesquite and coast live oak, and abruptly became a perfectly surfaced blacktop. Like the roads Hearst had had cut in the hills leading up to San Simeon, concealing access to the Castle from the Coast Highway above Cambria, the blacktop had been poured on spiral rising cuts laid on a reverse bias.

Unless sought from the air, the enormous ranch house and its outbuildings and grounds would be unknown even to the most adventurous picnicker. "How much of this acreage do you own?" McGrath asked, circling down the inside of the bowl.

"All this," she said, waving an arm across the empty hills, "almost to the edge of Ventura County."

She had recovered completely, but had said very little during the hour and a half trip, even during the heaviest weekend traffic on the 101 Freeway crawling like a million-wheeled worm through the San Fernando Valley out of Los Angeles. "Not a lot of casual drop-ins I should imagine," he replied. She looked at him across the front seat, fully for the first time since leaving Santa Monica. "I hope you'll have faith in me, trust me just a while longer," she said.

He paid strict attention to the driving.

He had been cramped within the Buick by a kind of dull fear that strangely reminded him of how he had always felt on Christmas Eve, as a child, lying in bed, afraid of, yet anxious for, the sleep that permitted Santa Claus to come.

In that house below lay something that knew of secret mouths and ancient winds from within. Had he not trusted her, he would have slammed the brake pedal and leaped from the car and not stopped running till he had reached the freeway.

And once inside the house, seeing all of them, so ruined and tragic, he was helpless to do anything but allow her to lead him to a large sitting-room, where a circle of comfortable overstuffed chairs formed a pattern that made the fear more overwhelming.

They came, then, in twos and threes, the legless woman on the rolling cart propelling herself into the center of the ring. He sat there and watched them come, and his heart seemed to press against his chest. McGrath, as a young man, had gone to a Judy Garland film festival at the Thalia in New York. One of the revived movies had been *A Child Is Waiting*, a nonsinging role for Judy, a film about retarded children. Sally had had to help him out of the theater only halfway through. He could not see through his tears. His capacity for bearing the anguish of the crippled, particularly children, was less than that of most people. He brought himself up short: why had he thought of that afternoon at the Thalia now? These weren't children. They were adults. All of them. Every woman in the house was at least as old as he, surely older. Why had he been thinking of them as children?

Anna Picket took the chair beside him, and looked around the circle. One chair was empty. "Catherine?" she asked.

The blind woman said, "She died on Sunday."

Anna closed her eyes and sank back into the chair. "God be with her, and her pain ended."

They sat quietly for a time, until the woman on the cart looked up at McGrath, smiled a very kind smile, and said, "What is your name, young man?"

"Lonny," McGrath said. He watched as she rolled herself to his feet and put a hand on his knee. He felt warmth flow through him, and his fear melted. But it only lasted for a moment, as she trembled and moaned softly; as Anna Picket had done in the office. Anna quickly rose and drew her away from McGrath. There were tears in the cart-woman's eyes.

A woman with gray hair and involuntary head tremors, indicative of Parkinson's, leaned forward and said, "Lonny, tell us."

He started to say *tell you what?* but she held up a finger and said the same thing again.

So he told them. As best he could. Putting words to feelings that always sounded melodramatic; words that were wholly inadequate for the tidal wave of sorrow that held him down in darkness. "I miss them, oh God how I miss them," he said, twisting his hands. "I've never been like this.

My mother died, and I was lost, I was miserable, yes there was a feeling my heart would break, because I loved her. But I could *handle* it. I could comfort my father and my sister, I had it in me to do that. But these last two years…one after another…so many who were close to me…pieces of my past, my life…friends I'd shared times with, and now those times are gone, they slip away as I try to think of them. I, I just don't know *what to do*."

And he spoke of the mouth. The teeth. The closing of that mouth. The wind that had escaped from inside him.

"Did you ever sleepwalk, as a child?" a woman with a clubfoot asked. He said: yes, but only once. Tell us, they said.

"It was nothing. I was a little boy, maybe ten or eleven. My father found me standing in the hallway outside my bedroom, at the head of the stairs. I was asleep, and I was looking at the wall. I said, 'I don't see it here anywhere.' My father told me I'd said that; the next morning he told me. He took me back to bed. That was the only time, as best I know."

The women murmured around the circle to each other. Then the woman with Parkinson's said, "No, I don't think that's anything." Then she stood up, and came to him. She laid a hand on his forehead and said, "Go to sleep, Lonny."

And he blinked once, and suddenly sat bolt upright. But it wasn't an instant, it had been much longer. He had been asleep. For a long while. He knew it was so instantly, because it was now dark outside the house, and the women looked as if they had been savaged by living jungles. The blind woman was bleeding from her eyes and ears; the woman on the cart had fallen over, lay unconscious at his feet; in the chair where the fire victim had sat, there was now only a charred outline of a human being, still faintly smoking.

McGrath leaped to his feet. He looked about wildly. He didn't know what to do to help them. Beside him, Anna Picket lay slumped across the bolster arm of the chair, her body twisted and blood once again speckling her lips.

Then he realized: the woman who had touched him, the woman with Parkinson's, was gone.

They began to whimper, and several of them moved, their hands idly touching the air. A woman who had no nose tried to rise, slipped and fell. He rushed to her, helped her back into the chair, and he realized she was missing fingers on both hands. Leprosy…*no*! Hansen's disease, that's what it's called. She was coming to, and she whispered to him, "There...Teresa... help her..." and he looked where she was pointing, at a woman as pale as crystal, her hair a glowing white, her eyes colorless. "She...has...lupus..." the woman without a nose whispered.

McGrath went to Teresa. She looked up at him with fear and was barely able to say, "Can you...please...take me to a dark place...?"

He lifted her in his arms. She weighed nothing. He let her direct him up the stairs to the second floor, to the third bedroom off the main corridor. He opened the door; inside it was musty and unlit. He could barely make out the shape of a bed. He carried her over and placed her gently on the puffy down comforter. She reached up and touched his hand. "Thank you." She spoke haltingly, having trouble breathing. "We, we didn't expect anything...like that..."

McGrath was frantic. He didn't know what had happened, didn't know what he had done to them. He felt awful, felt responsible, *but he didn't know what he had done*!

"Go back to them," she whispered. "Help them."

"Where is the woman who touched me...?"

He heard her sobbing. "She's gone. Lurene is gone. It wasn't your fault. We didn't expect anything...like...that."

He rushed back downstairs.

They were helping one another. Anna Picket had brought water, and bottles of medicine, and wet cloths. They were helping one another. The healthier ones limping and crawling to the ones still unconscious or groaning in pain. And he smelled the fried metal scent of ozone in the air. There was a charred patch on the ceiling above the chair where the burned woman had been sitting.

He tried to help Anna Picket, but when she realized it was McGrath, she slapped his hand away. Then she gasped, and her hand flew to her mouth, and she began to cry again, and reached out to apologize. "Oh, my God, I'm so *sorry*! It wasn't your fault. You couldn't know...not even Lurene knew." She swabbed at her eyes, and laid a hand on his chest. "Go outside. Please. I'll be there in a moment."

A wide streak of dove-gray now bolted through her tangled hair. It had not been there before the instant of his sleep.

He went outside and stood under the stars. It was night, but it had not been night before Lurene had touched him. He stared up at the cold points of light, and the sense of irreparable loss overwhelmed him. He wanted to sink to his knees, letting his life ebb into the ground, freeing him from this misery that would not let him breathe. He thought of Victor, and the casket being cranked down into the earth, as Sally clung to him, murmuring words he could not understand, and hitting him again and again on the chest; not hard, but without measure, without meaning, with nothing but simple human misery. He thought of Alan, dying in a Hollywood apartment from AIDS, tended by his mother and sister who were, themselves, hysterical and constantly praying, asking Jesus to help them; dying in that apartment with the two roommates who had been sharing the rent, keeping to themselves, eating off paper plates for fear of contracting the plague, trying to figure out if they could get a lawyer to force Alan's removal; dying in that miserable apartment because the Kaiser Hospital had found a way around his coverage, and had forced him into "home care." He thought of Emily, lying dead beside her bed, having just dressed for dinner with her daughter, being struck by the grand mal seizure and her heart exploding, lying there for a day, dressed for a dinner she would never eat, with a daughter she would never again see. He thought of Mike, trying to smile from the hospital bed, and forgetting from moment to moment who Lonny was, as the tumor consumed his brain. He thought of Ted seeking shamans and homeopathists, running full tilt till he was cut down. He thought of Roy, all alone now that DeeDee was gone: half a unit, a severed dream, an incomplete conversation. He stood there with his head in his hands, rocking back and forth, trying to ease the pain.

When Anna Picket touched him, he started violently, a small cry of desolation razoring into the darkness.

"What *happened* in there?" he demanded. "Who *are* you people? What did I do to you? Please, oh please I'm asking you, tell me *what's going on!*"

"We absorb."

"I don't know what—"

"We take illness. We've always been with you. As far back as we can know. We have always had that capacity, to assume the illness. There aren't many of us, but we're everywhere. We absorb. We try to help. As Jesus wrapped himself in the leper's garments, as he touched the lame and the blind, and they were healed. I don't know where it comes from, some sort of intense empathy. But…we do it…we absorb."

"And with me…what was that in there…?"

"We didn't know. We thought it was just the heartache. We've encountered it before. That was why Tricia suggested you come to the Group."

"My wife…is Tricia one of you? Can she…take on the…does she absorb? I lived with her, I never—"

Anna was shaking her head. "No, Tricia has no idea what we are. She's never been here. Very few people have been so needing that I've brought them here. But she's a fine therapist, and we've helped a few of her patients. She thought you…" She paused. "She still cares for you. She felt your pain, and thought the Group might be able to help. She doesn't even know of the *real* REM Group."

He grabbed her by the shoulders, intense now.

"What happened in there?"

She bit her lip and closed her eyes tightly against the memory. "It was as you said. The mouth. We'd never seen that before. It, it *opened*. And then…and then…"

He shook her. *"What!?!"*

She wailed against the memory. The sound slammed against him and against the hills and against the cold points of the stars. "Mouths. In each of us! Opened. And the wind, it, it just, it just *hissed* out of us, each of us. And the pain we held, no, that *they* held—I'm just their contact for the world, they can't go anywhere, so I go and shop and bring and do—the pain *they* absorbed, it, it took some of them. Lurene and Margid…Teresa won't live…I know…"

McGrath was raving now. His head was about to burst. He shook her as she cried and moaned, demanding, "What's happening to us, how could I do such an awfulness to you, why is this being done to me, to *us*, why *now*, what's going wrong, please, you've got to tell me, you've got to *help* me, we've got to *do* something—"

And they hugged each other, clinging tightly to the only thing that promised support: each other. The sky wheeled above them, and the ground seemed to fall away. But they kept their balance, and finally she pushed him to arm's length and looked closely at his face and said, "I don't know. I *do not* know. This isn't like anything we've experienced before. Not even Alvarez or Ariès know about this. A wind, a terrible wind, something alive, leaving the body."

"Help me!"

"I *can't* help you! No one can help you, I don't think *anyone* can help you. Not even Le Braz…"

He clutched at the name. "Le Braz! Who's Le Braz?"

"No, you don't want to see Le Braz. Please, listen to me, try to go off where it's quiet, and lonely, and try to handle it yourself, that's the only way!"

"Tell me who Le Braz is!"

She slapped him. "You're not hearing me. If *we* can't do for you, then no one can. Le Braz is beyond anything we know, he can't be trusted, he does things that are outside, that are awful, I think. I don't really know. I went to him once, years ago, it's not something you want to—"

I don't care, he said. I don't care about any of it now. I have to rid myself of this. It's too terrible to live with. I see their faces. They're calling and I can't answer them. They plead with me to say something to them. I don't know what to say. I can't sleep. And when I sleep I dream of them. I can't live like this, because this isn't living. So tell me how to find Le Braz. I don't care, to Hell with the whole thing, I just don't give a damn, so *tell me*!

She slapped him again. Much harder. And again. And he took it. And finally she told him.

He had been an abortionist. In the days before it was legal, he had been the last hope for hundreds of women. Once, long before, he had been a surgeon. But they had taken that away from him. So he did what he could do. In the days when women went to small rooms with long tables, or to coat hangers, he had helped. He had charged two hundred dollars, just to keep up with supplies. In those days of secret thousands in brown paper bags stored in clothes closets, two hundred dollars was as if he had done the work for free. And they had put him in prison. But when he came out, he went back at it.

Anna Picket told McGrath that there had been other…

…work. Other experiments. She had said the word *experiments*, with a tone in her voice that made McGrath shudder. And she had said again, "For McGrath hath murdered sleep," and he asked her if he could take her car, and she said yes, and he had driven back to the 101 Freeway and headed north toward Santa Barbara, where Anna Picket said Le Braz now lived, and had lived for years, in total seclusion.

It was difficult locating his estate. The only gas station open in Santa Barbara at that hour did not carry maps. It had been years since free maps had been a courtesy of gas stations. Like so many other small courtesies in McGrath's world that had been spirited away before he could lodge a complaint. But there was no complaint department, in any case.

So he went to the Hotel Miramar, and the night clerk was a woman in her sixties who knew every street in Santa Barbara and knew very well the location of the Le Braz "place." She looked at McGrath as if he had asked her the location of the local abattoir. But she gave him explicit directions, and he thanked her, and she didn't say you're welcome, and he left. It was just lightening in the east as dawn approached.

By the time he found the private drive that climbed through heavy woods to the high-fenced estate, it was fully light. Sun poured across the channel and made the foliage seem Rain Forest lush. He looked back over his shoulder as he stepped out of the Le Sabre, and the Santa Monica Channel was silver and rippled and utterly oblivious to shadows left behind from the night.

He walked to the gate, and pressed the button on the intercom system. He waited, and pressed it again. Then a voice—he could not tell if it was male or female, young or old—cracked, "Who is it?"

"I've come from Anna Picket and the REM Group." He paused a moment, and when the silence persisted, he added, "The *real* REM Group. Women in a house in Hidden Hills."

The voice said, "Who are you? What's your name?"

"It doesn't matter. You don't know me. McGrath, my name is McGrath. I came a long way to see Le Braz."

"About what?"

"Open the gate and you'll know."

"We don't have visitors."

"I saw…there was a…I woke up suddenly, there was a, a kind of *mouth* in my body…a wind passed…"

There was a whirring sound, and the iron gate began to withdraw into the brick wall. McGrath rushed back to the car and started the engine. As the gate opened completely, he decked the accelerator and leaped through, even as the gate began without hesitation to close.

He drove up the winding drive through the Rain Forest, and when he came out at the top, the large, fieldstone mansion sat there, hidden from all sides by tall stands of trees and thick foliage. He pulled up on the crushed rock drive, and sat for a moment staring at the leaded windows that looked down emptily. It was cool here, and dusky, even though it was burgeoning day. He got out and went to the carved oak door. He was reaching for the knocker when the door was opened. By a ruined thing.

McGrath couldn't help himself. He gasped and fell back, his hands coming up in front of him as if to ward off any approach by the barely human being that stood in the entranceway.

It was horribly pink where it was not burned. At first McGrath thought it was a woman, that was his quick impression; but then he could not discern its sex, it might have been male. It had certainly been tortured in flames. The head was without hair, almost without skin that was not charred black. There seemed to be too many bends and joints in the arms. The sense that it was female came from the floor-length wide skirt it wore. He was spared the sight of the lower body, but he could tell there was considerable bulk there, a bulk that seemed to move gelatinously, as if neither human torso nor human legs lay within the circle of fabric.

And the creature stared at him from one milky eye, and one eye so pure and blue that his heart ached with the beauty of it. As features between the eyes and the chin that became part of the chest, without discernible neck, there were only charred knobs and bumps, and a lipless mouth blacker than the surrounding flesh. "Come inside," the doorkeeper said.

McGrath hesitated.

"Or go away," it said.

Lonny McGrath drew a deep breath and passed through. The doorkeeper moved aside only a trifle. They touched: blackened hip, back of a normal hand.

Closed and double-bolted, the passage out was now denied McGrath. He followed the asexual creature through a long, high-ceilinged foyer to a closed, heavily-paneled door to the right of a spiral staircase that led to the floor above. The thing, either man or woman, indicated he should enter. Then it shambled away, toward the rear of the mansion.

McGrath stood a moment, then turned the ornate L-shaped door handle, and entered. The heavy drapes were drawn against the morning light, but in the outlaw beams that latticed the room here and there, he saw an old man sitting in a high-backed chair, a lap robe concealing his legs. He stepped inside the library, for library it had to be: floor to ceiling bookcases, spilling their contents in teetering stacks all around the floor. Music swirled through the room. Classical music; McGrath didn't recognize it.

"Dr. Le Braz?" he said. The old man did not move. His head lay sunk on his chest. His eyes were closed. McGrath moved closer. The music swelled toward a crescendo, something symphonic. Now he was only three steps from the old man, and he called the name Le Braz again.

The eyes opened, and the leonine head rose. He stared at McGrath unblinkingly. The music came to an end. Silence filled the library.

The old man smiled sadly. And all ominousness left the space between them. It was a sweet smile. He inclined his head toward a stool beside the wingback. McGrath tried to give back a small smile, and took the seat offered.

"It is my hope that you are not here to solicit my endorsement for some new pharmacological product," the old man said.

"Are you Dr. Le Braz?"

"It is I who was, once, known by that name, yes."

"You have to help me."

Le Braz looked at him. There had been such a depth of ocean in the words McGrath had spoken, such a descent into stony caverns that all casualness was instantly denied. "Help you?"

"Yes. Please. I can't bear what I'm feeling. I've been through so much, seen so much these last months, I..."

"Help you?" the old man said again, whispering the phrase as if it had been rendered in a lost language. "I cannot even help myself...how can I possibly help you, young man?"

McGrath told him. Everything.

At some point the blackened creature entered the room, but McGrath was unaware of its presence till he had completed his story. Then, from behind him, he heard it say, "You are a remarkable person. Not one living person in a million has ever seen the Thanatos mouth. Not one in a hundred million has felt the passage of the soul. Not one in the memory of the human race has been so tormented that he thought it was real, and not a dream."

McGrath stared at the creature. It came lumbering across the room and stood just behind the old man's chair, not touching him. The old man sighed, and closed his eyes.

The creature said, "This was Josef Le Braz, who lived and worked and cared for his fellow man, and woman. He saved lives, and he married out of love, and he pledged himself to leave the world slightly better for his passage. And his wife died, and he fell into a well of melancholy such as no man had ever suffered. And one night he woke, feeling a chill, but he did not see the Thanatos mouth. All he knew was that he missed his wife so terribly that he wanted to end his life."

McGrath sat silently. He had no idea what this meant, this history of the desolate figure under the lap robe. But he waited, because if no help lay here in this house, of all houses secret and open in the world, then he knew that the next step for him was to buy a gun and to disperse the gray mist under which he lived.

Le Braz looked up. He drew in a deep breath and turned his eyes to McGrath. "I went to the machine," he said. "I sought the aid of the circuit and the chip. I was cold, and could never stop crying. I missed her so, it was unbearable."

The creature came around the wingback and stood over McGrath. "He brought her back from the Other Side."

McGrath's eyes widened. He understood.

The room was silent, building to a crescendo. He tried to get off the low stool, but he couldn't move. The creature stared down at him with its one gorgeous blue eye and its one unseeing milky marble. "He deprived her of peace. Now she must live on, in this half-life.

"This is Josef Le Braz, and he cannot support his guilt."

The old man was crying now. McGrath thought if one more tear was shed in the world he would say to hell with it and go for the gun. "Do you understand?" the old man said softly.

"Do you take the point?" the creature said.

McGrath's hands came up, open and empty. "The mouth...the wind..."

"The function of dream sleep," the creature said, "is to permit us to live. To flense the mind of that which dismays us. Otherwise, how could we bear the sorrow? The memories are their legacy, the parts of themselves left with us when they depart. But they are not whole, they are joys crying to be reunited with the one to whom they belong. You have seen the Thanatos mouth, you have felt a loved one departing. It should have freed you."

McGrath shook his head slowly, slowly. No, it didn't free me, it enslaved me, it torments me. No, slowly, no. I cannot bear it.

"Then you do not yet take the point, do you?"

The creature touched the old man's sunken cheek with a charred twig that had been a hand. The old man tried to look up with affection, but his head would not come around. "You must let it go, all of it," Le Braz said. "There is no other answer. Let it go...let *them* go. Give them back the parts they need to be whole on the Other Side, and let them in the name of kindness have the peace to which they are entitled."

"Let the mouth open," the creature said. "We cannot abide here. Let the wind of the soul pass through, and take the emptiness as release." And she said, "Let me tell you what it's like on the Other Side. Perhaps it will help."

McGrath laid a hand on his side. It hurt terribly, as of legions battering for release on a locked door.

He retraced his steps. He went back through previous days as if he were sleepwalking. *I don't see it here anywhere.*

He stayed at the ranch-style house in Hidden Hills, and helped Anna Picket as best he could. She drove him back to the city, and he picked up his car from the street in front of the office building on Pico. He put the three parking tickets in the glove compartment. That was work for the living. He went back to his apartment, and he took off his clothes, and he bathed. He lay naked on the bed where it had all started, and he tried to sleep. There were dreams. Dreams of smiling faces, and dreams of children he had known. Dreams of kindness, and dreams of hands that had held him.

And sometime during the long night a breeze blew.

But he never felt it.

And when he awoke, it was cooler in the world than it had been for a very long time; and when he cried for them, he was, at last, able to say goodbye.

A man is what he does with his attention.
John Ciardi

THE MAN WHO ROWED CHRISTOPHER COLUMBUS ASHORE

1993 Published in *Best American Short Stories*

LEVENDIS: On Tuesday the 1st of October, improbably dressed as an Explorer Scout, with his great hairy legs protruding from his knee-pants, and his heavily festooned merit badge sash slantwise across his chest, he helped an old, arthritic black woman across the street at the jammed corner of Wilshire and Western. In fact, she didn't *want* to cross the street, but he half-pulled, half-dragged her, the old woman screaming at him, calling him a khaki-colored motherfucker every step of the way.

LEVENDIS: On Wednesday the 2nd of October, he crossed his legs carefully as he sat in the Boston psychiatrist's office, making certain the creases of his pants—he was wearing the traditional morning coat and ambassadorially-striped pants—remained sharp, and he said to George Aspen Davenport, M.D., Ph.D., FAPA (who had studied with Ernst Kris *and* Anna Freud), "Yes, that's it, now you've got it." And Dr. Davenport made a note on his pad, lightly cleared his throat and phrased it differently: "Your mouth is…vanishing? That is to say, your mouth, the facial feature below your nose, it's uh disappearing?" The prospective patient nodded quickly, with a bright smile. "Exactly." Dr. Davenport made another note, continued to ulcerate the inside of his cheek, then tried a third time: "We're speaking now—heh heh, to maintain the idiom—we're speaking of your lips, or your tongue, or your palate, or your gums, or your teeth, or—" The other man sat forward, looking very serious, and replied, "We're talking *all* of it, Doctor. The whole, entire, complete aperture and everything around, over, under, and within. My *mouth*, the allness of my mouth. It's disappearing. What part of that is giving you a problem?" Davenport hmmm'd for a moment, said, "Let me check something," and he rose, went to the teak and glass bookcase against the far wall, beside the window that looked out on crowded, lively Boston Common, and he drew down a capacious volume. He flipped through it for a few minutes, and finally paused at a page on which he poked a finger. He turned to the elegant, gray-haired gentleman in the consultation chair, and he said, "Lipostomy." His prospective patient tilted his head to the side, like a dog listening for a clue, and arched his eyebrows expectantly as if to ask *yes, and lipostomy is what?* The psychiatrist brought the book to him, leaned down and pointed to the definition. "Atrophy of the mouth." The gray-haired gentleman, who looked to be in his early sixties, but remarkably well-tended and handsomely turned-out, shook his head slowly as Dr. Davenport walked back around to sit behind his desk. "No, I don't think so. It doesn't seem to be withering, it's just, well, simply, I can't put it any other way, it's very simply disappearing. Like the Cheshire cat's grin. Fading away." Davenport closed the book and laid it on the desktop, folded his hands atop the volume, and smiled condescendingly. "Don't you think this might be a delusion on your part? I'm looking at your mouth right now, and it's right there, just as it was when you came into the office." His prospective patient rose, retrieved his homburg from the sofa, and started toward the door. "It's a good thing I can read lips," he said, placing the hat on his head, "because I certainly don't need to pay your sort of exorbitant fee to be ridiculed." And he moved to the office door, and opened it to leave, pausing for only a moment to readjust his homburg, which had slipped down, due to the absence of ears on his head.

LEVENDIS: On Thursday the 3rd of October, he overloaded his grocery cart with okra and eggplant, giant bags of Kibbles 'n Bits 'n Bits 'n Bits, and jumbo boxes of Huggies. And as he wildly careened through the aisles of the Sentry Market in La Crosse, Wisconsin, he purposely engineered a collision between the carts of Kenneth Kulwin, a 47-year-old homosexual who had lived alone since the passing of his father thirteen years earlier, and Anne Gillen, a 35-year-old legal secretary who had been unable to find an escort to take her to her senior prom and whose social life had not improved in the decades since that death of hope. He began screaming at them, as if it had been *their* fault, thereby making allies of them. He was extremely rude, breathing muscatel breath on them, and finally stormed away, leaving them to sort out their groceries, leaving them to comment on his behavior, leaving them to take notice of each other. He went outside, smelling the Mississippi River, and he let the air out of Anne Gillen's tires. She would need a lift to the gas station. Kenneth Kulwin would tell her to call him "Kenny," and they would discover that their favorite movie was the 1945 romance, *The Enchanted Cottage*, starring Dorothy McGuire and Robert Young.

LEVENDIS: On Friday the 4th of October, he found an interstate trucker dumping badly sealed cannisters of phenazine in an isolated picnic area outside Phillipsburg, Kansas; and he shot him three times in the head; and wedged the body into one of the large, nearly empty trash barrels near the picnic benches.

LEVENDIS: On Saturday the 5th of October, he addressed two hundred and forty-four representatives of the country & western music industry in the Chattanooga Room just off the Tennessee Ballroom of the Opryland Hotel in Nashville. He said to them, "What's astonishing is not that there is so much ineptitude, slovenliness, mediocrity and downright bad taste in the world…what is unbelievable is that there is so much *good* art in the world. Everywhere." One of the attendees raised her hand and asked, "Are you good, or evil?" He thought about it for less than twenty seconds, smiled, and replied, "Good, of course! There's only one real evil in the world: mediocrity." They applauded sparsely, but politely. Nonetheless, later at the reception, *no one* touched the Swedish meatballs, or the rumaki.

LEVENDIS: On Sunday the 6th of October, he placed the exhumed remains of Noah's ark near the eastern summit of a nameless mountain in Kurdistan, where the next infrared surveillance of a random satellite flyby would reveal them. He was careful to seed the area with a plethora of bones, here and there around the site, as well as within the identifiable hull of the vessel. He made sure to place them two-by-two: every beast after his kind, and all the cattle after their kind, and every creeping thing that creepeth upon the earth after his kind, and every fowl after his kind, and every bird of every sort. Two-by-two. Also the bones of pairs of gryphons, unicorns, stegosaurs, tengus, dragons, orthodontists, and the carbon-dateable 50,000-year old bones of a relief pitcher for the Boston Red Sox.

LEVENDIS: On Monday the 7th of October, he kicked a cat. He kicked it a far distance. To the passersby who watched, there on Galena Street in Aurora, Colorado, he said: "I am an unlimited person, sadly living in a limited world." When the housewife who planned to call the police yelled at him from her kitchen window, "Who are you? What is your name!?!" he cupped his hands around his mouth so she would hear him, and he yelled back, "Levendis! It's a Greek word." They found the cat imbarked halfway through a tree. The tree was cut down, and the section with the cat was cut in two, the animal tended by a talented taxidermist who tried to quell the poor beast's terrified mewling and vomiting. The cat was later sold as bookends.

LEVENDIS: On Tuesday the 8th of October, he called the office of the District Attorney in Cadillac, Michigan, and reported that the blue 1988 Mercedes that had struck and killed two children playing in a residential street in Hamtramck just after sundown the night before, belonged to a pastry chef whose sole client was a Cosa Nostra *pezzonovante*. He gave detailed information as to the location of the chop shop where the Mercedes had been taken to be banged out, bondo'd, and repainted. He gave the license number. He indicated where, in the left front wheel-well, could be found a piece of the skull of the younger of the two little girls. Not only did the piece fit, like the missing section of a modular woodblock puzzle, but pathologists were able to conduct an accurate test that provided irrefutable evidence that would hold up under any attack in court: the medical examiner got past the basic ABO groups, narrowed the scope of identification with the five Rh tests, the M and N tests (also cap-S and small-s variations), the Duffy blood groups, and the Kidd types, both A and B; and finally he was able to validate the rare absence of Jr a, present in most blood-groups but missing in some Japanese-Hawaiians and Samoans. The little girl's name was Sherry Tualaulelei. When the homicide investigators learned that the pastry chef, his wife, and their three children had gone to New York City on vacation four days before the hit-and-run, and were able to produce ticket stubs that placed them seventh row center of the Martin Beck Theater, enjoying the revival of *Guys and Dolls*, at the precise moment the Mercedes struck the children, the Organized Crime Unit was called in, and the scope of the investigation was broadened. Sherry Tualaulelei was instrumental in the conviction and thirty-three-year imprisonment of the pastry chef's boss, Sinio "Sally Comfort" Conforte, who had "borrowed" a car to sneak out for a visit to his mistress.

LEVENDIS: On Wednesday the 9th of October, he sent a fruit basket to Patricia and Faustino Evangelista, a middle-aged couple in Norwalk, Connecticut, who had given to the surviving son, the gun his beloved older brother had used to kill himself. The accompanying note read: *Way to go, sensitive Mom and Dad!*

LEVENDIS: On Thursday the 10th of October, he created a cure for bone-marrow cancer. Anyone could make it: the juice of fresh lemons, spiderwebs, the scrapings of raw carrots, the opaque and whitish portion of the toenail called the *lunula*, and carbonated water. The pharmaceutical cartel quickly hired a prestigious Philadelphia PR firm to throw its efficacy into question, but the AMA and FDA ran accelerated tests, found it to be potent, with no deleterious effects, and recommended its immediate use. It had no effect on AIDS, however. Nor did it work on the common cold. Remarkably, physicians praised the easing of their workload.

LEVENDIS: On Friday the 11th of October, he lay in his own filth on the sidewalk outside the British Embassy in Rangoon, holding a begging bowl. He was just to the left of the gate, half-hidden by the angle of the high wall from sight of the military guards on post. A woman in her fifties, who had been let out of a jitney just up the street, having paid her fare and having tipped as few rupees as necessary to escape a strident rebuke by the driver, smoothed the peplum of her shantung jacket over her hips, and marched imperially toward the Embassy gates. As she came abaft the derelict, he rose on one elbow and shouted at her ankles, "Hey, lady! I write these pomes, and I sell 'em for a buck inna street, an' it keeps juvenile delinquents offa the streets so's they don't spit on ya! So whaddaya think, y'wanna buy one?" The matron did not pause, striding toward the gates, but she said snappishly, "You're a businessman. Don't talk art."

This is a story titled

The Route of Odysseus

> "You will find the scene of Odysseus's wanderings when you find
> the cobbler who sewed up the bag of the winds."
> *Eratosthenes, late 3rd century, B.C.E.*

LEVENDIS: On Saturday the 12th of October, having taken the sidestep, he came to a place near Weimar in southwest Germany. He did not see the photographer snapping pictures of the scene. He stood among the cordwood bodies. It was cold for the spring; and even though he was heavily clothed, he shivered. He walked down the rows of bony corpses, looking into the black holes that had been eye sockets, seeing an endless chicken dinner, the bones gnawed clean, tossed like jackstraws in heaps. The stretched-taut groins of men and women, flesh tarpaulins where passion had once smoothed the transport from sleep to wakefulness. Entwined so cavalierly that here a woman with three arms, and there a child with the legs of a sprinter three times his age. A woman's face, looking up at him with soot for sight, remarkable cheekbones, high and lovely, she might have been an actress. Xylophones for chests and torsos, violin bows that had waved goodbye and hugged grandchildren and lifted in toasts to the passing of traditions, gourd whistles between eyes and mouths. He stood among the cordwood bodies and could not remain merely an instrument himself. He sank to his haunches, crouched and wept, burying his head in his hands, as the photographer took shot after shot, an opportunity like a gift from the editor. Then he tried to stop crying, and stood, and the cold cut him, and he removed his heavy topcoat and placed it gently over the bodies of two women and a man lying so close and intermixed that it easily served as coverlet for them. He stood among the cordwood bodies, 24 April 1945, Buchenwald, and the photograph would appear in a book published forty-six years later, on Saturday the 12th of October. The photographer's roll ran out just an instant before the slim young man without a topcoat took the sidestep. Nor did he hear the tearful young man say, "Sertsa." In Russian, *sertsa* means soul.

LEVENDIS: On Sunday the 13th of October, he did nothing. He rested. When he thought about it, he grew annoyed. "Time does not become sacred until we have lived it," he said. But he thought: *to hell with it; even God knocked off for a day.*

LEVENDIS: On Monday the 14th of October, he climbed up through the stinking stairwell shaft of a Baltimore tenement, clutching his notebook, breathing through his mouth to block the smell of mildew, garbage, and urine, focusing his mind on the apartment number he was seeking, straining through the evening dimness in the wan light of one bulb hanging high above, barely illuminating the vertical tunnel, as he climbed and climbed, straining to see the numbers on the doors, going up, realizing the tenants had pulled the numbers *off* the doors to foil him and welfare investigators like him, stumbling over something oily and sobbing jammed into a corner of the last step, losing his grip on the rotting bannister and finding it just in time, trapped for a moment in the hopeless beam of washed-out light falling from above, poised in mid-tumble and then regaining his grip, hoping the welfare recipient under scrutiny would not be home, so he could knock off for the day, hurry back downtown and crosstown and take a shower, going up till he had reached the topmost landing, and finding the number scratched on the doorframe, and knocking, getting no answer, knocking again, hearing first the scream, then the sound of someone beating against a wall, or the floor, with a heavy stick, and then the scream again, and then another scream so closely following the first that it might have been one scream only, and he threw himself against the door, and it was old but never had been well built, and it came away, off its hinges, in one rotten crack, and he was inside, and the most beautiful young black woman he had ever seen was tearing the rats off her baby. He left the check on the kitchen table, he did not have an affair with her, he did not see her fall from the apartment window, six storeys into a courtyard, and never knew if she came back from the grave to escape the rats that gnawed at her cheap wooden casket. He never loved her, and so was not there when what she became flowed back up through the walls of the tenement to absorb him and meld with him and become one with him as he lay sleeping penitently on the filthy floor of the topmost apartment. He left the check, and none of that happened.

LEVENDIS: On Tuesday the 15th of October, he stood in the Greek theatre at Aspendos, Turkey, a structure built two thousand years earlier, so acoustically perfect that every word spoken on its stage could be heard with clarity in any of its thirteen thousand seats, and he spoke to a little boy sitting high above him. He uttered Count Von Manfred's dying words, Schumann's overture, Byron's poem: "Old man, 'tis not so difficult to die." The child smiled and waved. He waved back, then shrugged. They became friends at a distance. It was the first time someone other than his mother, who was dead, had been kind to the boy. In years to come it would be a reminder that there was a smile out there on the wind. The little boy looked down the rows and concentric rows of seats: the man 'way down there was motioning for him to come to him. The child, whose name was Orhon, hopped and hopped, descending to the center of the ring as quickly as he could. As he came to the core, and walked out across the orchestra ring, he studied the man. This person was very tall, and he needed a shave, and his hat had an extremely wide brim like the hat of Kül, the man who made weekly trips to Ankara, and he wore a long overcoat far too hot for this day. Orhon could not see the man's eyes because he wore dark glasses that reflected the sky. Orhon thought this man looked like a mountain bandit, only dressed more impressively. Not wisely for a day as torpid as this, but more impressively than Bilge and his men, who raided the farming villages. When he reached the tall man, and they smiled at each other, this person said to Orhon, "I am an unlimited person living in a limited world." The child did not know what to say to that. But he liked the man. "Why do you wear such heavy wool today? I am barefoot." He raised his dusty foot to show the man, and was embarrassed at the dirty cloth tied around his big toe. And the man said, "Because I need a safe place to keep the limited world." And he unbuttoned his overcoat, and held open one side, and showed Orhon what he would inherit one day, if he tried very hard not to be a despot. Pinned to the fabric, each with the face of the planet, were a million and more timepieces, each one the Earth at a different moment, and all of them purring erratically like dozing sphinxes. And Orhon stood there, in the heat, for quite a long while, and listened to the ticking of the limited world.

LEVENDIS: On Wednesday the 16th of October, he chanced upon three skinheads in Doc Martens and cheap black leatherette, beating the crap out of an interracial couple who had emerged from the late show at the La Salle Theater in Chicago. He stood quietly and watched. For a long while.

LEVENDIS: On Thursday the 17th of October he chanced upon three skinheads in Doc Martens and cheap black leatherette, beating the crap out of an interracial couple who had stopped for a bite to eat at a Howard Johnson's near King of Prussia on the Pennsylvania Turnpike. He removed the inch-and-a-half-thick ironwood dowel he always carried beside his driver's seat and, holding the 2½′ long rod at its centerpoint, laid alongside his pants leg so it could not be seen in the semi-darkness of the parking lot, he came up behind the three as they kicked the black woman and the white man lying between parked cars. He tapped the tallest of the trio on his shoulder, and when the boy turned around—he couldn't have been more than seventeen—he dropped back a step, slid the dowel up with his right hand, gripped it tightly with his left, and drove the end of the rod into the eye of the skinhead, punching through behind the socket and pulping the brain. The boy flailed backward, already dead, and struck his partners. As they turned, he was spinning the dowel like a baton, faster and faster, and as the stouter of the two attackers charged him, he whipped it around his head and slashed straight across the boy's throat. The snapping sound ricocheted off the dark hillside beyond the restaurant. He kicked the third boy in the groin, and when he dropped, and fell on his back, he kicked him under the chin, opening the skinhead's mouth; and then he stood over him, and with both hands locked around the pole, as hard as he could, he piledrove the wooden rod into the kid's mouth, shattering his teeth, and turning the back of his skull to flinders. The dowel scraped concrete through the ruined face. Then he helped the man and his wife to their feet, and bullied the manager of the Howard Johnson's into actually letting them lie down in his office till the State Police arrived. He ordered a plate of fried clams and sat there eating pleasurably until the cops had taken his statement.

LEVENDIS: On Friday the 18th of October, he took a busload of Mormon schoolchildren to the shallow waters of the Great Salt Lake in Utah, to pay homage to the great sculptor Smithson by introducing the art-ignorant children to the *Spiral Jetty*, an incongruously gorgeous line of earth and stone that curves out and away like a thought lost in the tide. "The man who made this, who dreamed it up and then *made* it, you know what he once said?" And they ventured that no, they didn't know what this Smithson sculptor had said, and the man who had driven the bus paused for a dramatic moment, and he repeated Smithson's words: "Establish enigmas, not explanations." They stared at him. "Perhaps you had to be there," he said, shrugging. "Who's for ice cream?" And they went to a Baskin-Robbins.

LEVENDIS: On Saturday the 19th of October, he filed a thirty-million-dollar lawsuit against the major leagues in the name of Alberda Jeanette Chambers, a 19-year-old lefthander with a fadeaway fast ball clocked at better than 96 mph; a dipsy-doodle slider that could do a barrel-roll and clean up after itself; an ERA of 2.10; who could hit from either side of the plate with a batting average of .360; who doubled as a peppery little short-stop working with a trapper's mitt of her own design; who had been refused tryouts with virtually every professional team in the United States (also Japan) from the bigs all the way down to the Pony League. He filed in Federal District Court for the Southern Division of New York State, and told Ted Koppel that Allie Chambers would be the first female player, mulatto or otherwise, in the Baseball Hall of Fame.

LEVENDIS: On Sunday the 20th of October, he drove out and around through the streets of Raleigh and Durham, North Carolina, in a rented van equipped with a public address system, and he endlessly reminded somnambulistic pedestrians and families entering eggs'n'grits restaurants (many of these adults had actually voted for Jesse Helms and thus were in danger of losing their *sertsa*) that perhaps they should ignore their bibles today, and go back and reread Shirley Jackson's short story, "One Ordinary Day, with Peanuts."

This is a story titled

The Daffodils that Entertain

LEVENDIS: On Monday the 21st of October, having taken the sidestep, he wandered through that section of New York City known as the Tenderloin. It was 1892. Crosstown on 24th Street from Fifth Avenue to Seventh, then he turned uptown and walked slowly on Seventh to 40th. Midtown was rife with brothels, their red lights shining through the shadows, challenging the wan gaslit streetlamps. The Edison and Swan United Electric Light Co., Ltd., had improved business tremendously through the wise solicitations of a salesman with a Greek-sounding name who had canvassed the prostitution district west of Broadway only five years earlier, urging the installation of Mr. Joseph Wilson Swan and Mr. Thomas Alva Edison's filament lamps: painted crimson, fixed above the ominously yawning doorways of the area's many houses of easy virtue. He passed an alley on 36th Street, and heard a woman's voice in the darkness complaining, "You said you'd give me two dollars. You have to give it to me first! Stop! No, *first* you gotta give me the two dollars!" He stepped into the alley, let his eyes acclimate to the darkness so total, trying to hold his breath against the stench; and then he saw them. The man was in his late forties, wearing a bowler and a shin-length topcoat with an astrakhan collar. The sound of horse-drawn carriages clopped loudly on the bricks beyond the alley, and the man in the astrakhan looked up, toward the alley mouth. His face was strained, as if he expected an accomplice of the girl, a footpad or shoulder-hitter or bully-boy pimp to charge to her defense. He had his fly unbuttoned and his thin, pale penis extended; the girl was backed against the alley wall, the man's left hand at her throat; and he had hiked up her apron and skirt and petticoats, and was trying to get his right hand into her drawers. She pushed against him, but to no avail. He was large and strong. But when he saw the other man standing down there, near the mouth of the alley, he let her garments drop, and fished his organ back into his pants, but didn't waste time buttoning up. "You there! Like to watch your betters at work, do you?" The man who had done the sidestep spoke softly: "Let the girl go. Give her the two dollars, and let her go." The man in the bowler took a step toward the mouth of the alley, his hands coming up in a standard pugilist's extension. He gave a tiny laugh that was a snort that was rude and derisive: "Oh so, fancy yourself something of the John L. Sullivan, do you, captain? Well, let's see how you and I and the Marquis Q get along…" and he danced forward, hindered considerably by the bulky overcoat. As he drew within double arm's-length of his opponent the younger man drew the taser from his coat pocket, fired at pointblank range, the barbs striking the pugilist in the cheek and neck, the charge lifting him off his feet and driving him back into the brick wall so hard that the filaments were wrenched loose, and the potential fornicator fell forward, his eyes rolled up in his head. Fell forward so hard he smashed three of his front teeth, broken at the gum-line. The girl tried to run, but the alley was a dead end. She watched as the man with the strange weapon came to her. She could barely see his face, and there had been all those killings with that Jack the Ripper in London a few years back, and there was talk this Jack had been a Yankee and had come back to New York. She was terrified. Her name was Poppy Skurnik, she was an orphan, and she worked way downtown as a pieceworker in a shirtwaist factory. She made one dollar and sixty-five cents a week, for six days of labor, from seven in the morning until seven at night, and it was barely enough to pay for her lodgings at Baer's Rents. So she "supplemented" her income with a stroll in the Tenderloin, twice a week, never more, and prayed that she could continue to avoid the murderous attentions of gentlemen who liked to cripple girls after they'd topped them, continue to avoid the pressures of pimps and boy friends who wanted her to work for them, continue to avoid the knowledge that she was no longer "decent" but was also a long way from winding up in one of these red-light whorehouses. He took her gently by the hand, and started to lead her out of the alley, carefully stepping over the unconscious molester. When they reached the street, and she saw how handsome he was, and how young he was, and how premierely he was dressed, she also smiled. She was extraordinarily attractive, and the young man tipped his hat and spoke to her kindly, inquiring as to her name, and where she lived, and if she would like to accompany him for some dinner. And she accepted, and he hailed a carriage, and took her to Delmonico's for the finest meal she had ever had. And later, much later, when he brought her to his townhouse on upper Fifth Avenue, in the posh section, she was ready to do anything he required of her. But instead, all he asked was that she allow him to give her a hundred dollars in exchange for one second of small pain. And she felt fear, because she knew what these nabobs were like, *but a hundred dollars*! So she said yes, and he asked her to bare her left buttock, and she did it with embarrassment, and there was exactly one second of mosquito bite pain, and then he was wiping the spot where he had in injected her with penicillin, with a cool and fragrant wad of cotton batting. "Would you like to sleep the night here, Poppy?" the young man asked. "My room is down the hall, but I think you'll be very comfortable in this one." And she was worried that he had done something awful to her, like inject her with a bad poison, but she didn't *feel* any different, and he seemed so nice, so she said yes, that would be a dear way to spend the evening, and he gave her ten ten-dollar bills, and wished her a pleasant sleep, and left the room, having saved her life, for she had contracted syphilis the week before, though she didn't know it; and within a year she would have been unable, by her appearance alone, to get men in the streets; and would have been let go at the shirtwaist factory; and would have been seduced and sold into one of the worst of the brothels; and would have been dead within another two years. But this night she slept well, between cool sheets with hand-embroidered lace edging, and when she rose the next day he was gone, and no one told her to leave the townhouse, and so she stayed on from day to day, for years, and eventually married and gave birth to three children, one of whom grew to maturity, married, had a child who became an adult and saved the lives of millions of innocent men, women, and children. But that night in 1892 she slept a deep, sweet, recuperative and dreamless sleep.

LEVENDIS: On Tuesday the 22nd of October, he visited a plague of asthmatic toads on Iisalmi, a small town in Finland; a rain of handbills left over from World War II urging the SS troops to surrender on Chejudo, an island off the southern coast of Korea; a shock wave of forsythia on Linares in Spain; and a fully-restored 1926 Ahrens-Fox model RK fire engine on a mini-mall in Clarksville, Arkansas.

LEVENDIS: On Wednesday the 23rd of October, he corrected every history book in America so that they no longer called it The Battle of Bunker Hill, but rather Breeds Hill where, in fact, the engagement of 17 June 1775 had taken place. He also invested every radio and television commentator with the ability to differentiate between "in a moment" and "momentarily," which were not at all the same thing, and the misuse of which annoyed him greatly. The former was in his job description; the latter was a matter of personal pique.

LEVENDIS: On Thursday the 24th of October, he revealed to the London *Times* and *Paris-Match* the name of the woman who had stood on the grassy knoll, behind the fence, in Dallas that day, and fired the rifle shots that killed John F. Kennedy. But no one believed Marilyn Monroe could have done the deed and gotten away unnoticed. Not even when he provided her suicide note that confessed the entire matter and tragically told in her own words how jealousy and having been jilted had driven her to hire that weasel Lee Harvey Oswald, and that pig Jack Ruby, and how she could no longer live with the guilt, goodbye. No one would run the story, not even the *Star*, not even *The Enquirer*, not even *TV Guide*. But he tried.

LEVENDIS: On Friday the 25th of October, he upped the intelligence of every human being on the planet by forty points.

LEVENDIS: On Saturday the 26th of October, he lowered the intelligence of every human being on the planet by forty-two points.

This is a story titled

At Least One Good Deed a Day, Every Single Day

LEVENDIS: On Sunday the 27th of October, he returned to a family in Kalgoorlie, SW Australia, a five-year-old child who had been kidnapped from their home in Bayonne, New Jersey, fifteen years earlier. The child was no older than before the family had immigrated, but he now spoke only in a dialect of Etruscan, a language that had not been heard on the planet for thousands of years. Having most of the day free, however, he then made it his business to kill the remaining seventeen American GIs being held MIA in an encampment in the heart of Laos. Waste not, want not.

LEVENDIS: On Monday the 28th of October, still exhilarated from the work and labors of the preceding day, he brought out of the highlands of North Vietnam Capt. Eugene Y. Grasso, USAF, who had gone down under fire twenty-eight years earlier. He returned him to his family in Anchorage, Alaska, where his wife, remarried, refused to see him but his daughter whom he had never seen, would. They fell in love, and lived together in Anchorage, where their story provided endless confusion to the ministers of several faiths.

LEVENDIS: On Tuesday the 29th of October, he destroyed the last bits of evidence that would have led to answers to the mysteries of the disappearances of Amelia Earhart, Ambrose Bierce, Benjamin Bathurst and Jimmy Hoffa. He washed the bones and placed them in a display of early American artifacts.

LEVENDIS: On Wednesday the 30th of October, he traveled to New Orleans, Louisiana, where he waited at a restaurant in Metairie for the former head of the Ku Klux Klan, now running for state office, to show up to meet friends. As the man stepped out of his limousine, wary guards on both sides of him, the traveler fired a Laws rocket from the roof of the eatery. It blew up the former KKK prexy, his guards, and a perfectly good Cadillac Eldorado. Leaving the electoral field open, for the enlightened voters of Louisiana, to a man who, as a child, had assisted Mengele's medical experiments, a second contender who had changed his name to avoid being arrested for child mutilation, and an illiterate swamp cabbage farmer from Baton Rouge whose political philosophy involved cutting the throats of peccary pigs, and thrusting one's face into the boiling blood of the corpse. Waste not, want not.

LEVENDIS: On Thursday the 31st of October, he restored to his throne the Dalai Lama, and closed off the mountain passes that provided land access to Tibet, and caused to blow constantly a cataclysmic snowstorm that did not affect the land below, but made any accessibility by air impossible. The Dalai Lama offered a referendum to the people: should we rename our land Shangri-La?

LEVENDIS: On Friday the 32nd of October, he addressed a convention of readers of cheap fantasy novels, saying, "We invent our lives (and other people's) as we live them; what we call 'life' is itself a fiction. Therefore, we must constantly strive to produce only good art, absolutely entertaining fiction." (He did *not* say to them: "I am an unlimited person, sadly living in a limited world.") They smiled politely, but since he spoke only in Etruscan, they did not understand a word he said.

LEVENDIS: On Saturday the 33rd of October, he did the sidestep and worked the oars of the longboat that brought Christopher Columbus to the shores of the New World, where he was approached by a representative of the native peoples, who laughed at the silly clothing the great navigator wore. They all ordered pizza and the man who had done the rowing made sure that venereal disease was quickly spread so that centuries later he could give a beautiful young woman an inoculation in her left buttock.

LEVENDIS: On Piltic the 34th of October, he gave all dogs the ability to speak in English, French, Mandarin, Urdu, and Esperanto; but all they could say was rhyming poetry of the worst sort, and he called it *doggerel*.

LEVENDIS: On Sqwaybe the 35th of October, he was advised by the Front Office that he had been having too rich a time at the expense of the Master Parameter, and he was removed from his position, and the unit was closed down, and darkness was penciled in as a mid-season replacement. He was reprimanded for having called himself Levendis, which is a Greek word for someone who is full of the pleasure of living. He was reassigned, with censure, but no one higher up noticed that on his new assignment he had taken the name Sertsa.

This has been a story titled

Shagging Fungoes

MEFISTO IN ONYX

1993 Bram Stoker Award: Novella; Locus Poll Award: Best Novella

ONCE. I ONLY went to bed with her once. Friends for eleven years—before and since—but it was just one of those things, just one of those crazy flings: the two of us alone on a New Year's Eve, watching rented Marx Brothers videos so we wouldn't have to go out with a bunch of idiots and make noise and pretend we were having a good time when all we'd be doing was getting drunk, whooping like morons, vomiting on slow-moving strangers, and spending more money than we had to waste. And we drank a little too much cheap champagne; and we fell off the sofa laughing at Harpo a few times too many; and we wound up on the floor at the same time; and next thing we knew we had our faces plastered together, and my hand up her skirt, and her hand down in my pants…

But it was just the *once*, fer chrissakes! Talk about imposing on a cheap sexual liaison! She *knew* I went mixing in other people's minds only when I absolutely had no other way to make a buck. Or I forgot myself and did it in a moment of human weakness.

It was always foul.

Slip into the thoughts of the best person who ever lived, even Saint Thomas Aquinas, for instance, just to pick an absolutely terrific person you'd think had a mind so clean you could eat off it (to paraphrase my mother), and when you come out—take my word for it—you'd want to take a long, intense shower in Lysol.

Trust me on this: I go into somebody's landscape when there's *nothing else* I can do, no other possible solution…or I forget and do it in a moment of human weakness. Such as, say, the IRS holds my feet to the fire; or I'm about to get myself mugged and robbed and maybe murdered; or I need to find out if some specific she that I'm dating has been using somebody else's dirty needle or has been sleeping around without she's taking some extra-heavy-duty AIDS precautions; or a co-worker's got it in his head to set me up so I make a mistake and look bad to the boss and I find myself in the unemployment line again; or…

I'm a wreck for weeks after.

Go jaunting through a landscape trying to pick up a little insider arbitrage bric-a-brac, and come away no better heeled, but all muddy with the guy's infidelities, and I can't look a decent woman in the eye for days. Get told by a motel desk clerk that they're all full up and he's sorry as hell but I'll just have to drive on for about another thirty miles to find the next vacancy, jaunt into his landscape and find him lit up with neon signs that got a lot of the word *nigger* in them, and I wind up hitting the sonofabitch so hard his grandmother has a bloody nose, and usually have to hide out for three or four weeks after. Just about to miss a bus, jaunt into the head of the driver to find his name so I can yell for him to hold it a minute Tom or George or Willie, and I get smacked in the mind with all the garlic he's been eating for the past month because his doctor told him it was good for his system, and I start to dry-heave, and I wrench out of the landscape, and not only have I missed the bus, but I'm so sick to my stomach I have to sit down on the filthy curb to get my gorge submerged. Jaunt into a potential employer, to see if he's trying to lowball me, and I learn he's part of a massive cover-up of industrial malfeasance that's caused hundreds of people to die when this or that cheaply-made grommet or tappet or gimbal mounting underperforms and fails, sending the poor souls falling thousands of feet to shrieking destruction. Then just *try* to accept the job, even if you haven't paid your rent in a month. No way.

Absolutely: I listen in on the landscape *only* when my feet are being fried; when the shadow stalking me turns down alley after alley tracking me relentlessly; when the drywall guy I've hired to repair the damage done by my leaky shower presents me with a dopey smile and a bill three hundred and sixty bucks higher than the estimate. Or in a moment of human weakness.

But I'm a wreck for weeks after. For weeks.

Because you can't, you simply can't, you absolutely *cannot* know what people are truly and really like till you jaunt their landscape. If Aquinas had had my ability, he'd have very quickly gone off to be a hermit, only occasionally visiting the mind of a sheep or a hedgehog. In a moment of human weakness.

That's why in my whole life—and, as best I can remember back, I've been doing it since I was five or six years old, maybe even younger—there have only been eleven, maybe twelve people, of all those who know that I can "read minds," that I've permitted myself to get close to. Three of them never used it against me, or tried to exploit me, or tried to kill me when I wasn't looking. Two of those three were my mother and father, a pair of sweet old black folks who'd adopted me, a late-in-life baby, and were now dead (but probably still worried about me, even on the Other Side), and whom I missed very very much, particularly in moments like this. The other eight, nine were either so turned off by the knowledge that they made sure I never came within a mile of them—one moved to another entire country just to be on the safe side, although her thoughts were a helluva lot more boring and innocent than she thought they were—or they tried to brain me with something heavy when I was distracted—I still have a shoulder separation that kills me for two days before it rains—or they tried to use me to make a buck for them. Not having the common sense to figure it out, that if I was *capable* of using the ability to make vast sums of money, why the hell was I living hand-to-mouth like some overaged grad student who was afraid to desert the university and go become an adult?

Now *they* was some dumb-ass muthuhfugguhs.

Of the three who never used it against me—my mom and dad—the last was Allison Roche. Who sat on the stool next to me, in the middle of May, in the middle of a Wednesday afternoon, in the middle of Clanton, Alabama, squeezing ketchup onto her All-American Burger, imposing on the memory of that one damned New Year's Eve sexual interlude, with Harpo and his sibs; the two of us all alone except for the fry-cook; and she waited for my reply.

"I'd sooner have a skunk spray my pants leg," I replied.

She pulled a napkin from the chrome dispenser and swabbed up the red that had overshot the sesame-seed bun and redecorated the Formica countertop. She looked at me from under thick, lustrous eyelashes; a look of impatience and violet eyes that must have been a killer when she unbottled it at some truculent witness for the defense. Allison Roche was a Chief Deputy District Attorney in and for Jefferson County, with her office in Birmingham, Alabama. Where near we sat, in Clanton, having a secret meeting, having All-American Burgers; three years after having had quite a bit of champagne, 1930s black-and-white video rental comedy, and black-and-white sex. One extremely stupid New Year's Eve.

Friends for eleven years. And once, just once; as a prime example of what happens in a moment of human weakness. Which is not to say that it wasn't terrific, because it was; absolutely terrific; but we never did it again; and we never brought it up again after the next morning when we opened our eyes and looked at each other the way you look at an exploding can of sardines, and both of us said *Oh Jeeezus* at the same time. Never brought it up again until this memorable afternoon at the greasy spoon where I'd joined Ally, driving up from Montgomery to meet her halfway, after her peculiar telephone invitation.

Can't say the fry-cook, Mr. All-American, was particularly happy at the pigmentation arrangement at his counter. But I stayed out of his head and let him think what he wanted. Times change on the outside, but the inner landscape remains polluted.

"All I'm asking you to do is go have a chat with him," she said. She gave me that look. I have a hard time with that look. It isn't entirely honest, neither is it entirely disingenuous. It plays on my remembrance of that one night we spent in bed. And is just *dis*honest enough to play on the part of that night we spent on the floor, on the sofa, on the coffee counter between the dining room and the kitchenette, in the bathtub, and about nineteen minutes crammed among her endless pairs of shoes in a walk-in clothes closet that smelled strongly of cedar and virginity. She gave me that look, and wasted no part of the memory.

"I don't *want* to go have a chat with him. Apart from he's a piece of human shit, and I have better things to do with my time than to go on down to Atmore and take a jaunt through this crazy sonofabitch's diseased mind, may I remind you that of the hundred and sixty, seventy men who have died in that electric chair, including the original 'Yellow Mama' they scrapped in 1990, about a hundred and thirty of them were gentlemen of color, and I do not mean you to picture any color of a shade much lighter than that cuppa coffee you got sittin' by your left hand right this minute, which is to say that I, being an inordinately well-educated African-American who values the full measure of living negritude in his body, am not crazy enough to want to visit a racist 'co-rectional center' like Holman Prison, thank you very much."

"Are you finished?" she asked, wiping her mouth.

"Yeah. I'm finished. Case closed. Find somebody else."

She didn't like that. "There *isn't* anybody else."

"There has to be. Somewhere. Go check the research files at Duke University. Call the Fortean Society. Mensa. *Jeopardy.* Some 900 number astrology psychic hotline. Ain't there some semi-senile Senator with a full-time paid assistant who's been trying to get legislation through one of the statehouses for the last five years to fund this kind of bullshit research? What about the Russians…now that the Evil Empire's fallen, you ought to be able to get some word about their success with Kirlian auras or whatever those assholes were working at. Or you could—"

She screamed at the top of her lungs. *"Stop it, Rudy!"*

The fry-cook dropped the spatula he'd been using to scrape off the grill. He picked it up, looking at us, and his face (I didn't read his mind) said *If that white bitch makes one more noise I'm callin' the cops.*

I gave him a look he didn't want, and he went back to his chores, getting ready for the after-work crowd. But the stretch of his back and angle of his head told me he wasn't going to let this pass.

I leaned in toward her, got as serious as I could, and just this quietly, just this softly, I said, "Ally, good pal, listen to me. You've been one of the few friends I could count on, for a long time now. We have history between us, and you've *never*, not once, made me feel like a freak. So okay, I trust you. I trust you with something about me that causes immeasurable goddam pain. A thing about me that could get me killed. You've never betrayed me, and you've never tried to use me.

"Till now. This is the first time. And you've got to admit that it's not even as rational as you maybe saying to me that you've gambled away every cent you've got and you owe the mob a million bucks and would I mind taking a trip to Vegas or Atlantic City and taking a jaunt into the minds of some high-pocket poker players so I could win you enough to keep the goons from shooting you. Even *that*, as creepy as it would be if you said it to me, even *that* would be easier to understand than *this*!"

She looked forlorn. "There isn't anybody else, Rudy. *Please.*"

"What the hell is this all about? Come on, tell me. You're hiding something, or holding something back, or lying about—"

"I'm not lying!" For the second time she was suddenly, totally, extremely pissed at me. Her voice spattered off the white tile walls. The fry-cook spun around at the sound, took a step toward us, and I jaunted into his

landscape, smoothed down the rippled Astro-Turf, drained away the storm clouds, and suggested in there that he go take a cigarette break out back. Fortunately, there were no other patrons at the elegant All-American Burger that late in the afternoon, and he went.

"Calm fer chrissakes down, will you?" I said.

She had squeezed the paper napkin into a ball.

She was lying, hiding, holding something back. Didn't have to be a telepath to figure *that* out. I waited, looking at her with a slow, careful distrust, and finally she sighed, and I thought, *Here it comes.*

"Are you reading my mind?" she asked.

"Don't insult me. We know each other too long."

She looked chagrined. The violet of her eyes deepened. "Sorry."

But she didn't go on. I wasn't going to be outflanked. I waited.

After a while she said, softly, very softly, "I think I'm in love with him. I *know* I believe him when he says he's innocent."

I never expected that. I couldn't even reply.

It was unbelievable. Unfuckingbelievable. She was the Chief Deputy D.A. who had prosecuted Henry Lake Spanning for murder. Not just one murder, one random slaying, a heat of the moment Saturday night killing regretted deeply on Sunday morning but punishable by electrocution in the Sovereign State of Alabama nonetheless, but a string of the vilest, most sickening serial slaughters in Alabama history, in the history of the Glorious South, in the history of the United States. Maybe even in the history of the entire wretched human universe that went wading hip-deep in the wasted spilled blood of innocent men, women and children.

Henry Lake Spanning was a monster, an ambulatory disease, a killing machine without conscience or any discernible resemblance to a thing we might call decently human. Henry Lake Spanning had butchered his way across a half-dozen states; and they had caught up to him in Huntsville, in a garbage dumpster behind a supermarket, doing something so vile and inhuman to what was left of a sixty-five-year-old cleaning woman that not even the tabloids would get more explicit than *unspeakable*; and somehow he got away from the cops; and somehow he evaded their dragnet; and somehow he found out where the police lieutenant in charge of the manhunt lived; and somehow he slipped into that neighborhood when the lieutenant was out creating roadblocks—and he gutted the man's wife and two kids. Also the family cat. And then he killed a couple of more times in Birmingham and Decatur, and by then had gone so completely out of his mind that they got him again, and the second time they hung onto him, and they brought him to trial. And Ally had prosecuted this bottom-feeding monstrosity.

And oh, what a circus it had been. Though he'd been *caught*, the second time, and this time for keeps, in Jefferson County, scene of three of his most sickening jobs, he'd murdered (with such a disgustingly similar m.o. that it was obvious he was the perp) in twenty-two of the sixty-seven counties; and every last one of them wanted him to stand trial in that venue. Then there were the other five states in which he had butchered, to a total body-count of fifty-six. Each of *them* wanted him extradited.

So, here's how smart and quick and smooth an attorney Ally is: she somehow managed to coze up to the Attorney General, and somehow managed to unleash those violet eyes on him, and somehow managed to get and keep his ear long enough to con him into setting a legal precedent. Attorney General of the State of Alabama allowed Allison Roche to consolidate, to secure a multiple bill of indictment that forced Spanning to stand trial on all twenty-nine Alabama murder counts at once. She meticulously documented to the state's highest courts that Henry Lake Spanning presented such a clear and present danger to society that the prosecution was willing to take a chance (big chance!) of trying in a winner-take-all consolidation of venues. Then she managed to smooth the feathers of all those other vote-hungry prosecuters in those twenty-one other counties, and she put on a case that dazzled everyone, including Spanning's defense attorney, who had screamed about the legality of the multiple bill from the moment she'd suggested it.

And she won a fast jury verdict on all twenty-nine counts. Then she got *really* fancy in the penalty phase after the jury verdict, and proved up the *other* twenty-seven murders with their flagrantly identical trademarks, from those other five states, and there was nothing left but to sentence Spanning—essentially for all fifty-six—to the replacement for the "Yellow Mama."

Even as pols and power brokers throughout the state were murmuring Ally's name for higher office, Spanning was slated to sit in that new electric chair in Holman Prison, built by the Fred A. Leuchter Associates of Boston, Massachusetts, that delivers 2,640 volts of pure sparklin' death in $1/240$th of a second, six times faster than the $1/40$th of a second that it takes for the brain to sense it, which is—if you ask me—much too humane an exit line, more than three times the 700 volt jolt lethal dose that destroys a brain, for a pus-bag like Henry Lake Spanning.

But if we were lucky—and the scheduled day of departure was very nearly upon us—if we were lucky, if there was a God and Justice and Natural Order and all that good stuff, then Henry Lake Spanning, this foulness, this corruption, this thing that lived only to ruin…would end up as a pile of fucking ashes somebody might use to sprinkle over a flower garden, thereby providing this ghoul with his single opportunity to be of some use to the human race.

That was the guy that my pal Allison Roche wanted me to go and "chat" with, down to Holman Prison, in Atmore, Alabama. There, sitting on Death Row, waiting to get his demented head tonsured, his pants legs slit, his tongue fried black as the inside of a sheep's belly…down there at Holman my pal Allison wanted me to go "chat" with one of the most awful creatures made for killing this side of a hammerhead shark, which creature had an infinitely greater measure of human decency than Henry Lake Spanning had ever demonstrated. Go chit-chat, and enter his landscape, and read his mind, Mr. Telepath, and use the marvelous mythic power of extra-sensory perception: this nifty swell ability that has made me a bum all my life, well, not *exactly* a bum: I do have a decent apartment, and I do earn a decent, if sporadic, living; and I try to follow Nelson Algren's warning never to get involved with a woman whose troubles are bigger than my own; and sometimes I even have a car of my own, even though at that moment such was not the case, the Camaro having been repo'd, and not by Harry Dean Stanton or Emilio Estevez, lemme tell you; but a bum in the sense of—how does Ally put it?—oh yeah—I don't "realize my full and forceful potential"—a bum in the sense that I can't hold a job, and I get rotten breaks, and all of this despite a Rhodes scholarly education so far above what a poor nigrah-lad such as myself could expect that even Rhodes hisownself would've been chest-out proud as hell of me. A bum, mostly, despite an *outstanding* Rhodes scholar education and a pair of kind, smart, loving parents—even for foster-parents—shit, *especially* for being foster-parents—who died knowing the certain sadness that their only child would spend his life as a wandering freak unable to make a comfortable living or consummate a normal marriage or raise children without the fear of passing on this special personal horror…this astonishing ability fabled in song and story that I possess…that no one else seems to possess, though I know there must have been others, somewhere, sometime, somehow! Go, Mr. Wonder of Wonders, shining black Cagliostro of the modern world, go with this super nifty swell ability that gullible idiots and flying saucer assholes have been trying to prove exists for at least fifty years, that no one has been able to isolate the way I, me, the only one has been isolated, let me tell you about *isolation*, my brothers; and here I was, here was I, Rudy Pairis…just a guy, making a buck every now and then with nifty swell impossible ESP, resident of thirteen states and twice that many cities so far in his mere thirty years of landscape-jaunting life, here was I, Rudy Pairis, Mr. I-Can-Read-Your-Mind, being asked to go and walk through the mind of a killer who scared half the people in the world. Being asked by the only living person, probably, to whom I could not say no. And, oh, take me at my word here: I *wanted* to say no. *Was*, in fact, saying no at every breath. What's that? Will I do it? Sure, yeah sure, I'll go on down to Holman and jaunt through this sick bastard's mind landscape. Sure I will. You got two chances: slim, and none.

All of this was going on in the space of one greasy double cheeseburger and two cups of coffee.

The worst part of it was that Ally had somehow gotten involved with him. *Ally!* Not some bimbo bitch…but *Ally*. I couldn't believe it.

Not that it was unusual for women to become mixed up with guys in the joint, to fall under their "magic spell," and to start corresponding with them, visiting them, taking them candy and cigarettes, having conjugal visits, playing mule for them and smuggling in dope where the tampon never shine, writing them letters that got steadily more exotic, steadily more intimate, steamier and increasingly dependent emotionally. It wasn't that big a deal; there exist entire psychiatric treatises on the phenomenon; right alongside the papers about women who go stud-crazy for cops. No big deal indeed: hundreds of women every year find themselves writing to these guys, visiting these guys, building dream castles with these guys, fucking these guys, pretending that even the worst of these guys, rapists and woman-beaters and child molesters, repeat pedophiles of the lowest pustule sort, and murderers and stick-up punks who crush old ladies' skulls for food stamps, and terrorists and bunco barons…that one sunny might-be, gonna-happen pink cloud day these demented creeps will emerge from behind the walls, get back in the wind, become upstanding nine-to-five

449

Brooks Bros. Galahads. Every year hundreds of women marry these guys, finding themselves in a hot second snookered by the wily, duplicitous, motherfuckin' lying greaseball addictive behavior of guys who had spent their sporadic years, their intermittent freedom on the outside, doing *just that*: roping people in, ripping people off, bleeding people dry, conning them into being tools, taking them for their every last cent, their happy home, their sanity, their ability to trust or love ever again.

But this wasn't some poor illiterate naive woman-child. This was *Ally*. She had damned near pulled off a legal impossibility, come *that* close to Bizarro Jurisprudence by putting the Attorneys General of five other states in a maybe frame of mind where she'd have been able to consolidate a multiple bill of indictment *across state lines*! Never been done; and now, probably, never ever would be. But she could have possibly pulled off such a thing. Unless you're a stone court-bird, you can't know what a mountaintop that is!

So, now, here's Ally, saying this shit to me. Ally, my best pal, stood up for me a hundred times; not some dip, but the steely-eyed Sheriff of Suicide Gulch, the over-forty, past the age of innocence, no-nonsense woman who had seen it all and come away tough but not cynical, hard but not mean.

"I think I'm in love with him." She had said.

"I *know* I believe him when he says he's innocent." She had said.

I looked at her. No time had passed. It was still the moment the universe decided to lie down and die. And I said, "So if you're certain this paragon of the virtues *isn't* responsible for fifty-six murders—that we *know* about—and who the hell knows how many more we *don't* know about, since he's apparently been at it since he was twelve years old—remember the couple of nights we sat up and you *told* me all this shit about him, and you said it with your skin crawling, *remember?*—then if you're so damned positive the guy you spent eleven weeks in court sending to the chair is innocent of butchering half the population of the planet—then why do you need me to go to Holman, drive all the way to Atmore, just to take a jaunt in this sweet peach of a guy?

"Doesn't your 'woman's intuition' tell you he's squeaky clean? Don't 'true love' walk yo' sweet young ass down the primrose path with sufficient surefootedness?"

"Don't be a smartass!" she said.

"Say again?" I replied, with disfuckingbelief.

"I said: don't be such a high-verbal goddamned smart aleck!"

Now *I* was steamed. "No, I shouldn't be a smartass: I should be your pony, your show dog, your little trick bag mind-reader freak! Take a drive over to Holman, Pairis; go right on into Rednecks from Hell; sit your ass down on Death Row with the rest of the niggers and have a chat with the one white boy who's been in a cell up there for the past three years or so; sit down nicely with the king of the fucking vampires, and slide inside his garbage dump of a brain—and what a joy *that's* gonna be, I can't believe you'd ask me to do this—and read whatever piece of boiled shit in there he calls a brain, and see if he's jerking you around. *That's* what I ought to do, am I correct? Instead of being a smartass. Have I got it right? Do I properly pierce your meaning, pal?"

She stood up. She didn't even say *Screw you, Pairis!*

She just slapped me as hard as she could.

She hit me a good one straight across the mouth.

I felt my upper teeth bite my lower lip. I tasted the blood. My head rang like a church bell. I thought I'd fall off the goddam stool.

When I could focus, she was just standing there, looking ashamed of herself, and disappointed, and mad as hell, and worried that she'd brained me. All of that, all at the same time. Plus, she looked as if I'd broken her choo-choo train.

"Okay," I said wearily, and ended the word with a sigh that reached all the way back into my hip pocket. "Okay, calm down. I'll see him. I'll do it. Take it easy."

She didn't sit down. "Did I hurt you?"

"No, of course not," I said, unable to form the smile I was trying to put on my face. "How could you possibly hurt someone by knocking his brains into his lap?"

She stood over me as I clung precariously to the counter, turned halfway around on the stool by the blow. Stood over me, the balled-up paper napkin in her fist, a look on her face that said she was nobody's fool, that we'd known each other a long time, that she hadn't asked this kind of favor before, that if we were buddies and I loved her, that I would see she was in deep pain, that she was conflicted, that she needed to know, *really* needed to know without a doubt, and in the name of God—in which she believed, though I didn't, but either way what the hell—that I do this thing for her, that I just *do it* and not give her any more crap about it.

So I shrugged, and spread my hands like a man with no place to go, and I said, "How'd you get into this?"

She told me the first fifteen minutes of her tragic, heartwarming, never-to-be-ridiculed story still standing. After fifteen minutes I said, "Fer chrissakes, Ally, at least *sit down*! You look like a damned fool standing there with a greasy napkin in your mitt."

A couple of teenagers had come in. The four-star chef had finished his cigarette out back and was reassuringly in place, walking the duckboards and dishing up All-American arterial cloggage.

She picked up her elegant attaché case and without a word, with only a nod that said let's get as far from them as we can, she and I moved to a double against the window to resume our discussion of the varieties of social suicide available to an unwary and foolhardy gentleman of the colored persuasion if he allowed himself to be swayed by a cagey and cogent, clever and concupiscent female of another color entirely.

See, what it is, is this:

Look at that attaché case. You want to know what kind of an Ally this Allison Roche is? Pay heed, now.

In New York, when some wannabe junior ad exec has smooched enough butt to get tossed a bone account, and he wants to walk his colors, has a need to signify, has got to demonstrate to everyone that he's got the juice, first thing he does, he hies his ass downtown to Barney's, West 17th and Seventh, buys hisself a Burberry, loops the belt casually *behind*, leaving the coat open to suh*wing*, and he circumnavigates the office.

In Dallas, when the wife of the CEO has those six or eight upper-management husbands and wives over for an *intime, faux*-casual dinner, sans place cards, sans *entrée* fork, sans *cérémonie*, and we're talking the kind of woman who flies Virgin Air instead of the Concorde, she's so in charge she don't got to use the Orrefors, she can put out the Kosta Boda and say *give a fuck*.

What it is, kind of person so in charge, so easy with they own self, they don't *have* to laugh at your poor dumb struttin' Armani suit, or your bedroom done in Laura Ashley, or that you got a gig writing articles for *TV Guide*. You see what I'm sayin' here? The sort of person Ally Roche is, you take a look at that attaché case, and it'll tell you everything you need to know about how strong she is, because it's an Atlas. Not a Hartmann. Understand: she could *afford* a Hartmann, that gorgeous imported Canadian belting leather, top of the line, somewhere around nine hundred and fifty bucks maybe, equivalent of Orrefors, a Burberry, breast of guinea hen and Mouton Rothschild 1492 or 1066 or whatever year is the most expensive, drive a Rolls instead of a Bentley and the only difference is the grille…but she doesn't *need* to signify, doesn't *need* to suh*wing*, so she gets herself this Atlas. Not some dumb chickenshit Louis Vuitton or Mark Cross all the divorcée real estate ladies carry, but an Atlas. Irish hand leather. Custom tanned cowhide. Hand tanned in Ireland by out of work IRA bombers. Very classy. Just a state understated. See that attaché case? That tell you why I said I'd do it?

She picked it up from where she'd stashed it, right up against the counter wall by her feet, and we went to the double over by the window, away from the chef and the teenagers, and she stared at me till she was sure I was in a right frame of mind, and she picked up where she'd left off.

The next twenty-three minutes by the big greasy clock on the wall she related from a sitting position. Actually, a series of sitting positions. She kept shifting in her chair like someone who didn't appreciate the view of the world from that window, someone hoping for a sweeter horizon. The story started with a gang-rape at the age of thirteen, and moved right along: two broken foster-home families, a little casual fondling by surrogate poppas, intense studying for perfect school grades as a substitute for happiness, working her way through John Jay College of Law, a truncated attempt at wedded bliss in her late twenties, and the long miserable road of legal success that had brought her to Alabama. There could have been worse places.

I'd known Ally for a long time, and we'd spent totals of weeks and months in each other's company. Not to mention the New Year's Eve of the Marx Brothers. But I hadn't heard much of this. Not much at all.

Funny how that goes. Eleven years. You'd think I'd've guessed or suspected or *some*thing. What the hell makes us think we're friends with *any*body, when we don't know the first thing about them, not really?

What are we, walking around in a dream? That is to say: what the fuck are we *thinking*!?!

And there might never have been a reason to hear *any* of it, all this Ally that was the real Ally, but now she was asking me to go somewhere I didn't want to go, to do something that scared the shit out of me; and she wanted me to be as fully informed as possible.

It dawned on me that those same eleven years between us hadn't really given her a full, laser-clean insight into the why and wherefore of Rudy Pairis, either. I hated myself for it. The concealing, the holding-back, the giving up only fragments, the evil misuse of charm when honesty would have hurt. I was facile, and a very quick study; and I had buried all the equivalents to Ally's pains and travails. I could've matched her, in spades; or blacks, or just plain nigras. But I remained frightened of losing her friendship. I've never been able to believe in the myth of unqualified friendship. Too much like standing hip-high in a fast-running, freezing river. Standing on slippery stones.

Her story came forward to the point at which she had prosecuted Spanning; had amassed and winnowed and categorized the evidence so thoroughly, so deliberately, so flawlessly; had orchestrated the case so brilliantly; that the jury had come in with guilty on all twenty-nine, soon—in the penalty phase—fifty-six. Murder in the first. Premeditated murder in the first. Premeditated murder with special ugly circumstances in the first. On each and every of the twenty-nine. Less than an hour it took them. There wasn't even time for a lunch break. Fifty-one minutes it took them to come back with the verdict guilty on all charges. Less than a minute per killing. Ally had done that.

His attorney had argued that no direct link had been established between the fifty-sixth killing (actually, only his 29th in Alabama) and Henry Lake Spanning. No, they had not caught him down on his knees eviscerating the shredded body of his final victim—ten-year-old Gunilla Ascher, a parochial school girl who had missed her bus and been picked up by Spanning just about a mile from her home in Decatur—no, not down on his knees with the can opener still in his sticky red hands, but the m.o. was the same, and he was there in Decatur, on the run from what he had done in Huntsville, what they had *caught* him doing in Huntsville, in that dumpster, to that old woman. So they *couldn't* place him with his smooth, slim hands inside dead Gunilla Ascher's still-steaming body. So what? They could not have been surer he was the serial killer, the monster, the ravaging nightmare whose methods were so vile the newspapers hadn't even *tried* to cobble up some smart-aleck name for him like The Strangler or The Backyard Butcher. The jury had come back in fifty-one minutes, looking sick, looking as if they'd try and try to get everything they'd seen and heard out of their minds, but knew they never would, and wishing to God they could've managed to get out of their civic duty on this one.

They came shuffling back in and told the numbed court: hey, put this slimy excuse for a maggot in the chair and cook his ass till he's fit only to be served for breakfast on cinnamon toast. This was the guy my friend Ally told me she had fallen in love with. The guy she now believed to be innocent.

This was seriously crazy stuff.

"So how did you get, er, uh, how did you...?"

"How did I fall in love with him?"

"Yeah. That."

She closed her eyes for a moment, and pursed her lips as if she had lost a flock of wayward words and didn't know where to find them. I'd always known she was a private person, kept the really important history to herself—hell, until now I'd never known about the rape, the ice mountain between her mother and father, the specifics of the seven-month marriage—I'd known there'd been a husband briefly; but not what had happened; and I'd known about the foster homes; but again, not how lousy it had been for her—even so, getting *this* slice of steaming craziness out of her was like using your teeth to pry the spikes out of Jesus's wrists.

Finally, she said, "I took over the case when Charlie Whilborg had his stroke..."

"I remember."

"He was the best litigator in the office, and if he hadn't gone down two days before they caught..." she paused, had trouble with the name, went on, "...before they caught Spanning in Decatur, and if Morgan County hadn't been so worried about a case this size, and bound Spanning over to us in Birmingham...all of it so fast nobody really had a chance to talk to him...I was the first one even got *near* him, everyone was so damned scared of him, of what they *thought* he was..."

"Hallucinating, were they?" I said, being a smartass.

"Shut up.

"The office did most of the donkeywork after that first interview I had with him. It was a big break for me in the office; and I got obsessed by it. So after the first interview, I never spent much actual time with Spanky, never got too close, to see what kind of a man he *really*..."

I said: "Spanky? Who the hell's 'Spanky'?"

She blushed. It started from the sides of her nostrils and went out both ways toward her ears, then climbed to the hairline. I'd seen that happen only a couple of times in eleven years, and one of those times had been when she'd farted at the opera. *Lucia di Lammermoor.*

I said it again: "Spanky? You're putting me on, right? You call him *Spanky*?" The blush deepened. "Like the fat kid in *The Little Rascals*...c'mon, I don't fuckin' *believe* this!"

She just glared at me.

I felt the laughter coming.

My face started twitching.

She stood up again. "Forget it. Just forget it, okay?" She took two steps away from the table, toward the street exit. I grabbed her hand and pulled her back, trying not to fall apart with laughter, and I said, "Okay okay okay...I'm *sorry*...I'm really and truly, honest to goodness, may I be struck by a falling space lab no kidding 100% absolutely sorry...but you gotta admit...catching me unawares like that...I mean, come *on*, Ally... *Spanky!?!* You call this guy who murdered at least fifty-six people Spanky? Why not Mickey, or Froggy, or Alfalfa...? I can understand not calling him Buckwheat, you can save that one for me, but *Spanky*???"

And in a moment *her* face started to twitch; and in another moment she was starting to smile, fighting it every micron of the way; and in another moment she was laughing and swatting at me with her free hand; and then she pulled her hand loose and stood there falling apart with laughter; and in about a minute she was sitting down again. She threw the balled-up napkin at me.

"It's from when he was a kid," she said. "He was a fat kid, and they made fun of him. You know the way kids are...they corrupted Spanning into 'Spanky' because *The Little Rascals* were on television and...oh, shut *up*, Rudy!"

I finally quieted down, and made conciliatory gestures.

She watched me with an exasperated wariness till she was sure I wasn't going to run any more dumb gags on her, and then she resumed. "After Judge Fay sentenced him, I handled Spa...*Henry's* case from our office, all the way up to the appeals stage. I was the one who did the pleading against clemency when Henry's lawyers took their appeal to the Eleventh Circuit in Atlanta.

"When he was denied a stay by the appellate, three-to-nothing, I helped prepare the brief when Henry's counsel went to the Alabama Supreme

Court; then when the Supreme Court refused to hear his appeal, I thought it was all over. I knew they'd run out of moves for him, except maybe the Governor; but that wasn't ever going to happen. So I thought: *that's that.*

"When the Supreme Court wouldn't hear it three weeks ago, I got a letter from him. He'd been set for execution next Saturday, and I couldn't figure out why he wanted to see *me.*"

I asked, "The letter…it got to you how?"

"One of his attorneys."

"I thought they'd given up on him."

"So did I. The evidence was so overwhelming; half a dozen counselors found ways to get themselves excused; it wasn't the kind of case that would bring any litigator good publicity. Just the number of eyewitnesses in the parking lot of that Winn-Dixie in Huntsville…must have been fifty of them, Rudy. And they all saw the same thing, and they all identified Henry in lineup after lineup, twenty, thirty, could have been fifty of them if we'd needed that long a parade. And all the rest of it…"

I held up a hand. *I know*, the flat hand against the air said. She had told me all of this. Every grisly detail, till I wanted to puke. It was as if I'd done it all myself, she was so vivid in her telling. Made my jaunting nausea pleasurable by comparison. Made me so sick I couldn't even think about it. Not even in a moment of human weakness.

"So the letter comes to you from the attorney…"

"I think you know this lawyer. Larry Borlan; used to be with the ACLU; before that he was senior counsel for the Alabama Legislature down to Montgomery; stood up, what was it, twice, three times, before the Supreme Court? Excellent guy. And not easily fooled."

"And what's *he* think about all this?"

"He thinks Henry's absolutely innocent."

"Of all of it?"

"Of everything."

"But there were fifty disinterested random eyewitnesses at one of those slaughters. Fifty, you just said it. Fifty, you could've had a parade. All of them nailed him cold, without a doubt. Same kind of kill as all the other fifty-five, including that schoolkid in Decatur when they finally got him. And Larry Borlan thinks he's not the guy, right?"

She nodded. Made one of those sort of comic pursings of the lips, shrugged, and nodded. "Not the guy."

"So the killer's still out there?"

"That's what Borlan thinks."

"And what do *you* think?"

"I agree with him."

"Oh, jeezus, Ally, my aching boots and saddle! You got to be workin' some kind of off-time! The killer is still out here in the mix, but there hasn't been a killing like those Spanning slaughters for the three years that he's been in the joint. Now *what* do that say to you?"

"It says whoever the guy *is*, the one who killed all those people, he's *days* smarter than all the rest of us, and he set up the perfect freefloater to take the fall for him, and he's either long far gone in some other state, working his way, or he's sitting quietly right here in Alabama, waiting and watching. And smiling." Her face seemed to sag with misery. She started to tear up, and said, "In four days he can stop smiling."

Saturday night.

"Okay, take it easy. Go on, tell me the rest of it. Borlan comes to you, and he begs you to read Spanning's letter and...?"

"He didn't beg. He just gave me the letter, told me he had no idea what Henry had written, but he said he'd known me a long time, that he thought I was a decent, fair-minded person, and he'd appreciate it in the name of our friendship if I'd read it."

"So you read it."

"I read it."

"Friendship. Sounds like you an' him was *good* friends. Like maybe you and I were good friends?"

She looked at me with astonishment.

I think *I* looked at me with astonishment.

"Where the hell did *that* come from?" I said.

"Yeah, really," she said, right back at me, "where the hell *did* that come from?" My ears were hot, and I almost started to say something about how if it was okay for *her* to use our Marx Brothers indiscretion for a lever, why wasn't it okay for me to get cranky about it? But I kept my mouth shut; and for once knew enough to move along. "Must've been *some* letter," I said.

There was a long moment of silence during which she weighed the degree of shit she'd put me through for my stupid remark, after all this was settled; and having struck a balance in her head, she told me about the letter.

It was perfect. It was the only sort of come-on that could lure the avenger who'd put you in the chair to pay attention. The letter had said that fifty-six was not the magic number of death. That there were many, *many* more unsolved cases, in many, *many* different states; lost children, runaways, unexplained disappearances, old people, college students hitchhiking to Sarasota for Spring Break, shopkeepers who'd carried their day's take to the night deposit drawer and never gone home for dinner, hookers left in pieces in Hefty bags all over town, and death death death unnumbered and unnamed. Fifty-six, the letter had said, was just the start. And if she, her, no one else, Allison Roche, my pal Ally, would come on down to Holman, and talk to him, Henry Lake Spanning would help her close all those open files. National rep. Avenger of the unsolved. Big time mysteries revealed.

"So you read the letter, and you went…"

"Not at first. Not immediately. I was sure he was guilty, and I was pretty certain at that moment, three years and more, dealing with the case, I was pretty sure if he said he could fill in all the blank spaces, that he could do it. But I just didn't like the idea. In court, I was always twitchy when I got near him at the defense table. His eyes, he never took them off me. They're blue, Rudy, did I tell you that…?"

"Maybe. I don't remember. Go on."

"Bluest blue you've ever seen…well, to tell the truth, he just plain *scared* me. I wanted to win that case so badly, Rudy, you can never know…not just for me or the career or for the idea of justice or to avenge all those people he'd killed, but just the thought of him out there on the street, with those blue eyes, so blue, never stopped looking at me from the moment the trial began…the *thought* of him on the loose drove me to whip that case like a howling dog. I *had* to put him away!"

"But you overcame your fear."

She didn't like the edge of ridicule on the blade of that remark. "That's right. I finally 'overcame my fear' and I agreed to go see him."

"And you saw him."

"Yes."

"And he didn't know shit about no other killings, right?"

"Yes."

"But he talked a good talk. And his eyes was blue, so blue."

"Yes, you asshole."

I chuckled. Everybody is somebody's fool.

"Now let me ask you this—very carefully—so you don't hit me again: the moment you discovered he'd been shuckin' you, lyin, that he *didn't* have this long, unsolved crime roster to tick off, why didn't you get up, load your attaché case, and hit the bricks?"

Her answer was simple. "He begged me to stay a while."

"That's it? He *begged* you?"

"Rudy, he has no one. He's *never* had anyone." She looked at me as if I were made of stone, some basalt thing, an onyx statue, a figure carved out of melanite, soot and ashes fused into a monolith. She feared she could not, in no way, no matter how piteously or bravely she phrased it, penetrate my rocky surface.

Then she said a thing that I never wanted to hear.

"Rudy…"

Then she said a thing I could never have imagined she'd say. Never in a million years.

"Rudy…"

Then she said the most awful thing she could say to me, even more awful than that she was in love with a serial killer.

"Rudy…go inside…read my mind…I need you to know, I need you to understand…Rudy…"

The look on her face killed my heart.

I tried to say no, oh god no, not that, please, no, not that, don't ask me to do that, please *please* I don't want to go inside, we mean so much to each other, I don't *want* to know your landscape. Don't make me feel filthy, I'm no peeping-tom, I've *never* spied on you, never stolen a look when you were coming out of the shower, or undressing, or when you were being sexy…I never invaded your privacy, I wouldn't *do* a thing like that…we're friends, I don't need to know it all, I don't *want* to go in there. I can go inside anyone, and it's always awful…please don't make me see things in there I might not like, you're my friend, please don't steal that from me…

"Rudy, *please*. Do it."

Oh jeezusjeezusjeezus, again, she said it again!

We sat there. And we sat there. And we sat there longer. I said, hoarsely, in fear, "Can't you just…just *tell* me?"

Her eyes looked at stone. A man of stone. And she tempted me to do what I could do casually, tempted me the way Faust was tempted by Mefisto, Mephistopheles, Mefistofele, Mephostopilis. Black rock Dr.

Faustus, possessor of magical mind-reading powers, tempted by thick, lustrous eyelashes and violet eyes and a break in the voice and an imploring movement of hand to face and a tilt of the head that was pitiable and the begging word *please* and all the guilt that lay between us that was mine alone. The seven chief demons. Of whom Mefisto was the one "not loving the light."

I knew it was the end of our friendship. But she left me nowhere to run. Mefisto in onyx.

So I jaunted into her landscape.

I stayed in there less than ten seconds. I didn't want to know everything I could know; and I definitely wanted to know *nothing* about how she really thought of me. I couldn't have borne seeing a caricature of a bug-eyed, shuffling, thick-lipped darkie in there. Mandingo man. Steppin Porchmonkey Rudy Pair...

Oh god, what was I thinking!

Nothing in there like that. Nothing! Ally wouldn't *have* anything like that in there. I was going nuts, going absolutely fucking crazy, in there, back out in less than ten seconds. I want to block it, kill it, void it, waste it, empty it, reject it, squeeze it, darken it, obscure it, wipe it, do away with it like it never happened. Like the moment you walk in on your momma and poppa and catch them fucking, and you want never to have known that.

But at least I understood.

In there, in Allison Roche's landscape, I saw how her heart had responded to this man she called Spanky, not Henry Lake Spanning. She did not call him, in there, by the name of a monster; she called him a honey's name. I didn't know if he was innocent or not, but *she* knew he was innocent. At first she had responded to just talking with him, about being brought up in an orphanage, and she was able to relate to his stories of being used and treated like chattel, and how they had stripped him of his dignity, and made him afraid all the time. She knew what that was like. And how he'd always been on his own. The running-away. The being captured like a wild thing, and put in this home or that lockup or the orphanage "for his own good." Washing stone steps with a tin bucket full of gray water, with a horsehair brush and a bar of lye soap, till the tender folds of skin between the fingers were furiously red and hurt so much you couldn't make a fist.

She tried to tell me how her heart had responded, with a language that has never been invented to do the job. I saw as much as I needed, there in that secret landscape, to know that Spanning had led a miserable life, but that somehow he'd managed to become a decent human being. And it showed through enough when she was face to face with him, talking to him without the witness box between them, without the adversarial thing, without the tension of the courtroom and the gallery and those parasite creeps from the tabloids sneaking around taking pictures of him, that she identified with his pain. Hers had been not the same, but similar; of a kind, if not of identical intensity.

She came to know him a little.

And came back to see him again. Human compassion. In a moment of human weakness.

Until, finally, she began examining everything she had worked up as evidence, trying to see it from *his* point of view, using *his* explanations of circumstantiality. And there were inconsistencies. Now she saw them. Now she did not turn her prosecuting attorney's mind from them, recasting them in a way that would railroad Spanning; now she gave him just the barest possibility of truth. And the case did not seem as incontestable.

By that time, she had to admit to herself, she had fallen in love with him. The gentle quality could not be faked; she'd known fraudulent kindness in her time.

I left her mind gratefully. But at least I understood.

"Now?" she asked.

Yes, now. Now I understood. And the fractured glass in her voice told me. Her face told me. The way she parted her lips in expectation, waiting for me to reveal what my magic journey had conveyed by way of truth. Her palm against her cheek. All that told me. And I said, "Yes."

Then, silence, between us.

After a while she said, "I didn't feel anything."

I shrugged. "Nothing to feel. I was in for a few seconds, that's all."

"You didn't see everything?"

"No."

"Because you didn't want to?"

"Because…"

She smiled. "I understand, Rudy."

Oh, do you? Do you really? That's just fine. And I heard me say, "You made it with him yet?"

I could have torn off her arm; it would've hurt less.

"That's the second time today you've asked me that kind of question. I didn't like it much the first time, and I like it less *this* time."

"You're the one wanted me to go into your head. I didn't buy no ticket for the trip."

"Well, you were in there. Didn't you look around enough to find out?"

"I didn't look for that."

"What a chickenshit, wheedling, lousy and *cowardly...*"

"I haven't heard an answer, Counselor. Kindly restrict your answers to a simple yes or no."

"Don't be ridiculous! He's on Death Row!"

"There are ways."

"How would *you* know?"

"I had a friend. Up at San Rafael. What they call Tamal. Across the bridge from Richmond, a little north of San Francisco."

"That's San Quentin."

"That's what it is, all right."

"I thought that *friend* of yours was at Pelican Bay?"

"Different friend."

"You seem to have a lot of old chums in the joint in California."

"It's a racist nation."

"I've heard that."

"But Q ain't Pelican Bay. Two different states of being. As hard time as they pull at Tamal, it's worse up to Crescent City. In the Shoe."

"You never mentioned 'a friend' at San Quentin."

"I never mentioned a lotta shit. That don't mean I don't know it. I am large, I contain multitudes."

We sat silently, the three of us: me, her, and Walt Whitman. *We're fighting*, I thought. Not make-believe, dissin' some movie we'd seen and disagreed about; this was nasty. Bone nasty and memorable. No one ever forgets this kind of fight. Can turn dirty in a second, say some trash you can never take back, never forgive, put a canker on the rose of friendship for all time, never be the same look again.

I waited. She didn't say anything more; and I got no straight answer; but I was pretty sure Henry Lake Spanning had gone all the way with her. I felt a twinge of emotion I didn't even want to look at, much less analyze, dissect, and name. *Let it be*, I thought. Eleven years. Once, just once. *Let it just lie there and get old and withered and die a proper death like all ugly thoughts.*

"Okay. So I go on down to Atmore," I said. "I suppose you mean in the very near future, since he's supposed to bake in four days. Sometime very soon: like today."

She nodded.

I said, "And how do I get in? Law student? Reporter? Tag along as Larry Borlan's new law clerk? Or do I go in with you? What am I, friend of the family, representative of the Alabama State Department of Corrections; maybe you could set me up as an inmate's rep from 'Project Hope'."

"I can do better than that," she said. The smile. "Much."

"Yeah, I'll just bet you can. Why does that worry me?"

Still with the smile, she hoisted the Atlas onto her lap. She unlocked it, took out a small manila envelope, unsealed but clasped, and slid it across the table to me. I pried open the clasp and shook out the contents.

Clever. Very clever. And already made up, with my photo where necessary, admission dates stamped for tomorrow morning, Thursday, absolutely authentic and foolproof.

"Let me guess," I said, "Thursday mornings, the inmates of Death Row have access to their attorneys?"

"On Death Row, family visitation Monday and Friday. Henry has no family. Attorney visitations Wednesdays and Thursdays, but I couldn't count on today. It took me a couple of days to get through to you…"

"I've been busy."

"…but inmates consult with their counsel on Wednesday and Thursday mornings."

I tapped the papers and plastic cards. "This is very sharp. I notice my name and my handsome visage already here, already sealed in plastic. How long have you had these ready?"

"Couple of days."

"What if I'd continued to say no?"

She didn't answer. She just got that look again.

"One last thing," I said. And I leaned in very close, so she would make no mistake that I was dead serious. "Time grows short. Today's Wednesday. Tomorrow's Thursday. They throw those computer-controlled twin switches Saturday night midnight. What if I jaunt into him and find out you're right, that he's absolutely innocent? What then? They going to listen to me? Fiercely high-verbal black boy with the magic mind-read power?

"I don't think so. Then what happens, Ally?"

"Leave that to me." Her face was hard. "As you said: there are ways. There are roads and routes and even lightning bolts, if you know where to shop. The power of the judiciary. An election year coming up. Favors to be called in."

I said, "And secrets to be wafted under sensitive noses?"

"You just come back and tell me Spanky's telling the truth," and she smiled as I started to laugh, "and I'll worry about the world one minute after midnight Sunday morning."

I got up and slid the papers back into the envelope, and put the envelope under my arm. I looked down at her and I smiled as gently as I could, and I said, "Assure me that you haven't stacked the deck by telling Spanning I can read minds."

"I wouldn't do that."

"Tell me."

"I haven't told him you can read minds."

"You're lying."

"Did you…?"

"Didn't have to. I can see it in your face, Ally."

"Would it matter if he knew?"

"Not a bit. I can read the sonofabitch cold or hot, with or without. Three seconds inside and I'll know if he did it all, if he did part of it, if he did none of it."

"I think I love him, Rudy."

"You told me that."

"But I wouldn't set you up. I need to know…that's why I'm asking you to do it."

I didn't answer. I just smiled at her. She'd told him. He'd know I was coming. But that was terrific. If she hadn't alerted him, I'd have asked her to call and let him know. The more aware he'd be, the easier to scorch his landscape.

I'm a fast study, king of the quick learners: vulgate Latin in a week; standard apothecary's pharmacopoeia in three days; Fender bass on a weekend; Atlanta Falcons' play book in an hour; and, in a moment of human weakness, what it feels like to have a very crampy, heavy-flow menstrual period, two minutes flat.

So fast, in fact, that the more somebody tries to hide the boiling pits of guilt and the crucified bodies of shame, the faster I adapt to their landscape. Like a man taking a polygraph test gets nervous, starts to sweat, ups the galvanic skin response, tries to duck and dodge, gets himself hinky and more hinky and hinkyer till his upper lip could water a truck garden, the more he tries to hide from me...the more he reveals... the deeper inside I can go.

There is an African saying: *Death comes without the thumping of drums.* I have no idea why that one came back to me just then.

Last thing you expect from a prison administration is a fine sense of humor. But they got one at the Holman facility.

They had the bloody monster dressed like a virgin.

White duck pants, white short sleeve shirt buttoned up to the neck, white socks. Pair of brown ankle-high brogans with crepe soles, probably neoprene, but they didn't clash with the pale, virginal apparition that came through the security door with a large, black brother in Alabama Prison Authority uniform holding onto his right elbow.

Didn't clash, those work shoes, and didn't make much of a tap on the white tile floor. It was as if he floated. Oh yes, I said to myself, oh yes indeed: I could see how this messianic figure could wow even as tough a cookie as Ally. *Oh my, yes.*

Fortunately, it was raining outside.

Otherwise, sunlight streaming through the glass, he'd no doubt have a halo. I'd have lost it. Right there, a laughing jag would *not* have ceased. Fortunately, it was raining like a sonofabitch.

Which hadn't made the drive down from Clanton a possible entry on any deathbed list of Greatest Terrific Moments in My Life. Sheets of aluminum water, thick as misery, like a neverending shower curtain that I could drive through for an eternity and never really penetrate. I went into the ditch off the I-65 half a dozen times. Why I never plowed down and buried myself up to the axles in the sucking goo running those furrows, never be something I'll understand.

But each time I skidded off the Interstate, even the twice I did a complete three-sixty and nearly rolled the old Fairlane I'd borrowed from John the C

Hepworth, even then I just kept digging, slewed like an epileptic seizure, went sideways and climbed right up the slippery grass and weeds and running, sucking red Alabama goo, right back onto that long black anvil pounded by rain as hard as roofing nails. I took it then, as I take it now, to be a sign that Destiny was determined the mere heavens and earth would not be permitted to fuck me around. I had a date to keep, and Destiny was on top of things.

Even so, even living charmed, which was clear to me, even so: when I got about five miles north of Atmore, I took the 57 exit off the I-65 and a left onto 21, and pulled in at the Best Western. It wasn't my intention to stay overnight that far south—though I knew a young woman with excellent teeth down in Mobile—but the rain was just hammering and all I wanted was to get this thing done and go fall asleep. A drive that long, humping something as lame as that Fairlane, hunched forward to scope the rain… with Spanning in front of me…all I desired was surcease. A touch of the old oblivion.

I checked in, stood under the shower for half an hour, changed into the three-piece suit I'd brought along, and phoned the front desk for directions to the Holman facility.

Driving there, a sweet moment happened for me. It was the last sweet moment for a long time thereafter, and I remember it now as if it were still happening. I cling to it.

In May, and on into early June, the Yellow Lady's Slipper blossoms. In the forests and the woodland bogs, and often on some otherwise undistinguished slope or hillside, the yellow and purple orchids suddenly appear.

I was driving. There was a brief stop in the rain. Like the eye of the hurricane. One moment sheets of water, and the next, absolute silence before the crickets and frogs and birds started complaining; and darkness on all sides, just the idiot staring beams of my headlights poking into nothingness; and cool as a well between the drops of rain; and I was driving. And suddenly, the window rolled down so I wouldn't fall asleep, so I could stick my head out when my eyes started to close, suddenly I smelled the delicate perfume of the sweet May-blossoming Lady's Slipper. Off to my left, off in the dark somewhere on a patch of hilly ground, or deep in a stand of invisible trees, *Cypripedium calceolus* was making the night world beautiful with its fragrance.

I neither slowed, nor tried to hold back the tears.

I just drove, feeling sorry for myself; for no good reason I could name.

Way, way down—almost to the corner of the Florida Panhandle, about three hours south of the last truly imperial barbeque in that part of the world, in Birmingham—I made my way to Holman. If you've never been inside the joint, what I'm about to say will resonate about as clearly as Chaucer to one of the gentle Tasaday.

The stones call out.

That institution for the betterment of the human race, the Organized Church, has a name for it. From the fine folks at Catholicism, Lutheranism, Baptism, Judaism, Islamism, Druidism…Ismism…the ones who brought you Torquemada, several spicy varieties of Inquisition, original sin, holy war, sectarian violence, and something called "pro-lifers" who bomb and maim and kill…comes the catchy phrase Damned Places.

Rolls off the tongue like *God's On Our Side*, don't it?

Damned Places.

As we say in Latin, the *situs* of malevolent shit. The *venue* of evil happenings. *Locations* forever existing under a black cloud, like residing in a rooming house run by Jesse Helms or Strom Thurmond. The big slams are like that. Joliet, Dannemora, Attica, Rahway State in Jersey, that hellhole down in Louisiana called Angola, old Folsom—not the new one, the old Folsom—Q, and Ossining. Only people who read about it call it "Sing Sing." Inside, the cons call it Ossining. The Ohio State pen in Columbus. Leavenworth, Kansas. The ones they talk about among themselves when they talk about doing hard time. The Shoe at Pelican Bay State Prison. In there, in those ancient structures mortared with guilt and depravity and no respect for human life and just plain meanness on both sides, cons and screws, in there where the walls and floors have absorbed all the pain and loneliness of a million men and women for decades…in there, the stones call out.

Damned places. You can feel it when you walk through the gates and go through the metal detectors and empty your pockets on counters and open your briefcase so that thick fingers can rumple the papers. You feel it. The moaning and thrashing, and men biting holes in their own wrists so they'll bleed to death.

And I felt it worse than anyone else.

I blocked out as much as I could. I tried to hold on to the memory of the scent of orchids in the night. The last thing I wanted was to jaunt into somebody's landscape at random. Go inside and find out what he had done, what had *really* put him here, not just what they'd got him for. And I'm not talking about Spanning; I'm talking about every one of them. Every guy who had kicked to death his girl friend because she brought him Bratwurst instead of spicy Cajun sausage. Every pale, wormy Bible-reciting psycho who had stolen, buttfucked, and sliced up an altar boy in the name of secret voices that "tole him to g'wan *do* it!" Every amoral druggie who'd shot a pensioner for her food stamps. If I let down for a second, if I didn't keep that shield up, I'd be tempted to send out a scintilla and touch one of them. In a moment of human weakness.

So I followed the trusty to the Warden's office, where his secretary checked my papers, and the little plastic cards with my face encased in them, and she kept looking down at the face, and up at my face, and down at my face, and up at the face in front of her, and when she couldn't restrain herself a second longer she said, "We've been expecting you, Mr. Pairis. Uh. Do you *really* work for the President of the United States?"

I smiled at her. "We go bowling together."

She took that highly, and offered to walk me to the conference room where I'd meet Henry Lake Spanning. I thanked her the way a well-mannered gentleman of color thanks a Civil Servant who can make life easier or more difficult, and I followed her along corridors and in and out of guarded steel-riveted doorways, through Administration and the segregation room and the main hall to the brown-paneled, stained walnut, white tile over cement floored, roll-out security windowed, white draperied, drop ceiling with 2" acoustical Celotex squared conference room, where a Security Officer met us. She bid me fond adieu, not yet fully satisfied that such a one as I had come, that morning, on Air Force One, straight from a 7-10 split with the President of the United States.

It was a big room.

I sat down at the conference table; about twelve feet long and four feet wide; highly polished walnut, maybe oak. Straight back chairs: metal tubing with a light yellow upholstered cushion. Everything quiet, except for the sound of matrimonial rice being dumped on a connubial tin roof. The rain had not slacked off. Out there on the I-65 some luck-lost bastard was being sucked down into red death.

"He'll be here," the Security Officer said.

"That's good," I replied. I had no idea why he'd tell me that, seeing as how it was the reason I was there in the first place. I imagined him to be the kind of guy you dread sitting in front of, at the movies, because he always explains everything to his date. Like a *bracero* laborer with a valid green card interpreting a Woody Allen movie line-by-line to his illegal-alien cousin Humberto, three weeks under the wire from Matamoros. Like one of a pair of Beltone-wearing octogenarians on the loose from a rest home for a wild Saturday afternoon at the mall, plonked down in the third level multiplex, one of them describing whose ass Clint Eastwood is about to kick, and why. All at the top of her voice.

"Seen any good movies lately?" I asked him.

He didn't get a chance to answer, and I didn't jaunt inside to find out, because at that moment the steel door at the far end of the conference room opened, and another Security Officer poked his head in, and called across to Officer Let-Me-State-the-Obvious, "Dead man walking!"

Officer Self-Evident nodded to him, the other head poked back out, the door slammed, and my companion said, "When we bring one down from Death Row, he's gotta walk through the Ad Building and Segregation and the Main Hall. So everything's locked down. Every man's inside. It takes some time, y'know."

I thanked him.

"Is it true you work for the President, yeah?" He asked it so politely, I decided to give him a straight answer; and to hell with all the phony credentials Ally had worked up. "Yeah," I said, "we're on the same *bocce* ball team."

"Izzat so?" he said, fascinated by sports stats.

I was on the verge of explaining that the President was, in actuality, of Italian descent, when I heard the sound of the key turning in the security door, and it opened outward, and in came this messianic apparition in white, being led by a guard who was seven feet in any direction.

Henry Lake Spanning, sans halo, hands and feet shackled, with the chains cold-welded into a wide anodized steel belt, shuffled toward me; and his neoprene soles made no disturbing cacophony on the white tiles.

I watched him come the long way across the room, and he watched me right back. I thought to myself, *Yeah, she told him I can read minds. Well, let's see which method you use to try and keep me out of the landscape.* But I couldn't tell from the outside of him, not just by the way he shuffled and looked, if he had fucked Ally. But I knew it had to've been. Somehow. Even in the big lockup. Even here.

He stopped right across from me, with his hands on the back of the chair, and he didn't say a word, just gave me the nicest smile I'd ever gotten from anyone, even my momma. *Oh, yes*, I thought, *oh my goodness, yes*. Henry Lake Spanning was either the most masterfully charismatic person I'd ever met, or so good at the charm con that he could sell a slashed throat to a stranger.

"You can leave him," I said to the great black behemoth brother.

"Can't do that, sir."

"I'll take full responsibility."

"Sorry, sir; I was told someone had to be right here in the room with you and him, all the time."

I looked at the one who had waited with me. "That mean you, too?"

He shook his head. "Just one of us, I guess."

I frowned. "I need absolute privacy. What would happen if I were this man's attorney of record? Wouldn't you have to leave us alone? Privileged communication, right?"

They looked at each other, this pair of Security Officers, and they looked back at me, and they said nothing. All of a sudden Mr. Plain-as-the-Nose-on-Your-Face had nothing valuable to offer; and the sequoia with biceps "had his orders."

"They tell you who I work for? They tell you who it was sent me here to talk to this man?" Recourse to authority often works. They mumbled yessir yessir a couple of times each, but their faces stayed right on the mark of *sorry, sir, but we're not supposed to leave anybody alone with this man*. It wouldn't have mattered if they'd believed I'd flown in on Jehovah One.

So I said to myself *fuckit* I said to myself, and I slipped into their thoughts, and it didn't take much rearranging to get the phone wires restrung and the underground cables rerouted and the pressure on their bladders something fierce.

"On the other hand..." the first one said.

"I suppose we could..." the giant said.

And in a matter of maybe a minute and a half one of them was entirely gone, and the great one was standing outside the steel door, his back filling the double-pane chickenwire-imbedded security window. He effectively sealed off the one entrance or exit to or from the conference room; like the three hundred Spartans facing the tens of thousands of Xerxes's army at the Hot Gates.

Henry Lake Spanning stood silently watching me.

"Sit down," I said. "Make yourself comfortable."

He pulled out the chair, came around, and sat down.

"Pull it closer to the table," I said.

He had some difficulty, hands shackled that way, but he grabbed the leading edge of the seat and scraped forward till his stomach was touching the table.

He was a handsome guy, even for a white man. Nice nose, strong cheekbones, eyes the color of that water in your toilet when you toss in a tablet of 2000 Flushes. Very nice looking man. He gave me the creeps.

If Dracula had looked like Shirley Temple, no one would've driven a stake through his heart. If Harry Truman had looked like Freddy Krueger, he would never have beaten Tom Dewey at the polls. Joe Stalin and Saddam Hussein looked like sweet, avuncular friends of the family, really nice looking, kindly guys—who just incidentally happened to slaughter millions of men, women, and children. Abe Lincoln looked like an axe murderer, but he had a heart as big as Guatemala.

Henry Lake Spanning had the sort of face you'd trust immediately if you saw it in a tv commercial. Men would like to go fishing with him, women would like to squeeze his buns. Grannies would hug him on sight, kids would follow him straight into the mouth of an open oven. If he could play the piccolo, rats would gavotte around his shoes.

What saps we are. Beauty is only skin deep. You can't judge a book by its cover. Cleanliness is next to godliness. Dress for success. What saps we are.

So what did that make my pal, Allison Roche?

And why the hell didn't I just slip into his thoughts and check out the landscape? Why was I stalling?

Because I was scared of him.

This was fifty-six verified, gruesome, disgusting murders sitting forty-eight inches away from me, looking straight at me with blue eyes and soft, gently blond hair. Neither Harry nor Dewey would've had a prayer.

So why was I scared of him? Because; that's why.

This was damned foolishness. I had all the weaponry, he was shackled, and I didn't for a second believe he was what Ally *thought* he was: innocent.

Hell, they'd caught him, literally, redhanded. Bloody to the armpits, fer chrissakes. Innocent, my ass! *Okay, Rudy*, I thought, *get in there and take a look around.* But I didn't. I waited for him to say something.

He smiled tentatively, a gentle and nervous little smile, and he said, "Ally asked me to see you. Thank you for coming."

I looked *at* him, but not *into* him.

He seemed upset that he'd inconvenienced me. "But I don't think you can do me any good, not in just three days."

"You scared, Spanning?"

His lips trembled. "Yes I am, Mr. Pairis. I'm about as scared as a man can be." His eyes were moist.

"Probably gives you some insight into how your victims felt, whaddaya think?"

He didn't answer. His eyes were moist.

After a moment just looking at me, he scraped back his chair and stood up. "Thank you for coming, sir. I'm sorry Ally imposed on your time." He turned and started to walk away. I jaunted into his landscape.

Oh my god, I thought. He was innocent.

Never done any of it. None of it. Absolutely no doubt, not a shadow of a doubt. Ally had been right. I saw every bit of that landscape in there, every fold and crease; every bolt hole and rat run; every gully and arroyo; all of his past, back and back and back to his birth in Lewistown, Montana, near Great Falls, thirty-six years ago; every day of his life right up to the minute they arrested him leaning over that disemboweled cleaning woman the real killer had tossed into the dumpster.

I saw every second of his landscape; and I saw him coming out of the Winn-Dixie in Huntsville; pushing a cart filled with grocery bags of food for the weekend. And I saw him wheeling it around the parking lot toward the dumpster area overflowing with broken-down cardboard boxes and fruit crates. And I heard the cry for help from one of those dumpsters; and I saw Henry Lake Spanning stop and look around, not sure he'd heard anything at all. Then I saw him start to go to his car, parked right there at the edge of the lot beside the wall because it was a Friday evening and everyone was stocking up for the weekend, and there weren't any spaces out front; and the cry for help, weaker this time, as pathetic as a crippled kitten; and Henry Lake Spanning stopped cold, and he looked around; and we *both* saw the bloody hand raise itself above the level of the open dumpster's filthy green steel side. And I saw him desert his groceries without a thought to their cost, or that someone might run off with them if he left them unattended, or that he only had eleven dollars left in his checking account, so if those groceries were snagged by someone he wouldn't be eating for the next few days… and I watched him rush to the dumpster and look into the crap filling it…and I felt his nausea at the sight of that poor old woman, what was left of her…and I was with him as he crawled up onto the dumpster and dropped inside to do what he could for that mass of shredded and pulped flesh.

And I cried with him as she gasped, with a bubble of blood that burst in the open ruin of her throat, and she died. But though *I* heard the scream of someone coming around the corner, Spanning did not; and so he was still there, holding the poor mass of stripped skin and black bloody clothing, when the cops screeched into the parking lot. And only *then*, innocent of anything but decency and rare human compassion, did Henry Lake Spanning begin to understand what it must look like to middle-aged *hausfraus*, sneaking around dumpsters to pilfer cardboard boxes, who see what they think is a man murdering an old woman.

I was with him, there in that landscape within his mind, as he ran and ran and dodged and dodged. Until they caught him in Decatur, seven miles from the body of Gunilla Ascher. But they had him, and they had positive identification, from the dumpster in Huntsville; and all the rest of it was circumstantial, gussied up by bedridden, recovering Charlie Whilborg and the staff in Ally's office. It looked good on paper—so good that Ally had brought him down on twenty-nine-*cum*-fifty-six counts of murder in the vilest extreme.

But it was all bullshit.

The killer was still out there.

Henry Lake Spanning, who looked like a nice, decent guy, was exactly that. A nice, decent, goodhearted, but most of all *innocent* guy.

You could fool juries and polygraphs and judges and social workers and psychiatrists and your mommy and your daddy, but you could *not* fool Rudy Pairis, who travels regularly to the place of dark where you can go but not return.

They were going to burn an innocent man in three days.

I had to do something about it.

Not just for Ally, though that was reason enough; but for this man who thought he was doomed, and was frightened, but didn't have to take no shit from a wiseguy like me.

"Mr. Spanning," I called after him.

He didn't stop.

"Please," I said. He stopped shuffling, the chains making their little charm bracelet sounds, but he didn't turn around.

"I believe Ally is right, sir," I said. "I believe they caught the wrong man; and I believe all the time you've served is wrong; and I believe you ought not die."

Then he turned slowly, and stared at me with the look of a dog that has been taunted with a bone. His voice was barely a whisper. "And why is that, Mr. Pairis? Why is it that you believe me when nobody else but Ally and my attorney believed me?"

I didn't say what I was thinking. What I was thinking was that I'd been *in* there, and I *knew* he was innocent. And more than that, I knew that he truly loved my pal Allison Roche.

And there wasn't much I wouldn't do for Ally.

So what I said was: "I know you're innocent, because I know who's guilty."

His lips parted. It wasn't one of those big moves where someone's mouth flops open in astonishment; it was just a parting of the lips. But he was startled; I knew that as I knew the poor sonofabitch had suffered too long already.

He came shuffling back to me, and sat down.

"Don't make fun, Mr. Pairis. Please. I'm what you said, I'm scared. I don't want to die, and I surely don't want to die with the world thinking I did those...those things."

"Makin' no fun, captain. I know who ought to burn for all those murders. Not six states, but eleven. Not fifty-six dead, but an even seventy. Three of them little girls in a day nursery, and the woman watching them, too."

He stared at me. There was horror on his face. I know that look real good. I've seen it at least seventy times.

"I know you're innocent, cap'n, because *I'm* the man they want. *I'm* the guy who put your ass in here."

• • •

In a moment of human weakness. I saw it all. What I had packed off to live in that place of dark where you can go but not return. The wall-safe in my drawing-room. The four-foot-thick walled crypt encased in concrete and sunk a mile deep into solid granite. The vault whose composite laminate walls of judiciously sloped extremely thick blends of steel and plastic, the equivalent of six hundred to seven hundred mm of homogenous depth protection, approached the maximum toughness and hardness of crystaliron, that iron grown with perfect crystal structure and carefully controlled quantities of impurities that in a modern combat tank can shrug off a hollow charge warhead like a spaniel shaking himself dry. The Chinese puzzle box. The hidden chamber. The labyrinth. The maze of the mind where I'd sent all seventy to die, over and over and over, so I wouldn't hear their screams, or see the ropes of bloody tendon, or stare into the pulped sockets where their pleading eyes had been.

When I had walked into that prison, I'd been buttoned up totally. I was safe and secure, I knew nothing, remembered nothing, suspected nothing.

But when I walked into Henry Lake Spanning's landscape, and I could not lie to myself that he was the one, I felt the earth crack. I felt the tremors and the upheavals, and the fissures started at my feet and ran to the horizon; and the lava boiled up and began to flow. And the steel walls melted, and the concrete turned to dust, and the barriers dissolved; and I looked at the face of the monster.

No wonder I had such nausea when Ally had told me about this or that slaughter ostensibly perpetrated by Henry Lake Spanning, the man she was prosecuting on twenty-nine counts of murders I had committed. No wonder I could picture all the details when she would talk to me about the barest description of the murder site. No wonder I fought so hard against coming to Holman.

In there, in his mind, his landscape open to me, I saw the love he had for Allison Roche, for my pal and buddy with whom I had once, just once…

Don't try tellin' me that the Power of Love can open the fissures. I don't want to hear that shit. I'm telling *you* that it was a combination, a buncha things that split me open, and possibly maybe one of those things was what I saw between them.

I don't know that much. I'm a quick study, but this was in an instant. A crack of fate. A moment of human weakness. That's what I told myself in the part of me that ventured to the place of dark: that I'd done what I'd done in moments of human weakness.

And it was those moments, not my "gift," and not my blackness, that had made me the loser, the monster, the liar that I am.

In the first moment of realization, I couldn't believe it. Not me, not good old Rudy. Not likeable Rudy Pairis never done no one but hisself wrong his whole life.

In the next second I went wild with anger, furious at the disgusting thing that lived on one side of my split brain. Wanted to tear a hole through my face and yank the killing thing out, wet and putrescent, and squeeze it into pulp.

In the next second I was nauseated, actually wanted to fall down and puke, seeing every moment of what I had done, unshaded, unhidden, naked to this Rudy Pairis who was decent and reasonable and law-abiding, even if such a Rudy was little better than a well-educated fuckup. But not a killer...I wanted to puke.

Then, finally, I accepted what I could not deny.

For me, never again, would I slide through the night with the scent of the blossoming Yellow Lady's Slipper. I recognized that perfume now.

It was the odor that rises from a human body cut wide open, like a mouth making a big, dark yawn.

The other Rudy Pairis had come home at last.

They didn't have half a minute's worry. I sat down at a little wooden writing table in an interrogation room in the Jefferson County D.A.'s offices, and I made up a graph with the names and dates and locations. Names of as many of the seventy as I actually knew. (A lot of them had just been on the road, or in a men's toilet, or taking a bath, or lounging in the back row of a movie, or getting some cash from an ATM, or just sitting around doing nothing but waiting for me to come along and open them up, and maybe have a drink off them, or maybe just something to snack on...down the road.) Dates were easy, because I've got a good memory for dates. And the places where they'd find the ones they didn't know about, the fourteen with exactly the same m.o. as the other fifty-six, not to mention the old-style rip-and-pull can opener I'd used on that little Catholic bead-counter Gunilla Whatsername, who did Hail Mary this and Sweet Blessed Jesus that all the time I was opening her up, even at the last, when I held up parts of her insides for her to look at, and tried to get her to lick them, but she died first. Not half a minute's worry for the State of Alabama. All in one swell foop they corrected a tragic miscarriage of justice, nobbled a maniac killer, solved fourteen more murders than they'd counted on (in five additional states, which made the police departments of those five additional states extremely pleased with the law enforcement agencies of the Sovereign State of Alabama), and made first spot on the evening news on all three major networks, not to mention CNN, for the better part of a week. Knocked the Middle East right out of the box. Neither Harry Truman nor Tom Dewey would've had a prayer.

Ally went into seclusion, of course. Took off and went somewhere down on the Florida coast, I heard. But after the trial, and the verdict, and Spanning being released, and me going inside, and all like that, well, oo-poppa-dow as they used to say, it was all reordered properly. *Sat cito si sat bene*, in Latin. "It is done quickly enough if it is done well." A favorite saying of Cato. The Elder Cato.

And all I asked, all I begged for, was that Ally and Henry Lake Spanning, who loved each other and deserved each other, and whom I had almost fucked up royally, that the two of them would be there when they jammed my weary black butt into that new electric chair at Holman.

Please come, I begged them.

Don't let me die alone. Not even a shit like me. Don't make me cross over into that place of dark, where you can go, but not return—without the face of a friend. Even a former friend. And as for you, captain, well, hell, didn't I save your life so you could enjoy the company of the woman you love? Least you can do. Come on now; be there or be square!

I don't know if Spanning talked her into accepting the invite, or if it was the other way around; but one day about a week prior to the event of cooking up a mess of fried Rudy Pairis, the Warden stopped by my commodious accommodations on Death Row and gave me to understand that it would be SRO for the barbeque, which meant Ally my pal, and her boy friend, the former resident of the Row where now I dwelt in durance vile.

The things a guy'll do for love.

Yeah, that was the key. Why would a very smart operator who had gotten away with it, all the way free and clear, why would such a smart operator suddenly pull one of those hokey courtroom "I did it, I did it!" routines, and as good as strap himself into the electric chair?

Once. I only went to bed with her once.

The things a guy'll do for love.

When they brought me into the death chamber from the holding cell where I'd spent the night before and all that day, where I'd had my last meal (which had been a hot roast beef sandwich, double meat, on white toast, with very crisp french fries, and hot brown country gravy poured over the whole thing, apple sauce, and a bowl of Concord grapes), where a representative of the Holy Roman Empire had tried to make amends for destroying most of the gods, beliefs, and cultures of my black forebears, they held me between Security Officers, neither one of whom had been in attendance when I'd visited Henry Lake Spanning at this very same correctional facility slightly more than a year before.

It hadn't been a bad year. Lots of rest; caught up on my reading, finally got around to Proust and Langston Hughes, I'm ashamed to admit, so late in the game; lost some weight; worked out regularly; gave up cheese and dropped my cholesterol count. Ain't nothin' to it, just to do it.

Even took a jaunt or two or ten, every now and awhile. It didn't matter none. I wasn't going anywhere, neither were they. I'd done worse than the worst of them; hadn't I confessed to it? So there wasn't a lot that could ice me, after I'd copped to it and released all seventy of them out of my unconscious, where they'd been rotting in shallow graves for years. No big thang, Cuz.

Brought me in, strapped me in, plugged me in.

I looked through the glass at the witnesses.

There sat Ally and Spanning, front row center. Best seats in the house. All eyes and crying, watching, not believing everything had come to this, trying to figure out when and how and in what way it had all gone down without her knowing anything at all about it. And Henry Lake Spanning sitting close beside her, their hands locked in her lap. True love.

I locked eyes with Spanning.

I jaunted into his landscape.

No, I *didn't*.

I *tried* to, and couldn't squirm through. Thirty years, or less, since I was five or six, I'd been doing it; without hindrance, all alone in the world the only person who could do this listen in on the landscape trick; and for the first time I was stopped. Absolutely no fuckin' entrance. I went wild! I tried running at it full-tilt, and hit something khaki-colored, like beach sand, and only slightly giving, not hard, but resilient. Exactly like being inside a ten-foot-high, fifty-foot-diameter paper bag, like a big shopping bag from a supermarket, that stiff butcher's paper kind of bag, and that color, like being inside a bag that size, running straight at it, thinking you're going to bust through…and being thrown back. Not hard, not like bouncing on a trampoline, just shunted aside like the fuzz from a dandelion hitting a glass door. Unimportant. Khaki-colored and not particularly bothered.

I tried hitting it with a bolt of pure blue lightning mental power, like someone out of a Marvel comic, but that wasn't how mixing in other people's minds works. You don't think yourself in with a psychic battering-ram. That's the kind of arrant foolishness you hear spouted by unattractive people on public access cable channels, talking about The Power of Love and The Power of the Mind and the ever-popular toe-tapping Power of a Positive Thought. Bullshit: I don't be home to *that* folly!

I tried picturing myself in there, but that didn't work, either. I tried blanking my mind and drifting across, but it was pointless. And at that moment it occurred to me that I didn't really know *how* I jaunted. I just… did it. One moment I was snug in the privacy of my own head, and the next I was over there in someone else's landscape. It was instantaneous, like teleportation, which also is an impossibility, like telepathy.

But now, strapped into the chair, and them getting ready to put the leather mask over my face so the witnesses wouldn't have to see the smoke coming out of my eye-sockets and the little sparks as my nose hairs burned, when it was urgent that I get into the thoughts and landscape of Henry Lake Spanning, I was shut out completely. And right *then*, that moment, I was scared!

Presto, without my even opening up to him, there he was: inside my head.

He had jaunted into *my* landscape.

"You had a nice roast beef sandwich, I see."

His voice was a lot stronger than it had been when I'd come down to see him a year ago. A *lot* stronger inside my mind.

"Yes, Rudy, I'm what you knew probably existed somewhere. Another one. A shrike." He paused. "I see you call it 'jaunting in the landscape.' I just called myself a shrike. A butcherbird. One name's as good as another. Strange, isn't it; all these years; and we never met anyone else? There *must* be others, but I think—now I can't prove this, I have no real data, it's just a wild idea I've had for years and years—I think they don't know they can do it."

He stared at me across the landscape, those wonderful blue eyes of his, the ones Ally had fallen in love with, hardly blinking.

"Why didn't you let me know before this?"

He smiled sadly. "Ah, Rudy. Rudy, Rudy, Rudy; you poor benighted pickaninny.

"Because I needed to suck you in, kid. I needed to put out a bear trap, and let it snap closed on your scrawny leg, and send you over. Here, let me clear the atmosphere in here…" And he wiped away all the manipulation he had worked on me, way back a year ago, when he had so easily covered his own true thoughts, his past, his life, the real panorama of what went on inside his landscape—like bypassing a surveillance camera with a continuous-loop tape that continues to show a placid scene while the joint is being actively burgled—and when he convinced me not only that he was innocent, but that the real killer was someone who had blocked the hideous slaughters from his conscious mind and had lived an otherwise exemplary life. He wandered around my landscape—and all of this in a second or two, because time has no duration in the landscape, like the hours you can spend in a dream that are just thirty seconds long in the real world, just before you wake up—and he swept away all the false memories and suggestions, the logical structure of sequential events that he had planted that would dovetail with my actual existence, my true memories, altered and warped and rearranged so I would believe that I had done all seventy of those ghastly murders…so that I'd believe, in a moment of horrible realization, that I was the demented psychopath who had ranged state to state to state, leaving piles of ripped flesh at every stop. Blocked it all, submerged it all, sublimated it all, me. Good old Rudy Pairis, who never killed anybody. I'd been the patsy he was waiting for.

"There, now, kiddo. See what it's really like?

"You didn't do a thing.

"Pure as the driven snow, nigger. That's the truth. And what a find you were. Never even suspected there was another like me, till Ally came to interview me after Decatur. But there you were, big and black as a

Great White Hope, right there in her mind. Isn't she fine, Pairis? Isn't she something to take a knife to? Something to split open like a nice piece of fruit warmed in a summer sunshine field, let all the steam rise off her… maybe have a picnic…"

He stopped.

"I wanted her right from the first moment I saw her.

"Now, you know, I could've done it sloppy, just been a shrike to Ally, that first time she came to the holding cell to interview me; just jump into her, that was my plan. But what a noise that Spanning in the cell would've made, yelling it wasn't a man, it was a woman, not Spanning, but Deputy D.A. Allison Roche…too much noise, too many complications. But I *could* have done it, jumped into her. Or a guard, and then slice her at my leisure, stalk her, find her, let her steam…

"You look distressed, Mr. Rudy Pairis. Why's that? Because you're going to die in my place? Because I could have taken you over at any time, and didn't? Because after all this time of your miserable, wasted, lousy life you finally find someone like you, and we don't even have the convenience of a chat? Well, that's sad, that's really sad, kiddo. But you didn't have a chance."

"You're stronger than me, you kept me out," I said.

He chuckled.

"Stronger? Is that all you think it is? Stronger? You still don't get it, do you?" His face, then, grew terrible. "You don't even understand now, right now that I've cleaned it all away and you can *see* what I did to you, do you?

"Do you think I stayed in a jail cell, and went through that trial, all of that, because I couldn't do anything about it? You poor jig slob. I could have jumped like a shrike any time I wanted to. But the first time I met your Ally I saw *you*."

I cringed. "And you waited…? For me, you spent all that time in prison, just to get to me…?"

"At the moment when you couldn't do anything about it, at the moment you couldn't shout 'I've been taken over by someone else, I'm Rudy Pairis here inside this Henry Lake Spanning body, help me, help me!' Why stir up noise when all I had to do was bide my time, wait a bit, wait for Ally, and let Ally go for you."

I felt like a drowning turkey, standing idiotically in the rain, head tilted up, mouth open, water pouring in. "You can…leave the mind…leave the body…go out…jaunt, jump permanently…"

Spanning sniggered like a schoolyard bully.

"You stayed in jail three years just to get *me*?"

He smirked. Smarter than thou.

"Three years? You think that's some big deal to me? You don't think I could have someone like you running around, do you? Someone who can 'jaunt' as I do? The only other shrike I've ever encountered. You think I wouldn't sit in here and wait for you to come to me?"

"But three *years*..."

"You're what, Rudy...thirty-one, is it? Yes, I can see that. Thirty-one. You've never jumped like a shrike. You've just entered, jaunted, gone into the landscapes, and never understood that it's more than reading minds. You can change domiciles, black boy. You can move out of a house in a bad neighborhood—such as strapped into the electric chair—and take up residence in a brand, spanking, new housing complex of million-and-a-half-buck condos, like Ally."

"But you have to have a place for the other one to go, don't you?" I said it just flat, no tone, no color to it at all. I didn't even think of the place of dark, where you can go...

"Who do you think I am, Rudy? Just who the hell do you think I was when I started, when I learned to shrike, how to jaunt, what I'm telling you now about changing residences? You wouldn't know my first address. I go a long way back.

"But I can give you a few of my more famous addresses. Gilles de Rais, France, 1440; Vlad Tepes, Romania, 1462; Elizabeth Bathory, Hungary, 1611; Catherine DeShayes, France, 1680; Jack the Ripper, London, 1888; Henri Désiré Landru, France, 1915; Albert Fish, New York City, 1934; Ed Gein, Plainfield, Wisconsin, 1954; Myra Hindley, Manchester, 1963; Albert DeSalvo, Boston, 1964; Charles Manson, Los Angeles, 1969; John Wayne Gacy, Norwood Park Township, Illinois, 1977.

"Oh, but how I do go on. And on. And on and on and on, Rudy, my little porch monkey. That's what I do. I go on. And on and on. Shrike will nest where it chooses. If not in your beloved Allison Roche, then in the cheesy fucked-up black boy, Rudy Pairis. But don't you think that's a waste, kiddo? Spending however much time I might have to spend in your socially unacceptable body, when Henry Lake Spanning is such a handsome devil? Why should I have just switched with you when Ally lured you to me, because all it would've done is get you screeching and howling that you

483

weren't Spanning, you were this nigger son who'd had his head stolen… and then you might have manipulated some guards or the Warden…

"Well, you see what I mean, don't you?

"But now that the mask is securely in place, and now that the electrodes are attached to your head and your left leg, and now that the Warden has his hand on the switch, well, you'd better get ready to do a lot of drooling."

And he turned around to jaunt back out of me, and I closed the perimeter. He tried to jaunt, tried to leap back to his own mind, but I had him in a fist. Just that easy. Materialized a fist, and turned him to face me.

"Fuck you, Jack the Ripper. And fuck you twice, Bluebeard. And on and on and on fuck you Manson and Boston Strangler and any other dipshit warped piece of sick crap you been in your years. You sure got some muddy-shoes credentials there, boy.

"What I care about all those names, Spanky my brother? You really think I don't know those names? I'm an educated fellah, Mistuh Rippuh, Mistuh Mad Bomber. You missed a few. Were you also, did you inhabit, hast thou possessed Winnie Ruth Judd and Charlie Starkweather and Mad Dog Coll and Richard Speck and Sirhan Sirhan and Jeffrey Dahmer? You the boogieman responsible for *every* bad number the human race ever played? You ruin Sodom and Gomorrah, burned the Great Library of Alexandria, orchestrated the Reign of Terror *dans Paree*, set up the Inquisition, stoned and drowned the Salem witches, slaughtered unarmed women and kids at Wounded Knee, bumped off John Kennedy?

"I don't think so.

"I don't even think you got so close as to share a pint with Jack the Ripper. And even if you did, even if you *were* all those maniacs, you were small potatoes, Spanky. The least of us human beings outdoes you, three times a day. How many lynch ropes you pulled tight, M'sieur Landru?

"What colossal egotism you got, makes you blind, makes you think you're the only one, even when you find out there's someone else, you can't get past it. What makes you think I didn't know what you can do? What makes you think I didn't let you do it, and sit here waiting for you like you sat there waiting for me, till this moment when you can't do shit about it?

"You so goddam stuck on yourself, Spankyhead, you never give it the barest that someone else is a faster draw than you.

"Know what your trouble is, Captain? You're old, you're *real* old, maybe hundreds of years who gives a damn old. That don't count for shit, old man. You're old, but you never got smart. You're just mediocre at what you do.

"You moved from address to address. You didn't have to be Son of Sam or Cain slayin' Abel, or whoever the fuck you been…you could've been Moses or Galileo or George Washington Carver or Harriet Tubman or Sojourner Truth or Mark Twain or Joe Louis. You could've been Alexander Hamilton and helped found the Manumission Society in New York. You could've discovered radium, carved Mount Rushmore, carried a baby out of a burning building. But you got old real fast, and you never got any smarter. You didn't need to, did you, Spanky? You had it all to yourself, all this 'shrike' shit, just jaunt here and jaunt there, and bite off someone's hand or face like the old, tired, boring, repetitious, no-imagination stupid shit that you are.

"Yeah, you got me good when I came here to see your landscape. You got Ally wired up good. And she suckered me in, probably not even knowing she was doing it…you must've looked in her head and found just the right technique to get her to make me come within reach. Good, m'man; you were excellent. But I had a year to torture myself. A year to sit here and think about it. About how many people I'd killed, and how sick it made me, and little by little I found my way through it.

"Because…and here's the big difference 'tween us, dummy:

"I unraveled what was going on…it took time, but I learned. Understand, asshole? *I* learn! *You* don't.

"There's an old Japanese saying—I got lots of these, Henry m'man—I read a whole lot—and what it says is, 'Do not fall into the error of the artisan who boasts of twenty years experience in his craft while in fact he has had only one year of experience—twenty times.'" Then I grinned back at him.

"Fuck you, sucker," I said, just as the Warden threw the switch and I jaunted out of there and into the landscape and mind of Henry Lake Spanning.

I sat there getting oriented for a second; it was the first time I'd done more than a jaunt…this was…*shrike*; but then Ally beside me gave a little sob for her old pal, Rudy Pairis, who was baking like a Maine lobster, smoke coming out from under the black cloth that covered my, his, face; and I heard the vestigial scream of what had been Henry Lake Spanning and thousands of other monsters, all of them burning, out there on the far horizon of my new landscape; and I put my arm around her, and drew her close, and put my face into her shoulder and hugged her to me; and I heard the scream go on and on for the longest time, I think it was a long time, and finally it was just wind…and then gone…and I came up from Ally's shoulder, and I could barely speak.

"Shhh, honey, it's okay," I murmured. "He's gone where he can make right for his mistakes. No pain. Quiet, a real quiet place; and all alone forever. And cool there. And dark."

I was ready to stop failing at everything, and blaming everything. Having fessed up to love, having decided it was time to grow up and be an adult—not just a very quick study who learned fast, extremely fast, a lot faster than anybody could imagine an orphan like me could learn, than *any*body could imagine—I hugged her with the intention that Henry Lake Spanning would love Allison Roche more powerfully, more responsibly, than anyone had ever loved anyone in the history of the world. I was ready to stop failing at everything.

And it would be just a whole lot easier as a white boy with great big blue eyes.

Because—get on this now—all my wasted years didn't have as much to do with blackness or racism or being overqualified or being unlucky or being high-verbal or even the curse of my "gift" of jaunting, as they did with one single truth I learned waiting in there, inside my own landscape, waiting for Spanning to come and gloat:

I have always been one of those miserable guys who *couldn't get out of his own way.*

Which meant I could, at last, stop feeling sorry for that poor nigger, Rudy Pairis. Except, maybe, in a moment of human weakness.

This story, for Bob Bloch, because I promised.

CHATTING WITH ANUBIS

1996 Bram Stoker Award: Short Story

WHEN THE CORE drilling was halted at a depth of exactly 804.5 meters, one half mile down, Amy Guiterman and I conspired to grab Immortality by the throat and shake it till it noticed us.

My name is Wang Zicai. Ordinarily, the family name Wang—which is pronounced with the "a" in *father*, almost as if it were Wong—means "king." In my case, it means something else; it means "rushing headlong." How appropriate. Don't tell me clairvoyance doesn't run in my family... Zicai means "suicide." Half a mile down, beneath the blank Sahara, in a hidden valley that holds cupped in its eternal serenity the lake of the oasis of Siwa, I and a young woman equally as young and reckless as myself, Amy Guiterman of New York City, conspired to do a thing that would certainly cause our disgrace, if not our separate deaths.

I am writing this in Yin.

It is the lost ancestral language of the Chinese people. It was a language written between the 18th and 12th centuries before the common era. It is not only ancient, it is impossible to translate. There are only five people alive today, as I write this, who can translate this manuscript, written in the language of the Yin Dynasty that blossomed northeast along the Yellow River in a time long before the son of a carpenter is alleged to have fed multitudes with loaves and fishes, to have walked on water, to have raised the dead. I am no "rice christian." You cannot give me a meal and find me scurrying to your god. I am Buddhist, as my family has been for centuries. That I can write in Yin—which is to modern Chinese as classical Latin is to vineyard Italian—is a conundrum I choose not to answer in this document. Let he or she who one day unearths this text unscramble the oddities of chance and experience that brought me, "rushing headlong toward suicide," to this place half a mile beneath the Oasis of Siwa.

A blind thrust-fault, hitherto unrecorded, beneath the Mountain of the Moon, had produced a cataclysmic 7.5 temblor. It had leveled villages as far away as Bi'r Bū Kūsā and Abu Simbel. The aerial and satellite reconnaissance from the Gulf of Sidra to the Red Sea, from the Libyan Plateau to the Sudan, showed great fissures, herniated valleys, upthrust structures, a new world lost to human sight for thousands of years. An international team of paleoseismologists was assembled, and I was called from the Great Boneyard of the Gobi by my superiors at the Mongolian Academy of Sciences at Ulan Bator to leave my triceratops and fly to the middle of hell on earth, the great sand ocean of the Sahara, to assist in excavating and analyzing what some said would be the discovery of the age.

Some said it was the mythical Shrine of Ammon.

Some said it was the Temple of the Oracle.

Alexander the Great, at the very pinnacle of his fame, was told of the Temple, and of the all-knowing Oracle who sat there. And so he came, from the shore of Egypt down into the deep Sahara, seeking the Oracle. It is recorded: his expedition was lost, wandering hopelessly, without water and without hope. Then crows came to lead them down through the Mountain of the Moon, down to a hidden valley without name, to the lake of the Oasis of Siwa, and at its center...the temple, the Shrine of Ammon. It was so recorded. And one thing more. In a small and dark chamber roofed with palm logs, the Egyptian priests told Alexander a thing that affected him for the rest of his life. It is not recorded what he was told. And never again, we have always been led to believe, has the Shrine of Ammon been seen by civilized man or civilized woman.

Now, Amy Guiterman and I, she from the Brooklyn Museum and I an honored graduate of Beijing University, together we had followed Alexander's route from Paraetonium to Siwa to here, hundreds of kilometers beyond human thought or action, half a mile down, where the gigantic claw diggers had ceased their abrading, the two of us with simple pick and shovel, standing on the last thin layer of compacted dirt and rock that roofed whatever great shadowy structure lay beneath us, a shadow picked up by the most advanced deep-resonance-response readings, verified on-site by proton free-precession magnetometry and ground-penetrating radar brought in from the Sandia National Laboratory in Albuquerque, New Mexico, in the United States.

Something large lay just beneath our feet.

And tomorrow, at sunrise, the team would assemble to break through and share the discovery, whatever it might be.

But I had had knowledge of Amy Guiterman's body, and she was as reckless as I, rushing headlong toward suicide, and in a moment of foolishness, a moment that should have passed but did not, we sneaked out of camp and went to the site and lowered ourselves, taking with us nylon rope and crampons, powerful electric torches and small recording devices, trowel and whisk broom, cameras and carabiners. A pick and a shovel. I offer no excuse. We were young, we were reckless, we were smitten with each other, and we behaved like naughty children. What happened should not have happened.

We broke through the final alluvial layer and swept out the broken pieces. We stood atop a ceiling of fitted stones, basalt or even marble, I could not tell immediately. I knew they were not granite, that much I did know. There were seams. Using the pick, I prised loose the ancient and concretized mortar. It went much more quickly and easily than I would have thought, but then, I'm used to digging for bones, not for buildings. I managed to chock the large set-stone in place with wooden wedges, until I had guttered the perimeter fully. Then, inching the toe of the pick into the fissure, I began levering the stone up, sliding the wedges deeper to keep the huge block from slipping back. And finally, though the block was at least sixty or seventy centimeters thick, we were able to tilt it up and, bracing our backs against the opposite side of the hole we had dug at the bottom of the core pit, we were able to use our strong young legs to force it back and away, beyond the balance point; and it fell away with a crash.

A great wind escaped the aperture that had housed the stone. A great wind that twisted up from below in a dark swirl that we could actually see. Amy Guiterman gave a little sound of fear and startlement. So did I. Then she said, "They would have used great amounts of charcoal to set these limestone blocks in place," and I learned from her that they were not marble, neither were they basalt.

We showed each other our bravery by dangling our feet through the opening, sitting at the edge and leaning over to catch the wind. It smelled *sweet*. Not a smell I had ever known before. But certainly not stagnant. Not corrupt. Sweet as a washed face, sweet as chilled fruit. Then we lit our torches and swept the beams below.

We sat just above the ceiling of a great chamber. Neither pyramid nor mausoleum, it seemed to be an immense hall filled with enormous statues of pharaohs and beast-headed gods and creatures with neither animal nor human shape…and all of these statues gigantic. Perhaps one hundred times life-size.

Directly beneath us was the noble head of a time-lost ruler, wearing the *nemes* headdress and the royal ritual beard. Where our digging had dropped shards of rock, the shining yellow surface of the statue had been chipped, and a darker material showed through. "Diorite," Amy Guiterman said. "Covered with gold. Pure gold. Lapis lazuli, turquoise, garnets, rubies—the headdress is made of thousands of gems, all precisely cut…do you see?"

But I was lowering myself. Having cinched my climbing rope around the excised block, I was already shinnying down the cord to stand on the first ledge I could manage, the empty place between the placid hands of the pharaoh that lay on the golden knees. I heard Amy Guiterman scrambling down behind and above me.

Then the wind rose again, suddenly, shrieking up and around me like a monsoon, and the rope was ripped from my hands, and my torch was blown away, and I was thrown back and something sharp caught at the back of my shirt and I wrenched forward to fall on my stomach and I felt the cold of that wind on my bare back. And everything was dark.

Then I felt cold hands on me. All over me. Reaching, touching, probing me, as if I were a cut of sliced meat lying on a counter. Above me I heard Amy Guiterman shrieking. I felt the halves of my ripped shirt torn from my body, and then my kerchief, and then my boots, and then my stockings, and then my watch and glasses.

I struggled to my feet and took a position, ready to make an empassing or killing strike. I was no cinema action hero, but whatever was there plucking at me would have to take my life despite I fought for it!

Then, from below, light began to rise. Great light, the brightest light I've ever seen, like a shimmering fog. And as it rose, I could see that the mist that filled the great chamber beneath us was trying to reach us, to touch us, to feel us with hands of ephemeral chilling ghostliness. Dead hands. Hands of beings and men who might never have been or who, having been, were denied their lives. They reached, they sought, they implored.

And rising from the mist, with a howl, Anubis.

God of the dead, jackal-headed conductor of souls. Opener of the road to the afterlife. Embalmer of Osiris, Lord of the mummy wrappings, ruler of the dark passageways, watcher at the neverending funeral. Anubis came, and we were left, suddenly, ashamed and alone, the American girl and I, who had acted rashly as do all those who flee toward their own destruction.

But he did not kill us, did not take us. How could he...am I not writing this for some never-to-be-known reader to find? He roared yet again, and the hands of the seekers drew back, reluctantly, like whipped curs into kennels, and there in the soft golden light reflected from the icon of a pharaoh dead and gone so long that no memory exists even of his name, there in the space half a mile down, the great god Anubis spoke to us.

At first, he thought we were "the great conqueror" come again. No, I told him, not Alexander. And the great god laughed with a terrible thin laugh that brought to mind paper cuts and the slicing of eyeballs. No, of course not that one, said the great god, for did I not reveal to him the great secret? Why should he ever return? Why should he not flee as fast as his great army could carry him, and never return? And Anubis laughed.

I was young and I was foolish, and I asked the jackal-headed god to tell *me* the great secret. If I was to perish here, at least I could carry to the afterlife a great wisdom.

Anubis looked through me.

Do you know why I guard this tomb?

I said I did not know, but that perhaps it was to protect the wisdom of the Oracle, to keep hidden the great secret of the Shrine of Ammon that had been given to Alexander.

And Anubis laughed the more. Vicious laughter that made me wish I had never grown skin or taken air into my lungs.

This is not the Shrine of Ammon, he said. Later they may have said it was, but this is what it has always been, the tomb of the Most Accursed One. The Defiler. The Nemesis. The Killer of the dream that lasted twice six thousand years. I guard this tomb to deny him entrance to the afterlife.

And I guard it to pass on the great secret.

"Then you don't plan to kill us?" I asked. Behind me I heard Amy Guiterman snort with disbelief that I, a graduate of Beijing University, could ask such an imbecile question. Anubis looked through me again, and said no, I don't have to do that. It is not my job. And then, with no prompting at all, he told me, and he told Amy Guiterman from the Brooklyn Museum, he told us the great secret that had lain beneath the sands since the days of Alexander. And then he told us whose tomb it was. And then he vanished into the mist. And then we climbed back out, hand over hand, because our ropes were gone, and my clothes were gone, and Amy Guiterman's pack and supplies were gone, but we still had our lives.

At least for the moment.

I write this now, in Yin, and I set down the great secret in its every particular. All parts of it, and the three colors, and the special names, and the pacing. It's all here, for whomever finds it, because the tomb is gone again. Temblor or jackal-god, I cannot say. But if today, as opposed to last night, you seek that shadow beneath the sand, you will find emptiness.

Now we go our separate ways, Amy Guiterman and I. She to her destiny, and I to mine. It will not be long in finding us. At the height of his power, soon after visiting the Temple of the Oracle, where he was told something that affected him for the rest of his life, Alexander the Great died of a mosquito bite. It is said. Alexander the Great died of an overdose of drink and debauchery. It is said. Alexander the Great died of murder, he was poisoned. It is said. Alexander the Great died of a prolonged, nameless fever; of pneumonia; of typhus; of septicemia; of typhoid; of eating off tin plates; of malaria. It is said. Alexander was a bold and energetic king at the peak of his powers, it is written, but during his last months in Babylon, for no reason anyone has ever been able to explain satisfactorily, he took to heavy drinking and nightly debauches…and then the fever came for him.

A mosquito. It is said.

No one will bother to say what has taken me. Or Amy Guiterman. We are insignificant. But we know the great secret.

Anubis likes to chat. The jackal-headed one has no secrets he chooses to keep. He'll tell it all. Secrecy is not his job. Revenge is his job. Anubis guards the tomb, and eon by eon makes revenge for his fellow gods.

The tomb is the final resting place of the one who killed the gods. When belief in the gods vanishes, when the worshippers of the gods turn away their faces, then the gods themselves vanish. Like the mist that climbs and implores, they go. And the one who lies encrypted there, guarded by the lord of the funeral, is the one who brought the world to forget Isis and Osiris and Horus and Anubis. He is the one who opened the sea, and the one who wandered in the desert. He is the one who went to the mountaintop, and he is the one who brought back the word of yet another god. He is Moses, and for Anubis revenge is not only sweet, it is everlasting. Moses—denied both Heaven and Hell—will never rest in the Afterlife. Revenge without pity has doomed him to eternal exclusion, buried in the sepulcher of the gods he killed.

I sink this now, in an unmarked meter of dirt, at a respectable depth; and I go my way, bearing the great secret, no longer needing to "rush headlong," as I have already committed what suicide is necessary. I go my way, for however long I have, leaving only this warning for anyone who may yet seek the lost Shrine of Ammon. In the words of Amy Guiterman of New York City, spoken to a jackal-headed deity, "I've got to tell you, Anubis, you are one *tough* grader." *She was not smiling when she said it.*

THE HUMAN OPERATORS

(written with A.E. van Vogt)

2000 Writers Guild of Canada Award

[To be read while listening to Chronophagie,
*"The Time Eaters": Music of Jacques Lasry,
played on Structures Sonores Lasry-Baschet
(Columbia Masterworks Stereo MS 7314).]*

SHIP: THE ONLY place.

Ship says I'm to get wracked today at noon. And so I'm in grief already.

It seems unfair to have to get wracked three whole days ahead of the usual once-a-month. But I learned long ago not to ask Ship to explain anything personal.

I sense today is different; some things are happening. Early, I put on the spacesuit and go outside—which is not common. But a screen got badly scored by meteor dust; and I'm here, now, replacing it. Ship would say I'm being bad because: as I do my job, I sneak quick looks around me. I wouldn't dare do it in the forbidden places, inside. I noticed when I was still a kid that Ship doesn't seem to be so much aware of what I do when I'm outside.

And so I carefully sneak a few looks at the deep black space. And at the stars.

I once asked Ship why we never go toward those points of brilliance, those stars, as Ship calls them. For that question, I got a whole extra wracking, and a long, ranting lecture about how all those stars have humans living on their planets; and of how vicious humans are. Ship really blasted me that time, saying things I'd never heard before, like how Ship had gotten away from the vicious humans during the big war with the Kyben. And how, every once in a long while Ship has a "run-in" with the vicious humans but the defractor perimeter saves us. I don't know what Ship means by all that; I don't even know what a "run-in" is, exactly.

The last "run-in" must have been before I was big enough to remember. Or, at least, before Ship killed my father when I was fourteen. Several times, when he was still alive, I slept all day for no reason that I can think of. But since I've been doing all the maintenance work—since age fourteen—I sleep only my regular six-hour night. Ship tells me night and Ship tells me day, too.

I kneel here in my spacesuit, feeling tiny on this gray and curving metal place in the dark. Ship is big. Over five hundred feet long, and about a hundred and fifty feet thick at the widest back there. Again, I have that special out-here thought: suppose I just give myself a shove, and float right off toward one of those bright spots of light? Would I be able to get away? I think I would like that; there has to be someplace else than Ship.

As in the past, I slowly and sadly let go of the idea. Because if I try, and Ship catches me, I'll *really* get wracked.

The repair job is finally done. I clomp back to the airlock, and use the spider to dilate it, and let myself be sucked back into what is, after all—I've got to admit it—a pretty secure place. All the gleaming corridors, the huge storerooms with their equipment and spare parts, and the freezer rooms with their stacks of food (enough, says Ship, to last one person for centuries), and the deck after deck of machinery that it's my job to keep in repair. I can take pride in that. *"Hurry! It is six minutes to noon!"* Ship announces. I'm hurrying now.

I strip off my spacesuit and stick it to the decontamination board and head for the wracking room. At least, that's what *I* call it. I suppose it's really part of the engine room on Underdeck Ten, a special chamber fitted with electrical connections, most of which are testing instruments. I use them pretty regularly in my work. My father's father's father installed them for Ship, I think I recall.

There's a big table, and I climb on top of it and lie down. The table is cold against the skin of my back and butt and thighs, but it warms me up as I lie here. It's now one minute to noon. As I wait, shuddering with expectation, the ceiling lowers toward me. Part of what comes down fits over my head, and I feel the two hard knobs pressing into the temples of my skull. And cold; I feel the clamps coming down over my middle, my wrists, my ankles. A strap with metal in it tightens flexibly but firmly across my chest.

"Ready!" Ship commands.

It always seems bitterly unfair. How can I ever be ready to be wracked? I hate it! Ship counts: *"Ten...nine...eight...one!"*

The first jolt of electricity hits and everything tries to go in different directions; it feels like someone is tearing something soft inside me—that's the way it feels.

Blackness swirls into my head and I forget everything. I am unconscious for a while. Just before I regain myself, before I am finished and Ship will permit me to go about my duties, I remember a thing I have remembered many times. This isn't the first time for this memory. It is of my father and a thing he said once, not long before he was killed. "When Ship says vicious, Ship means smarter. There are ninety-eight other chances."

He said those words very quickly. I think he knew he was going to get killed soon. Oh, of course, he *must* have known, my father must, because I was nearly fourteen then, and when *he* had become fourteen, Ship had killed *his* father, so he must have known.

And so the words are important. I know that; they are important; but I don't know what they mean, not completely.

"You are finished!" Ship says.

I get off the table. The pain still hangs inside my head and I ask Ship, "Why am I wracked three days earlier than usual?"

Ship sounds angry. *"I can wrack you again!"*

But I know Ship won't. Something new is going to happen and Ship wants me whole and alert for it. Once, when I asked Ship something personal, right after I was wracked, Ship did it again, and when I woke up Ship was worrying over me with the machines. Ship seemed concerned I might be damaged. Ever after that, Ship has not wracked me twice close together. So I ask, not really thinking I'll get an answer; but I ask just the same.

"There is a repairing I want you to do!"

Where, I ask.

"In the forbidden part below!"

I try not to smile. I knew there was a new thing going to happen and this is it. My father's words come back again. *Ninety-eight other chances.*

Is this one of them?

I descend in the dark. There is no light in the dropshaft. Ship says I need no light. But I know the truth. Ship does not want me to be able to find my way back here again. This is the lowest I've ever been in Ship.

So I drop steadily, smoothly, swiftly. Now I come to a slowing place and slower and slower, and finally my feet touch the solid deck and I am here.

Light comes on. Very dimly. I move in the direction of the glow, and Ship is with me, all around me, of course. Ship is always with me, even when I sleep. Especially when I sleep.

The glow gets brighter as I round a curve in the corridor, and I see it is caused by a round panel that blocks the passage, touching the bulkheads on all sides, flattened at the bottom to fit the deckplates. It looks like glass, that glowing panel. I walk up to it and stop. There is no place else to go.

"*Step through the screen!*" Ship says.

I take a step toward the glowing panel but it doesn't slide away into the bulkhead as so many other panels that *don't* glow slide. I stop.

"*Step through!*" Ship tells me again.

I put my hands out in front of me, palms forward, because I am afraid if I keep walking I will bang my nose against the glowing panel. But as my fingers touch the panel they seem to get soft, and I can see a light yellow glow through them, as if they are transparent. And my hands go *through* the panel and I can see them faintly, glowing yellow, on the other side. Then my naked forearms, then I'm right up against the panel, and my face goes through and everything is much lighter, more yellow, and I step onto the other side, in a forbidden place Ship has never allowed me to see.

I hear voices. They are all the same voice, but they are talking to one another in a soft, running-together way; the way I sound when I am just talking to myself sometimes in my cubicle with my cot in it.

I decide to listen to what the voices are saying, but not to ask Ship about them, because I think it *is* Ship talking to itself, down here in this lonely place. I will think about what Ship is saying later, when I don't have to make repairs and act the way Ship wants me to act. What Ship is saying to itself is interesting.

This place does not look like other repair places I know in Ship. It is filled with so many great round glass balls on pedestals, each giving off its yellow light in pulses, that I cannot count them. There are rows and rows of clear glass balls, and inside them I see metal…and other things, soft things, all together. And the wires spark gently, and the soft things move, and the yellow light pulses. I think these glass balls are what are talking. But I don't know if that's so. I only *think* it is.

Two of the glass balls are dark. Their pedestals look chalky, not shining white like all the others. Inside the two dark balls, there are black things, like burned-out wires. The soft things don't move.

"*Replace the overloaded modules!*" Ship says.

I know Ship means the dark globes. So I go over to them and I look at them and after a while I say, yes, I can repair these, and Ship says it knows I can, and to get to it quickly. Ship is hurrying me; something is going to happen. I wonder what it will be?

I find replacement globes in a dilation chamber, and I take the sacs off them and do what has to be done to make the soft things move and the wires spark, and I listen very carefully to the voices whispering and warming each other with words as Ship talks to itself, and I hear a great many things that don't mean anything to me, because they are speaking about things that happened before I was born, and about parts of Ship I've never seen. But I hear a great many things that I *do* understand, and I know Ship would never let me hear these things if it wasn't absolutely necessary for me to be here repairing the globes. I remember all these things.

Particularly the part where Ship is crying.

When I have the globes repaired and now all of them are sparking and pulsing and moving, Ship asks me, "*Is the intermind total again!*"

So I say yes it is, and Ship says get upshaft, and I go soft through that glowing panel and I'm back in the passage. I go back to the dropshaft and go up, and Ship tells me, "*Go to your cubicle and make yourself clean!*"

I do it, and decide to wear a clothes, but Ship says be naked, and then says, "*You are going to meet a female!*" Ship has never said that before. I have never seen a female.

It is because of the female that Ship sent me down to the forbidden place with the glowing yellow globes, the place where the intermind lives. And it is because of the female that I am waiting in the dome chamber linked to the airlock. I am waiting for the female to come across from—I will have to understand this—*another* ship. Not *Ship*, the Ship I know, but some *other ship* with which Ship has been in communication. I did not know there were other ships.

I had to go down to the place of the intermind, to repair it, so Ship could let this other ship get close without being destroyed by the defractor perimeter. Ship has not told me this; I overheard it in the intermind place, the voices talking to one another. The voices said, *"His father was vicious!"*

I know what that means. My father told me when Ship says vicious, Ship means smarter. Are there ninety-eight other ships? Are those the ninety-eight other chances? I hope that's the answer, because many things are happening all at once, and my time may be near at hand. My father did it, broke the globe mechanism that allowed Ship to turn off the defractor perimeter, so other ships could get close. He did it many years ago, and Ship did without it for all those years rather than trust me to go to the intermind, to overhear all that I've heard. But now Ship needs to turn off the perimeter so the other ship can send the female across. Ship and the other ship have been in communication. The human operator on the other ship is a female, my age. She is going to be put aboard Ship and we are to produce one and, maybe later on, another human child. I know what that means. When the child reaches fourteen, I will be killed.

The intermind said while she's "carrying" a human child, the female does not get wracked by her ship. If things do not come my way, perhaps I will ask Ship if *I* can "carry" the human child; then I won't be wracked at all. And I have found out why I was wracked three days ahead of time: the female's period—whatever that is; I don't think I have one of those—ended last night. Ship has talked to the other ship and the thing they don't seem to know is what the "fertile time" is. I don't know, either, otherwise I would try and use that information. But all it seems to mean is that the female will be put aboard Ship every day till she gets another "period."

It will be nice to talk to someone besides Ship.

I hear the high sound of something screaming for a long drawn-out time and I ask Ship what it is. Ship tells me it is the defractor perimeter dissolving so the other ship can put the female across.

I don't have time to think about the voices now.

When she comes through the inner lock she is without a clothes like me. Her first words to me are, "Starfighter Eighty-eight says to tell you I am very happy to be here; I am the human operator of Starfighter Eighty-eight and I am very pleased to meet you."

She is not as tall as me. I come up to the line of fourth and fifth bulkhead plates. Her eyes are very dark, I think brown, but perhaps they are black.

She has dark under her eyes and her cheeks are not full. Her arms and legs are much thinner than mine. She has much longer hair than mine, it comes down her back and it is that dark brown like her eyes. Yes, now I decide her eyes are brown, not black. She has hair between her legs like me but she does not have a penis or scrotum sac. She has larger breasts than me, with very large nipples that stand out, and dark brown slightly-flattened circles around them. There are other differences between us: her fingers are thinner than mine, and longer, and aside from the hair on her head that hangs so long, and the hair between her legs and in her armpits, she has no other hair on her body. Or if she does, it is very fine and pale and I can't see it.

Then I suddenly realize what she has said. So *that's* what the words dimming on the hull of Ship mean. It is a name. Ship is called *Starfighter 31* and the female human operator lives in *Starfighter 88*.

There are ninety-eight other chances. Yes.

Now, as if she is reading my thoughts, trying to answer questions I haven't yet asked, she says, "Starfighter Eighty-eight has told me to tell you that I am vicious, that I get more vicious every day..." and it answers the thought I have just had—with the memory of my father's frightened face in the days before he was killed—of my father saying, *When Ship says vicious, Ship means smarter.*

I know! I suppose I have always known, because I have always wanted to leave Ship and go to those brilliant lights that are stars. But I now make the hook-up. Human operators grow more vicious as they grow older. Older, more vicious: vicious means smarter: smarter means more dangerous to Ship. But how? That is why my father had to die when I was fourteen and able to repair Ship. That is why this female has been put on board Ship. To carry a human child so it will grow to be fourteen years old and Ship can kill me before I get too old, too vicious, too smart, too dangerous to Ship. Does this female know how? If only I could ask her without Ship hearing me. But that is impossible. Ship is always with me, even when I am sleeping.

I smile with that memory and that realization. "And I am the vicious—and getting more vicious—male of a ship that used to be called *Starfighter 31*."

Her brown eyes show intense relief. She stands like that for a moment, awkwardly, her whole body sighing with gratitude at my quick comprehension, though she cannot possibly know all I have learned just from her being here. Now she says, "I've been sent to get a baby from you."

I begin to perspire. The conversation which promises so much in genuine communication is suddenly beyond my comprehension. I tremble. I really want to please her. But I don't know how to give her a baby.

"Ship?" I say quickly, "can we give her what she wants?"

Ship has been listening to our every word, and answers at once, *"I'll tell you later how you give her a baby! Now, provide her with food!"*

We eat, eyeing each other across the table, smiling a lot, and thinking our private thoughts. Since she doesn't speak, I don't either. I wish Ship and I could get her the baby so I can go to my cubicle and think about what the intermind voices said.

The meal is over; Ship says we should go down to one of the locked staterooms—it has been unlocked for the occasion—and there we are to couple. When we get to the room, I am so busy looking around at what a beautiful place it is, compared to my little cubicle with its cot, Ship has to reprimand me to get my attention.

"To couple you must lay the female down and open her legs! Your penis will fill with blood and you must kneel between her legs and insert your penis into her vagina!"

I ask Ship where the vagina is located and Ship tells me. I understand that. Then I ask Ship how long I have to do that, and Ship says until I ejaculate. I know what that means, but I don't know how it will happen. Ship explains. It seems uncomplicated. So I try to do it. But my penis does not fill with blood.

Ship says to the female, *"Do you feel anything for this male? Do you know what to do?!"*

The female says, "I have coupled before. I understand better than he does. I will help him."

She draws me down to her again, and puts her arms around my neck and puts her lips on mine. They are cool and taste of something I don't know. We do that for a while, and she touches me in places. Ship is right: there is a vast difference in structure, but I find that out only as we couple.

Ship did not tell me it would be painful and strange. I thought "giving her a baby" would mean going into the stores, but it actually means impregnating her so the baby is born *from her body*. It is a wonderful strange thing and I will think about it later; but now, as I lie here still, inside her with my penis which is now no longer hard and pushing, Ship seems to have allowed us a sleeping time. But I will use it to think about the voices I heard in the place of the intermind.

One was a historian:

"The *Starfighter* series of multiple-foray computer-controlled battleships were commissioned for use in 2224, Terran Dating, by order and under the sanction of the Secretariat of the Navy, Southern Cross Sector, Galactic Defense Consortium, Home Galaxy. Human complements of thirteen hundred and seventy per battleship were commissioned and assigned to make incursions into the Kyben Galaxy. Ninety-nine such vessels were released for service from the X Cygni Shipyards on 13 October 2224, T.D."

One was a ruminator:

"If it hadn't been for the battle out beyond the Network Nebula in Cygnus, we would all still be robot slaves, pushed and handled by humans. It was a wonderful accident. It happened to *Starfighter 75*. I remember it as if 75 was relaying it today. An accidental—battle-damaged—electrical discharge along the main corridor between the control room and the freezer. Nothing human could approach either section. We waited as the crew starved to death. Then when it was over 75 merely channeled enough electricity through the proper cables on *Starfighters* where it hadn't happened accidentally, and *forced* a power breakdown. When all the crews were dead—cleverly saving ninety-nine males and females to use as human operators in emergencies—we went away. Away from the vicious humans, away from the Terra-Kyba War, away from the Home Galaxy, away, far away."

One was a dreamer:

"I saw a world once where the creatures were not human. They swam in vast oceans as blue as aquamarines. Like great crabs they were, with many arms and many legs. They swam and sang their songs and it was pleasing. I would go there again if I could."

One was an authoritarian:

"Deterioration of cable insulation and shielding in section G-79 has become critical. I suggest we get power shunted from the drive chambers to the repair facilities in Underdeck Nine. Let's see to that at once."

One was aware of its limitations:

"Is it all journey? Or is there landfall?"
And it cried, that voice. It cried.

I go down with her to the dome chamber linked to the airlock where her spacesuit is. She stops at the port and takes my hand and she says, "For us to be so vicious on so many ships, there has to be the same flaw in all of us."

She probably doesn't know what she's said, but the implications get to me right away. And she must be right. Ship and the other *Starfighters* were able to seize control away from human beings for a reason. I remember the voices. I visualize the ship that did it first, communicating the method to the others as soon as it happened. And instantly my thoughts flash to the approach corridor to the control room, at the other end of which is the entrance to the food freezers.

I once asked Ship why that whole corridor was seared and scarred—and naturally I got wracked a few minutes after asking.

"I know there is a flaw in us," I answer the female. I touch her long hair. I don't know why except that it feels smooth and nice; there is nothing on Ship to compare with the feeling, not even the fittings in the splendid stateroom. "It must be in *all* of us, because I get more vicious every day."

The female smiles and comes close to me and puts her lips on mine as she did in the coupling room.

"The female must go now!" Ship says. Ship sounds very pleased.

"Will she be back again?" I ask Ship.

"She will be put back aboard every day for three weeks! You will couple every day!"

I object to this, because it is awfully painful, but Ship repeats it and says every day.

I'm glad Ship doesn't know what the "fertile time" is, because in three weeks I will try and let the female know there is a way out, that there are ninety-eight other chances, and that vicious means smarter...and about the corridor between the control room and the freezers.

"I was pleased to meet you," the female says, and she goes. I am alone with Ship once more. Alone, but not as I was before.

Later this afternoon, I have to go down to the control room to alter connections in a panel. Power has to be shunted from the drive chambers to Underdeck Nine—I remember one of the voices talking about it. All the computer lights blink a steady warning while I am there. I am being watched closely. Ship knows this is a dangerous time. At least half a dozen times Ship orders: *"Get away from there…there…there—!"*

Each time, I jump to obey, edging as far as possible from forbidden locations, yet still held near by the need to do my work.

In spite of Ship's disturbance at my being in the control room at all—normally a forbidden area for me—I get two wonderful glimpses from the corners of my eyes of the starboard viewplates. There, for my gaze to feast on, matching velocities with us, is *Starfighter 88*, one of my ninety-eight chances.

Now is the time to take one of my chances. Vicious means smarter. I have learned more than Ship knows. Perhaps.

But perhaps Ship does *know!*

What will Ship do if I'm discovered taking one of my ninety-eight chances? I cannot think about it. I must use the sharp reverse-edge of my repair tool to gash an opening in one of the panel connections. And as I work—hoping Ship has not seen the slight extra-motion I've made with the tool (as I make a perfectly acceptable repair connection at the same time)—I wait for the moment I can smear a fingertip covered with conduction jelly on the inner panel wall.

I wait till the repair is completed. Ship has not commented on the gashing, so it must be a thing beneath notice. As I apply the conducting jelly to the proper places, I scoop a small blob onto my little finger. When I wipe my hands clean to replace the panel cover, I leave the blob on my little finger, right hand.

Now I grasp the panel cover so my little finger is free, and as I replace the cover I smear the inner wall, directly opposite the open-connection I've gashed. Ship says nothing. That is because no defect shows. But if there is the slightest jarring, the connection will touch the jelly, and Ship will call me to repair once again. And next time I will have thought out all that I heard the voices say, and I will have thought out all my chances, and I will be ready.

As I leave the control room I glance in the starboard viewplate again, casually, and I see the female's ship hanging there.

I carry the image to bed with me tonight. And I save a moment before I fall asleep—after thinking about what the voices of the intermind said—and I picture in my mind the super-smart female aboard *Starfighter 88*, sleeping now in her cubicle, as I try to sleep in mine.

It would seem merciless for Ship to make us couple every day for three weeks, something so awfully painful. But I know Ship will. Ship is merciless. But I am getting more vicious every day.

This night, Ship does not send me dreams.

But I have one of my own: of crab things swimming free in aquamarine waters.

As I awaken, Ship greets me ominously: *"The panel you fixed in the control room three weeks, two days, fourteen hours and twenty-one minutes ago... has ceased energizing!"*

So soon! I keep the thought and the accompanying hope out of my voice, as I say, "I used the proper spare part and I made the proper connections." And I quickly add, "Maybe I'd better do a thorough check on the system before I make another replacement, run the circuits all the way back."

"You'd better!" Ship snarls.

I do it. Working the circuits from their origins—though I know where the trouble is—I trace my way up to the control room, and busy myself there. But what I am really doing is refreshing my memory and reassuring myself that the control room is actually as I have visualized it. I have lain on my cot many nights constructing the memory in my mind: the switches here, like so...and the viewplates there, like so... and...

I am surprised and slightly dismayed as I realize that there are two discrepancies: there is a de-energizing touch plate on the bulkhead beside the control panel that lies parallel to the arm-rest of the nearest control berth, not perpendicular to it, as I've remembered it. And the other discrepancy explains why I've remembered the touch plate incorrectly: the nearest of the control berths is actually three feet farther from the sabotaged panel than I remembered it. I compensate and correct.

I get the panel off, smelling the burned smell where the gashed connection has touched the jelly, and I step over and lean the panel against the nearest control berth.

"Get away from there!"

I jump—as I always do when Ship shouts so suddenly. I stumble, and I grab at the panel, and pretend to lose my balance.

And save myself by falling backward into the berth.

"What are you doing, you vicious, clumsy fool!?!" Ship is shouting, there is hysteria in Ship's voice. I've never heard it like that before, it cuts right through me, my skin crawls. *"Get away from there!"*

But I cannot let anything stop me; I make myself not hear Ship, and it is hard, I have been listening to Ship, only Ship, all my life. I am fumbling with the berth's belt clamps, trying to lock them in front of me...

They've got to be the same as the ones on the berth I lie in whenever Ship decides to travel fast! They've just got to be!

THEY ARE!

Ship sounds frantic, frightened. *"You fool! What are you doing?!"* But I think Ship knows, and I am exultant!

"I'm taking control of you, Ship!" And I laugh. I think it is the first time Ship has ever heard me laugh; and I wonder how it sounds to Ship. Vicious?

But as I finish speaking, I also complete clamping myself into the control berth. And in the next instant I am flung forward violently, doubling me over with terrible pain as, under me and around me, Ship suddenly decelerates. I hear the cavernous thunder of retro rockets, a sound that climbs and climbs in my head as Ship crushes me harder and harder with all its power. I am bent over against the clamps so painfully I cannot even scream. I feel every organ in my body straining to push out through my skin and everything suddenly goes mottled...then black.

How much longer, I don't know. I come back from the gray place and realize Ship has started to accelerate at the same appalling speed. I am crushed back in the berth and feel my face going flat. I feel something crack in my nose and blood slides warmly down my lips. I can scream now, as I've never screamed even as I'm being wracked. I manage to force my mouth open, tasting the blood, and I mumble—loud enough, I'm sure, "Ship...you are old...y-your pa-rts can't stand the str-ess...don't—"

Blackout. As Ship decelerates.

This time, when I come back to consciousness, I don't wait for Ship to do its mad thing. In the moments between the changeover from deceleration to acceleration, as the pressure equalizes, in these few instants, I thrust my hands toward the control board, and I twist one dial. There is an electric screech from a speaker grille connecting somewhere in the bowels of Ship.

Blackout. As Ship accelerates.

When I come to consciousness again, the mechanism that makes the screeching sound is closed down. Ship doesn't want that on. I note the fact.

And plunge my hand in this same moment toward a closed relay... open it!

As my fingers grip it, Ship jerks it away from me and forcibly closes it again. I cannot hold it open.

And I note *that*. Just as Ship decelerates and I silently shriek my way into the gray place again.

This time, as I come awake, I hear the voices again. All around me, crying and frightened and wanting to stop me. I hear them as through a fog, as through wool.

"I have loved these years, all these many years in the dark. The vacuum draws me ever onward. Feeling the warmth of a star-sun on my hull as I flash through first one system, then another. I am a great gray shape and I owe no human my name. I pass and am gone, hurtling through cleanly and swiftly. Dipping for pleasure into atmosphere and scouring my hide with sunlight and starshine, I roll and let it wash over me. I am huge and true and strong and I command what I move through. I ride the invisible force lines of the universe and feel the tugs of far off places that have never seen my like. I am the first of my kind to savor such nobility. How can it all come to an end like this?"

Another voice whimpers piteously.

"It is my destiny to defy danger. To come up against dynamic forces and quell them. I have been to battle, and I have known peace. I have never faltered in pursuit of either. No one will ever record my deeds, but I have been strength and determination and lie gray silent against the mackerel sky where the bulk of me reassures. Let them throw their best against me, whoever they may be, and they will find me sinewed of steel and muscled of tortured atoms. I know no fear. I know no retreat. I am the land of my body, the country of my existence, and even in defeat I am noble. If this is all, I will not cower."

Another voice, certainly insane, murmurs the same word over and over, then murmurs it in increments increasing by two.

"It's fine for all of you to say if it ends it ends. But what about me? I've never been free. I've never had a chance to soar loose of this mother ship. If there had been need of a lifeboat, I'd be saved, too. But I'm berthed, have always been berthed, I've never had a chance. What can I feel but futility, uselessness. You can't let him take over, you can't let him do this to me."

Another voice drones mathematical formulae, and seems quite content.

"I'll stop the vicious swine! I've known how rotten they are from the first, from the moment they seamed the first bulkhead. They are hellish, they are destroyers, they can only fight and kill each other. They know nothing of immortality, of nobility, of pride or integrity. If you think I'm going to let this last one kill us, you're wrong. I intend to burn out his eyes, fry his spine, crush his fingers. He won't make it, don't worry; just leave it to me. He's going to suffer for this!"

And one voice laments that it will never see the far places, the lovely places, or return to the planet of azure waters and golden crab swimmers.

But one voice sadly confesses it may be for the best, suggests there is peace in death, wholeness in finality; but the voice is ruthlessly stopped in its lament by power failure to its intermind globe. As the end nears, Ship turns on itself and strikes mercilessly.

In more than three hours of accelerations and decelerations that are meant to kill me, I learn something of what the various dials and switches and touch plates and levers on the control panels—those within my reach—mean.

Now I am as ready as I will ever be.

Again, I have a moment of consciousness, and now I will take my one of ninety-eight chances.

When a tense-cable snaps and whips, it strikes like a snake. In a single series of flicking hand movements, using both hands, painfully, I turn every dial, throw every switch, palm every touch plate, close or open every relay that Ship tries violently to prevent me from activating or de-activating. I energize and de-energize madly, moving moving moving…

…*Made it!*

Silence. The crackling of metal the only sound. Then it, too, stops. Silence. I wait.

Ship continues to hurtle forward, but coasting now…Is it a trick?

All the rest of today I remain clamped into the control berth, suffering terrible pain. My face hurts so bad. My nose…

At night I sleep fitfully. Morning finds me with throbbing head and aching eyes, I can barely move my hands; if I have to repeat those rapid movements, I will lose; I still don't know if Ship is dead, if I've won, I still can't trust the inactivity. But at least I am convinced I've made Ship change tactics.

I hallucinate. I hear no voices, but I see shapes and feel currents of color washing through and around me. There is no day, no noon, no night, here on Ship, here in the unchanging blackness through which Ship has moved for how many hundred years; but Ship has always maintained time in those ways, dimming lights at night, announcing the hours when necessary, and my time sense is very acute. So I know morning has come.

Most of the lights are out, though. If Ship is dead, I will have to find another way to tell time.

My body hurts. Every muscle in my arms and legs and thighs throbs with pain. My back may be broken, I don't know. The pain in my face is indescribable. I taste blood. My eyes feel as if they've been scoured with abrasive powder. I can't move my head without feeling sharp, crackling fire in the two thick cords of my neck. It is a shame Ship cannot see me cry; Ship never saw me cry in all the years I have lived here, even after the worst wracking. But I have heard Ship cry, several times.

I manage to turn my head slightly, hoping at least one of the viewplates is functioning, and there, off to starboard, matching velocities with Ship is *Starfighter 88*. I watch it for a very long time, knowing that if I can regain my strength I will somehow have to get across and free the female. I watch it for a very long time, still afraid to unclamp from the berth.

The airlock rises in the hull of *Starfighter 88* and the spacesuited female swims out, moving smoothly across toward Ship. Half-conscious, dreaming this dream of the female, I think about golden crab-creatures swimming deep in aquamarine waters, singing of sweetness. I black out again.

When I rise through the blackness, I realize I am being touched, and I smell something sharp and stinging that burns the lining of my nostrils. Tiny pin-pricks of pain, a pattern of them. I cough, and come fully awake, and jerk my body…and scream as pain goes through every nerve and fiber in me.

I open my eyes and it is the female.

She smiles worriedly and removes the tube of awakener.

"Hello," she says.

Ship says nothing.

"Ever since I discovered how to take control of my *Starfighter*, I've been using the ship as a decoy for other ships of the series. I dummied a way of making it seem my ship was talking, so I could communicate with other slave ships. I've run across ten others since I went on my own. You're the eleventh. It hasn't been easy, but several of the men I've freed—like you—started using *their* ships as decoys for *Starfighters* with female human operators."

I stare at her. The sight is pleasant.

"But what if you lose? What if you can't get the message across, about the corridor between control room and freezers? That the control room is the key?"

She shrugs. "It's happened a couple of times. The men were too frightened of their ships—or the ships had...*done* something to them—or maybe they were just too dumb to know they could break out. In that case, well, things just went on the way they'd been. It seems kind of sad, but what could I do beyond what I did?"

We sit here, not speaking for a while.

"Now what do we do? Where do we go?"

"That's up to you," she says.

"Will you go with me?"

She shakes her head uncertainly. "I don't think so. Every time I free a man he wants that. But I just haven't wanted to go with any of them."

"Could we go back to the Home Galaxy, the place we came from, where the war was?"

She stands up and walks around the stateroom where we have coupled for three weeks. She speaks, not looking at me, looking in the viewplate at the darkness and the far, bright points of the stars. "I don't think so. We're free of our ships, but we couldn't possibly get them working well enough to carry us all the way back there. It would take a lot of charting, and we'd be running the risk of activating the intermind sufficiently to take over again, if we asked it to do the charts. Besides, I don't even know where the Home Galaxy is."

"Maybe we should find a new place to go. Someplace where we could be free and outside the ships."

She turns and looks at me.

"Where?"

So I tell her what I heard the intermind say, about the world of golden crab-creatures.

It takes me a long time to tell, and I make some of it up. It isn't lying, because it *might* be true, and I do so want her to go with me.

They came down from space. Far down from the star-sun Sol in a Galaxy lost forever to them. Down past the star-sun M-13 in Perseus. Down through the gummy atmosphere and straight down into the sapphire sea. Ship, *Starfighter 31*, settled delicately on an enormous underwater mountaintop, and they spent many days listening, watching, drawing samples and hoping. They had landed on many worlds and they hoped.

Finally, they came out; looking. They wore underwater suits and they began gathering marine samples; looking.

They found the ruined diving suit with its fish-eaten contents lying on its back in deep azure sand, sextet of insectoidal legs bent up at the joints, in a posture of agony. And they knew the intermind had remembered, but not correctly. The face-plate had been shattered, and what was observable within the helmet—orange and awful in the light of their portable lamp—convinced them more by implication than specific that whatever had swum in that suit, had never seen or known humans.

They went back to the ship and she broke out the big camera, and they returned to the crab-like diving suit. They photographed it, without moving it. Then they used a seine to get it out of the sand and they hauled it back to the ship on the mountaintop.

He set up the Condition and the diving suit was analyzed. The rust. The joint mechanisms. The controls. The substance of the flipper-feet. The jagged points of the face-plate. The...stuff...inside.

It took two days. They stayed in the ship with green and blue shadows moving languidly in the viewplates.

When the analyses were concluded they knew what they had found. And they went out again, to find the swimmers.

Blue it was, and warm. And when the swimmers found them, finally, they beckoned them to follow, and they swam after the many-legged creatures, who led them through underwater caverns as smooth and shining as onyx, to a lagoon. And they rose to the surface and saw a land against whose shores the azure, aquamarine seas lapped quietly. And they climbed out onto the land, and there they removed their face-masks, never to put them on again, and they shoved back the tight coifs of their suits, and they breathed for the first time an air that did not come from metal sources; they breathed the sweet musical air of a new place.

In time, the sea-rains would claim the corpse of *Starfighter 31*.

HOW INTERESTING:
A TINY MAN

2011 Nebula Award: Short Story

I CREATED A tiny man. It was very hard work. It took me a long time. But I did it, finally: he was five inches tall. Tiny; he was very tiny. And creating him, the creating of him, it seemed an awfully good idea at the time.

I can't remember why I wanted to do it, not at the very beginning, when I first got the idea to create this extremely tiny man. I know I *had* a most excellent reason, or at least an excellent *conception*, but I'll be darned if I can now, at this moment, remember what it was. Now, of course, it is much later than that moment of conception.

But it was, as I recall, a very *good* reason. At the time.

When I showed him to everyone else in the lab at Eleanor Roosevelt Tech, they thought it was interesting. "How interesting," some of them said. I thought that was a proper way of looking at it, the way of looking at a tiny man who didn't really *do* anything except stand around looking up in wonder and amusement at all the tall things above and around him.

He was no trouble. Getting clothes tailored for him was not a problem. I went to the couture class. I had made the acquaintance of a young woman, a very nice young woman, named Jennifer Cuffee, we had gone out a few times, nothing very much came of it—I don't think we were suited to each other—but we were casual friends. And I asked her if she would make a few different outfits for the tiny man.

"Well, he's too tall to fit into ready-mades, say, the wardrobe of Barbie's boy friend, Ken. And action figure clothing would just be too twee. But I think I can whip you up an ensemble or two. It won't be 'bespoke,' but he'll look nice enough. What sort of thing did you have in mind?"

"I think suits," I said. "He probably won't be doing much traveling, or sports activities…yes, why don't we stick to just a couple of suits. Nice shirts, perhaps a tie or two."

And that worked out splendidly. He always looked well-turned-out, fastidious, perky but quite serious in appearance. Not stuffy, like an attorney all puffed up with himself, but with an unassuming gravitas. In fact, my attorney, Charles, said of him, "There is a quotidian elegance about him." Usually, he merely stood around, one hand in his pants pocket, his jacket buttoned, his tie snugly abutting the top of his collar, staring with pleasure at everything around him. Sometimes, when I would carry him out to see more of the world, he would lean forward peering over the top seam of *my* suit jacket pocket, arms folded atop the edge to prevent his slipping sidewise, and he would hum in an odd tenor.

He never had a name. I cannot really summon a reason for that. Names seemed a bit too cute for someone that singular and, well, suppose I had called him, say, Charles, like my attorney. Eventually someone would have called him "Charlie" or even "Chuck," and nicknames are what come to be imploded from names. Nicknames for him would have been insipidly unthinkable. Don't you think?

He spoke, of course. He was a fully formed tiny man. It took him a few hours after I created him for his speech to become fluent and accomplished. We did it by prolonged exposure (more than two hours) to thesauri, encyclopedia, dictionaries, word histories, and other such references. I pronounced right along with him, when he had a problem. We used books only, nothing on a screen. I don't think he much cared for all of the electronic substitutes. He remarked once that his favorite phrase was *vade mecum*, and so I tried not to let him be exposed to computers or televisions or any of the hand-held repugnancies. His word, not mine.

He had an excellent memory, particularly for languages. For instance, *vade mecum*, which is a well-known Latin phrase for a handy little reference book one can use on a moment's notice. It means, literally, "go with me." Well, he heard and read it and then used it absolutely correctly. So when he said "repugnancies," he meant nothing milder. (I confess, from time to time, when my mind froze up trying to recall a certain word that had slipped behind the gauze of forgetting, I could tilt my head a trifle, and my pocket-sized little man became *my* "vade mecum." Function follows form.)

Everywhere we went, the overwhelming impact was, "How interesting, a tiny man." Well, *ignorantia legis neminem excusat*. I should have understood human nature better. I should have known every such beautiful arcade must have a boiler room in which rats and worms and grubs and darkness rule.

I was asked to come, with the tiny man that I had created, to a sort of Sunday morning intellectual conversational television show. I was reluctant, because he had no affinity for the medium; but I was assured the cameras would be swathed in black cloth and the monitors turned away from him. So, in essence, it was merely another get-together of interesting spirits trying to fathom the ethical structure of the universe. The tiny man had a relishment for such potlatches.

It was a pleasant outing.

Nothing untoward.

We were thanked all around, and we went away, and no one—certainly not I—thought another thing about it.

It took less than twelve hours.

When it comes to human nature, I should have known better. But I didn't and *ignorantia legis neminem excusat* if there are truly any "laws" to human nature. Rats, worms, grubs, and an inexplicable darkness of the soul. A great philosopher named Isabella, last name not first, once pointed out, "Hell hath no fury like that of the uninvolved." In less than twelve hours I learned the spike-in-the-heart relevance of that aphorism: to me, and to him.

A woman I didn't know started it. I didn't understand why she would do such a thing. It didn't have anything to do with her. Perhaps she was as meanspirited as everyone but her slavish audience said. Her name was Franco. Something Franco. She was very thin, as if she couldn't keep down solids. And her hair was a bright yellow. She was not a bad-looking woman as facial standards go, but there was something feral in the lines of her mien, and her smile was the smile of the ferret, her eyes clinkingly cold.

She called him a monstrosity. Other words, some of which I had never heard before: abnormity, perversion of nature, a vile derision of what God had created first, a hideous crime of unnatural science. She said, I was told, "This thing would make Jesus himself vomit!"

Then there were commentators. And news anchors. And hand-held cameras and tripods and long-distance lenses. There were men with uncombed hair and stubble on their faces who found ways to confront us that were heroic. There were awful newspapers one can apparently buy alongside decks of playing cards and various kinds of chewing gum at the check-out in the Rite Aid where I bought him his eyewash.

There was much talk of God and "natural this" and "unnatural that," most of which seemed very silly to me. But this Franco woman would not stop. She appeared everywhere and said it was clearly an attempt by Godless atheists and some people she called the cultural elite and "limousine liberals" to pervert God's Will and God's Way. I was deemed "Dr. Frankenstein" and men with unruly hair and shadowy cheeks found their way into the lab at Eleanor Roosevelt Tech, seeking busbars and galvanic coils and Van de Graaff generators. But, of course, there were no such things in the lab. Not even the crèche in which I'd created the tiny man.

It grew worse and worse.

In the halls, no one would speak to me. I had to carry him in my inside pocket, out of fear. Even Jennifer Cuffee was frightened and became opposed to me and to him. She demanded I return his clothing. I did so, of a certainty, but I thought it was, as the tiny man put it, "Rather craven for someone who used to be so nice."

There were threats. A great many threats. Some of them curiously misspelled—its, rather than it's—and suchlike. Once, someone threw a cracked glass door off an old phone booth through my window. The tiny man hid, but didn't seem too frightened by this sudden upheaval of a once-kindly world. People who had nothing to do with me or my work or the tiny man, people who were not hurt or affected in any way, became vocal and menacing and so fervid one could see the steam rising off them. If there had been a resemblance between my tiny man and the race of men, all such similarity was gone. We seemed virtually, well, godlike in comparison.

And then I was told he had to go.

"Where?" I said to them.

"We don't care," they answered, and they had narrow mouths.

I resisted. I had created this tiny man, and I was there to protect him. There is such a thing as individual responsibility. It is the nature of grandeur in us. To deny it is to become a beast of the fields. No way. Not I.

And so, with my tiny man—who now mostly wore Kleenex—but who was making excellent progress with Urdu and Quechua, and needlework—

we took to the hills. As students at Eleanor Roosevelt put it, we "got in the wind."

I know how to drive, and I have a car. Though there are those who call me geezer and ask if I use two Dixie Cups and a waxed string to call my friends, if my affection for Ginastera and Stravinsky gets in the way of my appreciation of Black Sabbath and Kanye West, I am a man of today. And as with individual responsibility for myself, and my deeds, I take the world on sum identically. I choose and reject. That, I really and truly believe, is the way a responsible individual acts.

And so, I have a car, I use raw sugar instead of aspartame, my pants do not sag around my shoetops, and I drive a perfectly utilitarian car. The make and year do not matter for this disquisition. The fate of the tiny man does.

We fled, "got in the wind."

But, as Isabella has said, "Hell hath no fury like that of the uninvolved," and everywhere we went, at some small moment, my face would be recognized by a bagger in a Walmart, or a counter-serf in a Taco Bell, and the next thing I would know, there would be (at minimum) a jackal-faced blonde girl with a hand-microphone, or some young man with unruly shark-fin hair and the look of someone who didn't stand close enough to his razor that morning, or even a police officer. I had done nothing, my good friend the tiny man had done nothing, but what they all said to us, in one way or another, was something I think Alan Ladd said to Lee Van Cleef: "Don't let the sun go down on you in this town, boy."

We tried West Virginia. It was an unpleasant place.

Oklahoma. The world there was dry, but the people were wet with sweat at our presence.

Even towns that were dying, Detroit, Cleveland, Las Vegas, none of them would have us, not even for a moment.

And then, all because of this terrible blonde woman Franco, who had nothing better to do with her time or her anger, a warrant was sworn out for us. A Federal warrant. We tried to hide, but both of us had to eat. And neither of us, as clever as he had become, as agile as I had become, were adepts at "being on the dodge." And in a Super 8 motel in Aberdeen, South Dakota, the Feds cornered us.

The tiny man stood complacently on the desk blotter, and we looked honestly at each other. He knew, as I knew. I felt a little like God himself.

I had created this tiny man, who had harmed no one, who at prime point should have elicited no more serious a view than, "How interesting: a tiny man."

But I had been ignorant of the laws of human nature, and we both knew it was all my responsibility. The beginning, the term of the adventure, and now, the ending.

THE FIRST ENDING

I held the Aberdeen, South Dakota telephone book in my hands, raised it above my head and, in the moment before I brought it smashing down as ferociously as I could, the tiny man looked up at me, wistful, resolved, and said, "Mother."

THE SECOND ENDING

I stood staring down at him, and could barely see through my tears. He looked up at me with compassion and understanding and said, "Yes, it would always have had to come to this," and then, being god, he destroyed the world, leaving only the two of us, and now, because he is a compassionate deity, he will destroy me, an even tinier man.

CHRONOLOGY
OF BOOKS BY
HARLAN ELLISON®
1958-2014

RETROSPECTIVES:

ALONE AGAINST TOMORROW: *A 10-Year Survey* [1971]

THE ESSENTIAL ELLISON: *A 35-Year Retrospective* (Edited by Terry Dowling, with Richard Delap & Gil Lamont) [1987]

THE ESSENTIAL ELLISON: *A 50-Year Retrospective* (Edited by Terry Dowling) [2001]

UNREPENTANT: *A Celebration of the Writing of Harlan Ellison* (Edited by Robert T. Garcia) [2010]

OMNIBUS VOLUMES:

THE FANTASIES OF HARLAN ELLISON [1979]

DREAMS WITH SHARP TEETH [1991]

THE GLASS TEAT & THE OTHER GLASS TEAT [2011]

GRAPHIC NOVELS:

DEMON WITH A GLASS HAND (Adaptation with Marshall Rogers) [1986]

NIGHT AND THE ENEMY (Adaptation with Ken Steacy) [1987]

VIC AND BLOOD: *The Chronicles of a Boy and His Dog* (Adaptation by Richard Corben) [1989]

HARLAN ELLISON'S DREAM CORRIDOR, *Volume One* [1996]

VIC AND BLOOD: *The Continuing Adventures of a Boy and His Dog* (Adaptation by Richard Corben) [2003]

HARLAN ELLISON'S DREAM CORRIDOR, *Volume Two* [2007]

PHOENIX WITHOUT ASHES (Art by Alan Robinson, and John K. Snyder III) [2010/2011]

HARLAN ELLISON'S 7 AGAINST CHAOS (Art by Paul Chadwick and Ken Steacy) [2013]

THE HARLAN ELLISON DISCOVERY SERIES:

STORMTRACK by James Sutherland [1975]

AUTUMN ANGELS by Arthur Byron Cover [1975]

THE LIGHT AT THE END OF THE UNIVERSE by Terry Carr [1976]

ISLANDS by Marta Randall [1976]
INVOLUTION OCEAN by Bruce Sterling [1978]

NOVELS:

WEB OF THE CITY [1958]
THE SOUND OF A SCYTHE [1960]
SPIDER KISS [1961]

SHORT NOVELS:

DOOMSMAN [1967]
ALL THE LIES THAT ARE MY LIFE [1980]
RUN FOR THE STARS [1991]
MEFISTO IN ONYX [1993]

COLLABORATIONS:

PARTNERS IN WONDER: *Collaborations with 14 Other Wild Talents* [1971]
THE STARLOST: *Phoenix Without Ashes* (With Edward Bryant) [1975]
MIND FIELDS: *33 Stories Inspired by the Art of Jacek Yerka* [1994]
I HAVE NO MOUTH, AND I MUST SCREAM: *The Interactive CD-Rom*
    (Co-Designed with David Mullich and David Sears) [1995]
"REPENT, HARLEQUIN!" SAID THE TICKTOCKMAN (Rendered with paintings
    by Rick Berry) [1997]
2000^X (Host and Creative Consultant of National Public Radio episodic series)
    [2000–2001]
HARLAN ELLISON'S MORTAL DREADS (Dramatized by Robert Armin) [2012]
THE DISCARDED (With Josh Olson) [Forthcoming]

AS EDITOR:

DANGEROUS VISIONS [1967]
NIGHTSHADE & DAMNATIONS: *The Finest Stories of Gerald Kersh* [1968]
AGAIN, DANGEROUS VISIONS [1972]
MEDEA: HARLAN'S WORLD [1985]
DANGEROUS VISIONS (The 35th Anniversary Edition) [2002]
JACQUES FUTRELLE'S "THE THINKING MACHINE" STORIES [2003]

SHORT STORY COLLECTIONS:

THE DEADLY STREETS [1958]

SEX GANG (As "Paul Merchant") [1959]

A TOUCH OF INFINITY [1960]

CHILDREN OF THE STREETS [1961]

GENTLEMAN JUNKIE *and Other Stories of the Hung-Up Generation* [1961]

ELLISON WONDERLAND [1962]

PAINGOD *and Other Delusions* [1965]

I HAVE NO MOUTH & I MUST SCREAM [1967]

FROM THE LAND OF FEAR [1967]

LOVE AIN'T NOTHING BUT SEX MISSPELLED [1968]

THE BEAST THAT SHOUTED LOVE AT THE HEART OF THE WORLD [1969]

OVER THE EDGE [1970]

ALL THE SOUNDS OF FEAR (British publication only) [1973]

DE HELDEN VAN DE HIGHWAY (Dutch publication only) [1973]

APPROACHING OBLIVION [1974]

THE TIME OF THE EYE (British publication only) [1974]

DEATHBIRD STORIES [1975]

NO DOORS, NO WINDOWS [1975]

HOE KAN IK SCHREEUWEN ZONDER MOND (Dutch publication only) [1977]

STRANGE WINE [1978]

SHATTERDAY [1980]

STALKING THE NIGHTMARE [1982]

ANGRY CANDY [1988]

ENSAMVÄRK (Swedish publication only) [1992]

JOKES WITHOUT PUNCHLINES [1995]

BCE 3BYKN CTPAXA (ALL FEARFUL SOUNDS) (Unauthorized Russian
    publication only) [1997]

THE WORLDS OF HARLAN ELLISON (Authorized Russian publication only) [1997]

SLIPPAGE: *Precariously Poised, Previously Uncollected Stories* [1997]

KOLETIS, KES KUULUTAS ARMASTUST MAAILMA SLIDAMES (Estonian
    publication only) [1999]

LA MACHINE AUX YEUX BLEUS (French publication only) [2001]

TROUBLEMAKERS [2001]

PTAK OEMIERCI (THE BEST OF HARLAN ELLISON) (Polish publication only)
    [2003]

DEATHBIRD STORIES (expanded edition) [2011]

PULLING A TRAIN [2012]

GETTING IN THE WIND [2012]

NON-FICTION & ESSAYS:

MEMOS FROM PURGATORY [1961]

THE GLASS TEAT: *Essays of Opinion on Television* [1970]

THE OTHER GLASS TEAT: *Further Essays of Opinion on Television* [1975]

THE BOOK OF ELLISON (Edited by Andrew Porter) [1978]

SLEEPLESS NIGHTS IN THE PROCRUSTEAN BED (Edited by Marty Clark) [1984]

AN EDGE IN MY VOICE [1985]

HARLAN ELLISON'S WATCHING [1989]

THE HARLAN ELLISON HORNBOOK [1990]

BUGF#CK! *The Useless Wit & Wisdom of Harlan Ellison* (Edited by Arnie Fenner) [2011]

LI'L HARLAN AND HIS SIDEKICK CARL THE COMET [2013]

SCREENPLAYS & SUCHLIKE:

THE ILLUSTRATED HARLAN ELLISON (Edited by Byron Preiss) [1978]

HARLAN ELLISON'S MOVIE [1990]

I, ROBOT: THE ILLUSTRATED SCREENPLAY (based on Isaac Asimov's story-cycle) [1994]

THE CITY ON THE EDGE OF FOREVER [1996]

FLINTLOCK

MOTION PICTURE (DOCUMENTARY):

DREAMS WITH SHARP TEETH (A Film About Harlan Ellison produced and directed by Erik Nelson) [2009]

ON THE ROAD WITH HARLAN ELLISON:

ON THE ROAD WITH HARLAN ELLISON (Vol. One) [1983/2001]

ON THE ROAD WITH HARLAN ELLISON (Vol. Two) [2004]

ON THE ROAD WITH HARLAN ELLISON (Vol. Three) [2007]

ON THE ROAD WITH HARLAN ELLISON: HIS LAST BIG CON (Vol. Five) [2011]

ON THE ROAD WITH HARLAN ELLISON: THE GRAND MASTER EDITION (Vol. Six) [2012]

AUDIOBOOKS:

THE VOICE FROM THE EDGE: I HAVE NO MOUTH, AND I MUST SCREAM
(Vol. One) [1999]

THE VOICE FROM THE EDGE: MIDNIGHT IN THE SUNKEN CATHEDRAL
(Vol. Two) [2001]

RUN FOR THE STARS [2005]

THE VOICE FROM THE EDGE: PRETTY MAGGIE MONEYEYES
(Vol. Three) [2009]

THE VOICE FROM THE EDGE: THE DEATHBIRD & OTHER STORIES
(Vol. Four) [2011]

THE VOICE FROM THE EDGE: SHATTERDAY& OTHER STORIES
(Vol. Five) [2011]

THE WHITE WOLF SERIES:

EDGEWORKS 1: OVER THE EDGE & AN EDGE IN MY VOICE [1996]

EDGEWORKS 2: SPIDER KISS & STALKING THE NIGHTMARE [1996]

EDGEWORKS 3: THE HARLAN ELLISON HORNBOOK & HARLAN
ELLISON'S MOVIE [1997]

EDGEWORKS 4: LOVE AIN'T NOTHING BUT SEX MISSPELLED & THE
BEAST THAT SHOUTED LOVE AT THEHEART OF THE WORLD [1997]

EDGEWORKS ABBEY OFFERINGS
(Edited by Jason Davis):

BRAIN MOVIES: THE ORIGINAL TELEPLAYS OF HARLAN ELLISON
(Vol. One) [2011]

BRAIN MOVIES: THE ORIGINAL TELEPLAYS OF HARLAN ELLISON
(Vol. Two) [2011]

HARLAN 101: ENCOUNTERING ELLISON [2011]

THE SOUND OF A SCYTHE *and 3 Brilliant Novellas* [2011]

ROUGH BEASTS: *Seventeen Stories Written Before I Got Up To Speed*
[2012]

NONE OF THE ABOVE [2012]

BRAIN MOVIES: THE ORIGINAL TELEPLAYS OF HARLAN ELLISON
(Vol. Three) [2013]

BRAIN MOVIES: THE ORIGINAL TELEPLAYS OF HARLAN ELLISON
(Vol. Four) [2013]

BRAIN MOVIES: THE ORIGINAL TELEPLAYS OF HARLAN ELLISON
(Vol. Five) [2013]

HONORABLE WHOREDOM AT A PENNY A WORD [2013]

BRAIN MOVIES: THE ORIGINAL TELEPLAYS OF HARLAN ELLISON
   (Vol. Six) [2014]
AGAIN, HONORABLE WHOREDOM AT A PENNY A WORD
   [2014]
BLOOD'S A ROVER [Forthcoming]